PENGUIN BOOKS

CITY OF LIES AND LEGENDS

Kayla is the author of the House of Devils series – *City of Gods and Monsters, City of Souls and Sinners, City of Lies and Legends* and *City of Smoke and Brimstone*. She is also the author of the upper-YA romantasy novel, *Dreams of Ice and Iron*. She started writing *City of Gods and Monsters* when she was in high school, so the characters and the world they live in are very close to her heart. When she isn't writing, she enjoys traveling, spending time in nature, and binge-watching her favorite television shows with her husband.

BOOKS BY KAYLA EDWARDS:

Dreams of Ice and Iron

The House of Devils series

City of Gods and Monsters
City of Souls and Sinners
City of Lies and Legends
City of Smoke and Brimstone

CITY OF LIES AND LEGENDS

HOUSE OF DEVILS
BOOK THREE

KAYLA EDWARDS

PENGUIN BOOKS

PENGUIN BOOKS

UK | USA | Canada | Ireland | Australia
India | New Zealand | South Africa

Penguin Books is part of the Penguin Random House group of companies whose addresses can be found at global.penguinrandomhouse.com

Penguin Random House UK,
One Embassy Gardens, 8 Viaduct Gardens, London SW11 7BW

penguin.co.uk

First self-published by Kayla Edwards 2024
This edition published by Penguin Books 2025
005

Copyright © Kayla Edwards, 2024

The moral right of the author has been asserted

Penguin Random House values and supports copyright.
Copyright fuels creativity, encourages diverse voices, promotes freedom of expression and supports a vibrant culture. Thank you for purchasing an authorized edition of this book and for respecting intellectual property laws by not reproducing, scanning or distributing any part of it by any means without permission. You are supporting authors and enabling Penguin Random House to continue to publish books for everyone. No part of this book may be used or reproduced in any manner for the purpose of training artificial intelligence technologies or systems. In accordance with Article 4(3) of the DSM Directive 2019/790, Penguin Random House expressly reserves this work from the text and data mining exception

Interior border designs © Lila Raymond (@lettersbylila_)
Map design © Virginia Allyn
Printed and bound in Great Britain by Clays Ltd, Elcograf S.p.A.

The authorized representative in the EEA is Penguin Random House Ireland, Morrison Chambers, 32 Nassau Street, Dublin D02 YH68

A CIP catalogue record for this book is available from the British Library

ISBN: 978–1–405–98882–7

Penguin Random House is committed to a sustainable future for our business, our readers and our planet. This book is made from Forest Stewardship Council® certified paper.

*For anyone who feels trapped in a dark place—
May you find the light again.*

*And for Jeff—
My leap of faith.*

Welcome Back to Angelthene

As always, we hope you enjoy your stay. Please avoid going out after sunset, and keep a form of protection on you at all times. The use of Blood Staves is strictly prohibited. Darkslayers operate in the city, so exercising a high level of caution in all districts is highly recommended for residents and visitors. Avoid unnecessary travel to the Meatpacking District, Hooded Skullcap, Stone's End, Ebonfield, Oldtown, the Narrow Hills, and the Black Alder District. Travel to Angelthene National Forest is recommended only between the hours of seven a.m. and three p.m. All cell phones within city limits are programmed to receive alerts regarding Blood Moons. If a Blood Moon is in the forecast, stay inside the forcefield until dawn. Report any suspicious activity to the Magical Protections Unit immediately.

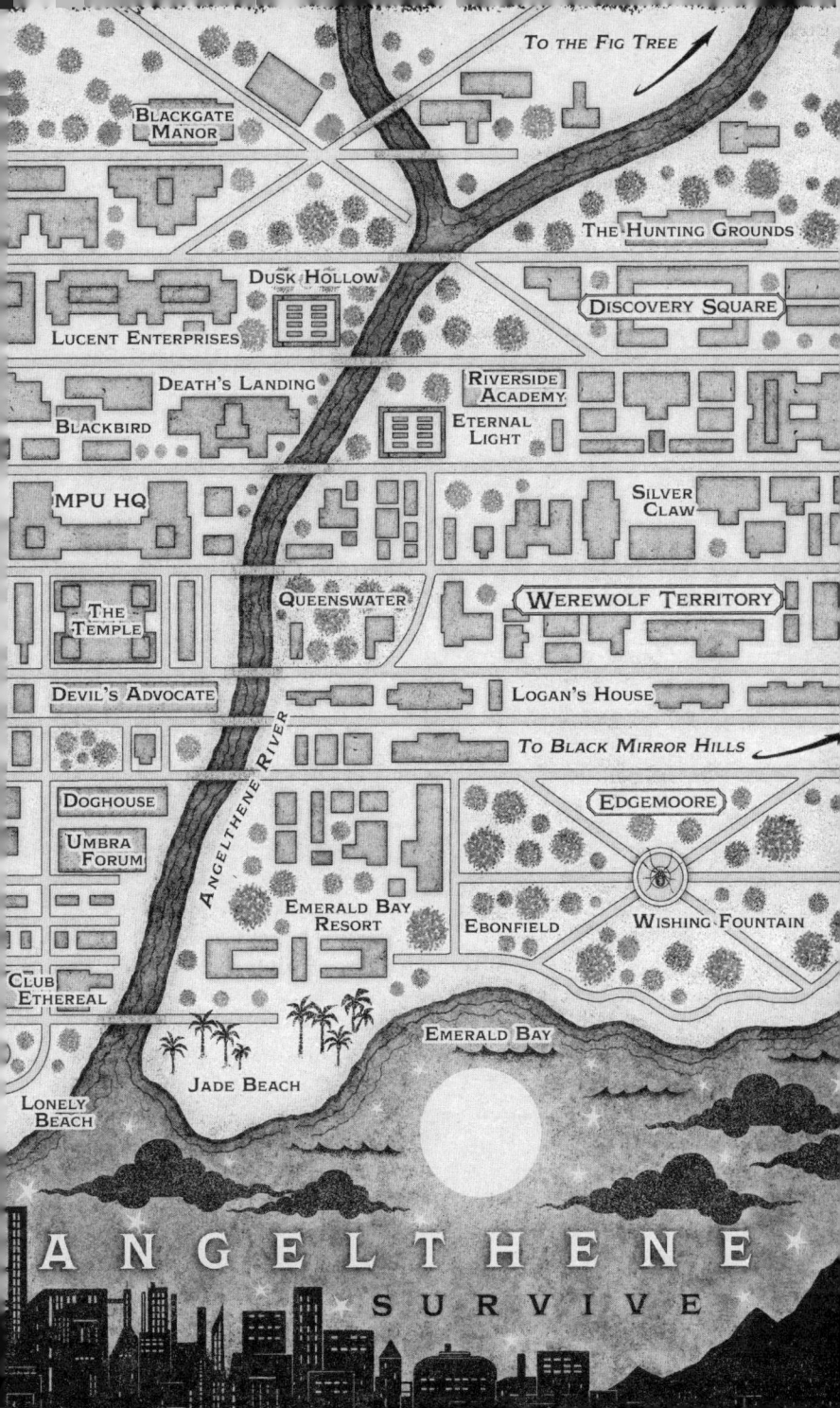

DARKSLAYING CIRCLES OF ANGELTHENE

THE SEVEN DEVILS

Marked with a horned letter S in the gothic script of an ancient world, they answer to Darien Cassel, Head of Hell's Gate

THE REAPERS

Marked with the cloaked and masked God of Death, they answer to Malakai Delaney, Head of the House of Souls and Right Hand of Darien Cassel

THE HUNTSMEN

Marked with a Hellhound, they answer to Lionel Savage, Head of the Hunting Grounds and former Right Hand of Randal Slade

THE ANGELS OF DEATH

Marked with overlapping wings in white ink, they answer to Dominic Valencia, Head of Death's Landing

THE WARGS

Marked with a crescent moon in luminescent ink, they answer to Channary Graves, Head of the House on the Pier

THE VIPERS

Marked with an animated striking serpent, they answer to Jude Monson, Head of the Den of Vipers

---

All Darkslaying circles in Angelthene answer to Darien Cassel, Head of all circles in the city. No one outside of these six circles may operate on Angelthene soil. To do so is punishable by death.

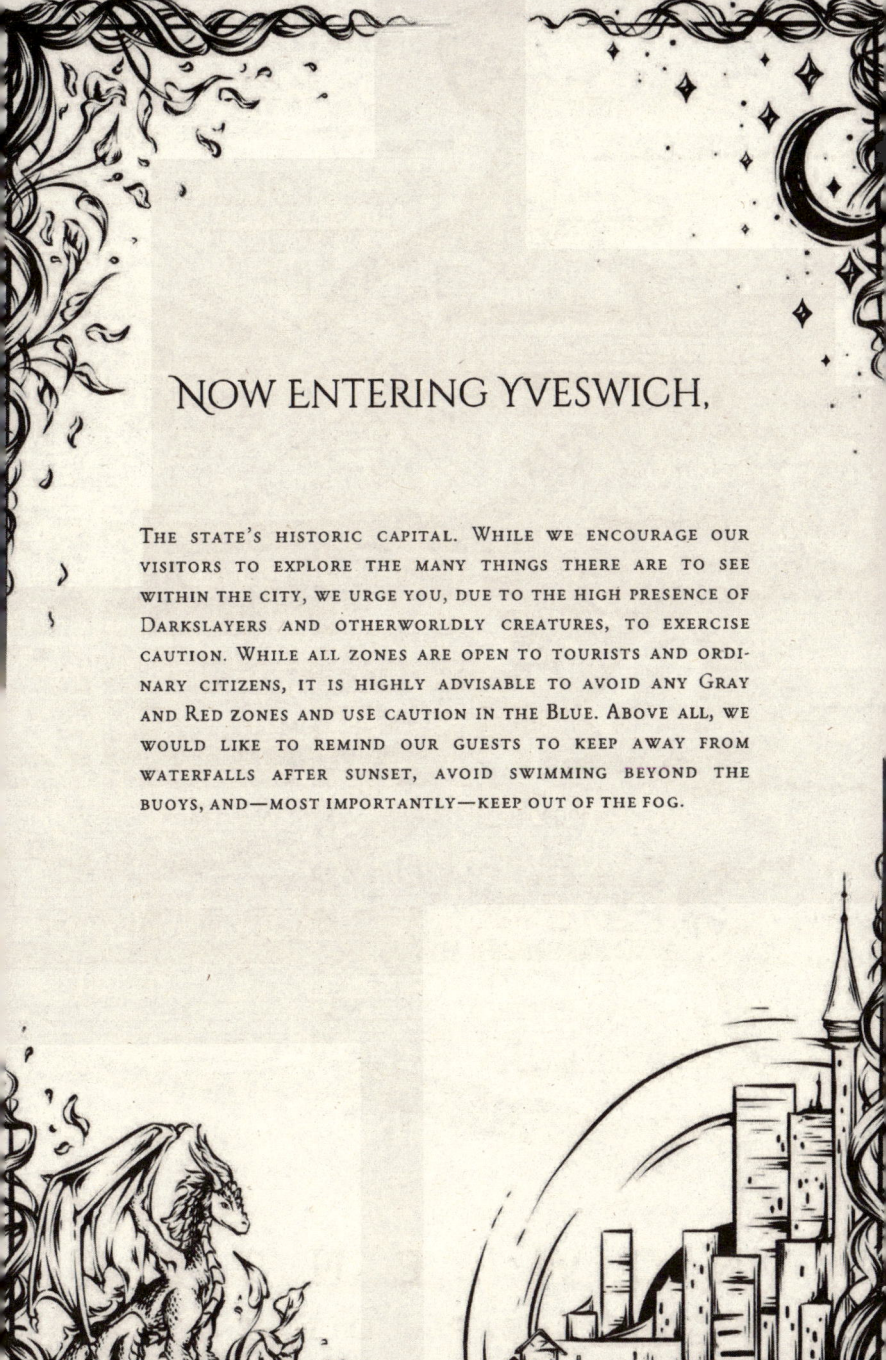

Now Entering Yveswich,

The state's historic capital. While we encourage our visitors to explore the many things there are to see within the city, we urge you, due to the high presence of Darkslayers and otherworldly creatures, to exercise caution. While all zones are open to tourists and ordinary citizens, it is highly advisable to avoid any Gray and Red zones and use caution in the Blue. Above all, we would like to remind our guests to keep away from waterfalls after sunset, avoid swimming beyond the buoys, and—most importantly—keep out of the fog.

DARKSLAYING CIRCLES OF YVESWICH

THE SHADOWMASTERS

Marked with the bleeding black skull of Obitus, god of death and the dying, they answer to Roman 'Shadows' Devlin, Head of the Hollow and the House of Black

In some parts of Terra, they are better known as 'Wraiths'

THE SELKIES

Marked with the teardrop of Caligo, goddess of water, mercy, and rebirth, they answer to Athene Cousens, Head of the Riptide and the House of Blue

---

THE WYVERNS

Marked with the flame of Ignis, goddess of fire and the Seven Circles, they answer to Cerise Brinton, Head of the Dunes and the House of Red

In some parts of Terra, they are better known as 'Flameweavers'

THE JACKALS

Marked with the eye of Tempus the Liar, outcast of the Terran pantheon and god of time, they answer to Griffin Brand, Head of the Labyrinth and the House of Sage

---

THE SYLPHEN

Marked with the white feather of Vita, goddess of the sky and flight, they answer to Raina Cruso, Head of the Eyrie and the House of Violet

---

All Darkslaying circles in Yveswich answer to Donovan Slade, Head of all circles in the city. No one outside of these five circles may operate on Yveswich soil. To do so is punishable by death.

For a full list of characters, flip to the back of the book

This book contains subject matter that might be difficult for some readers, including intense violence, violence against children, brutal injuries, graphic language, discussion of domestic violence, substance use disorder, drug dependence and symptoms of withdrawal, death, gore, suicidal ideation, and physical and psychological torture. This book also contains explicit sexual content. Please read with caution and prepare to return to Angelthene...

ELSEWHERE

In the heart of the universe, in the middle of nowhere, a great tree stood sentinel over a small body of water. While the surrounding land was shrouded in thick darkness and creeping mist, the tree and pond glowed with ethereal light. It filtered through the crystalline branches and teal leaves, casting dappled shadows across the water.

A young woman sat upon the gnarled roots that domed above the pond, the soles of her bare feet skimming the surface of the water as she swung her legs back and forth. Wind stirred her hair, but try as it may, its touch went unfelt. She felt nothing here—not the splash of the water under her feet, not the ridges of the tree bark against her palms, not the tiny legs of the luminescent fireflies as they alighted on her arms and knees.

The strapless dress that hugged her body was colored like an opal, with many small points of shifting color that looked like indecisive stars. The hem that fell to her ankles fluttered as though it were alive, looking every bit as otherworldly as the brooding tree.

There was no sun here, no moon. No way of telling how long she had sat below the shelter of this tree. She might have been content to stay here forever, had her heart not begged for the opposite.

It wanted her to remember, to leave this silent womb of the universe behind. *Go back,* her heart whispered. *You must go back.* Where, she didn't know. Even her own name escaped her. Her age, her past—everything was gone. At first, the fear of her empty mind had been so great that she had nearly succumbed to the force of it. Now, fear was simply another thing that did not exist here. It was just her, the tree, the pond, and an endless, starry night sky. But—

At the very edge of her mind was a face. It was blurry—nothing more than streaks of black and tan, with a smudge of steely blue.

Eyes. Those were eyes. Whoever she was seeing through the foggy lens of her memory had eyes like a stormy sea.

But soon, that face was gone too, just like her memories.

And her heart, just like her mind, went quiet.

PART ONE
THE RIPTIDE

I

OLDTOWN

ANGELTHENE, STATE OF WITHEREDGE

In just over twenty-four years, Darien Cassel had fought and defeated more monsters than he could count.

Except grief. Grief was the worst monster of all.

Twice, it had sunk its claws into him, both wounds so deep that he wondered how the fuck he was still breathing. The first time was when he'd lost his mother. The second was when the love of his life had fallen into a coma.

He recalled that horrible stretch of silence when Loren's heart had stopped beating, remembered how the brightness in her eyes had dulled, every muscle in her beautiful face falling slack as she slipped away from him. The memory was seared into his mind; awake or asleep, he saw it constantly. And every time he saw it, it felt like someone was driving a knife into his heart.

Dead. She'd died that night. Her heart had started again, sure, but she was still gone. She had never woken up.

Darien was still waiting. He would always wait.

For one split second, the memory was so debilitating that he forgot where he was. Forgot that he was in a back alley somewhere in Oldtown, beating the absolute shit out of one of Gaven's men.

Blood sprayed through the air. Bone snapped and cartilage crunched, but he kept hitting, even as the man he was pinning down with a knee to the chest begged between punches for him to stop. The air was hot tonight, the sunset bathing the city of Angelthene in thick, orange light. The heat clung to him like a wool blanket, warming up the black leather of his jacket as he struck—

Someone cleared their throat. Maximus Reacher, who stood with Jack Steele and Travis Devlin near the mouth of the alley, the three Devils observing from afar. The sound was a signal they had agreed upon—a simple noise meant to snap Darien out of a frenzy before he could go one punch too far.

Nights like tonight had become routine. A week straight of hunting, and Darien had no intention of stopping, not until one of these pigs finally squealed and told him where Gaven Payne was hiding.

Darien shook the blood off his right hand and used the left to push the loose strands of his sun-warmed black hair out of his face.

And then he grabbed the man by the collar and yanked his head up off the ground. "Where," Darien whispered, leaning in close to the man's ear, "is Gaven?"

The other targets Darien had tracked down had received a slightly different hand of cards, but the game still ended the same way—in death. Darien had asked those targets a few simple questions before he'd started doling out punches, but his patience had worn thin. Tonight, it was hit first, ask questions later. The monster inside him needed to feed, and it was tired of being caged, tired of being thrown measly scraps and bones.

It wanted flesh. Blood.

"He l-left," the man spluttered, spittle flying from his cut-up lips.

"Left town?" Darien prompted, pulling back a little. He tightened his grip on the man's collar, twisting the blood-dampened fabric with inked fingers.

Another of the poor fuckers he had tracked down had told him the same thing, but as for the others, they had refused to speak, even when Darien and his Devils had gotten a little more creative than usual with their interrogation tactics at the Chopping Block, going so far as to shatter a few knees and remove some limbs. The Butcher had been more than willing to lend Darien the same room as last time—'for the comfort of his victims', Casen had said with a booming laugh.

Gaven would be last. Initially, Darien hadn't planned it this way; all he'd wanted was to find and kill the man responsible for manipulating him and burning Blackbird 88 Above to the ground. But now, with Darien picking off Gaven's men one by one, the prick could see him coming—and was likely pissing himself with fear knowing he only had so much time left.

This was better. More rewarding. More tantalizing to someone with such an appetite for blood.

"Where did Gaven go?" Darien said, studying the man's puffy, blood-soaked face.

He tried to look away, but Darien wrenched his collar, making him whimper. "You're going to tell me where Gaven went," Darien hissed through bared teeth, "and you're going to tell me right now."

"O-okay, okay," the hellseher stuttered, a web of blood thickening his words. "H-he said," a heavy swallow, dark red blood oozing out of his clogged nostrils, "he was going back."

Back to whatever hellhole he'd crawled out of. Running away, maybe. Leaving, before Darien could catch up with him.

Good. It was more information than the others had given him.

Which meant his family would be safe—for now, at least. And even safer once he finished tracking down and slaughtering the last of Gaven's men, if there were any left in Angelthene. If they were smart, they would've already fled, but if this waste of skin pinned under his knee was any indication, they were stupid as could be.

"And where is 'back'?" Darien asked. Magpies squawked out a death prediction on the roof of the consignment store to his left.

"I don't know." His cheeks puffed with labored breaths. Both of his hands were broken, fingers bent and scabbed. Darien had taken his sweet time snapping all ten. "He never told me."

Darien drew a switchblade, his other hand still fisting the man's collar—holding him in place in case he tried anything stupid. "You sure about that?"

He flicked open the blade.

The coward's eyes widened, his pupils dilating as they fixed on the knife, the edge of that blade glinting in a streak of sunlight. *"Yes!"* he exclaimed, his voice cracking. "I swear it, I swear to you—he didn't tell me shit! I swear on my life, I've told you everything I know! *Please!*"

Darien let go of the man's collar with a shove. "Thank you," he whispered.

A tremor wracked the man's body. "Will you set me free now?"

"A promise is a promise, isn't it?" It certainly was.

He slashed the hellseher's throat.

Freedom—but in death instead of life.

The man's back arched in agony, the back of his head grinding into concrete, feet thumping. The sounds of his suffering sliced through the alley, the gurgling and gasping enough to make anyone physically ill. Anyone other than Darien—and the men watching from several feet away. Anyone who wasn't sick in the fucking head.

With a stare as dead as he felt, Darien watched his target fight for oxygen. Watched him die, just like he had the others. With mangled fingers, his victim clawed at his gushing throat in a feeble attempt to pinch it shut. A sea of red spread across the ground and seeped into Darien's knees, the black denim of his pants lapping it up like a thirsty beast.

It didn't take long before the man's body went limp. His hands collapsed to the ground, his bloodstained fingers curling with one final spasm. His aura dimmed like a lightbulb, until not one speck of color was left.

The smell of blood choked the air. The magpies quieted down.

And the monster inside him laid down to rest, its hunger sated once more.

Darien shut his eyes and tipped back his head, breathing in deeply through his nose as a rush of sick satisfaction crackled through his veins. He sensed the others watching, their concern hanging in the air, heavy as the heat, but he didn't turn.

Slaying gave him a high stronger than any drug. Spilling blood had always been his most addicting thrill, but in the ten days that had passed since Loren was admitted to the hospital, he had become more dependent on it than ever.

Without it, he didn't feel alive. With it, he felt vile. His self-loathing had reached a boiling point, and he avoided mirrors more than ever now.

At least the hatred he felt for himself was better than feeling nothing.

2

THE HOSPITAL
ANGELTHENE, STATE OF WITHEREDGE

Maximus Reacher had spent so much time in Angelthene General Hospital these past few days that he was beginning to forget what Hell's Gate looked like.

The hospital staff had moved Loren to a different room under Darien's command. She was on the fourth floor of the Healer's ward, her door facing a quiet waiting area where Max and the other Devils took turns keeping watch. But tonight, Max wasn't here to keep watch.

His boots pounded as he neared the ward. The hallways were quiet, save for a handful of exhausted nurses and Healers, who nodded in greeting. It had been an adjustment, but the staff had grown used to seeing Max and the others—not just the Seven Devils, but also the few Angels of Death and Reapers who popped in. They no longer gawked or stuttered over their words, though they still chose to keep their distance, their attempts at making conversation short-lived and half-hearted.

The edge of the curved desk that occupied a large portion of the waiting area came into view. Five steps later, Max rounded the corner.

Eight plastic chairs were set up along the perimeter of the room. Two were occupied.

Tanner Atlas was slouched by the windows, his ringed thumbs flicking across his phone screen. The music tinkling through the speakers told Max he was playing that same old frog game again.

In the chair closest to the vending machine sat Dallas Bright. The witch was fast asleep, an open bag of candy-covered chocolates in her loose grip, her Fleet wings draped across the empty chairs on either side of her. The steady rise and fall of her stomach threatened to scatter the candies across the floor.

Tanner looked up, blinking the glaze out of bloodshot eyes. "Hey."

Max gestured to Dallas. "Did she go to class today?"

Tanner's grimace was enough of an answer.

Max sighed. "Her parents are going to kill her if she keeps missing class." Not to mention training with the Fleet. Had Dallas's parents been anyone other than Roark and Taega—anyone *decent*—they would've been empathetic toward their daughter, would have even slept here, in this waiting area, the way Dallas had done so often, showing their support not just for their biological daughter, but the one they'd adopted too.

He sighed again and studied Dallas's sleeping form. Her copper eyelashes twitched, the thick hair she wore in an unruly knot atop her head fluttering in a draft of cool air blowing from a vent.

Her tangled, hadn't-been-washed-in-days hair. Even asleep, she looked exhausted. Ever since Loren had wound up in the hospital, Dallas only slept when she passed out, her body giving her no other choice. It was the reason Max was here right now: if Dallas was going to refuse to take care of herself, then *he* would take care of her.

Max closed the short distance to her chair. He looked down at her, waiting for her to wake up, but she didn't stir. He brushed a strand of hair off her face, the task made difficult by the patch of drool drying near the corner of her mouth.

Dallas jerked awake. "What—" Her bag of candy fell, spilling its contents across the floor. Witch Whoppers clattered and rolled, the noise causing one of the receptionists to peek over the desk.

Max turned in the direction the candies were rolling—

And saw Darien heading this way. He didn't slow down, nor make eye contact, not even when a couple of the candies bumped into his boots.

Darien had stopped at Hell's Gate to shower and change into a clean hooded sweatshirt and jeans. There wasn't one drop of blood on him, not even on his boots—a different pair than the ones he wore to collect or fight. It was one of the few requests the hospital staff had been daring enough to voice: that they come to the Healers ward dressed in clothes that were as clean as possible. Blood was a big, fat 'no', but expecting Darkslayers not to have *any* blood on them was...kind of laughable, really.

Max understood why, though. This part of the hospital was full of Tricking patients with heavily compromised immune systems, some on ventilators, others fed by IV lines. New strains of the Tricking were appearing almost weekly, so it was because of this and the rising number of cases that the Healers had been forced to make adjustments.

It was either that or the staff was trying their best to make the visiting Darkslayers appear less frightening for the other patients.

As if clean clothes had anything to do with that.

Darien disappeared into Loren's room without a backward glance.

"How's he doing?" Tanner asked, taking care to keep his voice down.

Max sighed. "How do you think?" he mouthed.

He had never seen Darien so...empty. And he'd known him for a long time—practically his whole life. Darien was now a shell of himself, but he wasn't brittle like one. If anything, Loren being in a coma had forged him into something else, something more dangerous than the old Darien, if that were even possible. He was a newly honed weapon still glowing red, his edges sharper than ever before.

Max had to admit, it scared him, and he wasn't the only one who felt this way. When Ivy had come to him two nights ago needing to vent, she had surprised him by speaking his thoughts aloud. She felt as hopeless as Max—as hopeless as *all* the Devils. Hopeless and utterly desperate to help Darien but not knowing how. All they could do was be there for him as best as they could. Even when there was nothing to say, nothing to do but listen if Darien was willing to speak, or sit with him in silence if he wasn't.

Dallas scrubbed her hands over her face and sat up. "How long was I out?" With a big yawn, she stretched her arms and fanned out her wings.

Max looked at Tanner for the answer.

The hacker shrugged. "Two hours, maybe?" He flashed them his phone screen, where pixelated frogs snatched flies into their mouths with pink tongues. "I've been busy."

Dallas glanced in longing at the Witch Whoppers scattered across the floor, a couple of them having already been crushed by the shoes of Healers bustling by. "I didn't even get to eat any of those," she mumbled, her eyes still watering from her yawn.

Her attention abruptly shifted to something—or someone—behind Max. She stiffened, the silver in her eyes flashing once before dimming.

Max turned, reaching for the gun that was tucked into his back waistband.

He froze at the sight of the man coming down the hallway.

The amber eyes. The tall, proud form. The harsh face. The swept-back hair, the smooth strands the same shade of polished copper as Dallas's.

Was he dreaming? Because Roark Bright was heading for Loren's room.

Hell if he was going to let *this* happen tonight.

Max crossed the room, hand drifting toward his gun again.

Was he really going to shoot the Red Baron? Gods, it would probably feel good as hell.

"What the hell do you think you're doing here?" Max's voice lashed out like a whip in the dead silence.

"Max!" Dallas hissed, stumbling out of her chair.

Max stepped in Roark's path before he could reach Loren's open door, his gun burning a hole in the waistband of his cargo pants.

The Red Baron slowed his pace to a smooth stop. "I need to have a word with Darien." His stare settled on Max, the reluctance in the action tangible.

Max's hand twitched toward his pistol again. "I'm not letting you in there."

Roark's upper lip curled like he'd stepped in dog shit. "Those are bold words to use on a general."

"That's a shit tone to use on a Darkslayer," Max countered. "If you set foot in that room, Darien will eat you alive, so you can either tell *me* what you want, or you can get the hell out." It may seem like an overreaction, but this man hadn't bothered to check in on Loren all goddamn week, and neither had Taega. He couldn't imagine what it had been like for the poor girl while growing up.

Same with the one standing at his side.

Erasmus, on the other hand, had tried to visit Loren several times, but Darien refused to let Erasmus—or *anyone,* really—get anywhere close to his girl, least of all the father who'd failed her, time and again. Max couldn't blame Darien for acting this way, but once in a while he'd feel a twinge of pity for the old guy. Sometimes, the man slept in the waiting area until Cyra came and urged him to go home. Two days had passed since Erasmus had last been here, two days since anyone had so much as heard from him or Cyra—two days since Darien had lost his temper and literally pulled a gun on Erasmus.

He'd left, of course. Literally ran out of the hospital as fast as his age would let him. Darien hadn't fired any shots, but with the way things were going, with no sign of Loren waking up, it was best if Erasmus stayed away.

Roark glanced at his biological daughter—just for a second. Not long enough to really *see* her—to see how gaunt and pale her face had become, how tired her eyes looked.

"Give us a minute, Dallas." Roark's dismissal was brusque.

Max grabbed Dallas by the wrist before she could step away, his thumb pressing on her racing pulse. "You've been telling her to give you a minute for the past twenty years," he growled at the Red Baron. "That's *her* family in that room, and if what you have to say has anything to do with Loren, then it's just as much Dallas's business as it is ours. She *stays.*"

Landlines droned with incoming calls. The receptionists let them ring, which meant they now had an audience.

Roark's eyes flicked toward the desk. Aside from a lone muscle ticking in his clean-shaven jaw, he showed zero emotion. No surprise there.

Max was debating blasting him in the head when Roark spoke.

"I know of a way we might be able to wake Loren up."

Max blinked. Well, *that* was unexpected.

Dallas stepped forward. "How?" Max knew the fresh skip in her pulse didn't have anything to do with her asshole of a dad.

A shadow moved in Max's periphery.

Darien filled the doorframe. He didn't say anything, his face sharper than shattered glass. He hardly spoke at all anymore. Never smiled, and sure as Ignis's tits never laughed.

When Max addressed Darien, he kept his voice down. "Roark thinks he knows how we can wake Loren up."

For several minutes, the Red Baron and the Devil sized each other up. With the two of them standing across from each other like that, Roark looked...small. Insignificant. Then again, Darien tended to have that effect on a lot of people.

Roark's attention strayed to the room that was partially blocked by Darien's menacing form.

And the girl lying unconscious on the bed inside.

Darien didn't move a muscle, but that perpetual threat in his eyes deepened. If Max hadn't known him so well, that deadly look would've made him hightail it out of the hospital—maybe even hightail it out of the goddamn city and never come back.

Darien had been dangerous his whole life—there was no doubt about that. But as a man in love, he was lethal.

The last of Roark's hesitation vanished as his attention returned to Darien. This time, there was no disdain in the Red Baron's stare, not even when the look Darien gave him in return was so sharp it would have sent a lesser man running.

Roark drew a deep breath. "You would have to go to Yveswich."

3

SIDUS

YVESWICH, STATE OF KER

Roman Devlin's equivalent to counting sheep was counting rabbits. Not the kind you bought from a pet store or chased out of your vegetable garden with a broom.

These rabbits were Darkslaying messengers. According to old stories, the first person to seek out a hellseher and hire them for a job wore a rabbit mask to hide their identity. The masks had instantly caught on, and soon the tradition had spread to every corner of Terra.

Here in Yveswich, there were more messengers than the local Darkslayers could keep up with. Endless messengers touting endless Darkslaying jobs in exchange for endless money, and still the city's crime level was at an all-time high.

While most people considered this a problem in immediate need of fixing, Darkslayers like Roman saw it as a good thing. More crime meant more money, more ways of entertaining his overactive mind. More ways of staying sane—or as close to sane as a person like Roman 'Shadows' Devlin could get.

"Twenty-two...," Roman murmured. He sat on the edge of the rooftop of the Onyx Skull, a nightclub with the best strippers in the city, his eyes shining with the black of the Sight as he scanned the district far below the soles of his dangling feet. This here was a Gray Zone—a section of the city owned and operated by the members of the Hollow. "Twenty-three..."

The rabbit masks in Yveswich were black instead of the white commonly found in other cities. The masks owed their dark shade to the rare material from which they were crafted, the magic in the masks allowing them to be seen with a hellseher's Sight. Inanimate objects didn't typically show up in a hellseher's vision—not unless they had some form of energy running through them, or were in contact with something that did, something that contained enough energy to spread beyond itself. Clothes were a good example; no matter how bright or strong the aura of the person who wore them, Roman never could see clothes.

He studied one of the masks now, watching the way the messenger's aura threaded through the material in bands of dull color. This messenger moved with apprehension—new to the job, probably. She walked the shadowed streets roughly four blocks from here, hoping for a Darkslayer to seek her out and accept the job she had to offer.

A different one caught Roman's eye, this one ducking in and out of buildings farther north. She passed under a mercury vapor street light, her mask reflecting green.

"Twenty-four..."

Roman knew it was a strange way to relax: counting rabbits on the rooftop of a nightclub, music thumping at his back. But *he* was strange, and so he did strange things.

The door that led into the club clanged open behind him, setting free the clamor of drunken voices, blaring song lyrics, and clinking glasses.

"There's a messenger here to see you," came a male voice.

How bold.

Roman kept his focus on the glimmering streets below. *Twenty-five... Twenty-six...*

The tangled streets of Yveswich were old and narrow, some of them seeming to meander without direction. In all its years since the city had been built, very little pavement had replaced the cobbles, and most of the buildings were so ancient they seemed to lean toward each other, gossiping about centuries past. The city had been built on sharply elevated terrain, and there was an abundance of waterfalls, the rapids draining into canals that bled into the nearby ocean. The waterfalls brought in droves of starry-eyed tourists year-round—thousands of souls foaming at the mouth for a glimpse of the unmatched beauty of the rapids.

The locals were smart enough not to fall for that trap. More waterfalls meant more Hounds—more monsters in general. And more monsters meant higher death tolls.

Tourists made up most of those deaths.

"Have Kylar take care of it," Roman clipped.

"She said her boss asked specifically for you."

Roman turned to look at Otto. He was a hellseher and a member of the

Hollow, someone who assisted the Shadowmasters in running the Gray districts and the many businesses within. "Who is she? You seen her around before?"

Otto shook his head. "Probably another new hire."

Not surprising. With too many messengers and not enough Darkslayers, the competition often led to an influx of turnovers. And, thanks to the turnovers, a lot of newbies toed the line of disrespect when interacting with Darkslayers, desperate to earn a job for their bosses so they could see a cut of that wealth.

No one had ever dared toe that line with Roman.

He got to his feet. The act of turning his back on the sheer drop to the street below sent a thrill of excitement up his spine. Maybe tomorrow he'd find a building to jump off of—one high enough to feed his appetite for adrenaline, but not quite high enough to kill him.

It was always the jumps that teetered on the brink of life and death that gave him the most satisfying rush.

Otto held the door open for him.

"Where?" Roman demanded as he descended the stairwell. Voices and music swelled to a cacophony, swallowing up the pounding of his charcoal combat boots.

"By the bar." The door clanged shut as Otto followed behind him. "I told her to wait by the Hollow Eyes sign."

The Onyx Skull was one of countless businesses that fed Roman's wallet, so between this and the simple fact that he was a Shadowmaster walking a Gray Zone, people gave him a wide berth. No amount of drugs or alcohol could make them stupid enough to get in the way of the Wolf of the Hollow.

As Roman crossed the room, he caught sight of four Shadowmasters standing in a group by the stage. Willow Adams and Kylar Lavin worked directly under him—the only two Shadowmasters who didn't first answer to his dad. The other two—Blaine and Larina, brother and sister—only came around when Donovan requested they keep an eye on him. Roman had decided he hated Blaine the moment he met him, and he'd quickly learned that his sister was just as awful. The only thing Larina had going for her was her looks—beautiful, blonde, and blue-eyed, the three B's most men fell to their knees over. The rest of her was as poisonous as cyanide.

Roman tore his eyes off the group and focused on the job at hand, trusting Kylar and Willow to get rid of those two within the hour.

Colorful lights oscillated through the smoky gloom of the building. Hundreds of people crowded the dance floor, their bodies oiled with sweat, eyes bleary with substance abuse. Everyone present was here because they wanted to be, so even if the rabbit messenger would've drifted from her post, she would've been easy for Roman to pick out in the crowd, simply due to the way she held herself.

She stood under a white neon sign featuring a pair of watchful eyes, hands gripping the straps of her backpack. Her posture was terrible—toes pointed inward, shoulders slumped. Her black rabbit mask and plain, all-black outfit gleamed under the strobe lights. The string that held the mask to her face had mussed up her hair—a thick and wavy fall of strawberry-blonde frizz that likely hadn't seen a brush in days.

Her head snapped his way as he approached, though she didn't budge an inch from her spot against the wall. Her shoulders curled forward, as if anticipating a punch to the stomach. Pathetic.

Roman stopped several feet from her, and Otto took his leave with a respectful dip of his chin. Roman assessed the rabbit messenger, wondering how much of his time she was going to waste before she finally spit out her words.

"Are you Roman?" The messenger's voice was high and timid, and although the mask hid the entirety of her face, Roman could feel her eyes on the small tattoo high up on his cheek.

"Breed, payment, and whereabouts," he instructed.

"Hound." Her voice was quiet; he had to strain to hear her. "One hundred thousand gold mynet. The canals on West Montgomery."

"One hundred thousand is a Green's pay," he said. "Grays charge double, and I charge triple."

Her hands twisted the straps of her backpack with a white-knuckled grip. "Three hundred thousand?"

"You know basic math," Roman clipped. She shrank back, hair slipping over one shoulder. "Yes or no?"

Her head bobbed. "Y-yes."

"My clients are to pay in full at the time of the agreement. Is your boss aware?"

Another nod.

Roman took out his phone. The messenger mirrored him, her hands trembling.

"Cold?" Roman smirked.

A light passed over them, turning her mask a vibrant shade of purple, the sharp grooves that accentuated the eyes sparkling.

"Nervous," she mumbled, bumping her phone against his. A beep sounded, indicating the wire transfer.

"At least you're honest." He glanced at the screen, making sure the right amount was there, and pocketed his phone. "Meet me back here tomorrow night. I'm assuming your boss wants the head?" It was the most valuable body part, but once in a while a client wanted more. A claw, the spine, sometimes the poisonous barbs on the tail—all ingredients for certain spells and potions. They fetched lower prices and catered to a limited clientele, but it was worth it for some, if the demand was there.

She gave another nod.

And then she paused, leaning forward a hair's breadth. Roman felt her attention on the pendants glimmering in the hollow of his throat. One in particular—and that made him stiffen.

"Is that the Skull of Obitus?"

"No," Roman lied, and walked away.

IN A BACK ALLEY in the district of West Montgomery, behind a thick wall of fog, Roman slayed the Hound.

The monster put up a good fight—they always did—but in the end it was no match for him. By the time he cut off its head, he had hardly worked up a sweat.

Blood sprayed as the head thumped to the ground. The body followed a moment later, crumpling like a boneless sack of flesh. The blood draining from the neck sizzled like acid as it trickled between the cobbles.

Roman took a moment to catch his breath. He pocketed his blade and wiped the lone drop of sweat off his forehead with the back of his wrist.

The alley was dark, the only street light on the block too far away to reach him. The fog was so dense, he could barely see the corpse of the Hound bleeding out on the street as he retrieved the canvas bag from the back pocket of his gray jeans and shook it open.

Tonight's fog was different than the kind that warranted the blaring of a civil defense siren. While just as utterly blinding, this fog was otherwise harmless. But the kind that caused city officials to sound an alarm? Now *that* was the type of fog that prompted every citizen in the area to get inside and *stay* inside. Even people as crazy as Roman knew better than to step outside during a fog warning.

Dropping into a crouch before the slain monster, Roman reached for the head with a gloved hand—

And froze. It was gone.

The hair on his scalp prickled with a warning.

He wasn't alone.

Adrenaline sparked in his veins, making him smile like a wolf. Oh, this was going to be *good*.

Slowly, Roman lifted himself to his feet. As he surveyed the soup of fog and darkness swirling around him, that predatory smile spread across his face until it was more a hungry baring of teeth.

"Little pig, little pig," he drawled, his husky voice growing louder with every word he sang. *"Come on outtttt!"*

Nothing. It seemed he'd stumbled into a game, and he had every intention of playing.

He walked slowly. Soundlessly. Turning in place, he picked apart the alley with eyes that were now black with the Sight. There was no aura, but he could feel that someone was here. Watching him.

Movement on his left.

Roman struck—not with his body, but with his magic. His shadows.

He could command the darkness as he saw fit, and his command tonight was for the shadows of the alley to apprehend this nosey little pig.

A tendril of blackness slashed through the air. It grabbed hold of an ankle, causing whoever it was to trip. They—*she* grunted and fell.

Roman reeled those shadows in, dragging the female back this way—

And slammed her up against the brick wall. Whoever it was, she gurgled and squirmed—his victims always did. And they always begged before he gutted them like fish.

A faint trickle of moonlight cut through the fog, and Roman stepped into it, shadows wreathing his fingers. "What do we have here?"

He paused. Cocked his head.

It was the rabbit messenger. The strawberry blonde who'd hired him not one gods-damned hour ago.

"Bold little bunny," Roman drawled. He glanced at the bag she'd dropped—the one containing the severed head of the Hound—and clucked his tongue. "Thieving little bunny."

The rabbit struggled, thrashing against the shadowy restraints. She smelled like apples—those green ones that were so sour they made him want to shave off his tastebuds.

"I didn't know you could—" She writhed and bucked, but his shadows didn't yield. "Control them," she concluded, panting.

A thrill of pleasure skittered up Roman's spine at the sight of her breasts rising with every inhale, at the sound of her pulse skipping like a flat stone on water. Fear, most likely. Maybe even a touch of excitement, if the feel of her aura was any indication. Both were turn-ons for him. Was she enjoying this?

Roman stepped up to where she was pinned. She tried to shrink away from his advance, but his shadows gave her no leeway. A wisp of black snaked around her throat, squeezing tight.

Her gulp carried through the alley. The sound made Roman smile—and his smile made the bunny hold her breath.

He was close enough now to touch her, to kill her. She knew it too—he could tell from her reluctance to expel the air from her lungs.

"They call me 'Shadowmaster' for a reason," Roman said, watching the freckled skin on her chest pebble with goosebumps. "How can I be the master of something if I cannot control it?"

He plucked the mask off her face.

Eyes the prettiest shade of green stared back at him. There was a split in her left iris, one portion a darker green than the other. With her sneakers dangling nearly three feet above ground, her head was slightly higher than his. Her brows, the same strawberry blonde as her hair, were straighter than they were arched, her mouth full, jawline soft. There were freckles all over her face, too, and just below her right eye was—

A small tattoo. A raindrop.

Roman's face twisted with a scowl. "You're a Selkie." He flung the mask over his shoulder. With a baring of teeth, he growled, "What are you doing working a Gray Zone?"

"None of your business."

He tightened his shadows around her wrists and ankles, splaying her limbs like a starfish. "No one talks to me like that." She was a doll on strings, and no doll was going to mouth him off like this.

"Looks like I just did."

"What do you want?"

"I wanted that Hound." Those brilliant green eyes flicked to the beheaded monster. The color was so bright and clear, her face so unthreatening, it was hard to picture this girl wearing the black of the Sight. A part of him wanted to see it—this pretty face with black eyes instead of green.

"Why not hunt your own?" Yveswich had more than enough Hounds to go around. Why was she insisting on pestering him?

She winced, her fingers spreading as the whips of his shadows flexed, digging into her pale flesh like wires. By the time she answered him, Roman had already figured it out. "I'm not strong enough," she muttered.

He smirked. Not strong enough, nor big enough to handle a Hound. What was she, five feet fuck-all? Pathetic little thing. Soft, too, by the looks of her, not nearly enough muscle on her frame to justify her occupation as a Darkslayer. Which meant—

There was only one slayer in the city who couldn't take down a Hound on her own.

"You're Shay."

She tensed, her stony expression lit up by a flash of lightning. A mist of rain started to fall, dampening Roman's dark hair.

"The 'miserable little wallflower', they call you. The 'baby seal of the Riptide'." Those were the nicer of the nicknames she'd earned. As the newest member of the Riptide, Shay Cousens had very few friends—aside from her sister, but siblings didn't count, not in the way that mattered. If anything, they were seen as a crutch—an undeserved boost to the top. As the eldest of three brothers, Roman knew that better than anyone.

Shay Cousens was an outcast.

Kind of like him, if he cared to admit it.

"I've heard a lot about you too, Roman Devlin."

Fuck, the way she said his name made him feel...weird. Like his skin was suddenly too tight.

Her ginger lashes dipped as her eyes skirted down his body. The longer she looked at him, the quicker her heart moved. "Some say you're a sadist," she went on. "Others claim it's a front—that you're not as unstable as you pretend to be."

"What do you believe?"

"I believe it's a bit of both." When her attention returned to his face, she angled her head like a bird, not seeming to care that his shadows were still forming a noose around her throat. "How do you plan on killing me, Shadows?"

Roman's jaw flexed as he watched a raindrop roll down her cheek.

Something about the way she'd voiced her question sounded more like an invitation than the kind of fearful inquiry a victim might ask her perpetrator. Was *he* in charge here, or was she?

He'd never had to ask himself that question before.

Roman gave her a cold smile. "I'm not going to kill you." No—for her, he had something much worse in mind than an easy kill. The shadows pinning her to the wall unraveled. "I'm going to send you back to the Riptide empty-handed." Back to the tyrant known as *Athene Cousens* empty-handed.

For a moment, Roman kept the shadows that were around her throat in place, listening to her heart stutter. Watched her choke, gag—just for a second. He was into that—breath-play. The kinkier the better. And maybe he was just plain fucking horny tonight, but he swore this bunny liked it too.

Roman reined in the last of his power, the tendrils of darkness melting into the alley.

The Selkie dropped and stumbled forward. She planted her palm on the wet ground to push herself back up, keeping her bright eyes on him all the while. Her breathing was shallow and rapid. Almost too rapid.

Was she faking it—her fear? It would be a first.

No, there was a definite skip in her pulse—hard to fake. That, and her aura had taken on a malleable feel that frequently accompanied submission. And auras never lied. Not without the aid of an illicit drug, anyway, and his intuition told him she wasn't on any.

"If I catch you anywhere near a Gray Zone again, seal pup, I will skin you alive. Understand?"

"Y-yes."

He leaned in, getting close enough to make her flatten her back against the wall. "Leave me alone," he whispered.

Head down, arms now hugging her middle, she inched away, staying as far from him as possible, and scurried down the alley, picking up her backpack as she went.

Roman watched her disappear around the corner—watched her glance over her shoulder at him, her long, thick hair fanning out with the movement.

And then she was gone, the pattering of her feet swallowed up by rain and thunder.

He shook his head. "Yeah, you're a pup, alright." She was bold, he had to give her credit for that. But she had no claws—only flippers. The few rumors about Shayla Cousens had proven true, but they'd failed to mention that she had a clever streak.

His boots swished through puddles of mud as he strode over to the canvas bag the Selkie had dropped. He stooped down, thunder rumbling overhead, and picked up the rain-dampened bag. Gods, these things stunk. They were his least favorite monsters to hunt, but they brought in fat pay cheques.

He was about to call it a night when something made him pause.

There was no blood on the canvas. And that tart scent, the one he hadn't noticed a moment ago, thanks to the Hound's corpse steaming in the rain—

He undid the drawstrings.

The bag was filled with apples—green ones.

Roman's scalp prickled.

When he pulled his phone out of his pocket to check the wire transfer, what he saw was so absurd, he couldn't even feel angry about it.

His account balance had dropped...by exactly three hundred thousand gold mynet.

Roman's cold laugh scraped against the alley walls. He tipped his head back with a groan, hand raking down his face. "Well, fuck me sideways," he muttered. "I've been played."

What else did she take? The question shot into his mind like a bolt of lightning—one of those random afterthoughts that usually didn't deserve an answer.

But his stomach dipped like he was in an elevator.

What else did she take?...

Roman patted his pockets, feeling for his wallet and keys. Both were exactly where they should be.

That dipping feeling came back as his hand flew to the chains he wore around his neck.

One was missing—the most important one. Not the bleeding black skull of Obitus, the pendant she had feigned interest in at the nightclub.

The pendant she had feigned interest in while she'd taken the time to inspect the piece of jewelry that had *really* caught her eye.

His face hardened into stone.

She was good. *Too* good.

A female voice spoke from within Roman's shadow. '*This is what happens when you let a pair of big goo-goo eyes distract you,*' Sayagul, his dragon Familiar, accused with a squawk and a hiss.

He hurled the bag into the shadows. It cracked against the wall, apples rolling out in pieces. Damn rights, he'd been played.

Roman groaned again, his hands squeezing into fists so tight his knuckles popped. "This isn't funny anymore," he growled.

4

THE HOSPITAL
ANGELTHENE, STATE OF WITHEREDGE

Darien stood at the foot of Loren's bed, arms folded across his chest, as he surveyed Roark, who stood facing him in the small room.

The Red Baron's wings were tucked away with a spell tonight, no trace of them visible. His distant, icy expression was exactly what Darien had expected from someone like him, but there was something about the man's aura that Darien had *not* predicted—an emotion his sixth sense could barely pick up on, that was how buried it was.

Roark Bright was hurting—for the girl lying behind Darien on that cold, uncomfortable bed. It was such a rare emotion for a man like Roark that Darien wondered if he was reading him correctly.

He decided he would allow Roark's next move to answer that question. Darien hoped, for the Red Baron's sake, that he had something to say that was worth his time, something worth the small but dangerous flame that had sparked inside his chest the moment Max had uttered that handful of words.

Roark thinks he knows how we can wake Loren up.

Fuck, if that wasn't enough to get his heart going again. This was the most alive he'd felt in ten days, and the contrast between now and before was staggering. Since the night Loren had said his name for the very last time, Darien had been on a downward spiral to madness, and now...now, he didn't know what to think.

Every day that passed was harder than the one that came before it. Whenever Darien inhaled, it felt like he had a bunch of glass in his lungs.

Now that she was gone, everything hurt—hurt so much more than it ever had in the years before he'd met and fallen for her. Physical pain was a drug for him—same as killing. But this? This glass-in-lungs sensation, this...this fucking *raw*, peeling soul...

He had no words for it.

Darien's attention flicked to Max, who entered the room next, followed by Dallas and Tanner.

"Shut the door," Darien said.

The hacker, looking equal parts intrigued and confused, closed the door and leaned back against it with crossed arms. Dallas took up position beside Max, her eyes bright with hope.

Darien's next command was for Max. "Spells, please."

Max acknowledged him with a sharp dip of his chin. A single, heavy blink darkened his eyes with the Sight as he pushed a wall of magic outside of his body, forming a sound barrier around the room.

Darien checked the magic for apertures with his own Sight. Only once he was certain that no one could hear them did he risk speaking to the Red Baron.

"What's so special about Yveswich?" Darien demanded.

"Caliginous chambers," was Roark's only reply. No elaboration—nothing. His amber eyes flicked to the monitor displaying Loren's heartbeat.

Darien drew a calming breath. Once he'd leashed the monster stirring inside him, the thing already hungering for more blood, he said, "Caliginous chambers are for *draining* magic."

Roark tore his attention off the array of equipment keeping Loren alive. "Those chambers are the most common, yes." The reply was loaded, and the time it took Roark to expand upon his statement made Darien's palms itch with the need to strike something. But he waited, every beep of the ECG machine cooling his blood.

For Loren. He had to stay level-headed for Loren. If he fucked this up, there was no telling if Roark would speak to them again.

"There is...another type of chamber," Roark finally explained. "One that has been kept secret from the general public." He drew a deep breath and clasped his hands before him. "While the most common type of chamber is used to drain magic, there is another that does the opposite. It funnels magic into a person's body instead of drawing it out."

"For what purpose?" Darien had a solid idea, but he was tired of guessing. And this man, who had been known as *Elix Danik* in a different life, had made them guess way too many times.

"The Fleet has utilized these chambers during wartime. As you can imagine, a person's magic gets spent very quickly when on the battlefield. The chambers have proven useful in helping restore depleted magic levels, allowing us to fight longer—"

"Wait," Darien interrupted. The monster inside him stirred again, and he felt a warning prickle up his spine, the edges of his vision flickering with the threat of a Surge. "Loren's human. Her body isn't built to handle magic." He gestured behind him with frustration—at the girl whose every breath tore him the fuck apart.

Breathing, but not living—that's what this was. And Roark spoke of Fleet soldiers, the most powerful people—aside from Darkslayers—in all of Terra. Not a mortal girl.

That glass-in-lungs feeling was back, but this time the shards were on fire.

"Right." Roark spoke with a surprising level of patience. "Which is the number one risk to trying this. Even magic-born people can have trouble with this chamber. If their body isn't strong enough to handle the chamber's supply of magic, their heart can give out."

Loren's body already couldn't handle magic, which was how she had gotten into this mess in the first place. She'd used her magic to seal the rip into the realm of the dead, and the amount it had demanded of her had stopped her heart. But...

He thought it through.

There had never been anyone like Loren before. She was human, sure, but she was also born from the Arcanum Well. And if there was even the slightest chance that this would work...

Darien needed her. Call him selfish, but he needed her more than he needed anything. She was his sun, and if he didn't have her, he'd be swallowed by the dark.

"Where is this chamber?" Max asked. "What's it called?"

Roark kept his eyes on Darien, refusing to look at his daughter's boyfriend. "The Fleet calls it the 'Reverse Chamber'. You would need to go to Caliginous on Silverway, on Yveswich's neutral ground, and request Chamber Number Five."

Request. Darien wouldn't request anything, he'd fucking demand it.

Caliginous on Silverway was a business name he'd heard before. It was the place where his cousin Roman Devlin went to deal with his Surges.

Roman—who'd called Darien after Angelthene had nearly been destroyed by the monsters of Spirit Terra. Roman had seen the horrors of that night all over the news. Darien hadn't been able to explain the situation to him in full, so Roman and the other Shadowmasters in the House of Black were under the same impression as the rest of the world: that Angelthene had suffered a security breach during a Blood Moon.

It was the farthest thing from the truth, but revealing such sensitive information over the phone wasn't a wise thing to do.

As for Roman, Darien knew his cousin suspected there was more to the story than he was willing to share. But Roman hadn't prodded—he never did. The only thing that mattered to him was that everybody was okay—especially his brother, Travis. Roman was the reason Travis was here in Angelthene; he had given him a way out years ago, all but forcing Travis to leave the House of Black so he wouldn't need to remain under their father's strict control. Part of the deal was that Darien would keep Roman in the loop regarding Travis's safety—and would make sure Travis never returned to Yveswich.

"Are there any chambers closer than Yveswich?" Dallas asked Roark.

"No," Roark replied. "One is being built at Lucent Enterprises, but it is strictly for government use. The chambers in Yveswich are the safer choice for Loren. The *only* choice right now."

"Has the chamber ever been tested in other ways?" Atlas asked. "Like seeing if it can heal the Tricking?"

"It cannot," Roark replied. "The magic it gives is temporary, sort of like a battery charge. It's not a miracle machine." Which explained why the imperator hadn't attempted to use the chambers, either to open a gate into Spirit Terra or to fuel his supply of aura ammunition, instead of going after Loren and the Elementals for his diabolical plans. Clearly, there were limitations—lots of them—surrounding the magic generated by these chambers.

There was only one miracle machine, and it was sealed away in Spirit Terra.

Darien said coldly, "Not like the Arcanum Well, then."

Silence.

Darien held Roark's stare. "You wouldn't finally be willing to discuss that with us, would you?"

Roark's unwillingness to speak prompted Max to mutter under his breath.

But then the Red Baron reached into the inside pocket of his jacket and took out a small, black-cloth carrying case with a zip closure. He opened it to reveal nine empty syringes and nine vials filled with luminescent teal liquid.

Darien straightened. "Where did you get those?" It was the serum the imperator used to enter Spirit Terra, the same serum Darien had injected into Loren's heart to get it beating again.

"Lucent Enterprises. It's the only place in the world that has it. They keep their supply under heavy surveillance, so this was the most I could take without raising suspicion." He zipped it shut and handed it to Darien. "They should keep her alive long enough to get her to the chambers for treatment."

Dallas said, "What happens if he runs out?"

Nobody answered.

"Monitor her closely," Roark said. "Clocks aren't a part of the makeup for these. They were an extra feature the imperator added to his own supply." Clearly, Roark had been digging since the night of the Blood Moon; Darien wondered what else he'd unearthed.

Tanner said, "What about all of this?" He gestured to the machines, the IV lines, the heart monitor.

"You won't need any of that when the serum's in her bloodstream. It'll keep her body in a state of limbo—frozen, in a sense, until she wakes up or —" He didn't finish his sentence. Darien watched as the Red Baron's eyes fell to the floor, his throat shifting with a swallow. He stepped toward the door. "That's all the information I have for you. It's rare for a person to survive in a coma for longer than two, maybe three weeks." Darien heard the implication behind his words.

It had already been ten days.

"Why did you wait this long to tell us?" Max called, following him to the door that Tanner was still blocking. "You haven't even been around. What do you care if she wakes up?"

Roark spun on his heel, a flush of anger reddening his face as he came within three inches of Max. "Don't ever ask me such a disrespectful question again, Reacher. I've been the closest thing to a father this girl has had for the past twenty years, and you haven't even been around for one."

He didn't wait for Max to reply; his next words were for Darien, fire still burning in his stare. "I had hoped she might wake up on her own. The chamber is a last resort—whether or not you risk using it is your choice. But as her *father*," he added, enunciating the word with a glare in Max's direction, "you have my support."

He made for the door again, waiting for Tanner to let him through.

The hacker didn't budge, face cold as stone. After a moment, Tanner looked at Darien for instruction.

Darien nodded once, and Tanner shrugged away from the door.

The Red Baron left. The room descended into quiet once more.

And then Dallas was hurrying into the hallway. It didn't take long before Max was following her.

Darien stayed where he was, but he listened, his Sight allowing him to sense that they were only several feet away, the Red Baron stilling midstride at his daughter's words.

"Why?" Dallas's voice might've been too quiet for mortals to pick up on, but not for hellsehers—not for immortals.

Roark said nothing, nor did he turn.

As Dallas persisted, Darien kept listening, ensuring no one said anything that might damn what they'd just discussed. "You could tell us." About the Arcanum Well, about the Phoenix Head Society. She tried to address her father with a respectful tone, but Darien heard the hint of betrayal that forever colored any words she said to, or about, her father. She added, "I know you could."

The hallway grew quiet. If Darien didn't have the Sight, he might have thought everyone had left.

Then Roark said, "You're a smart girl, Dallas."

That was it. And then he was gone, his polished shoes tapping with his brisk departure.

And Darien might have been the only one to pick up on the words Roark didn't say, the words that would've added so much more to that simple statement, had he merely voiced them.

Figure it out.

MAX SHUT the door to Loren's room. He faced Darien, who used his own magic this time to cover the walls, ceiling, and floor with spells that would mask their voices. They were alone in here, Dallas and Tanner having given them space to talk, as per Darien's request.

Max waited until the black in his friend's eyes faded away. And then he said, "We're leaving. Aren't we?"

Darien studied him for a long moment. Try as Max may, he couldn't read his expression. And then Darien said, *"I will be leaving."*

The clock on the wall ticked as Darien's words sank in.

"Fuck that," Max bit out. "If you think for one second that any of us are going to let you go alone—"

"Of course not." Darien's voice was softer than it had been in nearly two weeks, and Max sensed that he was trying very hard to control it. "I'll be taking Jack, Ivy, and Tanner with me. Joyce too, if she's willing." Darien drew a breath, the arms that were crossed over his chest tensing. "God, I hope she'll be willing, because I need Loren—" He paused, his throat shifting with a swallow. "I need this to work."

Max's head spun. He might've blamed it on a lack of sleep, coupled with the stress of these last few weeks, but the truth was, he didn't know what to think, how to feel. He'd been working at Darien's side for so long that the thought of him leaving made him feel...lost, if he wanted to admit it.

"And what about me?" Max asked, his words choked by emotion he suddenly found impossible to control. He'd managed to keep himself together since the Blood Moon, but now he could feel himself splintering, the glue that held him together finally snapping. "I'm your Second, Darien."

"Which is exactly why I want you here. I'm leaving you in charge of the Devils and Hell's Gate. You need to look after the others while I'm gone, make sure they don't get into any trouble—keep them safe, the way I've always done." The order was firm. Darien added, "And I want you working with Delaney—he'll be handling the other houses in my absence."

"You haven't even talked to him."

"I know he'll agree," Darien said. Max saw his next words coming before they were out. "I want you to find Maya, Max."

Max didn't know what to say.

"You've been a fucking amazing friend," Darien continued. "A better friend than I've deserved. I want you to find your sister."

Max wanted that too. He'd been fighting the urge to go looking for MJ since the night Blue had revealed to him that she was still alive. She might be known as 'Scarlet' now, but she was still his sister, and she was out there somewhere—had been out there this whole damn time. All these years, he'd believed she was dead, that she had died in a house fire—a drug lab explosion, really—a bunch of corrupt cops had decided was an accident.

But...Darien was Max's brother in his own right. They were family, and if Darien needed him, he'd be there, no questions asked.

Max swallowed. "Darien—"

"I'm not asking, Max. I'm telling."

"Fuck you," Max snapped.

A smile tugged at the corner of Darien's mouth. "Fuck you too."

Max smiled back, but it was soon fading as reality set in. "When are you leaving?"

"In the morning. I'll have to talk to Joyce first, make sure this can work." He looked over his shoulder at Loren, his hand tightening around the small black case Roark had given him. "If there's even a single risk..."

His voice trailed off, but Max knew Darien wouldn't do it—not if the time it took to get Loren from Angelthene to Yveswich would result in her death.

Max said, "So I guess this is goodbye."

It took Darien a moment to make eye contact again. "Unless I see you at the house before I leave, then yeah, this is goodbye." He pushed away from the bed and stepped toward Max. "But not forever." He extended a hand.

Max shook it, clasping tight. "You sure this is what you want?" He wasn't asking about Loren—that one was easy. He was asking about Darien giving him permission to find Maya.

Not that he'd ever needed permission. Darien was the type of person who wouldn't have hesitated to say yes, had Max merely asked him. But Darien had gone through so much shit lately that Max hadn't wanted to.

And besides, he didn't know where to begin in his search for Maya. Blue's ability to communicate was still somewhat shaky, her knowledge of her own past even more so, but going to her with his questions would be a good start.

Darien replied without hesitation. "When you find Maya, tell her I said hello."

5

THE HOUSE OF SOULS
ANGELTHENE, STATE OF WITHEREDGE

Travis Devlin couldn't remember the last time he had been on a date. Had he ever actually been on one? Did the school dance in seventh grade count? Maybe not...

As he waited in his car—a top of the line model he'd purchased fresh off the lot, since Darien had totaled the last one—out front of the gates to the House of Souls, he fidgeted with his collar, glancing continuously at the clock because he just couldn't fucking help it.

Was it hot in here? Was his shirt the right size? And where the hell was Jewels, anyway?

His phone buzzed in his back pocket. Half-expecting it to be Jewels bailing on their date, he lifted himself up in his seat to retrieve the device and saw a text message from Max.

MAX
> You with Jewels?

TRAVIS
> Waiting.

MAX
> What the hell does waiting mean? You suck at texting.

TRAVIS
> WAITING FOR JEWELS!!!!

MAX
> Tell Malakai that Darien needs to speak with him.

> **TRAVIS**
> Tell him yourself.

> **MAX**
> He's not answering his phone.

> **TRAVIS**
> I'm not talking to that psychopath.

> **MAX**
> Too bad. Boss's orders.

Travis sighed. He shut off the screen and threw his phone onto the dash.

His hellseher hearing picked up on the creak of the front door to the House of Souls swinging open, sounding every bit as haunted as that dark, towering mansion looked.

Travis leaned forward in his seat—and cursed under his breath at the sight of the Reaper storming through the gates.

The wrong Reaper.

It took Malakai Delaney exactly three seconds to reach the driver's-side door. And then—

Pound. Pound. Pound. The window quivered as the Reaper's heavily tattooed fist thudded against it.

Travis bit the inside of his cheek, stilling the words—none of them kind— that were clawing to come out as he flicked the button to lower the window.

As soon as the glass was down all the way, Malakai gave him a cold grin, silver canines gleaming in the street light. "Yeah, hi, it's me. Bet you weren't expecting to see me here."

"Nope," Travis lied, rolling his eyes again. He might not know Malakai very well, but he'd known *of* him long enough to suspect this might happen tonight. If his little sister Jewels went on a date, it didn't matter who with, Malakai would be having words with the guy before they left. And Travis, until proven otherwise, was exactly that: just a *guy*.

Travis had never wanted to be more than 'just a guy' to any girl. He had always been eager to learn their bodies, never their minds or hearts, but Jewels was…he didn't want to say *different,* considering he barely knew her. Maybe he had simply reached the age where getting to know someone's heart didn't make him cringe as much as it used to. And maybe, if he was willing to admit it, seeing Darien and Loren together had tempted Travis to find something like what they shared to call his own. Just a bit.

The fake smile on Malakai's face had faded, leaving only rage in its wake. "Just because she agreed to go out with you doesn't give you the green light for any first-date hanky-panky," he warned.

"Right."

"There are three things I need butt-heads like you to understand," Malakai continued. He held up his thumb. "Thing number one: no sex on the first date."

"Second's good then?"

Malakai's eyes flickered into black pits, his glare hotter than lava.

Travis held up his hands in a sarcastic show of innocence. "Third then, got it."

Malakai's pointer finger joined his thumb. "Thing number two: if you're going out with my sister, you're a listener, not a talker. The one thing I hate is a guy who can't shut up about himself. You'll show respect, you'll listen to her when she's talking, and you'll be a gentleman in every regard. Which means you'll hold doors open for her, you'll—"

"That's a lot more than two things."

"Onto thing number *three,* smartass," Malakai growled, his middle finger joining the pointer and thumb. "If she decides she likes you—emphasis on *if*—you will not, under any circumstances, break her heart. We clear?"

Travis couldn't hold back any longer. First date be damned, he would not take this shit for another second.

The words came out in a rush—and damn were they a heavy weight off his chest. "You seem to know a lot about relationships for someone with a track record of commitment issues and threesomes."

Malakai grabbed him by the collar and yanked him halfway out the goddamn window.

"Hey, guys!" a voice hollered. It was Jewels. She stood on her tiptoes on the front steps of the House of Souls, waving a pale hand in the air. "GUUUYYYSSSSSS!"

"She sure has lungs on her for someone so small," Travis said.

"All the better to yell at you when you piss her off," Malakai growled.

"Get in here!" she shouted. *"Both of you!"*

Malakai released Travis with a shove, practically throwing him back in the car. Travis rolled up the window and cut the engine. He opened his door, and when he was halfway out Malakai slapped it shut, nailing Travis in the knee.

Travis swore.

"Pussy," Malakai muttered as he made for the gates, his shoulder-length, reddish hair blowing behind him in a breeze.

"You look like you belong in a shampoo commercial!" Travis called. "You sure you're in the right line of work?"

Malakai gave him the middle finger.

It was cool tonight, but spring was coming up quick. With the Veil having nearly fallen not even two weeks ago, Travis and the other Devils found themselves on edge whenever the temperature dropped, or the sky decided to open with rain.

But this was normal. Angelthene had always experienced rain and cooler spells in the winter months.

Funny how a person could wind up fearing something that had once been so innocent.

Travis limped after the Reaper, barely making it through the gates Malakai tried to shut on him.

"Malakai!" Jewels snapped. "Quit being an ass and leave him alone, will you? This is important."

She disappeared inside the house, her short leather skirt swishing. She wore a cropped tee with a heavy metal band logo on the front, tour dates listed on the back. Travis didn't catch the name of the band, but he made a mental note to bring it up later. He loved that kind of music; it would be a good conversation starter for someone who loathed conversation.

Sex, he was good at. Really good at, if he felt like boasting. Talking? Ehhh...not his strong suit.

Malakai fell into stride beside him as they neared the steps. "You'd better hope it's important," the Reaper threatened, eyes flickering black again.

"Why are you such an asshole?" Travis demanded.

Malakai merely gave him the middle finger again before stalking up the front steps and through the door—another door he shut in his face.

Travis considered himself lucky that the asshole didn't lock it.

The inside of the house was quiet, save for the droning of voices on a television. Travis followed the sound into the living room, where he found Jewels standing in front of the TV, remote in hand. Her brother stood beside her, arms crossed, a muscle in his jaw ticking as he glared Travis down. Valen Hayes and Sylvan Wolfe were lounging on the leather couch, glasses of whiskey in hand, looking just as miffed as Malakai to see Travis here.

Jewels said, "Would you forget about protecting me for five minutes and take a look at who's on TV?" She used the remote to gesture to the screen in frustration.

Travis gave up on his staring contest with Malakai, the Reaper doing the same. Looked at the screen—

And blinked. Stepped closer.

Travis couldn't believe his eyes.

The Terran Imperator was on television. The imperator—who should have died in Spirit Terra when Loren shut the rip in the Veil.

"Is this live?" Malakai bit out.

"It was," Jewels said. "Earlier this evening. I recorded it."

Quinton Lucent was speaking about the losses and damages the city had sustained during the Blood Moon. Of course, he said nothing of Spirit Terra, nor his direct involvement in the whole mess.

Jewels hit the pause button on the remote. "Look!" She waved wildly at the TV. "Right there!"

Malakai's brow creased. "What am I looking for?"

She stepped up to the TV and jabbed her finger into the screen.

The imperator was looking to the left, the angle showing a sheen of teal in his pupils.

Valen said, "I still don't see what you're talking about."

"The teal!" she exclaimed.

"It might just be the lighting," Sylvan offered.

"Or," she said, pinning them all with an intense stare, "it's that glowing shit we saw coming out of the monsters."

Malakai prompted, "And that would mean...?"

Her face went blank. "I don't know," she admitted. She gestured to the screen. "But how the hell is he still alive?" She flicked her brows up. "Any ideas?"

"If he *is* alive," Travis said, "the others could be too." The imperator's men, his son Klay—the people they'd believed were inside Spirit Terra when the Veil was shut. Which meant— "We need to tell Darien." He patted his pockets—and cursed. "I left my phone in the car."

Malakai was already calling, phone at his ear. It rang several times before it went to Darien's voicemail—full, as usual.

He hung up. "He's not answering." He slipped his phone into his pocket and disappeared down the corridor that led to the front door.

"Where are you going?" Jewels called.

"To tell Darien." He poked his head around the corner, his eyes meeting Travis's with hesitation. "Where is he, anyway?"

Travis scowled. "Why should I tell you?"

Malakai held up a finger in thought. "The hospital," he concluded. *Damn.* "Duh!" He grabbed a jacket off the coat rack and swung open the front door.

Jewels snatched Travis's wrist and tugged him toward the corridor, her touch soft and warm on his skin. "Let's go."

"Where?"

"With Malakai, obviously." She slowed, studying him with big eyes that were lined with kohl. "Don't you want to talk to Darien about this?"

"Yeah, but...what about our reservation?" They were supposed to have a late dinner—everything Darkslayers did was late—at a new restaurant in the Financial District, and after that they had tickets to see a broadway play. The last one was Jewels's decision. Obviously.

"Are you kidding?" She grinned, letting go of his wrist so she could put on her black-and-purple platform sneakers, stuffing her feet in and lacing them quickly. "Trust me when I say this is way more fun than dinner, at least for me. I watch a lot of shows about unsolved mysteries—I practically live and breathe this stuff." She opened the door and clomped out into the night.

Travis tried not to groan. Maybe he would've been into it more if it didn't involve following her brother to the hospital.

Malakai was waiting in the driveway by his truck, one foot on the running board, a hand propping the driver's door open.

Why wasn't he leaving, for shit's sake?

Travis attempted to direct Jewels toward his car, nudging her with his arm like he was a herding dog and she the sheep, but they didn't make it past Malakai before a sharp whistle cut through the Reaper's lips.

Now who was herding who?

"Uh-uh," Malakai drawled, shaking his head. His cold stare was all for Travis. "You can get in my truck or you can drive yourself—*without* Jewels." Damn, was he controlling.

Jewels shot Travis a pleading glance. "Just come with us," she whispered. "We'll lose him later, I promise."

"I heard that," Malakai said darkly.

Travis relented. Using the remote to lock his car, he followed Jewels to the passenger's-side door and slid into the cab. There was no back seat, so he was stuck in a romantic sandwich with Jewels and her dickhead brother, who insisted he sit in the middle, refusing to make any of this easy on him.

So much for that date.

6

THE HOSPITAL
ANGELTHENE, STATE OF WITHEREDGE

Darien sat in one of the chairs in Loren's room, watching the green line of the electrocardiogram bob up and down.

It was nearly ten. Through the window on the west wall, the city lights glimmered, lines of traffic threading through streets that were mostly barren at this late hour.

Looking out at that city, it was hard to imagine it had faced such destruction not two weeks ago. Most of that destruction had already been repaired, thanks to the magic that allowed for the swift clearing of debris and the reconstruction of buildings. Magic could fix a lot of things, but it couldn't fix this.

He looked at Loren, at those eyes that had been shut for far too many days, at that perfect face that showed not a hint of emotion. She just...*was*. Existing, but stuck in place. Breathing, but not living.

Darien got up and shut the door partway. The staff would need access to the room during their nightly rounds, so he never fully closed it.

He crossed the room and laid down beside Loren, being mindful of the equipment keeping her alive. The bed was small and uncomfortable, but if she had to sleep in here, then so would he.

He'd spent every night with her since her heart had stopped. Stopped and started again. Tomorrow, they would both be on their way to Yveswich. He tried not to think about the Caliginous Chambers; those details would come tomorrow. Tonight, he had to try his best to shut off his mind in preparation for the long drive.

Talking to Doctor Joyce Atlas was the first step. As soon as she was on shift, Darien would find her and get this show on the road.

As he slung an arm across Loren's waist and closed his eyes, he felt a shift deep inside him, an ember burning in the ashes of his life.

It was hope.

Sleep claimed him with swift claws, and this time he didn't dream. He just slept.

DARIEN STIRRED. Sleep had gripped him tight, dragging him down deep, and he had trouble shaking it off. It weighed on him like a heavy blanket, and he fought to lift it, becoming aware of his surroundings bit by bit.

He registered the sound of the heart monitor first, the soft beeping floating through a room that smelled faintly of bleach and hand sanitizer. He felt the cool press of the hospital sheets next, and the plastic of an IV line pushing against the inside of his wrist.

He opened his eyes to a dark room. A nurse must've come in while he was asleep and turned off the light.

Angling his head to see the clock on the wall, the starchy pillowcase scratching his cheek, he read the time.

Witching Hour was coming up quick. He'd been asleep for less than two hours, but it was better than what he got most nights.

He studied Loren in the dark, the soft curves of her face illuminated by the light of the ECG machine. He imagined her opening her eyes and giving him one of her drowsy little smiles that made his heart flutter.

Sleep threatened to reclaim him as he let his imagination soar, envisioning Loren stretching her hands out above her head. She would ask him what time it was, her lips parting with a yawn.

Time to get up, sweetheart, he would say.

She would curl up against him, tucking her head against his chest. *Five more minutes.*

HE MUST HAVE FALLEN ASLEEP AGAIN. When he woke back up with a jolt, his face had broken out in a cold sweat.

Twenty minutes had passed, but it somehow felt like years.

He forced his ragged breathing to slow, matching his heartbeat to the one zigzagging across the monitor—Loren's heart. Fuck, tired wasn't a good enough word to describe how he felt right now.

As he laid there, he quarreled with the need to sleep, focusing instead on the ordinary sounds of the hospital, like he did so many nights. Checking to make sure everything was as it should be.

He listened to the familiar drip of the coffee machine at the nurse's station, the hum of the vending machine in the waiting area, the ticking of the clocks in different rooms. Phones droned a floor down; the calls never stopped coming, not in a city swarming with monsters and crime.

The hair on his scalp prickled. The stiff sheets rustled as he sat up, listening harder—not for those mundane, everyday sounds, but for something else, the reason why he was awake right now when he was so fucking exhausted.

Something seemed...off.

He got up, and as he moved, he slid free the pistol concealed near his hip. Bandit was slumbering in his shadow, but at the *click* of the safety being released, the dog began to stir.

Walking heel to toe, Darien crossed the room, checking the corners as he moved. He flipped on the light, blinking in the sudden brightness, and eased open the door.

The hallways and waiting area were dim and empty, not a nurse in sight, not even at the desk. The smell of roasted coffee beans filled the air, the drip of the espresso machine tapering off with one last *plink*, but no one came to pour themselves a cup.

Still shaking off the remnants of sleep, he drew in a deep breath and pushed the Sight into his eyes.

The auras of other sleeping patients filled his vision. There was a nurse five rooms down, swapping old bedding for new.

The attack came from behind him—from *inside* the goddamn room.

Darien shouted in surprise as the Familiar Spirit—a wolf with glowing white marks under its eyes—attacked him with enough force to send him flying into the door. It slammed back against the wall, ripping through plaster, as the wolf's teeth shredded the sleeve of his hooded sweatshirt.

'*Bandit, wake up!*' Darien bellowed. He kneed the wolf in the ribs, but it wouldn't let go. Sharp teeth latched into his muscle, drawing blood. Darien sensed the other presences in the room now—more Familiars, which explained how they'd got in without him noticing. '*Bandit, WAKE UP!*'

The dog jolted into consciousness—right on time to jump out of

Darien's shadow and intercept a different Familiar Spirit, this one a dog bigger than Bandit.

Darien wrenched his arm free of the wolf's maw and kicked it in the side of the head, sending it smashing into a shelf with a yelp.

An arm wrapped around his throat from behind, while another five men burst through the door, weapons drawn. Six more followed—all of them hellsehers, armed to the teeth, Familiars at the ready.

Fuck.

Darien surrendered himself to his rage, and for several minutes he blacked out—he just fought.

Every move he made was deadly. He never missed—slashing arteries, ripping open throats, and blasting bullets into skulls. But these men had come prepared, and Darien realized, as he fought to keep them from laying a single finger on Loren, that he was—truly, for possibly the first time in his life—outnumbered. There were too many men, even for someone like him, and he was half a-fucking-sleep.

Darien plunged a knife into an ear of one man and slashed another's throat, blood spilling to the floor like a waterfall.

He ducked under a blade and kicked the guy's feet out from under him. Shot him in the head. *Bang*. And then—

One of the men reached for Loren's IV—

And Darien lost it.

His magic erupted—and it was like a bomb went off.

He threw out a shield of protection, forming a bubble around Loren, as his magic laid waste to almost everything in sight.

Darien got down and covered his head as wood and glass and metal and plastic flew through the room. His magic obliterated his assailants, blood spraying what was left of the walls.

Turned out the hospital staff had made the right decision by keeping the rooms on either side of Loren's empty; Darien could see through the gaping holes in the walls now—the demolished furniture, the shattered windows and fluttering blinds, the broken televisions.

Slowly, he pushed to his feet, debris slipping off his clothes.

The first thing he did was check on Loren. Glass crunched under his boots as he crossed the room to her bed, Bandit trotting beside him. The dog's cropped tail twitched with pride.

'*I was having a very pleasant dream,*' Bandit said.

'*Yeah?*' Darien replied. '*What about?*'

'*Fetch.*'

Darien checked Loren. Not a mark was on her—not one glass sliver, nor one drop of blood. Even the heart monitor was untouched. He watched as her chest rose with even breaths, her heart beating out a steady rhythm on the monitor.

The sound of wet coughing filled the room.

One of the men was still alive, but barely. He was slumped against the wall by the shattered window, wincing in pain, hands clutching his guts that were spilling out onto the floor.

Hostility simmered in Darien's blood as he stalked around the bed like a predator, Bandit on his heels, and dropped to a crouch before the man.

"Who sent you?" Darien demanded, eyes like fire. He forced the man to meet his gaze with the muzzle of a gun jammed below the chin. "Gaven?" Bandit growled at the prick's name, hackles rising.

The man coughed again, blood filling his mouth. "Who the fuck's Gaven?"

Darien's scalp prickled.

They weren't here for him.

"You were after *her*," Darien growled. *"Why?* Can't you see she's in a fucking *coma?"*

The man choked, blood dribbling down his chin.

"Answer me, you piece of shit." Darien grabbed him by the shirt, yanking him forward and shaking him. *"Answer me!"*

But he was already dead. His mouth fell open with a croak, one last line of blood dripping down his chin.

Hurried footsteps sounded in the hallway.

Darien shot to his feet, taking aim as he turned—

Travis, Malakai, and Jewels appeared in the doorway.

With wide eyes black with Venom, Malakai took in the wreckage of the room—and swore. "What the hell happened?"

Darien put the safety on the gun and tucked it away. "What does it look like?"

Travis, still panting from running, said, "The imperator's still alive. We just saw him on the news."

"That's why we're here," Jewels explained, beads of sweat on her face. She was pale and winded, all thanks to the Tricking. "We thought we should warn you, but...looks like we're a little late."

"You should feel flattered that he felt the need to send eleven—wait, *twelve* guys?" Malakai gave a dark laugh as he finished counting the mutilated bodies.

Darien crossed the room and pushed his way through. Out the door, to the nurse's station. The waiting area was destroyed, the desk in pieces. The vending machine was absolutely shredded, as if by claws, candy and leaking soda cans spread across the floor, puddles fizzing with carbonation.

He found the two nurses on shift, hiding behind what was left of the far wall behind the desk. They nearly screamed when they saw him.

"I need you to page Joyce Atlas," Darien said. Her shift was supposed to start at Witching Hour; she should already be here.

They gaped at him, faces white.

Darien prompted, "You okay? Can you do that for me?"

The younger one recovered from her shock first. She got up on shaking legs and disappeared into a room in the back. A moment later, Darien heard the click of a landline being lifted off its receiver.

"Darien," said a male voice.

Darien turned to find Malakai standing several feet away in the destruction of the waiting room. Behind him, Jewels and Travis stood in the doorway to Loren's room. They spoke to each other in quiet tones, their eyes on Darien.

"What's going on?" Malakai asked.

"I'm leaving," Darien said. "Tonight."

"Cops are coming," Travis declared as he joined the others in Loren's destroyed room, stepping over dead bodies and puddles of blood.

Doctor Joyce Atlas was here now. She sat on the side of the bed, filling a syringe with glowing teal liquid. She set the empty vial aside and administered the serum via a vein in the crease of Loren's right arm.

Darien had filled Travis and the others in, his magic allowing them to talk without being heard. Roark Bright had stopped by several hours ago to tell Darien of the Caliginous Chambers, and he'd given Darien nine vials of serum from Lucent Enterprises. Travis hoped it would be enough to keep Loren alive while Darien got her from here to the chambers.

Travis focused on his cousin now, who spoke to Malakai.

"Tanner will be handling all the transactions, so there's not much else you'll need to do," Darien was saying. "But I trust you'll do a good job."

"Pfft." Malakai smiled. "I'll do a better job than you."

Travis said, "Will you be stopping along the way?" Darien was going to Yveswich—Travis's hometown.

And he would get to see Roman. Years had passed since Travis had last seen his brother; now, he barely knew him, barely even remembered what he looked like. The last time Travis had spoken to Roman was the day he'd left Yveswich, and all he knew of his brother now was whatever Darien and the others decided to share with him. But even their information was limited; Roman rarely called, and when he did he rarely spoke. He had never been much of a talker—that, Travis remembered vividly.

Darien said, "Only to charge the vehicles." His eyes flicked to Joyce. "How's it going?"

"She's stable, but we shouldn't delay." Joyce stuck the cap on the empty syringe, hurried over to the sharps container, and dumped it inside.

Sirens wailed. They weren't far away—a block or two, at most.

Darien stalked to the bed and picked up Loren, wrapping her legs around his waist. Joyce had dressed her in a pair of her own black workout pants from the trunk of her car and one of Darien's hooded sweatshirts— the only clothes they could find. She had no shoes on, just socks, but Darien would need to stop at Hell's Gate to grab some things before leaving.

Travis hoped he would get the chance to speak to his cousin in private. About Roman, about…about Paxton.

Joyce made for the door. "Follow me," she said, stepping over debris and into the hallway. "If we take that route," she said, gesturing to a hallway to her left, "we should be able to take the staff staircase to the ground floor and get out without being stopped."

Travis and the others followed Darien, who was already making his way to the door. In his arms, Loren looked like she was merely asleep, her cheek resting against his chest. Travis hoped, for both her sake and Darien's, that she would wake up soon.

Because Darien now spoke with a note of hope in his voice, the kind of pure, innocent longing that could spell destruction, should this plan they'd concocted end in death. "Good. Let's go."

7
ELSEWHERE

Something had changed.

The girl stood in the heart of the universe, looking down at the soft blue glow outlining her body.

Minutes or hours ago, she couldn't be certain how long, the crack of bullets and the shouting of male voices had severed the eternal quiet. The noise had startled her so badly that she'd leapt off the dome of tree roots and splashed through the shallow rim of the pool, her bare feet catching in her dress as she fled.

But no danger had come. And the echo of the bullets had rippled out across barren land, leaving her alone in silence once again.

Now, as she stood by the edge of the glowing pool, she stared out at the fireflies flitting across the still surface.

Something about her had changed—that much she knew for certain. Her skin, yes, but something else too. She didn't know what, but she could feel it.

In her peripheral vision, just behind the tree, something moved.

She stood tall, steeling herself for what might come. "Who's there?" she called, her soft words echoing far and wide.

A branch snapped. Dark grass rustled.

The girl held her breath—

A glowing white dog stepped out from behind the gnarled trunk of the tree. Slowly, he crept forward, bushy tail drooping between his legs.

Those floppy ears…she had seen those ears before. And those eyes—

She loosened her fists. "Singer?" Memories of this dog flooded her mind, like puzzle pieces falling into place, but everything in between was still shrouded in fog that wouldn't thin.

Singer gave a soft whine.

Slowly, she dropped into a crouch, being careful not to startle him away, and gently snapped her fingers. "Come here, buddy."

His tail rose with a wag, and he trotted over, tongue lolling out the side of his mouth. His eyes twinkled like diamonds, and there was love in them —so much love.

The girl sniffled as she pet the dog's ears, wishing she could feel their velvet softness. He pressed his head into her palm, back leg thumping with delight as he savored the feeling. "Look at you!" she blubbered. "You're all... wispy. Like a cloud." She hugged him. "My cloud."

He barked, the sound echoing so loudly that he cowered, ears flattening down. But he was soon forgetting all about it, and jumped up to lick her cheek.

She laughed, instinctively reaching up to rub the slobber off her skin, only to realize there was none there. "I missed you too, Singer," she whispered. "I missed you so much." If crying were possible here, she would have wept with joy.

Hollow quiet returned the moment the echo of her words faded away, reminding her just how alone she was. She had Singer now, but...

She rose to her feet.

She had to get out of here. There was a fresh sense of urgency in her soul—something that told her she didn't have time to waste. She had to leave.

Singer sat down in the black grass and looked up at her, as if expecting treats, tail swishing back and forth.

"Do you know where we are?" she whispered.

The dog merely canted his head to one side, ears pricking.

She sighed. "Me neither."

She started walking, toward the edge of the dome of light surrounding the tree, Singer keeping pace beside her as they neared the thickening darkness. She was grateful that her emotions, like touch, were dulled here; had they been at full strength, she wasn't sure she would have had the courage to keep walking.

When she reached the very edge of the bubble of light, she stopped, staring at her surroundings that looked very much like outer space—a galaxy that stretched on forever.

She drew a deep breath. "Here goes nothing."

And then she took her first step into the dark.

Water splashed underfoot, but it was shallow, and it didn't glow—not like the pool at her back.

A second step. A third. By the fifth, she was no longer uncertain.

This was the way—she could feel it.

Together, girl and dog walked below galaxies, on and on into the dark, until that blue tree was so far behind her that it no longer provided a source of light. It was just her, Singer, and the stars.

Several paces later, she heard ticking. She moved toward the sound, eventually stumbling upon the great gears of a clock embedded in the pitch-black earth, groaning and ticking with the passing of time.

An ancient, female voice floated through the fog of her thoughts. *You will find your answers in time.*

In time, as in *eventually*?

Or in Time, as in a *place*?

She took another step, her bare toes deathly close to the gears. There were more stars down below—she could see them in the tiny slivers of space between the rotating gears.

Suddenly, the world shook, and gravity shifted, nearly throwing her on her ass.

She flung her arms wide, attempting to balance herself, but the world tilted too sharply and swiftly for her to stand a chance at fighting it. The ground became sky—but, somehow, her feet were still rooted in place. She hung upside down, water dripping from the ground—the ground that was now sky—like rain.

Sunlight flooded the darkness, blinding her. She threw a hand up to block it, squinting her eyes shut tight.

Her feet lost purchase, and she and Singer fell, down and down and down.

They landed on a lush green hill.

"Oof!" She rolled several times, Singer doing the same beside her, until, eventually, they stilled.

She looked up at the sky, watching as the gears, the stars, and the darkness faded away, leaving a canvas of sunlit blue in its place.

She took a moment to catch her breath, and then she turned to Singer, who looked at her with curiosity, ears standing up.

"You okay?" she whispered.

The dog stood and shook himself off, blades of grass flying off his ghostly body.

She smiled. "I will take that as a 'yes'."

The girl stood too, and dusted off her opalescent dress. She turned, looking down the hill that was studded with jacaranda and palm trees.

An old, towering building sat at the base of the hill. A school.

Students were breezing in and out of the arched doors, a number of them sitting among the grounds, grimoires spread before them. A few ate lunch, and a small group of veneficae practiced spells, waving magic staves through the air.

A male student—a human—was heading this way, a heavy stack of books and papers in his arms.

She stepped aside as he trudged by. His short, wavy hair was the buttery shade of sunlight, and round glasses that were taped in the center were perched upon his freckled nose. He was tall and gangly, his bony arms shaking under the weight of all those books.

One of those books slid off the top of his stack and thumped to the grass, a few papers fluttering free.

"Dang it all to Ignis," he muttered. He chased after the loose papers, books teetering in his arms.

The girl rushed forward. "Here, let me help you."

As she reached for a sheet of paper on the grass, she froze, reading the name scribbled at the top of it.

Erasmus Sophronia.

He stomped over, muttering under his breath, and snatched the sheet from her reaching hand. He stacked it with the others and took a quick glance around the hill—

The girl froze as he made eye contact with her, but...something wasn't quite right. Instead of looking *at* her, he looked *through* her.

"Can you see me?" she whispered.

Erasmus Sophronia advanced on her, his speed too quick for her to step out of the way—

He walked right through her. She gasped as her body melted away like smoke and solidified again a moment later.

She stared after the student as he rushed down the hill, toward the towering building. The stone slab out front read ANGELTHENE ACADEMY FOR MAGIC, most of the letters embedded with moss.

Her eyes flicked up to the banner fastened above the door, the block letters proudly announcing *Graduate Class of 4793.*

"Singer," she whispered, glancing down at the dog standing at her side. "I think we've gone back in time."

Slowly, she lifted her left hand and inspected it, turning it from side to side. There was a transparency to her skin that hadn't been there before.

Her stomach dipped, and she recognized then how hollow it felt—how hollow *she* felt.

"I think we're dead."

8
HELL'S GATE
ANGELTHENE, STATE OF WITHEREDGE

Darien packed swiftly, taking more than he likely needed, but he didn't know how long he'd be away. The others were either packing their own things or were helping prepare the vehicles in the garage. They would be taking his truck and car, Ivy and Jack driving the latter while Darien, Loren, Tanner, and Joyce took the truck.

He threw on his leather jacket and checked for his wallet, keys, and phone. All were there, along with the last of his Venom and an extra bag of Stygian salts—just in case. Yveswich was a lot colder than Angelthene, so he grabbed a heavier jacket too—black sherpa-lined canvas with a hood—and dropped it on top of his bags.

'Did you remember to pack Cluckles?' Bandit's misty voice drifted into his thoughts.

Darien looked toward the door to see Bandit trotting in.

"Sadly, yes."

Bandit tilted his head. *'You're not lying?'*

"I wish I were." That rubber chicken was so damn loud, but it wasn't like he was getting much sleep these days anyway.

Darien zipped up his bags and dumped them outside the door to his suite.

Tanner was coming down the hallway, carrying a duffel in one hand, a backpack and laptop bag slung over his shoulder.

"I'm all packed," the hacker declared. "Need any help?"

"Take these to the truck, please," Darien said, gesturing to his bags. "Make sure everything's good with Loren and Joyce." Joyce had stopped at her house to pack before coming here. Now, she was in the truck, monitoring Loren. "I need a few more minutes."

"Sure thing."

Darien stepped past Tanner and into Loren's old suite just down the hall, bracing himself for the memories and emotions that would punch him in the gut the minute he saw it.

Ivy was already in there, juggling two suitcases as she flicked off the bathroom light and crossed the room. One was the bag Loren had used since the first day they'd met—the day Darien had brought her to the Bright penthouse to pack her things for a single weekend. That weekend had turned into a longer stay than either of them had expected.

Fuck, that seemed like a lifetime ago. Six months—that was it. Six months since he'd met Loren. Six months since she'd joined his family and filled in the cracks in his life, the damaged bits he had failed to heal in all the years that had come before her.

"I thought you might like some help," Ivy said, passing him the bag. "I packed several of her outfits, all her toiletries, her makeup, and some extra things I think she'll appreciate when she wakes up."

When. The ease with which his sister used this word thawed some of the ice in Darien's chest.

He hadn't realized he had looked away until Ivy stepped closer, forcing him to make eye contact. "She *will* wake up, Darien." Her tone was soft, but the conviction was firm.

"I know." He managed to sound believable, but he'd spent so much of his life getting kicked in the nuts that he wasn't sure of anything anymore.

But *this*...he had to trust that this would work.

"I packed some 'fun' things too," Ivy continued, waggling her brows. "Like lingerie and condoms—"

"Ivy."

She smiled and tucked a lock of dark hair behind her ear. "Just trying to lighten the mood." Darien didn't bother telling his sister that he and Loren didn't use condoms—they might be close, but they weren't *that* fucking close.

Darien glanced at the other bag in her hand. A small gray one—another of Loren's. "What about you? Where are your things?"

"I'm all ready to go. I've had years of practice packing for myself and a toddler, remember?"

A groggy male voice behind Darien mumbled, "What toddler?"

Darien turned to see Jack standing there, a bag in each hand, a third slung over his shoulder. His short brown curls were all mussed-up, and there were creases from a quilt on one side of his face.

"You," Darien said, and stepped around him.

"You guys all act like I'm so incompetent," Jack grumbled. He and Ivy followed Darien to the stairs.

"Because you are," Darien said, Ivy's voice mingling with his as she said the same thing.

They thumped down the steps, and when Darien got to the bottom, Travis met him there. Darien had lived with Travis long enough to tell when the redness in his eyes didn't have anything to do with being tired or high.

Travis rubbed the back of his neck. "Hey," he mumbled.

Darien acknowledged him with a nod. "Hey."

"I'll take that," Ivy said quietly, extracting the other bag from Darien's grip. She and Jack made their way into the garage.

Darien faced his cousin, giving him time to find his words.

Finally, Travis said, "This is really fuckin' weird, man." He gave a husky laugh, but he looked more concerned than anything.

"You're telling me," Darien said. "We'll be back soon." He had no idea if that was true, but it was better than offering his cousin nothing. He'd shut the door on all of them since Loren went into a coma—not just shut it, but slammed and locked it—and now it was time to crack it back open.

"When you see Roman, can you... Can you tell him—" Travis abruptly went silent, his throat shifting with a swallow.

Darien clapped him on the shoulder. "I'll tell him." He pulled his cousin into an embrace that was over quickly.

Travis stepped back and crossed his arms. "And Pax?" he said, looking away, his jaw clenched so tightly the muscles fluttered.

"I'll tell him you still suck at Rushin' Racers."

Travis snorted, but the humor was short-lived. "He probably doesn't even remember me."

"He does," Darien assured him, making for the garage. "And he understands."

Travis followed, their boots pounding in unison. "Mortifer should take a lesson on understanding, actually." Travis's words echoed faintly in the hallway. "He's having a hard time with this."

"Where is he?"

"Last I saw, he was in the garage. Probably fucking with your wires so you can't leave."

"I'll talk to him."

Darien pushed open the garage door and descended the concrete steps into the massive room. The other Devils waited by the truck and car, Malakai and Jewels among them.

Dallas and Sabrine were here too. The girls stood by the open back door of the truck, where Joyce checked Loren's pulse in the back seat.

And, sure enough, Mortifer was seated on the hood of Darien's car, getting an earful from Max.

"I'm serious, Morty," Max was saying, a stern finger raised before him. "You don't touch those. You *never* touch those."

"You got caught, didn't you?" Darien said to the Hob as he joined the group. Sabrine turned at the sound of his voice, her eyes red and puffy from crying. Dallas had called her right away, telling her to get to the house if she wanted to say goodbye.

Max said, "I fixed his doctoring before he could do any permanent damage."

Darien loaded the rest of his things into the truck bed and slammed the tailgate shut. "All good?" he called to Joyce.

"She's fine, Darien. Stable as can be."

"Good." He walked around the front of the car and faced Mortifer, who peeked up at him with stubborn reluctance.

"Why the long face?" Darien said quietly. "I'll be back soon."

"He wants to go with you," Lace said as she hugged Ivy goodbye.

Mortifer refused to look at Darien. His smoky arms were crossed, a big frown on his face. The Hob didn't get upset very often, but Darien had learned in his years of caring for Mortifer that if it wasn't ice that was upsetting him, it was the safety of his family. Usually, Darien's safety.

"I need you here, bud," Darien said, trying his best to make his voice sound not so...fuck, *flat*. Disinterested. Cold. But he could hear it in his own words—these past few weeks had changed him, and he wasn't fooling anyone. "I need you to look after the others and keep the house safe," Darien continued. "It's an important job, and I only trust *you* to do it for me. So what do you say? Can I count on the best Hob in the whole entire universe to handle this *very* important, very special task?"

It took him a minute, but Mortifer finally nodded and uncrossed his arms, bracing his tiny hands on the car instead.

"And when we get back," Darien added, "we'll go for some of that shave ice. How does that sound?"

The Hob was quicker at nodding this time, the black-and-red flames on his head rapidly flickering with the motion.

Darien looked between the others, all of them either ready to go or ready to say their goodbyes. Darien had already spoken to each of the Devils in private, Travis last, so there was nothing left to do except leave. And while he knew this change was only temporary, there was a part of him that felt—feared—it might somehow wind up being permanent.

Max said, "I guess we won't be talking to you for a while."

"No phones unless it's important," Darien confirmed.

"If you don't want to come back, I got it covered here," Malakai said, a smile tugging at his mouth. Darien sensed that the Reaper's attempt at lightening the mood was half-hearted. He could see the concern in Malakai's eyes, subtle as it was, though Darien knew he would never admit to caring about anyone but himself or the sister standing just behind him.

Darien smirked. "You'd like that, wouldn't you?"

That smile grew, the silver of his canines glinting like chrome under the fluorescents. "Just sayin'."

Lace snickered. "Say hello to Roman and Kylar for us." Her attention drifted to the truck. Quietly, she added, "And Loren when she wakes up." Lace had taken this whole thing just as hard as the others. Darien suspected Loren had started to grow on her, even if she, too, would never admit to her feelings.

They were all a stubborn bunch, but Darien suspected that was what had brought them together in the first place.

Ivy opened the driver's door of the car. "See you soon, fam." She blew a kiss over her shoulder and got inside.

"Hey," Jack complained, "I thought I was driving."

"We'll switch at the stronghold," Ivy said, already buckling up, a triumphant smirk on her face.

"Suuuure we will..."

Darien headed for the truck, Tanner taking the passenger's side while Joyce took the back with Loren.

As Dallas passed him, she stopped him with a pull of his sleeve.

"This is the first time I'll be away from her since we were kids," she said quietly. Her eyes were glassy, the silver rings around her pupils dim. "I know you'll keep her safe."

Darien vowed, "If anyone wants her, they'll have to get through me." It had been that way since day one, and it would be that way until the very last.

The witch let go. "Safe travels."

She stepped aside, and Sabrine came forward to take her place.

"Hey," Sabrine said with a sniffle. She dabbed at her eyes with the sleeve of her sweatshirt—one of Logan's, by the looks of it. Way too big for her—and way too ripped to not belong to a temperamental werewolf.

"I've never seen so many tears in my life," Darien joked. He glanced around the group to see that a few of the others were tearing up as well, though they tried to hide it—Lace, Dallas, Mortifer. Fuck, this was harder on them all than he'd thought it would be.

"There's no one I trust her with more than you," Sabrine whispered. "But please, take care of yourself too. I think it's pretty obvious that we all need you around."

"I will."

She offered him a hand, and he grabbed it and pulled her into an embrace instead. Her arms closed around him, squeezing tight.

"I'm going to bring her home," Darien promised.

Sabrine nodded against his shoulder, her body shaking with a sob. She stepped back, dabbing her cheeks again with her sleeve.

Darien made for the truck. "Keep that wolf of yours in line," he called.

Sabrine's laugh was choked by new tears. "I will."

Darien got in the truck and shut the door. The others stepped out of the way, and Max hit a couple buttons on the wall.

The garage doors rolled open, the rows of bright fluorescents quarreling with the heavy blackness of a starless night.

Darien started the truck and reversed out of the garage, gravel crunching under the tires. He spun around to face the gates that were already swinging open, the magic sensing his departure.

With one last look at Hell's Gate in the rear-view mirror, and his family and friends waving at them from inside the garage, he left, not knowing when or if he'd be back.

THE DRIVE from Angelthene to Yveswich would take about twenty-two hours if you drove the speed limit and made no stops along the way. While stopping was inevitable, the speed limit wasn't, especially if you were good at reckless driving without getting caught.

Darien merged into traffic on the interstate, truck engine giving a violent growl. Beside him, in the passenger's seat, Tanner had a number of programs open on his laptop, one of them scanning for speed traps. Loren was in the back, her socked feet in Joyce's lap. Joyce—who hadn't complained once, and who'd insisted on sitting in the back instead of taking the front seat when her son had offered it to her. For a woman whose life had been uprooted so suddenly, she sure was handling it well.

Jack and Ivy were following in Darien's car. He checked on them in the mirrors every few minutes, making sure all was good. Without the ability to call or text, they would all need to be more observant.

One last message landed in Darien's phone with a loud buzz that vibrated his pocket. The message he'd been waiting for, the confirmation he needed for ease of mind. He'd sent a single message to Malakai shortly after leaving Hell's Gate, and the Reaper had only just responded. Darien read them both now—his own message and the one from Malakai.

> DARIEN
>
> You'll remember what I told you?

> MALAKAI
>
> I'm not that forgetful, dumbfuck.

Darien almost smiled. It was the best consolation he'd get from someone like Malakai, and he accepted it gladly. Look out for the others at all costs—*that* was the deal. He'd have to trust that Malakai would see it done.

With a deep breath, he shut off his phone.

As he drove through the dark streets of Angelthene, he cracked open his window, breathing in the smoky hint of creosote and the cool bite of sage— the smells of home.

A swarming of vampire bats flew over the interstate as the truck and car sped under a road sign. This time, when Darien read those three words, printed in stark-white paint, they meant far more to him than they ever had before.

NOW LEAVING ANGELTHENE

9

S. COASTAL DISTRICT
YVESWICH, STATE OF KER

The overcast sky began to spit rain as Shay Cousens stapled a poster to a telephone pole in the South Coastal District.

This was poster number two hundred and forty-one. Shay had printed two hundred and fifty, and she'd put up the majority of them herself. She'd brought help in the form of three Selkies, but as it turned out her friends—if she could even call them that—were easily distracted.

Shay turned her back on the missing person poster—the image of her sister that would soon be blurred by the rain—and followed the chatter of voices and the rattle of spray paint cans.

It was mid-morning, and the South Coastal District was bustling with foot traffic. Shay dodged people on the sidewalk as she made her way, turning her body from side to side, others doing the same to keep from brushing shoulders with her. Here in Yveswich, physical contact was avoided just as much as eye contact, especially when you were alone. Especially when you were *female* and alone, a sad reality that stalked every city the world over.

Stranger danger had been nailed into Shay at a young age. Not by her mother, who'd barely had a hand in raising her, but by her older sister Anna. Shay had Anna to thank for most of what she knew, her street smarts being highest on the list. Anna had taught her practically everything—how to cook, how to sew, how to drive, how to throw a punch. The one thing Shay could say she had taught Anna was how to steal—and not get caught.

Stealing from Roman Devlin was the kind of milestone she and Anna would've celebrated by spending a night on the town. But Anna wasn't here anymore—a painful truth that was setting in deep, like claws curling into her stomach.

A fat drop of rain hit her cheek, in the same spot where the tear of the Riptide adorned her skin in blue ink. It was the closest she would come to crying. She never cried—not if she could help it.

And not when she was certain Anna would come back. She *always* came back.

Shay found the three Selkies halfway down a narrow alley a block over, laughing and talking over one another as they added a penis to the mural of Yveswich's governor. These murals were all over the city, painted on nearly every flat surface you could find—but the governor didn't usually have big, hairy dicks in his mouth.

Shay adjusted the straps of her backpack and cleared her throat.

The Selkies kept giggling, pushing each other out of the way to add more obscene details to their masterpiece.

Pia, Beatrice, and Kailani were three of the Riptide's finest Darkslayers. Pia, with her voluptuous figure, short black curls, and dark skin that seemed to glow, was the kind of beautiful that stopped people dead in their tracks. She was one of Anna's closest friends—and one of Shay's *only* friends.

The other two were here mostly because Pia had convinced them to come. Had Shay alone asked them, they likely would've declined. Beatrice was fair and slight, her eyes colored like the ocean. Kailani was raven-haired, honey-skinned, and soft around the middle—the most beautiful of all the Selkies.

But right now, 'beautiful' was the last thing Shay would call any of them, even Kailani. No, right now they were just annoying.

"Yoo-hoo!" Shay crowed, waving a gloved hand in the air. "You guys are supposed to be helping me, not tagging."

Pia looked her way, a lingering smile tipping her lips up. "We've been helping you for the past two weeks, Shay. Let us have some fun."

"Come on, let's go," she insisted. "We only have nine posters left—"

Laughter exploded as the Selkies kept spraying paint, not hearing a word Shay said.

With a roll of her eyes, she turned and left the alley, thick mud sticking to her running shoes and the hem of her pants.

It shouldn't surprise her that the others weren't even trying. Anna was Second to Athene Cousens, and if she didn't come back, her title would be up for grabs. In the world of Darkslaying, friends only stayed friends until one of them decided it didn't suit them anymore.

The rain fell harder, bringing a dull pulse to Shay's brow. Her medication rattled in her backpack, telling her it was almost time to toss back a pill before that ache became unbearable.

"Shay!" Pia called, but Shay didn't slow. "Shay, wait up!"

Shay pushed through foot traffic and stomped onto the crosswalk—

Tires screeched as a driver slammed on the brakes. Shay stumbled back, heart shooting up her throat as a white sports car with a streamlined body nearly flattened her like a pancake. The vehicle lurched to a stop, the engine's roar swiftly dulling to a quiet purr.

"Watch where you're going, asshole!" She kicked the front bumper, leaving a muddy footprint on the chrome.

Wipers swept across the tinted windshield, the spells on the car too thick to see the dumbass of a driver.

She flipped him off. "Learn how to drive," Shay muttered. She gave his bumper another kick for good measure before continuing across the road.

The car kept sitting there, even after she was well out of the way. Not quite off the road, but far enough for that particular lane to start moving again.

She heard the hum of a window being lowered, and felt compelled to look over her shoulder, steeling herself for an argument she hoped would be worth her time.

But the fight simmering inside her instantly cooled at the sight of him. She was not expecting to see him again so soon, if at all, and because of this she found herself taking in his features in a state of disbelief.

Tousled dark hair. Bold brows. A sharp jaw dusted with the barest hint of a five o'clock shadow. The arm he slowly slung over the unrolled window was covered in a patchwork of tattoos that appeared to have no rhyme or reason. Silver rings glinted on three of his fingers, partially concealing the wispy tattoos on the back of his hand—tattoos that were meant to look like shadows.

This morning just took a nosedive down the toilet—because she had just kicked Roman freaking Devlin's bumper.

She hurried away, wondering what the odds were that he didn't recognize her. Probably not good, she decided, a chill licking up her spine. Now that she was off the crosswalk, traffic began to move again, and it was easy to pick out the deep growl of Roman's engine among the many ordinary ones. She listened to it fade with distance, heart thumping in her ears.

Pia caught up to her, nearly startling her out of her skin. Shay wasn't easily frightened, but Anna's absence was weighing on her. And her altercation—make that *two* altercations—with the guy better known as 'Shadows' was only pushing her closer to the edge.

"Shay!" Pia grabbed her arm.

"What?" She whirled around, strands of damp, strawberry-blonde hair plastering her face. It was cold today, her breath hanging in the air before her, but the chill that lingered on her skin had more to do with that Shadowmaster than it did the weather.

Pia's brow creased with worry. "Are you okay?"

"I'm fine," she said, working to soften her tone. "Why?"

"Why?" she repeated in disbelief. *"Why?* You almost got run over!" She gestured wildly to the road at her back.

"Yeah, well, the guy was an asshole."

"That *asshole* was Roman Devlin, and you kicked his bumper."

She continued her trek, leaving Pia behind. "Thanks for reminding me," she mumbled.

Pia followed. "You're lucky you're alive and not roadkill—or worse. Trust me, I've heard rumors of what that guy's done to people." So had Shay. There wasn't a single person in this state who hadn't heard of Roman and his violent tendencies. "Shay? Did you hear what I—"

"Yeah, I heard you, Pia. That was Roman Devlin and I'm lucky I'm not roadkill. At least one of us listens to the other."

Pia's hurt was tangible. "Don't pull that crap with me, Shayla. I miss Anna just as much as you do."

Shay pivoted again, causing Pia to stop short before they could bump into each other. "Then tell me why I'm doing this by myself. Why do I spend every day since she's been gone putting up posters while my so-called friends giggle like a bunch of twelve-year-olds over the governor sucking dick?"

Pia flinched.

"Pia," Shay sighed, briefly shutting her eyes. Gods, her neck and shoulder were killing her. "I want to find my sister. That's all I want." Pia stepped toward her, but Shay held up a hand. "And some space. If you really feel like helping me with the posters next time, let me know."

Shay walked away, hands gripping the frayed straps of her backpack. She sensed Pia staring after her, but she didn't try to follow.

The harbor was the last place Shay wanted to go, but if she was going to leave tomorrow—which was the whole reason she had stolen from Roman Devlin, needing the money to fund the search for her sister—then she needed to pack up a few more of her things, so down to the harbor she went.

Nugget rolled out of her shadow and plopped onto the pavement. He was her Familiar Spirit, a glowing white seal pup with black whiskers and big black eyes. He bounced after her, and when she didn't slow he whined.

"Don't give me that. I know Pia didn't mean any harm, but I feel like no one is taking this seriously." She sighed. "Not even Mom seems to care that Anna's gone." Athene Cousens was known for being heartless—most Darkslayers were—but Shay hadn't expected her mother to show such little interest in finding her eldest daughter. Instead, it was like Athene was unwilling to admit that she was gone, lying to herself that the heir to the Riptide would soon return.

If she didn't return, Athene would have a problem on her hands. Anna had helped build the glowing reputation of the Riptide, and if she didn't come back, Athene would be put in the spotlight for all the wrong reasons, namely the kind that suggested Anna had either run away or not been strong enough to defend herself against whoever had harmed her.

Shay knew it wasn't the first one. Anna had planned to run away *with* her, not without her. She never would have left, not without Shay. They had been saving money for years, taking little bits here and there—nothing that would strike Athene as suspicious—and stashing it away in Anna's hidden bank account until it was safe to disappear with new identities. That time had nearly arrived when Anna had vanished, leaving Shay alone—and with no access to the money they'd worked so hard to save.

Nugget whined again. Nearly twenty years, and he had never said a word, never grown bigger than a pup.

"I know *you* care, Nugs. But...don't take this the wrong way, but you can't exactly help me put up posters with those flippers. I don't think you'd be very good at stapling." She smiled down at him. "Now get back in my shadow, your bouncing is slowing us down."

He rolled his eyes but got back inside, dramatically rolling onto his back and melting into her shadow.

Shay took one of many staircases down to the harbor. The water was choppy today, the boats that were moored along the stretches of dock constantly bobbing up and down.

As she walked onto the dock, soggy wooden boards flexing underfoot, she stared out at the island a short distance away that belonged to the House of Blue. Pelicans soared above the ocean, scouting for fish, and seals wended their way through the harbor on glossy backs, whiskered snouts pointing toward the gray sky.

Click.

Shay froze.

A nasally male voice said, "Try anything funny and we'll paint the dock with your brains."

Slowly, she lifted her hands and turned around.

There were four men, but she only recognized two—the stout warlock and the reedy hellseher pointing a gun at her. She'd stolen from them last week.

It had taken them long enough to find her.

"Before you kill me," Shay began as they spread out, fencing her in, "I want to apologize."

The reedy one smirked. "Better forget apologizing and start praying instead." He stepped closer.

"I want to apologize," she continued, "for how stupid you're going to look in about..." She glanced at her wrist. "Two minutes."

Shay was well aware that she was on the smaller side; she may not be able to take four men at once—or even one, if she was willing to admit it— but she had other ways of getting away from them.

The reedy hellseher smiled. "And why's that?"

"Because I'm about to disappear."

"We're not into party tricks," said another. "Give us back the money and we'll make this painless for you."

Shay batted her eyelashes. "Oh, I'm so scared," she pouted, laying on the sarcasm. "What *ever* will I do?"

The men didn't like her sense of humor. They dove for her, but they all missed by a mile, falling for the illusion she cast with her magic—tricking their eyes into believing she was standing three feet to the left of where she *really* stood.

Her assailants collided with surprised and angry shouts. By the time they hit the dock in a pile of limbs and raging faces, she was already halfway to the shore, the dock vibrating under her pounding feet.

"After her!"

Shots were fired. She dodged them, ducking behind moored boats and barrels of fish, leaping over stacked boxes and crates, backpack thumping against her spine.

With a heavy blink, she called upon her magic once more, using up what was left in the shallow reservoir to cast one more illusion—a false image of her sprinting down a branch of dock that would lead her pursuers to the left instead of toward shore.

As she ran, no one on her tail for the time being, she glanced down at the inside of her wrist. The small tattoo of a fish skeleton was faint, only the tip of the tail glowing white. She wouldn't be able to safely use illusion again until the whole meter was full—

Bam! She collided with something hard, the force of the hit rattling her bones. The wind rushed out of her lungs in a whoosh as she fell back on her ass. Looked up.

No. Freaking. Way.

Roman Devlin stood over her, his towering form silhouetted by the rain-washed sun. He, unlike her, wasn't winded from the collision, nor was he fazed. He stood, solid as a tree, as she slowly lifted herself off the dock.

How was it possible that he was even scarier in broad daylight? It wasn't even that he *looked* scary, not really, his energy was just...threatening. And there was something about his eyes—a shade of golden brown she'd never seen before—that warned her to stay the hell away from him.

"I don't believe it," he drawled in a low, husky voice. "The baby seal of the Riptide has a baby seal for a Familiar." His eyes flicked to Nugget, who had crawled out of Shay's shadow to peer at Roman from behind her leg.

"Out of my way." Shay made to step around him, knowing she only had minutes to spare before those men would be heading this way.

But he easily blocked her, sidestepping into her path. "Hold up just a sec, small fry. What's the rush?" Those eerie eyes shifted to the stretch of dock behind her—

"There she is!" one of the men shouted.

"Quick—after her!" said another.

Shay rolled her eyes. *Great.* Just what she needed!

"Tsk, tsk," Roman drawled with dark amusement. He shook his head, damp hair gleaming with rain. "You sure make a lot of enemies, don't ya, pup?"

She tried to step around him again, but he mirrored her, crowding her back the other way. Had he really been that tall last night?

Oh, that was right—his shadows had held her up against the wall. The recent memory sent a lick of cold up her spine. His actions last night had definitely lived up to his reputation.

Shay squared her shoulders and lifted her chin, forcing herself not to balk when she looked into his eyes. "What do you want?" Gods, she hated looking at him. Not just because of how much he freaked her out, but also because of how attractive he was. And being attracted to someone like him was a mistake. He was beautiful but he was also a threat. And Shay knew better than to let herself get close to threats.

Roman 'Shadows' Devlin, tall, dark, and devilishly handsome Shadow-master of the Hollow, said, "My necklace."

"I don't have it."

His smile was a baring of teeth. "Full of tricks and lies, you are." Yeah, she was, but the last thing she was going to do was hand it over. She'd managed to get good pay for the head of the Hound at the Black Market, but she'd need to sell his necklace the minute she ran out.

"I'm not lying. I would let you search me, but you're not my type, and as you can see, I got places to be."

She bolted, taking her chances at passing him, but he was faster than anyone she'd encountered.

His hand lashed out, fisting the collar of her rain jacket. With a sharp yank, he pulled her back around to face him. Shay's hands came up to grasp his sleeves, yanking on the worn leather, but he didn't yield. With how high he held her, she was barely able to balance on the tips of her toes.

"I've got a few questions for you," he said casually, completely unaffected by her struggles—and the men who were shouting commands at each other, devising a plan. The Shadowmaster was so close, she could smell him—mint, leather, and the warm spice of his cologne. "Do you got time? You look like you got time." He glanced at the men sprinting this way—and gave that same wolflike smile he'd worn in the alley. She hated to admit it, but that smile put the fear of the gods into her.

"Let me go," she gritted out.

"How did you do it?" he demanded, leaning in so close, she could count the freckles on his nose. "Change my phone screen. Are you a hacker?"

The pounding footsteps grew louder. She wasn't sure these people realized they were barreling toward Roman Devlin. If they did, they were stupid for not stopping—not just stopping, but also running the other damn way.

Shay discreetly tilted her wrist... Glanced at the inside of it.

The tattoo was half-full.

She started squirming. "Let me go—"

"Why don't you answer this question instead?" he drawled, licking his lips; she spotted a piercing in his tongue. "Where's my necklace?" Gods, he didn't actually care that much about a stupid necklace, did he? Why couldn't she have taken his watch instead?

Because it wasn't worth as much, *that* was why. But as she balanced on her tiptoes, facing off with one of the deadliest people in Ker, she found herself wondering what sort of value she placed on her own life. The question was worth consideration—because Roman Devlin looked like he was about to kill her where she stood.

"I sold it," she lied.

Those eyes immediately shifted into pits of deadly black. "You're fucking lying."

Shay's stomach quaked, the blood in her head draining down to her feet with dizzying speed. It had been...a while since she had felt an emotion so strong.

That tone in his voice... Was that...*fear?*

"So what if I am?" she squeezed out, backpedaling.

The black in his eyes dimmed—just a bit. "Then you can consider yourself lucky enough to live another day."

"If you let me go," Shay began, wiggling again—and calling upon her magic as discreetly as she could, willing her eyes not to give her away by turning black, "I'll tell you where it is, okay? But right now, we have to run—"

"I don't run from threats, I kill them."

"That's great, Shadows. Kill those men for me then, will you?"

"And why should I do th—" He choked on the last word as he realized his hand was now grasping open air.

Shay's magic had recharged, allowing her to slip away without Roman noticing. She now stood two feet behind him.

He whirled, his expression livid, the hand with the barbed-wire tattooed across his knuckles still forming a claw around open air.

"They're your problem now," she said with a smile as he blinked at her in disbelief. "Later, Shadows."

She gave him a little wave, and dove into the water.

10

S. COASTAL DISTRICT
YVESWICH, STATE OF KER

Shay could count on one hand the things she liked about essentially being a slave to the Riptide. But being able to use the bracelet—made of enchanted ocean glass—to shift into a Selkie was a highlight she couldn't deny.

She swam through the harbor, away from her attackers—away from Roman Devlin. She heard the splash of a body falling in, smelled blood in the water, but kept moving, twisting around marine plants and through schools of small fish.

The bracelet had transformed her legs into a long, fishlike tail, and it moved behind her with powerful strokes, propelling her through the cold, murky water. Iridescent scales dusted the backs of her hands and arms, her temples and chest. Her clothes and pack had vanished with magic, allowing her to swim freely without the hindrance of the extra weight. As she swam, she thought of a plan.

Going out to the House of Blue would have to wait. First, she would need to make sure Shadows was off her tail. She wouldn't chance being cornered by him again. Besides that, she wouldn't wager on surviving him for a second—make that third time. Luck had brought her this far, but she wasn't so foolish as to think that luck wouldn't soon run out.

She swam along the coast, toward the boundary of the South Coastal District and into the North.

Aside from the rhythmic chug of boat engines and the fascinating calls of various marine life, it was quiet under here. Peaceful. Light filtered weakly through the depths, gleaming off the fronds of tall kelp and the shiny bodies of multicolored fish. She passed a few seals who turned to look at her with curiosity, one booping her with its nose. She smiled and kept swimming.

Nugget came out to join her, easily keeping up now that they weren't on land. It was the one place where he felt as free as Shay. They sometimes came down here at night when they wanted to get away. The ocean was Shay's sanctuary, a place where she could pretend the rest of the world did not exist. A place where she could be alone. While many people feared the ocean, it was one of the safer places in Terra, sharks, serpents, and water monsters excluded.

Now that she'd put a safe distance between her and the bloodbath Roman had surely left in his wake, she broke the surface of the water. Pushing the wet hair out of her face, drops of rain splashing the choppy sea, she checked her surroundings to see how far she'd swum.

She was near the Squid Squad Seafood Market; she could hear traders hawking their wares and fending off food-nabbing gulls, could see families braving the cold for ice cream cones and real-fruit popsicles on the boardwalk. Deep in the North Coastal District, an ancient clocktower declared the hour, its chimes echoed by another in the south. It was almost noon.

Her aquatic form armored her against chill temperatures, the gusty wind that snatched at her dripping hair not nearly as biting as it would be if she took off the bracelet. She was already gearing herself up for that moment; it was the one thing she hated about the Shift.

She swam to the shallow end, and with a steeling breath, she tugged off the bracelet. The moment her clothes materialized, she stuffed the piece of jewelry into her jacket pocket and zipped it shut. Her feet tingled as they took the place of the scaled tail, her boots soaked through. Teeth chattering, she walked out of the water, shaking the wet hair out of her face—

And looked up to find Roman standing on the shore, his Familiar—a small black dragon—perched on his shoulder, long tongue slithering out.

Shay stopped short. "Shit."

He gave her another of those deadly half-smiles, the gold of his eyes engulfed with the black of the Sight. "Hiya, pup."

ROMAN WOULD NOT BE LETTING this little thief get away from him again.

He gripped her by the arm and towed her out of the water, toward where he'd parked his car. To his surprise, she didn't resist, and instead walked just behind him, slightly dragging her wet, squeaking boots.

"I'm not even going to bother asking how you did that," Roman said, referring to that trick of the eyes on the dock, "because I know you'll lie." It had to be a glamor—there was no other explanation for that shit.

"Gee, Mister," she fake-gushed, "you're really smart."

He yanked her close, snarling in her face, "You are *this* close to being cut up and stuffed into those fish barrels!" He pointed at the seafood market by the docks, where people ate lobster rolls and crab cakes at hightop tables.

The smell of those rolls and cakes twisted his stomach; Roman detested seafood.

The Selkie wasn't fazed—not even by the black that had fully engulfed his eyes for the second time in under ten minutes. This was a far cry from the show she'd put on in the club. "Shh, there are children present," she said.

He growled and pulled her along.

"Just so you know," she began, her tone all sweet and innocent and annoying, "your donation has gone to a very good cause—"

"Donation?" he repeated. He pulled her close again and snarled in her face, their noses nearly touching, "You *stole."* He kept moving, refusing to waste any extra time with this colossal pain-in-the-ass.

"And the money has gone to a very good cause," she crooned.

"And what cause is that?"

"Can't tell you."

He growled again. Sayagul—the small dragon Familiar on his shoulder—echoed it with a squawk, her forked tongue slithering through her sharp teeth.

'As soon as you turn her into a crab cake,' Sayagul hissed, *'I want a bite.'*

'A bite? You can eat the whole damn thing, as long as you don't burp on me afterward.'

'Deal.'

"I'm concerned about you, Shadows," Shay continued. "You don't seem to know how to smile or laugh. And you aren't good at conversation, since you keep growling like some sort of wild animal—"

"And you're not very good at shutting up, are you?"

He was rewarded with two seconds of glorious, peaceful silence before she opened her infuriating mouth again.

"Where are we going?" Now that his car was in view, she began to drag her boots, putting her whole weight—what she had of it—into pulling on his arm. He'd parked across the road, by an old cafe that made the best lattes and double-chocolate muffins—a place that always raked in excellent money, no matter the season or time of day.

He could really use one of those lattes and a muffin right about now. It was the better alternative to taking out his rage on a random bystander.

Or this tiny thief who was majorly testing his patience.

People on the sidewalk moved aside to let him through, a few of them turning to stare as the Shadowmaster dragged the Selkie across the road, forcing traffic to a standstill.

"You," Roman began, gritting his teeth as he fought the Surge, the emotions threatening to erupt like a volcano, "are going to return what belongs to me." With his free hand, he dug out the car remote from his pocket and unlocked the doors.

"And if I don't?"

Magic ripped through him like a rusty blade, that Surge creeping ever closer. With a roll of his shoulders and neck, he gritted out, "Then I kill you. Understand?"

"But you can't kill me," she said, blinking up at him with big, innocent eyes. "I'm a Selkie."

Sayagul squawked and beat her wings. *'Who does she think she is?'*

His eye twitched. "The rules of the New World don't apply to the Old. I can sell you to those seafood vendors if I want to." He pointed again at the Squid Squad Seafood Market. There were no rules in Yveswich that stated Darkslayers couldn't kill each other—not like in the newer cities, such as Angelthene. "Do you want to keep living your pathetic thieving life, or shall I do the honors of grinding you up into a tasty little crab cake?"

There she went with the lash-fluttering again. "Do you think I would taste good dipped in tartar sauce?"

And just like that, his eye twitch was back.

"Alright," Shay breathed, "let me get this straight so I can stop torturing your poor eye." She wet her lips that were pale from the cold. "If I give you back your necklace, you'll leave me alone?"

Roman winced as the Surge dug its claws in deeper. It looked like he'd be spending his afternoon at Caliginous on Silverway. "Yes," he ground out.

Shay sighed. "Fine, I'll go get it."

Roman's hand—the one grasping the Selkie's arm—suddenly closed around open air.

What—

Roman froze. Spun around in a circle.

He was alone. Shay was gone.

Laughter erupted out of him without restraint, the sound loud and maniacal. People stared, a few jumping in shock from the volume.

"Un-fucking-reaaaaal!" he bellowed, tipping back his head to project his voice.

More people stared. A scowling mother pressed her hands over her daughter's ears and hurried by.

'I told you to kill her while you had the chance!' Sayagul snarled, launching off his shoulder with a heavy beat of her shimmering wings. *'And you tell* me *not to play with my food.'* She disappeared into his shadow with one last lash of her pink tongue.

Eventually, Roman's wild laughter tapered off. He looked at the people staring from the outdoor seating of the cafe, a few of those people gaping with open mouths.

The edges of his vision flickered with colors that were quickly becoming vibrant.

Caliginous on Silverway, coming right up.

"What are you looking at?" he snapped at the gawking crowds.

And then he got in his car and sped away.

II

HELL'S GATE
ANGELTHENE, STATE OF WITHEREDGE

The gray light of a rainy day was creeping through the curtains in Max's suite when he woke Dallas up with a pillow to the face.

Smack!

"What the—!" The witch's eyes flew open. It took her a moment to find Max, where he stood, fully clothed, by the foot of the bed.

She blinked once. Twice.

And then she narrowed her eyes, the silver rings around her pupils glinting with a warning. "What the hell was that for?" she demanded, her glare slicing to the pillow still hanging in his grip.

Max tossed it onto the bed. "Payback," he replied, "for the last time you decided to wake me up with one of your pillow fights." If they were both in a playful mood, those pillow fights led to heated moments that were worth sacrificing sleep for. But right now, sex was the last thing on his mind—and the sour look on Dallas's face assured him it was the last thing on hers too.

"Get dressed," he said. "We've got shit to do." After the others had left Hell's Gate, they had gone back to bed, both of them too tired to start the day when it was still dark out. But Max hadn't meant to sleep until nearly noon.

Dallas, on the other hand, slept until noon quite often.

She looked out the window. "Now? The day's barely started."

"It's almost noon."

She threw the quilts over her face and burrowed deep.

"Get your ass outta bed, Dallas. Now."

Soft snoring was his only reply. There was no way she had fallen asleep again that fast.

Max sighed. She was asking for this.

He ripped the covers off the bed, sheets and all, exposing a half-naked Dallas to the crisp air.

She squealed, drawing her knees up to her chest. "You are such a jackass!" she hissed, goosebumps prickling across her legs. Damn, those legs looked good. So did the curve of her ass, visible under the hem of her oversized shirt...and her lacy black underwear.

Focus, Max.

"You have ten minutes to get ready if you want to come with me." He grabbed his keys and wallet off the dresser. "Go ahead and sleep the day away if that's what you want, but don't try to tell me I didn't offer to include you."

He vanished into the hall, walking slowly to see if she would take the bait.

A couple seconds later, she bit with a defeated groan. "Include me in what?" she called.

Max picked up his pace, and when he reached the staircase he thundered down the steps and into the foyer. With over half of the Devils gone, the house was quiet. Lonely. He was so used to a full house that anything less than that felt like an empty shell.

His sharp hearing picked up on the sound of his bed creaking as Dallas stood, followed by the slap of her bare feet on the floor.

"Include me in what?" she called again.

Max went to the closet to grab his jacket and boots.

He had been up nearly all night, thinking. About his past. About Maya. About the house that had burned down, and the mother he hadn't spoken to in years.

Now that Darien was practically forcing him to solve the mystery surrounding his sister, he would waste no time in looking for her. He wanted answers. More than that, he wanted to see her again, wanted to see for himself that Maya Jane hadn't died in that house fire seven years ago.

The situation had been believable. Perfectly fabricated, now that he thought about it. No one had suspected the truth back then, not even Max. But what he'd learned these past few weeks, not just about Maya but about himself as well, had changed things. Turned out, he didn't know himself nearly as well as he believed, and if that were possible then he hadn't known his sister as well either. Maybe even at all.

The thought irked him. But if Maya had been keeping secrets, then Max trusted she had a good reason for it.

Max shrugged into his brown leather jacket and zipped it up. He took his boots with him to the staircase and sat down on the bottom step. As he shoved his feet into his boots, he realized the reason the house sounded extra quiet today was because Mortifer wasn't eating his ice chips.

If he leaned forward, he could see the Hob from here, his silhouette tucked behind the cereal boxes on top of the fridge. His small back was facing Max, his shoulders slumped, head hanging low.

"He'll be back soon," Max called, knowing exactly whose absence was causing Mortifer to mope.

The Hob glanced over his shoulder, his sad red eyes meeting Max's. He slid himself over a few inches until he was fully hidden behind a box of fruit-flavored cereal.

Dallas hurried down the stairs in jeans and a t-shirt, a rain jacket slung over an arm. Her wings were concealed with a spell she'd purchased on the Avenue of the Scarlet Star—a *legal* one. Her days of visiting the Umbra Forum were behind her now.

"Alright, big guy," she said, side-stepping him as she went in search of her own shoes. "Time to fill me in."

"We're going to find Maya."

"Okay?" Dallas stuffed her feet into her shoes, not bothering to untie them first. "And how are we going to do that?"

"I was doing some thinking last night," Max began as he laced up his right boot.

"I knew it," Dallas said with a playful tone. She yanked the elastic off her wrist and tied up her hair. "You haven't slept at all, have you?"

Max ignored her. "I have fire magic. And if my family heritage is anything like Darien and Trav's, then there's a very strong chance that Blue is right, and Maya had fire magic too." He moved onto the left boot. "Which means," he said, pulling the laces tight, "that someone started that house fire on purpose."

Dallas blinked. "Who would do something like that?"

Max finished tying a knot and got to his feet. "My fucking mother."

Pamela Reacher had lived in many houses in Angelthene, but her current rental down by the airport took the cake for most disgusting.

It hadn't taken Max long to track her to this trailer park—a pigsty of a neighborhood whose view of the ocean was the only thing it had going for it. The homes were so close together they were practically stacked, and yards that should've been home to manicured lawns or flowerbeds were covered in junk.

He slowed the SUV to a stop out front of a single-wide home with a small covered porch. The number four was nailed to the siding next to the door, the iron rusted. The for-sale sign out front was bent, its sad appearance suggesting it had been ripped out of the dirt and thrown a handful of times.

His mother had been known to do such things. As a chronic tenant, she'd had to bounce around homes a lot, and whenever her landlords decided to sell, she never took the news gracefully.

Max blinked his Sight into his vision and scanned the interior of the house, looking for auras.

Two people were inside—a man and a woman, the former snoring in the recliner in front of the television. As for the woman, she was seated on the couch, smoking a cigarette while typing one-handed on a device that Max assumed was a cell phone.

Yeah, that was his mother alright. She'd never had enough money to hide her aura, and regardless Max knew she didn't value her life enough to bother. The spells over the house were evidence of that, the protection thinner than tissue paper. Barely enough to keep out the smaller of the storm-drain breeds. How she hadn't been eaten yet was a mystery.

And a tragedy.

"I wish *I* had the Sight," Dallas grumbled. She was in the passenger's seat, studying him with envy. Max was so distracted by the sight of the woman who'd done a shit job at raising him that he'd nearly forgotten Dal was there.

He cut the engine and pocketed his keys. "Another great mystery we haven't solved yet."

Double-checking that his weapons were in place, he undid his seatbelt and opened his door. A sprinkle of rain swept into the vehicle, and Max breathed it in, the fresh air filling his lungs.

"What do you mean?" Dallas opened her door as well, checking for the third time that morning that the pistol he'd given her was tucked into the back of her acid-washed jeans, safety on. Max had to admit, the sight of his gun on her—tucked into her pants, no less—was a major turn-on.

"You're a witch, but your parents have hellseher blood from the Well," he explained, forcing himself to focus before he got a raging hard-on.

"So you think I should've been born part hellseher?" Judging from the way she said it, the thought had crossed her mind before—several times.

"Looks like your coffee's finally kicking in," Max joked. Two vanilla cappuccinos sat in the cupholders, both of them drained to the dregs. Dallas wasn't a morning person—or an afternoon person, really—so her stipulation for coming with him today was a drink from her favorite café.

"Ha-ha," she said flatly as she exited the SUV, Max doing the same on his side.

He led the way through the white picket fence and across the yard, past a dried-out birdbath, a set of old tires, and a couple soggy rolls of newspapers no one had bothered picking up.

The porch steps sagged under his boots as he ascended to the door, Dallas following on his heels. Recent life events and her training with the Fleet had served her well; her aura was steady and determined, a drumbeat that never faltered.

Max wasted no time in knocking. *Bang. Bang. Bang.* The pounding of his fist rattled the unit number that was nailed to the siding.

Inside, the man stirred but kept snoring. The woman was the one who came to the door.

She approached with hesitation, her rail-thin arms crossed tightly over her chest. "Who's there?" she called in a croaky voice.

Max didn't answer; he simply watched her silhouette walk down the hallway, remembering all those years he'd spent under the same roof as this woman. Years that had managed to both shape and destroy him.

As she stepped into the faint wash of light, her bare feet sticking to the floor, recognition flickered across her tired face. "Oh, it's you." His mother's lip curled with a sneer. She leaned against the wall inside the door, her bony, cigarette-stained fingers grasping the sleeves of her ratty housecoat.

"Is that all the greeting I get after seven years?"

Pamela's mouth became a thin line. "You shouldn't be here."

"Pam?" called a deep, raspy voice. The kind of voice that sounded like it had been run through a blender a thousand times, likely thanks to chain-smoking. "Who's at the door?"

Pam eyed her son with contempt. "No one."

Max smirked. No one, indeed.

A man appeared behind her—also dressed in a ratty housecoat, this one with no string to hold it shut, and plaid pajama pants that were equally as ratty. His upper half was bare, and there were bruises healing on his abdomen, just like the one on Pamela Reacher's cheek. What a fantastic pair these two made.

"What do you want?" the man barked as he stomped down the hallway.

"I want to talk to my mother."

He sneered. "Well, she don't wanna talk to you."

Max kicked the screen door off the hinges. His mother screamed and stumbled back as the door literally fell on her.

The man tried to retreat, but Max grabbed him and threw him to the floor, flattening his cheek against the grimy tile.

"Stop!" his mother bellowed. She whaled on his back, screaming and cursing her lungs out. "Get off him!"

Dallas froze the bitch in place with the muzzle of a pistol pressed against the back of her head. "I'm going to need you to stop hitting your son, Mrs. Reacher," Dallas said, her cool, smooth voice filling Max with pride.

Slowly, Pam straightened, lifting her hands above her head.

Max focused on the panting man pinned beneath his knee. "Did my sweet and loving mother forget to tell you that she has a Darkslayer for a son?" He tightened his fist in the man's grubby hair. "I kill people for a living, but sometimes I just kill for fun. What's your name?"

"Tim."

"Tim. Hi, Tim. I'm Maximus Reacher."

Tim's aura turned piss-yellow with fear.

"Yeah, you've heard of me, haven't you?" He yanked on his head, forcing him to answer. "Haven't you?"

Tim nodded as best as he could while his head was ensnared.

"Would you like to be killed for fun, Tim?" Max drawled.

"No!" he cried, snot dripping from his nose. "No, please!"

"Then you're going to leave me to chat with my mother in peace. And you? You're going to take a walk—a long one. Nice day for a walk, wouldn't you say?" He twisted the guy's head, forcing him to look through the busted screen door at the rain falling in sheets on the gray ocean. Max gave Tim's head a shake. "Wouldn't you say?"

"Yes," the man blubbered.

"Good." He got to his feet and let him go. "Now get out of here."

Tim pushed himself up, nearly falling into the wall. "I need my shoes."

"Bare feet work just as well." Max fisted the shoulder of Tim's housecoat and shoved him toward the busted door. "Don't come back until my vehicle is gone."

Max watched as the man hurried down the front steps and staggered through the yard.

And then he turned around and faced his mother.

Pamela was barely breathing. Her hands were frozen in the air, Dallas still pointing the gun at her head.

Max gestured for Dallas to lower it. She did, clicking the safety into place.

Slowly, Pamela crossed her shaking arms.

"Well?" Max said.

Pamela stared. "Well what?"

"Aren't you going to invite me in?"

"You look like shit," Max said.

He sat across from his mother at the shabby kitchen table, Dallas at his right. The room was filthy and stank of mold. Dishes were stacked by the sink, the overflowing garbage was oozing onto the tile, and the counters were cluttered with illicit ingredients for Blood Potions and other drugs. As for food, what little he could see was rotting, including the spotted bananas and withering grapes in the fruit bowl. Yet another habit of his mother's that hadn't changed.

Pamela took another drag on that rancid cigarette—laced with a hallucinogenic called Black Crystal. Its acidic tang burned his airways whenever he inhaled.

She tapped the ash into a glass tray. "What do you want, Maximus?"

"Maya is still alive."

Silence. Pam's aging face shifted with a heavy frown. Max watched her, holding her stare. After a minute, she clucked her tongue and turned her head, looking toward the door, as if searching for help and not finding any.

"Don't you dare look away from me or I'm going to flay that barefoot asshole right before your eyes," Max snarled. That barefoot asshole was standing outside; he could see him through the tiny kitchen window. Max waited for Pamela to look at him again before he spoke. "Maya is still alive," he said again, speaking in a carefully measured tone.

"So what?"

"So what?" he repeated, grinding his teeth. *"So what?* So you lied to me for seven fucking years. You made me believe that Maya was dead."

"I never made you believe anything." Her voice was as cold and detached as Max remembered it. "You were just a teenager, Max. You wouldn't have understood. Besides—" She took another drag with chapped lips and blew a stream of smoke in his direction. "I didn't want to bother my child with my problems." She said it with pride, the bitch.

"Oh yeah?" Max scoffed. "Is that why you didn't do shit when your ex boyfriends took me out back to beat the daylights out of me? Is that why you always spent your money on drugs instead of making sure Maya and I had enough to eat? Is that why you sold my fucking bed that one time, forcing me to sleep on the floor, so you could pay for your drugs? Because I didn't need to be bothered with *your problems?*" He drew a breath, filling up his lungs that had shrunk too small, the pungent bite of Black Crystal reminding him of his tainted childhood. "It was never about us—*that* was the problem. It was always about *you.*"

Pamela said nothing. With a trembling hand, the skin speckled with unsightly sores, she ground the cigarette butt into the ashtray.

"I want you tell me the truth," Max said, as calmly as he could. "What *really* happened that night?"

"There was a fire."

"But it wasn't an accident."

She looked at him with hard, watering eyes, her pupils pinpoints.

"You pretended it was an accident so the cops wouldn't look into her death. You faked it. You *sold* Maya." Even saying the words made him sick to his stomach, bile burning his throat. "Didn't you?"

Nothing.

Max banged a fist on the table, making Pamela jump. *"Didn't you?"* he bellowed.

"Yes," she whispered.

"To who?"

"I don't know."

"What the fuck for?"

"Her magic."

"What bloody magic?" He wanted answers, and he was going to damn-well get them—no more guessing. *"What. Bloody. Magic?"* he repeated through clenched teeth.

"She had fire magic." There it was. "They told me they would keep her safe, that she would have everything she needed—"

"What she *needed* was a loving family. A mother who supported her, not one who sold her! And for what? What did you use the money on, huh?" He banged his fist on the table again. *"What did you use the money on?"*

"To pay the bills."

"To pay for your fucking drugs."

Silence fell. Max took a moment to breathe.

"I need you," he began in a level voice, "to tell me everything you remember about the people who took her."

"I don't know anything. The deal was done in secret—I didn't even know their names."

"There must be something. If you've felt even the smallest amount of regret for what you've done, then you will tell me."

Max waited, staring down his mother as she looked at the floor and picked at her bloody hangnails. Dallas reached under the table and gave his arm a comforting squeeze.

Finally, Pam said, strands of greasy hair fluttering in her face, "There's an envelope in the drawer behind you. Pass it to me."

Max got up, shoved his chair aside, and threw open the drawer with a *bang*. He sifted through layers of junk until he found a white envelope. "The seal is broken," he said.

"Tim opened it; he thought it was money." Of course he did. She beckoned with a hand.

He passed it to her. She ripped it open, shaking its contents into her palm.

A business card was the only thing inside.

"This is all I have—all they gave me." She slid it across the table. Max grabbed it, not bothering to sit down again. He was nearly done here.

There was no lettering on the business card, no contact information. There was only a symbol. A phoenix head with three overlapping circles behind it.

"This is it?" Max prompted.

She nodded. "That's it."

"Let's go, Dal."

Dallas stood immediately.

Pamela shut her eyes.

As they left, Max turned, one last time, to look at his mother. "How long did the money last?"

Pam opened her eyes but kept her focus on the table. Max watched as a single tear splashed on the wood.

He felt no sympathy.

"Don't make me ask you again," he warned.

Her answer was a ragged whisper. "Three months."

He shook his head. "You're a disgrace."

The rain was beginning to let up when Max joined Dallas in the SUV. He was still parked out front of his mom's house; he'd needed to have a smoke before driving again, his rage threatening a full-blown Surge for the first time in years.

He shut his door and placed the last of his cigar in the center console, slapping the lid shut.

"You okay?" Dallas asked.

"As okay as I can be." He stared out at the ocean, his ragged breathing gradually smoothing out. "I bet that makes you feel better about your parents." He tried to laugh to lighten the mood, but it sounded forced.

Dallas shook her head. "No," she whispered. "It doesn't make me feel better at all."

Max swallowed. "It should've been me." His lungs still ached, as if someone were squeezing them. "If my magic had manifested before Maya's, my mom would've sold me instead." He said again, "It should've been me."

Dallas reached across the SUV and loosened his fist, interlocking her fingers with his. "You can't do that to yourself—blame yourself for your mom's actions. That was all her, Max. There was nothing you could have done." Maybe she was right, but it still felt like he had failed. Big brothers were supposed to protect their younger siblings, and he hadn't been there for her. Maya hadn't even trusted him enough to tell him about her magic.

Where had everything gone so wrong?

In the corner of his eye, Max caught sight of the barefoot asshole his mother was dating. Tim was heading toward the house, but stopped and pivoted on a mud-caked heel the moment he realized Max was still here.

He started the engine. "I might have to take up fighting," he muttered. Maybe Darien was onto something with that outlet.

"I don't mean to be a negative Nancy, but how are we going to find out what that symbol is, without Tanner here to help us?"

"I've got plenty of hacker friends, remember?" But none as good as Atlas. And, considering how elusive that symbol was, he wasn't so sure that even someone as gifted as Tanner would be able to trace its origin. "We'll talk to the Butcher," Max said. "See if he can find anything on that rental car, maybe talk to Blue—go from there."

It would be a long road—he could feel it now. But he wouldn't give up until he found Maya—Scarlet, whatever her name was, it didn't matter. She was still his sister, and she deserved not to be lost anymore.

12

BORDER STRONGHOLD
PARADISI, STATE OF KER

"Hey, Menace." Darien spoke into the quiet of the truck, hoping Mortifer was listening—and wasn't too upset with him to answer. "You there?"

In the back seat, a sleeping Joyce stirred at the sound of his voice, but quickly drifted off again. As for Tanner, he was still wide awake, monitoring multiple programs on his laptop in the passenger's seat, one foot propped up against the dash. Twilight was falling, and the cars on the interstate were desperate to get out of the dark and under the protection of a forcefield.

The radio came on, the buzz of static filling the vehicle, interrupted by blips of audio from multiple stations as Mortifer flipped through them.

Finally, the Hob found a station with a man's voice saying, "Yes."

The radio flicked off again.

Darien felt the ghost of a smile on his mouth. "Do me a favor and see if you can find out what this traffic jam is all about." They hadn't reached it yet, but it was showing on the navigational system displayed on the screen—and it was right by the entrance to the city of Paradisi, the border stronghold between the states of Witheredge and Ker. It was the last major city on their route to Yveswich.

Tanner murmured, "I told you I can find it, if you'd just give me a second."

"You're doing enough. Let Mortifer feel involved."

"He's got his hands full with Hell's Gate."

Darien grunted. "That house is safer without me there."

It was Tanner's turn to grunt his disagreement. "The rest of us beg to differ."

Mortifer began flipping through the radio stations. He found one and cranked it to the highest volume. Static exploded in the truck—but with bits of audio from intercepted police radios coming through.

"...directing traffic into Northern Paradisi..."

Another burst of static. "...there have been multiple casualties. Paramedics are on site, with a helicopter on the way..."

"...demon attack. There was a security breach in the Desert Canyon district..."

One last bit of audio came through, and Darien swore he heard them say—

"Angelthene." He and Tanner said the name of their city in unison.

They shared a loaded look.

"You don't think..." Tanner began.

Darien merged into the farthest left lane, Ivy and Jack doing the same behind him. "You bet I fucking do."

They needed to stop here anyway to charge their vehicles, so taking a look at what had caused these multiple casualties would be worth their time, especially now that Darien had heard the cops make a connection to their home city.

Darien took the eastern road into Paradisi—a sprawling, desert metropolis protected by a forcefield and walls. He'd hoped to evade the traffic jam, but the roads eventually connected, causing the vehicles to bottleneck once more.

There was a collection of cars with flashing blue and red lights parked just ahead, a few cops directing traffic. Darien caught sight of a brawny warlock standing among them, the badge on his plain black jacket glinting.

Well, isn't this a coincidence? he thought.

He turned in his seat, unbuckling his belt to reach his hat on the floor.

Joyce was awake now, though still groggy. She passed the sports hat to him. "Here."

He put it on and lowered his window, whistling sharply to get the attention of the warlock—the Head Detective of Angelthene's Magical Protections Unit.

Finn Solace turned, looking mildly surprised at the sight of Darien beckoning him to his truck. He excused himself from the group and jogged over.

As soon as he was in earshot, Darien spoke. "What are you doing here?" he demanded. "And make it quick."

"I was called in to take a look at a security breach. A demon killed several people before escaping into the sewer system. They asked for my help in identifying it because..." The look in Finn's eyes became guarded, his voice tapering off.

"Finn," Darien warned.

He sighed. "Because they thought it looked just like the monsters that were in Angelthene during the Blood Moon."

Shit.

Tanner prompted, *"Was* it the same?"

Finn sighed. "Yes." He studied Darien, his eyes briefly flicking to Jack and Ivy in the car behind him. "What are you doing here?"

"Just passing through." It wasn't exactly a lie, but from the way Finn nodded, Darien understood that the detective knew it wasn't the full truth.

He would accept it without prodding for more. Darien had blacklisted Finn after he'd lied to him about Gaven, so trusting Finn again wasn't something Darien was willing to do just yet—maybe even ever. Darien had taken some time to think through Finn's actions these past few days, and although he understood his motivations, he didn't like liars—especially not when those lies put the safety of his family and friends on the line.

Darien inched the truck along, Ivy and Jack following on his tail.

Finn walked alongside the truck. "Listen, if you have any pointers for how my team can handle this thing if it shows up again—"

"I don't," Darien said. "They're hard to kill."

"But you've done it before," Finn insisted, still walking beside the truck. Night had thickened, and the city glimmered with lights, LED lamps flaring to full brightness.

"Right," Darien said, *"I've* done it before." Seeing the desolate look on Finn's face, Darien added, "My best suggestion is to stay away from those things. If your men see one, tell them to run the other fucking way."

"Running isn't something we encourage in the MPU." Horns blared as Darien held up traffic.

"Then you'll have to find yourself a new team because your old one will be dead in seconds." Traffic started to move quicker. Darien added, "Find out where it got in and reinforce the spells." He stepped on the accelerator, leaving Finn behind.

Finn cupped his hands over his mouth. "It materialized in a hardware store!" he called.

Darien flicked the button on his window, rolling it up. He drove into the city, not wanting to acknowledge what that meant, but knowing full well that it was exactly as he feared.

The monster had materialized inside the city. Which meant it hadn't come from Angelthene—it was new.

Darien leaned against the driver's door of his truck and watched the needle on the energy gauge of the cristala charging station tick upward.

They were in the parking lot of a grocery store, charging their vehicles at the small group of cristala stations at the far end of the lot—the first place they'd come across that didn't have a lineup.

Despite the late hour, the city was booming with traffic, the citizens and people who were passing through having been pushed behind schedule by the security breach. Those who were unwilling to risk traveling to their destinations were rushing to find accommodations, and those who were daring enough to try were quickly charging their vehicles and leaving again.

Paradisi, being a border stronghold, was one of the safest cities in the state. But the fall of night brought a sense of urgency to any community, no matter how protected—it was the same all throughout Terra, the massive amount of nocturnal demons forcing most people to retire to their homes before sundown.

Darien kept his eyes on the gauge as he sifted through his jacket pockets, searching for a packet of smokes. He found one and opened it, extracting a cigarette with his teeth.

A soft whistle floated through the warm desert air. "Can I bum one of those, big boy?" Jack called from where he charged the car at the next station. He was grinning like an idiot—he always grinned like an idiot. Darien swore he'd still be smiling when he died.

Darien held the packet out in offer.

Jack pushed away from the car with an even wider grin, walked over, and slid one out of the packet. He helped himself to another with a wink, and tucked it into his jacket pocket.

"Since when did you start smoking again?" Darien asked, his words slightly muffled by the cigarette in his teeth. He put the packet away and lit the smoke.

"Since the Blood Moon," Jack said with a new smile, as if anything about that night was funny. He returned to the car and leaned against the back of it. Darien tossed him the lighter, and he caught it with ease. "Thanks."

Darien blew a stream of smoke through pursed lips, the nicotine already loosening his tense muscles. "Does Ivy know?"

"Nope."

"Is that why you're smoking while she's in the store?" She and Tanner had vanished inside to grab a few things, leaving Darien and Jack to charge the vehicles, and Joyce to monitor Loren.

"Yup."

They smoked in silence for a while. Darien kept his eyes on the needle that was inching toward half-full. Another fifteen minutes and they'd be ready to go—and they wouldn't be stopping again until they made it to Yveswich. It was just after eight; they would arrive mid-morning, if all went according to plan. And once they arrived, they would need to find Roman.

This all felt exactly how Travis had described it back at Hell's Gate: fucking weird. Darien knew his cousin would agree the moment they showed up at his door, after years of hardly even speaking.

As Darien waited, he listened to the sounds of the city—cars starting up in the parking lot, grocery store doors sliding open and shut, vampire wings beating overhead, power flowing up from the anima mundi. The latter was a sound too quiet for mortal ears, but Darien was so used to its steady buzz that whenever it vanished during an outage, the resulting silence felt too eerie to be peaceful.

Jack said, "I'd be doing the same thing as you, you know." Darien looked up to see that his brother-in-law was no longer smiling. "If it were Ivy," he finished, a haunted look in his eyes. That look was so rare, Darien could count on one hand the amount of times he'd seen it since meeting Jack—since he'd come onto Ivy at a casino and dared to kiss her right in front of Darien. Back then, Darien hadn't wanted to admit it, but he'd liked Jack right away. He was cocky and stupid sometimes, sure, but he was fearless and loyal to a fault.

He took one last drag on the cigarette before putting it out and flicking it into the ashtray by the charging station. "I'd expect nothing less from you, Jacky."

Darien looked over his shoulder, through the tinted window of the truck, to see Joyce checking Loren's pulse. "All good?" he called.

It took Joyce a moment to answer, and when she did she didn't turn—she just nodded.

Darien's brow creased, and he was about to prod when she called, "All good."

Jack suddenly pushed off the car. "Whoa whoa whoa." Panic choked his voice. "Darien—"

Darien followed his line of sight across the parking lot.

The lights inside the store were flickering. People were fleeing and screaming. Glass was shattering—

And the truck wasn't charged.

Darien swore. "Is that done?" he called to Jack as he stalked toward him.

"Is what done?"

"The car—is it fucking done charging?"

"I fucking think so!"

Darien was at the driver's door of the car in under half a second, ripping out the charging cables as he moved. "Stay with Loren and Joyce!" he barked, whipping open the door and throwing himself into the seat.

"What about Ivy? She's—"

"I'll take care of her." He started the engine and slammed the door. "Do *not* leave them!" he shouted through the glass.

Jack gave a faint nod, but Darien barely saw it.

He was already ripping the car across the parking lot at one hundred miles an hour, flying around vehicles and fleeing pedestrians.

He screeched to a stop by the doors just as the windows lining the front of the store exploded, glass showering the pavement.

Darien got out, not bothering to shut off the car. He sprinted through the sliding doors—

And skidded to a halt among the wreckage inside.

Blood—everywhere. Most of the people were already dead, body parts scattered across the floor. The few who were still alive were hiding in the aisles, in storage closets and bathrooms, most of them injured. Darien felt like he was going to throw up as he looked for Ivy and Tanner, hoping like hell that he wouldn't find any pieces of them on the floor.

He spotted Ivy by the tills, but the sight of her did little to ease the tightness in his chest. She was dragging herself across the floor with one hand, the other clutching the gaping wound in her thigh, as the creature— the same breed Darien had killed at the carnival, though slightly smaller— stalked toward her, blood dripping from its maw.

Darien attacked.

He threw the beast into the wall with his magic, the force of the hit splitting the concrete. The creature roared, thrashing under his hold as he pinned it there.

Darien held firm, though sweat was already beading on his skin, his heart pounding out a frantic rhythm that warned him he wouldn't be able to do this for long.

Venom—he needed to get Venom into his bloodstream.

With slow and steady breaths, he made his way to his sister, blood sticking to his boots, and stepped in front of her, putting himself between her and the thrashing monster. The lights flickered again, threatening to plunge the store into darkness.

The stone embedded in the creature's forehead was glowing amethyst. A monster of the Aether.

"Took you long enough," Ivy joked, wincing in pain. She ripped the bottom of her shirt with blood-soaked hands and made a tourniquet for her leg.

"Where's Atlas?"

"Here." The hacker limped out of aisle three, clothes all torn up and bloody. Something colorful had splattered the front of his shirt and pants.

Lines of sweat dripped down Darien's back as he focused on keeping the creature in place. With his free hand, he felt around in his jacket pocket until his fingers closed around the bottle of Venom.

Darien called into the store, "I would get out now if I were you."

Those who were capable of walking hurried out, a pregnant woman and her crying children among them.

"Atlas, take the cap off, please," Darien said, offering up the bottle of Venom.

Tanner twisted it off, though he had to try twice, the blood on his skin making his fingers too slippery.

There were barely two drops of Venom left—one for each eye. Darien tipped his head back and dripped them in, blinking as the drug stung the corneal surface of his eyes.

The creature's roar shook the building, the rows of fluorescent lights sparking. Darien's arm trembled with the strain of keeping it contained by his magic—magic that was once again invisible, now that the Veil was shut.

He blinked, long and hard. Black engulfed his eyes, arriving far slower than he'd like, thin lines that looked like tree roots sprouting to his temples and the tops of his cheeks.

Three deep breaths and a quick motion with both hands, as if he were ripping something open, and Darien tore the demon's head in half. The *crack* of severed bone cut through the sudden silence.

Its body fell to the ground with a thud that shook the store, the stone in its forehead dimming. One pulse, two, and then the violet shade of the Aether faded away until it was completely clear.

"You're getting really good at that," Tanner said, bracing his hands on his knees with a wince.

"I've had more practice than I'd like." He gripped Tanner by the upper arm. "You alright?"

Tanner straightened. "Yeah, just...got hit pretty hard."

"You bleeding?"

"Nothing fatal."

"Good." Darien gave himself three more seconds to catch his breath, and then he stooped down to pick up Ivy.

"You okay?" he asked her, being careful not to apply pressure to her bad leg as he slid his arms beneath her.

"I'll be fine," she said around tense, panting breaths. She slung an arm around his neck, hand in a tight fist. "But I think I need stitches."

Darien gave a pointed look at the wound in her leg. "You don't say," he joked as he pushed himself to his feet.

She tsked and swatted his arm. "My bag, Darien." She gestured to the grocery bag nearby, and he grabbed it on the way.

Darien and Tanner were walking out of the store just as the cops were arriving, Finn among them. The warlock gave him a probing look as they passed each other, but said nothing.

As they neared the car, Darien glanced at Tanner. "You smell like formaldehyde," he said, nostrils flaring. He eyed the splotches of color on the hacker's clothing—the few on his face, too.

"It's nail polish," Tanner mumbled, scraping a dried speck of it off his cheek. "Don't ask." He rounded the car with a limp.

Tanner got in the passenger's seat as Darien put Ivy in the back. As soon as he was in, door shut, he put the car in drive, ripped over to the charging stations—

And screeched to a halt before he could run over Jack.

Jack was shouting, fear written all over his face. Through the spells on the vehicle, Darien couldn't hear what he was saying, but it looked like—

Loren.

The blood in Darien's veins turned to crackling ice.

He threw himself out of the car. "Jack?"

Jack's eyes were bolted wide, his face whiter than bone. "It's Loren—Darien, Joyce said she's not breathing. *She's not breathing!*"

13
ELSEWHERE

In the heart of the universe, over two thousand years in the past, a girl and her dog followed a student named Erasmus Sophronia through a school for magic.

Erasmus was a straight-A student with a truly brilliant mind. He'd received an impressive number of scholarships—more than most veneficae and vampires were offered—and every university he'd applied to had immediately written back with an acceptance letter. The teachers and headmaster at Angelthene Academy adored him, taking every opportunity they had to place him in education's spotlight.

But his classmates were another matter entirely.

He had very few friends, which came as no surprise for a mortal. Of course, the few he did have were human too. His very best friend, a handsome redhead with amber eyes, called himself 'Elix Danik'.

Elix, too, was exceptionally smart. He had seen the end to most of his bullying when he'd graduated secondary school, going on to join multiple sports teams, and even found himself the object of admiration to three half-human girls. For Elix, life had improved.

Erasmus, however, wasn't so lucky.

The girl and her dog had followed Erasmus to his classes for three consecutive school days. They watched him now, as he stomped across the dark grounds surrounding the school, toward a small, dark building tucked away behind a chain-link fence.

Erasmus trembled with anger, his flushed face streaked with dried tears. Splotches of purple marked his cheeks and jaw. He'd had a run-in with a few of the students who bullied him nearly every day, and, like always, had limped away afterward with two black eyes and pride so wounded, it was a wonder he had any left.

A shadow stepped out of the trees by the old building.

"Who was it this time?" said Elix Danik.

Erasmus paced in the grass. His hands were balled into fists, the tendons in his slender arms standing out in stiff lines. "Who do you think?" he snapped.

"If you don't stand up to them, they'll never stop."

"Easy for you to say!" Erasmus fumed. "They don't even bother you anymore. Look at you!" He waved an angry hand. "You're practically a whole different person."

"I'm still your friend," Elix said gently. "And as your friend, I am telling you that you are never going to see the end of it if you don't stand up to them."

Erasmus took a moment to breathe, every inhale ragged. "They'll kill me," he whispered.

Elix did not deny it. Instead, he said, "They might try."

Voices bounced across the dark school grounds—the same male voices Erasmus had hoped not to hear again for a while. Ever, even.

His face paled in the moonlight. "They're coming!" he hissed.

Elix pulled his friend toward the chainlink fence. "Quick." He let go of his arm so he could pry up the broken bottom of the fence, and waved him under. "Get inside."

Erasmus ducked under the chainlink, and Elix followed.

They hurried up the steps and into the shadowy building, past the rows of old desks that were covered in dust and cobwebs. They wheeled a chalkboard aside and pushed open a hidden door in the far wall.

The girl and her dog followed them inside, slipping through the door as Elix pushed it shut. Down a pitch-black stairwell they walked, the walls lined with cold torches that hadn't been lit in years. Upstairs, male voices shouted out in anger at the sight of the empty building, but the noise was soon swallowed up with distance as they gave up their search.

In the basement, there was more storage, including an old clawfoot bathtub with solid gold faucets, the porcelain riddled with cracks. The room was lit with candles dripping hot wax into brass holders, the assortment of flames casting flickering orange light on the dank walls.

Something in the bathtub stirred—

It was a young woman.

Erasmus and Elix froze as she startled awake. She sat up with a soft gasp and spun to face them, clutching a ratty blanket to her chest.

Her long hair was tangled, the strands too dirty to tell the color. There was dirt on her freckled face too, and her eyes—a shade between blue and green—were bright with fear.

Erasmus was the first to speak. "Who are you?" His whisper traveled far, like the hiss of a serpent.

She didn't reply.

"How did you get in here?" he tried again.

Still, nothing.

Elix said, "Are you a student here?"

She just sat there, clutching the blanket to her chest, her eyes wide and unblinking. She was very pretty, and...human? She looked human, but there was something...*off* about her.

The two friends leaned in close to whisper.

"I think we should tell someone," Elix said.

"No." The rebuke came from the dirty, trembling girl in the bathtub. "Don't." In a softer voice, she added, "Please."

It was the boys' turn to be silent.

And then Erasmus stepped forward—slowly. "My name is Erasmus Sophronia. And this is my friend, Elix Danik."

"Friend." She tested the word on her tongue, as if trying a new piece of fruit for the first time.

Elix said, "Do you need help?"

Before she could reply, Erasmus, who was glancing around the room at the takeout containers and blankets, said, "Have you been living in here?"

The woman remained silent.

Erasmus said, "What's your name?"

She pulled the tattered sleeves of her sweatshirt over her fingers—fingers that looked like they had been burned several times, likely from lighting all those candles. "Helia," she whispered.

"Like the goddess." Erasmus's voice was as quiet as hers.

The woman gave him a funny look, but nodded. "Like the goddess."

Rain began to fall from the ceiling. At first, the girl and her dog did not notice it, too distracted by what was going on in the old building to care about a little bit of rain. But soon, the water drops were growing in size, and the basement was flooding.

Erasmus, Elix, and Helia didn't notice. They kept talking, unaffected by the water rising past knee-height.

The girl and her dog began to panic. "Help!" she called to them, Singer echoing her plea with a bark.

She sloshed through the water, moving as fast as she could toward the group of three peculiar people, but it was like moving through quicksand. No matter how hard she ran, she couldn't reach them, and soon the water was too deep to stand in.

"We have to get out of here!" she shouted. But they did not hear her. She could see them, but they couldn't see her. She was alone.

She treaded water to stay afloat, but it just kept getting deeper, pushing her head closer to the ceiling. Erasmus, Elix, and Helia were down below, unaffected by the rising water. They kept talking, their faces obscured by the dark, rippling depths.

The girl swam up the stairwell, her dog paddling behind her, but the door was sealed, and they couldn't get out. Her head neared the ceiling, and soon Singer went under.

"No!" she cried out on a broken breath. She dove under the surface, attempting to grab him, but he was already gone.

She came up for air, gasping, and bumped her head on the ceiling.

"Help!" she called again, but it was no use.

The space in which she had air left to breathe kept getting smaller, and smaller, and smaller...

And the girl began to drown.

14

BORDER STRONGHOLD
PARADISI, STATE OF KER

Darien barked to Tanner, "Clean the wound and stitch her up!"

The hacker acted without delay, hurrying to Ivy's side as Darien pushed past Joyce, who was leaning on the seat over Loren, back door open.

"What happened?" Darien demanded.

"I don't know, she just stopped breathing," Joyce said. "I gave her more serum—"

"How much?"

"One vial."

He lifted Loren out of the truck and laid her down on the ground. Joyce rushed after him, clutching the case that held the vials of serum.

Darien grabbed it from her and pushed the hem of Loren's sweatshirt —one of his—up to her chin. He unzipped the case, bit the cap off a syringe, and filled it with one of the vials.

"Come on," he muttered, watching the teal liquid fill the tube too goddamn slowly. To Loren, he said, "Stay with me, baby, stay with me. *Come on.*"

The moment it was full, he slammed the needle into her heart and pushed down on the plunger, dispensing every last drop.

"You're not doing this," Darien gritted out. "You're not fucking doing this, Loren." He threw the syringe aside and began chest compressions. "You're not leaving me. You are *not* leaving me. I haven't come all this way —all this fucking way—for *nothing!*"

He pinched her nostrils shut and breathed into her mouth. Behind him, sirens wailed, people wept, and Ivy cried out in pain as Tanner disinfected her wound, the pungent bite of alcohol choking the air.

"Breathe," Darien said, pumping her heart. "I need you to breathe, sweetheart. *Breathe.*"

Again, he blew into her mouth—the mouth he'd kissed a thousand times. Her lips were icy, her skin pallid and waxy. Even her hair had lost its luster, as if Death had already claimed her.

No. Darien chanted the word, every breath sawing his lungs apart. *No. No.*

Fucking *no.*

"*Loren!*" he called out to her, a broken sob that cleaved the air, heart splitting in two. "Come on, baby. Come on, baby—*breathe! BREATHE!*"

This wasn't happening—this couldn't be happening. If he'd made a mistake, if he'd chosen the wrong path, the path that had led to her death—

If he was responsible for this, he would never forgive himself.

He would never survive this.

"Breathe, goddamn it!" Again, he pinched her nose and blew into her mouth. Pumped his hands harder. *Harder.* She had to wake up—she had to stay with him. "Breathe, sweetheart! *BREATHE!*"

IN THE HEART of the universe, in the middle of nowhere, the girl began to fade away. The water was heavy, and she could no longer tell up from down, could no longer see the old school building. It was dark here, and she was alone, not even her Familiar Spirit by her side.

But then she heard a voice. A male voice, shouting at her to breathe.

She didn't know who it was, who was calling out an unfamiliar name on raw, broken breaths, but suddenly, she was overcome with the will to live—to fight.

Somewhere, far above, she saw a light. It was so soft, it was barely visible through the dark, rippling water, but she swam toward it, kicking her feet as hard as she could. Her hands had grown transparent, but she could still see them, and she clung to this fact as though it were a life raft as she swam, following the sound of his voice—so strong and deep. Stronger, perhaps, than the water that threatened to crush her.

"Breathe!" shouted that deep, rich voice. *"Breathe!"* There was such power in that voice, she would have wept from the emotion choking every word, had she been able.

She wished she knew why he was so upset.

She wished she could see him.

Harder, she swam. Faster. Her chest was tight and aching, and her hands were fading, quickly now, but she fought. Gods damn her, she fought.

One more kick, one more stroke of her transparent arms, and she broke the surface of the water, coughing and gasping for air.

She sat up—in the clawfoot bathtub in the schoolhouse.

Erasmus and Helia sat on the floor nearby, speaking quietly among a collection of candles. Helia was wrapped up in a plaid blanket, picking through an emergency kit that was open before her. Elix was gone—it was just the two of them now. Helia began to tend to Erasmus's wounds, gently dabbing at the split in his lip. He watched her with affection, the blood on his face gleaming in the candlelight.

The water in the bathtub drained with a noisy gurgle. The girl kept breathing breaths she didn't need, her ghostly body cold and shaking.

That powerful male voice was gone. But there was a part of her now that didn't feel as alone as she had before.

"BREATHE!" Darien shouted, his throat so raw it felt bloody. He pounded a fist on Loren's chest. *"Breathe!* Breathe, *god-fucking-DAMNIT!*—"

Loren's chest rose with a shuddering breath drawn through her mouth. Those eyes were still shut, but she was breathing again.

She was *breathing*—

And then she coughed.

Darien held his breath, staring at her face, hoping and praying with every goddamn shred of his soul that she was finally waking up.

She had coughed up a mouthful of water, he realized. That was water dribbling down the sides of her face.

What the *fuck*.

Carefully, Darien wiped it away, not knowing what this meant, what to do, how to feel. But—

She was still breathing. It was enough—for now.

Darien fell back on the concrete, bracing a hand behind him, his own breathing shallow and rapid. He tipped his head back, gulping down air, not able to get enough.

He felt like he was drowning.

"Fuck." He was *this* close to breaking, but he would bend right in half before he let himself snap.

Night number fucking one, and they were already down to seven syringes.

"You suspected something was going wrong with her when I checked in with you," Darien said, speaking quietly. "Didn't you?"

He stood behind the truck with Doctor Atlas, out of earshot of the others. He hadn't planned on berating Joyce for failing to act quicker, but once the fear of losing Loren tonight had subsided, Darien had recalled her behavior while they'd charged the cars.

Joyce had told him that everything was good, but she'd lied—he could see that now. For whatever reason, she'd withheld the truth, and it had almost cost Loren her life.

"I thought everything was fine," Joyce whispered.

"But it wasn't." Rage began to simmer below Darien's skin, and he fought the heat. "It wasn't fine, and you didn't tell me."

She swallowed. "I didn't want to concern you, Darien. You're under a lot of stress—"

"She *is* my concern," he said, pointing at the truck. "She is my concern," he repeated. "The next time anything happens, I don't care how minor you think it is, I want you to tell me. Even if I'm busy, even if I'm fighting a goddamn Veil monster, I need you to come and get me. Can you do that, Joyce?"

Another swallow, her gray eyes shining in the street lights. "Yes."

"I'm grateful that you're here," he said, softening his tone, "but I need you to do your job."

"With all due respect, Darien," she hissed, "my job usually involves a team of hospital support staff and equipment designed to keep people alive."

"I understand and respect that. I'm not asking you to work miracles, Joyce, I'm asking you to tell me when something's going wrong, so that I can help you." The edge in his voice was back, and he worked at softening it again. "So I can help you help *her*." He pointed at the truck again. "I need you to communicate with me, and I need you to act quicker when something doesn't feel right. Does that make sense?"

Her swallow was audible. "Yes."

"Can you do this?"

It took her a minute, but she finally looked him in the eye. "Yes," she said. "I can."

"Thank you."

He turned and joined the others. They were gathered around the vehicles, catching their breath and bandaging wounds. "Everyone good to keep going?" he asked them.

"Fine with me," Tanner said as he pulled a clean shirt over his head. His eyes flicked between his mom and Darien as he smoothed the hem. "Everything good?"

"Fine," Darien said.

Tanner's mouth shifted into a thoughtful frown, his attention shifting back to Joyce. "Mom?"

"We're all good, Tanner," Joyce assured him. She breezed passed Darien, heading for the truck. "All good and ready to roll." She swung open the back door. Darien had placed Loren inside after monitoring her for several minutes, ensuring she was stable. No more inexplicable water coming out of her lungs.

He watched her now, making sure her chest was rising with even breaths.

It was.

He faced Ivy. She was leaning against Jack, supported by the arm he'd wrapped around her waist. "Are you good to continue?" Darien asked her.

"Of course." She gestured to her bandaged leg. "It's just a scratch." She forced a smile, but Darien saw through it.

"You look pale." He headed for the driver's door of the truck. "Make sure you eat something."

"Least I get to drive now," Jack joked. He laughed when his wife smacked him in the head.

They were behind schedule now, though not by much. Come tomorrow, they'd be in Yveswich.

Come tomorrow, they'd be paying a visit to Caliginous on Silverway. Roark might've said the Reverse Chamber couldn't work miracles, but Darien hoped with everything he had that it would work a miracle for him.

THE REST of the ride to Yveswich was quiet and tense. Darien pushed the truck as fast as it could go, ripping through red lights and stop signs whenever he could, his eyes continuously flickering to the rear-view mirror and the girl lying on the seat in the back.

At one point during the journey, Bandit crawled out of Darien's shadow. The Familiar said nothing as he crept between the front seats and into the back, moving with far more care than usual.

Darien watched in the rear-view mirror, Tanner turning in his seat to watch too, as the dog lay down beside Loren, stretching his mist-lined body out to fit. He laid his head down on her stomach and watched her for a few minutes before closing his eyes.

Tanner shared a look with Darien, but neither of them said anything. Sometimes words just weren't enough.

15

SOLESTIA
YVESWICH, STATE OF KER

"This some kinda joke, lady?"

Shay Cousens tore her gaze from the grimy window of the mechanic shop and looked for the source of the grumbling voice.

A burly man in grease-coated coveralls was frowning down at her. Part warlock, mostly human.

Shay shifted in her seat, the uncomfortable plastic chair creaking beneath her. The waiting area by the front entrance was empty aside from herself and an old witch reading the newspaper, but the humid shop that stank of tires and oil was alive with activity.

"I'm sorry, what?" She'd already had two cups of coffee, but she still felt like she was half-asleep.

The man's frown deepened. "You got no engine." He chucked her keys into her lap with a filthy hand.

"Excuse me?" she snapped. "What do you mean I have no engine?"

"We don't like pranks around here," he scolded.

She grabbed her keys and flung herself out of her seat. "This is outrageous! You're telling me my car won't start because I have no bloody *engine?*"

For the first time since this wretched morning had gone sideways—since she'd tried to start up her car to go looking for her sister, only to be met with a hollow *click* when she'd turned the key in the ignition—the man looked at her like she might actually be telling the truth.

As politely as possible, she asked him, "Where's your boss?" This had to be some kind of mistake—a joke, or something.

Or a thief had decided to steal her engine.

What kind of thief stole an engine? Of course this would happen to her, of all people! Shay was a master of theft—which meant *she* was supposed to do the thieving.

Oh, this was ironic! Ironic and plain stupid.

"The boss ain't here today," the man said, "but the owner just pulled up." He nodded toward the big window behind her. "Talk to him if you want, but there's nothing I can do about your missing engine, unless you want to buy a new one."

That wasn't an option—she couldn't afford a new one, not when she needed to spend all this money she'd stolen on her search to find Anna—but before she could say so, he lumbered away.

The bells on the door chimed, signaling someone's entry. Shay's scalp prickled with the familiar feel of the aura she had hoped never to sense again, and when that husky, bass voice filled the room, she felt all the blood in her head rush down to her feet.

"Heard there's a rogue engine on the loose."

This could *not* be happening.

Slowly, Shay turned around to face Roman Devlin, who looked all kinds of pissed—and all kinds of stupidly attractive in his tattered gray jeans, black combat boots, and a baggy, heavy metal band shirt with the sleeves ripped at his shoulders.

With a swallow, Shay forced herself to look at his face—at that pissed-off expression that spelled murder.

Roman drawled, "Wonder why that could be."

She lifted her chin. "How big a raise did you give your employees to steal my engine?" This mechanic shop was on neutral ground; she'd thought it would be safe to be towed here, but it seemed Roman had spread his shadows beyond the Gray Zone.

Why did that not surprise her?

She had royally screwed up by choosing to steal from him. Anyone else —literally *anyone*—and she guaranteed she wouldn't be in this mess right now. But this man—this absolutely infuriating Darkslayer—was relentless. He just wouldn't let it go, would he?

He made a sound of disapproval. "Oh, I can't give them the credit for that. That was all me, pup."

Her cheeks splotched with anger. "You son of a bitch."

Roman's frown deepened into something very deadly. Was it just her, or did the gold in his irises darken right before her eyes? Even the warm cast to his tousled dark hair was suddenly absent.

Was it the fluorescents? Was it the sunlight streaming in through the window that was in dire need of washing?

Roman said, "Where's my necklace?"

She scoffed. "You think I'm going to give it to you after this?"

"Where's my necklace?"

"What are you, a parrot? I need my car so I can find my sister."

A moment of silence. And then, "Fine."

Shay blinked. "Really?"

"Sure. I'll trade you: your engine for my necklace."

She bared her teeth at him, the spark of hope in her chest doused by the ice-cold waters of this perpetual raincloud. That's what Roman was: a raincloud, darkening her life everywhere he went with his sour mood, eye-twitch, and silly ripped clothes.

"You're a big stupid-head!" she snapped.

"That's creative." His humorless snicker confirmed Shay's suspicions that he didn't know how to laugh. "Deal or no deal?"

"No deal," she said, talking over him. "How about this?" She crossed her arms and tipped her weight to one leg. "You help me find my sister, and then you can have your necklace back." He didn't bat an eye at her mention of her sister; every Darkslayer House in Yveswich knew she was missing now, no thanks to anyone but Shay.

Of course, Athene was trying her hardest to cover it up, but, much to her extreme disappointment and anger, her least favorite daughter had decided to staple missing person posters all over the city, drawing attention to the problem her mother should've acknowledged weeks ago.

Anna had been abducted—of that, Shay had no doubt. She needed help, and it seemed the only one who was willing to give it was Shay. She wouldn't let her down—and she definitely wouldn't let this brooding, idiotic Darkslayer get in her way.

That Darkslayer was staring at her. "Fine," Roman bit out.

And then he turned and walked out the door, the keys that were carelessly half-stuffed into the front pocket of his jeans jingling.

Shay blinked. *What?*

She pushed through the door and ran after him, bells clanging as they thwacked against the glass. The sun beat down on her head, sending a flush of heat through her body. Despite the warm spell, there were storm clouds brewing on the horizon. Not surprising. The cold always won in Yveswich.

"Where are you going?" she called.

"To tell mommy seal what her bratty little pup is doing." He ripped his keys from his pocket and unlocked the door with the remote.

Shay tripped, one of her boots crossing over the other, but she caught herself before she could fall. "You *wouldn't!*"

Oh but he would—she didn't doubt it for a second.

"You know, Cousens," Roman began, not deigning to look at her as he kept walking. The bands of muscle in his arms rippled as he constantly flexed them, no doubt fighting a Surge. "I'm a bit concerned about your level of intelligence, after you didn't even think to pop the hood on your car. A missing engine?" He tsked, sparing her half a glance over his broad shoulder. "Come onnnn. That's easy. Anyone with half a brain would've figured it out before wasting money—*stolen* money—on a tow."

"You know," Shay countered, voice saccharine as she followed close on his heels, "I'm a bit concerned about your level of intelligence after you failed to stop me from stealing your necklace, your last kill, and—oh, looky here, your wallet." She dangled it before her.

He froze.

And then he spun around on a heel, his rage exploding out of him as he spat in her face, *"Give me back my fucking necklace, or you—"* He grabbed her by the collar before she could retreat, tugging her so close their lips nearly touched, his other hand lashing out to snatch his wallet out of her fingers. *"—are dead!"*

Fear, strong and true, rocked through her, but she didn't fight him, didn't try to pull away. She held his cold stare, and she decided to try again —one last time. She had never been a quitter, and she wasn't about to start now. There was far too much at stake for that.

"I know what I did was wrong, but I'm desperate. My sister is all I have—the only person who cares whether I live or die." Her breathing turned ragged, and she was well aware that he could feel it on her mouth— that was how close he was. "I have no idea where she is, no idea what's happened to her, who she's with, or if she's even safe, and it's *killing* me. I don't know if you have any siblings, but I would do anything in the world to protect mine—*anything."* She dared to look at him harder, even as the last of the tiny gold flecks in his irises winked out. "Even travel into the desert to find her by myself. Even cry—which I never, *ever* do." She could have sworn the corner of his mouth twitched. But she was telling the truth —the burning behind her eyes hadn't happened in so long that at first she didn't recognize it. She added in a whisper, that face of his still deadly close to hers—close enough to bite or kiss, "Even steal from Roman Devlin."

Even *blackmail* Roman Devlin, but she wasn't about to say that; she didn't think he would appreciate having a statement like that shoved in his face, especially not when it suggested she had succeeded in doing such a thing.

He looked at her—*really* looked at her, this time with a level of intensity that made her want to cover herself up, regardless that his eyes never strayed from her face. It might've been minutes that passed or hours, she couldn't be certain. The sun blazed down, hotter than before, and she began to sweat in the thick humidity, her heart racing and tripping, just like her feet that had decided moments ago to be clumsy.

No, they hadn't decided anything—it was *Roman* turning her into this pile of useless putty. Stupid, aggravating Roman in his stupid, ripped shirt.

Finally, he spoke. "Don't do it."

Shay blinked. "Do what?"

"Cry. I hate criers."

"Well, I'm warning you now, I'm an ugly crier. Trust me—you don't want to see it." There was that mouth twitch again—the one that made her think this bastard might actually smile. "So you should probably just agree," she added, "and spare us both the ugly mess."

A beat of silence. And then: "You were going to drive your piece of shit car into the desert?" He was still so close, his nearness allowed her to smell him—the cologne on his skin, and the mint on his breath.

For a moment, she didn't know what to say. She hadn't expected him to ask her a question like that. What did a heartless Shadowmaster like Roman care if she drove it into the desert?

"I said I'd do anything, and I meant it," she stated.

The skin around his eyes tightened; there was a freckle by the left and two by the right. "That tin can wouldn't make it five miles in this heat."

She eyed his vehicle, shining just behind his tall form. "Yours would," she said cheerfully. "I bet it also has air conditioning." Her eyes flicked up to meet his again, and a muscle ticked in his sharp jaw. "It's nice," she offered.

"It was nicer before someone kicked the bumper." He wasn't wrong—her shoe had left a scuff mark.

"Five days," Shay offered. "Help me look for my sister for five days. If we don't find anything, we'll come back, I'll give you your necklace, and you'll never have to see me again."

Two minutes passed—exactly two. Shay counted every second.

"Never?" he gritted out.

"Cross my heart." That heart was skipping every second beat, but her magic kept him from noticing. To him, she was steady as ever—a rock unmoving in a river current.

She wished that were true. There was a part of her that was stronger than most people, she had to give herself credit for that, but underneath was a layer as soft as silt—and that silty layer won over all the others whenever she was around Roman.

Finally, he released her—not with a shove, but with a gradual loosening of his hand, a gesture that somehow felt more threatening than if he'd pushed her. He'd stretched her shirt—crumpled it into the shape of his fingers. Scarred, tattooed fingers that were nice to look at. She had always liked hands.

"Five days," he said, the pale gold flecks in his eyes winking out again, "if I don't kill you first."

PART TWO
THE HOLLOW

16

SOLESTIA
YVESWICH, STATE OF KER

Roman Devlin might kill her.

Shay had come to terms with this simple truth the moment she'd opened the passenger's-side door of his car and got inside. For her sister, she would risk it—would risk death at the hands of one of the deadliest Darkslayers in the state of Ker.

Anna had always been the safe one, the logical sister who calculated how high up she was before making a jump. Shay was different in all the worse ways. She was reckless and stupid—flaws, maybe, but without them she wouldn't stand a chance at following through on this plan that was both reckless *and* stupid.

The plan involving the raincloud of a Darkslayer in the driver's seat. How in the gods' names had she managed to get this far? She decided it was best not to question it, and instead concentrate on making sure it lasted—and keeping herself alive. She was no good to her sister if she wound up dead.

What would Anna think if she saw her now?

Shay buckled her seatbelt. "If you keep glaring at me, your face is going to get stuck like that," she warned.

Roman was indeed glaring at her. She met that glare with a narrowing of her own eyes.

After a few seconds that felt like years, he put the car in drive and sped out of the parking lot of the mechanic shop. The momentum flattened Shay's spine against the leather seat. It was very clean in here—no gum wrappers on the floor, no takeout cups tossed into the back seat, no dog hair from volunteering at the local animal shelters. It was...*too* clean. Maybe he *was* a psychopath.

As Roman sped through the neutral districts of Yveswich, Shay gripped the bottom of her seat with both hands, leading him to believe she was afraid of his daredevil speed, when in reality she was keeping her hands closer to the weapons concealed on her person.

"I need to stop at home and get my bag," she said. She had her most important things in the purse by her feet—medication, phone, wallet—but she had no extra sets of clothes, no toothbrush, no sanitary products for her time of the month, which was unpredictable at best and nonexistent at worst.

Roman said nothing. Seconds ticked by, and he still didn't speak.

She decided to hold her tongue and give him the benefit of the doubt. Maybe he'd stalked her longer than she thought, and he already knew where her apartment was. She wouldn't doubt it; rumor claimed there wasn't a living thing Roman couldn't find.

She stared through the windshield, watching the highway get eaten up by the tires as he wove through lanes of traffic, across and under overpasses, and past multiple waterfalls.

But she couldn't keep quiet any longer as he veered away from the city and took the exit onto the interstate.

She shot him a look of accusation, but he spared her nothing—not even that tic in his jaw made an appearance. "Ahem—excuse me. Did someone stuff cotton in your ears or something? I said I need to get my bag."

Again, she was met with silence. She was about to repeat herself another time when he spoke.

"I think it's best if you keep quiet for most of this trip."

"Why?"

His hand tightened on the wheel and twisted, making the hard muscles in his biceps bulge. "Because if you pluck my last nerve, Shay, I am going to kill you." He speared her with a hard look. "And I don't have many nerves left that you haven't touched yet." He turned on the radio and cranked the volume. "I like music, and I like silence." His words were barely audible over the noise. "When I choose music, I expect whoever I'm with not to talk. And when I choose silence, I mostly prefer whoever I'm with not to talk. Think you can handle keeping your mouth shut unless it's to tell me where to go?"

"I just told you to go to my apartment and you didn't listen!" she shouted.

"Your apartment?" Oh hell. The curious tone of his question told her he had no idea about the apartment.

She broke eye contact and stared straight ahead. "There you go with your parroting again," she muttered. The noise pounding through the speakers was giving her a headache. "Your taste in music sucks, by the way." It was a lie—she liked this band, but she wasn't about to give him the satisfaction of knowing that—especially not when that tic in his jaw amused her so much.

"Shay," he warned.

"We need to get to Motel 58."

He lowered the volume—just a bit. "Where is it?"

"About a four-hour drive." It was a lie—the drive would take closer to eight, but she wasn't about to admit that. She'd already pushed her luck as it was, and if she managed to make it all the way through the desert and to Motel 58 without being thrown out of the vehicle, she would be surprised.

He stepped on the accelerator. "Bet I can cut that in half." The needle on the speedometer flew to the right as they shot like a bullet down the interstate.

Motel 58 was Shay's only hope of finding Anna. She had chased every lead in the weeks following Anna's disappearance, and the only clue she'd managed to find involved Motel 58. It wasn't much, but it was better than nothing.

She only hoped it wouldn't lead to a dead end.

Roman turned up the music until the bass rattled the frame and pounded into her eardrums. As they raced away from Yveswich, Shay couldn't help but steal another glance at the man the general public called *Shadows*. The man she'd somehow managed to manipulate—or so she thought.

This whole thing almost seemed too easy, especially for someone of his reputation. Was there more going on here? She had always prided herself on her guile and guts, but she wasn't stupid enough to think that Roman wasn't a threat. In nearly twenty years, no one had been able to keep up with her the way he had these last couple days—and now she was waltzing into the middle of the desert with him.

Uneasiness settled heavily in her stomach like a stone.

She studied Roman out of the corner of her vision. That look on his face—that dead cast to his eyes that no longer showed a hint of gold—told her she had made a terrible mistake.

Roman rarely left Yveswich, and if he did it was only for a day or two, tops. And his dad always, *always* knew about it.

So driving out of the city with a Selkie was a first. Not telling his dad was another first.

And allowing himself to be manipulated by anyone other than said dad was definitely a first. But the truth was, he needed a breather. Don and his men had been suffocating him since he was a kid, so it was high time he came up for some air. And although this Selkie had stolen something important from him, he had to admit he was looking forward to getting away for a few days until he managed to get it back.

As he sped down the interstate, he allowed himself to pretend, just for one second, that he was leaving Yveswich for good. Of course, if that were true, he'd have Pax in the passenger's seat with him instead of Shay Cousens.

'I hope you know what you're doing,' Sayagul said from where she was curled up in his shadow.

Paxton had school for the next few days. Roman would make sure Kylar kept an eye on him—and would contact him if Donovan tried anything vile. Kylar, Roman trusted, not just with his life but Paxton's too. If Don tried anything, Roman knew Kylar would take the brunt of it and hide Paxton while it happened. Keeping their little brothers safe was the one thing they both excelled at—and the one thing they had both agreed to do for each other.

The thought didn't sit well with Roman, though. He didn't want Kylar getting hurt any more than he wanted Paxton to, but Roman had stepped in for all of them—Paxton, Kylar, Eugene, Willow—so many times that he hardly had any skin left to scar.

But Roman had a good feeling about this. Not about the Selkie, but about his choice to get away at this particular time. Last weekend was... rough. Terrible, actually. But he refused to think about the details. And when one rough weekend happened, his dad usually didn't try anything again until a week or two had passed. He still made their lives a living hell in ways that didn't involve fists and different methods of physical torture, but...this weekend, they should be safe.

Still...

As he drove, Roman thought about it. He could feel Shay Cousens watching him, but he paid her no attention. He stared at the road as he wove through traffic, idly dragging his tongue piercing across the roof of his mouth.

Five days—max. And he'd make sure his dad believed he was out on a job that would pay him very well.

If anything happened before then, Roman would race back to Yveswich, no questions asked. Even if this time, his dad finally broke him.

17

YVESWICH CITY LIMITS
YVESWICH, STATE OF KER

Yveswich was the kind of city that used its age to its advantage, becoming more visually appealing as decades passed. The ancient houses, temples, and serpentine rows of businesses had never been updated, never been torn down if there was even the slightest chance of saving them. Instead, they were preserved with the utmost of care, so Yveswich throughout the centuries had remained mostly the same, aging like fine wine.

Every time Darien came here, it felt like stepping through a time portal. And today, as the truck began its descent into the sprawling maze of a city, felt no different. The only thing that seemed to change every few years was the level of traffic and the number of lanes—always more, never less.

The forcefield over Yveswich extended farther past the outskirts of the city than the one above Angelthene, so Darien felt the magic ripple over the truck several miles before they reached the sign proudly welcoming them to the state's historic capital. A faint wash of acid-green passed over his vision, becoming more subtle the farther he drove.

"Where to first?" Tanner asked, clicking away on his laptop.

"We'll go downtown. I'll track Roman from there." Downtown was neutral ground, which was the safer and less conspicuous choice for outsiders. Besides, they had nowhere to go, no accommodations yet, so pulling over at the side of the road in a Gray or Red Zone was a bad fucking idea. The last thing Darien wanted was to draw attention to themselves before Roman and the few people the Shadowmaster trusted knew they were here.

As Darien approached the exit that led downtown, the sun began to tuck itself behind a layer of clouds that promised rain. Unlike Angelthene's dry heat, it was always uncomfortably muggy here, even during prolonged periods of sun.

A white sports car blew by on the interstate—heading out of town. The deep growl of the engine was orgasmic.

Darien's eyes flicked to the rear-view mirror in time to see the car—candy-coated with white rims—zip around the bend. "Fuck, that's a nice car."

Tanner chuckled. "They're going to get slapped with a ticket in two minutes if they don't watch it," he said, monitoring the speed traps. Darien had barely slowed down in time to not get dinged himself a few minutes ago.

He drove across a stone bridge that arched above a canal. The canals here were even greater in number than the waterfalls, both adding to the city's constant wet feel.

Congested traffic in the downtown core pushed them behind schedule by about an hour. By the time Darien found a casual neighborhood to pull over in, and Jack and Ivy vanished inside the doors of a pizza joint to grab everyone lunch, it was past noon.

Darien shut off the truck and took out a resealable bag of Stygian salts. He shook some onto the lid of the center console and slid them into a line with the edge of an empty cigarette packet. He snorted the salts through a rolled-up banknote and sat back in his seat, waiting for them to take affect.

The drug burned his nose and made his skin tingle as if he'd been stung by bees. He closed his eyes and focused, Joyce and Tanner keeping quiet as Darien searched for his cousin, using the memory of Roman's face as a target. Several years had passed since he'd last seen him, but not long enough to make a difference.

Minutes passed and he found nothing, not one trace of him. He wasn't surprised—if anything, he was frustrated. He would need to find Roman another way now.

Darien blinked the Sight out of his eyes, the drug preventing the black from leaving them for several blinks. "Nothing," he declared.

Tanner was focused on his screen, a hand pressed to his chin while the other scrolled on the navigation pad. "Doesn't surprise me," he murmured.

The back door swung open on Joyce's side. Jack and Ivy were back with a stack of pizza boxes and bottles of water.

"Any luck?" Ivy asked, passing out the waters.

Darien took one and twisted the lid open. "He's invisible."

Jack helped himself to a slice of pepperoni and bit into it, eating half in one go. "What do we do now?" he asked, mouth covered in tomato sauce.

Darien thought about it. "We track Pax instead." The kid had likely changed enough in appearance that he'd have to get Tanner to find a photograph online, but that should be easy enough with the amount of social networking sites the kids were using nowadays.

Joyce shuffled through the pizza boxes, Ivy balancing the stack carefully, and selected a different flavor. "Who's Pax?" she asked.

Darien took a swig of water. "Roman's half-brother." Pax shared a dad with Roman and Travis, but he had a different mom.

Ivy checked her watch. "What's the day today?"

"Wednesday," Tanner said.

"He'll still be in school."

"Which gives us enough time to find a place for the rest of you to lie low," Darien said. "I'll be going by myself to find Pax." It was a precaution, in case Paxton's dad had any plans to pick his kid up after school. Darien highly doubted it, but he wouldn't chance being seen by the wrong people. And Donovan Slade was the wrong fucking person.

"What kind of pizza did you get?" Darien asked his sister.

"Pepperoni, ham-and-pineapple, and triple-meat."

Darien beckoned for Ivy to pass him the pizza boxes. "Give me the pepperoni before Jack eats it all."

YEARS HAD PASSED since Darien had last seen his cousin Paxton Slade. Back then, the kid must have been... Shit, he couldn't remember how old. *Young*. Darien wasn't sure Pax would even recognize him now.

With a photo of Paxton fresh in his memory, Darien tracked him to a part of town not far from his school. This area, being on neutral ground, had a safer and more laid-back feel. As he drove, the people he observed on the sidewalks didn't feel the constant need to look over their shoulders or keep their hands in reach of the weapons they carried—concealed, of course. Unless you were a Darkslayer, you didn't open carry here, same as in Angelthene.

Darien slowed at a stop sign out front of a bakery with a violinist playing out front. The tiny business made this whole block smell divine. Using his Sight, he looked through the relatively weak spells on an antique shop to his left, where five boys stood in an alley beside it.

Paxton.

Darien pulled a sharp U-turn and parked a few stalls down from the entrance to Oswald's Antiques.

He got out and made his way to the alley, pulling his hood up as he moved. A light rain fell from the sky, and there was a chill in the air that made everything smell like the first bite of winter—something Darien hadn't experienced since the last time he'd gone snowboarding.

As he neared the mouth of the alley, he made the decision to take Pax for one of those cinnamon buns he could smell baking in the ovens. Based on the auras crowding around his cousin in that alley, the kid would deserve it.

He passed the antique shop, tinny old music floating through the open doors. Rain dribbled off the plastic awning, the drops drumming on Darien's hood as he stepped out front under it and rounded the corner into the alley.

Paxton Slade had changed, though not by a lot. Instead of a gangly little kid, he was now a gangly preteen—and he was pinned against the brick wall by one of the three boys fencing him in. A fourth rifled through Pax's backpack, pocketing the spare change he found inside.

Fuck, did kids really steal each other's lunch money still?

None of those boys, not even Paxton, had noticed him yet.

A sharp whistle cut between Darien's lips.

The kids turned, the thieving one rising out of his crouch. The one pinning Paxton to the wall, however, did not let go.

Darien acknowledged his cousin with a dip of his chin. "Hey, Pax." Molten anger rolled through him, spiking his body temperature. Too bad these kids were just that: *kids*.

Paxton stared at him like he'd seen a ghost. "Hi." With that mop of dark hair and the splash of freckles on his nose, he was looking more like Roman the older he got.

"These boys giving you trouble?"

The leader pinning him to the wall said, "This is between us and him, so mind your own goddamn business."

"Three things," Darien snapped. His tone made the kid pale. "One—watch your tongue, kid. Two—he's my cousin so he *is* my business. Three—this is between you and me now. You get two choices: let him go...or see what happens if you don't."

It took three seconds. Only three, and then the leader let go of Paxton with a shove that knocked his head into the wall.

Darien's temper sparked, but he leashed it as they hastily picked up their backpacks and stomped out of the alley.

Darien stopped the thief as he passed. He pulled on his backpack, dragging him back this way. "Empty your pockets."

Quickly, he turned them inside out. Change clattered to the cobbles and rolled.

Darien stared the kid in the eye. "He take anything else?" His question was for Paxton.

When Paxton replied, his voice wavered. "Don't think so."

Darien pushed the kid toward the mouth of the alley. "Scram."

He did.

Darien faced his cousin, who still stood by the wall, his scraped hands hanging awkwardly at his sides. "Remember me?" Darien said.

The kid smiled, bullies instantly forgotten. "You kidding? I still want to be you when I grow up!"

"Get your things, we gotta go."

He picked up his backpack and threw the discarded contents—books, apple, pens—back inside. "Where are we going?"

"We'll talk in private."

He went for the spare change next.

"Leave it," Darien said. "I'll get you more."

"It better be more than five gold mynet." He slid his arms through the straps of his backpack and hurried to Darien's side. "It's pizza day at school tomorrow."

"How about a hundred and a cinnamon bun?" He gestured to the bakery across the street with a jerk of his chin.

"Sold!"

The rain was really coming down as they crossed the street and ducked into the bakery. Fuck, that smell was orgasmic. Darien's mouth was watering.

"So, what are you doing here?" Paxton asked cheerily as he followed Darien to the counter, backpack thwacking against empty chairs. The place was warm and quiet, only a handful of people snacking at barstools and a table by the counter. Darien kept his hood up to avoid anyone seeing his tattoo, though he could feel several sets of probing eyes tracking his movements.

"I'm here for one of those cinnamon buns," Darien replied.

Pax rolled his eyes. "No, really."

"I'm not lying. I could smell them all the way from Angelthene."

He snorted a laugh. "You're such a dork."

They stopped at the counter and perused the menu board above the till. Their selection was solid gold—cinnamon buns and twists, double-chocolate tarts and muffins, chocolate croissants, chocolate donuts. Chocolate, chocolate, chocolate. It was heaven. But it was the cinnamon buns that were calling Darien's name.

A young woman came to take their orders. Darien placed his, then looked down at his cousin, who gaped up at the board with an open mouth.

"You're drooling," Darien said.

Pax closed his mouth.

"What do you want?"

"Same as you, but with extra icing."

Darien placed the order, asking for extra icing on both.

Five minutes later, they were seated at a table by the door, gorging on the pastries. Darien took his time, letting the cinnamon sugar dissolve on his tongue, the kid doing the same across from him.

When they were finished, Darien stacked the paper plates and plastic forks and slid them to the side of the table.

"So what's up, dude?" Paxton said with a dimpled grin, folding his string-bean arms on the yellow plastic tablecloth. "What's hanging? What are you, like thirty now?"

Darien chuckled. "Fuck off. What are you, like five?"

"Twelve, actually."

"You look five."

"You look thirty."

"You're a dumbass, and you've got icing all over your face."

Paxton grabbed a crumpled napkin and scrubbed it clean.

"I need to see Roman," Darien said.

He licked the stray crumbs off his lips. "You're fresh outta luck. I haven't talked to him all day, and when Roman goes MIA like this, he can be gone for days."

Fuck. Looked like he'd have to do this on his own, then.

"How's Travis?" Paxton asked with a mumble, eyes downcast as he picked at a tear in the tablecloth. "He okay?"

"He's fine. He still sucks at Rushin' Racers."

Paxton grinned. "Really?"

"Really."

The smile vanished, and he returned to picking at the tablecloth, eyes down again.

Darien said, "He also misses his little brother."

Paxton sighed. "I miss him too. But I'm glad he's gone." Finally, he stopped fiddling with the tablecloth and folded his arms on the table. "You'll tell him I'm not mad? That I understand?"

"He knows," Darien said. "But I'll still tell him."

Paxton nodded. "Cool."

Darien reached into his pocket and pulled out a twenty. "Here—"

Paxton snatched it out of his hand. "You said a hundo, but I'll take it!" He snapped it and held it up to the light, as if checking for signs of counterfeit.

"It's not for you. Go order a twelve-pack to go."

Paxton pushed out from the table and stood. "Extra icing?"

"On the side," Darien called. Ivy didn't like anything too sweet.

Paxton skipped up to the counter and placed the order.

As Darien waited, he stared out the window, at the rain dribbling down the cobbled road. There was a florist across the street, a specialty tea shop beside it, and two doors down from the florist was a spa that prided themselves on their selection of all-natural skincare. *Face jellies.* Darien couldn't help but smirk at the memory. There was even an ice cream parlor with over a hundred flavors, and a coffee shop ran by a witch who served everything from drinks that sparkled with gold dust, to cupcakes with decorations that talked or moved.

This block felt just like the Avenue of the Scarlet Star. Loren would love it here; the moment she woke up and felt well enough to come here, he'd show her this place.

Paxton returned, bumping into an empty chair hard enough to make it groan, the sound snapping Darien out of his daydream.

"I also got a pop," Paxton said. "Hope you don't mind." He slurped from a can of grape soda, his upper lip already stained purple.

"You won't be getting any sleep tonight with all that sugar." He glanced out the window again. "What's this street called?"

He took another slurp. "Avenue of the Waning Moon."

"You serious?"

"Mm-hmm."

No wonder it reminded Darien so much of the Avenue of the Scarlet Star; it was practically a dupe, though this one had two differences that stood out to him the most: motor vehicles were allowed to drive down the Avenue of the Waning Moon, and there was no marble sundial dedicated to Tempus, chronic liar and fucked-up outcast of the Terran pantheon.

And part of the reason why Angelthene was still standing. When Darien considered the other part—the girl who'd shielded the city with her aura—he felt that glass-in-lungs sensation return.

"You okay?" Paxton was staring at him, soda can frozen in hand.

"Yeah," he lied.

"You looked like you went somewhere else for a sec."

"I'm back now." He blinked. "Here, I'll take those." He grabbed the box of pastries from Pax's sticky hands and got to his feet. "Get your things, we're leaving."

They headed out into the damp afternoon. Darien pulled up his hood and slid his free hand into his pocket, the chill in the air biting his knuckles.

"How's your dad?" Darien said.

"You mean the tyrannosaurus rex?" Paxton shrugged his hood on. "Still stomping around, biting everyone's heads off."

"I'm glad to hear you're still obsessed with dinosaurs."

"No way, dude!" He looked up at Darien in horror, rain pelting his pale face. "Dinosaurs are for nerds."

Darien raised a brow.

It took Paxton exactly three seconds before he caved under the scrutiny, a contagious grin lighting up his face. "I have this huge collection of old fossils and figurines!" he exclaimed. "All my friends are insanely jealous. Wanna see?"

"Later. You got a phone?"

"*'Do I got a phone'!*" Paxton mocked. He promptly produced one from the side pocket of his backpack. "Tah-dah!"

Darien waved a hand. "Give it here."

He held fast. "Are you calling Roman?"

Darien pried the device out of his hand. "Yes."

"Why don't you just use *your* phone? Did you break it?"

"Because no one can know I'm here. What's your passcode?"

"If I tell you, I'll have to change it."

"Pax," Darien warned.

"Fine," he sighed, rolling his eyes. He stomped in a mud puddle, splashing both of their pants. "1 2 3 4."

Darien deadpanned. "Wow. I never would've guessed."

Paxton shoved him in the arm. "Shut up."

"Do you talk to Roman like that?" He punched in the passcode and scrolled through Paxton's contacts.

"All the time—he's the one who gave me the 101 on how to be a lippy little shit." He waggled his brows.

Darien smirked. "'Lippy little shit'. That's what he calls you, isn't it?"

"Yup."

Darien found Roman and hit call.

It didn't even ring—it went straight to voicemail.

He hung up and gave the phone back to Pax. "Voicemail," he explained. "Told ya."

Darien started walking again, and Paxton followed. They passed Oswald's Antiques, the smell of old furniture and wood polish floating through the doors.

"You want to talk about that bullshit I saw in the alley?"

"Nope."

Darien shook his head. "I don't know what they think they're going to gain by bullying Donovan Slade's kid."

"Dad doesn't care. He thinks I need to stick up for myself."

"Your dad knows about this, and Roman doesn't?"

Paxton shrugged. "I can't tell Roman or he'd kill them, and you can't kill underage kids."

"You actually can't murder anyone, but that's besides the point."

"*You* murder people," Pax challenged.

Darien smiled, and Paxton's face turned a shade paler.

Darien's brows flicked up. "Your dad's Donovan Slade, and my killing people makes you shit your pants?"

"I'm not shitting my pants."

"Then why's your face all white?"

He scowled. "I'm cold, *okay?*"

"Stand up straight—don't slouch."

"I'm not."

"You are. Own your height. You're tall, and you're going to get taller. Wear your height with pride."

Paxton straightened and thrust his shoulders back, comically exaggerating every movement.

Darien laughed and shook his head. "Where do you live?" he asked.

"With my dad, where do you think?"

"Alright, that's enough attitude for one day."

"Sorry, but *seriously?* Dad would *never* let me go anywhere else! Soon as I turn eighteen, I'm moving out and changing my last name to 'Devlin'."

Devlin was Roman's mom's last name. Paxton had no connection to her, since she had died before he was born, but Darien understood that Pax's connection to Roman was enough of an incentive to claim the last name as his own. Anything to get away from his tyrannical father and the name 'Slade'.

If Randal and Don had succeeded at anything in life it was guaranteeing their kids would do anything in their power to get away from them, severing all ties in the process.

Darien said, "What about Roman? He live at the House of Black too?"

"Technically, yeah."

"What do you mean 'technically'?"

"I mean he technically lives at the House of Black, but he's got his own place too. Dad's not allowed to know about it, though."

"You wouldn't happen to have a key to that place, would you?"

"'Course, but it's at home. There's no way we'll get in without being seen. " He picked at the split in his lip; those bullies had really done a number on him. A splotch of purple and yellow was blooming by his eye too, and there was a ring of bruises around his throat that looked like fingerprints.

'Should've killed them,' Bandit hissed.

'You can't kill underage kids,' Darien replied. *'Weren't you listening?'*

Bandit grumbled. *'They'd make good chew toys.'*

"Wait," Paxton said, snapping his fingers, "I got an idea." He took out his phone again, found a name in the contacts, and hit call.

"Wait, wait, wait." Darien stopped short, forcing the other people on the sidewalk to maneuver around them. "Who are you calling?"

"Relax. His name's Eugene—he's Kylar's little brother." Kylar 'Ky' Lavin was Roman's Second and hacker. Darien had met him a handful of times, but he hadn't seen him in years.

The line rang three times before a young male voice—slightly nasally—picked up. "Hello?"

"Eugene," Paxton began, "meet me at the clubhouse in half an hour. And bring Kylar, 'kay?"

"What's going on?" The kid had a thick lisp that made understanding him a little more difficult, especially at this volume.

"I'll tell you when you get there. Make sure you bring your keys, I forgot mine."

"Pax, what is—"

"No questions!" He hung up.

"Well done," Darien said.

Paxton beamed up at him, a picture of pride.

"Where's this clubhouse?" Darien asked.

Paxton fumbled his phone away. "Technically, it's on Roman's property, but he doesn't know about it." That was highly doubtful.

Darien stepped off the curb and rounded his car, the black paint glistening in the rain.

Paxton was stumbling down the sidewalk, struggling to zip the pocket on his backpack shut.

"What are you doing?" Darien asked.

"Zipper's stuck." He yanked it closed. "Fixed it."

"More like broke it."

Paxton skidded to a halt and gaped at the car, the astonished look on his face comical as hell. "Whoaaa, sick whip! Is this thing yours?"

Darien merely unlocked the doors.

Paxton grinned. "Can I drive?"

"When you get your license."

"Awe, man!" He stepped back to admire the car and gave his best attempt at a whistle. "Gee, it's almost as nice as Roman's!"

Bandit growled. *'Did he really just say that?'*

'Be nice,' Darien replied. He raised a brow at Pax. "Almost?"

Paxton smiled and shrugged. "Sorry to hurt your feelings."

Darien opened the driver's door. "Get in. I'll show you how fast this thing can go."

18

ELSEWHERE

In the heart of the universe, over two thousand years in the past, the girl and her dog continued to observe the three peculiar students as they went to and from their classes at the academy.

Erasmus was a genius who excelled at any task that came his way, so it was with ease that he created a fresh identity for his unlikely friend, Helia.

Of course, in order to create a new identity, Helia would need to change her name. But she loved her name, so she decided she would choose one that shared the same meaning as Helia—sunlight—but was different enough to never raise suspicion.

She would call herself 'Cyra'.

Helia, under the new name of Cyra, began taking classes at Angelthene Academy, where she was sorted into the same house as her two friends: the House of Salt. Helia and Erasmus grew close quickly, and soon they were spending every waking moment possible by each other's side. Elix, too, was with them often; Helia loved Elix as well, but in a different way than she loved Erasmus. While the love she felt for Elix was friendship, the kind she felt for Erasmus was far stronger.

One day, Erasmus and Elix left the school with Helia. For three days they journeyed to their destination—a bustling city built by the water, just like Angelthene.

But this city was older and colder, and its history bled even deeper into the past than Angelthene's.

Helia brought her two friends to see a Nameless being, where they discovered that Helia was not just named after the goddess—she *was* the goddess.

The night prior, Erasmus had been made aware of this in secret; Helia had confessed to him by candlelight in the Old Hall, and Erasmus, because he loved and trusted her, had believed her, regardless of how unlikely it sounded, like something out of a fairytale book. Even now, he found himself in awe as he watched his new friend converse with the Nameless being in a cavern deep below an ancient city—a serpent king of old who never showed its face. Erasmus hadn't told Elix about Helia's true identity; Helia had asked Erasmus not to—she wanted to tell Elix herself.

Now, Elix watched with a mixture of awe and fear as they stood in that cavern, deep below the earth. The Nameless serpent slithered in the shadows as it spoke to Helia, who, just a moment ago, had offered the creature a trade. Nothing could be seen of the massive serpent but glimpses of its long, limbless body shifting continuously under the blueish glow of bioluminescent insects, its rippling scales gleaming. The cavern was filled with statues of humans, vampires, werewolves, and veneficae—past visitors the monstrous serpent had deemed unworthy of a bargain and turned to stone.

"If I give you access to the prima materia," the serpent said, its voice ancient and hushed, "you may only use it to create one thing. Do you understand?"

"I understand." Helia's words were firm and fearless.

When the snake spoke again, its voice came from somewhere behind them, words skittering like skipped stones across the walls. "What is it that you would like to create?"

Erasmus said, the lenses of his eyeglasses reflecting the bluish tone of the bioluminescence, "When a phoenix dies, it is reborn. It will live forever. We would like to create something that can do the same for people—something that can...remake them. Turn them into something stronger."

"Only a mortal would wish for such a thing," the serpent hissed, that horrible voice coming from elsewhere now. "Why would a goddess be willing to trade her powers for a mere mortal?" The question was for Helia.

"I am willing to trade my powers for love," Helia replied, her strong voice echoing. "Erasmus and Elix are my friends—I would like to give them the gift of eternal life, so that they shall live by my side forever."

"Very well," the snake whispered. "You may create a life-granting machine, and in exchange you will give to me your magic, Goddess of Doorways and Passages. You shall give me all of your power, but a drop you may keep for yourself."

"Thank you."

"Do not thank me." The snake's voice was a hushed whisper that raked up Erasmus's spine. "All magic comes with a cost—a sacrifice. Every time you use your creation, you must make a trade. Life and death are the natural order of things—one cannot exist without the other. Do you understand?"

"Yes." Her answer held no uncertainty, but Erasmus and Elix shared a glance, the both of them one step behind their new friend.

"You must choose wisely when you do your bidding," the snake said. "Every life given will yield different results. Do you wish to continue?"

"Yes."

"Erasmus—" Elix tried.

"It's okay," he whispered back.

The serpent said, "Say it, then. Say it, Goddess of Doorways and Passages, and it shall be done."

THE CAVERN VANISHED in a cloud of smoke, and the girl and her dog found themselves back at Angelthene Academy on a brand new day.

And they continued to watch.

Erasmus and Helia befriended a student who spent most of his time alone in the library. This student, like Erasmus, had been bullied nearly all his life. Other students tripped him in the hallways and called him names. If he ever made eye contact with the people who bullied him, they would accuse him of staring, and they would call him a freak. They called him strange. They called him dumb. The bullying eventually became so bad that he stopped wanting to look at anyone at all. He just stared at his books—his only friends.

Until, one day, Erasmus and Helia approached his table in the library, where he sat alone, those books that were his only friends spread before him.

His name was William, and he, like Erasmus, had a brilliant mind. He was part-warlock, part-human.

At first, the girl and her dog thought Erasmus and Helia were kind to reach out a hand to another outcast, someone who was clearly struggling to find his footing in a world that favored immortals.

But it wasn't long before she understood that the gesture was insincere. And she watched in horror as something that appeared on the surface to be an innocent attempt at friendship spiraled into something sinister.

19

ARDESIA
YVESWICH, STATE OF KER

"What'th the path-word?" A young, nasally voice floated through the intercom out front of the gates to Roman's property.

Darien sat in the car, an arm slung across the open window, fingers drumming the door that was slippery with rain. Pax, having insisted that he should be the one to speak to Kylar's little brother, stood in front of the intercom, jacket and hair soaked.

Paxton jammed his finger into a button on the pad. "Black Dragon."

"Wrong!" Eugene's shout crackled through the speaker.

Paxton threw his arm wide. "What do you mean 'wrong'?"

"Password's changed."

Paxton shot a glare at the windows of the mansion—even bigger than Hell's Gate, which was saying something—that sat at the end of a long, gravel driveway. The house was white, the roof, shutters, and doors dark blue. There was a massive courtyard ringed with trees out front, a fountain in the center.

"You can't change the password, dipshit!" Pax exclaimed. "It's MY clubhouse!"

"Language," Darien scolded.

A heavy pause. "Wait juth-t a minute!" Eugene squawked. "Who's out there with you? You're not supposed to bring new people here when Roman's not home, Pax!"

"Eugene," said a different voice. This one was bass and husky, and sounded like he was about *this* close to disowning his little brother. "What's going on?"

"Nothing."

Darien revved his engine. "Kylar, open the gate!" he called.

There was a loaded pause. And then Kylar said, "No way is that who I think it is. Gene, go open the gate."

"But—"

"*Go,* you termite!"

A heavy sigh. "Fine." The intercom crackled once before falling silent.

Darien studied Pax, who was still glowering, rain dripping off his nose. "Roman lets them on the property while he's gone?"

"He lets *Kylar* on the property. Eugene's just here 'cause he's cool enough to be my friend." He frowned and toed the gravel, eyes on his shoe. "And Kylar's brother, I guess," he admitted.

"Am I cool enough to be your friend?" Darien joked, attempting to lift the kid's spirits.

It worked; his face lit up with a smile. Good—he didn't need to feel any more unworthy after the horseshit Darien had seen in that alley.

"Pfft, just look at ya!" Paxton waved a hand that was drowning in his floppy jacket-sleeve. "You're cool enough to be everybody's friend."

The gate rolled open, and the thick layers of spells protecting the property mellowed.

Darien beckoned to Pax. "Get in the car."

"I'll walk. The house is like *right* there."

"You'll get in the car so you can show me around. I don't want to have to wait for your slow ass to get up the driveway. Besides, it's pouring out, and you look like a rat that just crawled out of the sewers."

Pax sighed dramatically, but stomped around the front of the car and opened his door. "You are *just* like Roman." He got in, muddy shoes squeaking.

The car growled as Darien looped around the fountain and drove up to the house. He parked as close to the front doors as he could get, cut the engine, and put his hood on, still damp from when they'd walked the Avenue of the Waning Moon.

He got out, and Paxton followed, dragging his backpack across the driveway.

Kylar Lavin stood on the front steps—grinning. The Shadowmaster was lean and tall, his skin a rich shade of brown, black hair buzzed short. His cheekbone was marked with a small tattoo of the black skull of Obitus, god of death and the dying.

Standing beside Kylar was a mini version of him—more gangly, with an unruly mop of black hair, a mouthful of braces, and glasses with thick lenses, the frames too big for his face. Darien figured the kid was only part-hellseher; no pureblood would have a prescription that terrible, let alone a prescription at all.

Half-brother, then. The one Darien had heard about but never met.

Kylar stepped forward. "Darien fucking Cassel," he said, shaking his hand. "Long time no see."

Darien dipped his chin in greeting. "Kylar."

"How the hell are you?"

"Surviving."

"You sound like me." He cracked a grin that showed off the tiny diamond embedded in his eyetooth. His gray eyes scanned the courtyard. "Sheesh, it's still pissing out here." He shivered. "I hate winter. Come inside, I'll show you around."

"Wait!" Paxton shouted, hurrying forward to wedge himself between Darien and Kylar. "I want to show him the clubhouse."

Eugene hissed, "The *secret* clubhouse, Pax?"

"This is Eugene," Kylar sighed. "My paranoid, geeky brother."

Eugene scowled.

"This your house or Roman's?" Darien asked. The kid didn't pick up on the jest.

"He wishes it was his," Kylar said. "Come on in, it's cold as balls out here."

Kylar led the way into the house—the really fucking impressive house —and gave him a quick but thorough tour. Roman had everything from a gym, training rooms built to withstand magic, a theater, multiple panic rooms, an indoor swimming pool, a shooting range, a wine cellar, and a rec room with a bar that had enough liquor on the shelves to last two lifetimes.

This place could easily feel like home. It reminded Darien of Hell's Gate, but with extras bells and whistles that made Darien want to renovate. He knew exactly why Roman had decided to keep this place to himself—a spot to call his own, unsoiled by the greedy hands of his dad.

"The bedrooms are all on the second and third floors," Kylar said, voice echoing as they strolled through the humid pool room. "That's a sauna." He pointed at a wooden door. "And that one's a steam room." He pointed again.

Darien snorted. "A sauna *and* a steam room? Un-fucking-real."

"Roman's nothing if not ostentatious."

They rounded the swimming pool, passing a bubbling hot tub, a rushing waterfall that kept the water in the pool moving, and a line of stone rain-showers.

Darien whistled. "Impressive."

"*Now* can I show you the clubhouse?" Pax said as they neared the frosted glass doors that led into the house.

"Now you can show me the clubhouse," Darien said. "Get going."

Paxton hurried ahead with a skip in his step. Out the pool room doors, up the stairs, past the spacious living room and kitchen, all the way to a split staircase by the front doors—another feature that reminded Darien of home. They went up to the third floor and down the hallway, where Paxton stopped underneath a latch in the ceiling.

"I'm too short," Paxton said, gazing up at the latch. "I usually use a chair." He eyed Darien. "But you'll do."

Darien reached up and opened the latch; even at his height, he could barely reach it. "You said you use *a* chair or three?"

Paxton laughed.

A folding ladder swung down, and Paxton climbed it into the attic with wet socks. Eugene followed, muttering to Paxton again about how the clubhouse was supposed to be top secret.

Darien gave Kylar an amused look. "This is hilarious."

Kylar smirked. "You're telling me. I wish my childhood was half as cool." Neither of them would mention that Paxton and Eugene's childhood managed to be this cool because they had older siblings who shielded them from their asshole fathers.

They followed the kids into the attic—the clubhouse. Rows of arched windows kept the place from feeling dark and claustrophobic, and there was a television mounted under a peak in the ceiling, a collection of worn furniture spread around it. There were racks filled with movies and board games, and a big round table with a chess set shoved to one corner. *Cryptic Crypts* was set up mid-game, tiny figurines and cards spread across the board. All the kids were playing that one nowadays.

"Well?" Paxton grinned. "What d'you think?"

"I think I'm going to have to move in," Darien said.

Paxton pointed at the larger sofa. "That one's a pull-out."

"I don't pull out."

Kylar barked a laugh.

Paxton and Eugene shared a look of bewilderment. "What does that mean?" the former asked.

"It means I prefer beds," Darien lied. "But thanks anyway."

Paxton shrugged. "Suit yourself."

Darien stepped up to the shelves of video games. He scanned the countless titles, some of them so old they had probably cost a small fortune to collect.

His gaze snagged on a movie poster on the wall. A young actress—eighteen, maybe nineteen—took up most of it. She had long, black hair, a school crest embroidered on her shirt. "Who's this?"

Paxton blurted, "No one."

"Doesn't look like no one." Darien turned. "You got a crush?"

"No!" Paxton's face turned red.

Eugene said, "Yeth, he does."

"I do not!" He pushed Eugune in the shoulder. "I just like the show."

Darien scanned the poster again. The girl held her right hand aloft, wisps of black, violet, and green lacing through her pale fingers. Behind her loomed a school bigger than Angelthene Academy, lightning forking through the sky above it. A cat peeked over her shoulder with ghostly eyes.

"Project Shadow," he read. "Nice."

Another two posters were taped beside the first. The second sported supernatural beings with wings both leathery and feathered. Vampires, he guessed. The third poster showcased a city that reminded Darien of Angelthene but in far worse condition, and fuck if that wasn't saying something.

He turned to face the kids, resisting the urge to pester Paxton further about his little crush. "So, you basically commandeered Roman's attic and turned it into a clubhouse?"

The boys glanced at each other. In unison, they said, "I guess?" They shrugged—again, at the same time. Did these kids share a brain, or what?

"And you think Roman doesn't know about it?"

"Oh, he knows," Kylar chuckled. "They just like to pretend he doesn't."

Eugene crossed his arms. "Well, now we're *definitely* going to have to tell him, since you two have seen it."

"Gene," Kylar rebuked. "He already knows—it's *his* attic, you delusional termite." He shot Darien an eyeroll. "Let's leave these two dweebs to their geekery and have a drink, shall we?"

"Sure." He followed Kylar to the ladder. As he passed the couches, he reached into his pocket, pulled out a hundred, and dropped it in Paxton's lap.

Paxton snatched it up. "Sick!" He tipped his head back to give him an upside-down grin. "Thanks, dude."

"Later, Pax."

The TV came on, volume on full. "Later!"

They went down to the ground floor, where Kylar made an immediate beeline for the kitchen.

"Kylar," Darien called. "Hold off on that drink."

Kylar turned. "It's almost four o'clock—still too early for you?" He flipped on the kitchen lights. The room was almost all white with steel appliances, the backsplash sparkling black tile. "I can make you a virgin, if you want."

Darien snorted. "Fuck, no."

Kylar pulled a bottle of whiskey off the rack and grabbed a glass from the cupboard. "What made you come to Yveswich, anyway? We've got—what, *five* years to catch up on?"

"Something like that." It was probably more like four years for Darien. He remembered coming here with a few of the Devils to go snowboarding about a year after Travis left this place, and of course Roman hadn't allowed him to go. The ski hill was far too close to Donovan for Roman to be comfortable with his brother making an appearance.

"How's Lace?" Kylar asked.

"Single."

Kylar gave him a sheepish look. "That's not why I was asking."

Darien smirked. "I don't care, Ky. That was a long time ago, and we're both over it."

Kylar merely grunted. He filled the glass with ice, the clatter of the frozen cubes causing a small, dark shape on top of the fridge to stir.

"Shit," Darien chuckled. "Don't tell me Roman has a Hob too."

Kylar peered at the top of the fridge. "That's Itzel. She likes to sleep during the day, but she's noisy as fuck at night. If you're here for a good night's rest, I'd consider a hotel if I were you." He poured the whiskey and took a swig. "Everything okay back at home?"

"Not exactly." Darien sighed. "I didn't come alone."

That made Kylar freeze, his long, dark fingers tightening around the glass. "You didn't bring Travis, did you?"

"Of course not. But—" He glanced at the doors. "I need to leave, but I'll be back in a bit. You'll still be around?"

"I'm not going anywhere."

"Good—I've got a lot to tell you."

20

THE DESERT
STATE OF WITHEREDGE

"Pull over," Shay said. "I need to go pee."

They'd been driving for just over four hours, and Shay had been holding her pee for nearly two. She'd hoped for a bathroom with toilet paper and proper plumbing, or at the very least an outhouse, but once they had left the small community of Foxhill, the land had turned into endless desert. No businesses, no houses, no people, and no bathrooms. The land out here was every shade of gold and russet, the vegetation sparse, the wildlife even sparser. Aside from some lizards and what she swore was an armadillo, there was no sign of life out here, at least not from the viewpoint of a vehicle.

That vehicle rolled onto the shoulder of the road and came to a gradual stop in a cloud of dust.

Shay reached for the door handle, her bladder about ready to pop, but froze before she could pull it open.

She eyed Roman over her shoulder. "Turn off the car," she said.

Roman squinted. "Why?"

"Because I'm scared you'll drive away and leave me here while I'm peeing behind that bush." She pointed at the shrubbery nearby.

There was that jaw tic again. It was either his jaw or his eye—his face never seemed to get a break when she was around.

Shay fought the smile pulling at her mouth.

"Do you want to know how angry you make me, Cousens?"

"Don't tell me, you'll hurt my feelings." She gave him exaggerated baby-eyes.

He smirked, but he clearly wasn't amused. "You're so full of it. You act like you're this sweet, innocent little thing who's all scared and woe-is-you, but I remember what you were like in that alley. You can conceal your emotions."

Damn, he was good.

"You're cunning," he went on. "You're a liar and a thief."

"Thank you."

"Those aren't compliments," he clipped. "Is there even one side of you that's real?" He leaned toward her, placing one tattooed elbow on the steering wheel. "Or are you just one big fake?"

"I have a real side," she said, refusing to bat an eye—not at that cold-as-ice stare, and certainly not at the impressive bands of corded muscle in his arms. "But you'll never meet her." She held out her hand, palm up. "Keys, Shadows." She looked pointedly at the sun-bleached sky. "It's getting dark."

He shut off the car, that ever-present frown on his face growing more intense. "It's three o'clock." He dropped the keys in her hand.

With a smug smile, she thanked him and hurried out of the car, unable to hold it any longer.

Sand crunched under her shoes as she rushed to a creosote bush. She squatted behind it, hoping Roman would be decent enough not to spy on her. If he did, he wouldn't see much, except she *did* nearly pee on her shoe. That would've sucked.

Shay buttoned her pants and shielded her eyes from the sun, looking out across the desert land rippling under the heat.

It was smouldering. Not even five minutes out here, and she could already feel her pale skin reddening.

The desert was peaceful and quiet, and so empty that she began to fear they wouldn't find anything out here. When she envisioned kidnapping scenarios, a desert didn't seem like the best place to hide someone. Maybe that was precisely why someone would choose to come out here.

She scanned the landscape one more time, sweat beading between her breasts and on her lower back. There were no other cars in sight, no people. The only movement came from the heatwaves and the few tiny lizards weaving between rocks and shrubs.

When she made it back in the car, it took until they had already driven two miles before she realized she still had the keys in her pocket.

Her head turned toward Roman in a flash, but he spoke before she could voice her surprise.

"I have another set," he said. "Guess you're not the only one who's full of tricks." His heavy stare settled on her. There was a flutter in her stomach and a tightness in her chest that told her she wouldn't like what he said next. "But you might be the only one who fucks someone over for your own agenda." He nodded at the keys in her pocket. "You can keep those. We'll see which of us leaves the other one first."

'Stop staring,' Sayagul said to Roman roughly thirty minutes later, glaring up at him from his shadow.

He tore his eyes off Shay and focused on the straight stretch of road ahead. It was seemingly endless, large tracts of desert land shimmering all around them, no buildings or people in sight. *'I wasn't,'* he grumbled.

'I don't know what it is with you and this Selkie,' Sayagul huffed. Neither did Roman. *'Has the heat already boiled your brain?'* Maybe it had. At least then he'd have an excuse for staring at Cousens as if she were stark naked in his passenger's seat.

'I'm just keeping an eye on her,' Roman lied.

'It doesn't matter how many eyes we keep on her. She's already tricked us three times. I'm certain she can do it again.'

Roman twisted the wheel. *'What's it going to take to get you off my case?'*

A beat of silence, and then the dragon said, *'Gummy bears.'*

'Fine.' He opened the center console, trying his damned hardest not to meet Shay's curious gaze, and found a fresh bag of gummy bears.

"Are those Sugar Squishies?" Shay had barely got the question out before Sayagul tore out of Roman's shadow with an angry squawk.

The dragon planted all four feet on the gearshift, perching on it like an eagle might sit at the very top of a towering tree, and glared up at Shay, who glanced at Roman with raised strawberry-blonde brows. Fuck, that rose-gold hair color did shit to him that he didn't want to admit.

"What did I say?" she asked him.

"'Sugar Squishies'." He tore open the bag with his teeth. "Sayagul's asserting her claim." He tossed the bag onto the dash, a yellow gummy bear rolling out.

Sayagul wouldn't stop glaring at Shay, her eyes narrowing into slits.

"I'm not going to steal them," Shay promised, the effort to suppress her laugh drawing attention to a dimple in her cheek—another thing Roman knew damn well he shouldn't be noticing. Just like those tan lines peeking out under the thin straps of her black tank top. "What's your name?"

'My name is not for the utterance of lying Selkies,' Sayagul hissed, her words audible to both Roman and Shay.

"It's Sayagul," Roman said.

The dragon's small head whipped around to face Roman, neck twisting, a screech slicing through the car.

"Sayagul," Shay said politely, causing Sayagul to face her again, smoke puffing from flared nostrils. "Pleased to meet you."

Sayagul's thin, forked tongue slipped out between her teeth, fluttering in Shay's direction. *'Not pleased in the slightest.'* With one final glare, the dragon scuttled up onto the dash to gorge, the smell of fruit and the sound of smacking teeth soon filling the vehicle.

"What's his name?" Roman asked Shay. When she stared at him in confusion, he clarified, "Your Familiar."

Her hands that were clasped in her lap tightened, just barely. She always seemed to keep her hands either tucked between her thighs or clasped in her lap, as if she didn't want to touch anything. "Nugget."

"I've never seen a white one before." Most Familiars were black, with less than three percent of the world's magic-born population having white.

Shay hummed. "You're fishing, aren't you?"

"What?"

"For information."

"It's only a question."

"From the guy who said he didn't want to talk."

He grunted and stared out at the road. She was right—he was fishing. He couldn't give a shit what her Familiar was called, but he *did* give a shit about those mysteries she kept so carefully buried.

"Roman 'Grunting' Devlin," Shay said, watching the desert plants pass by the car. "Another name to add to my list."

"Oh, you're making a list, are you?" Roman said icily.

"I am. Roman 'Grunting' Devlin, Roman 'Secretive' Devlin, Roman 'Teeth-Clenching' Devlin, Roman 'Glaring' Devlin…" She gave him a cheeky smile, the sun that fell through the windshield lighting up the green of her eyes. "Shall I continue?"

With a black look, Roman reached for the volume on the stereo and cranked it.

Shay grinned with triumph. "Roman 'Likes Loud Music' Devlin!" she shouted, looking far too pleased with herself.

Roman ignored her.

And vowed to quit staring at those fucking tan lines and the dimples in her cheeks.

21

ZIMA
YVESWICH, STATE OF KER

"These lobster rolls are so freaking good," Ivy said, stuffing another bite in her mouth. "They literally melt on your tongue."

They were in the district of Zima, an oceanfront neutral zone where people came to stroll the wooden walkway, bundle up in blankets on the rocky beach, or gather around bonfires. Darien and the others stood by the car and truck—all except Joyce, who sipped on a bottle of sparkling water in the passenger's seat of the truck, door open.

"Want a bite?" Ivy offered the roll to Darien, melted butter dripping to the damp sidewalk. The rain had stopped, but it was cold as hell outside.

"No thanks," Darien said, breath fogging before him. "I'm full."

"Apparently, the pizza didn't cut it for her," Tanner said from where he leaned against the back door of the truck, arms crossed to keep out the cold.

"Guess I shouldn't tell you about the cinnamon buns, then," Darien said to Ivy, "or you'll wind up in a food coma."

"Cinnamon buns? *Food coma?*" Ivy's brows shot up. "Not with my bottomless stomach."

"I don't know where she hides it," Jack said. He slid a finger between her breasts. "In here, I think."

She swatted his hand away. "Ewwww, there's butter on your finger!" He merely laughed. "I know where you hide *yours.*" She poked him below the ribs with a manicured nail.

"What's that supposed to mean?" He pulled up his shirt. "My stomach is a washboard."

"Which is exactly why I just baited you into showing me that man-candy." She ran her free hand down the grooves.

Darien fought the urge to bleach his eyeballs. "*Really* don't need to see this right now—ever, preferably."

Ivy snickered. "Sorry." She took another bite, nearly eating the red-checkered paper that barely contained the roll. "So, you found my sweet little Pax?"

"And Kylar. Soon as you're finished with that, we're going." He owed Kylar an explanation, but after that, his first stop was Caliginous on Silverway—and, hopefully, waking Lola up.

His eyes flicked to the tinted windows of the truck. Fuck, he wished she would just open that door now so he could forget about all of this and have her back.

Ivy stuffed the last bite in her mouth and dusted the crumbs off her hands—and then wiped the butter on the front of Jack's shirt, leaving grease stains on the black material.

"Hey!" he protested.

"Would you rather have licked it off?" Ivy waggled her brows.

"I'd rather lick it off those sweet tits." He dove for her, and Ivy squealed.

Darien cursed, looking away. Anyone other than his sister and he wouldn't give a shit.

Tanner stifled a laugh. "Where to?" the hacker asked as he pushed off the truck, shifting his hands into the pockets of his gray jacket.

Darien got out his car keys and tossed them to Ivy, who barely caught them with her butterfingers. "Roman's house," Darien said.

Jack shot him an intense look. "Not the House of Black!"

"Roman has his own place," Darien clarified.

"Oh thank god." Jack clutched his chest. "No Don for one more day."

"His house isn't in the Hollow, I hope," Tanner said. He handed Darien the truck key as they passed each other.

"No, but it *is* in a Gray Zone." He rounded the truck and got in the driver's seat. "Follow me—it's about a twenty-minute drive."

"Damn." Tanner leaned forward in his seat to see the house better as Darien drove up the driveway, Ivy and Jack following in the car. "Tell me Roman's well off without telling me Roman's well off."

Darien smirked. "No kidding."

His cousin had done well for himself, though it came as no surprise to Darien. Roman had a smaller crew behind him, only two Shadowmasters working directly under him while the rest answered to his dad. He may run the House of Black, but that didn't mean Don didn't sink his claws into Roman's cash cow whenever he pleased. And, last Darien heard, Donovan was slowly infiltrating the House of Black, taking this and that from the Darkslayer circle that had risen above the others since Roman's promotion.

Clearly, Roman had never allowed his dad's greedy hands to set him back—though Darien would love to remove the asshole's hands as a favor to his cousin. He'd killed Randal; maybe crossing another Slade off the list was in his future. For Pax, too—they both deserved to be free.

"You okay?" Tanner asked. He was studying Darien, gray eyes flicking to the steering wheel—and Darien's white-knuckled grip. Whenever Atlas put away the electronics, he noticed everything.

Darien loosened his hands. "Just getting a little antsy."

"This'll work," Tanner said. "I have a good feeling about it."

Darien tried to smile, but it felt more like a grimace.

The garage doors rolled open as Darien approached. He drove in, parking beside an impressive selection of quads, motorcycles, and flashy hotrods, a few older models among them. Roman had a thing for rebuilding old classics.

Jack and Ivy pulled up beside him, and they cut the engines. A moment later, the garage doors rolled shut, and the lights came on full, bathing the room in a bright wash that made the paint on the hotrods shine like liquid gold.

Darien got out, the others following. Kylar was crossing the garage, a big smile on his face, Paxton and Eugene right on his heels.

"Welcome back," Kylar said. He gestured to the kids. "I can't get rid of these two. Might have to call the exterminator."

Darien chuckled.

Kylar greeted the others with hugs and handshakes, introducing himself halfway through to Joyce.

"And this is my annoying brother, Eugene," Kylar said, settling a heavy hand on Eugene's curly head. Eugene pushed it away with a scowl. Kylar added, "And this is Roman's little brother, Paxton." He flicked Paxton in the ear.

"Ow!" Paxton's hand shot to his reddening ear.

"Darien said you have a lot to tell me," Kylar continued, addressing all of them now. "I hope Travis is still alive?"

"Unfortunately," Jack said, to which Ivy tsked.

Darien opened the back door of the truck. "We're here for...a different reason," he began.

Curiosity creased Kylar's face as he took note of the girl lying in the back seat. "You brought a human girl?" he asked.

Darien said, "She's the reason I'm here."

"I'm going to simplify this as best as I can," Darien began as he joined the others in the living room.

Everyone was seated on the couches and armchairs, but Darien made the decision to stay standing. Kylar, Paxton, and Eugene's attention flickered between Darien and the girl in his arms—sleeping, for all they knew. It was hard to tell the difference if you weren't already aware of what'd happened to her.

"This is my girlfriend, Loren. She's in a coma. Her dad is Roark Bright, the Red Baron—he adopted her when she was a baby. He told me about the Caliginous Chambers—said there's a chamber that puts magic into a person's body instead of removing it. He thinks it's worth a try, to see if it wakes her up."

Silence choked the room for several long minutes. It had started raining again; the sound of the droplets pelting the big windows was the only sound for what felt like a lifetime.

Finally, Kylar spoke. "She's human?"

"Yes, but she's different." So much shit had happened that Darien barely knew where to start explaining it. "Have you ever heard of the Arcanum Well?"

Kylar shifted, lacing his tatted fingers between his knees. "Isn't that kind of like a fountain of youth? I heard stories of it when I was a kid."

"Sort of. Her biological father is the creator of the Well. And he used it to create her."

Kylar's jaw slackened. "You shitting me?"

"No."

"You and Roman aren't playing some massive joke on me?" He looked at the others, who stared back at him with solemn expressions, a couple of them—Tanner, Joyce—shaking their heads.

"No," Darien replied. "Ever heard of Spirit Terra?"

Kylar shook his head, but it wasn't in reply to his question—it was in disbelief. "This just keeps getting better, doesn't it?"

"Spirit Terra is real, and so is the Veil. The security breach in

Angelthene—the one you saw on the news? That was the Veil nearly falling."

Kylar rubbed his chin. "Shit."

"Yeah: shit. And Loren is the reason it didn't fall—she used her magic to seal a rip in the dimensions."

"Her...*magic,*" Kylar repeated. "Did she get it from the Well?"

Jack, whose arm was slung across Ivy's shoulders, pulled her close and whispered in her ear, "He catches on quickly."

"Yes," Darien said, answering Kylar's question. "Her dad hid the Arcanum Well in Spirit Terra, but when he hid it he didn't know his daughter would grow up to inherit its powers and could find and use the Well again if she wanted to. People have been hunting her ever since they dug up the history of the Well and its creators." He glanced down at Loren's face—so beautiful, even now, with her features slack, as if with an exhaustion she couldn't shake.

"And Darien has been protecting her," Ivy cut in, tossing a proud smile his way. "We've all been protecting her, but mostly him. And he's done such a great job." Darien appreciated his sister's compliment, but with Loren in a coma, alive only because of that serum coursing through her blood, it no longer felt like he'd done a great job of protecting her.

Paxton said, "She's like that sleeping lady from old fairytales."

"Did you try kissing her?" Eugene's question earned him a light slap on the back of the head from his brother.

Tanner said, "You wouldn't happen to know where Roman is, would you?"

"He texted me a few hours ago," Kylar replied. "Said he'll be out of town for a few days and won't be answering his phone. He gave me termite duty." He went for Eugene's head again, but the kid ducked right on time.

"Did he say why he decided to piss off?" This question came from Jack.

"He didn't tell me anything." Kylar's eyes found Darien's. "Getting back to the Caliginous thing. You need to use the chambers so you can try and wake her up?"

"Yes. Think you can take us there?"

Kylar checked his watch. "They close at nine every night. I think we should wait until the last hour; it's usually pretty deserted by then. I'm guessing you don't want to be seen?"

"By as few people as possible," Darien confirmed.

"Then let's do it that way. Tanya should be working—she's kind of a friend of mine and Roman's. I don't think she'll have a problem with us using...what did you call it?"

Tanner said, "Roark called it a 'Reverse Chamber'."

"Reverse Chamber," Ky repeated. "Alright. Usually, it's hard to get appointments there unless you're a member, but Tanya should be able to help us out."

"Is Roman a member?" Ivy asked around a yawn. She leaned into her husband, looking like she could use a nap.

Paxton piped up. "Can't they just use Roman's spots, then?"

"Doesn't work that way, termite," Kylar said. His eyes flicked up to Darien's. "But, like I said, I think we can work something out with Tanya. Roman's lent her some money in the past, and hasn't asked for anything in return except some free treatments, so she's not really in any position to refuse."

If she did refuse, Darien had a few ideas, and he planned on exhausting all his options until he found one that bloody well worked.

They had several hours to kill, but the moment eight o'clock rolled around, he'd be at the doors of Caliginous on Silverway.

And he wouldn't leave until he got what he wanted.

22

THE DESERT
STATE OF WITHEREDGE

Shay leaned forward in her seat, peering at the map displayed on the screen that was set in the dash of Roman's car. Twilight was gaining on them with swift heels, but the sun dipping toward the horizon still shone so brightly it made it hard to see the screen.

"I swear that dot keeps getting farther away." Shay slumped against her air-conditioned seat with a sigh.

"I swear I've heard you say that like six times already," Roman replied.

She scowled at him.

He spared her half a glance. "Your face is going to get stuck like that."

"That's *my* line." She picked up her purse off the floor and took out her medication.

"What's that?"

"Medication."

"I have eyes, you know. What's it for?"

She shot him a hard stare. "Do you always go around asking people what their medication is for?"

He shrugged. Back to silence, then.

She sighed, figuring she might as well talk to him, or this car ride was going to feel *that* much longer. "It's for my migraines. Indecisive weather doesn't exactly agree with my body." Not that the weather was indecisive out here; there wasn't a cloud in sight, not even the slightest chance of a storm or a sprinkle of rain.

And yet that pain still crept up on her, persistent as ever.

"Barometric pressure, right?"

She blinked at him, unable to hide her surprise. "You're the first person to not stare at me like I'm a freak for saying that."

He grunted. "People have been staring at me like I'm a freak my whole life." He kept his eyes on the road. "I've also had my own...challenges. Nothing really surprises me anymore. Especially not barometric pressure—that one's easy."

"Not easy to deal with, though." She shook a chalky pill into her palm, closed the cap, and threw the bottle into her purse before dumping it on the floor again.

"What else helps?" he asked, surprising her again. "Aside from medication."

"Water." She grabbed her bottle out of the cup holder. It was nearly empty, barely enough to swallow her pill. "And ice." She added, "Massages help too."

He snorted. "Don't even think about it."

"Eww!" she gasped. "As if I'd let *you* touch me!"

When he glared, she took her shot.

"Your face is going to get stuck like that," she warned.

He shook his head, muttering too quietly for her to hear as he returned to staring at the stretch of road.

Silence resumed. The hum of the tires on flat, sunbaked pavement was relentless. Shay watched the red dot on the screen, wondering if that damned motel was ever going to show up. She was so parched, it felt like the pill had lodged itself halfway down her throat. Anxiety began to breathe down her neck, filling her thoughts with worries about Athene and the other members of the Riptide finding out where she was and what she was doing.

And who with.

She eyed Roman. "Is your aura hidden?"

He snaked his finger under the collar of his shirt and pulled up a chain with a tiny pendant attached, a closed eye engraved in the center. "You really think I'd be that stupid?"

Shay shrugged.

He tucked it back under his shirt. "I've had a price on my head since I was sixteen. My aura hasn't been visible for a day since."

"That must cost you a fortune."

"Would you put a price on your life?"

"Some people say you don't care whether you live or die." It was one of the many, many rumors she'd heard about him.

"Do they?" The question was flat.

"Yup."

Roman thought about it. "I'll say Pax's life, then."

"Pax?"

"My little brother. Until he turns eighteen, he needs me. So I need to stay alive until then."

"Where is he now?"

"Probably wondering why his brother ditched." The way he said it told Shay that he was worried about Pax, though from the look on his face, you'd never guess.

She stared out the windshield that was covered in dust, the bright sun highlighting every speck of dirt. "I didn't realize..."

"What?" His cold, hard laugh raked across her bones. "That I have a family? That I have someone who depends on me? Typical selfish thought train."

Silence prevailed for several minutes, and then Shay said, "Is he your only family? Aside from your dad?" For someone who was frequently talked about throughout the state and beyond, she knew next to nothing about him.

"My dad isn't family. I've got Paxton and Travis. Pulled Travis out a long time ago. Threw him far away."

"Can't you do that for Paxton too?"

"It's...complicated. He's technically my half-brother, the son of my father's newest whore. My dad couldn't give a rat's ass if Travis was gone, but Pax... Pax, he's got on a really tight leash."

Quiet returned once more. Shay didn't know what else to say. While she found the silence between them tense and unnerving, there was something about peeling back Roman's many layers that unsettled her just as much.

And then Roman circled back to their earlier topic. "Speaking of dots getting farther away on screens."

Shay stiffened, the movement causing the pain blooming on one side of her neck and head to worsen. The waves of nausea would be coming soon, which meant she had to get into a dark, quiet room as soon as possible, so she could deal with the pain in peace. "I thought you didn't like talking."

"I like to talk when it suits me."

"Well, this topic doesn't suit *me,* so tough luck, pal."

"How'd you do it?" he persisted. "I know what I saw on that screen."

She shook her head, gritting her teeth against the pain worming into her muscles. "Uh-uh. You're not the one who gets to dictate every conversation we have. It's *my* turn to say we're done talking."

"If you're a hacker, you can just admit it."

"I'm not a hacker."

"Then it was magic."

Shay didn't know what to say, so she ignored him. She could practically hear him mulling it over and realizing the mainstream knowledge on magic didn't add up. Cameras and screens never lied; not even veneficae glamors worked on them.

Shay's magic, on the other hand...

A small building appeared up ahead. Shay leaned forward, squinting to read the sign.

It was a store. The faded letters on the big windows out front declared they sold everything from pool floaties and hiking boots to snacks and over-the-counter drugs. There was a group of cristala charging stations too, thank gods, though they looked like they hadn't received maintenance in a while, maybe even years—decades, if she was pessimistic.

Shay unbuckled her seatbelt. "Pull over."

But Roman didn't slow. He drove right by in a cloud of dust, and soon the store was only a speck in the side mirror.

She swung her head around to glare at him. "You got cotton in your ears again, Shadows? I said pull over!"

He pointed up ahead, and Shay looked with reluctance. "There's your motel."

Sure enough, there was a flashing red sign welcoming them to Motel 58. Below it was another: VACANCY.

Perfect. But—

"I'm thirsty." The steady pulse on one side of her head told her she was way past dehydrated. "Just turn around real quick—"

"'I'm thirsty', 'I have to pee', 'the dot keeps moving'," Roman mimicked. "Can you lay off the whining for five fucking minutes?"

She bristled. "Can you lay off the assholery?"

He veered into the tiny parking lot of Motel 58 and lurched to a stop out front of the office. There were a few other cars parked in front of the handful of numbered doors, and Shay saw a sign to the right of the office, directing guests toward a swimming pool.

Oh, thank gods. It was hot as sin out here, even this late in the day.

Roman shut off the car and opened his door.

"Where are you going?" Shay squawked. She was going to murder his belligerent ass. "We need to think of a plan."

"The plan is to get a room. The sun's setting, so it's either the motel or the car. And it's pretty tight in here, so unless you want to sleep on top of me—"

Shay opened her door. "Let's go."

She had hoped to find some answers before calling it a day, but searching in the dark wasn't a good idea. Aside from this motel and that tiny, rundown store a mile back, there was nothing around but desert and the open road—and a whole lot of darkness once the sun went down. And darkness always equaled monsters.

Shay followed Roman through the baking heat, into a tiny office that smelled strongly of pine-scented air freshener and lemon floor-cleaner. A fan blew in one corner, rustling the papers on the desk.

The way Roman dramatically glanced around, looking for an employee, was a bit comical, Shay had to admit. As if someone could possibly be hiding in a room as small as this one.

Roman stepped up to the desk, dark hair blowing as he entered the path of the fan, and slammed his hand down on the bell. *Ding!*

Shay cringed. "Was that really necessary?" she hissed.

"What? I'm in need of assistance." He rang it again.

"Shadows, stop it. Someone will come—"

Ring. He dropped his hand down again, his unblinking eyes fixed on her. *Ring. Ring, ring, ring, ring, ringringringringringring—*

She lunged forward and planted her hands on top of his. "Would you *stop it?*" she snapped, gripping his hand tightly. "You're going to wreck our chances of getting a room!"

"If you wanted to sleep with me that badly, pup, all you had to do was ask." His hand under hers was warm and rough; she could feel scars on his knuckles.

"You are unbelievable!" she fumed.

The door behind the desk swung open, and a heavyset, half-human warlock walked out. He had a black moustache, a balding head, and a nametag that said, *Omar*. "My apologies," he mumbled. He took a sip from a cup that smelled of weak coffee.

Shay removed her hands from Roman's and laced them behind her back, not liking how the feel of his skin lingered on hers. The warmth of his hand was more intense than the desert heatwaves.

"No, *I* am sorry," Shay began, "for my...*friend's* behavior." She glared up at Roman.

Omar looked the Shadowmaster over. "You like the bell," he said, moustache twitching. He set down his mug.

Roman dinged it again. "I love it," he said with one of those deadly smiles that showed no humor or joy. Slowly, he turned his head to look at Shay, and said through his teeth, "I just *love* loud, obnoxious things."

Shay cleared her throat. "We're looking for a room. Two, actually." She held up two fingers. *Please, please, let there be two.*

The man sat down at the desk and clicked a few keys. The computer made grinding noises that gave away its age.

After a moment, Omar sighed. "No can do."

"But your sign says 'vacancy'." Shay pointed over her shoulder, at the sign that indeed said VACANCY in glowing red letters.

Omar kept his focus on the screen.

Shay persisted. "Listen, if my friend here was too rude—"

"I like the bell," Roman cut in with a defensive tone.

She forced herself to smile and said through her teeth, "Yeah, well I would like a place to sleep, *Shadows.*"

"You're Shadows?" Omar asked, his dark eyes flicking to Roman.

Roman didn't say anything.

"That shadow guy, right? Roman. You work for the House of Black."

"I *run* the House of Black."

Omar returned to his screen. "I don't have two rooms, I have one. It's being cleaned."

Roman said, "Great, we'll take it."

Omar clicked the mouse. "You want it under her name?"

"Shay Cousens," Shay replied before Roman could open his stupid mouth. She stepped up to the desk. "There are two beds, right?" Her scalp prickled at the thought of being in the same room as Roman, let alone having to share a bed with him.

She wouldn't do it. She would sooner sleep on the floor than put herself that close to him. The car, even—anything was better than getting under the covers with that man.

Nope, not doing it. Roman was one hundred percent off-limits.

The shadow-asshole smirked. Shay shot him a glare—

Omar was smirking too. What was this, some kind of joke?

She narrowed her eyes on Roman. "If there's only one bed, you're sleeping on the floor."

The owner was still smiling as he handed Roman a key with the number nine on it. "Two beds."

The door to room number nine creaked as Roman pushed it open, the knob hitting the wall. He felt for a light switch and flipped it on.

Dim. No surprise for a cheap motel.

Cousens pushed her way into the room, bumping Roman's shoulder with hers. "I'm taking the bed closest to the door," she declared.

Roman scowled at the back of her head as he followed her inside, slamming the door shut behind him. "Why?"

She dumped her bag on the bed. "In case you try to sneak past me in the night." She gave him a fake smile.

"You have major trust issues."

She made for the door again—the one Roman was blocking. "Come on, move." She waved her hands in a 'shoo' motion. "Out of the way—let's go." She poked him in the chest.

He recoiled—and so did she. "Where? We just got here."

"Back to the store so we can buy some things." Roman didn't miss that she held her hands behind her back now, as if afraid to touch him again.

"Like what?" he demanded.

"Toothpaste, deodorant, water. Maybe you're okay with wearing the same pair of underwear for five days in a row, but I'm not."

He lifted the duffel in his hand. "I came prepared."

She regarded him with suspicion, the eye that had a portion of darker green in the iris tightening. Roman hated how those eyes compelled him to look at them more than he needed to. "Do you always drive around with a suitcase in your car?" she asked him.

"Yes." He wouldn't expect her to understand. Her mom was a bitch, but rumor said the Cousens girls were spoiled. Shay was sheltered, and likely would be her whole life.

"Well, *I* need some things, and you're going to come with me."

"Why?"

She batted those ginger eyelashes at him. "Because you're scary and tough, and that's why you're here."

"I thought I was here to chauffeur your thieving ass around and help you find your sister."

"Yeah, well, throw 'bodyguard' into the mix." She seemed to think of something, and snapped her fingers. "Before I forget."

She rushed over to the beds and grabbed the throw pillows—there was an unnecessary amount of them for two beds—and created a barrier on the floor, separating her bed from his.

"What're you doing, pup?"

"See this?" Shay pointed at the pillows. "This is the Roman Doesn't Cross Line. The Anti-Roman Line. The If-Roman-Sticks-So-Much-As-A-Toe-Over-This-Line-He-Dies Line."

"Me? You're the one who dragged me to this flea-bitten motel."

She snorted. "'Flea-bitten'."

"I should be worried about *you* crossing that line."

Confusion flitted across her face. "And why would I do that?"

Roman gave a smile as she walked right into his trap. "Because you want to fuck."

His answer caught her unprepared, and he didn't think he was imagining the pink dusting her cheeks.

Fuck. That reaction did something to him that he didn't want to admit. In fact, *she* did things to him that he didn't want to admit.

Which was probably why he'd made it this far without slitting her throat and dumping her body on the side of the desert road like he would anyone else. Her tight little body, with those perky tits and beautiful ass—

Fuck.

Sayagul gave a derisive snort. '*You need to start thinking with the right head, pal. Either that, or you need to get laid. Not with her, might I add.*'

'*Not a good time, Sayagul,*' Roman replied.

'*Kill the girl and be done with this nonsense.*'

'*I'm not killing her.*'

Sayagul hissed. '*Is that your decision?*'

'*For now.*'

Shay was watching him. "What's she saying?"

He set his bag on the nearby table. "She thinks I should kill you."

She cleared her throat. If she felt any fear, she did an excellent job of not giving it away. "And? Do you think you should kill me?"

Roman studied her. To her credit, she maintained eye contact, not even breaking it to blink. "Not today."

She tucked her hair behind an ear and made for the door again—the one he was still blocking. "Well, if today's my last day, then I'd at least like some clean underwear and deodorant. Let's go."

Roman prowled across the room, brushing his arm against hers, and headed for the barrier of pillows on the floor. "Get these out of the way, or we're going to trip."

She backed up and blocked him. "Do not," she growled, pointing a finger at him, "touch the pillows."

He bared his teeth. "Try to stop me."

She took the bait—foolish girl.

Before she could land a blow—she had zero fighting skills, and even if she did, she didn't have weight or size on her side—he kicked her feet out from under her.

She fell—

But she took him down with her—not what he was expecting.

And he landed on top of her—also not what he was expecting.

Fuck.

SHAY SUSPECTED Roman had purposely landed on her in a way that his weight wouldn't completely obliterate her lungs.

But that was the last coherent thought in her head as she stared up at him—at the six-foot-ginormous Shadowmaster lying heavily between her thighs, her hips pinned by his. She could feel every muscle in his impressively chiseled body, every weapon. It was too much—too close.

"Get off," she growled.

He brought his face in close to hers. "Make me."

"Do you like intimidating girls by squeezing the breath out of them?"

"Just you."

She didn't know why, but those two words did something weird to her stomach and heart.

"What's that?" His voice was a croon. He tilted his head to one side, the corner of his mouth twitching.

She tried to shove him off, but he grabbed her wrists and pinned them to the floor on either side of her head, the scrape of his calluses making her shiver. "What's what?" she squeezed out. Gods, she was *panting*, her breasts flattening against his chest with every ragged inhale.

"Are those butterflies?" He was so close, she could count every speck of gold in his eyes. "Am I giving you butterflies?" His mouth formed an almost-smile—cold and deadly, like usual. "Is Shayla Cousens enjoying this?" That smile widened—and gods, it made her stomach quake.

She focused on calming her heart—and beating those wild butterflies into submission. "No."

"You're a terrible liar, pup," he breathed, the words caressing her mouth. His hands—so big and rough—squeezed her wrists. "What's the matter? Have you already lost your edge?"

"Get. *Off.*"

"Show me first. Show me how you'd get someone off of you if they attacked you." Her mind was so far in the gutter that at first she thought he was saying 'get someone off', as in get *him* off.

Gods.

"You mean *you?*" she spat.

"I'm not attacking you. I'm giving you a lesson. Flashy little magic tricks won't always save your life." He pressed his warm, solid body into hers and tightened his hold on her wrists. Gods, she could feel things she shouldn't be feeling—and she could have sworn he was enjoying this as much as he accused *her* of enjoying it. Roman commanded, "Now show me."

She knew a lot about combat, but her size and old injury usually put her at a disadvantage. Still, she showed Roman—thrusting up her hips and sweeping her wrists out from under his, causing him to lose his grip on her and fall forward. Purposefully, she knew. There was no way she'd win against him in combat—not in a real fight.

The change in position brought his lower half *way* too close to her face for her liking.

And then she drove her knee up into his groin—but, of course, he was waiting and blocked it.

He got to his feet and stepped over her. "Good."

She glared up at him. "You let me win." She stood on legs that—to her horror—wobbled.

"Of course I did." He adjusted the big gun tucked into the front of his jeans. "We would've been here all night, and the look on your face tells me only one of us would've enjoyed ourselves." He winked and headed for the door. "Let's go, pup."

Face red, heart pounding, Shay grabbed her key, not clueing in until she'd left the room...

The gun Roman adjusted?...

Yeah, that wasn't his gun.

THE STORE really did sell everything it advertised and more. Shay thought it was truly impressive how much they managed to stock in such a small building—no magic or trick of the eyes here.

Shay flitted through the racks of clothing in the back corner of the shop. There were some really good deals on shorts and tops, which was a godsend. Wearing the same pair of pants the whole time was out of the question; it was way too hot for pants, and besides, the motel didn't have laundry machines.

"Oooh!" She pushed the hangers aside and grabbed one that showed off the cutest yellow bikini. "This is cute." She felt the clerk—a half-witch in her late thirties—watching from the counter; she probably thought she was going to shoplift.

Shay gladly would have—if she didn't need to keep a low profile while she was out here.

Okay, *and* if she didn't pity the store owners, who probably struggled for business in a place as deserted as this one.

She flipped the hanger around to inspect the bikini bottoms—ruched in the center. These would make her ass look really good.

"Are you in trouble?" a voice hissed.

Shay nearly jumped out of her skin.

The clerk was standing right by her elbow.

Shay backed up a step. "Pardon?"

The woman leaned in. "Are you in trouble?"

"Why would I be in trouble?"

"I sense tension between you and that...that man you came in with." She cupped a hand over the side of her mouth. "He won't stop watching you."

Shay looked over her shoulder to see Roman fumbling with a snow globe. There were three whole shelves of them, right next to spinning racks stuffed full with keychains, pens, and postcards. He caught the globe before it could smash on the floor, and eyed it with irritation as he set it back on the shelf—as if the snow globe's near-demise was the fault of its own and not the clumsy idiot who shouldn't be touching breakable things.

"Do you need me to call someone?" the woman persisted.

Shay blinked. "What? No! I'm fine, really. It's funny, actually—you'll never believe me, but *I* kidnapped *him.*"

The lady eyed her with uncertainty.

"How much is this?" Shay held up the yellow bathing suit.

"If he's paying, forty-five. If you're paying, it's half-price."

Shay grinned. "Oh, he's definitely paying, if I have anything to say about it." She placed a hand on the woman's shoulder. "Thank you for looking out for me."

She patted her hand, her palm dry and cracked from living in constant heat. "It's the most I can do, especially out in these parts."

"What do you mean by that?"

"Women disappear around here all the time. I like to keep an eye out, especially for young lookers like yourself." She shot another wary glance at Roman.

"Have you heard of anything suspicious happening around here lately? Seen anything? Anything at all?"

She shook her head. "Nothing since the cops came around looking for that young woman who went missing in Yveswich."

Shay swallowed the lump in her throat. "Anna."

"Yeah, that's the one. They kept their search quiet and quick—they were out of here within a day. Which tells me they didn't find much."

A sharp whistle cut between Roman's lips.

"I'm not a dog!" Shay called.

"Let's go, pup." He whistled again—this time, as if actually calling a dog to heel, and he beckoned her by patting a tattooed hand against his muscled thigh, the asshole.

She rolled her eyes. "Thank you again for looking out for me," she told the clerk.

"Any time, darling." She led the way to the counter, and Shay followed, picking up her basketful of items along the way.

As Shay neared Roman, she said, "I keep warning you your face is going to get stuck like that, but you won't listen."

His glared only deepened. "While you were busy splurging on cute outfits," Roman said, directing his stare to the bathing suit, "I found some things that are actually useful."

She smiled from ear to ear, knowing exactly how much her next words would ruffle his feathers. "You really think this is cute?" She held up the bikini.

He ignored her. "Such as water, trail mix, hiking boots."

"I found useful things too. Deodorant, toothpaste, underwear." The only thing she couldn't find was shampoo and conditioner, which would be a Star-damned tragedy for her frizzy hair. "What do you think of these?" She held up a cherry-print thong with red sparkles on the cherries. "Sexy, hey?"

"Let's go, small fry." He waved an impatient hand.

"Wait, I need boots too."

She hurried over to the shoe rack and selected a brown pair in size six and a half—the most expensive pair, but in her defense they were the only ones left in her size.

Shay returned to the counter, set her boots down among her other things, and smiled at the clerk, who was still looking at Roman as if he might bite.

"He's paying," Shay declared. She smiled at Roman. "Aren't you, Shadows?"

A twitch of his left eye was her only answer.

Shay's smile grew. "I'll take that as a 'yes'."

23

HELL'S GATE
ANGELTHENE, STATE OF WITHEREDGE

The silver glow of a cloudless night was creeping through the curtains in Max's suite when Dallas woke him up with a pillow to the face.

He jolted into consciousness with a snort, batting aside the pillow Dallas had abandoned on his face. "Red," he mumbled, his voice thick with sleep. He clutched the pillow and rolled onto his stomach. "Come back to bed."

"You have exactly five minutes to get ready if you want to come with me."

Max groaned. "This is payback, isn't it?" He blinked away the last of the sleep that clung to his mind and took in the room—and the spitfire witch glaring down at him from the side of the bed.

"Four minutes and forty seconds," she warned.

He redirected his tired gaze to the alarm clock on the nightstand—and swore. "There's no way I slept for four hours." Casen had told them to stop by the Umbra Forum at seven p.m., so Max, suspecting they'd be spending most of the night out, depending on the information the Butcher gave them, had opted for a power nap.

And now they were late—by over an hour.

Max threw the covers aside and got to his feet. "Did anyone call?" he slurred, looking for his phone.

"Yeah, Big Daddy Butcher—wondering if we're alive, clearly."

He swore again. "Did you answer?" Adjusting his boxers that were all twisted up from sleeping, he thumped over to the dresser and started throwing open drawers. He rifled around inside until he found a pair of jeans and a white shirt.

"I didn't know we had reached the stage in our relationship where I'm allowed to answer your phone." Dallas's voice turned all fluttery as she watched him pull up his jeans and button them.

"I never said you couldn't." He picked up on the flush of desire coursing through her—and felt arousal of his own stir awake. "What are you looking at?" he breathed, the words coated in an invitation.

"Nothing."

He stepped close, wrapped a hand around the back of her neck, and pulled her in for a kiss.

The taste of her was intoxicating. When she parted Max's lips with her tongue, a groan rose in his throat, his cock stiffening in his pants.

By the time he broke the kiss, she was out of breath. "Nothing, hey?" he breathed, the words fanning her mouth. His gaze drifted down her body...

And narrowed at what he saw.

Dallas was fully clothed in tight blue jeans and a black leather jacket that showed her midsection—and the jewel sparkling in her belly button.

Not appropriate attire for a place as dangerous as Angelthene's black market.

"What are you wearing?" He stepped back and pulled his shirt over his head.

She threw up her hands in confusion. "Jeans and a jacket—what does it look like I'm wearing?"

"That's not a jacket, that's a garbage bag you shrunk in the wash." He didn't deny that it looked good on her—too good. "You're not wearing that to the Umbra Forum."

"Garbage bag?" she spat.

He made for the nightstand and grabbed his wallet and keys.

"Garbage bag?" she said again.

"Put another jacket on or you're not coming," Max said. "Those are my conditions." Anyplace other than the Umbra Forum and he wouldn't care—would welcome any sexy outfit she put on. But there? No way. Not when he had more important things to do than rip people apart for leering or trying to touch her. Clearly, she had gotten a little too comfortable with going to places like the Umbra Forum, and it was comfort that got you killed.

She mumbled to herself before stomping into the closet and yanking one of Max's hooded sweatshirts off the hanger.

"Garbage bag," she said one last time. But she took off the leather jacket and slipped into the baggy sweatshirt instead.

Maximus chuckled and swung open the bedroom door.

"'It's Witching Hour Somewhere'," Dallas read as she and Maximus passed by the many neon signs leading to the Butcher's office at the Umbra Forum. She snorted a laugh and smiled up at him. "That's a good one. I'm going to use that on you the next time I want a cocktail at nine a.m."

Max chuckled. "Then you'll be getting no sympathy from me when you get knocked on your ass with a wicked hangover."

They stopped at the Butcher's closed door, and Max pounded a fist against the chipped wood.

"Who is it?" grumbled a familiar voice.

"Your favorite Devil," Max crooned.

The Butcher stomped to the door and swung it open. "That'd be Darien, but you're a close second, Maxy." He stepped aside and beckoned them in with a large hand. "Have a seat."

Max stepped into the cramped room that was choked with Boneweed smoke. He angled one of the chairs for Dallas, and she sat down, pushing back her too-long sleeves.

The Butcher smiled in approval. "Chivalry, I like it." He shut the door, lumbered across the room, and threw himself into the chair on the other side of the desk, nearly snapping it under all seven feet of him. "We waiting for anyone else?" He reached behind him to grab a laptop off a filing cabinet.

"Just Dominic and Blue, but we can start now," Max said. The Angel and his blue-haired sweetheart had slept for longer than they'd meant to.

The Butcher opened the laptop on the desk, and soon the clicking of keys filled the room.

Max drummed his fingers on the armrests of his chair. "Tell me you found something."

"Patience, Maxy." A few clicks more, and the Butcher spun the laptop around so they could see the screen. "Here's your rental."

Max leaned forward. "Foxhill Rentals?" he read.

The Butcher opened the left desk drawer, took out a joint, and lit it with a lighter that was shaped like a naked woman. "That's the one."

The door opened behind them, and one of the Butcher's men appeared in the doorway.

"What'd I say about knocking?" Casen growled around a mouthful of smoke.

"Sorry," the young warlock muttered, cheeks ruddy and speckled with craters. "Got a couple people here to see you, but I can tell them to come back—"

"Who are they?"

The warlock turned toward the hallway—and the people he was escorting.

"It's Dom," called the Angel of Death.

The Butcher beckoned with a giant hand, the motion sending curls of smoke above the desk. "Send them in."

The young warlock stepped aside, leaving room for Dominic and Blue to enter, and shut the door behind them.

Max slid his chair aside. "Take a look at this, will you, Blue?" He gestured to the screen.

She stepped up to it, waving aside the heavy smoke that was making her cough. She leaned down to see the screen better, the hair that had grown to her collarbones slipping forward to partially conceal her face. "What is this?"

"You ever been here before?" Max asked, his heart beating faster. "This is Foxhill Rentals—the place where those men who took you rented their car."

"I have never been," she said, squinting at the screen. "But..." She pointed at a thumbnail of another photo, and the Butcher enlarged it. "I recognize the name—the..."

"Logo?" Dominic prompted.

She nodded.

A bubbly pop song exploded into the room.

"Shit," Dallas muttered. She fumbled to get her phone out of her pocket and checked the screen. "My bad."

The Butcher gave a gravelly chuckle. "Now *that's* something you don't hear at the Chopping Block every day," he said. He blew a smoke ring at the ceiling.

Dallas stood and walked to the corner of the room before answering the call. "Hello?"

Max turned to Casen. "Foxhill Rentals—where is it?"

Casen angled the laptop so he could see it better. A couple clicks, and he found the address. "Foxhill—would ya look at that? A town in the middle of butt-fuck nowhere." He enlarged a map and zoomed in. Max had never been there before—never even heard of it. Casen studied Max's expression—whatever it was. "That's quite the drive."

"Max?" Dallas called.

He turned.

"That was Sabrine—she said to get down to the school."

"Why?"

"She didn't say."

"Is it an emergency?"

"She said it's important."

Dominic shared a look with Max. "How are we supposed to get into AA without Atlas?" the Angel asked.

Max sighed. He made a good point; Atlas was the only person Max knew who was skilled enough in hacking to get through the protective spells over Angelthene Academy.

"I have an idea," Dallas said. She studied Dom with a smile that spelled trouble. "You probably won't like it, though."

Dom frowned. "Delaney?"

Dallas's grin showed all her teeth. "How'd you know?"

MALAKAI DELANEY WAS HAVING the best dream. The kind that involved multiple women and wet pussy.

Which meant he'd probably be waking up soon with a raging hard-on. Which meant he'd have to whack off. Which meant it must be morning.

Bang. Bang. Bang.

He flipped onto his stomach and grumbled into the pillow. Bent a knee to help with that raging hard-on. Gods—when was the last time he'd taken a girl to his bed?

Bang. Bang. BANG.

His eyes snapped open. "What," he began, "is going on?"

His giant room was still dark. Through the open curtains, stars glimmered in a clear sky.

The banging began again. Was someone at the bloody door?

He flung the blankets aside and got up, nearly falling over with exhaustion as he pulled on a pair of jeans and a t-shirt.

And then he threw the door open and stomped down the hallway. "Anybody going to answer that?" he called into the quiet mansion. He scowled and walked faster. When he spoke again, he amplified his voice with every word. "I have to do everything *myself, DON'T IIIII?*"

The banging came back.

His bare feet slapped the stairs as he thundered down to the ground floor.

"Whoever it is better fucking run!" he howled. "Because I'm a grumpy son of a bitch, my cock's half-hard, and I'm horny for blood."

TRAVIS DEVLIN STOOD in the dark front yard of the House of Souls as Max rapped a fist against the solid wood door. Dallas hovered on the steps behind Max, and waiting on the street out front of the house were Lace, Dominic, and Blue, the latter two unable to get past the spells on the gate.

It took a few minutes before they heard the thunder of approaching footsteps.

Yeah, that was Malakai motherfucking Delaney alright.

Travis scowled and shook his head. He was not looking forward to this.

Malakai swung open the door with such force that it blew his shoulder-length hair back. "What?" he gritted out. Max was in the way of Travis getting a good look at the Reaper's face, but the tone of his voice was a dead giveaway for his irritation.

Travis felt his hands twitch of their own accord. Ever since his botched date with Jewels—his *only* date, thanks to her dickhead brother—he'd been aching to take it up with Malakai. Not with talking, but with fists.

Max spoke before Malakai had a chance to. "We need a favor."

The Reaper peered around Max—

And scowled when he spotted Travis. "The answer's no." He shut the door—

Max blocked it with a hand. "Listen—"

Malakai stormed through the doorway, eyes flickering into orbs of shining black. "You did *not* just stop me from closing my own door."

Travis threw his arms wide in welcome. "You got a bone to pick with me, Malakai, I'm right here!"

He bared his teeth, silver canines gleaming. "You're not worth my time or Jewels's."

Travis scoffed. "It was you, wasn't it? I *knew* it. You're the reason she ghosted me!"

Malakai charged down the steps like a bull. "Say that one more time, Devlin, I dare you."

"Least you could do is admit it like a grown man."

"There's nothing to admit because I didn't do it. If Jewels hasn't talked to you, that's her decision, not mine."

"That's rich, coming from the brother who controls everything she does."

Malakai punched Travis in the mouth.

First blood. Now, he was free to draw second—and third, and fourth, and hopefully last.

Travis laughed around the blood coating his teeth. "Finally! I've been waiting for this." He punched Malakai back, splitting his brow open.

Max rushed down the stairs and attempted to step between them. "Alright, that's en—" He was silenced by Malakai's fist—hitting him hard enough in the mouth to make his gums bleed.

Dallas ran inside, calling for Aspen and Jewels.

Max swore under his breath. Rubbed his jaw.

Malakai advanced on Travis. "I don't control her."

"Words of a chronic denier and narcissist."

Malakai swung, and Travis ducked. He tackled Malakai to the ground hard enough to knock the wind out of them both. Travis landed several hits, blood spraying, before Malakai pushed him off with a knee to the chest.

The Reaper pinned Travis this time and struck. Again, again—

Travis whipped his head up, the move lightning-fast, and head-butted the Reaper.

Malakai fell back, but stumbled to his feet before he could hit ground.

Travis got up and attacked again, fist landing in his gut. Another two strikes to Malakai's ribs, and they were falling.

They rolled, hitting and kneeing and kicking, neither of them slowing down—

And then Dallas, Aspen, and Jewels were there.

"Malakai!" Aspen shrieked. She launched herself forward, latching onto Malakai's shoulders. She had to try several times, her grip on him slipping as he and Travis kept hitting— "I'm calling halftime! Malakai, stop it!"

Malakai let go, but not before he spat a gob of blood and saliva on Travis's face.

Travis wiped it off—and spat out a mouthful of his own on the ground. "You're a disgusting pig, Delaney." He got to his feet, wincing, only now just feeling the pain of their brawl.

Everyone took a second to breathe, including the girls, who wore expressions ranging from surprise and relief to fury.

"Okay, three things," Jewels began. Her words were strained, her face paler than usual. "One." She faced her brother and held up her thumb. "You *are* controlling, and you really need to lighten up. Two." She turned to Travis, adding her pointer finger. "You baited him. And three." She kept her stare on Travis, ticking a third item off on her fingers. "He's not the reason I haven't called you."

Travis stared, blood running down his throat. He nudged a back tooth with his tongue—loose, the prick. "He's not?"

"No!" She crossed her arms, her gaze ducking to the side. "I haven't been feeling well."

Shit—the Tricking. Of course Travis remembered, but he'd jumped to conclusions by blaming Delaney for her abrupt silence.

Malakai stomped closer. "And you—" He pointed at Travis. "Are a selfish prick who's clearly not helping—"

"What did I just say?" Jewels fumed.

Everyone took another second to breathe in the cool night air.

And then Aspen said, "Max said you need a favor?"

Max, looking thoroughly pissed, rubbed at his jaw again. "And some ice."

"One, two, three ice packs," Jewels said, passing the last one to Travis.

"Thanks." He pressed the ice that was wrapped in a cloth against his mouth—and winced.

Aspen eyed Malakai—and the ice pack dangling from his fist. "If you don't use that, you're going to have trouble keeping your eye open tomorrow."

He grumbled, but pressed the pack to the bruised skin.

Clover was seated at the dining room table, three laptops open before her. Aspen stood just behind her, offering suggestions whenever she needed them.

Travis wasn't surprised by how well the two worked together. They were twins, their faces nearly identical, their thought patterns and movements too. The only way you could tell them apart was by their hair; while Aspen's was shorter and poker-straight, Clover's fell to the middle of her back in perfect waves.

Jewels stepped up to Travis's side, so close her arm nearly brushed his. "How are you feeling?" She kept her voice low.

"Like a blueberry." He shifted the ice on his lip.

She smiled up at him. "You're starting to look like one."

Travis nearly smiled back, but stopped before the cut on his lip could split back open. "How about you? How are you feeling?" He felt dumb for even asking. He couldn't begin to imagine what it was like to live with a disease like the Tricking.

"I'm doing better today, all things considered." She directed her next words over her shoulder. "Malakai, quit glaring."

Travis made to turn—

Jewels stopped him with a hand gripping his arm. "He's less likely to attack if you don't make eye contact," she whispered.

Malakai drawled, "I can hear you."

"Well aware," she shot back.

About an hour later, they finally cracked the system. Travis realized how spoiled they were to have Tanner Atlas working for Hell's Gate; he was way faster than most hackers.

Aspen and Clover whooped and clapped. The latter slumped in her chair and said, "I need a drink."

Aspen faced the group. "I'll stay here with Clover. When do you need the spells down?"

Max said, "We'll call." He checked his watch. "But probably thirty, forty minutes from now."

"Speaking of calling," Dallas sighed, flashing them her phone screen. "It's Sab again." She stepped away from the group and answered the call.

Travis glanced down at Jewels. Maybe he was imagining it, maybe he was being too hopeful or plain fucking desperate, but he thought she might've been peeking at him out of the corner of her eye. "You coming?" he asked her.

She pursed her lips in thought. "You know what? I think I will. I want to live my life, and I've been stuck inside for the past three days. I'll go get changed—I'll be right down." She disappeared down the corridor.

Travis watched her go, and when he turned back around he was met with Malakai's icy glare. "You look worse than me," Travis said.

"Fuck you, Devlin."

24

THE FINANCIAL DISTRICT
YVESWICH, STATE OF KER

Caliginous on Silverway was on the top floor of a skyscraper in the Financial District of Yveswich.

It was just past eight. The block was quieting down, employees heading to their vehicles in groups of at least two as the darkness thickened. Street lights flared to life, and security systems came on, extra layers of spells rippling over windows and doorways. In the alleys, parking facilities, and subway system, predators began their hunt, eyes shimmering in the gloaming.

Kylar and Tanner worked together to mask the live video feeds with old footage. They were in the truck with Darien, Kylar squished up against the door in the back to give more room to Loren and Joyce, Tanner in the passenger's seat. Cords were tangled across the dash and the center console, the floor and the back seat.

"You got the cameras in the elevator?" Kylar asked Tanner as they finished hacking, keys clicking.

Tanner closed his laptop. "And the hidden one behind the mirror." He grabbed his laptop bag from the floor and stuffed the computer inside.

Kylar shot Darien a grin in the rear-view mirror. "Now I know why he's so famous."

"We ready?" Darien asked. Ivy and Jack were waiting in the car that was parked behind the truck; Darien could see them watching in the mirrors.

Everyone answered in unison. "Ready."

Darien carried Loren into the building, Kylar leading the way while the others took up the back. There were a few people leaving the building and the many businesses within, but most of them were employees who appeared so done with their shift that they didn't spare them a second look.

They rode the elevator to the top floor, a song that had to be thousands of years old floating through the speaker.

Darien was careful not to look at his reflection in the glass. He knew that if he looked, he'd see the monster pacing hungrily in his soul. He'd managed to go this long without a Surge, but it was only a matter of time before the beast went for his throat and pulled him under.

The elevator doors slid open with a hiss. On the wall straight ahead was a sign welcoming them to Caliginous on Silverway.

Kylar got out first, Darien second, Tanner third. Jack, Ivy, and Joyce walked together at the back of the group, Ivy carrying one of Loren's bags. She'd insisted on bringing it, in case Loren woke up after her first treatment. Darien hadn't argued with her; he hoped—prayed—it would be that easy. He'd never been the type to pray often, but he prayed for her.

Footfall clapped on spotless floors as they crossed the spacious room. A massive desk sat at the back, too tall to see if anyone was there. Salt lamps and diffusers were grouped together on either end of it, the latter scenting the air with peppermint and lavender. Loren had set up one of those things in the bedroom a little while ago; the scents and gentle gurgling helped her sleep.

Come to think of it, they helped Darien sleep too. Not enough to combat the nightmares and Surges, but enough to notice the benefits. Funny how something as simple as a plant could do so much.

"Tanya," Kylar said as they neared the desk, greeting the young, red-haired witch who sat behind it.

She looked up from the computer and smiled. "Kylar." She glanced among their group. "What can I help you with?"

Kylar took in the empty waiting area behind them. "Are you the only one working?"

"I have closing duty, yes. Is there—"

"We need to use the Reverse Chamber," Darien said, hoisting up Loren as her legs began to slide down his waist. She felt so small in his arms, like a bird with broken wings.

The open and friendly expression on Tanya's face cleared, and in its place was apprehension; Darien could sense it coloring her aura, and with it was the shade of fear. She spluttered, "I'm sorry, I'm not sure what you mean."

"Tanya." Kylar spoke softly, a patient smile on his face. "This is Darien

Cassel, Roman's cousin. We need you to do us a favor and let us use the Reverse Chamber."

Tanya's throat bounced with a tight swallow. "I'm not supposed to—"

"It's an emergency," Darien said. His arms tightened around Loren, hugging her to him. "This is my girlfriend. She fell into a coma during the security breach in Angelthene, and the only way we can save her is if you let us try the Reverse Chamber."

"A coma," Tanya repeated, looking lost. "I don't know if the chamber can work...that sort of..." *Miracle,* Darien knew she was about to say, but didn't.

Darien held her stare. "Please. Just let us try it."

"I could get in a lot of trouble," she whispered fiercely.

Kylar said, "We're taking precautions. We've already masked the cameras."

"I could lose my job, Kylar."

"I'll pay you," Darien said. Her attention snapped to him. "What's your annual salary?"

Her eyes darted about. "That's not—"

Darien said firmly, "Your annual salary, Tanya."

Her hesitation was brief. "Fifty-five thousand."

"I'll double it," Darien said. Tanya's mouth parted in surprise. "A hundred and ten thousand cash the moment we're done sessions."

She lifted her chin. "And if it doesn't work?"

"You'll still get the money."

Tanya studied Darien. There was compassion in her stare as she glanced between him and the unconscious girl in his arms. She might've been swayed by the money, but Darien could tell from her aura that it wasn't for greed. Everyone had shit they had to pay for, and this woman was probably barely scraping by.

She grabbed a coil of keys off the desk and got to her feet. "Come with me."

TEN MINUTES LATER, Loren was dressed in a white one-piece bathing suit with *Caliginous on Silverway* embroidered on the left breast.

Darien followed Tanya through a heavy door that led to a single narrow corridor. Above the door was a silver plaque with the number five etched into it. Loren was back in his arms, the others following behind him. The hallway was shiny and white, the walls curved like a tunnel. At the end was a door with a small round window in the center. There was another door halfway down that had a window too, but the glass on that one was frosted—*Change Room,* the plaque beside the door read.

"This is a private change room," Tanya said, tapping the wood of the door as they passed it. "You are welcome to use it when you are ready to leave today." There were more change rooms in the main area; they'd used one before coming into this corridor. But a private room was better; Darien would make sure to use it, so none of the other guests who might be in the building would see more than they needed to.

Tanya stopped at the end of the hallway and flattened her hand on a scanner. She hit a few buttons, and the chamber beyond the door lit up with bright light.

The chamber was white too, but the walls were made of material with points of shifting color, like an opal. The only piece of furniture inside was a floating tabletop in the very center—made of glasslike material that glowed like a holographic projection.

"What color magic?" Tanya asked, her eyes drifting to Loren.

Darien thought about it. "Try white."

She hit a few more buttons on the panel until the screen displayed a color wheel. Every color was on it—all except black or gray. With a few swift taps, she disabled all but white.

Tanya opened the door. "No one is allowed inside the chamber once it's on. You need to take off her jewelry."

Ivy stepped forward and removed Loren's solar conduit and the Avertera talisman. The spells on the building were so thick, Darien knew it would be a challenge for anyone to find her here, if they were looking.

Tanya said, "Does she have any conduit tattoos?"

"Just a medical one for her blood sugar."

"Good." She held the door open for Darien, and he walked in, footsteps echoing. It was warm in here, but not uncomfortably so, and it smelled faintly of citrus and rain. "Lay her down on her back on the table," Tanya said.

Darien did as she asked, and leaned down to press a kiss to Loren's forehead, her skin cold and chalky white.

He fucking hated this—how empty and emotionless she looked. Lifeless. Loren had always been bright and happy. Colorful. Sunshine in the flesh.

He wanted his girl back.

"I'm still here, baby," he said quietly, smoothing her hair back from her face. "I'll be right on the other side of that door." As he stepped back, he slid his hand down her arm, his fingers lightly squeezing hers.

He left the chamber, looking back over his shoulder twice as he went. He didn't like the idea of leaving Loren in here, but he'd do what he had to.

Tanya shut the door and hit a few more buttons.

The chamber shuddered to life with a whir that vibrated the floor beneath Darien's boots. Tiny balls of soft light winked awake all around Loren, and rain began to drip from spouts in the ceiling and floor, the levitating droplets shivering in the air, slowly moving up and down in vague lines. Soon, the floor was covered in two inches of water, but it didn't get any deeper than that.

Darien held his breath. He watched through the window, the others crowding behind him. Loren's hair floated above her as though she were underwater, her face peaceful and undisturbed. Minutes passed, and Darien barely breathed the whole time. Sweat beaded on his palms, that beast in his soul beginning to pace again.

"Come on, baby." The words he uttered were so quiet they were barely audible. *"Come on."*

But Loren didn't open her eyes.

25

ANGELTHENE ACADEMY
ANGELTHENE, STATE OF WITHEREDGE

"It's the Scarlet Star," Travis said.

"It's a sun," Malakai replied, as though he were stupid.

"It's. The. Scarlet. Star." It was obvious—the engraved face with eight rays. The shape had been carved into the wall behind a bookcase in the library of Angelthene Academy.

Their group was crowded, shoulder to shoulder, around that bookcase. Logan was here too, towering behind Sabrine, the wolf so tall it was hard for even Travis to see around his massive fucking head. Max, Malakai, Jewels, and Dallas made up the rest of their group, and Dominic, Blue, and Lace were keeping watch in the corridors so the security guards who were making their rounds wouldn't catch them.

Malakai bared his teeth. "It's. A. Sun."

"They're the same bloody thing," Travis growled.

"Ah." Malakai gave him an idiotic grin, canines glinting in the flickering lantern light. "So you're saying I'm right."

"I'm saying you're a dumbass."

Dallas stepped forth, wedging herself between them, elbows knocking them each in the gut. "Alright. Time out. We don't need two brawls in a single night."

Malakai said, "I usually prefer multiple."

Maximus cut in. "You brought us all the way here for...an engraving?" He didn't say it rudely; he said it with question. They'd all learned that if Sabrine had something to say, it was usually important.

"It's not just an engraving, Maximus," Dallas said. "This is the same symbol that's in the Old Hall." She turned to Sabrine. "The same one Loren wears on her necklace. Right?"

"Right," Sabrine said. "I was studying, and when I went to grab some potion books, I found a book shelved in the wrong section—a history book in the potions section, can you imagine?" She shuddered, and Travis smirked. "Had it not been there, I never would've spotted it, so we owe a massive thanks to the lazy fool who put it there." She patted the book bag that was slung across her shoulder; it was stuffed so full, books were bulging through the fabric. "I also have my preference for organization to thank for that."

"She's a neat freak," Logan said. "My house has never looked so clean."

"But what *is* it?" Malakai asked again, the idiot. "The sun—what is it?"

"Scarlet. *Star!*" Travis barked. Dallas and Sabrine shushed him.

Malakai continued as if he hadn't spoken. "So Loren wears this around her neck. So what?"

Dallas sighed. "I keep forgetting some of you are new here. Loren's had this necklace since my dad adopted her at the Temple of the Scarlet Star. It's a key, but it was also enchanted with a wish her dad bought from Tempus."

"And," Sabrine added, "that wish is what saved all of us on Kalendae."

"When the city blew up?" Malakai asked. The Reapers had been filled in on everything that'd happened that day, Darien choosing to trust them after they'd fought at their side during the Blood Moon—and after Malakai had helped resuscitate Loren. Travis supposed it was the one good thing the Reaper had done.

But he still wasn't sure trusting Malakai was a good idea. Arguing with Darien about it was out of the question, though. Darien, he trusted. Even if he didn't always agree with his decisions.

Jewels squeezed between the group, the chains on her black skinny jeans jingling. She ducked down, reaching between the fourth and fifth shelves from the bottom, and traced the shape of the Scarlet Star with her index finger. "Yeah, that's definitely a keyhole. I can feel the little ridges on the inside."

Travis bent his knees and dipped his head, peering past Jewels to see between the shelves. It was so small, and so heavily shadowed by the bookcases, it was crazy Sabrine had spotted it at all. "How are we supposed to get in there without Loren's necklace?" he said.

Sabrine piped up. "I have an idea. Erasmus obviously left that symbol in the Old Hall on purpose, right?"

The group echoed her with a "Right," though a few of them sounded lost, Travis included.

"And," she continued, "he gave her that key—the necklace—on purpose. Not just for a wish, but so that she would have a way to find the things he'd hidden—the things that would explain where she came from and what the Phoenix Head Society did. Such as the scroll."

She was met with several confused stares.

"The Master Scroll?" she prompted with wide eyes. "The Dominus Volumen?" She clapped her hands. "Come on, keep up."

Travis said, "Okay, so what are you getting at?"

"My guess is that Erasmus has another one."

"Another key?" Jewels asked.

"Yes."

"So..." Max rubbed his chin. "His townhouse, then."

Malakai said, "Another break-in?"

Sabrine shrugged. "We could try knocking and see if he gives it to us."

"The man's spelled," Dallas said. She chewed on her lip. "Pretty sure he can't say shit, and maybe can't even give it to us, if he even has it."

"He *does* have it," Sabrine insisted. "No room for pessimism right now, Dal." She glanced about the group. "Okay, so, who's going and who's staying?"

"I'm going," Malakai said. "If any break-ins are happening, I want to be involved."

"I'll stay," Travis said. Anything to get away from Malakai.

Jewels said, "I'll stay too." When her brother shot a look her way, she rolled her eyes. "Malakai..." Her tone was a warning. Travis bit the inside of his cheek to keep from laughing. "What did I say?"

He scowled. "Fine. Who else is coming with me? I don't even know where this townhouse is."

"I'll go," Max said. "Dallas?"

"Right behind you." She linked arms with Sabrine, who looked over her shoulder at Logan.

"Stay with them?" Sabrine asked him.

Logan's wolf eyes were the same shade as the lantern light. "You got it."

Sabrine winked. "Don't get caught."

"I don't think anyone's home," Dallas said.

Max knocked again—quietly. It was late, and this neighborhood in Oceana was filled with the kind of people who would call the cops on you for not putting your garbage bin on the curb at the right time. There were neighborhood watch signs everywhere; Max wouldn't be surprised if cops were already on their way.

Malakai was texting, the screen light limning his beard and accentuating the harsh lines of his face. "Asp says the spells will be down in two minutes."

Max stepped back and craned his neck to see the windows on the second floor. All were dark. "If they *are* home, we're going to put the old fuck into cardiac arrest."

Malakai shut off his screen and slid the device into his pocket. "Who cares? He's nothing but problems. Maybe it's time he did us a favor and croaked."

Max felt the spells come down. The sudden absence of magic raised a prickle on his skin and erased a layer of white noise that made everything eerily quiet.

"Step aside," Malakai said, pushing his way through. He had a long, thin piece of metal in hand.

Sabrine said, "You're going to pick the lock with a bobby pin?"

"It's Aspen's." He slid it into the lock in the knob.

Max gave Dallas a look of amusement. "Says the guy whose hair is longer than hers," he said around a huff of laughter.

Malakai glowered over his shoulder. "It's not a regular bobby pin, dumbass, it's her special lock pick."

There was a faint click, and the knob turned with ease.

"Told ya," he whispered.

Malakai crept into the house first—

A dark shape swung at his head.

The Reaper ducked, that shape nearly taking out Max next.

He reared back right on time, his boot squashing Dallas's foot.

"Mother trucker!" she exclaimed.

The shape hurtled for the Reaper's head again—

Malakai dodged the hit. "It's me, you old fucker!" he hissed.

"And th-that is s-supposed to make me f-feel better?" Erasmus's voice wavered in the dark. He stood in the foyer, weapon held before him in shaking hands.

Malakai's hand closed around the broom before Erasmus could swing again. "It's supposed to make you stop trying to decapitate me!" He forced his way into the foyer, hand still gripping the broom.

Erasmus held onto his end, though he stumbled back as Malakai advanced on him. "Wh-who's with you?"

Max stepped in, the girls following. He felt for a light switch by the door and flipped it on. Light flooded the foyer, blinding them all for several seconds.

"Relax," Dallas crooned, wings twitching. "We won't let the big bullies hurt you."

Malakai was still gripping one end of the broom. "Can I let go now, or are you going to swing at me again like I'm a fucking flightball?"

"He won't," Max said. Erasmus looked his way, breathing heavily, eyes wide behind round glasses that needed cleaning. "He's already caused enough damage. Haven't you, Erasmus?"

A beat of silence passed before Erasmus let go. Malakai leaned the broom against the wall—out of reach of Erasmus.

"What made you think I was here to kill you?" Malakai asked, his jaw still flexing with irritation.

"Y-you're a Darkslayer. It's your j-job."

"Fair point."

He assessed the four of them. "If you're not here to k-kill me, then what do you w-want? Is Loren—"

"She's fine," Max said quickly.

"She's n-not at the hospital anymore." None of them said anything. His eyes filled with fresh dread. "Is she—"

"She's fine, and that's all you need to know." Max's voice was firm. "We're here because we need you to help us."

Sabrine stepped forward. "We need to know if you have another necklace like the one you gave to Loren. The Scarlet Star."

Erasmus's only answer was a noisy gulp.

"We know it's a key," Max added. "And if you care at all about your daughter and the mess you've put us all in, you'll help us find the answers we need."

Erasmus looked like he was going to throw up, his mouth tightening into a grimace. Max had seen that same look on Loren, back before Darien broke the spell on her.

Footsteps sounded on the carpeted stairs. Cyra appeared, freezing on the third step from the bottom. She wore satin pajamas, her eyes puffy with sleep. She blinked, shielding her eyes against the light—and gaped at the sight of the group in the foyer, and Erasmus cowering against the wall.

"Erasmus?" she said. "Is everything okay?"

Sabrine stepped forward and pulled up an image on her phone—the photograph she'd snapped of the symbol in the library. She showed it to Cyra. "We found this in the library of Angelthene Academy. We need to know—do you have another key?"

Cyra's hand went to the chain she wore around her neck. Only the top of the chain showed, the rest hidden under her pajama shirt. But she didn't speak, didn't remove it.

Fuck, this was infuriating as all hell.

"Take it off," Max said. His words were for Sabrine, who turned to look at him. "If she's bound to secrecy, then she probably can't remove it herself." He looked at Cyra. "I don't think I'm wrong, am I?" He was met with the barest shake of her head.

Sabrine stepped forward, easing up onto the first stair.

Cyra let go of the necklace. "It is…ordinary." She came down to Sabrine's level and dipped her head, allowing the wolf to remove it.

"Not a conduit or a wish?" Max asked, for the best clarification he could get.

Cyra nodded once.

"That's all we need. Let's go."

They made their way out, and Max wondered if he was the only one who found it odd that Cyra wore the necklace—the key—instead of Erasmus.

The library was quiet.

Logan and Dominic were keeping watch now, giving Lace and Blue a break. The girls sat on the table across from the one Travis was lying on, old tomes spread before them. Nearby, Jewels flitted around the shelves, picking up a fairytale book here, a potions book there. They were all getting bored—not to mention tired.

Travis's eyelids began to slide shut as he stared up at the high, vaulted ceiling, watching the lantern light dance with shadows and glint off cobwebs—

The table shook under him as Jewels climbed up to sit beside him. "That ghost is giving me the creeps," she said.

Travis lifted his head to see the ghost with pit-like eyes floating between the shelves on the other side of the room.

Lace said, "They call him 'The Staring Teenager'. Apparently, he likes getting the students in trouble." She pursed her lips in thought and leaned forward to see the ghost better, her hair slipping over her shoulder like platinum silk. "Wonder why he hasn't bothered us yet."

Jewels shuddered. "Let's stop talking about him, or he might come over here," she whispered.

Travis studied Jewels, the soft curves of her pale face kissed with firelight. She wasn't wearing any makeup, and although Travis thought she looked amazing when she was all dolled up with the dark eyeshadow and lips, she was very pretty without all that stuff too. He was glad Malakai wasn't around to catch him staring.

"I didn't mean to act all crazy earlier," Travis said. "I wasn't upset with you, I was pissed at your brother. He annoys the hell out of me. No offense."

Jewels trilled a laugh. Her smile was contagious; it made Travis want to smile. "You handle him a lot better than the other guys I've dated. Honestly, I am really impressed. Most don't even make it past the first date."

"Wonder why."

She laughed again. "He means well. We're each other's only family, so Malakai has trouble letting me go."

"Yeah, but does he have to be such an asshole about it? Doesn't it make you feel...suffocated?" He couldn't imagine making it to the age of twenty-three and still having someone control him.

He had Roman to thank for that reality.

The thought of his brother brought a deep frown to Travis's face. While Travis had managed to escape the control and abuse of his father, Roman had been fed on by sharks for the past few years, and he'd thrown himself into the water willingly. It was realizations like these that made Travis feel a hell of a lot less powerful, less capable, less grown up. Roman might've forced him to leave Yveswich, but a part of him still felt like he'd run away like a coward.

Jewels shrugged and picked at her glossy black nails. "Sometimes, but... Malakai's played the role of big brother and dad for years. He's watched over me since we were kids. We didn't have a good home life."

Travis grunted. "Neither did I." It seemed to be a common theme with Darkslayers. But then again, did people who came from good, wholesome upbringings typically seek out jobs that involved killing people and monsters?

Probably not.

"Do you have any siblings?" she asked him.

"Two. Roman and Paxton. Roman's my older brother, Paxton's younger than me. He's my half-brother." The half-brother he'd left behind. Another twinge of guilt speared his heart. Thank god Roman was still there, or that kid would probably be dead by now. "They live in Yveswich—that's where I'm from."

"Wait...," Jewels said, holding up a pale hand. "Roman *Devlin* is your brother."

He nodded.

She shook her head. Squinted at him. "Why didn't I make the connection before?"

He shrugged. "It's not like you and I have ever really talked."

It was her turn to shrug. "Guess not. Do you have a good relationship with Roman and...?"

"Paxton," he finished for her.

"Paxton."

"I don't really have one at all. Roman got me out of Yveswich years ago, so I wouldn't have to be around my dad anymore. Pax was so young back then, I don't know if he even remembers me. He'd be twelve now, I think."

"Have you never gone to visit?"

"Can't. Roman would murder me." When Jewels's brow creased with question, Travis explained, "My dad's Donovan Slade."

Her eyes widened. "Oh shit." There were a lot of people who never made the connection, since their last names were different. There were even a few people in Angelthene who'd never known that Darien and Ivy were Randal's kids, having never heard of them until they'd changed their surnames and became Devils—became important.

"Roman's waiting until Paxton's eighteen and can legally live on his own," Travis said. "Then, they'll both leave Yveswich."

"Roman runs the House of Black, though. He'd leave all of that behind?"

"The only thing Roman cares about is his family. He doesn't care about all that other stuff."

The doors to the library creaked open. The others were back.

Sabrine was at the head of the group. She gave them a wolfish grin and held up a necklace identical to the one Loren wore. "Good thing we've got a bunch of muscleheads here. We're going to need to move that bookcase."

26

MOTEL 58
STATE OF WITHEREDGE

The yellow bikini was even cuter than Shay had thought.

She turned to look at the curve of her backside in the bathroom mirror, her long hair brushing against the small of her back. Yup, the ruched center in the bottoms made her ass look really good.

"Time to swim, Nugs," she said with a smile.

Where he lay on the bathroom floor, the Familiar looked up at her with big eyes. It was late, but both of them were itching for a swim after that long, hot drive with that big, cranky Darkslayer.

She grabbed a white towel off the rack, wrapped herself in it, and bent to scoop up Nugget. He was extra warm and limp in this baking heat.

The television was on in the room, but Roman was nowhere to be found.

Good riddance.

"Do you think he left us?" she asked Nugget. She wouldn't be surprised; his grouchiness had doubled after their store visit a couple of hours ago. She had no idea what the hell was wrong with him, aside from the whole blackmailing thing, but it made her want to smack him.

She parted the curtain on the window and looked out at the dirt parking lot. Under the moonlight, his car gleamed like bone.

She let the curtain fall. "Nope, still here," she declared.

Before leaving the room, she grabbed her key in case Roman decided to lock her out and walked barefoot to the pool.

There was no one else out here, the pool lit by the warm glow of a few string lights. She set down Nugget and threw her towel on a pool chair—

"Might want to look before you dive," said a gravelly voice from the shadows of the building.

Shay spun, hand shooting to her racing heart. "Are you trying to *kill* me?" she hissed, her pulse pounding under her fingertips.

Roman was leaning against the wall by a door that had a maintenance sign nailed to its surface. One of his booted feet was braced against the wall at his back, cigarette in hand. "If I tried to kill you, pup, you'd be dead before you realized what I was doing." He motioned to the pool behind her, the silver rings on his fingers glinting. "That would've given you one nasty concussion."

With reluctance, she turned—

The pool was bone-dry. Debris and an old buoy sat at the bottom.

"You've got to be kidding me," she muttered. It was boiling out, even at night, and even when she was dressed like—

She spun back around in time to see Roman's eyes slowly moving up her body, lingering on the slope of her backside...and the ruched center in the bottoms of her swimsuit. Males had shown interest in her since she'd hit puberty, but for some reason it felt different when the attention was coming from Roman Devlin.

She couldn't decide if it was a good different.

Shay crossed her arms over her breasts, well aware that her nipples were poking against her bathing suit—and well aware that he was now looking right at them, his stare potent enough to burn. "What are you doing out here?" she said tightly.

"Smoking. What's it look like?" He lifted the cigarette to his mouth. He was so buried in shadows, she could hardly see him. They clung to him like pets to their master, as if magnetized to him.

Shay cleared her throat. "Can I have some?"

A beat of silence.

And then he pushed off the wall and stalked toward her, not stopping until he practically walked right into her. With his stare still fixed on her, he offered up the cigarette. Smoke streamed between them, curling up toward the stars.

She took it from him, being careful not to touch his hand, and took a drag. Roman watched her mouth the whole time, even after she'd blown out the smoke and offered the cigarette back. Her eyes stung and watered, and she had the prickling urge to cough.

He didn't even try to make an effort not to touch her as he took it back, his hand closing over hers. He pinched the cigarette out of her fingers and took another drag. As Shay watched him, she couldn't help but think how they'd both had their mouths on the same thing.

Nope, that was bad. A very bad thought.

Smoke puffed out his nose. "You're not a smoker," he observed.

Her lips parted in surprise.

His attention fell to her mouth again, and the corner of his twitched, deepening a nearby scar in his cheek. "You can't hide everything from me, Shayla." He wet his lips, the stud in his tongue flashing like a tiny silver star.

And then he left, and Shay watched him go.

Just before he disappeared around the corner, she felt the string of her bathing suit bottoms lift on one side—

And snap back down, stinging her flesh.

Her hand flew to her ass. *"Roman!"* she shrieked. What in the hells—

Her only answer was a dark, sinful chuckle from around the bend, the sound quickly fading along with the crunch of his footsteps.

She shook her head, rubbing the stinging skin, wondering how it was possible that it suddenly felt less dark out here than it had a moment ago, as if the shadows had followed him. "Did he just do that?" she said to no one.

His shadows, maybe? Could he—they—*do* that?

She shook her head, her thoughts drifting aimlessly about.

Nugget was staring up at her from the ground, accusation in his round, glittering eyes.

"Don't even start," Shay warned.

And then she collapsed in one of the poolside loungers, not wanting to go back in the room and be near Roman again so soon.

"What?" Shay hissed to Nugget, who still watched her with implication. She threw up her hands. "I didn't do anything."

The Familiar merely shook his fuzzy head, looking like he knew something Shay didn't.

ROMAN SLAMMED the door to room number nine and locked the deadbolt, the chain. His blood was thrumming, electrifying with thoughts of Shay in that bathing suit.

That yellow fucking bathing suit.

He should keep the door locked. Whenever she decided to come back in here, there'd be no telling what would happen, what he might do.

He'd wanted to do a lot more than snap the string of her bathing suit, that was for goddamn sure.

'You will absolutely not be doing more,' Sayagul cut in, her words coated with warning. The dragon fluttered out of his shadow and onto the bed, where she'd stashed her half-eaten bag of gummy bears under one of many throw pillows.

'I know that,' Roman grumbled.

The dragon eyed him as she pried the candy bag out from under the pillow with a claw. *'Don't make me use these on you,'* she warned, holding up a sharp claw in illustration.

Roman stared at the locks. Said, "Fuck my life," and unlocked them.

He'd control himself. Would stay the fuck out of Shay's pants—or bikini, whatever the hell she wore the next time he let these thoughts poison his head again—or his mistake would get them both killed.

27

CALIGINOUS ON SILVERWAY
YVESWICH, STATE OF KER

"It's not working."

Darien pushed away from the door to the Reverse Chamber and started pacing.

The others—Ivy, Jack, Tanner, Kylar, and Joyce—kept quiet as they observed him. He was about to tip into the deep end of a Surge—he could feel it, the beast breathing hungrily down the back of his neck.

Ivy was the first to speak. "It will."

"It might take a few treatments." This came from Tanya, who spoke from the end of the corridor, a hand propping open the door behind her. "Even people with very depleted magic levels don't always leave here afterward with a full reservoir. Sometimes it takes two, maybe even three treatments."

Darien appreciated the effort everyone was making, but they all spoke from zero experience. Never had anything like this—anyone like Loren—happened before.

Tanya said, "I recommend we pause treatment after twenty minutes."

Darien stopped pacing, the violent storm in his soul shifting into a hurricane. *"Twenty minutes?"* he growled. "That's fucking *it*?"

Tanner said quietly, "You don't want to push it, Dare."

Darien started pacing again, eyes flickering black. "Twenty minutes, then." He blinked away the Sight. "But we'll be back here tomorrow." His tone left no room for argument.

Tanya left, and the corridor fell silent.

Darien stepped up to the window in the door and looked in, at the floating balls of light and the trembling water droplets. Loren's hair kept floating. Her chest kept rising and falling.

And she kept sleeping.

He curled his hands into fists, knuckles cracking.

Kylar said, "You want to try one of the chambers?"

Darien didn't turn.

"If they work for Roman's psycho ass, they'll do something for you."

"Maybe another time," Darien muttered.

Ivy said softly, "It might be a good idea."

"I'm fine."

"Or," Jack said, "you could try jerking off. Works for me when Ivy's not in the mood."

"What is wrong with you?" Ivy hissed in horror. "I'd prefer not to be widowed so young."

Darien pinned Jack with a glare. "I can't stand you sometimes."

Twenty minutes was over quickly. Tanya shut off the chamber from the control panel behind the desk.

Darien watched through the window as the balls of light winked out. The last of the rain splashed to the floor, and Loren's hair fell to the floating table in golden strands that immediately dulled, cheeks bleaching of color.

The buzzer sounded, indicating the chamber was off.

Darien pushed through the door, boots splashing through water, and checked Loren's pulse.

Steady, but not strong. Same as fucking before.

He scooped her up and joined the others in the corridor. "Ivy, let's get her changed." Ivy pushed open the change room door and held it open for him. "We'll bring her back to Roman's."

Tanner picked up on the words Darien didn't say. "Where are you going?"

Darien faced Kylar. "Is there anyone in this city who sells Venom?"

"Sure. What do you need it for?"

Darien glanced between the faces of his family, felt Loren's chest rise with an even breath—the people he'd sworn to protect.

"Precaution," he said, and stepped into the change room.

YVESWICH'S black market was far bigger than the Umbra Forum in Angelthene. It was also much more crowded.

And yet, despite not being able to see his face and tattoos in the deep shadows of his hood, the clusters of people in the area kept themselves at a wise distance, their reluctance to get too close making it slightly easier to traverse the vast place.

Nightfall had given the air a sharper edge, and the sodden coat of rain that had plagued the city all day had frozen nearly to hail. Drops of it plinked off tin roofs and splashed into the canals, hard enough to sting when those half-frozen beads pelted your skin.

The cold and the wet didn't bother Darien, though, not when it gave him an excuse to wear the kind of clothes that kept his identity secret. Heads turned, and gazes pried at their trio—just him, Jack, and Kylar were here—but no one drew a connection. The only person they might've recognized was Ky, who felt zero need to hide his face.

Kylar led the way now, not faltering once, no matter how many times the path they were walking branched out, meandered, or stopped entirely, becoming a dead end. He always knew where to go, which stalls to cut through when met with brick or wooden walls. It would be really easy for lesser people to get lost in a place like this. Lost and never found. It made Darien think of Loren, made his gloved hands curl into tight fists as he recalled the day he'd tracked her down on the Avenue of the Scarlet Star. A girl of light, who'd known nothing of darkness.

When Kylar tipped the brim of his invisible hat to yet another merchant, Darien said, "Come here often?"

"All the damn time, Cassel," Kylar said, throwing him an over-the-shoulder grin. He ducked under another tent and edged around the firepit crackling in the center of the shop. "This market might be neutral ground, but when night falls in this city, and you're a member of the Hollow, places like this become your playground. It's not technically a Gray Zone, but it might as well be with how often we come here." He gestured to a narrow path tucked between two tin shops, one painted an ugly shade of yellow, the other a gaudy green. "This way."

The route Kylar led them down was hardly big enough to squish through. Darien had to angle his body sideways to avoid knocking hanging lanterns off their hooks. Jack did the same behind him, taking extra care after the warning Darien had given him regarding not touching, breaking, or setting fire to anything while they were here.

The many stores and freestanding, haphazardly erected walls stopped the wind of the evening from guttering out the lanterns, but Darien could hear the gusts howling through the cobbled streets several blocks away. On the surface, the air here smelled of charcoal, drenched wood, and the perpetual brine from the ocean. The second layer revealed secrets no mortal would pick up on: blood that belonged to animals and humans, herbs and foul ingredients bottled into magic potions, and hot, bubbling tar.

Venom. They were getting close.

The path spit them out in a stretch of the market that was sheltered by a patchwork of roofs—tin and plastic and wood, the mismatch of material creating a raucous piece of music from the rain clattering down like gemstones.

Kylar waved them forward, and they continued on, past vendors promising all kinds of things—spell-protections, miracle potions, healing tonics. A dense wall of bodies was packed in a circle up ahead, watching the fights taking place in a cage very similar to the Chopping Block. The men inside were covered in blood, their faces concealed by black masks that were typically worn to stave off the cold, leaving only their eyes and mouths exposed.

"Shadows tells me you like to fight," Kylar said with a smile, the small Darkslayer tattoo on his cheek crinkling. "Fair warning: the magic barriers on that one are the kind that incinerate. It's exciting the first couple times, but after that it gets pretty boring. The matches don't last long when people disintegrate after a hard enough punch. If you want a real fight, I recommend the Snake Pit." He pointed to their right. "You'll find it down that way." He gave Darien another of those wide smiles, the diamond embedded in his tooth flashing. "You want to go for a round? You look like you want to kill someone."

Jack grinned, his own teeth sparkling in the lantern light. "He always looks like that."

Darien pushed him away with a palm to the side of the head, sending him slamming into a werewolf twice the size of him. The wolf grumbled before shoving a laughing Jack back their way.

Kylar was still eyeing Darien. "We can make a stop," he offered.

Even the simple thought of ripping off someone's limbs electrified his blood, he had to admit, and he felt that bloodthirsty beast inside him begin to pace. But Darien said, "I always *want* to kill someone, but when I *need* to, I'll let you know." It was getting to that point, but he would hold back his Surges for as long as he could.

Kylar merely chuckled.

Darien scanned the endless maze of shops that stretched far into the distance. "How much further?"

"Could be a minute, could be an hour—never can tell in this place. Might want to keep that dog of yours in your shadow." He lowered his voice, his eyes cutting to Darien. That ever-present glint of humor on his face was gone. "And whatever you got," he said, now looking at Jack, "keep him hidden."

"Why?" Darien's voice melded with Jack's as they asked the question simultaneously.

"Familiars have been going missing. They fetch high prices, and the sellers can't keep up with the demand. See those cages?" He gestured with a brown hand to a tent nearby, where a surly-looking warlock puffed on a cigar, his round, ruddy face gridded by the shadows of steel bars as an assortment of hanging cages swayed around him. "Two nights ago, those cages were full. Every single one."

"Of Familiars?" Darien pressed. He'd never heard of such a thing.

"Wearing glowing collars," Kylar said. "Their people nowhere in sight."

"Wait, wait, wait." Jack slowed down. He craned his neck to see better, firelight driving away the shadows of his hood. "You're telling me—"

Kylar grabbed him by the sleeve. "Keep walking. If you look like you don't have a purpose here, someone will turn you into a purpose of their own."

"You're telling me," Jack continued, entirely unconcerned, "that someone's found a way to *steal* Familiars?"

"Keep your fucking voice down," Darien hissed.

Kylar stopped at a tin box of a shop with a red wooden door. The circular window in the center was made of bubbled glass too foggy with condensation to see through. "Familiar Spirits are the hottest item on the market right now," Kylar said, grabbing the door handle, "and no one knows why."

He swung open the creaking door and stepped inside.

DARIEN STOOD between Kylar and Jack inside the tiny drug-dealing business in Yveswich's black market. The reek of hot tar made Darien's eyes burn as they waited for the dealer to come back.

None of them said anything, though Jack had tried opening his mouth a few times, only to shut it after Darien shot stern glances his way. You didn't talk in a place like this—not about anything personal, but preferably not at all.

Finally, the heavyset warlock returned. "Most I can do is thirty mil," he said, wiping the sweat off his forehead with a meaty wrist.

"What do you mean?" Darien asked. "You're out?"

"Right." He set the bottle on the high counter—behind the wall of spells that protected him from clients. "That'll cost you three thousand GM."

"That's three times the usual price."

"Right." He wiped at his forehead again. "You paying or no?"

Jack said, "Why's your supply so low?"

"And why the upcharge?" Kylar added.

"The demand is high," he said, eyes darting around, "and the ingredients are slim-pickings right now."

"Will you be getting more?" Darien pressed.

"Depends on if anyone deals with the infestation by the tar pits."

Jack and Kylar glanced at Darien. "What infestation?" Darien asked.

"Bunch of Hounds and the like by the tar pits. Can't make Venom if we can't get the ingredients, and can't get the ingredients if no one wants to go near the tar pits."

Darien took out three thousand gold mynet and slapped it down on the counter. The guy picked up the money and nudged the bottle through the spells.

"If we get you your tar," Darien said, "you'll give me more and you'll discount it."

The dealer opened his mouth to reply—

"That's not a question," Darien said. He grabbed the Venom and walked out.

By the time they got back to Roman's house, Darien was glad to see that the others had made themselves comfortable. Ivy and Joyce had spent the evening baking cookies with Itzel, the House Hob, while Tanner played video games in the living room on the ground floor with Paxton and Eugene.

After checking on Loren in one of the spare bedrooms upstairs, Darien took a shower—a long one. He was sore as hell, his muscles so tense he swore he would use up all the hot water before they would have a chance to loosen. When he got out, he found a pair of gray sweatpants and a white tee in his duffel and put them on, hating how quiet the room was. Loren had always been a quiet sleeper, but this silence was unsettling.

He checked on her for the third time in under an hour, pressing his thumb against the inside of her wrist—still beating. "I'm right here, baby," he said with a whisper. "I've got you." He smoothed a strand of sun-bright hair off her face and pressed a kiss to her brow before making his way down to the kitchen.

Ivy was cleaning up, wiping the counter with a damp rag. Jack and Atlas were playing Rushin' Racers in the living room, eyes glued to the screen.

"Where's Pax?" Darien asked. "Sleeping?"

"Ky took him home," Tanner replied, his bloodshot eyes still fastened on the screen. Home to the House of Black—poor kid. Tanner cursed under his breath as Jack took first place in the race with a loud, "Whoop!". Tanner continued, "He has school tomorrow."

"Is Kylar coming back?"

"In an hour."

Jack added, "Said something about Pax being fine at the house 'cause it's a school day." Darien didn't like the sound of that.

He joined Ivy in the kitchen as she was rinsing the rag and squeezing it dry. Joyce must have gone to sleep, and as for the Hob, she was nowhere to be seen. "Need any help?"

"Absolutely not, you do enough," Ivy said. She draped the rag across the faucet. "Besides, I'm all done."

Darien spotted the box of cinnamon buns on the counter by the fridge. He crossed the room and flipped the lid open, the scent of cinnamon sugar wafting across his face. "Started with twelve, down to one."

"That one's for you," Ivy said. "I had to literally beat Jack away with a spatula, so make sure you enjoy it."

Darien picked it up and bit into it, eating half of it in a single bite.

A kettle on the stove began to whistle.

Ivy hurried over and shut off the burner. "How'd it go at the Black Market?" She poured hot water into a mug on the counter, tea bag already in it.

"I could only get thirty mil, and for triple the price. Apparently, there's a demon infestation by the tar pits."

"Tar? Is that what they use to make Venom?" She bobbed the tea bag up and down, the scent of spearmint and chamomile floating through the air.

"Apparently, it's the key ingredient."

She shot him a worried glance. "You really think you'll need to use it again?"

"Hope not. But better to have it on hand than not, if one of those fuckers shows up again." He finished off the cinnamon bun and rinsed the sticky residue off his hands. "Keep Soot close." He flicked off the tap and dried his hands. "Kylar said Familiars are going missing."

"Is that even possible?"

Darien shrugged. "Apparently."

"How? And why?"

"I don't know. But keep your guard up—always. Especially when you go jogging. I'd prefer if you took Jack with you, but he's too damn lazy." Darien increased the volume of his voice, directing it at Jack.

Jack waved a dismissive hand. "Get out of here."

"I'll be careful," she said. She discarded the tea bag and returned to her mug, leaning down to inhale the steam drifting out of it. "I feel so bad for Pax." She shuddered. "Staying at that house with that...psycho."

"Woo-hoo!" Jack cheered, throwing his hands in the air. "Four for five! You suck, Atlas."

Tanner tossed his controller aside and got up to join them in the kitchen, Jack soon following. "You don't think he beats Paxton, do you?" Tanner wondered.

Darien's brows flicked up. "A Slade? Beating one of their kids? Yeah, I fucking think that. And whatever he's doing to Pax, you can guarantee he's doing to Roman tenfold."

"So what do we do about it?" Jack said. He walked to the counter and helped himself to a cookie.

Ivy scowled. "I just made those!"

"They're for eating, aren't they?" He bit into it with an overly sexual groan, eyes rolling into the back of his head.

"Sharing. You ever heard of sharing?"

"If I find out Don's physically abusing either of them," Darien said, "he's dead."

"He had a bruise by his eye," Tanner said. "Did anyone else notice that?"

"He's got a problem with bullies at school," Darien explained.

Ivy gasped, her elbow knocking the mug and nearly spilling her tea. "Not my sweet little Pax!"

"He was being picked on in an alley when I found him today. Kids stealing his lunch money—that bullshit."

"So," Jack said, polishing off the cookie. "What are we gonna do about *that?*" He dusted the crumbs off his hands. As they pattered to the floor, Twitch crept out of his shadow to lap them up with his tongue.

"Do you think Donovan knows?" Tanner asked.

"Pax said he does," Darien said. "Don thinks it builds character and he needs to toughen up."

"Wait," Jack said. "Are *you* saying Pax needs to toughen up, or is Donovan saying that?"

"Donovan, you idiot."

Tanner cut in. "Wouldn't be a bad idea to teach him how to defend himself, though." Darien had a feeling Roman had already taught him a few things, but learning how to throw a punch meant nothing if you couldn't follow through when it came down to it.

"What about Roman?" Ivy asked, taking a sip of tea. "Do you think he knows?"

"Paxton doesn't want him to."

The kitchen fell silent as they mulled it over.

"Well, we've got two choices," Ivy said. "Intervene, or mind our own business."

"We teach Pax how to deal with the bullies on his own," Darien decided. "I'll take care of his dad."

Darien had just announced that he was going to bed and was halfway to the staircase by the front door when Atlas caught up to him.

"Hey, Darien?" Tanner called quietly.

Darien turned.

Tanner slid his hands into his pockets. "Can I talk to you for a minute?"

"Sure." They faced each other in the dark foyer. Darien waited for Tanner to speak, but he seemed unable to find words. "Tanner, if this is about what happened at the stronghold—"

"What, between you and my mom?" Tanner chuckled. "Shit happens, Darien. She made a mistake, and you've both moved on. I'm not going to hold something that minor against you." The sudden apprehension on his face told Darien where this conversation would go. "This is about you," Tanner began. "You need to cut yourself some slack."

"Atlas—"

"You've been blaming yourself for everything. You're blaming yourself for Loren being in a coma, you're blaming yourself for her nearly dying in Paradisi, and now you're blaming yourself because she didn't wake up after one treatment."

That glass was in his lungs again. "Tanner, I promised to protect her—"

"And you've been doing a great job." Before Darien could argue, he continued, his words rushing together, as if he'd waited days to get this off his chest. "Darien, she would've died six months ago if you hadn't found her in that alley." The reality of his statement was a blade skewering his heart—and it lit that glass in his lungs on fire. "Randal and the imperator would've put her in the Well replica a lot sooner, the city would've blown up a lot sooner, and none of us would even be here right now." Maybe that was true, but he couldn't take full responsibility for that miracle on Kalendae—*any* of the responsibility, really, when you got down to the details.

"*Loren* saved Angelthene on Kalendae—"

"Because you put that suit on her," Tanner said. Darien swallowed. "She's alive right now because of you—we *all* are alive right now because of you. So you need to cut yourself some damn slack and trust that this is going to work."

Darien inhaled, the sound as ragged as he'd felt for the past ten days. "I feel like I failed."

"That girl is still breathing because of you. And guess what? When she wakes up, it's gonna be because of you."

Silence fell between them. The television droned in the background as Ivy and Jack watched a movie. Darien knew his sister well enough to sense that she wasn't watching the screen.

"Can you at least try?" Atlas asked.

Darien nodded. "I'll try."

"One more thing." He smiled a little. "You look like shit."

Darien smirked. "Thanks."

"You need sleep. When was the last time you slept for more than two hours?"

Darien grimaced.

"Exactly." He drifted down the hall, heading toward the kitchen—probably straight to the cookies, if he knew Atlas at all. "Try to sleep—you're no good to any of us if you die of exhaustion."

Ivy added in a singsong voice, "He's right, you know."

Yeah, he was. And it was for them, not himself, that Darien pulled himself up the stairs and collapsed on the bed in his guest suite, an arm slung across Loren's waist. Because he was no good to any of them if he died.

Loren still wore the Avertera talisman—they all hid their auras now, to prevent the imperator from finding out what they were doing, where they were. But when Darien was this close to Loren, he could feel her aura, muted as it was. Soft as the salt lamp glowing on the nightstand.

Her aura was growing dimmer every day. He hadn't wanted to admit it, but he could sense that she didn't have much time left.

If she didn't wake up soon, she wouldn't wake up at all.

28

ANGELTHENE ACADEMY
ANGELTHENE, STATE OF WITHEREDGE

Angelthene Academy was situated above a network of tunnels that looked like they hadn't been accessed in centuries.

Max used his Sight as they walked through the darkness, nothing to guide them but the beam of a flashlight he'd found in the SUV. He'd given it to Dallas, who walked at the head of the group, the flashlight illuminating the tunnels ahead.

The traces of auras down here were so old and dull, he couldn't get a firm read on them. Many souls had walked this ground—he could see the colorful streaks they'd left behind, like swipes of watercolor paint. The souls of people who were probably very old now; a person's aura vanished the minute they died, so the colors that were still down here belonged to people who must still be alive.

"What is all of this?" Dallas's voice echoed as she pointed the flashlight at the walls. The tunnels were coated in a glossy black crust that reminded Max of volcanic glass.

Malakai said, "It looks like the same shit they use to make the rabbit masks in Yveswich."

Max glanced at Malakai, seeing nothing of the Reaper's face but the colors of his aura, like threads of glowing yarn outlining his features. "What do you mean?"

"You've never heard of their masks? They're made of this crazy-expensive shit that lets a person's aura enter the mask, so Darkslayers can go looking for a messenger instead of waiting for one to come to them. Yveswich has way too many messengers and not enough Darkslayers, so they handle their jobs differently. Messengers aren't supposed to approach Darkslayers, they're supposed to wait for one to come to them." The way Malakai said it suggested he'd prefer it worked that way in Angelthene too.

Dominic said, "How do you know that?"

"I've been to the city before, and a couple of my friends worked for Cerise Brinton years ago."

"The Wyverns," Dominic said.

"Cerise is a cunt. They don't work for her anymore."

The tunnels continued for what felt like a long time. Some led all the way outside the gates, but most zigzagged through the property of Angelthene Academy. No matter how many tunnels they walked, however, they never found anything interesting.

Until they wound up in a circular room with a bunch of old candles cluttered upon a stone ledge at the far end. Taped above the ledge were grainy, black-and-white photographs.

Dallas pointed the flashlight at the ceiling. "Where are we?"

Max looked up with his Sight. "Below an old building, by the looks of it." A spell-protected one, surrounded by chainlink fences with loops of barbed wire at the top.

Dallas and Sabrine shared a loaded glance. "The Old Hall?" they said in unison.

"Wait," Dallas said, chewing on her lip. "That doesn't make any sense. Darien searched the Old Hall. There's no way he wouldn't have noticed these tunnels down here."

Malakai walked up to the wall and tapped his knuckle against the glossy surface. "Not with this." He was met with several confused stares, Max included. Since when was Delaney an annoying know-it-all? "If you're looking at adamant while using the Sight," the Reaper explained, "you can only see one side of it. The other is totally invisible. So if Darien was looking from that angle up there—" He pointed up through the earth. "He wouldn't have seen it. It would've looked like nothing was down here."

"Why don't they use that on buildings?" Jewels wondered aloud.

"That would suck if they did," Travis said. "None of us would have jobs anymore." He smirked. "Time to do up the old résumé."

"The material's too rare," Malakai explained to his sister, totally ignoring Travis. "There's not enough of it, and besides, it's expensive as shit." He scanned the ceiling. "You think they'd be able to afford upgrading all the buildings in a city this size? No chance in hell."

Max crossed the room, gesturing for Dallas to follow with the flashlight.

Soon, the others were joining them as they gathered around the ledge of candles, photographs above it.

Dallas pointed the beam at a photograph of a group of people, staring stony-faced at the camera.

"The Phoenix Head Society," he and Dallas murmured, voices melding together.

"Mother trucker," Dallas muttered, pointing a finger at two faces in the center of the group. "That's my mom and dad."

"And there's Erasmus," Sabrine said, coming in at her left. In the photo, he was very young but easily recognizable. His hair was wavy, his glasses round.

"Yeah, that's him alright," Travis said. "The source of all our problems."

Malakai said, "Wait just a goddamn minute." He wasn't the only one now looking at the woman in the center of the photo.

It was Cyra. Cyra, standing between Erasmus and Roark. She was obviously the heart of the group, the two dozen others in the photo situated around her like planets orbiting around the sun. She looked almost exactly the same as she did now, as if she hadn't aged a day.

"Cyra was a member of the Phoenix Head Society?" Dallas whispered.

"Guess so," Max replied.

"But..." Sabrine pointed between Cyra and Erasmus. "Why is Erasmus mortal again, and so...old? And Cyra's not."

No one had the answer to that.

"Roark and Taega," Sabrine insisted, her words frantic—desperate for an explanation. "All of them are young still." She shook her head, looking as lost as Max felt. "I don't get it."

They scanned the faces of the other members. Max didn't recognize anyone else. Except... Was that—

Logan stepped closer, his shaky breaths audible. "Is that..." His nostrils flared, and his arms began to tremble with the threat of the Shift. The temperature of the room spiked several degrees, causing sweat to prickle across Max's back. "Is that my dad?"

Bleddyn Sands—so young, Max had failed to recognize him at first.

Max scanned the group again. Six of them—the people in the front row—wore fine silver chains around their necks, but the pendants were too small to tell what they were. They looked like thin, rectangular pieces of metal. "What are they wearing?"

"Keys?" Jewels guessed. "Like the solar amulet, maybe?"

Max turned to face Logan, who was having trouble getting a handle on the Shift. "What would you be willing to bet your dad was killed for this?"

He jabbed a finger at the grainy face of Bleddyn Sands—and the pendant he wore around his neck.

"Jaden...," Sabrine breathed. "What if Jaden and Calanthe knew about this, about his involvement in the society, and that's why they've been planting dead vampires in Werewolf Territory? Because they *want* something. *This*, maybe." She pointed again at the photo.

"Sab," Dallas warned quietly. She wasn't the only one now watching Logan with vigilance.

Max angled his body, shielding Dallas from Logan.

Sabrine settled a calming hand on Logan's trembling arm. "It's okay," she whispered, rubbing his arm. "Breathe, okay? Breathe, honey. We're all here with you."

Everyone stood in silence for a few minutes, waiting for Logan's shaking to subside, and the fire in his eyes to dim. Max stayed on high alert, keeping his body partially shielding Dallas. Werewolves as powerful and unpredictable as Logan were ticking time bombs. The amount of destruction he'd wreak if he lost control, even for only a few seconds...

Finally, Logan calmed down. As the temperature in the room cooled, he murmured, "Darien said the same thing. He thinks they need an excuse to attack—to come onto my land and..."

Sabrine pointed at the pendant—key, maybe—that Bleddyn wore around his neck. "Go looking for this?" she finished gently.

"Maybe." Logan swallowed. "My dad...he never told me."

"Doesn't mean he was keeping secrets, bud," Max said. "If Erasmus and Cyra are spelled and can't speak, it might've been the same for your dad."

"What are these over here?" Lace asked. She was looking at a collection of photographs taped to the wall. All of them were individual student photos.

The group moved over to look.

"Oh my god," Sabrine said, her gaze snagging on a young man—the first photo in the top row. "Is that—"

"Holy shit," Dallas breathed. "Is that the Staring Teenager?"

"He was a member of the Phoenix Head Society?" Lace guessed.

Dallas shook her head. "No, *these* are the members of the Phoenix Head Society." She pointed at the group photograph to their left.

"Then who are all of these people?" Sabrine's voice wavered; she was likely drawing the same conclusion Max had just drawn.

"Sacrifices," he said, remembering the many rumors they'd uncovered about the society—the act known as the Initiation. Several of the people in their group turned to look at him, their eyes brimming with questions. Max whispered, "These are the people who died in the Well."

"LET ME SEE THAT BOOK," Travis said to Sabrine. "The one you found in the library." With all the shit they'd just uncovered, with having no excuse to come down here but a book randomly shelved in the wrong area, Travis had a thought. He might be wrong, but it was worth checking, anyway.

Sabrine opened her book bag, took out the heavy tome, and handed it to him.

He opened the front cover. There was a manila sleeve taped to the inside. He thumbed the library sign-out card free and checked the names listed in different handwriting. The last person to sign this book out was—

"T. Isley," he read aloud. He recognized the last name.

Dallas and Sabrine said in unison, "Tamika?" They shared a glance.

Tamika Isley—the optometrist. The woman who'd come to Hell's Gate not long ago to share her information about Spirit Terra.

"You think she left that book in the wrong spot on purpose?" Sabrine asked.

Travis said, "I'm starting to think nobody does anything on accident anymore."

"It could've been someone else who left it there," Dominic pointed out.

Malakai snorted. "Yeah, like the old fucker. Leaving clues everywhere like we're in a goddamn egg hunt."

Sabrine shrugged. "If it was him, then at least he's not being totally useless."

"What do we do now?" Lace wondered. "Try talking to Tamika?"

Max faced Travis. Travis had seen that look before—whatever Reacher was about to say, it would set this path into motion. "I want you to find Tamika," Max said. "Ask her why she signed this book out—find out if it was her who put it in the wrong spot. And I want you with Lacey—I'm not okay with leaving Hell's Gate with only one of us in town."

Travis's brow creased. "Where are you going?"

"Foxhill Rentals." Right—Maya. "I'm following that lead the Butcher gave me, but I could use some company." His eyes flicked about the group.

"I'll go," Dom offered.

Blue grabbed his hand. "Wherever he goes, I go." Her accent was thick, but she was getting really good at speaking their language. Dom sometimes spoke hers too, the Angel deeming it only fair that he learn her language if she learned his.

Max dipped his chin. "Perfect. I was hoping you might be willing." It was with visible reluctance that Max turned to the leader of the Reapers. "Malakai?" His voice was tight.

Malakai's retort came without delay. "No."

"Yes!" Jewels cut in, her sharp tone echoing against the shining walls. "You're going."

"And leaving you here?" Malakai growled through clenched teeth. "With Devlin?"

Travis's hands curled into fists. Fuck him.

"Yes." Jewels spoke firmly. Gods, Travis loved it when Jewels gave him a run for his money.

Malakai looked like he wanted to throw some punches—but so did Travis. The wounds in his knuckles were still healing, but his palms tingled with the desire to hit. And this fucker's face would be his target again.

The Reaper cursed under his breath.

"Come on, Malakai," Max said. "Darien left you in charge, which means you're not allowed to be useless and sit around on your ass."

He literally growled like a dog. "Fine, but I'm taking my bike." He looked at his sister again, his jaw shifting as he ground his teeth. "You'll be okay while I'm gone?"

Jewels rolled her eyes. "I think I can manage."

"I'll look after her," Travis said, his words more for Jewels than they were her idiot brother.

"If she winds up with so much as a scratch on her," Malakai warned, "you can say goodbye to your precious dick."

"Malakai!" Jewels fumed. "Enough with the attitude!"

Max looked at Dallas. The witch was already watching him, the rings around her pupils glinting in the glow of the flashlight.

"You didn't really think I'd forget about you, did you?" he asked her.

Dallas answered him with a grin.

"Pack your things, Red. We're going for a drive."

29

ELSEWHERE

In the heart of the universe, over two thousand years in the past, the girl and her dog watched as the Phoenix Head Society began to take form. And as she watched, she began to understand what the great serpent had meant when it warned them that each life they gave would yield different results.

With access to the prima materia, the three students created an invention using the bathtub Helia had slept in below the Old Hall. It was their base material, and they turned it into a giant well that fused with the floor, sinking into it and turning the basement into a glowing pond, the bottom of which shone like volcanic glass.

They called their invention 'The Arcanum Well'.

Then began the sacrifices. What they did was horrible—tricking that first student, William, into joining their friendship club, promising him that the otherworldly magic of the Well would transform him into something Other. Something better and stronger than his old self. After all, it was all he'd ever wanted.

But it was a lie. They planned to take from William his life and his magic, robbing him of everything, and in doing so, *they* would become something Other, something better and stronger than their old selves. All the things they'd promised to William—the things he'd never see.

William, being part warlock, yielded a venefica result. Sacrificing him to the Well would turn Erasmus, who would enter the fires of the Well after William, into a warlock.

From there, the three students—killers, all of them—performed so many procedures with the Well, so many deaths, that they became something the world had never seen before.

They were gifted with superhuman strength and speed; an unmatched sense of sight, touch, hearing, and smell. But their real gift came in the form of a magical, all-seeing ability they called 'Sight'. The Sight turned their eyes black and allowed them to see auras and spells that were invisible to the naked eye.

At last satisfied with what they were, and no longer ashamed of the mortality they viewed as a curse, they began to add to the Phoenix Head Society, initiating new members they deemed worthy and granting them life as a hellseher. Once in a while, if a member acted out, they would throw them into the Well, using their monstrous creation to steal their life and powers.

Twelve members of the Phoenix Head Society held positions higher than the others. Erasmus, Helia, and Elix were at the top, of course. As the original members and creators of the Arcanum Well, their decisions went undisputed.

Then came Xinia Rose Croft, Bleddyn Sands, and Taega Tine, followed by the final six of the twelve.

And six of the twelve held the title of *Keyholder*, or *Keeper of the Keys*. The keys were created to protect what they had made—to keep anyone outside of the Phoenix Head Society from using or stealing their invention.

Changing themselves into something Other wasn't easy to hide. Soon, people began to take notice. They were no longer the same as they once were, thus suspicions began to arise.

They made the difficult decision to drop out of school—to create new identities for themselves and hide the Well from the people who began to look for it.

By then, Elix's conscience was so bothered by everything they'd done that he wanted no part in the society. And his girlfriend, Taega Tine, had already left—the first person to leave without facing repercussions for doing so.

The Phoenix Head Society broke apart. The friendships they'd built crumbled with distance and time, though most of all from regret. Society eventually accepted hellsehers like they did new breeds of monster, and the burning question of where they came from dulled with the passing of decades, allowing hellsehers to live without morbid curiosity nipping at their heels everywhere they went.

One day, many years down the line, Erasmus and Helia, now married and deeply in love, grew lonely. They used the Well—the machine that was being hunted by desperate people who'd dug up the secrets of the society, people who wanted a taste of power and immortality for themselves—to create a child. Helia, being born a goddess, was unable to have children, and the Well was powerless to change this.

After creating a precious mortal baby with the Well, they revisited the ancient serpent that had blessed them with their ultimate gift—

The world began to glitch. The girl and her dog stumbled back from fog and static that swept into that age-old cavern, and two blinks later they were teleported back to the first meal that had been devoured by the Well.

William—the one who later generations would call 'The Staring Teenager'.

The Arcanum Well went up in flames, and William began to scream.

A death for a life.

The girl and her dog couldn't stomach seeing it for a second time—couldn't stomach watching any of this horrifying history any longer.

They fled, out the doors of the Old Hall. Across the dark and deserted school grounds. Through the gates, their spiritual bodies melting around the wrought-iron bars, and into the sprawling city glimmering with lights.

She wanted to cry. Cry and scream her lungs out, but no tears wet her eyes.

It wasn't fair. They had tricked that poor student—killed him so they could take his life and magic and turn themselves into something Other.

And they did it again. And again. And again. So many lives taken, so many people gone. All for greed.

The girl ran, Singer at her side, her opalescent dress swishing about her legs. Through the dark and dirty streets of Angelthene's upper districts and into the south, past the Meatpacking District and the hollow eyes that peered at her from thick shadows.

The monsters were out, but they paled in comparison to the ones who called themselves The Phoenix Head Society.

She did not stop running until she made it across town and into the district of Ebonfield. Only then did she slow her pace. With careful steps, golden blades of grass crunching under her bare feet, she approached the two dirt roads that intersected to form an X.

Not far from the roads sat a stone wishing fountain, its shape barely visible in the blur of night.

She approached slowly, picking up the hem of her dress by habit as she maneuvered the tall grass.

Stopping before the fountain, she glanced down at her transparent hand.

There were old scars on her palm that told her she had done this before—cut herself to speak to bargaining beasts.

Except she could no longer bleed.

She looked at the bucket that sat upon the fountain's edge, its bottom speckled with holes.

Slowly, she crept up onto the edge, one bare foot at a time, and crouched upon it. It was too dark inside to see anything—just a seemingly bottomless black pit, waiting to devour her.

Behind her, where he stood on the grass, Singer whined. He tucked his ears back against his head, tail drooping between his legs.

"We have to, buddy," she whispered. She reached down to grab him, pulling him up onto the stone ledge with her. "You have to trust me." With Singer now at her side, she stared into the fountain's depths.

And then, with a deep breath, she held on tightly to Singer and jumped inside the belly of the beast.

30

MOTEL 58
STATE OF WITHEREDGE

Shay woke up shortly after midnight to see Roman smoking a cigarette in his bed. He was lying flat on his back, fully clothed, the bed still made. The glow of the clock on the lone nightstand outlined his stupidly attractive profile with soft red light.

As she watched him bring the cigarette to his mouth for another drag, she questioned how sane she was for establishing that boundary earlier that evening—the wall of throw pillows she'd placed between her bed and his.

There was no denying that he was handsome—stupidly hot, if she wanted to admit it. But getting involved with someone like him, even if for only a one-night stand, would be bad, for multiple reasons. The most obvious was the fact that they came from different circles, but *which* circles they came from added to how utterly bad it would be if they got under the covers together. Athene and Donovan had been rivals for years; the Shadowmasters and the Selkies positively loathed each other.

Which reminded Shay of the little oopsie she'd made in coming out to Motel 58 with a Shadowmaster. Not just *a* Shadowmaster, but Roman freaking Devlin. If her mom found out, she'd be toast.

Better not add banging Roman to the list of mistakes she'd made, no matter how tempting that particular mistake may be. Especially when she was this tired—and never mind the fact that it had been...*months* since she'd last had sex?

Yup—months. And the last time wasn't even good. No big O involved.

Nope, didn't matter. It wasn't happening. Roman was off-limits, no questions asked.

No matter how hot he looked while smoking in that bed.

"I took down your little barrier," Roman said, as if reading her quarreling thoughts. His husky voice filled the dark room until it felt like the walls might pop like balloons. That voice made Shay shiver, the skin on her arms pebbling. "After I tripped on one of the pillows," he finished. Shay swallowed a laugh; so *that* was the sound she'd heard shortly after falling asleep.

"What's the matter," she crooned, her voice thick and crackly with sleep, "the Prince of Shadows can't see in the dark?"

Slowly, Roman turned his head to face her, and blew a mouthful of smoke her way. It hit a wall of magic, clawing its way up toward the ceiling, where it hung like the tiny clouds of a brewing storm.

"This is a non-smoking room," Shay said.

Those unnerving eyes continued to watch her in the dark as he brought the cigarette to his lips once more, the end glowing bright red.

Point taken.

Seconds passed, and Roman wouldn't stop staring at her. The room was so dark, it made his eyes look like black pits, though she could see just enough to tell that he wasn't using the Sight.

She squirmed, the sheets tangling about her feet that were suddenly sweating, despite the air conditioning. "You really don't like talking, do you?"

More silence, and then, "What's there to say?"

"Conversation is key to getting to know someone." She had a feeling there was a lot to know about Roman Devlin, and she hated to admit that she was just slightly curious about him.

Slightly. Especially after what little information he had revealed about himself during the drive. He had a younger brother—someone he cared for. What else was he hiding?

"Who said I want anyone to know me?" Roman drawled.

She rolled her eyes. "Fine," she sighed. "Go ahead and be a brick wall for all I care." Tugging the scratchy blanket over her shoulders, she began to turn her back on him—

"I've never done well with people, pup," Roman said.

Shay stilled. After deliberating, she faced him again and settled back down, tucking the blankets around her to keep out the chill. She wondered if that was all he would offer her, but to her surprise he kept speaking.

"My mom called me her lone wolf. Even as a kid, I was more likely to be found playing by myself than with others my age. I was the shadow that stuck to the corners at social gatherings." He took another drag and blew out a mouthful of smoke. Shay watched as his magic molded the cloud into a small, rippling wolf. "The oddball," Roman went on. "The freak." He stretched an arm out above his head in illustration, fingers splaying, eyes feverish and wide with intensity. His magic animated the wolf; it trotted forward and threw its head back with a howl.

Shay tore her eyes from the mesmerizing image to study Roman again in the dark. "That sounds kind of sad."

The red light of the clock glinted on his teeth like fresh blood as he smiled, looking very much like the wolf of smoke evaporating above their heads. "Sad?" He pursed his lips, still watching the smoke. "Nah. I never wanted friends. Don't even want them now. I decided, if people were going to call me a freak and an outcast, I would own whatever labels they gave me. And when they started calling me a homicidal maniac, I became exactly that: a homicidal maniac." Shay wasn't sure homicidal maniac was the same thing as being a Darkslayer, but there were people who would argue that statement.

"And how do you fare, now that you're older? Being a Shadowmaster and all. Aren't any of them your friends?" She couldn't imagine getting through life without anyone. If Shay hadn't had Anna to lean on, she never would've lasted this long.

"If you're smart, you don't make friends in this business, you form alliances. That's all we Shadowmasters are: allies. If you have friends, you have weaknesses. And weakness never got anybody anywhere."

Shay pondered his words, and then tasted her own before speaking, choosing them carefully. "I don't believe you live entirely by your own rules. There's no way you made it this far without caring about anyone." Without thinking, she blurted, "Haven't you ever been in love?"

Roman rolled onto his side to face her and propped himself up on an elbow. Looking directly at her, he opened his mouth and put the cigarette out on the flat surface of his tongue, the sight of his piercing making her gulp.

Shay's insides clenched with unease, as if she was the one feeling the pain of that fire scorching her flesh. Roman, on the other hand, didn't so much as flinch, as if he put cigarettes out on his tongue every single day.

He tsked, discarding the cigarette butt in the ashtray on the nightstand with long, tattooed fingers. Where he'd found that ashtray in a non-smoking room, she had no idea. "Love, Miss Thief," Roman said, "is the biggest weakness of all."

31

ELSEWHERE

The girl and her dog plummeted into the water inside the Wishing Fountain with a noisy splash. Gravity sucked her into the dark depths, yanking her down, down, down...

She resurfaced with a gasp, her opalescent dress ballooning around her like flower petals peeling open to drink from the sun.

She pushed the wet hair out of her face and tipped her head back, peering up at the starry sky way, way above. The mouth of the fountain was barely a pinprick from here.

It was far deeper than she'd thought.

Beside her, Singer grunted and paddled, the dark and grungy water lapping against his nose.

"We have to dive," she told him. She had no idea how she knew that—she could just...feel it.

Singer whined, his ears flattening back.

"I know, buddy," she whispered, her teeth chattering with phantom cold. "I'm scared too. But we have to." She pulled him close, wrapping her arms around his glowing white neck, wishing she could feel the comfort of his warm, soft fur. His glow spilled across the water like milk, highlighting stray leaves and slimy algae.

Singer kept paddling, paws churning the water, each ripple glowing white.

"On the count of three." Her words echoed, reminding her of what it felt like to have someone speak to her, instead of just speaking to herself or an animal. "One...two...three." With a deep breath she didn't need, she dove under the water, pulling Singer down with her.

She swam—deep, deep, deeper. The fountain swallowed her up like a ravenous serpent, and soon she could no longer tell where the surface was. As she kicked her feet, she trusted that she was going the right way, her left arm reaching out blindly before her while the other hand hung onto Singer's scruff with a tight fist.

Gravity tilted, and suddenly she swimming up instead of down. She spotted a bluish glow up ahead—a new surface.

She burst out of the depths with a gasp—and found that she was treading water in the opposite end of the Wishing Fountain—one that sat in the middle of a gloomy room with curved, windowless walls.

If her heart had been capable of beating, it would have skipped as she took in the skulls and bones piled around the room, sticky with dirt and sheets of web. And if she had been able to smell, it would have reeked in here—of death and foul, rotting things.

An eight-legged, shadowy beast squatted in an alcove.

"Liliana Sophronia," the spider hissed. "What a truly splendid surprise."

The girl and her dog crawled out of the fountain, dripping water onto the floor. "Is that my name?" The girl's voice echoed as she wrung out the bottom of her dress, water splashing on concrete. "Liliana Sophronia?"

The spider gave a thoughtful hum. "Most call you 'Loren'."

"Loren," the girl repeated. Quieter, she mouthed, "Loren..."

"I feel as though we've had this conversation before," said the Widow. She paused, as if realizing something, her many eyes shining like black eggs. "Oh my dear sweet child, you seem to have misplaced your memories. And would you just look at your hands!" She tutted.

Loren held them up—and sucked in a quiet gasp.

Both of them were transparent now. And the rest of her felt like...a broken eggshell. Brittle and empty, no life left inside.

"Am I dead?" The question was a hollow whisper. She peered into the darkness, squinting to see the Widow, but all she could spot of her were eight thick legs and a monstrous mound of a body.

The Nameless being carefully considered her answer before giving it. "You are teetering on the precipice of life and death," she said, her childlike voice echoing.

"Is there anyone waiting for me?" Loren swallowed. She couldn't feel the cold here, but she was suddenly shivering, "Back at home?"

"Many a person waits for you," the Widow said gently. "They fight for you to return. You are in very good hands, child." If only she knew who those people were. The only ones who came to mind were Dallas and Sabrine; she doubted Roark and Taega would fight for her to come back. She remembered them now—remembered bits and pieces of her childhood, however sparse.

And it was that broken childhood that told her that her adoptive parents were not fighting.

"How did I get here?"

"You made an incredible sacrifice for your city and those you love. An act of selflessness—a true one." That didn't sound like her. Selfless? Maybe. An incredible sacrifice?

Definitely not her. If there was one thing she wasn't, it was brave, courageous. She had always dreamed of having the right to call herself those things, but she knew herself, and she was no hero.

"How do I get back?"

"You are the Skeleton Key." Skeleton Key? "If you cannot find a door, you need simply to make one."

"Can you help me?" Emotion choked her words, and her stomach twisted with urgency. "Please, I—I want to go home. I feel like I...like I miss people and I can't even remember who they are." Her breath hitched in her throat, sticky as those webs clinging to the ceiling, where long-dead insects hung in iridescent cocoons. She said again, "I want to go home." The last word broke on a sob that echoed against the walls. Her features pinched with sadness, but no tears came. To be unable to cry was a very strange cage.

"Start by placing your hand on the wall to your right."

Loren picked up the hem of her sodden dress and stepped over rocks and bones. When she reached the wall, she brushed aside a curtain of webs, unveiling smooth stone beneath, and flattened her hand on its surface.

"Close your eyes," said the spider. "Listen to your heart."

Loren shut her eyes and concentrated. There was no heartbeat to listen to—just a deep and silent void in her chest, in her very being.

But she tried—she tried really hard, casting a line to the heart that had ceased to beat.

In her mind, she saw darkness. After a few moments, it began to ripple, as if she were peering through water.

Beyond the waves, there was a face. She couldn't see much of it, but it was male. Male and very, very handsome. Obscured as it was, this fact was clear.

"Who is he?" she whispered, studying the sharp line of his jaw, the night-dark gleam of his hair.

The Widow merely said, "Forever your protector."

Her brows pulled together as she tried to force the water to clear. She wanted to see him, but the depths just kept rippling, stopping his features from clarifying.

"What do I do now?"

"Continue to follow your heart. He who wishes to return to life must take a leap of faith."

The Widow's last word echoed into the distance as Loren's surroundings abruptly melted away, magic pitching her into the unknown. Her breaths quickened, and she cast that silver line inside her toward Singer, hooking him with it and pulling him along with her.

When she opened her eyes again, she was standing upon a narrow path that floated above endless black space—a night sky studded with colorful stars and swirling motes of light. The dark, grassy path she stood upon was speckled with glowing flowers, the petals all colors of the rainbow.

There was only one way to go now, and that was forward.

She started walking.

32

THE HOUSE OF SOULS
ANGELTHENE, STATE OF WITHEREDGE

Malakai stood across from Aspen in the corridor outside of her bedroom, waiting for a swift kick to the nuts the moment she processed what he was asking her to do.

"And I want you to come with me," he concluded with a noisy clearing of his throat.

She blinked her green eyes up at him. Poked herself in the chest with a long, red nail. "Me?"

He nodded. Crossed his arms. Shifted on his feet. The floorboards creaked under his weight.

It took her a long time to fully process what he'd said, and as the silence stretched on, Malakai began to feel something fluttery in his gut. What the hell *was* that? Was this what those hopeless romantics called 'butterflies'?

Eww.

How many minutes had passed? He was beginning to sweat. He ran his tongue across a silver canine, fingers squeezing into fists.

Finally, she said, "What about Sylvan and Valen?"

"I want you." He clarified, "To come with me, I mean."

He wasn't expecting her to smile at him, but her face lit up like the sun.

"Okay!" she exclaimed. "When do we leave?"

That was...entirely unexpected. But wildly welcomed.

Malakai cleared his throat again. "In the morning. Pack tonight and be ready to go whenever Reacher calls."

She was still grinning. "Okay. Sure." She edged around him and drifted through her bedroom door, her Familiar curling around her ankles, the fennec fox blinking her big eyes at Malakai. "Thanks, Malakai."

"No, thank you," he said tightly.

He disappeared downstairs, mimicking himself in a squeaky voice. "'No, thank you'. Could you sound any more *stupid?*" he asked himself with a shake of his head. "Bearded fucking buffoon is what you are."

'You're too hard on yourself,' Creature said, flitting out of Malakai's shadow to perch on his shoulder. *'And we're out of bananas.'*

"You already told me." Creature had an insane obsession with bananas, even more so than he did grapes.

'I'm telling you again,' the bat said. *'We need to pick some up on our way out.'*

"Need, hey?"

'Need.'

He found Sylvan and Valen watching the sports station in the living room. The antique clock chimed out the hour; it was late. He needed to sleep, or tomorrow would be brutal.

"I'm going with Reacher out to Foxhill to look for his sister," Malakai declared.

Only Valen heard him. Sylvan's glazed eyes remained glued to the flatscreen.

Malakai grabbed the remote off the arm of the couch and shut it off.

Sylvan blinked and slowly looked his way. "You're going out to Foxhill with Reacher?" Leather groaned as he turned his body to face him.

"So you *did* hear me," Malakai said.

"Which of us is going with you?" Valen asked.

Sylvan asked him, "Want to flip a coin?"

"Neither of you," Malakai cut in. "I'm taking Asp."

They both gave him stupid grins.

"So *that's* what's happening here!" Valen said.

"What? No! Nothing's happening, shut up." He glanced toward the stairs. "I want you guys to keep an eye on Jewels. Make sure she doesn't let Travis stay the night here, and make sure she doesn't stay at Hell's Gate. Got it?"

Sylvan said, "There's such a thing as daytime sex, you know."

"You want us to spy on her?" Valen asked.

"Not spy," Malakai hissed. "Just watch her, make sure she stays safe."

Sylvan got up and turned the TV back on, using the button on the corner instead of the remote Malakai still held in his hand. "And has safe sex, got it."

"I think he said no sex," Valen said with a smirk. He winked at Malakai.

Malakai rolled his eyes and threw the remote at Valen, hitting him in the knee hard enough to make a thud. He walked away. "I'm counting on you," he called over his shoulder.

33

ROMAN'S HOUSE
YVESWICH, STATE OF KER

Darien had just started to drift off in his room at Roman's house when the television on the ground floor came on, the volume so loud it literally shook the bed he was lying on.

"What the hell?" he muttered. He lifted his head off the pillow and glanced around the room—dark apart from the orange glow of the salt lamp on the end table. That lamp was the reason he'd claimed this room; he knew Loren would love that little glowing rock. As soon as she saw it, she'd probably want to take it home like she did the dented cans in the grocery store.

It was by habit that he got up slowly, trying not to jostle her. With sleep weighing heavily on him, demanding he soon pass out if he wanted to live another day, he could almost fool himself into thinking she was merely asleep.

The television got louder, vibrating the windows.

Darien remembered Kylar's warning from that afternoon as he swung open the bedroom door, not bothering to put on a shirt or pants overtop of his gray boxers. It was unlikely that anyone was up at this hour—though they would be soon if that noise kept up.

If he had anything to say about it, it would stop right the fuck now.

He stomped out the door and down the hallway, to the split staircase that would take him to the ground floor. He thundered halfway down the steps, just far enough to see the tiny Hob—smaller than Mortifer—sitting on the leather couch, television remote in hand. Her glowing eyes were hot-pink, and the black-and-blush flames on her head were swirled like cupcake frosting. Beside her sat a bowl overflowing with ice chips.

What the hell was her name again?...

"Itzel!" Darien barked.

The Hob glanced his way.

"That is *way* too loud. Turn it down."

The Hob poked a button on the remote.

Well, that was easy.

"Thank—" Darien shut his mouth as the volume didn't go down—it went up. *"Down!"* he growled. "Turn. It. *Down."*

Itzel merely leaned back against a throw pillow, crossed her legs, and turned her attention to the movie, tiny hand reaching for an ice chip. Slowly, she put the chip in her mouth and chewed.

She didn't look his way again.

Darien shook his head. "Unbelievable."

Bandit stirred in Darien's shadow. *'Shall I eat her?'*

"Tempting," Darien muttered.

Bandit licked his chops. *'Say when.'*

A husky laugh came from behind him. Darien turned to see Kylar standing at the top of the stairs.

"Told you she's loud," said the Shadowmaster.

"Is she like this every night?"

"Without fail. You should see her on Tuesdays."

"What happens on Tuesdays?"

"Pots and pans orchestra."

Darien dragged a hand down his face. "My gods."

"Want some earplugs?"

"Do I."

He followed Kylar upstairs and into the washroom, where he threw open a drawer to reveal packs upon packs of brand-new earplugs.

"These are all here because of Itzel?"

"Yup."

Darien scanned them. "Which are best?"

"They're all pretty well the same. I'd recommend using these and also putting up some magic until you fall asleep."

"Don't tell me you can still hear her through these things."

Kylar smiled, the diamond in his tooth sparkling in the bathroom light. "I won't tell you."

Darien grabbed a couple packs and made for his room. "Thanks, Kylar."

"See you in the morning."

"If I'm still alive by then."

Kylar's chuckle chased him into his room as he shut the door. He checked on Loren, and then ripped open the pack of earplugs and stuffed them in as far as they could go.

He laid down, and he concentrated on matching his breathing to the rise and fall of Loren's chest until, eventually, he fell asleep, the bed still shaking under him—but he was too tired to care anymore.

The next morning, Darien felt like he hadn't slept at all.

He walked—more like staggered—into the kitchen at ten to seven. His whole body ached like someone had beat the shit out of him, and his eyes felt like there were grains of sand in them. When he'd looked in the mirror shortly after getting up, they were bloodshot. He hadn't looked this haggard in years.

Kylar was at the counter, pouring himself a bowl of cereal. He looked over his shoulder at the sound of Darien's entry. "Morning."

Darien's reply was hardly more than a grumble.

Kylar smiled. "I take it you didn't sleep well."

"'Well'?" Darien echoed. "I don't think I slept at all."

"Cereal?"

"Sure."

Kylar slid the box his way. "Bowls are in the cupboard to your left." He opened a drawer by his hip. "Spoons are in here." He pushed a carton of milk his way.

"Thanks." Darien found a bowl and filled it with cereal and milk. He dunked a spoon inside, poured himself a cup of coffee, and sat down at the table with Kylar. He took a sip of the coffee—and *moaned*.

Kylar chuckled. "Good?"

"This is the only thing keeping me from turning into a demon right now." He took another sip. "Where are the others?"

"Still sleeping. Aside from Ivy."

"Is there any way to get that Hob to shut up?"

A piece of cereal bounced off Darien's forehead and plunked into his coffee cup. He couldn't see the Hob, but he could tell from the direction it was thrown that she was either on the fridge or on top of the cupboards *above* the fridge. Were all Hobs the damn same?

"Get Paxton to sleep here," Kylar said around a mouthful of cereal.

"Itzel's quiet when he's here 'cause he's got school the next day. She doesn't give a shit about the rest of us." He laughed.

As if the kid heard them, the front door swung open, and Paxton walked in. He was dressed for school—backpack on, hair combed.

"Sup, dudes!" He waved with his jacket sleeve.

Ivy came in behind him, her eyes immediately finding Darien's as she removed her jacket and hung it up. "Don't worry," she said, "he walked several blocks from the House of Black, and I picked him up from there."

"Pax," Darien called. "You want to sleep here tonight?"

He toed off his shoes and shimmied his arms out of his backpack. "You'll have to drive me to school in the morning." His bag thumped to the floor.

"Deal."

"Which means you'll have to get up early." He smiled up at Ivy. "Unless Ivy wants to drive me again."

"I said 'deal'," Darien said.

Paxton's curiosity was tangible. "What's going on?"

Darien and Kylar responded simultaneously. "Itzel."

"Oh." He made for the kitchen and helped himself to cereal—the sugary kind. No surprise there.

Darien watched as the kid sat down and immediately tore into his cereal like a wild animal. "Your dad doesn't feed you or what?"

"Pfft—I don't want to eat with the Shadowmasters!" he said with disgust, milk dribbling down his chin. "They're all mean. Except for Kylar and Willow." He smiled at Kylar.

Darien set down his mug and took a bite of his own cereal before it could get soggy. "Why don't you take off your jacket?" he asked Pax. Darien had noticed that he didn't take it off yesterday, either.

"I'm good. I gotta leave soon, anyway." He glanced at Ivy. She was in the kitchen, making coffee. "How long do we have?"

She checked the clock. "Fifteen minutes."

Darien said, "I can drive him, Ivy."

"It's fine, I don't mind. Plus, I haven't seen my little Paxy in years." She pulled out a chair at the table and sat down. "What are your plans for today?" she asked Darien.

Darien hadn't thought about it much. His only goal was waking up Loren, but if he had to wait until the evening to get her in the chamber again, that meant he had several hours to kill.

He faced Kylar. "Where are those tar pits?"

34

MOTEL 58
STATE OF WITHEREDGE

Shay opened her eyes to a dawn-lit room and the sound of water running in the shower. Slowly, the events of the previous day and night came back to her in pieces.

She was at Motel 58. None of yesterday was a dream, and Roman Devlin was in the shower—which meant he hadn't left her yet.

She had to admit, it was a bit of a surprise.

Fifteen minutes passed and she started to grow antsy, her bladder about ready to burst as she waited for Roman to hurry the hell up. She tossed and turned under the covers, watching the numbers on the clock fall away.

What was he *doing* in there?

She scrubbed the possibilities from her mind as quickly as she thought of them—one naughty image in particular that involved his hand—and got out of bed. She padded across the room, the air conditioning making her shiver.

"Roman?" she called through the closed door.

Nothing. She knocked. Knocked again—louder, this time.

Still nothing. Uneasiness quaked in her stomach.

Suddenly, the possibility of him jacking off in there sounded a whole lot better than her new suspicion: that he had started the shower, left it running, and had driven away without her.

She pounded on the door. "Roman, are you in there?" Gods, she had to pee so badly, she was about to march in there and just *go*. She reached for the door handle—

The faucet squeaked as the shower was shut off.

Oh, thank gods. She waited, trying to be patient but bouncing from foot to foot.

At least he's still here, she told herself. *He's here. He didn't leave you. He's here, he didn't leave you.*

She heard the squeal of the shower curtain being drawn, followed by a towel being yanked off the rack.

"Roman?" Her tone turned desperate. She crossed her legs and squeezed her thighs together. Damn her tiny bladder. "If you don't get out here, I'm going to pee my pants—"

The door opened, revealing billowing steam, golden light, and a half-naked, dripping-wet Darkslayer.

She turned away in a flash. The last thing she saw was Roman's perpetually unimpressed face—well, okay, *and* his muscles. Okay, fine, maybe more of his muscles than anything else.

"You knocked?" The question was flat.

"Yes." She refused to look at him. "I have to pee." Out of the corner of her eye, she saw him tighten the towel around his waist.

He stepped around her, close enough for her to feel the heat coming off his skin. "It's all yours." He gestured to the bathroom.

She hurried inside and shut the door, the humid air scented with Roman's shampoo or body wash—whatever it was. When she peeked in the shower, she saw that it was both. Why was she surprised that a guy like him would bring his own stuff? As for Shay, she would need to use the motel's crappy shampoo—the bottles that were sitting untouched in the metal rack below the shower-head, promising dry, tangled hair. She grimaced.

Or...she could steal some of Roman's. That was probably the better option; he *did* have a really good head of hair.

She was finishing up and about to wash her hands when she heard the door to the motel room open.

Oh no.

She rushed out into the room, now silent and empty with Roman's departure. Cursing under her breath, she stuffed her bare feet into her shoes and sprinted out the door—

To find Roman standing right there. Sparking a cigarette.

"Who hurt you, pup?" His words were slightly muffled by the cigarette hanging from his mouth. He still didn't have a shirt on, but at least he'd put on a pair of gray sweatpants. Shay tried not to let her eyes drift downward, to the sweats that would draw attention to something she definitely shouldn't look at. But the effort it took not to look at *that* only caused her to notice more things about his upper half—the scars, the tattoos. There were a lot of both.

And a lot of muscle. His stomach was so defined, she swore there were muscles there that didn't even *exist* in hellseher anatomy.

She blinked rapidly, her failure to answer his question suddenly occurring to her. "Pardon?"

He blew out a mouthful of smoke. "You are way too untrustworthy to not have abandonment issues."

She crossed her arms. "Why aren't you smoking inside?"

"I wanted some fresh air."

She eyed the cigarette with amusement.

Roman ignored the pointed look. "I promised you five days," he said, taking another drag. "This is day two. Better not waste it."

She drifted toward the open door, blindly feeling for the threshold with her foot. "Don't go anywhere," she warned.

He stared out at the sunrise. "Time's ticking."

She went back inside and slammed the door.

THE STORE where they'd stocked up on supplies last night—*Everything but the Kitchen Sink,* it was called—even had a tiny mom-and-pop diner tucked into a corner at the front of the building.

After skipping dinner last night, Shay was desperate for a proper meal, so she'd dragged Roman here as soon as she was finished getting ready. Her hair was freshly washed and dried, her body scented with the motel's floral soap—not the best, but it was better than the sweat she could smell on herself yesterday.

Now, she sat across from Roman in one of five booths. He was staring at her in tense silence, and she was doing the same to him.

The only waitress on shift came to their table with a couple of ice waters, a cup of coffee for Shay, and a teapot and mug for Roman. After jotting down their orders, she left.

As soon as she was gone, the silence and the staring resumed.

Shay sipped her coffee. "Aren't your eyes dry?"

Roman was staring really hard. "What?"

"You haven't blinked in like five minutes."

"I didn't sleep last night, either."

"Why not?"

"Because I don't trust you."

"Weren't you just accusing *me* of having trust issues?" She took another sip of coffee, the liquid warming her empty stomach.

"I was making an observation." He poured himself a cup of tea—green. "If either of us should have trust issues, it's me." His gold eyes—the color so warm for someone with such an evil stare—flicked to her mug. "Are you drinking black coffee?"

She ignored him and glanced at the cat-shaped clock above the sit-down counter. "I've gone almost a full twenty-four hours without tricking you." She smiled. "I think that calls for a medal."

"I still want to know how you did it." He sipped his tea.

She mirrored him, bringing her own mug to her lips. "Tough luck, pal."

Roman's eye-twitch was back. And gods, did it amuse her.

Twenty minutes later, their food arrived. They'd both ordered the pancakes, but Roman's came with the toppings—berries, whipped cream—on the side. Even the butter had its own dish.

"You're a picky eater," she observed as she dug in.

He ignored her.

"How do your shadows work?"

"We're gonna talk about my magic but not yours?"

"Who said I have magic?" She took another bite, already halfway done and Roman hadn't even started.

"I can control the shadows in any room," he said. "The bigger the area, the harder it is to control them."

"So they're not, like, *in* you?" She waved her fork at him.

He merely looked at her, his expression impossible to read, as always. "I can also fuck with them."

She choked on her pancake. Banging her chest with a fist, she reached for her water and drank, feeling the chunk of pancake shimmy down her throat. She set down the glass, eyes watering, and said, "Excuse me?"

He simply ate in silence.

Shay didn't ask him anything else.

After the waitress collected their empty dishes, Roman downed his water and said, "That's one way to get you to shut up."

She glared, realizing she had no idea if he'd lied or not, and that she'd managed to let him out of the conversation way too easily.

The waitress returned with the bill. Before she could give it to Roman, Shay handed over a fifty. "Keep the change," Shay told her.

"Thanks, doll." She winked. "Enjoy your day."

Roman was staring again.

"You're welcome," Shay crooned.

The way his mouth twitched reminded her of a wolf about to bite. And when he spoke, his voice was a growl. "Thanks, *Roman*."

SUNBAKED dirt crunched under Shay's hiking boots as she crossed the small lot of Motel 58. Roman walked several paces behind her; she could feel his chronically pissed-off stare drilling a hole in the back of her head.

But she paid him no mind and offered him no explanation as to what she was doing as she breezed into Omar's office.

The bells on the door chimed, and Shay stopped short at the sight of the mortal woman in her sixties sitting at the desk—the kindest-looking lady Shay had ever seen, with a ruddy complexion, graying hair tied up in a curly updo, and a friendly smile. A pair of eyeglasses hung from her neck on a gold chain.

"You're not Omar," Shay blurted.

The door opened behind Shay, a wave of heat blasting in as Roman crowded her into the small office.

The hair on Shay's scalp prickled, but she didn't turn, resisting the urge to step away from Roman's overwhelming presence.

The lady trilled a laugh. "Oh gosh, no! And thank heavens for that. My name is Priscilla. I am Omar's assistant, bookkeeper, and barista all in one." She smiled, cheeks like rosy apples.

"I hope you make better coffee than what he was drinking last night," Roman said.

Shay elbowed him in the abs; how hard those abs were didn't escape her notice—as hard as they'd looked when she'd ogled them this morning. "I'm Shay. We're staying in room number nine."

"Oh, how lovely! You just came from the diner, didn't you? We offer a light breakfast in the communal kitchen, if you'd prefer for next time. Muffins, croissants, coffee, tea. Free of charge." She beamed.

"Thank you," Shay said. "That sounds lovely."

"How is your stay so far? Is your room comfortable?"

Roman said, "It's a little warm, and there seems to be a pest I can't get rid of."

"The room is fine!" Shay fumed, her face flushing. Why couldn't he have waited outside? "Actually, I was hoping to ask you a few questions."

"Oh, I'd be happy to help!"

Shay took out the folded poster from the back pocket of her jean shorts and stepped up to the desk. She unfolded the paper, placed it on the wood, and flattened the creases. "Have you ever seen this woman before?" She spun it around to face Priscilla.

Priscilla put on her glasses and gingerly picked up the paper, peering down her nose through thick, rectangular lenses. "She's that missing hellseher from Yveswich?"

"Yes. She's my sister, and I have reason to believe she was staying here not too long ago."

Priscilla nodded solemnly. "Indeed, she was. In room number three."

Shay's stomach twisted. "Who was she with? Did you get a good look at them?"

"I was here when they checked in. She was with three men—she stayed in the vehicle with the younger two while the older one came inside to book the room."

Three men. Shay felt like she was going to hurl.

Roman said, "What name did they register the room under?"

"A 'Samuel Spence'." She tutted. "Fake name, if you ask me. Police came by a few days ago, asking the same thing."

"Did they seem interested in anything in particular?" Shay pressed.

"Nothing really jumped out at me. You know how the police are with this sort of thing."

Shay looked up at Roman, defeat sinking her shoulders. He didn't look at her.

"Can you tell us anything else?" he asked Priscilla.

"When they checked out, they drove that way." She pointed a wrinkled finger.

"Toward Angelthene?" Roman asked.

"Mm-hmm. But by then, this poor girl wasn't with them anymore. Just the blue-haired one."

Shay's brow furrowed. "The blue-haired one?"

"Oh, I'm sorry." She gestured to her head—her forgetfulness. "There was a second female in the group. She had blue hair."

Roman said, "I saw that chick on the news."

"The wanted one?" Shay asked, glancing between Roman and Priscilla. Gods, Roman was tall—it hurt her neck to look at him.

"They say she's trouble," Priscilla said. "But before I forget, I wanted to say that the last I saw of this other poor girl, they were driving that way." She pointed the opposite direction—toward the massive stretch of desert and dry, craggy hills. According to the maps Shay had studied, there wasn't much out there.

Shay wet her lips, heart pounding. "Can you tell us anything else about this blue-haired girl?"

She hummed. "Not much, I'm afraid. All I know is the police have been looking for her since those three men turned up dead."

Dead? Why hadn't Shay heard about this?

"Where?" Roman asked.

"They seem to be keeping the whole thing hush-hush, but...I heard it was somewhere in Angelthene."

Shay gripped the desk. "What about Anna? They didn't..." She swallowed. "Find her?"

Priscilla shook her head and took off her glasses. "They only found the men."

SHAY HEADED out into the blistering heat and shut the door to room number nine behind her. She could feel Roman watching from where he leaned against his car as she locked up, but she didn't turn to see what he was looking at—she didn't need to. She'd caught him staring only a few minutes ago, when they'd left the motel office to briefly return to the room for backpacks, water, and supplies.

She wore a white tank and frayed denim shorts that barely covered her ass. If he was looking anywhere but at the latter, especially after she'd caught him flat out leering when they'd left the office, she'd be surprised. She was still too distracted by what they'd learned to call him out on it, but the urge was creeping up on her quickly.

Shay plunked the key into her backpack and zipped it shut. She slung one of the straps over her shoulder and walked to the car, gravel crunching under her boots.

Roman was still staring. He looked...pissed off? Yeah, that was his '*I'm pissed*' face. It was a far cry from the look he'd given her earlier, and the sight of it took her by surprise more than the lust.

"What's with you?" she demanded.

"Could you have worn shorter shorts?"

She flashed him a saccharine grin. "Could you be any more annoying?"

He opened his door. "You're going to fry out there in the desert. You got sunscreen?" Why did that question—and the genuine concern in his stare—make her feel funny inside? It was...definitely not what she had expected him to say.

"Why do you care?" She opened her door and threw her bag into the back seat next to his.

"I don't—I'm just trying to avoid another of your whining episodes."

They got in, and Roman started the car. Shay reached for the A/C, only for Roman to block her, his knuckles knocking into hers with a spark that felt like static electricity.

Shay pulled away and tucked her hand between her thighs.

"Don't," he began in a hard voice, seemingly unaffected by the electric jolt, "touch my dials." Shay was surprised that he seemed so...blasé about the charge, considering her skin was still prickling. It felt like a bunch of tiny teeth were nibbling her fingers.

"Don't look at my ass," she countered, discreetly rubbing the back of her hand against her thigh.

"I wasn't looking at your ass."

"I caught you."

A muscle feathered in his jaw, and his eyes dipped downward—to the hand that was clamped between her bare thighs. His attention stayed there longer than necessary. The more he looked, the hotter Shay felt—not to mention embarrassed as the beginnings of a pulse formed between her legs.

Slowly, Roman lifted his gaze. When his eyes locked on hers, there was no gold in the irises—they were just black, like the Sight, except not. It was...odd. And now she knew she wasn't imagining the change.

Shay whispered sweetly, "Maybe, if you resist staring, you'll find that my choice of shorts won't bother you so much."

They glared each other down for what felt like *years*. Time seemed to do weird things when she was around him. Like suddenly not exist anymore.

Finally, Roman said, "I can't stand you."

Shay buckled up. "Likewise."

He sped out of the parking lot, car drifting to one side, and took off down the stretch of highway, the sun beating brightly through the windshield.

35

THE TAR PITS
YVESWICH, STATE OF KER

The tar pits in Yveswich reminded Darien of the ones in the suburbs of eastern Angelthene, though there were more here than there were back at home.

The pits were in a Neutral Zone north-east of Yveswich's Financial District. While the place had once been a bustling park with a museum and other attractions, the area was now crumbling and deserted, the museum nothing but a dark and empty shell of its former self. The tar pits were scattered across the park, and there were waterfalls nearby, the fresh scent of water mingling with the oily, earthen reek of tar.

The thing about Hounds, unlike many other breeds of demon, was that they could come out in the daylight. They just preferred to do their hunting at night—unless someone disturbed them.

Darien parked the truck near the entrance to the old museum and cut the engine. Jack and Kylar were with him, both of them filling their handguns with ammunition.

Darien flipped open the center console and found a box of bullets that were fortified with morstone powder.

"I can't remember the last time I slayed a Hound," Jack said.

Darien drew his handgun from the waistband of his black cargo pants and ejected the magazine. "Probably because you haven't."

Jack bristled. "Yeah, actually, I fucking have," he retorted.

"Then why'd you just fill your pistol with regular bullets?"

"Because I don't have any morstone ones."

Darien tossed him the box of bullets. "All you had to do was ask."

"Thanks," Jack muttered.

"You didn't get much sleep last night, did you?"

Jack started swapping out the old bullets for morstone ones. "I maybe got two hours. That Hob is loud as hell."

Kylar chuckled. "I warned you guys." He gazed out at the bubbling tar pits. "The House of Black gets hired to slay Hounds all the time. They're a bitch to kill but not impossible."

"All the time?" Darien echoed. He finished with the ammunition and slapped the magazine back in. "You got that many?"

"Yveswich is infested with them, I swear."

"Since when?"

Kylar shrugged. "We've always had a fair number, but there have been more lately."

Darien turned in his seat. "Define 'lately'."

Kylar blinked. "Shit, Cassel, I don't know. Does it matter?"

Darien stared out at the waterfalls, remembering words spoken in his house not too long ago. "I think it does."

Jack and Kylar both stared at him. Kylar said, "Maybe a few weeks, at most? Where's your mind at?"

"The waterfalls," Darien murmured. He faced Jack. "Remember what Tamika said about the waterfalls? What was it?"

Jack's brows shot up. "You're asking *me?*"

Darien swore. "You're right—you're useless." Jack laughed, and Darien opened his door. "Let's go." He shifted in his seat, about to get out, when he remembered his gloves. "Jacky, the glove compartment—open it and pass me my gloves."

He opened the latch. "Is that why they call it a glove compartment?" He tossed them to Darien, and they all got out, shutting their doors quietly.

They walked across the park, moving with caution. Hounds typically lived in the rocky crevices behind and near waterfalls, sometimes choosing to sleep in the pools of water directly below the rapids. Darien counted on the Hounds being there now, too tired to notice as they approached the closest tar pit.

Darien motioned for Kylar and Jack to stand by as he walked quietly to the edge of the pit. It was raining again, the air so cold his breath fogged before him. The area was eerily quiet, not one bird chirping. Not even magpies dared to linger here.

He had nearly made it to the edge when the pit rumbled, and Darien caught sight of the dripping spikes rising out of the tar.

Are you kidding me? Darien thought, holding very still.

Bandit stood at attention in his shadow. '*If there's* one *sleeping in there,*' the Familiar whispered, '*there's bound to be more.*'

Darien scanned the park, noticing the thin, sharp spikes protruding from every single pit. Covered in tar, he'd thought at first glance that they were branches or roots.

And he hadn't expected Hounds to be able to breathe while submerged in thick, viscid tar.

'*This is an all around bad idea,*' Bandit said.

'*Thanks for being positive.*'

'*Positive? I can be positive. I am* positive *that this is a bad idea.*'

Darien crept closer, easing his free hand into his jacket pocket. Another step, and his fingers closed around the glass vial. One vial would probably get him enough Venom to last at least a month, worst case scenario.

He looked over his shoulder at Jack. "If they wake up," Darien mouthed, "distract them."

Jack's eyes widened. "Do you hate me that much?" he mouthed back.

"What do I pay you for?"

Jack looked like he wanted to shout, but didn't. "To be bait, apparently!"

Darien knelt beside the pit and bit the cap off the vial. With gloves protecting his hands, he slowly dipped it into the tar. The pits got hotter the closer you got to the center, so here, at the edge, the tar was warm but not hot, though no less sticky. If you fell into one of these things, you'd have a hell of a time trying to get back out, not to mention the damage it'd do to your skin. It would trap you like a fly and rapidly burn you to death, if you didn't first fall in and suffocate.

A roar shook the whole damn park.

The Hounds in the other pits were awake, more by the waterfalls rising from the noise. Darien heard Kylar and Jack swear. Sensed them releasing their safeties and taking aim.

Another roar. A shout. The crack of morstone bullets and bloodcurdling snarls rent the air. Behind him, bone snapped and crunched, and the bodies of Hounds hit the grass as Jack and Kylar felled them.

"Shit—*Darien!*"

Darien had just filled and closed the vial when he looked over his shoulder—

Just in time to see Jack being dragged into a tar pit.

Darien moved, Kylar at his back. They sprinted for Jack as the tar-covered Hound—eyes glowing red, horns dripping black—dragged Jack to the edge of a massive tar pit in the center of the park.

With the layer of tar covering the Hound, the bullets Jack emptied from his gun did shit. The Hound was unaffected; it wouldn't let go.

Darien opened a switchblade and hurled it at the Hound. The force behind his throw—more power and speed than a bullet—embedded the knife in the creature's head. It roared and let go, but there were a dozen more where that came from.

"Truck!" Darien barked as he skidded to a halt next to Jack. He pulled him to his feet by the shoulders of his jacket and shoved him toward Kylar. "Get in the truck—now!"

They ran, and Darien took off after them, hanging back far enough to intercept any attacks that came their way. There were a few, and he had to use bullets and knives to fend them off, aiming for the Hound's eyes—anywhere that wasn't completely covered in crusts of old tar and oozing layers that were fresher, the dark color glistening in the overcast light.

Jack and Kylar made it to the truck before Darien—

Something hit him in the side of the head. He fell, tasting dirt, vision turning white.

It cleared right on time for him to see the Hound that had attacked him —diving right for his throat.

Before the jaws could close, a black blade blasted through the Hound's head. Blood and tar sprayed, and Darien rolled through the grass right on time, the blade anchoring the demon to the ground. Had he acted one second later, it would've skewered him too.

Darien leapt to his feet. Pulled out the blade of black adamant—the blade Jack had thrown—from the corpse.

And turned, lashing out in time to decapitate another Hound, the power in the blade ripping through his blood and making his teeth sing.

The head fell to the ground, tar spraying, and rolled, the body crumpling in a gory heap.

Another Hound lunged at his left. Darien leapt and twisted, slamming the blade into the back of the monster's skull. Skin and bone severed, the sound like boulders smashing together. Fizzing black blood exploded from the wound, soaking Darien's front.

He hit the ground on his feet, ducking under a brutal claw, and ran for the truck, breath sawing apart his lungs. Without a proper hilt, the blade was hard to hold, the tar on his right hand making his grip slip, as if the blade was trying to reject it. The unholy magic singeing from hilt to tip continued to vibrate Darien's eardrums and blood, the power so intense it nearly buckled his knees.

Jack had started the truck, the passenger's-side door open for Darien. He waved frantically, Kylar shouting from the back seat.

He dove inside and shut the door on claws that were singed by the protective spells. The Hound roared in pain as the bones in its hand were shattered.

Jack peeled away from the park and screeched onto the interstate, narrowly missing the barricade separating lanes. Horns blared, and cars swerved, several spinning in complete circles down the interstate.

Jack straightened the truck and reduced speed.

For several minutes, none of them said anything, their ragged breathing filling the silence.

And then Kylar leaned between the front seats. "Tell me you got the tar," he said, still catching his breath.

Darien felt around in his pockets until he found the vial. He held it up, the tar shining like liquid night.

"So if you're on Venom," Kylar said, "you can kill Hounds more easily?"

"Far more easily."

"And what about the Veil monsters?"

"It's about a fifty-fifty chance."

Jack chuckled. "Sixty-forty if you're lucky." His eyes met Darien's, the black fading out of them. "Thanks for saving my ass, by the way. That would've been a shitty way to die."

"What, drowning in tar while a Hound disembowels you? There are plenty worse ways to die, Jacky."

Only Jack would laugh at that.

THEY WERE PASSING through the north end of the Financial District when Darien told Jack to stop the truck.

He pulled into a stall by the curb. Across the street sat a massive hotel, the building shades of cream with gilded accents. The sign read 'The Blood Queen', the cursive font forming a sharp contrast with its name. Darien had spotted this hotel on billboards when they'd first driven into the city, the advertisements priding itself on its five-star rating as 'luxury gem of the state'. Two security guards stood in uniform by the revolving glass doors. But it wasn't the hotel, nor the security guards that had caught Darien's attention.

He leaned forward in his seat, watching the two men making their way down the sidewalk, toward the doors of the hotel. They were dressed in heavy coats, hands in their pockets. Despite the hoods at their disposal, neither of them made an attempt to put them on and hide their faces—rookie mistake. Their breath fogged before them, and even from this distance, Darien could see their features clear as daylight.

"I'll be damned," he murmured.

Kylar leaned between the front seats. "What's going on?"

"Those are Gaven's men."

"You serious?" Jack said. "What are they doing in Yveswich?"

"Who's Gaven?" Kylar cut in.

"Gaven Payne," Darien replied.

"*The* Gaven Payne?" Kylar asked. "You mean the weapons dealer?"

"That's the one." Darien watched as Gaven's men disappeared through the revolving glass doors. These two had been in the warehouse with Darien that time Gaven had killed several of his own men and threatened the rest. The day Darien had held his men aloft and nearly strangled them to death with his magic. "He and I have...a score to settle."

Jack explained, "He burned down Darien's restaurant."

"My mom's restaurant," Darien clarified. He opened his door. "Kylar, wait here. Jack, come with me."

Jack left the truck running and unbuckled his seatbelt. "We're going to kill them in broad daylight?"

"We're going to watch them," Darien said. "I want to see where they're going, who they're with." Gaven—he wanted to see if they were with Gaven. He wasn't so stupid as to think he could kill them in a city that wasn't his, and with so many people around, but if he found out Gaven was hiding out here, in this fancy as shit hotel...

Then the man was fucking dead.

There was a plus side to Yveswich being so cold; no one questioned hoods, heavy jackets, or gloves. Darien pulled on the hood of his sweatshirt, Jack doing the same at his side as they crossed the road. It was still raining, the wind pelting their faces with half-frozen drops.

They had just made it across the road and were nearing the sidewalk when the hotel exploded.

36

THE FINANCIAL DISTRICT
YVESWICH, STATE OF KER

Darien and Jack were thrown backward by the blast.

The first and second floors of the hotel exploded, an eruption of fire, brick, broken glass, and burning wood tearing down the street, slicing telephone poles clean in half and overturning cars.

Darien struck the ground in the middle of the road, bricks shattering into red dust all around him, and rolled. The moment he stopped spinning, he pushed himself up onto his hands and knees. Pain lanced through every bone, but he shook it off, flexing his jaw to pop the pressure in his ringing ears.

Fuck, he couldn't stand up. His vision was spinning, blood dripping out of his ears and nose. The impact had torn his clothes and filled them with mud and gravel.

Traffic screeched to a stop. In the distance, beyond the bubble of destruction, people got out of their vehicles to stare. Several feet away, Jack was recovering where he'd slammed into a parked car. He was bleeding from the side of his head, and there was a bunch of glass and mud on his clothes. He'd set off the car alarm, headlights flashing, horn blaring.

Darien spat out a mouthful of blood and pushed to his feet just as a fleet of cop cars, ambulances, and fire trucks came flying around the corner.

He caught sight of Kylar getting out of the truck—

"Stay there!" Darien barked, knuckling away the blood leaking from his nose. He waved for Kylar to get back inside. He did, moving to the driver's seat instead. The spells and tinted windows hid every trace of him from view.

Good.

Several cops and detectives got out of their cars and stormed this way, hands on their guns, while paramedics and firefighters headed toward the building. The warlock detective at the head of the group had a shaved head, a scar by his mouth. He was tall—almost taller than Darien, but with less muscle on him. He was dressed in typical MPU getup—suit jacket and pants, badge engraved with the symbol of the YMPU glinting on his hip.

"Turn around!" the detective bellowed. "You're under arrest."

Jack said, "What the fuck for?"

A cold smile pulled at Darien's mouth as he watched the dickhead detective advance on him. "For being in the wrong place at the wrong time," Darien said, breath fogging before him.

The detective gestured to one of the cops, who stepped forward and cuffed them, Darien first and then Jack.

Jack fought against their hold. "We didn't do anything!"

"Jack," Darien warned.

The detective came within three inches of Darien, a condescending sneer on his face. "Then I'm sure you wouldn't mind answering some questions down at the station," he clipped, eyes cold as the air, *"Darien Cassel."*

"I'm going to ask you one more time."

Darien sat in a chair in one of several interrogation rooms at Yveswich Law Enforcement Headquarters. His hands rested on the table, the long chains of his cuffs threaded through an opening in the middle of the wood, where they looped through a ring bolted to the underside.

The detective stood on the other side of the table. Hands on his hips, face as cold as stone. "What were you doing at The Queen?"

"I already told you," Darien said in a level voice, staring with hard, unblinking eyes at the asshole who'd ordered him arrested outside of the hotel. "We were looking to book a couple rooms."

The detective slammed a hand down on the table. "Lie one more time," he growled, stooping to Darien's eye level, "and you'll be looking through bars for the rest of your worthless goddamn life!"

Darien ignored the threat and glanced behind the detective—looking through the reflective window that separated this room from the one Jacky was in.

Jack grinned and held his index and middle fingers up to his mouth, tongue waggling between them.

Darien smirked.

"What's so goddamn funny?" the detective fumed.

"My brother in law thinks you're a pussy." His eyes snapped back to the detective's cold stare. "Your spells are a little weak." He winked.

The guy rounded the table, stopping right by Darien's chair. "I don't like having to repeat myself," he said, nostrils flaring. "What were you doing at The Queen?"

"I already told you. We were looking for rooms."

"Innocent people just died," he spat.

"You ran background checks already?"

The detective punched him in the face.

The impact whipped Darien's head to the side. Pain bloomed through his jaw, but he welcomed it. *Finally*, he was feeling something that wasn't soul-crushing heartbreak.

The monster inside him stood up and paced. It foamed at the mouth, thirsting for blood. Darien prepared to unleash it. He flexed his jaw—

And laughed, the sound quiet, deadly, and short-lived. "You're one of those dirty cops." Darien's smile turned into a baring of teeth. "I fucking hate cops. Especially dirty ones."

"And I hate piece of shit criminals like you."

"You don't have the best control for someone in a position of authority." And he was also stupid for getting this close.

Darien swept out his leg and kicked the guy's feet out from under him.

He landed on his ribs on the side of the table with enough force to knock the wind out of him. The detective reached for his gun, but before he could draw it or get back up, Darien acted, breaking the chains of his cuffs with one hard snap—

And lunged, grabbing the broken end of the chains with one hand and wrapping them around the prick's throat. Looping the ends around his hands for better grip, Darien spun the detective around and pinned him to the table with a knee to the spine. Pulled hard on the chains, cutting off his airways.

The door banged open.

Voices shouted. Hands drew guns. Five officers, all for him.

"Step back!" one of them barked. "Put your hands in the air!"

Darien addressed the detective thrashing under his hold. "No one talks to me like that," he murmured. He pulled tighter, making him gag. *"No one."*

"Let him go, Cassel!" Darien recognized that voice—it was Finn.

Darien's smile was deadly. "Hold on, I'm almost done."

Another said, "Let him go, or I'll shoot!"

Darien pulled harder, the chains cutting into the detective's throat. He heard skin split. Felt the warmth of the man's blood slipping over his fingers. Darien looked up with eyes that flickered black, pinning the other officers in place with a hard stare. Daring them to make one fucking move. The room was silent save for the gurgling coming from the man in his grip and the tinkling of his fingernails on the chains as he clawed at them.

Three more seconds, and then he let go of the detective with a shove. "So touchy," he tsked. He glanced at the purple-faced detective, who gasped for air, both hands braced on the table. "Might want to get that checked out," Darien said. He acknowledged Finn with a nod. "Afternoon, Finn."

"Take off the cuffs," Finn said. His voice was strained, and sweat beaded on his forehead. The officers stared at him with blank looks.

"Solace?" one ventured.

"Take off the cuffs! You've got the wrong guys."

"How do you know?"

When Finn replied, his eyes were on Darien. "Because they're not that fucking messy. Let them go, you're wasting everyone's time."

Darien smiled and held his hands out in offer, broken chains dangling.

One of the officers pulled out a set of keys and stepped forth. He unlocked the cuffs and pulled them off, stepping back as soon as he was able.

Darien rubbed at the lines in his wrists. "My brother-in-law, if you please."

The detective to the left stepped up to Finn's side. "But we haven't talked to him yet," he hissed in Finn's ear.

Finn exploded. *"For god's sake, would someone go un-cuff Steele?"*

The lone female officer in the group left. A moment later, she returned with Jack in tow.

Darien nodded. "Jacky."

A smile pulled at Jack's lips as he took in the scene. "Looks like all the fun was happening in here."

The detective, still gasping and rubbing the vicious red lines in his throat, squeezed out, "He's full of shit. They can see through the mirrors."

"They're Darkslayers," Finn retorted. "What'd you expect?" The term 'Darkslayers' was a bit broad and understated their reputations, but Darien would take it. Finn's dark eyes snapped to Darien's face. "Come with me."

One of the officers tried to follow. "Solace?"

"Leave us." Finn made for the door, glancing over his shoulder at Darien and Jack as he went, the look probing.

They followed. Darien sensed a few officers trailing them, but they soon stopped, finally listening to Finn's orders.

Finn paused at a room on the way out and grabbed their things—jackets, weapons—and gave them back.

Darien checked his wallet before sliding it into his jacket pocket.

Finn said, "No one took anything."

"I'll be the decider of that." He holstered his weapons and put on his jacket, Jack doing the same.

When they were done, Finn led the way out of the room.

Darien walked at his side down the corridor, Jack just behind them. "If you think this makes us even, you've still got a long way to go, Finn," Darien said, voice low.

"I wasn't trying to get even. Just trying to right a wrong."

"How orderly of you." They walked in silence for a minute. "Any more demons since Paradisi?"

Finn shook his head. "None yet—knock on wood." He glanced at their surroundings. "Anybody got any wood?"

Jack grinned. "Not right now."

They passed the desks scattered throughout the big room at the front of the building, and Finn rapped a knuckle against the side of the first. "Thought you'd like to know the one you killed wasn't the same as the first."

"What do you mean?"

"The one that materialized in the hardware store," Finn clarified. "We never found that one."

Darien frowned. "What are your thoughts?"

"Don't fucking know. I'm guessing they covered a lot of ground since the security breach."

That was right—Finn still had no idea that the Veil had nearly fallen; had no idea that it existed at all, aside from in history books.

Finn was giving Darien the side-eye. "What *were* you doing at The Blood Queen, anyway?"

"Don't tell me this was some good cop, bad cop ploy to get me talking."

"My questions are my own. Why are you in Yveswich, and why The Queen?"

"How many casualties?"

Finn's jaw flexed. "It's too early to tell."

"Got any names yet?" Something told him that Finn and the others were aware that at least two of the people who'd died in the blast were wanted criminals.

Finn repeated, "Why The Queen?"

They were at the entrance to the building now. Darien pushed through the doors, turning to walk backward. "It's like I told that prick detective before he punched me: We were looking for a place to stay." He turned back around and left, Jack at his side. To where Kylar waited in the truck in the parking lot that was slashed with rain.

Finn watched him go; Darien didn't turn around, but he could sense him watching.

He had a feeling there would be more where that came from, once word got around that he was in Yveswich.

And he'd have to watch his back a hell of a lot more now.

BY THE TIME they got back to Roman's, the heat in Darien's veins was just beginning to calm down when he felt it crank up again with a vengeance.

A vehicle he didn't recognize—a black jeep—was parked by the fountain out front of the house.

"Who the fuck is that?" Darien barked as Kylar rolled the truck to a stop at the gates.

"Shit." Kylar's voice was a whisper, his eyes bolted so wide the whites all around his irises were showing.

Darien shot him a hard look. "Kylar? Who is that?"

"Shadowmasters." He swallowed. Wide eyes snapped to Darien's face. "And not Roman's."

37

THE INTERSTATE
ANGELTHENE, STATE OF WITHEREDGE

Maximus slammed on the brakes and cursed under his breath as Malakai Delaney zipped his bike in front of the SUV to take the lead.

He twisted the face of the watch on his wrist and growled into the microphone, "What the hell are you doing?"

"Taking the lead," Malakai replied, his voice barely audible over the earsplitting rumble of that bike. "What's it look like?" He somehow managed to talk into the watch without tipping that heavy motorcycle over, which was a goddamn shame. Aspen was perched on the back of it, red hair blowing like a flame in the wind.

Max grumbled under his breath and flicked the watch off. "He doesn't even know where we're going," he said, glancing at Dallas, who sat in the passenger's seat, for backup. Dominic and Blue were in the back, the former teaching the latter more about their language, a book open between them. She was getting really good at it.

Dallas was smiling down at her phone, her painted nails clinking on the screen. She didn't appear to have heard what Max said, but when he saw her dimples fluttering, he found that he didn't care. This many months into dating her, and she still took his breath away. She was looking a lot better than before Darien had taken Loren out of town; her cheeks had that healthy glow to them again, her eyes bright with life.

Hope could do a lot to a person. He only crossed his fingers that they wouldn't be let down by whatever happened in Yveswich.

Not being able to message or call Darien was weird. But he figured everything was going okay; if something had gone wrong, Darien would've contacted them by now. While he and the others had their phones shut off and blocked from being tracked by any hackers who might sneak past Tanner's protection, Max and the rest of the Devils who were still in Angelthene had no reason to stop cell phone use.

Max glanced at Dallas again. "What are you smiling about, Red?"

"I'm making a dating profile for Casen," she said proudly.

"For the Butcher?" He snorted a laugh.

"Uh-oh," Dominic drawled. "That's not going to go over well."

"Relax," Dallas said, her smile stretching into a grin as she clicked away, typing way faster than Max could ever hope to. "I know what I'm doing."

"How are you going to create a dating profile when you can't use his photo?" Max asked. A photo of the Butcher online? Announcing that he was looking for single women in their late thirties and early forties? That would be a sight.

He signaled to get into the fast lane. Malakai beat him to it, cutting him off again.

Max cursed him under his breath.

"I'm using one of his side profile. See?" She showed him the screen. Yeah, you could barely even tell it was him. Surprising, considering he stood out everywhere he went like a sore thumb.

"How'd you get that?"

"I'm sneaky." She started clicking again. "I'm texting Sab for ideas—she's helping me. What do you think his interests are?"

Dominic said, "You mean aside from drugs and alcohol?"

"And fighting rings and porn?" Max added.

"You guys are being very negative. I think he deserves to find happiness, don't you?" She'd come a long way from the girl who'd called him a 'BP dealing piece-of-shit' at the Umbra Forum. From the look on her face, Max knew she was still feeling guilty about that. Dallas was a pro at hiding her emotions, but Max had been with her long enough to know how to read her. She might not be quick to apologize, but she had other ways of showing that she was sorry.

"Shake it up a bit," Dominic suggested. "Instead of fighting rings, say he's into wrestling."

"And concerts," Max offered. "You could also mention that he likes to travel, but don't say anything about the drug runs." His laugh was soon echoed by Dominic. Blue glanced at the Angel in question, but he didn't explain.

Dallas snickered, and Grim laughed in Max's shadow. *'She is going to be in major trouble,'* said the mountain lion.

'Yeah, probably,' Max replied. *'But it'll be funny to watch.'*

"You know he's going to shut that down the minute he finds out about it, right?" Max said to Dallas.

"I'm hoping I can get a few phone numbers before then. Maybe line up a dinner date or two."

Max had to admit he felt proud of her for thinking of this. And she was right about one thing: Casen deserved happiness. Everyone did, no matter where they'd come from or what hand of cards they'd been dealt. Max didn't know much about the Butcher's past, but he remembered Darien mentioning that he had a daughter he hadn't seen in years.

It was already hot out, the sun beating through the windshield. He turned on the air conditioning for the first time since last fall and stripped off his long-sleeve, leaving only the black muscle shirt he had on underneath.

They were heading out to Foxhill. It would be a long drive, especially with Malakai nearly causing accidents every few miles with his aggression, but Max had faith that soon they'd find answers about Maya. And with Blue here, getting better at communicating with them every day, he had even more faith.

He just hoped the others would be fine in Angelthene. Not once had they been scattered like this—not since before Darien had formed the Seven Devils and turned them all into a family—so it felt weird to split up.

He glanced at his watch. It was early afternoon. Soon, Travis and Lacey would be leaving Hell's Gate to follow their lead. He hoped they'd all be served a healthy dose of luck today.

And answers. Lots of them.

TRAVIS DEVLIN TRIED NOT to grimace as he scanned the assortment of vintage dolls in Jewels Delaney's bedroom.

He felt like all those glass eyes were watching him. Especially when Jewels headed to her dresser to grab something from her jewelry box and her hip knocked into one of the dolls, causing its eyes to roll.

He shivered. "Yeesh."

She glanced at him in question as she pushed a stud into each ear. "Something wrong?"

"I feel like I'm being watched." He scanned the dolls in their frilly dresses. "By a lot of glass eyes."

She grinned. "That's why I like them. They freak Malakai out too—his fear kept him from coming into my bedroom when we were kids." That was hilarious—Malakai, the leader of the Reapers, afraid of dolls? Gold. Pure gold. Jewels continued, "I used to tell him the dolls could talk, and he insisted I was lying." She slid her feet into a pair of black platform sneakers.

Travis's eyes flicked to the dolls again. *"Can* they talk?"

She merely smiled and shrugged.

Travis scanned her room again, avoiding the dolls this time. A framed painting of a giant purple jellybean hung above her four-poster bed. Her nightstand was cluttered with essential oils, a music box shaped like a carousel, and a bunch of bright-colored silicone objects—

"Are those vibrators?" he blurted.

She turned to grab her keys and phone off the dresser. "Yes."

Travis's blood electrified, his imagination instantly running wild. "Which is your favorite?" He couldn't help it, especially not after he'd first walked into this house and glimpsed her nipples—pierced—under that white shirt she was wearing. No bra. And her heart-shaped ass in those painted-on jeans?

Damn.

Jewels snickered. "Whoa there, tiger, I think we'll wait a bit longer before we discuss that." She looked him over, a hint of scarlet lingering in her cheeks, her teeth worrying her full bottom lip. "Ready?"

His eyes strayed to the vibrators again—damn, was he weak. "What's the rose-shaped one do?"

She breezed past him, her face a shade darker than usual. "Let's go."

"If you didn't want me to ask about them, you should've hidden them." He flicked off her bedroom light.

"I don't mind being asked about them, I just want to keep my secrets a bit longer."

"Hard to get—I like it."

She rolled her eyes but smiled.

He followed her into the black-and-cobalt hallway. The only reason he'd been in her bedroom was because she'd invited him in while she finished getting ready. And the only reason he'd been allowed in at all was because Malakai wasn't here.

Travis was looking forward to having a few days alone with Jewels to hopefully get to know her better. He'd have to thank Max for getting rid of that asshole. He knew it wasn't the reason Max had invited Malakai to go with him to Foxhill, but to Travis it was as good a reason as any.

Jewels led the way down to the front door, shoes thumping on creaky floorboards. The house was constantly dark, even in the middle of the day, the narrow maze of hallways and limited amount of windows forcing them to keep the wall sconces lit with enchanted flames.

When they reached the front door, Jewels peeked through the small, grimy window beside it that was cut into the shape of a sickle moon. "Where are the others?"

"Lacey's in the car. Logan and Sabrine are meeting us there."

She swung open the door—and grinned. "Finally!" She skipped down the steps, tipping her head back to look at the blue sky. "A warm, sunny day." She inhaled the fresh air with an audible breath.

Travis pulled the door shut behind him; it was so old, he had to slam it, the warped bottom catching on the threshold. "You like the sun?"

She snickered. "What, just because I'm pale and like the color black, you assumed I was some nocturnal creature that hisses every time someone mentions summer?"

He fought a smile and followed her across the yard. "Guess I was wrong."

Lace was leaning against the back of the car, cigarette burning in her fingers, her other hand typing on her cell phone. She looked up as they approached. "Aspen said they stopped for a rest at Oaklyn," she said. She blew a stream of smoke at the sky. "But it's a straight shot from there to Foxhill."

"No brawls?" Travis asked.

Lace gave him a crooked smile. "Not yet."

"Front or back?" Jewels asked her.

She butted out the cigarette and pushed off the car, tucking her phone into the pocket of her jeans. "You can have the front, I'm fine in the back. Anyone heard from Logan and Sabrine?"

"They said they'd meet us there," Travis replied, heading for the driver's door. He checked his watch. "It's almost three."

"What time does that place close?" Jewels asked as she slid the seat forward so Lace could get in.

"Three." Travis got in his side and started the car. "Buckle up—we're going to have to hurry."

38

ROMAN'S HOUSE
YVESWICH, STATE OF KER

Kylar went into the house first, Jack second, Darien third. Darien listened to the voices—Ivy and Tanner, no Joyce, and two others he didn't recognize—coming from the living room and kitchen as they walked down the hallway that led out of the garage.

He catalogued the scene before him the minute it came into view—the two Shadowmasters who stood in the living room, isolated from Ivy and Tanner, who stood closer to the kitchen. Closer to the front door. Paxton and Eugene sat on the couch—bodies tense, eyes bolted wide.

The female Shadowmaster made Darien nearly stop dead in his tracks, his breath catching in his throat. From this angle, she could almost pass for Loren. She wasn't quite as slight and delicate-looking, but she had the same proportions, the same narrow waist and toned legs, the same golden-blonde shade of hair that fell to the small of her back in soft waves. A hellseher, but a near goddamn twin.

For one split second, he thought it was her. The cruel lie the universe was feeding to him kicked the air right out of his lungs and made him drag his boots for several steps.

Darien forced himself to draw a breath. To get a grip.

She turned to look at their trio as they walked in, the face that was definitely not Loren's dousing the idiotic flame that had kindled in his chest.

Not her. He had known better than to think it was, but for one second it had damn well looked like it. Could've fooled him.

The man standing beside her was brawny and tattooed, his features and the shade of his hair giving away their relation. Brother and sister, Darien would guess. Both in their mid-twenties.

The female Shadowmaster was still staring at him. Even her eyes were a vivid blue—ocean-blue, a shade he hadn't seen on many people. A shade he'd only started noticing after meeting Loren.

"You're back," Ivy said with a smile. Her voice was strained, but she hid her stress well. "Blaine, Larina, this is Darien, my brother. And Jack, my husband. Darien, Jack—meet Blaine and Larina Barlowe."

They kept it formal and brief, Jack first and then Darien stepping forward to shake hands. Darien knew the guy—Blaine—was squeezing harder than he needed to, but it was his encounter with the girl that put him more on edge. She wouldn't stop staring at him, and she held onto his hand for longer than he'd like. *He* was the one who had to pull away first.

"We've heard a lot about you guys," Blaine said. "Would've been nice if Pax and Eugene had introduced us sooner." Darien didn't miss the cold glare he shot at the kids, nor did he miss the way Pax shrank a size.

"Funny," Darien said, shifting to catch Blaine's eye when he dared to stare at Pax for too long. "We've never heard of you."

Kylar cleared his throat and made for the kitchen. "You guys want a drink?"

"I'd love one," Blaine said, still staring at Darien with a threat in his eyes.

Kylar started grabbing glasses from the cupboard. "What can I get you?"

Darien tore his eyes off Blaine and left the room.

He needed to get the hell away from here before he became violent. No one called after him; they knew better than that. After what just happened with the cops, he was closer to being assaulted by a Surge now than before he'd left Angelthene.

He kept an eye on the auras on the floor above as he made his way down to the shooting range, through the heavy metal doors that trapped sound inside. There wasn't a trace of Loren in the house, no trace of Joyce. He counted on the Shadowmasters not figuring out that anyone else was here, if they even were—Ivy and Tanner might've hidden them elsewhere, if they'd had time—and headed to the rack of guns to let off some steam.

Roman's selection of firearms was solid gold. There were so many to choose from, Darien had trouble deciding. But he picked one that stood out to him more than the rest, grabbed a pair of electronic earmuffs off a hook on the wall, and stalked up to the barrier, not bothering with eyewear. He didn't wear any in the streets, so why'd he wear any here?

The gallery stretched on for an impressive distance—the whole of Roman's property, which was a fucking lot. The paper targets set up at the farthest end were the ones that caught his eye.

He put on the earmuffs and fitted the gun to his shoulder. Took off the safety and aimed. Squeezed the trigger.

Bullets cracked through the room, the pop of each muffled. The familiar feel of the gun kicking back against his shoulder eased some of the tension in his muscles, and at the sight of the targets he'd hit, each a bull's eye, he almost smiled.

Movement to his right.

Darien swung the gun around, aiming at Larina Barlowe's golden head as she walked into the range.

She skidded to a stop and lifted her hands, though her fear was quickly replaced with blatant interest—not just in him, for once. Her eyes roamed the room, scanning the targets he'd shot. Her full mouth formed a word he couldn't hear.

Darien pulled off the earmuffs and hooked them around his neck. "What?"

"I said 'impressive'." She came closer, turning her head to scan the targets that were farther away—the ones she wouldn't have been able to see from the door. "Very impressive," she corrected. She came to a stop right beside him, close enough that her arm nearly brushed against his. She'd taken off her jacket; he could see the tattoos on her arms now, a full sleeve on the left and a single tattoo on the right. "You're definitely Roman's cousin."

Darien loaded more rounds into the gun. "What do you want?"

"You're not very polite, are you?"

"Manners aren't my strong suit." He moved the slide to the rear of the firearm and slammed it shut. "What do you want?" he said again.

"To get to know you better. It's not every day Roman brings home guests, especially not Darkslayers from other cities." She shrugged and crossed her arms. "Call me curious."

"Or nosey." Darien aimed the gun and fired, ignoring the *pop* of the bullet without the earmuffs to tone it down. "Intrusive." He fired again. "Meddlesome." Another three shots. *Crack. Crack. Crack.* Another three perfect bull's eyes.

She snickered. Cleared her throat. "Maybe I'm wrong, but I find it a little strange that you came to visit Roman and he's not even here."

"Nosey, intrusive, meddlesome," he repeated.

"Where is he?"

"Working," Darien clipped. "And in case you didn't notice, Roman's not our only family. We're here for Kylar and Paxton too."

"It's funny." She studied him closely, eyes narrowing. "Paxton's never mentioned this place before. Neither has Roman." Her lips twisted with a frown. "Same with Kylar." The last one sounded like a threat. If she or her brother went anywhere near Kylar, Darien would slit their throats from ear to ear.

Darien lowered the gun. "Do you keep such close tabs on them that they need to tell you everything about their lives?"

She smiled tightly, though her brow creased and she shook her head, as if realizing that he made a good point.

"Am I right or am I right?" Darien prompted.

"I can admit," she began, "that sometimes we keep a closer watch on the other Shadowmasters than maybe we should—"

"Roman," Darien corrected, firing another shot. "You keep a close watch on Roman."

"Not by choice. We work for Donovan."

"That's no excuse to turn into a stalker."

"We take orders, and we get paid to follow through."

He squeezed the trigger, the sudden release of a new bullet making her jump. He glanced down at the goosebumps pebbling across her arms. Said through his teeth, "Still no excuse."

She drew a breath. "Okay, so...is that why you just stomped out on us when we were about to have a drink?" She tossed her head to get the hair out of her face. "Because you think we're out of line for coming here?"

"Yes." He fired the last of the bullets until the gun gave a hollow *click*.

"Fair enough." She looked him over with the kind of assessment he could feel. "I've heard a lot about you, you know." Her voice was slightly muffled by the dull ringing in his ears.

"Have you?" he said flatly. He reloaded the gun.

"I have," she began, tucking a strand of gold hair behind her pierced ear, skull-shaped studs lining the arch. "And I must admit, I'm a little curious about the infamous Darien Cassel. Or 'meddlesome', as you might call it."

He snorted a laugh. Slammed the slide back in.

She mistook the sarcastic sound for an invitation to say more. "I hope I'm not crossing a line when I say this, but...you're very attractive."

Bandit huffed in his shadow. *'She's got nerve.'*

"Thanks." He fired another few rounds, forcing the conversation to a standstill. He'd never been so grateful for the pop of bullets slicing into his eardrums before.

But she spoke again as soon as the crack of the last shot faded away. "I take it you get that a lot."

"Not usually so blatantly stated."

"May I?" She gestured to the gun.

Darien handed it over. Of course she would choose to grab onto the gun exactly where his hand was still holding onto it.

He pulled his fingers out from under hers and took a step back.

The way she chose to handle the gun was an invitation in itself. He'd familiarized himself with guns at the age that most kids were still playing with toys, so he knew damn well when her hands lingered on places they had no business lingering.

She grabbed a pair of earmuffs that hung from the barrier and put them on. Aimed. Fired. She hit every target square in the center, but she didn't go for the ones at the far end of the room.

"Impressive," Darien said, forcing himself to be civil. He decided he didn't want this chick and her dickhead brother using his assholery as an excuse to come back or—worse—tell Don. Having them here one time was bad enough, and Darien refused to be responsible for their tattling. "Try the far one."

She hesitated for a beat before firing, her shoulder jerking from the kickback. The bullet landed two inches to the left of where she'd aimed.

She sighed. "Damn."

"Close."

She took off the earmuffs and handed him the gun. "So... You looked at me a little funny when you first walked in." She draped the earmuffs across the barrier. "Care to explain why?"

"You looked like someone else from behind."

Larina hummed. "If you'd prefer to take me from behind," she said, her voice saccharine, "that can be arranged." When she literally batted her eyelashes at him, Darien barely stopped himself from barking a laugh. She wasn't even just shooting *a* shot, she was shooting multiple—location and gun aside.

Bandit growled, though he had the sense not to make the warning audible to anyone but Darien.

"The only thing you'll be taking," Darien said, leaning in slightly, the action making her stiffen and hold her breath, "is a hint."

"Ouch. I would wonder if I'm not your type, but you were practically drooling over me not even fifteen minutes ago. What changed?"

"I'm taken."

"Your relationship status changed that quickly?" she teased.

"I was taken when I walked in, and I'm still taken now."

"Who's the lucky lady?"

"Not here."

"Something tells me it isn't going well between you two. Every time you talk about her, you look like you're in pain." She scanned him from head to toe. Wet her lips. "I can help with that."

"You're being a little forward, considering we just met."

"The rumors I've heard suggest you prefer it that way." To hell with those rumors and his old way of life. Sure, he'd spent many years accepting invitations just like this one, not having the least bit of interest in getting to know girls before he got into their pants, but not anymore.

"I'm really trying not to be rude right now," Darien said, his tone now razor-edged, manners be damned. "But you need to back off."

She held up her hands in a show of innocence. "Hey, I meant no harm." A smile that warned him she liked the challenge he was giving her fluttered across her mouth. "If you change your mind, you know where to find me." She backed up, turning on a heel. As she headed for the door, she swished her hips, her hair teasing the small of her back. "Pleasure to meet you, Darien Cassel." She fluttered her fingertips and pushed the door open.

Darien put the earmuffs on, aimed at the farthest target, and fired.

Bull's-fucking-eye.

DARIEN SLAMMED THE FRONT DOOR. "What the hell was that all about?" he barked, turning to face the group gathered in the foyer. The Shadowmasters had just left, the gate closing behind their jeep. "Who let them in?"

Every pair of eyes in the room went to Paxton and Eugene, who stood farthest from the group.

Paxton's shoulders curled forward, and he tugged on the sleeves of his baggie sweatshirt. "They followed us here."

"And you led them right to the goddamn house?" Darien worked at controlling his voice and failed.

"Eugene," Kylar growled, jaw clenching. "Explain."

"We didn't notice they were following us until we were at the gates. We had nowhere else to go, and it was too late."

Darien dragged a hand down his face. "So you let them in."

"You don't get it." Paxton's voice was a ragged whisper. "That was Blaine and Larina. They answer to my dad. If we didn't let them in, they would've taken us to the House of Black." The fear choking every word told Darien that being taken to the House of Black wasn't what they were afraid of; it was what would've happened once they got there.

Ivy stepped up to Paxton and slid an arm around his shoulders. When she spoke, she spoke to Darien. "They don't know about Loren. Tanner hid her and Joyce with spells in your room." Darien breathed a sigh of relief. No heartbeat, no breathing, no auras detected.

Darien glanced at Tanner. "Thank you."

He merely nodded.

"Did you show them the house?" Kylar asked, his throat bobbing with a swallow. Sweat shone on his temples.

"They asked for a tour," Ivy said. "But that was right before you guys walked in." When her steel eyes flicked to Darien's, she frowned. "Good thing Larina was so distracted by Darien."

"Yeah," Darien said flatly, "good thing."

Jack ran a hand—scraped and still filthy from all the shit that'd happened earlier—through his hair. "Roman is going to be pissed."

Yeah, he was. Darien knew Roman wouldn't have minded that they were staying here, but they'd gone and exposed the one safe place he'd kept for himself, untouched by the corruptive hands of his dad.

His haven was gone now. Whenever he finally got back to the city, he wouldn't have a home to go to anymore.

39

ANGELTHENE OPTOMETRY
ANGELTHENE, STATE OF WITHEREDGE

They'd made it to Angelthene Optometry with minutes to spare.

Travis waited at the front of his car with Lace and Jewels as Tamika Isley finished her shift. He could see her aura flitting around in there, grabbing her bags and shutting off lights.

What a surprise she'd be getting.

In the parking stall next to his, Logan cut the engine of his pickup truck —a vintage classic, that peppermint-and-oil smell that new cars just couldn't replicate lingering in the leather seats. While a hellseher's sense of smell certainly had its drawbacks, the perks often outweighed them.

Travis credited Roman for his appreciation of old vehicles. He wondered if his brother still took the time to restore them. While Roman kept some of the models to add to his growing collection, he resold the ones that weren't his favorites for a pretty penny.

Logan and Sabrine got out of the truck and joined their group, the shutting of their doors gusting more of that smell Travis's way.

The brawny male wolf said, "You sure she's working today?"

"I can see her in there," Travis said.

"I got Clover to hack their schedules," Jewels added. She checked the pocket watch she wore on a gold necklace—a lot of vintage eye candy today. Creepy dolls excluded. "She gets off at three."

"What time is it now?" Sabrine asked her.

"Quarter after."

Travis stared at the building. "Hopefully they're not taking forever because they're waiting for cops." He wouldn't doubt it. Tamika had only been involved with them once, when she'd shown up at Hell's Gate with info about Spirit Terra. It was possible that she regretted getting involved with them and had resorted to calling the emergency number.

Another five minutes passed before the front door opened. Three female employees emerged wearing scrubs; the one in mint-green was Tamika. Her sleek, dark hair was tied up in a ponytail, glasses on. Darien was right; this witch would look really good on Tanner's arm. Too bad neither of them seemed to want anything to do with each other. Atlas was stubborn like that, though; he was married more to his job than any of them.

The other two employees spotted their group first and started whispering as Tamika locked up. One of them reached into her bag—probably for pepper spray or a cell phone.

Travis heard the one lady mutter the names 'Darien Cassel' and 'Travis Devlin'. It seemed she couldn't figure out who he was.

Did they really look that much alike? Darien was bigger than him and had darker hair, but he supposed their features and eye color were close enough to make telling them apart a challenge. Travis's hair had grown out a bit too; it was closer to Darien's length now, and he'd recently got the back and sides faded. He highly doubted a haircut made that much of a difference, though.

Tamika dropped her keys into her small handbag and evaluated their group from across the lot. She whispered to her panicked employees, *"Don't call anyone. They just want to talk to me."*

"You?" one of them hissed. "Why?"

"Tamika!" the other begged. She looked like she might faint.

"It's fine," Tamika said. "I'll see you both at work tomorrow." She started heading this way, the other two drifting toward their cars.

"Yes, tomorrow!" one of them called. "We'll make sure you're here for your shift!"

Tamika cupped a hand to her brow and rolled her eyes.

She stopped several feet away, both hands moving to grasp the strap of her bag. "Why are you here?" Her eyes flicked about the parking lot that was now empty aside from them and their cars. A third that Travis figured must belong to Tamika sat in the corner of the lot.

Sabrine took the history book out of her book bag that was constantly strapped to her body like an extra limb. "Any particular reason why you shelved this in the wrong section?"

Travis added, "And why you loaned it at all."

Her eyes flicked about the parking lot. She pushed the eyeglasses that were sliding down her small nose back up. "Follow me." She took out her car keys and made for her vehicle.

Tamika Isley lived in the Victoria Amazonica District in a mansion nearly as big as Hell's Gate.

Travis was surprised by this. He hadn't expected someone so well-off to work at a tiny, humble business like Angelthene Optometry.

After parking their vehicles in the long driveway, Tamika brought them inside and gave them a tour of the ground floor. There were a lot of polished wood accents in here, a lot of marble-and-gold statues that looked like they'd cost almost as much as the house.

"Do you live here by yourself?" Travis asked as they followed her into a study. Sunlight brightened up the patterned rug, the behemoth of a desk, and the collection of brown leather furniture by the window.

"I live with my mother and our butler, Harold."

Travis shared a look with Lace and tipped up an eyebrow. "I've always wanted to get me one of those."

She smirked. "Hire Arthur."

"He'd be good at it."

One whole wall in the study was covered with a glass display case of spectacles, some of the frames so old they looked like they might crumble to dust.

Logan drifted toward the display case, his size dwarfing it. "You really like your job, hey?"

"I love my job," Tamika said. "I don't usually tell people this, because it sounds a bit pompous, but I don't have to work. My dad left me with a large enough fortune, but the years go down better if I have something worthwhile to spend my time on." Emotion flickered in her eyes as she studied the display case. "That's my dad's collection. Some of those are very rare."

"What are the red ones for?" Jewels asked, pointing a pale hand at the gold frames with red lenses.

"They block blue light."

Logan said, "And the green?"

"Those help with migraines and light sensitivity."

Travis said, "The red ones would probably be good for Atlas."

Lace smirked. "You'd never catch him wearing those."

Tamika gestured to the armchairs and long, deep-buttoned couch. "Have a seat, if you'd like."

Travis and Logan stayed standing. Tamika, too. Lace claimed an armchair and crossed her legs, one arm slung across the back of the chair, while Jewels and Sabrine took the couch.

Tamika was silent for a few moments, as if searching for the right words. "I rented that book after everything that happened during the Blood Moon," she began. "Like I told you before, my dad was obsessed with the legends of Spirit Terra and how our worlds were split. I never took him seriously as an adult, which is something I deeply regret now that he's gone, but as a child I was a dreamer. I had a fascination for the fantastical." Her quick smile was wistful. "I guess I still sort of do. When the Veil nearly fell, my interest was piqued for the first time since I was a teenager. The first time since my dad died. I wanted to familiarize myself with the old legends in case it ever happened again."

"And what did you find?" Sabrine prompted.

"Well, for one, that symbol in the library. It's the Scarlet Star. I put the book there so I'd remember where to go once I talked to you guys."

Travis said, "We were just down there last night. It's a bunch of old tunnels the Phoenix Head Society used to use."

Lace asked her, "You know what the Phoenix Head Society is, right?"

"I do. I also found old charts and maps in that book." She pointed at the tome in Sabrine's lap. "Maybe even the same ones Arthur found. I remembered what he did with the color wheel, so I created my own to study."

She strode over to the mahogany desk, scrubs swishing, and rolled down a world map that was secured to the wall behind it. Overtop of the map, she had stapled a transparent color wheel the same size as the map.

"When our worlds were separated," she began, "the goddess who'd completed the act had to create sealing points to hold the Veil in place, kind of like staples." She dragged a light brown finger down a row of staples in the map. "Or thread holes. She couldn't do it all in one go, so creating these areas to affix her power made the act less of a strain on her body. There are six, I think." She pointed to each on the map. Major capital cities sprinkled clear across the globe.

Travis crossed the room, the others soon following. "Why'd you put a star over Yveswich?" he asked.

"Because it's the most important one. It was the first sealing point." Her swallow was audible. Travis could feel her sudden fear as if it were a jacket he'd shrugged on when she added quietly, "The city is also directly on top of the Void."

Travis could have sworn the room dropped several degrees.

Roman. Roman was living directly overtop the Void. Paxton. And now Darien was there too. Ivy, Jack, Tanner—they were all there, and they had no fucking idea—

"Why didn't you come tell us this sooner?" Logan asked.

"Because..." Tamika's eyes flicked about. "I feel like I'm being watched."

40

THE DESERT
STATE OF WITHEREDGE

The desert felt infinite.

They'd been driving this one stretch of road for hours and had found nothing. Roman was a speed demon, so Shay had to keep reminding him to slow the hell down so she could get a good look at the surrounding land.

His foot crept onto the accelerator again—

"Shadows," Shay growled with a heavy blink. "Slow. Down."

He let off the pedal. "I hate driving slow." He gripped the steering wheel with restraint and twisted, his tattooed skin—wisps of shadow on one hand, ancient numerals on the other—pulling across his knuckles. "It's torture."

"Yeah, well, if you keep speeding, we're never going to find anything, and I'm not about to have you ruin my five days out here."

She leaned forward in her seat, bracing a hand against the sun-warmed dash, and scanned the desert mountains and flat, rocky terrain. The desert lilies, creosote, and yucca. So many plants, and so many lizards, but not one hint of Anna.

Something shiny peeked around a bend up ahead.

The cristala power plant.

"Didn't we already pass that?" Shay said, jutting her finger across the car.

Roman leaned away as if she had germs. "I can't tell when your hand keeps getting in my way every five minutes."

She scowled but dropped it. "Are you sure we aren't going around in circles?"

He shot her an irritated look, the gold in his eyes glinting. "This is a flat, straight road, pup. Have you *seen* the map?" He tapped the edge of the screen set in the dash.

"Pull over."

He eyed her. "Don't tell me you need to pee again."

"If you'd rather I piddle in your nice, fancy car—"

He abruptly pulled to the side of the road, the rough shoulder jostling the car and making her bounce. Dust billowed across the hood in a cloud—the only cloud in the whole area, not a single one marking the sky of perfect eggshell-blue.

She waited for it to clear before unbuckling her seatbelt and opening her door. "Let's go."

"I thought you said you needed to pee."

"I lied. We're going to take a walk."

He cut the engine and got out, grabbing their backpacks from the back seat. He tossed Shay's at her without warning, and she fumbled and dropped it.

"Very smooth," he crooned.

She glared but picked it up and put it on.

"Where to, pup?" He put his arms through the straps of his pack, and Shay tried not to stare at the muscles in his arms that shifted with the movement—way too visible, thanks to the ripped sleeves of his band tee.

What a stupid shirt.

"Higher ground," Shay replied, tucking a strand of hair behind an ear. Using Roman's shampoo was a colossal mistake she would not repeat. She now smelled like him, so whenever he wasn't hovering behind her like a cloud she couldn't get rid of, he still haunted her, his scent everywhere. It didn't help that she liked it. Damn these cologne and shampoo companies for making men smell so mouth-watering. "I want a better view." She pointed at the rugged red mountains to the west. "Let's start there."

They started walking, the crunch of dry ground under their hiking boots the only sound for over an hour. Even with the wide distance they managed to cover, there was nothing to report but more desert plants—more creosote, prickly pear, mesquite...

The quiet out here was unsettling, especially with Roman looming behind her, his shadow falling across hers every now and again on the cracked and parched earth. The dry air crusted Shay's hair with grit, and sweat made her clothes cling unpleasantly wherever they touched.

The toe of Shay's boot snagged on a bump in the earth, and she pitched forward, catching herself with tired, quivering legs.

She cursed under her breath, her toe aching where she'd stubbed it.

"You okay there, pup?"

She adjusted her lopsided pack and kept moving. "Fine." She wiped the sweat off her brow before it could run into her eyes. "I think we should talk to pass the time."

"Talk?"

She looked over her shoulder to see Roman taking a swig of water as he scanned the horizon. He moved smoothly and effortlessly, as if they hadn't been walking for what seemed an eternity in heat so dry it sucked the life out of you.

"Yes, talk," she said, turning back around before he could notice her staring. She might've caught him ogling her ass earlier that day, but she looked at him as often as he seemed to look at her. Maybe even more. "We might as well get to know each other better if we're going to be stuck out here for the next five days."

"Four."

She rolled her eyes. "I'll make it easy on you and start with the basics. What's your favorite color?"

A pause. She thought for sure he wouldn't answer, when suddenly he told her, "Green."

"Mine's yellow."

"I didn't ask."

She rolled her eyes. "Quit being an ass."

A brief pause. And then: "Why yellow?"

"It's happy and bright," she said.

"It's the color of piss."

"It's the color of sunflowers and lemons—"

"And piss."

When she scowled over her shoulder, he scowled back. "You already made that abundantly clear," she huffed. This wasn't going well at all. Maybe it was a good thing he was such a jerk; it'd kept her from jumping his bones this long, and she counted on it lasting.

But she was starting to learn that she had a thing for toxic assholes. Not that she'd ever been with one—she had never let herself get anywhere close to that point, though they seemed to be the type she was drawn to the most.

Every man Shay had slept with had been...careful with her. As if she were made of porcelain. Which was nice, at first. Romantic, even. But it hadn't taken long to discover that gentle wasn't what she wanted. She would've communicated this, had she felt any desire to pursue longer relationships with those men. But her goal was to sever all ties to her city. Yveswich would not be her future—she wouldn't let it. And it was for this same reason that she'd never taken a Darkslayer to her bed. Darkslaying wasn't in her future, either. She may be a hellseher, but she didn't fit in with that crowd.

Something told her Roman would give her what she wanted in bed, without her having to spell it out for him—

She cut off the thought before she could continue with this ridiculous, toxic fantasy. What was *wrong* with her? The heat was getting to her head! Roman Devlin was completely and utterly off-limits, even for one night.

One night that she would probably never forget.

It took her a minute to realize that she was scowling at the man troubling her thoughts—and another minute to realize he was watching her with a frown.

"What's twisting your panties, Miss Thief?"

"You," she blurted. Well, it was the truth.

The smile that stretched across his face reminded her of a baring of teeth—a shark's mouth.

"You are so annoying." She trudged along, leaving him behind.

Silence fell again. She debated asking him another question, but decided against it. He'd probably just say something stupid or mean. As stupid as his shirt, or as mean as the mug he constantly wore.

"Why'd Anna leave, anyway?"

Shay twisted the straps of her backpack, the fabric damp with sweat. "She didn't leave. She was abducted."

"You sure about that?"

"I'm not in the mood for your assholery and farfetched conspiracy theories. I know my sister better than anyone, and she never would have left me."

"Sounds like you trusted her a whole lot."

"I still do."

"Trust is dangerous. It gives the other person power over you. Better to be your own support; at least you can count on yourself."

"For the last time, Shadows, she did not leave me." If she'd had even the slightest shred of doubt, the information Priscilla had given them had wiped it away. Anna had come here with three men and a strange, blue-haired convict—that didn't sound like her at all.

Shay welcomed the silence this time as they reached steeper terrain and began picking their way up the mountainside. Some of the rocks were so big, she had to maneuver them with care, finding handholds farther up and pulling herself to the top like a monkey.

As time went by, and the climb continued, the muscles in Shay's legs began to scream, and her arms shook so badly they felt like rubber. The scar tissue in the muscles of her shoulder and neck began to ache, like little bolts of lightning prickling into her head and one side of her face. Another migraine was coming—*joy*. She tried to ration her water, but she was parched. The sun only seemed to get hotter, even as afternoon rolled around and it began its descent, gradually turning the trees and rocks studding the landscape into stark silhouettes.

"You sure you can make this one, short legs?" Roman said from right behind her. Shay assessed the rock she would need to climb to get up to the next level—higher than any of the others she'd scaled.

She dried her sweaty palms on her shorts, the material stiff with salt. "I got this."

Sucking in a breath of dry air, she scaled the rock, the ridges digging into her skin. The rock was so hot, it nearly burned her, and there were blisters on her palms that threatened to burst and bleed.

She was nearing the top when she slipped, the rock slicing deep into her palm.

A muffled cry tore out of her, and her stomach plummeted beneath her feet as she fell, straight into open air—

She hit something hard, but it wasn't ground or rock—it was Roman. His arms wrapped around her, and he cursed, staggering from the impact as he braced himself against a rock lower down—stopping both of them from falling to certain death.

He held her for a minute, her chest rapidly rising and falling under his arm. The fall had taken her by such surprise, her body so fatigued from walking, that she was suddenly shaking—*all* of her was shaking, not just her arms and legs. Even her lungs were quivering, and a metallic taste coated her tongue.

"You alright?" Roman's question was tense.

"I'm fine."

"You're bleeding." He lowered her down, setting her on her ass as though she were a doll, and ripped a strip off the bottom of his shirt.

"If you keep ripping your shirt, you're not going to have any shirt left," she warned, eyeing his sleeves.

"We forgot bandages."

"It's just a scratch—"

"Oh please, you're bleeding enough to attract every monster in the whole fucking desert." He squatted before her. "Now give me your hand so I can deal with this and we can get going." He held his out, palm up. He had a lot of scars on that hand, a lot of calluses.

She relented, placing her hand in his. It was warm and dry and as rough as it looked, and Shay hated to admit it but...she liked the size difference between her hand and his.

Uh-uh—no way. Scratch that right now. There was no way she was letting herself *like* anything about Roman, even just his hands.

He poured water on the cut first—from his bottle, not hers, she noticed—clearing away the grit that was embedded in the wound. That wound was deeper than she'd realized, but her hellseher healing would fix it in a matter of hours. Didn't stop the pain, though. He swiftly tied the strip of fabric around her palm, his movements far more gentle than she'd expected from someone like him.

"You should've told me about your hands," he scolded.

"What about them?"

He grabbed her other one and turned it palm-up. "They're all peeling and covered in blisters."

"I'm fine."

"You're resilient," he corrected. She'd take that as a compliment. He helped her to her feet, taking hold of her forearms instead of her hands. "For someone so small," he added.

Shay extracted her arms from his grip and stepped up to the rock that had nearly killed her. This jackass was going down.

Instantly, Roman was there, shadowing her like an eclipse of the sun. "What do you think you're doing?"

She threw up a hand. "Climbing—duh!"

"Nice try, Shay." The sound of her name on his tongue—instead of 'small fry', 'pup', or 'Cousens'—sent a prickle up her spine. "We're not about to have an instant replay of that bullshit that almost killed us." Shay highly doubted the fall would've killed him; he might've called her resilient, but she knew her limits. And it was *his* body that was durable. Her size and the pain she lived with daily had limited her in ways most hellsehers never had to contend with.

She licked her cracking lips. "What am I supposed to do then?"

He took off his backpack and set it on the ground.

And then he pulled off his shirt, stuffing it in the largest compartment and zipping it shut. Before she could ask him what in the hell he was doing, he dropped to a crouch before her, turning so his back faced her. The tops of his shoulders were reddened by the sun, his freckles more prominent. And his tattoos...gods.

The ink on his back was divided by his spine—there were no tattoos on the right, but the left was completely covered with a grayscale masterpiece, filled with far too many details to notice with only one glance.

Okay, maybe not a glance but a hard stare. One really hard stare.

"Get on," Roman said.

Shay blinked down at him. Was he really doing this? "Shadowmaster *and* camel?" she gasped. "Who *are* you?" His back was full of scars and weird little puckered marks that almost looked like...the top of a lighter.

"My offer expires in three, two, one..."

She got on, wrapping her arms around his neck and her legs around his waist. "At least give me your backpack," she said.

"I can carry it—"

"Shadows, give me the damn backpack! You won't be able to balance me properly if you have to carry it too."

He passed it to her, and she held it by one of the straps. This would be awkward, but it would work. He stood with ease, his hands gripping her beneath her thighs, and scaled the rock. It was impressive—the way he could move. But she found it difficult to focus on much else when his warm hands were gripping such an intimate part of her body, his hold never faltering.

Nope, not thinking about his hands.

"Scratch the whole camel thing," Shay said. "You're a mountain goat." That earned her a small chuckle. With her chest pressed against his back, she could feel the brief spell of laughter rumble through him. "Roman 'Mountain Goat' Devlin—I like it."

He kept walking, covering ground quickly. "No one is to hear about this, pup. Got it?"

She zipped her mouth shut and tossed away the key.

Twenty minutes later, they reached the top. The moment Roman set her on her feet, she hurried to a flat, horizontal rock by the edge, one that gave her an utterly breathtaking view of the desert valley down below. She tried to convince herself that she had practically run away from Roman because she was eager to see the land below, and while that was partially true, she mostly wanted to put some space between them —immediately.

Roman joined her shortly after, bringing that rippling cloud of dark energy with him. She studied him out of the corner of her eye as he took a swig of water, a couple drops dripping down his chin.

Gold eyes locked on hers. "Have some water, pup. I don't feel like carrying you all the way back."

She didn't want to be carried by Roman again either, so she let her pack slide to the dusty earth and took out her canteen. She stole a moment to stretch out her aching shoulders before unscrewing the lid and drinking the last of the lukewarm water.

For several minutes, they caught their breath as they stood together on that mountain, looking down at the red desert.

It was beautiful. When Shay thought of the desert, she pictured barren, lifeless land, but it was anything but that. It was alive in a way that only the desert could be, and so stunningly beautiful that it literally took the last of her breath away.

She shielded her eyes from the sun and looked harder, utilizing her sharp hellseher eyesight to scan for anything that might tell her where Anna could be.

There was the cristala power plant—gleaming like liquid silver.

"There's nothing out here," she sighed. What a waste.

But something glimmered in her periphery. She craned her neck, looking farther north—

There was another one.

"I knew we passed that plant twice!" She pointed. "See?"

Roman was already looking. "Yeah, I see."

"Why do you think there's two?" And so close together.

"It's just a power plant, Shay."

"But why two?" It was the only thing about this whole damn desert that stood out to her as being weird, and she wasn't about to write it off. "Are there ever two in a single area like this?"

Roman thought about it. "We'll look them up on the map when we get back to the motel." He watched her as she scanned the desert again, that stare of his more unsettling than the swiftly falling night.

Night! Shit—they'd lost track of time.

"Have you seen what you wanted to see?"

Shay dropped her hand. "For today." Even if she wanted to continue looking, they didn't have a choice.

"Good, because it's getting dark." There was a new edge to his voice that didn't stem from irritation, an edge she'd heard only once before—on the dock when she'd lied about selling his necklace. Was that...fear? "Let's go."

Together, they hurried back the way they'd come. She had no choice but to let Roman help her down from the ledges that were too steep for her to navigate on her own, but she accepted without argument, unable to stomach the idea of pitching headfirst off the cliff.

Or of being out here past sunset. If night fell, and they weren't in the car by then, they would both be dead. It didn't matter that she was with Roman Devlin—there were far too many monsters out here for him to handle on his own.

They developed a routine quickly, Roman jumping down first before twisting back around and helping Shay down, either with a hand for her to hold, or by gripping her by the waist and lifting her down. No matter how many times he performed the last move, his arms never shook.

"I can see the car," Shay panted as they finally reached level ground.

They picked up speed, running side by side, their breaths rasping through the air that was scented with sage and sunbaked dirt.

A howl cut through the quiet, shooting a prickle up Shay's spine.

Darkness fell swiftly, the last of the sun's rays peeking through the splits in the mountain like glowing fingers. There wasn't much daylight left.

Shay began to sense them—the demons that dwelled in these parts, sleeping by day and hunting by night. They were awake.

And there were a lot of them.

"We have to move faster." Roman's words were strained, and he was panting now too. "Give me your hand." He held his out.

"I'm fine."

"Shay, you're slow." He pointed at the setting sun, not slowing his pace. "See that? We have five minutes at best before we're both fucking dead!"

Behind them, deep in the hills, the monsters began their hunt, driven by ravenous appetites. Another howl rang out, this one echoed by countless others. Hungry snarls cut through the cliffs, and rocks clacked down the steep bluffs as the monsters pursued them.

Roman thrust his hand closer, still never slowing. He was just ahead of her, and she had to speed up to get her hand into his. His warm fingers closed around hers, gripping tight, and he pulled her along, the both of them running so quickly it felt like her legs were barely touching ground.

The monsters were coming—she could hear them moving in packs.

She made the mistake of looking over her shoulder.

Hundreds of eyes—yellow and red—glowed among the hills, deadly and feverish with hunger. Those hills were cloaked in shadow now, not one bit of light left to keep the monsters at bay. While some were horned with cloven feet, others looked like wolves, their backs rippling with something akin to shadow. Worse even than these were the beasts whose bodies were a mix of hound and serpent, their streamlined, canine physiques lined with scales that shifted continuously over grotesque, otherworldly muscle.

Shay tore her eyes off the walking nightmares, pushing her legs faster.

The last of the sunlight fell across the ground before them, an orange curtain of protective light. But the darkness was gaining on them; it was at their heels now, cooling the sun-scorched ground right under their feet.

"I have to carry you." Roman's voice was choked with fear that blindsided her. He took off his backpack and tightened his hold on her hand, and before she could react, he was pulling her close and lifting her up until she was on his back like before, her legs wrapped around his waist.

Roman kept running, faster now that she was no longer hindering him, staying in the protection of the fading sunlight as shadows nipped at his heels. He supported her with one hand under her right thigh, his left gripping his backpack. That curtain of light kept fading, growing dimmer and smaller with every second that passed. The shadows were winning.

"Can't you make them go away?" Shay panted.

"Make what go away?"

"The shadows!"

"I can't stop night, pup. I'm not that powerful."

Barks and growls rent the air. They were no more than three feet behind them, chasing them in the cover of the shadows while Shay and Roman fled in the protection of the light.

"Roman," she gritted out.

"I know."

They were almost there. Shay's heart thundered, and her head pounded like an anvil. With her arm wrapped tightly around Roman's neck, she could feel his heart beating just as hard.

One of the demons took a chance and dove for them, only to fall back with a yelp as the waning sun burned its flesh.

Roman panted, "Not today, asshole."

There was the car—glinting in the very last of the day's light.

Roman skidded to a halt beside it in a cloud of dust. He practically threw Shay into the passenger's seat with the bags and then got in his side. He started the engine, his movements blindingly fast.

Shay turned to look out the back window—but stopped herself before she could see anything, not wanting to glimpse the foul things that were hunting them.

"Roman," she choked out. They were surrounding the car—she didn't have to see them to know this. She could feel them.

They were hungry.

He spun the car around and raced down the highway.

For several long minutes, their rapid breathing and the hum of the engine were the only sounds. Shay hoped like hell that none of those creatures would attack the car; spells only offered so much protection. If the car was flipped over or destroyed just enough, the spells would fail to function.

Roman broke the silence first, his voice still tense. "Pup?"

"Yeah?" She couldn't catch her breath.

"Do me a favor."

"Sure." After he'd just saved her life? *Twice?* She'd do just about anything he asked.

"Don't look in the mirrors," Roman said.

She didn't.

41

FOXHILL RENTALS
FOXHILL, STATE OF WITHEREDGE

"Max?" Dallas called. "I don't think it's the brightest idea for a well-known Darkslayer to keep yanking on the door of a closed building." He rattled the handle again, prompting Dallas to noisily clear her throat. "Security cameras!" she hollered. "*Hello?*"

He pushed away from the glass doors of Foxhill Rentals and ran a hand through his hair. "What kind of business closes at five o'clock?"

"Uhhhh," Malakai drawled, giving Max an are-you-stupid look, "lots of them. Nighttime big problem, remember?" He pointed a tattooed finger at the twilit sky.

Max swore. "It's inconvenient." With one last glare at the hours of operation taped to the glass, he stomped over and joined the group standing by the bike and SUV.

"We'll come back first thing in the morning," Aspen said, fighting a hand through the tangles and knots the wind had put in her mahogany hair. "But we should probably figure out where we're staying, or we're going to have to dog-pile in the SUV."

Dominic said, "I vote Malakai takes the bottom."

"Anybody spot any vacancy signs on the way in?" Max asked. He wasn't hopeful; they hadn't passed many hotels, and the town wasn't so big that he would've missed them.

Blue's brow creased. "Vacancy?" She looked up at Dominic, the low brim of her sports hat forcing her to tip her head farther back to see the Angel's face.

"Free hotel rooms," he explained.

"Oh."

Dominic pointed south. "There was a place just down the highway. Desert Haven Something-Or-Other."

"Sounds promising," Malakai muttered, looking like he was trying not to say something rude—or punch Dominic out for what he'd said about dog-piling.

Max headed for the SUV. "It'll do. Let's go."

Desert Haven Hotel was right on the highway. The rooms would probably be noisy, but he wasn't about to be picky. They would hopefully only be here for one night.

Max waited in the SUV, window down, as Dallas and Blue, the latter glamored, went inside to book three rooms. Malakai and Aspen stood by the bike, talking quietly to one another, while Dominic leaned against the back door of the SUV, wiping sweat off his forehead with the back of his wrist.

They were parked in the back corner of the lot, avoiding being seen by the people who ran the hotel. It wasn't as if they weren't allowed to do normal things like rent hotel rooms, but it was best if they didn't draw attention to themselves. And three Darkslayers from three different houses were bound to attract attention.

Especially when they'd nearly broken into Foxhill Rentals without disabling the security cameras first. Having to wait until tomorrow to continue his search was torture, but he had to admit it was the wise thing to do.

Besides, hacking wasn't the answer Max wanted. He wanted to speak to someone, wanted more information than he could get from the database of the tiny business. The only thing the system would likely reveal was the fake name the rental car was registered under—something a hacker like Atlas could easily obtain. Max wanted to talk to someone with a brain and a pair of eyes—not a computer.

"Life's been crazy lately, hey?" Dominic said, coming to lean his forearms on Max's open window.

"Very." He'd just about had enough excitement to last two hellseher lifetimes.

"What are you going to do when you find her?"

Max stared out at the cars breezing down the highway, tires clunking over the raised pavement markers separating the lanes. "I haven't really thought that far ahead." He didn't want to jinx it—didn't want to get his hopes up anymore than he should. And they were already sky-high.

"You're not doubting that you're gonna find her, are you?"

Max shrugged with one shoulder. "Still feels wild to me that she's somewhere out there. That she isn't...dead like I'd thought." He swallowed.

"Blue said she liked Scarlet—Maya. They got along, apparently."

"Did she say anything else?"

"I would've told you." He took the black elastic off his wrist and tied his hair back. "She still reacts funny whenever I try to ask her about the facility." He looked toward the office of the hotel, wings drooping. "She's probably scared that if she talks about it, it'll make it real again." That was how Max felt about the night his house burned down and he'd lost Maya. For a while he'd been reluctant to see a therapist, afraid that he'd wind up remembering that night clearer than he was already forced to.

Max's attention snagged on Malakai and Aspen. "What are you two whispering about?"

Malakai turned his head dramatically slowly. Said through clenched teeth, "Does it matter?"

"No keeping secrets."

Malakai gave him the middle finger, his ring glinting in a street light that flared to life.

Aspen grabbed his wrist and lowered it. "We're talking about Jewels."

"What about her?" Max's eyes flicked between the two Reapers. "Everything okay?"

"Quit pretending to care," Malakai retorted.

Max bared his teeth. "I'm not pretending, you jackass! Not everyone is as much of an asshole as you."

Aspen said, "We're just worried about her." She looked at Malakai, who was busying himself with watching the vehicles on the highway. Night was falling fast. More street lights flickered on, spreading pools of light across the sidewalks. "Don't want to be away for too long."

"Is it that bad?" Dominic asked.

"It's the Tricking," Malakai said. "Bad is all there is."

The front doors to the hotel opened, bells clanging against the glass.

"Gross, it's still hot as Ignis out here," Dallas said as she headed this way, Blue at her side. She pinched her shirt with one hand and billowed it, using the other to hand Blue a key. "Let's hope the rooms have A/C."

As soon as they got closer, Max said, "How'd it go?"

"As well as it can." She handed Aspen a different key. "The rooms are a bit spaced apart, but we're all on the ground floor."

Max held his hand out for the key—

Dallas gripped it in a fist. "They only gave us one, so I claim key privilege."

"What kind of hotel only gives you one key? I should have it, I'm the smoker."

"Fair point." She tossed it at him, and he caught it.

"What are we doing for dinner?" Dominic asked. "I'm starving."

Malakai got on his bike. "Aspen and I are gonna take off. We'll see you guys in the morning." Aspen got on behind him, and the bike rumbled to life. He was ripping it away, toward the parking spot in front of room number twenty-three, before anyone could reply.

Dominic said, "I don't think I've ever met such an arrogant, stand-offish prig."

Max gestured for Dom and Blue to get in the SUV. "Let's unload, and then we'll go for dinner." He was starving too. And angry. So he decided he'd take out his anger on a burger instead of looking for something to hit.

42

CALIGINOUS ON SILVERWAY
YVESWICH, STATE OF KER

Night number two had rolled around, and Loren still hadn't woken up.

Darien paced in front of the door to Chamber Number Five, fingers curling and uncurling. Inside the chamber, Loren slept upon the glasslike tabletop, her shimmering hair floating above her. Lines of raindrops drifted from floor to ceiling and ceiling to floor, and multicolored lights bobbed around her like fireflies, a few clinging softly to her limbs.

Night number fucking two, and Darien was about to lose it.

Tonight, Darien had instructed Tanya to activate every color on the screen. White hadn't worked last time, so he was trying all of them now—every color of the rainbow.

And it still wasn't working.

He glanced at the clock next to the door. They were nearing the thirty minute mark.

At twenty-eight minutes, Darien broke.

He grabbed the handle and swung open the door. None of the others tried to stop or follow him as he stalked into the chamber. Opening the door triggered the alarm, its keening wails slicing through the building. The door slammed shut behind him, and red lights flashed in warning as he crossed the room, water splashing under his boots. Bandit came out of his shadow, walking at Darien's side as they approached the floating tabletop—and the girl they both loved.

Darien stopped beside it and gripped the edge, the grids of magic in the transparent material flaring and fluttering under the pressure. The siren kept wailing, rattling his eardrums, the red streaks of warning light passing across his face and Loren's.

"I know you're in there, Loren," he bit out. "I know you're in there, because I can feel you. And I know you're scared. You're scared and you think you're alone but you're not." He smoothed the golden hair away from her face, thumbs grazing her cheeks. Warm—her skin was warm, but it lacked the usual flush she had when she was around him. Life—it lacked life. "You're not alone, because I'm here—I'm right here, sweetheart. And I need you to fight. I need you to wake up, baby." He banged a fist on the levitating tabletop, causing the magic to sputter and crackle. "I need you to come back to me—please."

Behind him, the door handle rattled. Tanya banged on the wood and shouted through the window, her shouts muffled by the barrier.

Her pleas were soon silenced by the others restraining her—blocking her from coming in or leaving the corridor. Atlas must've figured out how to lock it—how to stop even a registered employee from getting in.

Darien kept his focus on Loren, his chest growing tighter the longer he called out to her and she didn't answer. A Surge was building inside him, his own magic threatening to come out. He fought it, if only to protect Loren.

"I need you to fight, baby, I need you to fight." He dropped his fist again. Harder. Shuddering the table. The rain and balls of light in the room shivered and bounced. "I need you to *fight!*" *Bang!* The siren kept wailing, and Darien kept hitting the table. *"I NEED YOU TO FUCKING FIGHT!"*

Bandit started barking, not in argument but encouragement. The sound volleyed sharply off the walls.

"I need you, baby. I need you—I need you so badly." Emotion choked every word—threatened to choke *him*. "Please, baby—please."

Bandit barked. *'I can see her!' Bark! Bark! 'I see her!'*

Darien's head whipped toward the dog, vision swimming. "What do you mean you can see her?"

'She's fighting!' Bandit barked again. *Bark! Bark!* The alarm kept wailing, red lights oscillating through the room, lighting up Loren with streaks of vermilion. *'She's trying to come back! She's trying to come back to us!'*

A sob caught in Darien's throat. "Go, Bandit—*please!*" Moisture stung his eyes. "Bring her home!"

The dog disappeared into Loren's shadow with a bark.

And Darien struck the table again, veins of magic zipping through the transparent material. "Don't give up, sweetheart. Don't give up. I'm here. I'm here, and I'm waiting. I'm waiting for you, baby—I'm waiting. I know you can hear me—I know you fucking can." The next strike of his fist sent wisps of shadow through the room. *"WAKE UP!"*

IN THE HEART of the universe, somewhere between life and death, the girl and her dog stopped walking.

"No." Loren's soft whimper was swallowed up by outer space as she glimpsed the end of the path up ahead.

It just...stopped. Another three hundred yards, perhaps, if she was measuring correctly, and after that there was nowhere to go.

It was far too quiet here.

Singer whined and pawed at her foot—another thing she could not feel.

She was hollower now than before—she could sense it, as if she were a cup with a chip in the bottom, the last of her life dripping through the crack far too quickly.

"What do we do?" She had barely got the question out when the path beneath her shuddered so violently, she nearly fell on her ass.

She threw her arms out to steady herself. Looked over her shoulder—

The path was crumbling away. The dirt and grass was just *falling away*, and the destruction was moving toward her—rapidly.

"Run!" she shouted. She bolted down the path as fast as she could, Singer sprinting just ahead of her, his ghostly white body lighting the way. "Don't slow down! Keep running!"

Behind them, the ground continued to fall away, quicker now, the dirt crumbling under her heels.

Up ahead loomed the end—the space where her path ended, leaving nothing but a dark and gaping mouth full of stars, waiting to swallow her whole.

She had no choice but to keep going, sprinting toward that mouth of endless sky.

Another dog was running this way—body black and misty, ears and tail cropped, eyes red. He was barking, the noise generating sound waves she could feel—the first thing she had felt in forever. She would have wept with joy, had she been able.

The strange dog fell into stride beside her, running with her now, the powerful muscles in his body shifting with every bound. '*You have to keep going,*' he told her.

The girl cried out in frustration—exhaustion. "I don't know if I can."

'*If you don't, you will fall.*'

"I'm so tired," she gasped. Tired was not a good enough word to describe how she felt. She wasn't tired, she was hurting. Maybe not the physical kind, but it hurt all the same.

'Keep going! Faster.'

"I can't!"

'You must. He is waiting for you.'

"Who?" she asked. But his face flashed into her mind, and as she ran, she sobbed.

43

THE IN-BETWEEN

'*Run!*' The dog barked and barked. '*Run, Loren! Don't stop. You need to keep running!*'

"Where?" she panted. There was nowhere to go. Another seven feet, and she would be out of path. Down she would fall, into the unknown. It terrified her.

The Widow's otherworldly voice, ancient yet young, shot into her mind. Words spoken in a blue-lit cavern. 'He who wishes to return to life must take a leap of faith.'

A new light shone ahead—brighter than all the stars. Brighter than the moon, if there had been one. Was she imagining it? The light? Creating a way out for herself?

Was it all a lie?

But then she heard a voice. A powerful male voice, calling out her name.

"I need you to fight, baby," the voice was saying. "I'm right here—I'm not going anywhere." Loren sobbed, and for the first time since she had awoken in this strange place, she could have sworn she felt the splash of tears on her cheeks.

That voice—it was so broken, yet so strong, and the emotion in it nearly shattered her, nearly buckled her knees. She picked up her dress with both hands and ran faster.

"I'm not leaving you," the voice said, "not now—not ever. Come on, Loren. I believe in you—you can do this!"

Behind her, the last few feet of path fell away.

And up ahead, the path ended.

With a ragged inhale, she pushed off the ground and threw herself into the unknown, a dog on either side of her, aiming for that voice—

Her leap of faith.

Darien dropped his fist again.

And again.

And again.

And again—

Bandit materialized in a swarm of black mist, tumbling out of Loren's shadow and splashing through the water on the floor.

Darien kept shouting, kept pounding his fist on the table. "Wake up!" Bang. "Wake up!" Bang!

Bandit scrabbled to his feet and sprinted to Darien's side. '*Keep going!*' he shouted. Strained barks tore through the room. The alarm kept wailing. '*Come on!*' Bandit begged, leaping to see better. *Bark! Come on!*

"Wake up!" Bang. "Wake." Bang! "The." *Bang!* "Fuck!" *BANG!* "UPPPPPPPPPPPPPPPPP!"

Magic tore through the room in a rainbow hurricane, blinding him and covering everything with effervescent color and light.

A breathy, broken sob that didn't belong to Darien cleaved the room.

Bandit stopped barking.

Darien held his breath.

The colors and shadows dropped to the floor in a fog and curled away—

And Loren opened her eyes.

PART THREE
THE DUNES

44

SOMEPLACE UNFAMILIAR
TERRA

It was too bright in here. Too crowded.

She had jolted into consciousness with a ragged gasp that tore apart her lungs, and although several minutes had passed since then, she still couldn't catch her breath.

The walls of the room were curved like a fishbowl and colored like an opal. She sat upon a floating tabletop, her hands braced behind her on the smooth, glassy material. Several inches of water covered the floor, sloshing under the feet of five people who drifted into the room to join the sixth.

She didn't recognize a single person. Several of those people were calling her 'Loren'.

Was that her name? *Loren?*

It was the only word she could pick out. The rest confused her, too many people speaking at once. Or maybe it just felt that way because her ears were ringing, her head weighed a thousand pounds, and her heart was jackhammering in her chest.

And then she recalled the spider—how the Nameless being had told her that her name was 'Loren'. Recalled how she'd run toward life in another dimension, Singer at her side—

Singer. Where was he?

She was going to throw up. There were too many colors in here, too many sounds, too many faces. The lights were too bright. She was dizzy and nauseous and—

Her attention snagged on the man closest to her.

For a moment, she forgot everything else, everything and everyone except him.

This was the face that had kept her going in that strange world, when she had come so close to giving up. The face she had run to.

Tattooed hands gripped the edge of the floating platform. There were a lot of scars on those hands. Some on his arms too, though she couldn't see past the sleeves that were pushed up to his elbows, the muscles in his forearms rigid. He was leaning toward her, but still giving her room to breathe. His face was lined with concern, his dark brows thrown low over eyes that were a stormy mix of gray and blue. Smooth black hair was styled back from his face, though a defiant strand had fallen loose, fluttering with every labored exhale.

He was breathing as heavily as she was.

She wished she knew why.

A symbol was inked below his ear. A small one. It was a letter—an S with a devil's horn on each end. She looked at the symbol for only a moment before her eyes were magnetized back to his face.

She couldn't decide which of his features was the most captivating: his eyes or his mouth.

"Who are you?" Her voice was barely a croak.

All sound in the room ceased.

Her skin prickled. The silence pressed harder. "Did I say something wrong?" she ventured.

The dark-haired one with the tattoos and scars turned very still.

And then his hands that were gripping the edge of the table tightened, squeezing the glass. The magic inside it flared, light crackling under his hold. Black flickered in his eyes—the Sight, she realized—but he fought it with fierce blinks until it disappeared again.

A different man stepped forward. This one had very short brown hair and gray eyes, his tall frame leaner than the one who'd captured her attention so thoroughly. His features were sharp and severe, yet somehow still managed to look kind if you paid close enough attention, his mouth framed by a five o'clock shadow. His bracelet and necklace were designed to look like circuit boards, and a full sleeve of similar designs was inked on his left arm.

"You...," he began, his eyes skating her face. "You don't recognize him?" He gestured to the black-haired one with the stormy eyes.

The one who still wasn't moving. He didn't appear to be breathing anymore, either.

She glanced about the room. A breathtakingly beautiful, dark-haired woman stood behind the heavily tattooed male; she looked like she could be his twin. Beside her were three more hellsehers—one with brown skin, a small tattoo of a bleeding black skull on his cheekbone, and another male with curly brown hair and brown eyes. The third was a female hellseher in her thirties, her gray eyes nearly identical to the man who wore the circuit board jewelry. His mother, maybe. None of them were smiling.

The silence was heavy. Suffocating.

"Should I?" she whispered.

That was when he walked out—*him,* the heavily tattooed one with all the scars.

The door banged open, and he vanished out of sight.

No one said anything. They just glanced at each other, looking as lost and confused as Loren felt.

"I'm sorry," she whispered.

She didn't know what she was apologizing for, but something told her it was a lot.

DARIEN COULDN'T BREATHE.

He rode the elevator to the roof of the skyscraper, hands curling and uncurling at his sides as he watched the small black screen finally announce that he'd reached the roof. With Caliginous on Silverway being the last business at the top, it was a short ride, but to Darien it felt like a million years.

The elevator dinged, and the doors slid open. He walked out onto the roof, sucking down the cold night air. His lungs were screaming, and his heart was beating so hard he felt like he was going to pass out.

He fought it—fought all the emotions. If he had to deal with a Surge right now, he wouldn't be of any use to Loren.

It was why he'd come up here. Why he'd stomped out barely five minutes after she'd woken up. He'd needed to get away from her—for her safety, and the safety of his family.

But also because he couldn't stomach what just happened.

Loren couldn't remember him. Not only had she asked him who he was, but she had looked at him as if he were a complete stranger.

As if the last six months hadn't happened.

As if they hadn't fallen so wildly in love with each other that they could barely handle being separated for more than two days' time.

As if they hadn't been to hell and back together.

As if he didn't love her so goddamn much that it sometimes physically hurt.

As if he wasn't planning on spending his whole life loving her the way she deserved to be loved.

Darien paced across the roof, boots pounding, hands tensing into tight fists that he had to consciously loosen every few seconds. The stars winked above, and throughout the city, monsters roared and scrapped, tires clattered over cobblestones, and wings beat as vampires soared between buildings, hunting for prey.

'We need to go back,' Bandit whispered. The dog crept out of Darien's shadow on timid paws.

"I can't go back right now."

Bandit's head drooped. *'She just got home.'*

"She doesn't fucking know who you are!" Darien shouted.

Bandit's head bowed further, and Darien hated himself for it.

His next words were broken whispers. "She doesn't know who I am, either."

Bandit whined. *'I missed her.'*

Heat pushed at the backs of Darien's eyes. "So did I." He still missed her. She was finally back, and he still missed her.

The elevator doors shot open.

Darien froze.

Tanner walked through, Silver trotting at his side.

Darien's hands curled into fists again. "Atlas—"

"Don't tell me to go away," Tanner said, though he stopped several feet from him. "You want us to keep our distance, I'm fine with that. I'll stand right here and we'll talk."

"I got nothing to say."

"I know this is hard—"

"I finally get her back and she can't even remember me." Alright, so maybe he did have things he wanted to say. "I finally get her back and I can't even kiss her. I finally get her back and I can't even touch her because she doesn't know who I am and would probably push me the fuck away if I tried."

He started pacing again. Bandit sat down, head hanging low. Silver crept toward him and sat down too, the wolf leaning his head against the dog's shoulder.

Tanner gave Darien a couple minutes before speaking. "You know this is normal, right?"

"What's normal?"

"Not being able to remember anything after being in a coma."

Darien stopped pacing. "What's the...the likelihood that her memories will come back?"

Tanner hummed. "Depends on the person. But usually memories return slowly over the course of a couple, few weeks. You need to give her time. And support. Patience—all things you're good at."

Darien took out a smoke and lit it. "Did she say anything else? After I left?" He took a drag.

"She asked what she did wrong." Darien was pretty sure she'd said that while he was still in the room, but he wasn't sure.

"She never does anything wrong. She does everything right, and life just hands it to her all the damn time." He'd always believed he had some of the worst luck in the world, but Loren? Loren had been through it these past six months—more shit than most people saw in a lifetime. And it killed him that he'd been unable to stop so much of it.

"Look," Tanner began. "I know you prefer to barricade yourself in a corner and fight your way out without accepting anyone's help, but we came to Yveswich to help you, Darien. And we're going to help you with Loren. Her memories are going to come back—you just gotta trust it."

Darien walked up to the ledge, stopping when the toe of his boots just about went over. He'd stood on buildings like this one countless times—mostly in the months after Elsie Cassel had passed away. After she'd fallen to her death from the roof of the apartment building where the broken Slade family had once lived. In the months afterward, he'd stood on ledges high up and tried to imagine how she had felt in her final moments. The moments before she'd supposedly jumped.

Maybe she *had* jumped. Maybe she'd been pushed. Either way, she'd died by falling from a great height. No matter how it'd happened, she'd died a brutal death.

There weren't many buildings tall enough to kill a hellseher, but there were plenty tall enough to take the life of a mortal.

This one, though... This was tall enough for anyone.

"Dare?" Tanner called. Boots scuffed as he approached.

Darien took one last drag on the cigarette, and then he held it out before him and dropped it. Down it fell, to the road below. He watched as the glowing red end faded with distance. Heard the sickening sound of his mother's body smacking against concrete. Felt his lungs ache as his teenaged self screamed his bloody heart out. Saw the oscillating red and blue lights of the cop cars when they'd finally pulled up, too late to do anything.

Darien blinked. He turned, every trace of the Surge and the many emotions that were ripping him apart now gone, and made for the elevator. Tanner, Bandit, and Silver were all watching him with emotions that ranged from fear to alarm.

"Are you..." Tanner cleared his throat. "...okay?"

"I'm fine." For many years, Darien had said those two words, but seldom had they ever been true. "Let's go. It's fucking cold out here."

45

CALIGINOUS ON SILVERWAY
YVESWICH, STATE OF KER

Loren Elizabeth Calla—that was her name.
Loren Elizabeth Calla.
Bits and pieces of her life had returned to her in the time since the dark-haired male Devil had left, but everything that'd happened since last Septem was still...gone. As if she had dropped off the planet for the past six months. It both infuriated and scared her.

Infuriated—because, based on what the people in this room had told her, pretty much everything interesting in her life had taken place in those six months. If everything they'd said was true, it was a shame she couldn't remember any of it.

Scared—because it was hard to believe what they were telling her, hard to digest the fact that these people—Ivyana Cassel, Jack Steele, the other two who'd left the chamber—were protecting her, which went against everything rumor claimed about the most dangerous and feared Darkslaying circle in Angelthene.

She was friends with the Seven Devils—how very bizarre. And she had magic—even more bizarre.

And she was in Yveswich, a place she had only ever dreamed of seeing. Of course, when she'd dreamed of it, she'd hoped she might be visiting as a tourist instead of a...patient at...

What was this place called again?

Caliginous on Silverway. Some sort of medical facility?

The other Darkslayer in the room was Kylar Lavin, a member of the Shadowmasters and the Hollow. Loren had heard as many rumors about this Darkslaying circle as she had the ones in her hometown. Ivy was quick to tell her that she'd never met Kylar before—finally, a person she didn't recognize, but for good reason. A real introduction this time, instead of those fake, awkward ones that made everyone stare at her like she had antlers growing out of her head.

The door to the chamber opened, and the man with the cropped brown hair and tech jewelry walked in. Behind him was the other—the black-haired one who'd stormed out.

It wasn't cold in here, but Loren felt goosebumps prickle across her half-naked body as that man's eyes immediately locked with hers, as if he felt that same magnetic pull that gathered in her chest every time he was around. With cold, weak hands she gripped the floating tabletop she sat upon, her heart pounding loudly.

Those eyes—a stormy, steely blue—were the kind of feature you'd never forget after seeing them, even just once. This was the face she had glimpsed while lost below the glowing tree—the last thing she remembered before all her memories had faded. Even with partial amnesia, her mind had clung to this one tightly, not wanting to let go of the memory of that face, even in death.

That mouth. That jawline.

Loren shivered.

Ivyana Cassel stepped forward, gesturing to the one with the brown hair that was buzzed short. "Loren, this is Tanner Atlas."

Tanner Atlas—she'd heard plenty about him. He was the hacker for Hell's Gate—the best hacker in Terra. He was very smart and very well-known.

He stepped forward and shook hands with her. "Welcome back, Loren." A smile twitched at one corner of his mouth.

"Thanks," she said in a small voice.

Ivy took a deep breath. "And this...is Darien Cassel." Her chipper voice was suddenly strained. "Your—"

"Friend." Darien Cassel's rich, deep voice made the chills on Loren's body intensify. He stepped forward and extended a large, scarred hand, the back of it covered in tattoos. "We're friends."

Everyone in the room was suddenly very quiet.

Loren eyed him, but slid her hand into his. His grip was solid and warm, and his hand all but swallowed hers. "Friend," she repeated, squinting at him. "I'm...friends...with Darien Cassel." She glanced about the room, her hand still in Darien's. His steel rings were cold; he must've gone outside. "I'm...friends with the Devils."

"And a few Angels of Death," Darien said, that voice doing weird things to her body again. It was the nicest voice she'd ever heard—she didn't need to remember the last six months to know that.

"Wow, who *am* I?" Loren laughed, the sound breathy, and as she smiled she saw Darien's attention dip to her mouth. The sudden shift in where he was looking made those chills come back, though this time they were accompanied by a rush of heat that made her head spin. "I sound a lot more interesting than I remember."

Darien's mouth twitched with a smile. "May I help you up?" That hand was still grasping hers.

"Okay." She slid to the edge of the levitating tabletop and slowly lowered one foot, toes pointing downward.

Gods, could this ridiculous thing be any higher? The ground seemed unnecessarily far away—or maybe she was simply too short, her leg stretched to its limit. Darien's hold on her never faltered, and she found herself leaning into his arm for support—and felt impressed when that arm didn't shake.

Finally, her toes met ground. The water on the floor was a comfortable temperature, like bath water. Slowly, she lowered her other foot and eased off the table.

As soon as she was standing, her legs folded under her like a fawn's.

Darien's heavily muscled arms circled her waist, catching her before she could fully fall. "Are you okay?" His face was *right there*—so close to her own that she could see the flecks of silver and darker blue in his eyes. There wasn't much air in her lungs, and he was stealing the last of it.

"I think so," she squeezed out, overly aware of how she was awkwardly half-crouching in the water, Darien's solid arms keeping her from fully sitting. She was grateful for that; she didn't want to get all wet.

"Do you mind if I carry you?"

Did she? She didn't think so, but her stomach felt all wiggly, and her mouth was suddenly bone-dry. "Okay."

He picked her up and hooked her legs around his waist. When he'd offered to carry her, this wasn't exactly what she had expected, but...she felt safe. Secure. And she didn't need to walk, which was probably for the best right now.

Darien carried her into the hallway, the others trailing behind them. Loren was so close to Darien, there wasn't really anywhere else to look but at his face.

Her eyes drifted to the small tattoo below his ear. Yup, that was real, all right. She couldn't believe this was happening. She was being carried by Darien Cassel; she felt like pinching herself.

Darien stopped at a private change room with a frosted window in the door. "Ivy?" he called. "Joyce."

Ivy stepped around him and into view. "I've got her bag."

Darien's eyes found Loren's. His eyelashes were so dark, they almost made his eyes look kohl-lined. "Ivy and Joyce will help you get changed."

Slowly, he lowered her. She hadn't realized how tightly her legs were gripping his waist, her knees catching on his belt and pockets as he placed her on her feet. Ivy immediately linked her arm with Loren's right, Joyce coming to the other side to take hold of the left—the one Darien was still holding onto.

He hesitated, his fingers tightening slightly on her wrist.

After another second, he let go, his touch leaving little bursts of heat on her skin.

Ivy and Joyce helped her into the small room. With one last glance in Loren's direction, Darien shut the door.

The light in here was mellow—easy on the eyes. Loren sat down on the bench that was anchored to the wall, her legs still shaking like a newborn deer's, even now. She placed her hands on her knees, trying to still the tremors.

"This is so embarrassing," she muttered. Even walking that short distance had sprinkled her vision with stars.

"You've been in a coma for almost two weeks," Ivy said. She set down the bag and unzipped the main compartment. "Embarrassed is the last thing you should feel right now."

"She's right." Joyce sat down on the bench beside her. "It's normal for your energy levels to be low, and your body weak. You'll be back to normal in no time." Her 'normal' wasn't much better, but she would take it over this any day. Joyce took out a juice box, stabbed it with a straw, and passed it to her. "Drink as much as you can. Your blood sugar is low."

Loren drank the whole thing—a blend of different berries—in several long gulps, watching as the serpent-entwined rod that was tattooed on her forearm shifted from a glaring red to a soft blue.

Joyce took the empty carton from her. "Better?"

She nodded. "Yeah, a bit better." The stars were fading now, thank gods. She watched as Ivy started pulling clothes out of the bag and set them on the bench. Her favorite hooded sweatshirt, a lacy bra and underwear, stretchy black pants, a pair of socks. "Please tell me you have deodorant in there."

Ivy smiled. "Sure do."

"I probably smell."

Joyce laughed, her gray eyes twinkling. "Your body has been kept in a magical state of limbo. Trust us when we say you don't smell." That was a relief, though she still had to resist the urge to smell herself. The first thing she'd do when they got to wherever they were going was shower and brush her teeth.

Ivy passed her a stick of deodorant anyway. "Tah-dah!"

Loren popped off the lid and put on several swipes. "Thanks." As soon as she was done, Ivy put it away again. Loren recognized her toiletry bag, her hairbrush, her cell phone and charger. There was even a romance novel with a bookmark in it. Pretty much her whole life was in that bag, and these people had managed to pack it all up for her.

"You're all so kind," Loren said. "It's..."

"Not what you expected?" Ivy smiled, one inky brow tilting up.

"I guess so. And I didn't really expect the...leader of the Seven Devils to carry me around like I'm a stuffed animal."

Ivy's smile grew; her features looked so much like Darien's, though she smiled a lot more than he seemed to. "Neither did we."

"Does he do that a lot?" Her stomach fluttered.

"Only when he needs to. And when you don't mind, of course."

"And we're...friends?"

"Mm-hmm." Something seemed off about her tone, but Ivy was speaking again before she could prod. "Let's get you out of that bathing suit." She eyed her up, her attention flicking from the one-piece to the clothes folded on the bench. "This might be a little tricky."

DARIEN WAITED on the other side of the change room door, an arm propped up against it, his forehead resting against the wood.

Standing here like a possessive psychopath might've been an overreaction, but Loren could barely walk, for fuck's sake. And besides that, she hadn't even been awake for one measly hour. He refused to take chances.

"I know you're staring," Darien said. He sensed Jack, Tanner, and Kylar peeling their eyes off him in unison.

Tanner said, "We're just looking out."

"And worried as balls that you're gonna snap," Jack added.

Darien lowered his arm and turned around to face them. "No one," he said quietly, "is to tell her the truth about her and I."

Kylar said, "Isn't that a bit counter-productive?"

"She's going to figure it out," Jack said. An ill-timed smile pulled at his mouth. "You can't stop touching or staring at her."

"If she figures it out, fine," Darien said. "Great. But she's barely been awake for an hour. Did you see how she reacted to being friends with me? With us? I'm not about to give her a heart attack by telling her she's fucking me too."

Jack snorted.

Darien gave him a dark look. "What about this is funny?"

Jack's smile vanished.

"What about taking her to see a Healer?" Kylar asked. "They've been known to help people who suffer from amnesia."

"If we check her into a hospital, the imperator will know we're here," Darien said.

"What about Atlas fucking with the records?" Jack asked.

"I can," Atlas offered.

"Let's give it a few days," Darien decided. "Give her a chance to settle down, see if any memories come back on their own. And in the meantime, keep your mouths shut." He shot Jack an extra-long stare. "I'm not asking you to agree with me, but I *am* asking you to respect my decision."

Tanner offered, "I think it's a good idea, for now. Her heart already gets all weird when you're around."

"And her heart's already delicate," Darien said. "So let's not push it, shall we?"

"Are you ever going to tell us what you traded the Widow?" Jack blurted.

Darien glanced between the three solemn faces of his friends. Tanner had tried asking him this question—once. So had a couple of the others.

Kylar said, "Traded? What'd you trade?" His eyes flicked to Jack and Tanner. "What happened?"

"Now's not the time," Darien said. Joyce and Ivy's voices grew louder with their approach. Darien raised a finger at Jack. "Not a word." Jack held his hands up in surrender.

The change room door opened behind Darien, and he stepped out of the way.

Loren was walking on her own now, though Ivy and Joyce were still holding hands with her. She wore her favorite hooded sweatshirt—the baby blue one she'd worn to his house that first time—black leggings, socks, and—

No shoes. Shit.

"We forgot her shoes at Roman's," Ivy said.

Darien stared—and stared and fucking *stared*—at Loren. Fuck, Jack was right, he couldn't take his eyes off her. But she was looking at him too.

This was the best thing that had happened to him in two weeks—her being awake. A part of him feared he was dreaming.

"Roman?" Loren echoed, her big, ocean-blue eyes still glued to Darien. They were both bad as hell at not staring. "Have I met him?"

"Not yet." Ivy was the one who answered, and Darien was glad for it, since his tongue had turned into a useless deadweight. He just kept staring at Loren like a lovesick puppy.

She was going to figure it out. He'd be surprised if they lasted a full twenty-four hours without her confronting him. But overwhelming her was the last thing he wanted to do.

And goddamn, her heart skipped every time she looked at him. The heart that had stopped twice in the last two weeks. Had he not been so hopelessly in love with her, he might've left out of fear that he'd be the one to stop that beautiful heart from beating again.

Darien managed to find his voice. "If you're okay with me carrying you, I will."

Loren's hesitation was brief. She nodded, and then slowly let go of Joyce and Ivy's hands.

The door to the corridor opened, and Tanya walked in, her face lighting up with surprise at the sight of Loren being awake. But she didn't have a chance to say anything.

Because Loren's legs gave out. And her heart sped up to a rate that Darien instantly knew was fatal.

46

CALIGINOUS ON SILVERWAY
YVESWICH, STATE OF KER

Darien dove, catching Loren before her head could hit the ground. "Syringes!" he barked. *"Now!"*

The others launched into motion at once. Joyce passed him the case containing the serum, while Ivy took his place supporting Loren's head. Lightning-fast, Darien unzipped the case and filled a syringe with a vial of serum.

Loren hadn't passed out yet. Her eyes were still open—glued to his face and wide with fear.

But her heart was too fast.

He rolled up her sleeve and inserted the syringe into a vein in the crease of her arm. "Just keep breathing, Loren," he said, pushing his thumb down on the plunger. "Keep breathing. Eyes on me." He pulled the syringe out, threw it aside, and rubbed the glowing spot in her arm, urging the serum to move through her bloodstream quicker. And then he shifted his hands to support her head, instead of Ivy doing it.

"Darien," Loren squeezed out. "My heart—"

"I know, sweetheart, I know. Just breathe. *Breathe.*"

She tried, but it wasn't fucking working. Her heart was getting faster—it was practically one long beat.

Tanya stood near the back of the group, murmuring frantically to Tanner—something about calling an ambulance.

"No fucking ambulances, no cops!" Darien shouted—

His own heart sped up as he heard Loren's pulse fade. The pulse point beneath his thumb was so weak, he could barely feel it.

Loren's eyes glazed over, her lids fluttering shut—

"Turn the chamber on!" Darien thundered over his shoulder.

Tanya's face went white.

Darien's next words were so loud, they shredded his throat. "TURN THE FUCKING CHAMBER ON—*NOW!*"

THEY SAY that when a person's time arrives, a part of them knows.

Loren couldn't remember anything from the past six months, but she remembered what death felt like—how desperate she was to stay alive while on the other side.

And she knew that this moment might be her last.

When she blinked, she saw that tree again, glowing above a pond. Saw that endless sky full of stars, and the path that went everywhere and nowhere at once.

She fought against those images, forcing herself to stay here, *right here* with these people. These people who cared for her, the people who deserved to be remembered—

Darien Cassel was carrying her into the chamber. She was so far gone that it took her a minute to realize that he was running—running and cursing and screaming his lungs out.

He set her down on the table on her back. Rain began to float through the room, followed by tiny balls of light that looked like fireflies.

The door banged shut, and Darien took one of her hands into both of his. "I've got you, Loren. I've got you. I'm right here—"

A broken sob shuddered through her teeth. "I don't want to die."

"You're not going to die."

Warm tears slid down her cheeks. She felt cold, and the edges of her vision were turning white and foggy. "I don't want to die, Darien." Her voice echoed and faded, and she saw that tree again, calling out to her. She recoiled, a frantic sob clawing up her throat. She didn't want to go back— she wanted to stay here. "I'm not ready—"

"I'm right here, sweetheart," Darien said. "I'm right here, Loren, and I'm not leaving. I'm not leaving you, okay?" He leaned closer, flattening her shaking hand over his thumping heart. "Feel that?"

She nodded. Blinked. More tears slipped down her face.

"Focus on my heart," Darien said. "On my breathing. I want you to breathe with me, Loren. Can you do that?"

She nodded again, clinging to the feel of his warm chest under her palm. She tried to blink away the fog obscuring his face, but the motion only set free more tears, salty moisture on her lips.

Darien drew a deep breath, accentuating the movement for her, and she copied.

Wisps of light, color, and shadow danced through the room like woven thread. They reminded Loren of the natural phenomenon that crossed the northern skies once every one hundred years—a sight she had always wished to see in person. But no matter how beautiful, she kept watching Darien, copying his breathing, her hand rising on his solid chest with every determined inhale.

She couldn't look away from him. Even if she'd wanted to, she couldn't, and she didn't want to. She wanted to keep looking at him.

"Breathe, sweetheart." Darien's voice—strong and commanding attention, but still managing to be gentle for her—worked wonders at relaxing the tension in her body, even more than the dancing lights and the breathing technique and whatever the humming chamber around her was doing. The opalescent walls shone and rippled with colors. "Just breathe." He inhaled again, and she copied.

In. Out.

In. Out.

In... Out...

In...

Out...

Eventually, her heart regained a steady, strong beat. No longer was it weak, fluttery, or too fast. She felt rejuvenated, like she'd had the best sleep of her life, or had finally found water after a long stretch of time spent in dry heat.

Another few minutes, and Darien spoke. Very quietly, this time. A whisper meant for only her. "Loren?"

She nodded. Swallowed—or tried to, her mouth and throat too dry. "I'm okay."

He gathered her to him, lifting her upper half off the table so he could wrap his arms around her. Hugging her, she realized later than she should have. Darien Cassel was hugging her. His chest was pressed against hers, his body warm and solid and strong. In his arms she felt...safe. Really safe.

He was a really good hugger.

"You're good at this," she mumbled into his shirt, her hands grasping his arms. She took a deep breath, testing her heart, the inhale filling up her lungs with the scent of him. He smelled really good. Was there anything about this man that wasn't appealing? That didn't call out to her? She'd been around him for less than an hour, and there didn't seem to be anything that didn't make her react all funny around him.

Friends. Maybe she had developed a crush on him these past six months, and this was why she felt this way. She wouldn't doubt it; it seemed like something she would do—crush on the man who'd decided to be her superhero instead of her villain.

"Mmm." Darien's voice rumbled through her chest. "I don't hug very often, but whenever you want one, I'd be happy to oblige."

Her arms closed around his muscular back, her fingers curling in his shirt, gripping the soft material in fists. For several minutes, they just breathed together. All around them, the rain and the lights kept shivering, even long after Loren's body had stopped its own violent trembling. She was calm now, her heart a normal, steady rhythm, and she was no longer cold.

Darien had a lot to do with that.

No—he had *everything* to do with that.

"Thank you," she whispered, gripping him tighter.

They both knew she wasn't referring to the hug, but Loren kept clinging to him, because that hug was pretty great too.

He was pretty great.

"I dreamed of you," Loren whispered, remembering that awful night in the Old Hall, when it had started raining. Flooding.

Darien pulled back a little—just enough to see her face. There was a crease between his dark brows, and she fought the urge to smooth it, to trace his features with the tips of her fingers.

Loren swallowed, tears flooding her eyes. "I was drowning, and you... you helped me breathe again."

47

MOTEL 58
STATE OF WITHEREDGE

Shay had jumped into the shower the minute they'd made it back to the motel, using the hot water to ease the tension in her muscles, a migraine splitting her skull in two.

Not just that, but she also used the water to calm herself down. Her heart was still racing from the close encounter in the desert, the sight of all those eyes peering at them from the darkness haunting her every blink.

Now, as she stepped out of the shower, her body wrapped up tightly in a towel, she breathed a sigh of relief that the migraine was gone.

But something arguably worse hit her like a battering ram.

A Surge.

She stumbled forward and gripped the counter, knocking over a few of her things.

"Shit," she hissed. Magic surged through her, causing her muscles to bunch up and her eyes to blacken with the Sight. "Shit, shit, *shit.*"

Why here? Why now? Why, with Roman right there in the motel room—

"Shay?"

"Shitballs," she mouthed, eyelids slipping shut. He was right on the other side of the door now—she could feel him.

He rapped a knuckle against the wood. "Everything okay?"

"Fine." The word was a strangled gasp. Another wave of magic ripped through her, and she panted, gripping the counter, unable to stop the embarrassing, breathy whimper that slipped out of her.

A heavy pause.

"Shay." Roman's voice had a different tone this time. "Pup, are you touching yourself?"

"What?" she shrieked. "No!"

"Then what's going on?"

"Go away, Roman." She stumbled over to the toilet, lowered the lid, and sat down, shaking in her towel. Wet hair dripped down her back, making her shiver harder. "Please, just...go away."

Gods, she hated this! It felt like her body was burning up inside, like an electrical fire had started in her veins—

She was able to fend off the Sight long enough to see wisps of shadow sneaking under the door.

"Roman!" She fisted the towel to her chest, her knees knocking together. "What the hell do you think you're *doing?*"

A tendril of black turned the lock on the knob. A moment later, the door swung open, and Roman appeared in the doorway. He leaned against the side jamb, hands in the pockets of his tattered gray jeans.

Shay spoke through her teeth. "Just so you know, when a girl barricades herself in the bathroom, it means she wants to be left alone." She winced as another wave of magic coursed through her.

"You sounded like you were dying in here." He studied her face—the eyes that were flickering black again. "You're having a Surge, pup. Nothing to be ashamed about."

"You need to leave."

He eased his hands out of his pockets and stepped into the room—

She shot to her feet. "Shadows," she bit out, burying her hands in the towel. "Stay away from me."

"What's going on with you?"

She tried to back away, but there was no room left. The backs of her legs hit the bathtub, and she fell—

Roman made the mistake of catching her. He launched himself forward, his hands closing around her forearms.

"Roman!" she shouted. *"Don't!"*

Lightning surged out of her body and into his.

He swore. Let go and stepped back—but it was too late.

Veins of lightning crackled up his arms, snaking into his shoulders and neck. It sparked up the sides of his face and wove between his teeth, lighting up his eyes with ghostly silver light—

"Shadows!" she cried. She reached for him, but froze before she could make the mistake of touching him again. Gods, if she'd killed him—

The crazy bastard suddenly started laughing—actually *laughing,* even as his eyes watered from the pain. "Wooooo!" he howled, throwing his head back like a wolf and rolling his shoulders. "That's the most alive I've felt in years!" His mouth stretched into a feral grin that showed off all his teeth.

Shay couldn't help but laugh herself, though hers was breathy and strained. "Usually, a zap smaller than that brings men like you to their knees."

He clucked his tongue and flexed his jaw until it popped. "Pup, there are no men like me."

She held up a hand and backed up—as far as she could go without falling again. "Don't come any closer." She curled her fingers into a tight fist, and when lightning sparked in her palm, pricking her skin like a hundred little knives, she quickly lowered it. "Please."

He leaned against the wall. "So...storm magic." His eyes now danced with amusement instead of lightning. "Is that what causes your headaches?" Damn, he was smarter and more observant than she'd given him credit for.

"The medication takes the edge off the pain, but it also...hides it." Gods, she'd never told anyone this. "My magic."

"You don't want Athene to know."

She shook her head. "If she finds out I'm more powerful than Anna, she'll never let me leave the Riptide."

A crease formed between his brows. "You want to leave?"

"Both of us do. It was the plan, until..." She swallowed. The pulse on the side of her head intensified, and she felt prickles of warning in her palms. She uncurled her fingers, looking down to see tiny little silver sparks dancing across her skin like stars.

Roman was studying her closely, with the kind of empathy in his eyes that she would never have expected from someone like him. "Is there anything I can do to help?"

She closed her hands and looked at him, closer than she *should* look at someone who was so damn appealing.

The bands of muscle in his arms. The edge of his sharp jaw. The angle of his cheekbones. The shape of his mouth, the left corner flecked with a small scar... Her own mouth dried out at the sight of his, and she felt her core tighten with hot, pulsing need. Her body was coiled like a spring, and before she knew it, that pulse between her thighs doubled in intensity.

Roman immediately picked up on the shift in her body. "Shay—"

"I want to be alone."

He shrugged away from the wall. "Oh please, you're not going to hurt me, Shayla."

She waved him toward the door. "Out, Shadows!"

"Shay—"

"Out!" Lightning crackled in her palms, singeing the air between them and making him flinch.

Finally, a *normal* reaction from this lunatic!

"Out!" she said again, waving.

He stepped back, and as soon as he was through the door, she slammed it shut and collapsed on the toilet lid, hanging her head between her knees.

That was a close one—not just her lightning, but...

She had nearly thrown herself at him. And throwing herself at Roman Devlin was a mistake she couldn't afford.

A moment later, she saw his shadows creep under the door again, only this time he locked it for her.

"You're welcome." His voice was a husky croon.

And damn was that voice sexy.

She refused to think about it, instead clamping her legs together and squeezing the towel in tight fists, hoping—praying—the Surge would pass quickly.

It didn't.

Three hours later, Shay tossed and turned in bed, unable to fall asleep. Usually, when a Surge this bad decided to assault her, she was lucky enough to be alone and able to deal with it in privacy.

Tonight, she had two problems, neither of which she could get rid of. One: taking care of the Surges that peaked her sexual drive usually involved a vibrator; she'd gotten so used to those little silicone miracles that she didn't have nearly enough practice with her hand. The problem? Her vibrator was miles away, lying uselessly in the drawer of her nightstand. Problem number two: Roman Devlin was in the same room as her.

As the minutes ticked by, and she tossed and turned in bed, desire burning hot in her core, she rolled onto her side and slipped a hand between her legs.

In the bed beside hers, Roman was quiet and still. Sleeping, she hoped. She also hoped that damn dragon of his was sleeping too, or Sayagul would get her in trouble immediately with her squawking.

Slowly, she eased her hand into her underwear and began to tease her clit.

Desire swarmed her in a hazy wave, even stronger than before, and she had to bite down on the blanket to keep quiet.

Gods, it already felt so good. But she was afraid to move any faster, and the longer she kept rolling that sensitive bundle of nerves under the tip of her finger, the piercing in her clit applying pressure that was so good—but not quite enough to get her off—she realized she was in over her head.

She couldn't do this. Maybe she should go out to Roman's car, where she could take care of herself in private—

"Shay." Roman's deep, husky voice filled the room.

Her hand froze. Her clit pulsed with need.

Damn it. Did he *ever* sleep?

She tried to peer at him through the dark without moving, and saw that he was lying on his back. Clothes still on, one knee propped up. One of his hands lay palm-up on the bed beside him while the other brought a cigarette to his mouth, his focus on the ceiling. He took a deep drag, the cigarette burning bright red.

"What?" she bit out.

A pause. And then: "Come here."

Goddamn it, why did that have to sound so inviting?

So inviting, in fact, that she found herself getting up and moving to the side of his bed.

"What?" She scowled into the dark. She was so tired and agitated, she felt dizzy just standing here.

He patted the bed beside him.

She laid down on her side—facing him. There was enough distance between her and Roman that it would—should—be easy not to touch each other.

Roman brought the cigarette to his mouth for another drag, and blew a stream of smoke at the ceiling. "Keep going," he said.

She stopped breathing. Maybe it was the cold quilt, but she found herself shivering. What did he mean 'keep going'? He wanted her to touch herself right in front of him while he stared at the ceiling like some kind of psychopath? Could this trip be any more mortifying?

"Don't be shy." He dragged out the three words.

And goddamn her, she was so turned on by the invitation, so in need of release, that her hand skimmed down the plane of her stomach, her fingers inching toward the pulse between her legs. With Roman lying so close to her, looking more attractive than anyone had a right to, her own touch made her shiver, promising a taste of the pleasure that had eluded her moments before.

She slid her hand into her underwear—the cherry-print thong she'd purchased yesterday—and began to touch herself.

Roman didn't look at her. He just kept smoking, entirely unaffected by her. This was—

Stupid. Embarrassing. It could've been a really hot moment, but instead he was ignoring her. Was this some sort of game? Seeing how easily the seal pup would obey the Shadowmaster like some mindless idiot?

Maybe she *was* a mindless idiot. It sure felt like it. But then again, the desire that assaulted a hellseher's body during a Surge could make them do all sorts of embarrassing things in the name of desperate arousal.

She was about to stop when Roman abruptly turned to face her and propped himself up on an elbow. With his free hand he grabbed her by the chin, fingers digging into her flesh, and kissed her—

Well, kind of. His mouth was on hers, his pierced tongue pushing her lips apart. He blew softly into her mouth, velvet smoke filling hers. It didn't feel romantic, not one bit, but it felt...

Good. It felt good. Especially with her fingers rolling that metal ball into her clit.

A soft whimper climbed up her throat as the taste of Roman and tobacco filled her mouth. Smoke streamed out her nose, and as she touched herself, she arched her body against Roman's, her nipples hardening against the press of his solid chest. She moved her fingers faster, desperate for the release that was building with rapid speed—

He broke the sort-of kiss, but stayed close enough that their noses were touching. And then he let go of her face and drew her hand out of her pajama shorts. Nudged her knees farther apart.

"Roman." His name was a strangled gasp on her tongue, but her protests tapered off at first contact—at the feel of his hand intruding in her underwear, lace digging into her ass cheeks as he pulled on the front band. She was hot and tight, and she needed release now.

Roman said, "Yes or no?"

"You're asking for my consent when you just put your mouth on mine without permission?"

He tugged on her underwear again. "Yes or no?" His eyes burned with an intensity that scorched her to the bone.

She nodded.

"Say it, Shayla." His use of her full name caused her core to pulse with a vengeance. She wanted him to touch her, and she wanted it right now. Her clit was hot and wet and pulsing, and if he didn't touch her this goddamn instant, she might start begging.

So she told him, "Yes."

That hand wasted no time in slipping into her panties. She had never been so grateful for her medication having contained her lightning magic as his warm, rough fingers circled her swollen clit—

And stilled when they found the metal ball.

"What's this?" His face was too close to hers. Close enough to kiss. She felt seen—*too* seen.

"I'm not going to answer that."

His laugh was dark; it reminded her of the very shadows he wielded.

She squirmed, urging his hand to move.

His thumb stilled—teasing. Taunting. She couldn't take it. "So needy," he crooned.

"Shut up and touch me, Shadows."

She felt, more than she saw, him smile in the dark. But he started touching her again, thank gods, circling that spot, using the piercing to apply more pressure. The way every movement, no matter how slight, caused her legs to twitch told her he'd had a lot of practice with his hand between women's legs.

"Stop staring at me." She meant for her words to come out strong, but they were punctuated by gasps that told him exactly how little effort it would take for him to bring her over the edge.

"If I'm going to touch you, I'm going to look at you."

Again, her legs twitched around his hand. Why did he have to be so good at this? Then again, maybe his skill level was for the best—it meant less time spent with that wicked hand between her legs.

Because this was bad. So bad. He was a Shadowmaster, and she was a Selkie, and they shouldn't be doing this, shouldn't be together at all—

She wet her lips. Roman kept staring at her, that hand moving sinfully, that tiny ball grinding into her sensitive flesh.

"Bet that feels good." His deep, husky voice raked across her skin as he came closer, passing his mouth over hers. "Doesn't it?" He rubbed her harder, kneading that little ball into her flesh. Bolts of pleasure zipped through her, making her legs twitch, her stomach muscles fluttering.

Her body tightened, and she bit down on her lip, rolling her hips in tune with his hand. But he just kept edging her, the sadistic bastard, lightening his touch every time she got close—

"Beg." The one word was like gravel.

And the word Shay said in return was as weak and fluttery as she felt. "What?"

"I want you to beg."

"Fuck you!"

A dark, quiet chuckle raked across her skin, the sound causing her nipples to tighten. "Right now, *I'm* fucking you, pup. And you're going to beg me to let you come."

"I'll leave," she threatened.

"No, you won't." He increased pressure, and she arched her back, her legs trembling. "You won't, because you want this. You want to come so badly, you're fucking dripping." He slid two fingers down, teasing her entrance, and back up, swirling them around her clit. It felt so good, she fucking *whimpered*—and she swore she saw Roman's eyes turn black. "Now, beg," he commanded, that deep, rough voice giving her full-body chills. "Say 'please'."

"Please."

"Louder."

"Please." She rolled her hips, but he didn't give her what she wanted.

"Say, 'Please, Roman'."

"I hate you!"

"Say it, and I'll give you the best orgasm of your life." He lightened up again—

"Shadows," she gasped, her body begging for release. "Gods—*please.*"

"You're not very good at obeying, are you?"

"Please, Roman."

"Good pup," he praised. She scowled. "Very good. Say my name when you come." He picked up speed, and gods it was so good, she could feel herself dripping on the bed—exactly like he'd said. "My real name, Shayla." With his free hand, he pushed up her shirt, exposing her breasts, and bent over her, strands of his hair skimming her chest. As he rubbed her clit, his mouth found her nipple, and he tugged on it with his teeth, making her moan.

"Roman," she cried. Gods, she wasn't even there yet, and she'd already called his name—

"That's it, Shayla," he crooned. "Just like that." He rubbed her harder. Faster. That tongue circled her hard nipple, his piercing pressing deep, teeth grazing the tip. And his fingers...gods, his fingers—

She fractured like a lightning bolt. A breathy moan slipped through her lips, followed by his name, just like he'd asked. Pleasure cascaded over her in a hot wave, causing her whole body to tense and release like a bowstring.

"Ooooh, there it is." That damned voice was rich with approval, the cadence drawing out her orgasm until it was almost too much.

He eased off the pressure and speed, but kept touching her, the sensitivity making her legs twitch like lightning was shooting through them.

"You're a quiet thing," he accused, bowing his head to kiss the skin between her breasts. The gesture made her heart skip in a different way.

His eyes flicked up, locking on hers. No doubt he'd heard the skip.

"Sorry to disappoint," she panted. Another whimper slipped out of her as he hit an ultra sensitive spot. She didn't want him to stop, didn't want this to be over, and it didn't seem like he did either.

"Want another one?" Did he really just ask her that?

She wet her lips that still tasted like him; Roman tracked the movement in the dark. "Please." Gods, she'd never begged for a man before.

But no man had ever made her come this hard before.

He pushed up onto his knees, so he was hovering directly over her instead of beside her...and moved his hand lower, teasing her slick entrance.

Her breathing hitched. Was he going to—

Yep, he sure was. He pushed his middle and index fingers inside her, as deep as they could go. She hadn't realized how badly she wanted him inside her—any part of him, fingers or cock, she didn't care—until he was filling her up, stretching her heat.

And then he began to move—to fuck her with that hand. And damn was he rough.

Her hands went behind her head, fingers grasping the headboard for dear life. As his fingers thrust in and out of her, she drew her feet up, her knees inching toward her chest—both from pleasure and the momentum of his hand as he fucked her. Hard. Fast.

"Someone's greedy," he breathed, his voice extra husky.

Her toes curled. "I hate you," she said again. Because it was better than admitting that she liked this—easier than admitting that she liked him.

She did, didn't she? She liked Roman Devlin.

She was so fucked.

"I hate you too," Roman growled through teeth that glinted in the dark like a wolf's. "Do you want it harder or faster?"

"Both." She wanted him to fuck her until she passed out.

He obliged her. The headboard slammed into the wall, and gods—her whole body was shaking. Again and again and again, his fingers delved in and out of her, deep as they could fit.

"Such a wet, tight little slut." His free hand flattened on her pelvis, pressing down as his other fingers worked inside her. "Aren't you? Shayla Cousens, coming on my fingers, like a tight, wet little slut—" That filthy mouth and the added bit of pressure from his other hand made her come again, just like he'd said, her insides fluttering around his fingers.

The release was so intense, she cried out his name again. A series of breathy moans escaped her as the throes of that second orgasm finished her off; okay, so maybe she wasn't as quiet for Roman as she was for the men she'd been with before him. She couldn't see him in the dark, but she felt appraisal rolling off of him, as tangible as the honey-sweet pleasure coursing through her body and making her limbs twitch.

"Fuck," Roman growled, "I love when you say my name." He slowed his movements gradually, as if savoring the moment, before stilling.

Shay was breathless and spent, her body limp, the slam of her heartbeat filling her ears. Roman stayed right where he was, staring at her as if she was the most tantalizing thing he'd ever seen.

"Still hate me?" His fingers were still inside her, filling her up.

"More than before."

A laugh scraped out of him. He pulled his fingers out of her—

Something was burning her ass cheek. She shrieked and bucked her hips.

Roman snatched up the cigarette that was burning her flesh before it could light the bed on fire. And then he leaned across her body, his shirt draping across her bare breasts as he butted out the cigarette in the ashtray. The scent of his cologne or body wash, whatever it was, rolled over her, and she was ashamed when she breathed it in.

She pulled her shirt back down to cover herself.

And then he rolled onto his back, as if *he* was the one who'd just experienced two mind-blowing orgasms.

"Go to sleep," he said.

She rolled her eyes. "What a kind dismissal."

But she got up on shaking legs and returned to her own bed, crawling under the covers and pulling them up to her chin.

"You're welcome," he drawled.

"I could've handled that on my own." But the Surge was gone now, and she was so grateful she could kiss him.

Of course she wouldn't. That was a terrible idea. And it would be her second terrible idea of the evening if she turned it into a reality.

He was a mistake. A very gorgeous mistake. The kind she'd make over and over again because she just couldn't resist.

Roman said, "It would've taken you three hours, seal pup."

In the corner of the room, where he slept upon her backpack, Nugget stirred awake, peering at him with wide eyes.

"Not you," Roman said.

Nugget curled up and went back to sleep.

Shay refused to think about what just happened. That was a problem for the morning.

"Promise me something," Roman said out of nowhere.

"What?" she asked, still panting, staring up at the ceiling with eyes bright with pleasure.

"Don't get attached."

"Don't flatter yourself," she scoffed. "There's no chance of that."

A beat of silence, the atmosphere impossible to read, and then the Wolf said, "Good."

Now that her body was spent, her heart still slowing, she fell asleep quickly, parts of her still throbbing from Roman's touch.

48

CALIGINOUS ON SILVERWAY
YVESWICH, STATE OF KER

Loren kept her arms around Darien Cassel's neck as he carried her out of the chamber. He'd put on a leather jacket, the worn material cool under her palms. The gun that was tucked away by his hip pressed into her with every stride, but she didn't try to shift to get away from it—she only hoped she wouldn't accidentally nudge the safety off. That would be the cherry on top of a fantastic night.

Singer was finally awake and walking beside them, nipping playfully at Bandit's cropped ears. Like Bandit, Singer was now as black as a silhouette.

Loren had yet to find the courage to ask how and why Singer was a Familiar. She would save that for another day, when she didn't feel so...overwhelmed.

She stared in wonderment at her surroundings as Darien carried her down the white hallway that looked more like a tunnel and into the main room of Caliginous on Silverway. The others followed, surrounding them in a protective half-bubble, the assortment of different footwear clapping against the walls. The air in here smelled of peppermint and lavender; Loren breathed it in, her attention drifting to the cone- and sphere-shaped diffusers on a big desk, cool mist spiraling out of the spouts.

A redheaded witch sat behind the desk in a swivel chair, keys clacking under her fingers. She rose as they entered, her hands smoothing down her black pencil skirt. The place was empty of other clients, but the janitors were here, paying them no mind as they vacuumed and mopped the floors, earbuds in.

Darien spoke to the witch as they crossed the room, making a beeline for the exit, his bass voice bouncing through the room. "I'll wire you the money later tonight, but we might need to come back."

"Whatever you need," she said, "I'll be here." She smiled at Loren; she was very pretty. "I'm glad to see you're awake."

"Thanks." Her legs began to slip, and Darien hoisted her up, tightening her thighs around his waist. It still seemed strange that he preferred to carry her like this, but she decided it was the better option. She felt more involved this way, though it felt very intimate, and every time he had to adjust her, she felt the twitch of butterfly wings in her stomach, and her heart pounded loudly enough, there was no way he couldn't hear it. "Have I met her before?" she asked him.

"No." He pushed the button to open the elevator, and they all filed in. He knuckled another couple buttons on the panel on the inside, and the doors slid shut with a hiss.

"Where are we going?"

"Roman's," Darien said. "How are you feeling?"

"I'm okay right now."

"Your heart sounds stable," he agreed.

The elevator lurched, dropping down to the ground floor at a speed that was jarring. Loren avoided looking at herself in the mirrors—surrounded by four of the Seven Devils, their leader carrying her, his hands wrapped around her thighs. This all still felt like one really long, really bizarre dream.

A dream she hoped she wouldn't wake up from.

"We should get her some food," Joyce said. "I gave her some juice when she got changed, but I think she should have more." Gods, listening to them talk about her like this made her feel like a child, but she was well aware that she needed as much help as she could get, and she wasn't about to refuse it.

Darien glanced down at her, their faces so close that she had to duck her head to keep her nose from skimming his. "Let's see your tattoo."

With Darien balancing her, she unwound her arms from around his neck and pushed up her sleeve. The serpent-entwined rod was glowing red again.

"You'll need to eat straightaway," he said.

"I think I'll be okay until we get to Roman's." Wherever that was. She had so many questions but didn't know where to start.

"If you feel faint or off in any way, I don't care how minor, you'll let me know. Okay?"

She wound her arms around his neck again, pulling the sleeves up to cover her fingers—avoiding direct skin contact. Touching him made her feel all funny inside, and truth be told she was worried about her heart. It was already unpredictable, and it seemed to act out of line whenever Darien was around. She wished she could control it. "Okay."

The elevator doors slid open with a hiss, and they walked out into the bottom floor of the skyscraper. A wet floor sign sat in the center of the big open space, water shining around it.

Darien carried her through the revolving doors at the front of the building, to the two vehicles that were parked by the curb. One was a big black truck with matte-black rims and smoked taillights. The other was a black sports car with a stream-lined body—beautiful and aggressive, the model clearly very expensive. The windows of both were heavily tinted.

It was rainy and cold out, the wind nipping at her cheeks and ears. The buildings on this street were very new and tall, skyscrapers piercing a sky studded with stars. Traffic zipped down a multi-lane road, tires clacking on cobbles that were drenched with rain.

"We'll take the car," Darien said, letting go of one of her thighs so he could retrieve a set of keys from the pocket of his jacket. He tossed them to Tanner. "We'll meet you back at the house."

He set her down on her feet beside the car and opened the passenger's-side door. She got in, breathing in the scent of leather and the same mouth-watering cologne she could smell on Darien.

Once she was buckled in, he shut her door. Loren peeked at him as he rounded the car, street lights gilding his hair, and got in his side. As he started the engine, Loren noticed a succulent keychain attached to his keys.

"Are you cold?" he asked her, his fingers moving to the dials.

"A little."

He turned on the heat and tilted a couple vents so they were facing her.

And then he put the car in drive and ripped out into the street, the others following in the truck. The glow of street lights pulsed through the sunroof.

Loren tucked her numb fingers between her thighs. "Where are Dallas and Sabrine?"

"Angelthene."

"Do they know I'm here?"

"Yes."

"What about Roark and Taega?"

"Roark supported my decision to bring you here. He was the one who told me about the Caliginous Chambers." Loren found that hard to believe, but she knew Darien was telling the truth.

A lot more than new and unlikely friendships seemed to have happened these last six months.

Yveswich was a beautiful place. The majority of the buildings were old, most of the roads cobbled instead of paved. The blend of new technology with old architecture turned the urban sprawl into a sight to behold; she couldn't pull her eyes off her window. There were waterfalls on higher terrain, a few draining into the ocean at lower levels, and canals wove like water serpents through the districts, permeating the air with the fresh scent of water.

Loren was so distracted by how much there was to see that the drive to Roman's house was over in no time. She had a sneaking suspicion that Darien was watching her very closely, but every time she turned to look at him, he was purposely staring elsewhere.

Darien rolled the car to a stop in front of a wrought-iron gate. A giant white house with a dark blue roof sat at the end of a driveway that glistened with rain.

He lowered the water-streaked window and flicked a button on the dial pad of the intercom. "Pax," he called, "open the gate."

A young, nasally male voice said, "What'th the path-word?"

Darien rolled his eyes. "Eugene, for fuck's sake, it's Darien. Open the gate, it's pissing out here."

"So bossy," Eugene grumbled. The line disconnected with a squeal, and a moment later, the gate rolled open.

Darien drove around a fountain, the others inching up behind him, and came to stop in front of the garage. The doors groaned open, and he pulled in, the others claiming the spot on the right.

"I want you to feel comfortable here," Darien said as he shut off the headlights and cut the engine. "Roman isn't here, but his little brother Paxton is. That was Eugene who just spoke to us—he's Kylar's brother and Paxton's friend. You can trust everyone in this house—I promise."

"Okay."

He unbuckled his seatbelt and opened the door. "Wait right there, I'll help you get out."

Loren undid her belt. "I think I'd like to try to walk on my own."

But Darien was already out of the car, his hellseher speed allowing him to reach her door far quicker than any mortal.

He opened it, and she stepped out, moving carefully. She still felt so weak that even the slightest movements sprinkled her vision with stars. It was frustrating, to say the least. She had spent her whole life dealing with problems that involved low blood sugar and fainting spells, but never anything quite this bad.

Darien shut her door for her and walked at her side. He moved at her pace, one hand extended toward her. "I'm going to keep my hand like this," he said, his deep voice echoing in the cavernous garage. "If you feel like you're going to fall, or if you need the support, don't be afraid to hang onto me."

She was so focused on walking, on willing her muscles to obey her commands, that she nearly didn't answer. She managed a very subtle nod—and a glance at Darien's hand. Callused and flecked with silvery scars.

The others were behind them—murmuring and lingering by the vehicles. Waiting for her to get in first, she realized. When she reached the few steps that led up to the interior door, she grasped the rail and climbed them.

As she moved, she peeked up—and up and up—at Darien. Gods, he was massive. She wondered how tall he was.

The inside of the house was even more beautiful than the outside. A couple pre-teens stood just down the hall—both of them gangly, one with white skin, the other brown. The first one had freckles on his nose and dark, messy hair. The second had a mop of black curls and thick, round glasses that were too big for his face.

"She's awake!" the freckled one exclaimed with a dimpled grin.

"Loren, this is Paxton," Darien said, still moving at her pace, that hand ready to catch her. He gestured to the other kid. "And that's Eugene, the paranoid termite."

"Holy smokes!" said Eugene with a thick lisp. "I didn't think she was going to wake up!"

"Eugene," called a gravelly, unimpressed voice from somewhere behind Loren. Kylar Lavin. "Shouldn't you be sleeping?"

"We're hungry," Paxton pouted. "You guys have been gone for hours."

The kids stepped aside, making room for the group to get down the rest of the hall and into the house. The high ceilings were vaulted, and there were a lot of big windows, making the house feel open and impossibly more spacious. The rooms were very clean, and what she could see of the furniture appeared new, hardly any wear on anything. Straight ahead was a massive living room and kitchen, candles that smelled of vanilla glowing on the coffee table and kitchen counters. The light above the stove was on, but aside from that, it was pretty dim in here.

Darien flicked a switch in the living room, brightening the low lights above the television and fireplace.

Loren's head spun. She stopped by the fireplace, hand moving to grasp the corner of the wall.

Darien was at her side immediately. "May I?" He held his arms out toward her in offer.

She nodded, and he scooped her up again, though he picked her up differently this time—one arm behind her back, the other under the backs of her legs. He carried her into the kitchen, used his boot to kick out a chair at the table, and sat her down, waiting to make sure she was balanced before letting go.

She cleared her throat. "Can I have a shower?" She really wanted a few minutes alone to process everything—and scrub her hair. Ivy and Joyce might have claimed she didn't smell, but she would feel better if she had a proper shower—her first in two weeks. What she could see of her hair was tangled and frizzy; she wasn't looking forward to trying to fight a brush through it.

"Eat first, and then you can shower." Darien stalked to the fridge and pulled open the door. He rummaged through the contents, the glow from inside reflecting on his boots, jacket, and the rings that were shaped like skulls and horned monster heads. "What would you like to eat?"

"It doesn't matter." She watched him continue to look through the fridge. "You're not actually going to cook me a whole meal at this hour, are you?"

"I can help," Ivy offered as she walked in, the others trailing behind her. She shed her trench coat and hung it up in the foyer just down the hall.

Darien straightened, those remarkable eyes meeting hers. "You need to eat."

"Yeah, but we could just...order something?"

"Is that what you want?"

Eugene hissed, "That's what I want."

"I want whatever's easiest." Her eyes flicked to the others who were now scattered throughout the kitchen and living room. Everyone was watching her, even the young boys. "And whatever everyone else wants," she added.

"And I want you to stop trying to please other people," Darien said. He shut the fridge door and took out his phone. "Name a food and I'll order it for you."

She nibbled on her lip. "A chicken burger, please." That should be easy enough to find. And relatively cheap. "And maybe a salad?"

"Communication's still disabled?" Darien's question was for Tanner.

"I never lifted it," Tanner replied. He pulled out a chair at the kitchen table.

"I'm going to need that other credit card number."

Tanner paused in the midst of sitting down. He dug his wallet out of the back pocket of his jeans, found a paper card tucked in one of the slots, and handed it to Darien.

It didn't take Darien long to find a restaurant that had chicken burgers on the menu. "Extra pickles?" With his focus on his phone, it took Loren a second to realize his question was for her.

As he waited for an answer, his eyes flicked up to meet hers.

She chewed on her lip. "Does it cost extra?"

He didn't answer, and as soon as he was done placing her order, he added the others' to the bill.

"Did anyone remember to pack my wallet?" Loren asked.

Jack sat down on the couch and turned on the TV. "Darien's your wallet." He laughed, and Kylar, who'd grabbed a video game controller off the coffee table, punched him in the arm. "Ow!"

Loren's face warmed. "Absolutely not."

Darien was staring at her, his phone frozen in those heavily tattooed hands. "You can pay me back when we get home. But for now, you won't worry about any price tags. Deal?" She supposed she could live with that.

"Okay." She nodded. "Deal."

The food arrived after thirty-five minutes.

Once that first bite was in her mouth, the flavors exploding across her tongue, Loren realized just how hungry she was. She ate the burger—and the extra pickles—faster than she'd consumed anything in her life, for once not caring that everyone was stealing glances at her, all of them more interested in her than they were their own food. Especially Darien, who was the last to dig into his food. Loren was one of the first to finish, beat only by Jack and Tanner, who were quick to retreat into the living room and continue their game. A racing one, by the looks of it. *Rushin' Racers,* the screen said.

Now that everyone was finished eating, Kylar stood and cleaned up the takeout containers. "Pax, Gene—off to bed. Right now."

Paxton had nearly made it to the living room. "Aww, man!" he complained, tossing his head back. "Do we have to?"

Eugene said, "Can we play just one race?"

"It's almost Witching Hour," Kylar pointed out. He dumped the takeout containers into the trash. "Bed—now."

The kids dramatically stomped to the staircase and made their way upstairs, calling "Goodnight" over their shoulders with a grudge.

Loren looked across the table at Darien. He was already watching her, like always.

He spoke before she had a chance to. "Would you like to see where you're staying?"

Loren got to her feet. "Yes, please."

HER ROOM WAS on the second floor.

The bed was a king, the back wall covered in a floor-to-ceiling window that showed off the backyard and the night sky. The furniture was made of light-colored wood, the bedding puffy like a cloud. An adorable salt lamp sat on the end table, glowing orange.

That glow was drowned out by the ceiling light as Darien flipped it on. "Ivy's grabbing your bag from the truck," he said. He stood just behind her, his presence electric. "If you need any help, she'll be there." Loren knew he was referring to the effort it would take her to shower, but she was feeling better after eating. Stuffed, actually. And energetic. She hoped that meant she'd be able to fully make it through a nice, hot shower without falling down or fainting. Or worse.

"The bathroom's two doors down," Darien said. "It's all yours."

She turned to face him. "Where are you staying?"

"Right across the hall."

"In that room?" She pointed.

Darien nodded.

She nodded, too. "Okay. Umm—thank you. For...everything."

The corner of his distracting mouth twitched, but it wasn't a real smile —not at all. "You're welcome."

"Are you..." She swallowed. Cleared her throat. "Are you okay?"

A beat of silence. And then: "Just worried about you."

Silence stretched between them. The honesty and raw emotion in his statement made her forget, for a moment, how to speak. And the way he was looking at her, his eyes roving her face... He looked like he was afraid he might never see her again.

Finally, she found her voice. "I'll let you know if I need anything?"

He nodded once. "Please do."

And then he was gone, shutting the door softly. She listened as he crossed the hall and entered the room across from hers. Heard the sound of a light switch being flipped on.

Now that he was gone, she felt...a little empty. She chalked it up to nerves and the fact that he'd hardly left her side since she had woken up in this foreign place, with these people who were strangers yet not, and headed into the bathroom to shower.

"You look exhausted," Ivy said as she walked into Darien's room.

He sat on the side of his bed, elbows on his knees, hands clasped between them. Staring across the hall at Loren's partially closed door. She'd taken a long shower, but had managed to get through it without any help.

He considered that a win.

"I am," he admitted.

Ivy sat down beside him. "Here's what's going to happen." She folded her hands in her lap. "I already talked to the others—we're all going to take turns watching Loren. And you—" She poked him in the shoulder with a glossy black nail. "—are going to sleep. If anything out of the ordinary happens, I promise we will wake you up."

He just kept staring at Loren's door, the orange glow of the salt lamp outlining the sides of it. He hadn't even taken off his jacket yet, or his boots. Had kept them on throughout dinner, in case he had to race her back to Caliginous on Silverway. "I don't know if I'll be able to sleep, even if I try."

"Try," she insisted. "You're no good to her if you're dead on your feet. She's alive, Darien. She's breathing. You need to live with this reality right now, and take the opportunity to get some rest. I promise nothing is going to happen tonight, and if it does—"

"You'll wake me up."

"You got it."

He nodded. "Thanks, Ivy."

She stood. "You're welcome." When she made it to the open door, she paused. "By the way, I removed a few things from her bag." It took Darien a second to understand what she meant—that she was talking about condoms and lingerie. His sister was a sharp one.

"Good thinking."

She smiled. "Night, Darien."

He kept sitting there for nearly thirty minutes, listening to Loren's heartbeat. Her Avertera talisman was back on, so he couldn't see her, but she was breathing.

She was alive, and she was breathing.

Eventually, he grew too tired to stay awake. He took off his boots and clothes and climbed under the covers in nothing but his boxers.

Fuck, it felt good to not have anything restricting him, to feel the soft press of clean sheets on his skin. He rolled onto his side so he was facing the door—staring out into the hallway as his eyelids grew heavy.

He passed out quickly. And for the first time since Loren had fallen into a coma, he slept through the night.

No nightmares. No dreams.

49

DESERT HAVEN HOTEL
FOXHILL, STATE OF WITHEREDGE

Max tipped his head back into the pillow with a groan as Dallas's tongue flicked against the head of his cock.

She knelt between his legs on the bed in their hotel room, her fingers wrapped firmly around his cock. Her soft hand stroked him up and down, matching the beat to the movements of her mouth.

Goddamn, was she good at this. Every day she got on her knees for him was the best day.

He thrust his hips up, driving himself deeper into her wet, perfect mouth, his hand fisting the silken hair at the back of her head. "Fuck, don't stop, Dallas," he growled. He kept thrusting, and she took him in deeply each time like a champ. "Don't stop."

His legs quivered, and his heart thundered in his chest. The hot, wet slip of her mouth and the flick of her tongue drove him wild. He was almost there—

A sharp knock came at the door.

He cursed, forcing himself to slow. Dallas began to slide her mouth back up to the crown, but he stilled her with a hand tightening in her hair.

"Go the fuck away, Delaney!" he yelled. There was no way he'd let that prick ruin this.

He picked up speed again, each thrust desperate and determined. Dallas obliged him with a tightening of her lips around his cock, teeth grazing just enough—

Another knock. Max bit down on a new retort as an unfamiliar female voice called through the door, "Police. Open up."

MAX WOULD'VE TOLD Dallas to answer the door, had he not already announced to the cop that a male was in the room.

Another knock came as he finished pulling on a pair of jeans, his cock still hard and throbbing beneath the denim. Talk about blue balls.

Dallas hung back, fixing her hair and wiping her mouth as Max stalked up to the door, not bothering with a shirt as yet another impatient rap of knuckles vibrated the wood.

He unlocked the deadbolt and opened the door, angling his body in a way that would hide the Devils tattoo below his ear.

A cop in her late thirties greeted him with a smile, entirely unaffected by his naked, scarred, and tattooed upper body. She was in uniform, her reddish-blonde hair tied back in a slick bun. "Evening." She took in the room behind him with sharp, green eyes, her smile inching toward a grin. "I apologize for the interruption."

The LED lights in the parking lot behind her bathed the pavement and cars in white. The rooms they had rented were on the ground floor, the doors accessible from the outside. The sun had set hours ago, but it was still hot and dry out, the towering palm trees lining the roads standing still as statues.

"It's not a problem," Max said tightly. "What can I help you with, Officer?" He glanced at the police car parked nearby—an undercover one, blue-and-red lights flashing.

"We're hoping you might be able to tell us if you've seen this individual." She held up a photograph.

The girl was about the same age as Dallas—beautiful, too. Her strawberry-blonde hair was long and thick, her eyes green, skin pale and lightly freckled. No tattoos or piercings, from what he could see—nothing that would make it super easy to recognize her if she came around. She would probably wind up being thrown into the infinite pile of missing young women who never found their way back home.

"I haven't," Max said.

"Perhaps your lady friend wouldn't mind having a look."

"Red," Max called quietly. He turned, keeping his tattoo out of sight.

Dallas stepped up to his side. She hooked her hair behind an ear and checked the photo, her wings tucked away with a spell. "I'm sorry," she said, shaking her head. "I've never seen her before."

The officer slipped the photo into her jacket. "She went missing three days ago. Her family is worried sick about her. You'll be sure to call the station if you see her."

"Sure thing," Max said.

She dipped her head in farewell. "Thank you for your time."

Max watched her leave. She got in the passenger's seat of the cop car, her partner heading to the driver's side. As the man got in, he glanced up at Max, just for a second, before disappearing inside, the edge of his mouth curving with the hint of a smile. They were both hellsehers, though they moved with the kind of confidence he strictly saw on Darkslayers.

Lights oscillated through the parking lot as they drove out. But—

Max thumped out of the hotel room, loose bits of gravel digging into his bare feet. The pavement was still warm from the day's heat.

The stop sign the car passed didn't reflect any light except the beams from the headlights. Neither did the glass of the dark windows across the street.

"Max?" Dallas stepped over the threshold. "What's going on?"

"The lights," he whispered, wondering what it meant and if he'd lost his mind sometime during the drive here. "They weren't reflecting."

She took a step closer. "What?"

Max's phone buzzed on the table inside the room. He stomped back inside, Dallas trailing behind him. He grabbed it and read the message from Malakai.

> **MALAKAI**
> That cunt cop come to your door too?

> **MAX**
> Get out here.

Max waited by the door, leaning out of it to see if Delaney would listen for once in his life and get the hell out here. As he waited, he sent a message to Dom, asking him and Blue to come outside too.

Two minutes passed, and then they were all there. All except Aspen, who was in the shower.

Malakai walked over in bare feet, no shirt on, damp hair tied back in a low knot. Dominic and Blue came from a room on the opposite side of Max's door and joined the group.

"What?" Malakai bit out, stopping a couple feet away.

"The cop. Describe her to me."

"Reddish-blonde hair, green eyes, full cop getup. What's going on?"

"What about the car?"

"What about it?"

"What did it look like?"

"Like a fucking cop car. Fuck's sake, Reacher, are you on drugs?"

"Just describe it to me."

Malakai lifted his hands in exasperation. "Black. Bars separating the front seats from the back. Lights were on."

"Did you notice anything funny about the lights?"

Malakai widened his eyes with exaggerated intensity. "No, but maybe that's because I'm not on drugs."

"That would be a first," Dominic said.

Malakai bared his teeth at him.

"If you knew Max at all," Dallas cut in, "you'd know he would never take drugs." She looked up at him, her eyes soft with understanding. "He's telling the truth."

"It was like a glamor or something," Max said.

"Glamor?" This question came from Blue.

Dominic explained, "It's when a person uses magic to trick people into seeing something else."

"That's what I did to you earlier—when I disguised you," Dallas said. "Here—watch." She took her stave out of the back pocket of her jeans and waved it through the air. She spoke an incantation in a low, robotic voice, and a moment later the color of her lips changed to ruby red.

"Like the Eye," Blue said, squinting at Dal's face.

"The Eye?" Max repeated. "Isn't that a place in—"

"Spirit Terra," Dallas finished. "Maybe that's the type of magic that gives veneficae the ability to use glamors?"

Dominic cut in. "But glamors only work on *people.*"

"Unless," Dallas insisted, "someone's figured out how to use it on objects too?" It was a stretch, Max knew. Glamors had been around for far longer than any of them could hope to live. There was no way someone could have suddenly figured out how to do something that seemed so... simple. It would've already been done.

"Or," Malakai said with an edge of frustration, "he's reading into it too much."

"Did you make sure she didn't see your tattoo?" Max's question was for Malakai; he trusted Dominic would've taken the necessary precautions to hide his identity, but Malakai could be so cocky that Max never knew what to expect from him. And from the sounds of the text he'd sent before coming out here, Malakai had given the cop enough attitude to warrant calling her a 'cunt'.

Malakai narrowed his eyes. "No, I pointed right at it and said 'I'm

Malakai fucking Delaney'!" he snapped. "What was so funny about the lights, anyway?"

Max looked out at the stop sign. "They weren't reflecting."

"And this is your great mystery?"

"Piss off, Malakai," he growled.

Malakai walked away. "Thanks for the dismissal. Call me if anything actually important happens." He disappeared into his room and shut the door.

Dominic smirked and fluttered his wings. "He's a dick, hey? Why'd you even invite him?"

"Darien wanted me to work with him." Max sighed. "And because he's a tough motherfucker." With Darien and the others gone, there was a shortage of tough people around, and he had no idea what he might encounter out here, in this place so far from home.

"If it's any consolation," Dominic said, "I believe you." He turned his head to look at the road just beyond the parking lot, black hair gleaming like fresh tar. "I don't really get it, but I believe you."

Max shook his head. "Maybe Malakai's right. But...something about that cop seemed...I don't know. Odd." He chewed on his lip as he looked out at the stop sign again. "I just don't know what."

MALAKAI SLAMMED the door to his hotel room and reached for the deadbolt.

'Scaredy-cat,' said a misty voice. Creature was on the bed closest to the door, chewing noisily on a chunk of banana.

Malakai glared over his shoulder. "Are you making a mess in my bed?"

Creature merely kept smacking with his mouth open.

Malakai reached for the deadbolt again. Paused. Curled his fingers into a fist. Behind him, Creature snickered.

"Ah, fuck it," he muttered, relenting. He turned the deadbolt, feeling stupid for doing it when so many spells were on the room.

"I think that's the first time I've ever seen you use locks," Aspen said from behind him.

He turned to see her standing in the bathroom doorway. A white towel was wrapped around her damp body, and she was using a smaller one to squeeze the excess water out of her hair.

He forced himself to stop gawking and said, "A cop came to the door. Looking for a girl who went missing three days ago."

"And?" She leaned against the doorjamb. "You're not usually this rattled about a cop. Or about anything, really." She flashed him a pretty smile.

The corner of his mouth tipped up, but soon the trace of humor was fading. "Max thinks it was weird. He said the lights on the cop car weren't reflecting."

Her copper brows pulled together. "Has he been drinking?"

"He claims he's sober, but now I've got the heebie-jeebies." He shook his shoulders as a chill crawled up his spine. Walked to the end of the bed—the one closest to the door—and sat down. "I think I was a little hard on him." He braced his hands behind him on the mattress.

Aspen clucked her tongue. "You?" she teased with a gasp. "No!"

He smirked. "Are you wanting to go to sleep right away?"

"I was thinking of watching a show." She discarded the hand towel on the bathroom counter behind her.

He reached for his backpack that sat on a chair by the door and took out a bag of sour candies. "Get over here then and share these with me." He tore the bag open and popped one into his mouth, feeling the sugar dissolve on his tongue—

And grimaced as his taste buds freaked out from the acidity.

Aspen laughed. "Sour?" She crossed the room, a knee peeking through the slit in her bath towel with every stride.

"Very," he squeezed out.

She shook her head and climbed onto the bed. "You and your sweet tooth."

50
HELL'S GATE
ANGELTHENE, STATE OF WITHEREDGE

Travis shoved a heaping handful of popcorn into his mouth. It was so salty, he needed water, pronto.

Lace sat beside him on the couch, partially watching the movie on the flatscreen as she sketched in her pad of paper. The side of her hand was blackened with graphite.

She looked over her shoulder. "Is that your phone?"

"Is what my phone?"

"That buzzing."

He craned his neck, following her line of sight to the kitchen—

And the Hob hiding behind the cereal boxes, his form silhouetted by a mysterious, bluish glow.

Travis set aside the bowl of popcorn. "Morty?" He got to his feet, wiping butter on his sweatpants. "What are you doing?" He walked into the kitchen.

It was late, and all of Hell's Gate was quiet and dark, aside from the television.

And the clicking of tiny fingers on a device that didn't belong to him.

Shit.

"Hey!" Travis hurried up to the fridge. "Mortifer, you'd better not be texting Darien, or he's going to be very mad—"

The Hob was nattering into the microphone—little bleating sounds that none of them could ever understand.

And then he literally chucked Travis's phone at him.

Travis fumbled it, barely catching it before it smashed on the ground.

He was about to scold Mortifer when he saw the name on the screen, and the timer on the ongoing call ticking away.

He lifted the phone to his ear. "Max?"

"I have no idea what he just said," Max replied, every word tense. "What's going on? Why'd he have your phone? Scared the piss out of me."

"I don't know, Lace and I are watching a movie. He took it when I wasn't looking. Did you call me, or did Morty call you?"

"I called you. I wanted to check in. Everything good?"

"Uhhhhh..." He remembered the time they'd spent with Tamika today; her fear of being watched; her obsession with Spirit Terra. Remembered the hidden tunnels used by the Phoenix Head Society, and the group photograph with Cyra, Bleddyn Sands, and Roark and Taega Bright in it.

"Trav?"

"Everything's...good...," Travis began slowly, "in the sense that nothing...bad...is happening at present."

A beat of silence. "What the hell does that mean? Should I be worried?"

"No, not worried," Travis said quickly. "We learned some things, but they're not really important ATM, you know?"

Another beat of silence. "Whatever it is, can it wait until we get back?"

"Yeah." He ran his fingers through his hair, the strands still damp from his shower. "Yeah, I think it can. How's it going over there?" He grabbed a glass from the cupboard and filled it with water from the fridge.

"A couple weird things, but what else is fucking new. Can't really complain. Have to wait until morning to continue, though."

"You sound pissed about that." Travis drank.

"How'd you know?" he joked. "You'll call if whatever it is turns into an emergency, right?"

"Yeah, you bet." He set the empty glass by the sink. "Have you...heard from you know who?"

"Nothing. I'm assuming that means everything's okay."

"Yeah. Hope so." Whenever Travis wasn't busy, his mind strayed to Roman and Paxton. A part of him felt envious that the others got to see his brothers instead of him. He wondered what Paxton looked like now, how much he'd grown. Wondered how Roman was. Wondered if they both thought about him as much as he thought about them.

Max said, "I'll see you soon, then. In a few days, I hope."

"You got it."

"Catch you later."

Travis hung up. Turned toward the fridge. "Morty?"

The Hob didn't turn. He sat on the fridge with his knees tucked up to his chest, arms wrapped around him.

"You don't need to be that way," Travis scolded softly. "They're going to be back soon. You're overreacting."

He disappeared in a puff of smoke.

Travis sighed. "Can't say I didn't try." He turned around to see Lace peering at him over her shoulder, the glow of the television flickering across her features.

"He left, didn't he?" she asked.

"Yup. Probably hiding in the upstairs fireplaces again."

She returned to sketching. "As long as no monsters come out of them," she muttered.

Travis grimaced. "I have nightmares about that now."

He crossed the room and sat back down. He rarely had nightmares, but he'd had several since the Blood Moon, and he knew what Loren had told them about the fireplaces was to blame. Hell's Gate was their home, the one place where they never had to look over their shoulders. And now, Travis often found himself staring into the gaping mouth of the fireplace in his suite in the late hours of the night, wondering if anything lurked in there. Watching. Waiting to devour him.

He grabbed the remote and turned up the volume. "I don't think I'll be going to sleep for a while now." Not until he was too tired to keep his eyes open. Ever since Darien and the others left, he awoke several times throughout the night, the lack of group protection putting him on edge. The Seven Devils functioned best as a unit, and since the day they'd formed, they had never been separated like this.

Lace kept drawing, but Travis knew her well enough to spot the tension in her shoulders. "Want to sleep on the couches?" she asked.

Call them cowards, but those creatures in Spirit Terra were the kind of monsters everyone should fear.

Travis nodded. "Absolutely."

51

MOTEL 58
STATE OF WITHEREDGE

Dawn poured into the motel room.

Shay slowly stirred awake, stretching her limbs and groaning softly into the pillow.

She'd had a really good sleep. Which was unexpected, given the gods-awful Surge that had assaulted her mind last night—

Wait a minute...

She bolted up in bed, clutching the covers to her chest. Glanced about the room.

Roman wasn't in here.

Had last night actually happened? Had she dreamt it?

The longer she sat there, fully waking up, she realized that she had not dreamt it at all. She was slightly sore between the legs, and when she dared to look, she saw a tiny burn mark on her ass cheek.

Shay hung her head in her hands. *"Seriously,* Shayla?" she hissed into her palms. She thrashed her feet under the blankets and squeezed her hair in tight fists. She wanted to rip it out! Maybe that would teach her not to do such...such *idiotic* things. "Why are you so *stupid?*"

She'd let Roman touch her, and she'd enjoyed it—two big mistakes.

"Okay, don't freak out," she told herself. She lifted her head and took several slow, deep breaths. "Don't freak out. He probably doesn't think it was a big deal. And it *wasn't*—it wasn't a big deal. It. Won't. Happen. Again." She took another few breaths—and groaned. "You are such an idiot!"

She threw the blankets aside, swung her legs over the side of the bed, and headed into the bathroom to get ready—and hide from Roman before he came back.

Maybe he'd truly left this time. The thought didn't make her panic as much as it used to. If he *did* leave, it was probably for the best.

Once she was showered and dressed, her hair and teeth brushed, she put on her shoes, gave Nugget a pat on the head as she left, and made her way to the communal kitchen. She half-expected Roman to be in there already, stuffing his face with the double-chocolate muffins and croissants he ate as if he might die tomorrow. But he was nowhere to be found.

She made herself a cup of green tea, sweetened it with honey, and loaded up a paper plate with fresh-cut melon, sliced strawberries, a bunch of grapes, and a couple of those mini chocolate-drizzled croissants Roman loved so much. But hey, she liked them too. She grabbed the tea and plate and made her way through the parking lot.

It was boiling out, her shirt clinging to her back. Her lungs felt heavy, and although the sky was blue as could be, she felt the beginnings of a migraine prickling at the back of her neck. Joy.

There was no sound out here but the buzz of cicadas and the hum of air conditioning units as she passed by the other motel rooms.

She went inside room number nine—still no Roman—and kicked the door shut.

"Hungry, Nugs?" The Familiar had moved from the chair to the bed. He was lying on his belly, cooling himself in front of the streams of air conditioning. He looked at her with a shrewd gaze as she toed off her shoes and sat down beside him. "I brought you some grapes." She plucked one off the vine and set it on the mattress in front of him.

The way the seal pup was eyeing her told her exactly what he was thinking. Having a Familiar meant having an animal to answer to—all. The. Time. Nugget knew all her mistakes, and he didn't always let her off the hook easily.

She rolled her eyes. "I made a mistake, okay? I won't be making it again." She popped a square of cantaloupe into her mouth.

Nugget refused to eat. His eyes narrowed.

She nudged the grape closer. "I promise."

He slowly lowered his head, eyes still on her, and sucked the grape into his mouth, swallowing it whole.

Shay cringed. "I don't know why you do that," she said, eating—and chewing, like a normal being—a sliced strawberry. "You can't taste anything if you're not chewing." She gave him another grape. This time, he rolled it around on his tongue before swallowing it—whole, again.

Strange animal.

When she was finished eating, she got up and went to her bags, the prickling of her headache intensifying, and dug around inside the pockets until she found her medication. Checked to make sure Roman's necklace was exactly where it should be, in one of the side pockets—

Uh-oh.

She poked around inside, searching for the fine silver chain and pendant. The necklace that she had made sure, every single day since she'd left Yveswich, had *stayed. Put.*

There was a tiny hole in the bottom of the pocket. A hole just big enough for Roman's favorite pendant to slip through.

Her heart gave a painful thump. "Oh no," she mouthed. She lifted a shaking hand to her lips.

Nugget blinked at her with round eyes.

"I'm fucked," she told him. Nugget whined.

The motel room door swung open, and sunlight flooded the room.

Shay dropped her bag and straightened.

Roman stood in the doorway in a ripped shirt—no surprise there—and gray jeans, his tall form silhouetted by sunlight. He tipped his sunglasses down and looked her over. Closely. "You alright?"

"Fine," she croaked. She cleared her throat.

He nodded slowly, looking like he didn't believe her. "I don't want you to get all weird about last night. That was just a friend helping out a friend. No big deal."

Right. Roman had probably helped out a lot of friends.

She didn't know why that made her stomach twinge like someone was shoving a fishhook through her belly button.

"Come here for a sec." He started to walk out the door again, but paused and turned back around, looking at her over his sunglasses again. "What were you doing?"

"Nothing."

"It doesn't look like nothing."

"I was getting changed," she stammered.

He slid his sunglasses into place. "Come with me." And then he walked out into the sunlight. The sound of gravel crunching under his boots gradually faded with distance.

Shay hurried over to her hiking boots and stuffed her feet into them. She laced them quickly, grabbed her key off the table, and left, telling Nugs that she would be right back.

Roman was waiting for her by the dried-out swimming pool. Feet braced apart, arms crossed.

She stopped several feet away from him. "What?"

"Have you taken your medication yet today?"

"No, why?"

He gestured to the pool, the rings on his fingers reflecting the bright sunlight. "Fill it up."

She blinked. "What?"

"I'm giving you a magic lesson."

"That's what you call a magic lesson?"

He merely inclined his head toward the pool. "Fill it up," he repeated.

"You're going to just stand there and bark orders at me? No instructions, nothing?"

"Fill it up."

"Gods, you are such a parrot!" she snapped.

He walked to one of the poolside loungers, plopped himself down, and retrieved the beer he'd left on the ground.

"It's eight in the morning," she pointed out.

He took a swig. Rested the bottle on his thigh. "Fill it up."

"You get to drink while I bust my ass practicing magic?"

"Quit complaining and fill it up."

"If I hear you say that one more time—"

"Fill. It. Up."

The blood in her veins boiled. It felt like her head was going to explode.

"Fill—"

"Roman," she warned. Lightning prickled in her palms. So much for all that work they'd done last night.

All the work *he'd* done. With that hand that was wrapped around the beer bottle. That big, rough hand.

Gods.

"It," Roman continued, a wicked glint in his golden eyes. Her blood became scalding, and the lightning in her palms crackled up her forearms. *"Up—"*

A crack of thunder severed the sky. The sound was so loud, Shay's stomach and heart leapt in unison, a chill skittering across her skin.

She looked up in disbelief—at the clouds that were gathering above a landscape that never saw rain.

When Roman smiled, Shay couldn't help but smile back.

He lifted his beer to her in a toast. And then he drank, long and deep, as the first drops of rain fell from the sky.

"I cannot stand you!" Shay thundered.

The rain had stopped after only a few minutes, and Roman had immediately taken to berating her for her 'indolence'. They stood across from each other by the pool, nearly chest to chest, both red in the face from screaming at each other.

She continued, "You are annoying and obtuse and—and—"

"And what?" Roman growled.

"And a pain in my ass!"

"That's one thing we have in common."

She shoved him in the chest and stomped away.

"I believe you owe me a thanks!" he called.

She whirled back around, her hair fanning out over her shoulders. "For what? For barking orders at me and calling it a lesson?"

He shrugged one shoulder. "Yup."

"You," she pointed at him, "are a stuck-up asshole."

"Did you not touch me just now without zapping me?"

"Can you be *quiet?*" she hissed, eyes darting around.

"Answer the question."

She crossed her arms. "I might've," she gritted out.

"You don't need medication, Shayla. Unless it's the kind that'll help with the pain. What you need is to learn how to control your magic. You need outlets. Keeping all that power pent up inside you is only going to wind up hurting you in the end."

She started pacing.

"Magic is not meant to be caged," he went on. "Whether this is about Athene or not, you're going to have to face it eventually. And when you do, you can't be afraid of it."

"My doctor told me quitting cold turkey is dangerous."

"So wean off of it."

She stopped pacing. "I caused it to rain after being off of it for less than twenty four hours," she whispered. "Who knows what'll happen if days pass. Weeks."

"So find out."

"All it takes is one little lightning bolt in front of my mom, and she'll lock me up like she did Anna." She stared out at the horizon—bright again. No clouds, no rain. No one had even noticed—no one but them. Her and Roman, the slayer who knew too much. "I'll never get away from the Riptide."

"Tell me why Nugget's still a pup."

She blinked at him. "What?"

"Why's he still a pup and you're—what, nineteen? Twenty?"

"I turn twenty next month." She studied him. "What are you getting at?"

"How long have you been taking your medication?"

"Since I was eight, I think. My dad got me on it when he was still alive. He told me to never stop taking it and to never tell anyone that I'm on it. And I don't want to stop taking it because..." She swallowed. Admitted, "It hurts too much. The headaches."

"That's the pent-up magic."

"Not all of it. I have scar tissue in my shoulder and neck muscles." Her hand drifted toward the left side of her neck—to the pain no one could see. The pain that was so bad some days that she was forced to stay in bed with an ice pack. "I had a swimming accident when I was very young. I tore the muscles, and they never fully healed."

"And they act up from the weather?"

She nodded; even that simple action caused a new bolt of pain to zip through the muscles and into the base of her skull. "The tissue swells up and hurts. Makes the migraines worse."

Roman came closer. One step. Two. "It's your choice." His voice was softer now. "I understand if you don't want to live with the pain, but I don't think you should run from your magic forever. If you want my suggestion, I say find an alternative that doesn't suppress the magic but helps with the pain and the swelling." He walked away, his shirt brushing against her arm as he passed. She hated herself for breathing in the scent of his cologne as it washed over her like a tidal wave. "Of course, it's only my opinion," he called over his shoulder. "What do I know?"

Shay stared at the few drops of rain that were drying in the pool—the pool that had been cleared of debris and dirt, likely thanks to Roman. It didn't escape her that he'd had enough faith in her to clean it out.

And she'd barely caused a sprinkle.

"Shayla?"

She turned just in time to catch the apple he tossed her way. A green one.

Roman flashed her a handsome grin that showed off a dimple she'd never seen before. "Nice catch, small fry."

52

ROMAN'S HOUSE
YVESWICH, STATE OF KER

When Loren woke up, it took her a few minutes to remember where she was.

Sunlight filtered weakly into the room, the rays falling across the puffy, cream-colored blankets she was bundled up in. Through the window, she could see the craggy hills of Yveswich piercing a sky of slate gray. Magpies bickered in the yard, but Loren refused to count them.

Paws padded on the hardwood. She rubbed the sleep out of her eyes and sat up. Singer stood on the floor beside the bed—looking up at her with floppy ears, one drooping more than the other.

"Hey, buddy," she whispered.

He wagged his tail, the motion sending tendrils of black mist curling through the room.

Loren braced herself before throwing the blankets aside, the cool air raising a chill on her skin. She stood and tiptoed to where her bags sat on the dresser.

"Let's go get ready," she said to Singer, who continued to watch her, tilting his head from side to side whenever she spoke. "I'm starving." It smelled like someone was already making breakfast—waffles or pancakes, if the toasty, buttery smell was any indication. And coffee. Her stomach growled.

She pulled on a white sweatshirt overtop of her pajama top and made her way to the bathroom to go pee and brush her teeth. Her hair was still partially damp from her shower last night, making her feel even colder. She dried the last of it with a blow dryer and fought through the tangles with her paddle brush. Before she went downstairs, she found her slippers tucked into a side pouch in her bag and slipped her feet into them.

And she might've passed Darien's partially closed door at a slower pace than necessary. She wondered if he was up yet.

The kitchen was alive with activity. Paxton, Kylar, Joyce, and Eugene were eating breakfast at the table, while Ivy, Jack, and Tanner made waffles—well, more of them. The table was cluttered with pitchers of juice, bottles of maple syrup, bowls of fresh blueberries, and plates stacked with hot waffles.

Loren drifted into the room, unsure how to go about announcing herself. This whole situation still felt so bizarre.

And the Darkslayers looked more like an ordinary family than they did the heartless killers rumor spoke about.

"Morning, Loren!" Ivy said. Her cheery smile made Loren immediately feel more at home. "Hungry?"

"Very."

"Have a seat. We're making blueberry waffles. There's some on the table already—go on and help yourself." She dipped her finger in the batter and poked Jack in the nose with it.

He wiped it off with the back of his hand. "Gross."

"Can I help you with anything?" Loren asked.

"Relax—you're our guest!" Ivy shooed her toward the table, bits of batter flinging off her fingers. Technically, they were all guests here, but Loren wasn't about to argue.

"Coffee?" Tanner offered. "There's also tea."

"Tea, please. But I can get it."

"So can I," he countered. "Have a seat, I'll make it for you."

Kylar was flipping through the newspaper. "Tea's in the cupboard two doors to your left."

Loren sat down beside Paxton, who was shoveling huge bites of waffle soaked in syrup into his mouth, a long-limbed puppy Familiar draped across his lap. Eugene sat beside him, watching a video on his tablet. He was so distracted by the screen that he missed his mouth when he tried to take a bite, soaking his cheek in syrup.

Tanner opened the tea cupboard and sifted through the many boxes inside. "What kind of tea would you like?" he asked her.

"What kinds are there?"

"Peppermint, orange pekoe, jasmine green, hibiscus, a boatload of white tea, and...matcha." He pulled a tiny tin out of the cupboard and held it up.

"That one, please." She couldn't remember the last time she'd had a good matcha latte.

Kylar said, "Do you even know how to make it?" He flipped to the next page of the newspaper. The front-page headline spoke of new strains of the Tricking and the desperate need for more healthcare workers.

"I can read instructions," Tanner said, already scanning the label with sharp, gray eyes. He grabbed the eyeglasses that were perched atop his head and put them on. Loren fought a smile, knowing he didn't need those to see. "Who's the tea drinker?" he asked Kylar.

"Roman. He needs an intervention—he's a junkie."

Tanner began making the tea, even using the little wooden whisk to break apart the lumps in the hot water. The only time he seemed unsure was when he opened the fridge—staring into it with a frown. "Roman's only got dairy milk," he said, leaning around the door to see her.

"That's fine." She wasn't about to be picky at a guest's house—especially not when the hacker of the Seven Devils was making her tea. And especially not when he seemed to know that she preferred a plant-based milk, her stomach sensitive to lactose.

Yup, these people definitely weren't trying to kill her. She started to wonder again if she was dreaming.

A few minutes later, Tanner set the mug of steaming matcha in front of her.

"Thanks," Loren said.

"You're welcome."

She rested her elbows on the table and cupped the warm mug. Her fingers were cold and stiff, but she hoped it didn't mean anything bad. She was used to far warmer climates; aside from on television, she had never even seen snow. Yveswich was a lot colder than Angelthene, and the house was big and prone to the morning chill.

Joyce slid the plate of waffles her way. "Please, eat. No one wants to see you faint again."

She served herself up a waffle and spooned some fat blueberries on top. "Where's Darien?" She took a sip of the hot, velvety matcha, the taste like heaven. For someone who'd never made matcha before, Tanner was a pro.

"Still sleeping," Ivy said.

Still sleeping at nine thirty in the morning. But last night he'd seemed so tired. So...distraught.

And mysterious. There was a lot to figure out about that one, and Loren had to admit she was a little curious about him.

A little.

Darien slept like the dead.

By the time he woke up, he could hardly remember what day it was or what planet he was on.

He stirred, slowly taking in the room. The dresser, the closet, his bags that sat on a cushioned bench at the end of the bed, sunlight streaming in through the curtains.

This was Roman's house, but it wasn't the same room he'd slept in before. Not the same bed.

He jolted up, kicking off the sheets and blankets, and crossed the room, bare feet pounding on the icy floors. His heart started thundering, his vision spinning like he was stuck in the heart of a hurricane—

Voices floated up from the ground floor. Kylar, Jack, Tanner, Ivyana, Joyce, the kids, and—

Loren.

Darien exhaled through his mouth.

Last night was real. It wasn't a dream.

The relief that flooded his body was so intense, he nearly passed out right there, where he leaned against the doorjamb, listening to the sound of Loren's sweet, bubbly voice. She was speaking to Bandit—about his rubber chicken, by the sounds of it. He was asking her to throw it. *Demanding* was more like it, the little shit.

Darien went to his duffel and dug around inside until he found some clean clothes and his leather bag of toiletries.

As soon as he was done getting ready for the day—well, almost, his hair still messy, his face in need of a shave—he went downstairs.

She might not be able to remember him, but he couldn't fucking wait to see her.

"If you want me to throw it," Loren said, gripping the rubber chicken by its neck while Bandit held onto it by its soft belly, his sharp teeth making it squeal, "you have to let go." She was still in her spot at the kitchen table, the others feasting on blueberry waffles all around her, the house fragrant with butter and coffee. She was so full, she could burst.

'Promise you'll throw it,' Bandit said from where he stood under the table between her knees, his misty voice audible to everyone in the room. He tugged on the rubber chicken again, the top of his head bumping the

table. A bottle of syrup tipped over, and Tanner leaned across the table to pick it up.

Loren held on tight. "Have I ever lied to you before?" She seriously wondered if she had. Wondered how many times she'd interacted with this sassy Familiar and his prized rubber chicken—the toy he'd named 'Cluckles'.

Bandit's red eyes shifted from side to side as he considered her question.

And then he let go of the toy, drool stringing out of his chops.

"Ready?" She prepared to throw...

Bandit took off, squeezing between her chair and Paxton's and nearly knocking the kid over.

"Hey!" Paxton exclaimed, righting himself. The lanky puppy Familiar that was curled up in his lap whimpered.

Bandit bounded across the kitchen, his steps so heavy he shook the house.

Loren threw the rubber chicken, aiming for the living room—

And hit Darien in the side of the face with it as he walked in.

She shot to her feet. "I am so sorry!"

Darien caught the chicken before it could fall.

'You ruined it!' Bandit exclaimed, his nails scrabbling on the floor as he screeched to a stop. *'You ruined our play time! You ruin everything!'*

"Everything?" Darien drawled, the question coated with amusement. His night-dark hair was all messy, a few of the strands hanging in his face. He lifted the chicken. "Who bought you this thing?"

Bandit barked and jumped, trying to grab the chicken Darien held out of his reach. *Bark! 'Throw it!' Bark! 'Throw it, damn you!'*

"You want me to throw it?"

Bark! Bark! 'Quit teasing!' Bark! 'Throw it!'

Darien crossed the living room. Opened the door to the deck, cold breeze blowing in. Wound his arm back. Threw—

And cursed when he realized he'd thrown too hard.

Loren watched out the window as the chicken soared threw the air— and hit the wall of spells protecting the property with a pop and a sizzle.

'You scalded it!' Bandit cried. The dog thundered across the deck and down the stairs that led into the yard.

Jack and Kylar were trying not to laugh.

"You really don't like that chicken, do you?" Tanner said.

"That wasn't nice," Ivy scolded.

Darien headed for the kitchen, leaving the patio door open for Bandit to get back in. "That thing is so goddamn loud. The next toy he gets will be a quiet one."

Loren sat back down and picked up her fork. She stabbed her last bite of waffle, swirled it in syrup, and popped it into her mouth.

A minute later, Bandit trotted inside, rubber chicken in his mouth. It smelled a bit like burnt rubber. *'I am happy to report that Cluckles is fine. He's just missing his comb.'* He glared up at Darien, who stood at the counter, pouring himself a cup of coffee. *'Because* someone *singed it off.'*

"Watch it, or I'll singe off the squeaker next."

Bandit bit down on the chicken, making it wheeze.

Darien fake-lunged at the dog, sending Bandit bounding into the living room again. Bandit growled and whipped his head back at forth, rubber chicken flapping.

Loren was so busy watching the dog that she jumped a little when Darien pulled out the chair beside her and sat down.

"How'd you sleep?" he asked, taking a sip of coffee.

"Like the dead."

He frowned. "Don't say that."

"Like the...living...dead?" she tried again.

Darien's mouth twitched—another almost-smile.

Jack snorted. "I'm not sure that's any better."

"I slept really well," Loren corrected. "I feel great."

"Good. You'll let me know if anything changes."

Ivy cut in. "Of course she will." She reached across the table and set a plate of waffles in front of Darien. "And you're going to eat."

"You made all this?"

"I helped," Jack said.

Ivy tipped up a brow. "He kept getting in the way, dropped a bunch of eggs, and ate half the batter."

"Mmm," Darien said. "Salmonella."

Tanner finished off the last of his breakfast, readjusted the band of his sweatpants, and sat back in his chair. "What's on the schedule for today?"

Several of them looked at Darien, Loren included—and Darien was already looking at her.

"You need a winter jacket," Darien said.

"I don't have any money."

"And I told you not to worry about price tags."

She frowned. But...she really did need a jacket. It was bitterly cold here, and...come to think of it, she didn't even own a proper winter jacket.

"And," Darien said, reaching under the table to drag his thumb across her forearm, "how do you feel about another one of these?"

She glanced down at her tattoo. It didn't escape her that he didn't need to touch her to ask that question.

And it also didn't escape her that his touch left a trail of heat on her skin, one that lingered long after he pulled away.

She covered the tattoo—and the lingering heat—with her own hand. "Another tattoo?"

"I think it would be a good idea," Darien said. "Yours only tells us when your blood sugar is low. I think we should get you something that'll tell us when you need to get to Silverway." His eyes flicked over her head—looking at Kylar. "Which parlors do you recommend?"

"Roman's," Kylar replied. "The owner's a goddamn genius, but...it's in a Gray Zone. And Donovan likes to go there."

"So we'll need to watch our backs," Darien said.

"Ho yeah."

"Who's Donovan?" Loren asked.

Silence pulsed through the kitchen. Not even the kids nattered at each other anymore.

Darien said, "Roman's dad. And someone you don't need to worry about as long as we're around." Loren didn't miss when Darien's eyes flicked to Paxton, who stared down at his puppy with a long face.

Loren didn't like the sounds of this *Donovan,* but she trusted Darien when he said she wouldn't need to worry about him.

53

FOXHILL RENTALS
FOXHILL, STATE OF WITHEREDGE

The rental shop was supposed to open at nine.

"It's almost ten o'clock!" Max fumed. He pushed away from the same door he'd rattled yesterday and joined the others in the empty parking lot.

Today was a holiday, which none of them had clued into until they'd arrived and seen that the place was closed. They'd figured it out after Dallas, the lone person in their group who operated on a normal schedule, had the sense to check her calendar. Foxhill Rentals had failed to update their hours for the holiday, but if they opened any later than ten, or didn't open at all, Max might have to resort to ripping out his hair.

Another five minutes passed before a single vehicle puttered into the sunlit parking lot. The white hatchback drove to the side of the building and parked in one of the stalls marked with a sign that read EMPLOYEE PARKING ONLY.

The guy sat in his car for a while after he'd cut the engine. The vehicle didn't have the best spells; Max could see inside even without the Sight. The man—warlock—kept glancing this way.

Dallas cleared her throat. "Maybe you ruffians shouldn't stare," she whispered.

Fuck, they were all staring, but mostly Max, Malakai, and Dominic—the ruffians.

This wasn't going well.

A few minutes later, the warlock got out of his car, coffee cup and lunchbox in hand, and approached with a tentative smile. It was already hot as sin, the palm trees casting long shadows across the pavement. "You folks looking to rent a car?"

"We have a few questions for you, actually," Max said.

"I can...do my best to help." He tucked the lunchbox under his arm and retrieved a set of keys from his pocket. "What's this concerning?"

"My sister," Max said. Honesty was the best option here, especially with the warlock's aura telling him he was close to pissing himself. "She's missing, and I just want to find her—that's it."

He took a second to process Max's words. And then he unlocked the doors and opened one. "Come on in. We don't technically open for another hour, but I'll do my best to help."

Max faced the others. "Dal and I will go in. You guys wait here."

The guy walked in and held the door for them. "I'm Paul," he said as Max and Dallas walked in. He shut the door and locked it. "Foxhill Rentals is the wife's and my baby. Family owned and operated for the past thirty years."

Max pointed at himself. "Max." He gestured to Dallas. "Dallas."

"Pleasure to meet you." He gestured across the room. "If you'd follow me to my office—it's right this way."

Paul led the way to a door at the back. There was nothing inside but a simple desk with three chairs, an old computer, one filing cabinet, and a painting of an old hotrod. He sat down behind the desk. "Anna Cousens, right?" He placed his coffee cup and lunchbox by the monitor.

Max paused in the midst of sitting down. "Come again?"

"That's who you're looking for, isn't it?"

Max sat, Dallas doing the same. "No," he said. "My sister's name is Maya."

Dallas said, "Who's this Anna girl?"

"She's a missing Darkslayer from Yveswich."

"A Darkslayer?" Max asked. That explained why Paul had jumped to conclusions; a Darkslayer looking for another Darkslayer made a lot of sense.

What *didn't* make sense was how and why a Darkslayer would've gone missing. Darkslayers didn't go missing—*they* did the abducting. They died sometimes, sure, but their deaths were almost always swept under the rug, not broadcasted all over the news as missing people in need of being found. And if their deaths weren't swept under the rug by the underworld, the bodies were left right out in the open. Darkslayers weren't afraid of killing, nor were they afraid of facing law enforcement for first-degree murder. Of course, law enforcement rarely bothered with murder trials for Darkslayers; they preferred to turn the other cheek. While some cops and court judges hated Darkslayers with a passion, most tolerated them with a grudge, knowing full well they wouldn't be able to handle the massive amount of demons and criminals in every city without them.

Paul held up his hands in innocence. "It's just what I heard. Police were poking around town not too long ago, but I'm not sure if they found anything." He clicked onto the computer and typed in a passcode. "How can I help? I'm assuming you'd like to see some records?"

"Three men rented one of your cars and drove it to Angelthene a few weeks ago. It turned up in a lake in Vampire Territory. Were you aware of that?"

Paul clicked the mouse several times. "We had one car that never made it back. It was probably the same one; all other rentals from the past month have made it back except for that one." He scrolled. "Was your sister with them?"

"No, but I have reason to believe they're connected to her disappearance."

He sighed through his nose and shook his head. "I can't imagine what that feels like. I have a sister, too." He kept scrolling. "And a daughter." He clicked a couple times and turned the computer screen so they could see it. "This was the model."

Max studied it. It was basic—just a black sedan, no bells or whistles.

Paul said, "We take photocopies of all driver's licenses, if you'd like to have a look."

"They're probably fake," Max said. "What about cameras that face the highway? I want to see where they went."

"There's only one." He clicked around again, keeping the screen facing them this time, until a bunch of live feeds appeared. The footage wasn't great—it was grainy and black and white, but it was better than nothing. "Hold on, I have to check that date again."

It took about twenty minutes, three pairs of squinting eyes, and a whole lot of zooming in, but they finally caught the barest glimpse of the car's tires—heading out into the middle of nowhere.

Literally.

"What's out there?" Max asked.

Paul exhaled. "Honestly? A whole lot of nothing. There's a bunch of desert out there, a motel, wildlife. Not a lot of people travel there, unless it's for work or hiking."

The perfect place to hide someone, then.

Max stood, took an envelope out of his back pocket, and offered it to Paul. "For your trouble and the almost-heart attack."

Paul blinked up at him. "Oh no, I can't accept that."

"Please, man, just take it." Max held the envelope there until Paul's fingers closed around the edge. "No one is to know about this. We were never here."

Paul nodded. "I won't tell anyone."

They left the office. "Thanks, Paul," Max called.

Soon as Max was outside, he studied Paul's aura to make sure he'd made the right call—by trusting him, paying him, and not attempting to erase his memories from today.

Paul's aura was wide open and bright—no secrets. This was a man who wore everything on his sleeve.

"Well?" Malakai's voice was nearly a bark. "It's hot as Ignis's fucking asshole out here!"

"It's not gonna get any colder," Max said, opening the driver's door to the SUV. "We're going into the desert."

54

GIOVANNI'S TATTOO
YVESWICH, STATE OF KER

Loren sat in the truck, watching as Darien bit the tags off her new winter jacket—a puffy white thing that promised warmth in this bitterly cold city. It was nearly spring, but that didn't seem to matter in Yveswich. The day was overcast, and the sprinkle of rain that misted the streets was half-frozen, the dip in temperature fogging up the truck windows.

They were parked out front of Giovanni's Tattoo. Jack and Kylar had come along for the ride and were in the back seat, talking about the time they'd all gone snowboarding at a winter sports resort called Frostfire Ridge.

Darien handed her the jacket, and she put it on. The outer material was cold and slippery, but the inside was fuzzy and well insulated. She zipped it up and tucked her hands into the sleeves.

"Better?" Darien asked her, his eyes more gray than blue in this light.

She nodded.

"Good." He opened his door, Jack and Kylar doing the same, the former still laughing as they recounted a memory of the Devil named Travis bailing on a black diamond slope. She'd always wanted to try snowboarding, but they were making it sound petrifying. Loren undid her seatbelt and got out too.

She'd learned from all their driving that the districts in Yveswich were divided into zones, and you could tell which one you were in by the way they chose to design it. In Neutral Zones, bits of all of them could be seen —traffic lights that were shaped like flames, lightning bolts, and trees; water fountains with elaborately carved statues of Caligo, goddess of water, mercy, and rebirth; street lamps crafted from ancient bone for the Hollow. There were bridges of red brick lined with enchanted torches for the Dunes; sidewalk art of Obitus for the Hollow; creeping ivy for the Labyrinth; lightning displays in shopping centers for the Eyrie; and artificial waterfalls for the Riptide, as if the city didn't already have enough of those.

But right now, they were in a Gray Zone, so the architecture was dark and eerie, the roads lined with the arching bones of some long-dead leviathan.

Of course, there were also monuments to honor the mayor himself—a few statues and a lot of murals. Most of the ones Loren had glimpsed were vandalized. City workers were gathered around to fix them, either with magic if they were magic-born, or with paintbrushes if they were mortal and unfortunate enough to be assigned such a painstaking duty.

It was a truly fascinating city, but it didn't stop Loren from missing home. From missing Dallas and Sabrine and her classes at Angelthene Academy. She still couldn't remember that part of her life—the months that she had supposedly spent studying at the school for magic—but because she had always dreamed of going there, ever since she was a little girl, she found herself missing it anyway. She wondered what the headmaster and professors thought of her absence, if they would be forgiving enough to let her come back.

Surrounded on all sides by Darkslayers, Loren crossed the slick sidewalk and entered Giovanni's Tattoo. The warmth that wrapped around her as soon as she stepped over the threshold was welcoming, but the buzzing of the guns immediately made her heart skip a beat. All her loathed tattoo appointments that stretched back to when she was a little girl were, unfortunately, unforgettable.

A male hellseher with a gray ponytail and beard stood behind the desk, his weathered hands flipping through an appointment book. He looked up at the sound of their entry and greeted them with a kind smile. "Welcome. Kylar, nice to see ya."

"Hey, Giovanni," Kylar said with a smile equally as bright, the diamond in his tooth winking like a tiny star. "Guys, meet Giovanni, ink master and goddamn genius."

Jack grinned. "Giovanni the Genius. Has a nice ring to it."

His curled moustache lifted with a smile. "Who's getting the old stick and poke today?"

Kylar and Jack stepped aside like curtains parting.

When Giovanni caught sight of Loren, no longer hidden by the wall of

Darkslayers, his head tilted ever so slightly, but he maintained his amicable smile.

Darien's hand slid across the small of her back. "This pretty lady right here." This time, when Loren's heart skipped, it had nothing to do with the buzzing of the guns, and she found herself disappointed when Darien pulled away and shifted his hands into his jacket pockets. The coat he wore today was made of black canvas, a heavier and warmer article compared to his usual leather one.

"Come on in." Giovanni stepped out from behind the desk and beckoned them to follow. "I can squeeze you into my schedule right now, as long as you don't want a back piece."

"No, not a back piece, thank you," Loren said. She moved with the guys as they followed Giovanni to a private room in the back. He patted the headrest of a big leather reclining chair in the center of the room. "Have a seat. Make yourself comfortable." As soon as she had her jacket off and sat down, he rolled over a stool and started gathering his things—tray, ink, gloves, disinfectant. "What are we doing today, Miss?" He took a seat on the stool and wheeled himself closer.

Darien said, "She has a medical tattoo that tells us when her blood sugar is low. We need another that'll tell us when she needs a treatment at Caliginous on Silverway."

Giovanni's gray eyes widened ever so slightly. He glanced at Kylar, who gave the barest shake of his head.

"And conduit tattoos," Loren added. Four pairs of eyes were now staring at her. The conduit tattoos were her idea. She hadn't told anyone that she wanted them, or why.

According to what her unlikely new friends had told her, she had magic. And it was her body's inability to handle it that had nearly killed her. What if an emergency happened, and she had to use her magic again? She couldn't remember how, but...it wasn't a bad idea to take precautions.

Darien shifted on his feet. "Loren, your solar amulet is a conduit."

Giovanni's eyes flicked about the group, the crease in his brow deepening.

Loren knew it was a conduit; they'd told her so her first night out of her coma. But unless you were a venefica using a stave, tattoos were more effective than physical conduits—everyone knew that—thanks to the ink's direct contact with the skin and bloodstream.

Darien's expression was impossible to read. He looked...like he was being tortured or something. His reaction was so extreme and so...unexpected...that she didn't know how to respond.

"I really want conduit tattoos," she told him. "Is there a reason why you think I shouldn't get them?"

"Is concern for your safety a good enough reason?" His answer sent a ripple of heat up her spine. Suddenly, she knew exactly why he looked so tortured, and the realization only made the heat that was spreading through her body more intense.

"I won't use them," she said softly, "unless it's an emergency. I promise." She didn't want a repeat of her time spent in a coma any more than Darien seemed to want it.

Darien said, "You can do whatever you want, and I'll support it." That hint of concern in his eyes still lingered, but his tone was resolute. He shifted his attention to Giovanni. "Do whatever she says."

She turned to look at Giovanni, who suddenly appeared more torn than anyone, his eyes brimming with suspicion.

"Will that be a problem, sir?" she asked him. Gods, she'd had no idea this would cause such a scene—and would make her feel all sorts of funny over Darien's unexpected reaction.

Giovanni cleared his throat and rolled his tray closer. "My tools will let me know if it is." He put on a pair of black nitrile gloves.

Loren glanced about, avoiding Darien's stare this time—she wasn't sure she could bear the intensity again. "What does that mean?"

"Giovanni's tools are enchanted," Kylar explained. "The guns decide what type of ink you get and where it goes. It'll react to your aura and the messages it gives off." Loren had to admit, it sounded kind of cool.

Until Giovanni put on a blindfold.

"What's that for?" she asked.

"Being able to see is not part of the process," he said, grabbing things with the kind of confidence that a person who wasn't blindfolded would have. "The tools will guide me." He held out a hand, palm up. "Your wrist, please, Miss."

The first tattoo was small, consisting only of basic line work in black ink. It went on the same arm as her medical tattoo and was shaped like a calligraphic C, the tail looping into a heart that ended in a zigzag, like a line on a heart-rate monitor. As she stared at the finished tattoo, a bead of light budded at the start of the C, looped through the heart, and zigzagged into the tail before sinking into her skin and dimming.

C for Caliginous on Silverway.

Giovanni switched ink pots and held his hand out again. "Your palm now, my dear."

The palm hurt the most. It felt like her skin was on fire, and it became so intense as he shaded in the small symbol with metallic ink that her eyes started to tear up, and her breathing grew shallow.

Darien was at her side in an instant. He dragged a free chair over and sat down. Despite the lingering intensity between them, having him closer oddly made her feel more relaxed.

And when the burning sensation turned into stabbing pain, her hand lashed out, as if with a mind of its own, and grabbed onto his jacket sleeve.

Gods, how embarrassing was this?

Especially when Darien pried her fingers off the canvas.

"I'm sorry," she said, preparing to pull away—

But he laced his fingers with hers.

Something flickered in her mind. A broken memory of a blinding white hospital room, crepe paper crinkling under her, and the feel of this Darkslayer's big hand cradling her own. The sound of his rich voice murmuring words she couldn't remember but wished she could.

Loren blinked rapidly, and the memory vanished like the little ball of light that had sunk into her wrist. "Have we done this before?" Her words were strained and breathy.

Darien's swallow was visible. His eyes were still guarded like before, but in a different way now. "Yes."

Giovanni declared, "Next hand." He and Darien switched places.

And Loren could hardly handle the butterflies in her stomach anymore than she could handle the pain when the Darkslayer gently cupped her other hand, being careful not to touch the inflamed skin around the new ink.

The buzzing resumed.

"Why did you do it the last time?" she asked Darien, flinching as the gun worked away. "Hold my hand, I mean."

"Because you were in pain, and I wanted to comfort you," Darien said, his voice a quiet rumble. "I didn't know you very well back then, though."

She studied him, wishing she could read his expression, but she never really could. He was a walking mystery with far more layers than anyone could ever hope to unpack. "And how well do you know me now?"

"Enough to tell when you're in need of support but are too stubborn to ask for it." The edge of his alluring mouth quirked with a smile. "But my middle name is 'Stubborn', so I don't blame you."

She smiled through the pain. "What is it, really? Your middle name."

"I don't have one."

"It's 'Fucking'," Jack joked. "Darien Fucking Cassel." He chuckled.

Neither Loren nor Darien looked at or responded to Jack; they just watched each other.

When Giovanni was finished, Loren had to force herself to let go of Darien. It didn't escape her that he wasn't the one to do it first. She could feel herself getting in deep with this man, and she barely remembered him.

A crush—she must have had a crush on him these past six months. That would explain where all these emotions were coming from.

Loren held up her hands to look at the ink on her palms.

On one hand was a small sun, drawn with gold ink that shimmered whenever she moved. On the other was a crescent moon in glittering, metallic silver. They were such simple shapes, but that didn't stop them from being beautiful.

Jack's exhale was audible. He murmured, "Sun. Moon." He said it as if it the tattoos were far more important than they looked.

Darien was still watching her. "The same but different," he said, his voice as awed as Jack's. "Different but the same."

TEN MINUTES LATER, Darien held the door to Giovanni's open for his girl. She walked out into the cold, hands bundled in her pockets. As she walked, she stole glances at him the same way he stole glances at her, but while she could never catch him doing it, he caught her every single time.

Until she'd put that jacket back on, Darien had found that he couldn't stop looking at the tattoo on the inside of her wrist.

The C stood for Caliginous on Silverway, but Darien had imagined, when he'd first seen it, that it stood for Cassel instead.

It was just a letter, and it was just his imagination running wild with a foolish idea, but it made his heart so fucking full.

He was fucked. Well and truly fucked.

He managed to hide every trace of his emotions as they got in the truck and went back to Roman's house.

Loren didn't speak for the whole drive, but she looked at him whenever she had an excuse to—like when Jack or Kylar said something that required he say something back. He could sense that she was on edge, but he couldn't get a firm grasp on her feelings.

A memory had come to her in that room—he'd seen it in her eyes. And he knew it scared her.

It made him wonder which of their many moments together had come back to her today, and how much time would pass before other, far more important memories found their way back to that beautiful mind of hers.

Maybe he should tell her, but...he didn't want to jump the gun. The way she'd looked at him with fear and surprise, the way her heart had stumbled in her chest, made him worry for the day when those other, much more important memories came back to her.

Patient. He just had to be patient and have faith that this would be over soon.

But pretending made him feel like he was losing his mind. He wanted his girl back, and he wanted her right fucking now.

55

THE CRISTALA POWER PLANT
STATE OF WITHEREDGE

Roman sat in the driver's seat of his car as daylight shifted to dusk. He was well aware of Shay stealing glances at him every few minutes—she had done it all day—but he kept his eyes on the cristala plant just up the road.

He wasn't avoiding her for the same reasons he knew she was avoiding him. Instead of feeling awkward about their encounter last night, his reason for putting distance between them involved attraction—because he'd enjoyed having his hand between her thighs a little too much.

He'd told her not to make a big deal out of it, but he was beginning to think he should take his own advice.

She was just another girl. Another beautiful body he'd had the pleasure of touching. He'd been with plenty of women, had done all kinds of kinky shit in the bedroom that made last night look like nothing, so he wasn't sure why he was so hung up on the little details of their hookup, like the breathy sounds she made when she came, or the way she'd arched into him, her nipples pressing into his chest.

And that little metal ball in her clit.

Fuck.

"They're starting to leave." Shay's voice filled the car—the first sound in over an hour.

Roman cleared his throat. "Yup."

Where she hid in his shadow, Sayagul hissed and lashed her arrowhead tail. *'Quit being such a horn-dog! It makes me detest sharing a mind with you.'*

'I haven't been laid in like a month,' he shot back. Maybe that was his problem. Even just the thought of getting laid put him in a state of semi-arousal.

'Oh boo-hoo,' Sayagul huffed. *'So hard done by. Get this investigation over with so we can go home. We've been away from Pax for three days.'*

'Pax is fine,' Roman said. Kylar would have found a way to contact him if anything was wrong. Itzel had control over his car; she could send a message through there, if need be.

But he still didn't want to be away for long. Five days felt like forever when he had a younger brother to take care of, but he was already over halfway through those five days. Only two left now.

Of course, when those five days were up, he wouldn't see Shay again. Not that he wanted to. She'd stolen his necklace and blackmailed him. What he *should* want to do was kill her, like he would anyone else.

Like he should've done that first night in the alley. He'd killed people for far less than what Shay had done.

"Is something bothering you?" Shay said quietly.

Roman blinked. "Just tired." He watched the cars begin to stream out of the gates to the plant as employees ended their shifts.

"I'm glad you're here," Shay said, her voice hardly a whisper. He glanced at her, but she was staring straight ahead, hands clasped between her bare knees. "I know this thing between us started badly with the manipulation and threats and stuff, but I don't know if I could have done this on my own."

Roman felt an unbidden smile pull at his mouth. "Is Shay Cousens thanking me?" The girl could flip like a light switch; this was a far cry from the Shayla who'd fumed at him by the empty swimming pool.

But fuck if that attitude didn't turn him on.

"No," she said quickly. "Just acknowledging."

It was getting dark. Nearly all the employees were gone, but the road beyond this plant was quiet, not a single pair of headlights lighting it up.

"Why are there no cars coming from the other plant?" Roman said, leaning forward in his seat. He couldn't see the other plant from here, but it wasn't far. Maybe thirty, forty minutes if you drove the speed limit. They'd come to this plant first, deciding to tackle them one at a time, but it seemed they'd chosen the wrong one.

He started the car and ripped out onto the road.

Being out here this late, when the shadows were poised to devour them, sent a near constant prickle up his spine. But he fought it, focusing on the white of the headlights bleaching the pavement and the feel of the air in his lungs as he breathed in deeply and exhaled slowly.

At the speed he drove, they made it out to the other plant in no time. As Roman downshifted and rolled the car to a stop out front of a busted chain-link fence, he cursed himself for not coming here first—for not getting to this one before nightfall.

Roman pulled the car around the far side of the building and parked behind a part of the desert mountain that jutted out farther than the rest. No one would be able to see the car from the road or the lot.

The building looked like parts of it had suffered an explosion. Windows were shattered, debris littered the empty parking lot, and parts of the exterior walls were blackened, as if scorched by flame.

There was no one out here. And of course, there were no lights on inside.

Gods.

Shay opened her door.

Roman's head whipped her way. "Hold up, small fry. Shut the door."

She did with reluctance. The dull thump of her door seemed unbearably loud. "This is obviously worth investigating, wouldn't you say?" she asked.

Probably, but— "There are no spells." His mouth was so dry, he could hardly speak. "We don't know what's in there."

"So look," she prompted. He stared out at the dark building, so distracted by all the shadows that he forgot for a moment that she was watching him. "Are you okay?" she asked him.

"I'm fine."

"I can look instead—"

"I will." He blinked the black into his eyes and scanned the building thoroughly. The traces of auras here were a few days old, and he didn't pick up on any that belonged to monsters.

Safe, then. But it still didn't erase that it was almost full dark out.

"Shadows?" Shay said quietly, tipping her head to try to catch his eye. "I really want to have a look around, but if you think it's not safe—"

"It's clear." He opened the center console, grabbed a handgun, and tucked it into the waistband of his pants. He grabbed another and handed it to Shay. "Be aware," he said as she took it, her fingers grazing his. "Don't get distracted, no matter what we find."

She checked the safety before tucking it into the back of her denim shorts.

They got out, softly closing their doors behind them, and crossed the parking lot, moving carefully to lessen the crunch of gravel under their feet.

"I'll go in first," Roman mouthed as they approached the worn, concrete steps that led to the front doors. "Cover me." They drew their guns and crept up the steps.

Roman eased open the door, the creak of the hinges scraping against scorched walls. It smelled of burning flesh and chemicals in here, the scents fairly new.

As they began to look around, it quickly became apparent that this wasn't a cristala plant—it was a front for something else.

There was no company name on anything, but there was a symbol: a Phoenix with three overlapping circles behind it.

"What is all this?" Shay stepped up to a giant, free-standing room that looked more like a chamber or a metal box. The door had a small window in it, the kind that reminded Roman of a sauna. A symbol was bolted above the door—a red metal flame. There were warning signs all over the walls, telling people to keep their distance and the door shut.

Down the hall sat a similar chamber, but this one looked more like a tank. You'd have to climb the ladder on the side of it to reach the door in the top. The glass was cracked, so no water was inside, but there was a symbol by the warning signs, just like the flame. This one was a water droplet, though.

Roman watched as Shay brought her fingers to the tiny tattoo on her cheekbone.

"What do you think all this is?" she whispered, dropping her hand.

Roman was about to speak when sound came from behind them—the creak of the front doors, and the crunch of glass under shoes.

He instructed Shay to hide, and then he rallied his magic with a hard blink, nostrils flaring.

A lone man strode past the fire-resistant chamber, but he didn't get any farther than that before Roman's shadows lashed out, ensnaring his limbs and pinning him to the wall.

SHAY WAITED IN THE DARKNESS, disguised extra well by her illusion magic, as Roman stepped up to the man he'd pinned to the concrete wall with his shadows.

Watching the scene unfold before her—the man struggling under Roman's immovable grip, and the Shadowmaster who approached with vicious, drawn-out movements that hinted at how much he enjoyed killing people—reminded Shay of that night several days ago, when Roman had done that very same thing to her.

Had it really happened such a short time ago?

"Who are you?" Roman's voice was low and deadly. It was strange to watch him slip this mask back on, after she'd got a glimpse of the man behind the smoke. "And what are you doing here?" Gods, that voice was so cold and remote, it sent a prickle up her spine.

"I'm Doctor Brennan Rowe," the man squeezed out. The smell of his sweat permeated the air. "I used to work here."

"What is this place? And don't even think about lying to me." Roman tightened his shadows. "I know it isn't a cristala plant. What are those tanks and chambers for?"

"This was an undercover magic facility. That was its name: *The Facility*. We used the chambers to hone a person's magic."

"Willing or unwilling?"

No answer.

Roman's shadows squeezed, making the man gasp. "Willing," Roman repeated in a razor-edged voice, "or unwilling?"

"Most of the subjects were not volunteers."

"That's a nice way to say you kidnapped them. What happened here? Why's everything destroyed?"

"A few of the stronger subjects staged a breakout. I was told to come back and make sure we'd covered our tracks."

"The subjects—name them."

Silence. Shay held her breath.

"Names, Doctor Rowe," Roman warned. The man flinched away from the volume of his voice.

"Gold, Violet, Sage, Magenta, Aurora, Blue, Blaze..." He paused, panting. Sweat dribbled down his jowls. "And Scarlet." Shay's brows knitted together.

Roman growled, "Do you think this is a joke?" He flexed his magic, the shadows digging into the doctor's skin, nearly cutting to the bone. "Do I look like a joke to you?"

"No, no, I—"

Shay stepped out of the shadows. "Anna?"

The facility fell silent.

She moved closer; the man watched her with vigilance, his eyes flicking between her and Roman. "Was there an Anna here?"

He shook his head. "No one by that name. The people I just listed—

they were all that was left. The others..." He swallowed. Grimaced. His chest heaved with noisy, labored breaths. "The others died."

Shay's stomach sank.

Not here. Anna wasn't here.

"Let him down, Shadows," she said softly.

Roman's shadows pulled the man off the wall, setting him down on his feet so his back faced the front doors.

Shay glanced at Roman, nodding once. He immediately knew what she was trying to tell him—to erase the man's memories of his encounter with them tonight.

Roman said, "I'm going to need you to hold very still, Doctor Rowe." He breathed in, nostrils flaring, eyes swallowed up by a shining black. "This'll take just a moment."

The man waited, lifting his hands in a gesture that welcomed what Roman was about to do. "I'm not going anywhere—"

The doctor's last word turned into a gurgle as claws burst through his stomach from behind. Blood sprayed through the air, the droplets misting Shay's face.

Doctor Rowe gasped and dropped to his knees.

Shay's eyes fell upon the monster looming behind him in a preternatural mist as it clinked its blood-coated claws.

56

THE FACILITY
STATE OF WITHEREDGE

The monster moved with blinding speed.

It was massive—a breed Roman had never seen or heard of before. The body reminded him of bone, its physique beastly, the spine and tail lined with long, black-tipped spikes he'd bet were poisonous. Its head was smooth and dry, like a skull or sun-beaten stone, and it had a mouthful of serrated teeth black as onyx. But the strangest thing about it was the stone in its forehead—glowing right above the terrifying pair of narrow eyes.

The creature threw Roman into the wall with brutal, blood-soaked claws, the force behind the attack knocking the wind out of him. As he landed on his feet, its long, spiked tail lashed through the air.

He blocked the attack with his magic, wincing as the spikes cracked along the invisible barrier. His magic was an extension of himself, so he could feel everything it touched—every hit, every drop of blood, every cutting drag of a claw.

Another lash of that deadly tail, and his magic bent and thinned. He stumbled back, barely managing to parry the attack. One more hit, and his shields would be done for.

Shots cracked through the air as Shay emptied her gun. Each landed true, but—

Nothing could penetrate the monster's skin. Not *one* of Shay's bullets did anything but bounce right off, the demon not even fazed.

With a sweep of his hand, Roman lashed out with his shadows, winding them like whips around the beast's meaty wrists and ankles.

Roman pulled them taut, miming the act of stretching those dark, wispy ropes—

With a bellow that shook the building, the thing snapped the bindings as though they were made of brittle glass, and Roman felt each of them breaking like the reddening sting of a rubber band.

He stumbled back, his heel catching on a chunk of rock.

"Shay," Roman ground out, sweat beading on his forehead, "I can't fucking kill this thing. You need to run—"

So quickly he hadn't a prayer of stopping it, the monster threw him into the wall, pinning him there with a giant claw around his throat, razor-sharp nails scraping off the top layer of his skin. Trickles of blood warmed his neck, pooling in the hollow of his throat.

The creature huffed at the air—scenting him with a baring of sharp, lipless teeth. Each was long and hooked like a shark's, saliva and blood stringing between jaws that were speckled brown with age.

"Yoo-hoo!" Shay hollered. The sound of her voice made Roman's heart stumble. And it stumbled again when she waved her hands in the air and started jumping up and down like a goddamn rabbit. "Over here, you ugly piece of monster-ass!"

"Shay!" Roman could barely choke out the warning, that brutal claw crushing his trachea. He'd told her to get the hell out of here, and she wasn't listening, goddamnit. *"Don't—"*

But the monster dropped him and made for Shay—

Who was suddenly standing on the opposite side of the room.

Roman landed on his feet in a crouch. Blinked. What the hell?

She waved for him to follow, mouthing, "Come on, come on," as the monster went the other way.

Roman moved. Together they ran, deep into the building, breaths rasping against the walls. The scuff of their shoes was unbearably loud.

Behind them, the monster bellowed an angry roar.

Shay grabbed his hand. "Under here." She pulled him down with her, and they slid across the ground and flew under a broken slab of concrete flooring that jutted upward, creating a hiding spot underneath. Dust choked the air as they struck ground in the dark, narrow space.

And held still. Quickly, Roman used his magic to create a sound barrier—

The creature approached. Snuffled around. But somehow, even as visible as Roman feared they were, it didn't see them.

A lifetime passed before it left with one last thunderous roar that shook the facility, pebbles clacking down around them like hail.

They took several minutes to breathe. Just breathe. Roman's lungs were on fire, lines of blood drying on his throat. He'd spent so many years as a Darkslayer that he'd had a few close calls, but this?

This was different. Worse than any of the others.

He owed the girl breathing heavily beside him a thank-you.

He glanced down at the tattoo on Shay's wrist—the fish skeleton that he'd never paid much attention to before. A conduit.

"So," he said, still panting. "Illusion."

SHAY TURNED VERY STILL as Roman spoke her secret aloud, right there underneath that cold slab of concrete in this horrible place called the Facility. The secret she had never told anyone except Anna and Dad.

Slowly, she turned her head toward him. Offered up the best smile she could manage. "Yup."

He was staring at her as if he'd won the lottery, the flecks in his irises glinting like gold in a riverbed. "That's incredible. I've never heard of that before."

"Not many people have," she whispered. "It's...a very rare type of magic. Hardly any books about it exist. I first learned I had the ability when my dad and I were playing hide-and-go-seek when I was five."

"How does it work?"

"Kind of like glamors, but with less limitations. I can trick people into seeing something different on screens."

His face smoothed with realization. "That was how you changed my phone screen."

She nodded. "I'm not very powerful, though. I need this tattoo to tell me when it's safe to use my magic again." She showed him the fish skeleton tattoo, the tail just beginning to glow. "It's very short-lived. I can only fool people for a few minutes before the illusion wears off."

"The dock," he mused.

She couldn't help but grin, remembering that day too. "You should've seen the look on your face."

His mouth twitched, but he was still looking at her as if she were a walking money sign. It made her stomach clench and twist as she wondered if she was reading him correctly.

"Are you going to tell anyone?" she whispered, a pit opening in her stomach.

Roman searched her eyes. Shook his head. "No."

"Do you promise?"

"I'll tell you a secret of my own, if you want." She waited, and after he swallowed a few times, he glanced around and said, the words barely audible, "I'm afraid of the dark."

Shay blinked—several times. "What?"

"I know," he mumbled. "Go ahead and laugh." Roman 'Shadows' Devlin—afraid of the dark. She never would have guessed.

Shay cleared her throat. "I'm afraid of being trapped in small places."

He smirked, glancing pointedly at their surroundings—cramped and dark. "I guess we're both at a disadvantage right now, aren't we?"

She noticed it, then—his heart. It was racing. There didn't seem to be much that scared him, but this?

Roman Devlin, Prince of Shadows and Wolf of the Hollow, was afraid of the dark.

As quietly as she could, Shay slid over to his side, nestling in close. They were both lying on their stomachs, barely able to see each other under here.

Shay liked risks, so she decided to take one. Roman's eyes were already on her, and hers were already on him as she leaned in slowly, the tip of her nose grazing his—

She paused, their faces so close together she could feel the heat on Roman's skin. "Is the wolf going to bite?" she whispered.

Roman was the one to lean in this time. And when he murmured his answer, she felt his breath on her mouth. "Not today."

She tipped her head, brushing her lips over his.

He didn't pull back. In fact, he waited with patience, as if captivated by every move she made. As she explored his mouth with a featherlight touch, her breath hitched in her throat, her heart thumping as swiftly as his. Butterflies stirred in her stomach, and her blood warmed.

And then Roman leaned in even closer, and pressed his soft lips solidly against hers.

He tasted everything and nothing like she'd imagined. Without smoke in his mouth, like that night in the motel room, she was able to experience the real him. And she found that she liked the taste so much, she desired the full meal.

When they broke the kiss, far sooner than Shay liked, Roman watched her, his face so close to hers that their noses were touching.

"Your heart is beating very fast," he murmured, his breath fanning her mouth. The feel of it made her want to kiss him again. "Is it the tight space or my expert kissing skills that's making your ticker freak out?"

She whisper-laughed. "A bit of both. But mostly..." Unable to resist him, she leaned in for another kiss, and he met her halfway.

Their second real kiss.

He spread her lips with his tongue, his piercing rubbing against the roof of her mouth in a way that promised ecstasy elsewhere. A groan rose in his throat, and his hand came around to the back of her head as he deepened the kiss. Gods, he was good at this—even better than she imagined. That night in the motel room, when he'd covered her mouth with his? That wasn't a real kiss. This, though?

This was real. Real, and all hers. She might not be able to have him forever, but she had him right now.

They explored each other's mouths, right there in the dark, tight space, where they'd both whispered secrets they trusted few to hear. Shay was well aware that she was giving more than just a single piece of herself to Roman, and even more aware that she would never get those pieces back.

But in that moment, she didn't care. She forgot that she was afraid of small spaces. Forgot that she was Shayla Athene Cousens and he was Roman Donovan Devlin, and they could be killed for doing this.

For the first time in her life, she felt alive and free. And from the way Roman held her, kissing her as if he had never desired anything or anyone more than he desired her, she knew he felt the same way.

Roman got out first.

He moved slowly, a sound barrier still wrapped around their little hiding spot. Moving more carefully than ever before, he lifted himself to his feet.

Behind him, Shay waited on her stomach in the dark, invisible aside from the occasional gleam of her eyes whenever she tilted her head.

Roman sensed that the monster wasn't here. But they shouldn't linger —not at night like this. They'd come back in the morning and continue their search under the protection of daylight.

He motioned that the coast was clear. Shay shimmied out, and he helped her up, lacing his fingers with hers.

Neither of them said anything as they left the building. Part of Roman's reason for keeping silent was the demon who couldn't have gone far. The other part was because Shayla Cousens had kissed him.

Usually, shit like that didn't affect him. But tonight had taken him by surprise. He was starting to realize that Shay Cousens was the farthest thing from predictable.

If he was ever lucky enough to have a woman like her, he'd never be bored.

When they made it back to the motel, Shay took a shower while Roman had a smoke. She scrubbed her body until not a trace of dust and blood was left, and then she moved onto her hair, using Roman's shampoo again.

Would it be weird of her to go looking for this brand on the shelves once all this was over?

Probably.

As she rinsed the suds out of her thick hair, she mulled over what they'd learned at the Facility.

It was a magic facility—a place where they honed the abilities of the subjects who were, for the most part, unwilling. A place that had been destroyed when some of those subjects had staged a breakout.

But the man hadn't listed Anna. Had claimed that a woman by that name had never been in the Facility. Shay's hellseher senses had allowed her to read him, and she hadn't picked up on anything that told her he was lying. No flicker or change in shade.

But a part of her felt like Anna was still connected to the Facility in some way. Anna, like Shayla, had very powerful magic, though Anna had only one type, and that was storm. Lightning, wind, rain.

Had they abducted her and tried taking her to the Facility? To use her storm magic to their advantage? Whatever it was. Perhaps she'd fought them, and...

She didn't finish the thought. She shut off the water and got out of the shower. After drying herself off, she wrapped her body in the towel and blow-dried her hair. She didn't like sleeping when it was all wet; it took forever to dry.

When she was done, she opened the door and found the motel room still empty. Nugget was lying on a pillow on Shay's bed, watching a cartoon on the television.

"Have you seen Roman?" Shay asked.

Nugs shook his head.

She put on clean clothes—the outfit she'd wear tomorrow too, since she was running out of options—and went looking for Roman.

She found him sitting out back by the empty pool, his feet draped over the side. Staring up at the cloudless sky of stars, his hair gleaming under the string lights like volcanic glass. He looked like he was having a conversation with the night, and Shay had a strange feeling that she was interrupting.

"This is the night my mom died." His quiet, gravelly voice brought her to a stop. She stood just by the pool steps, unsure how to respond.

"How did she die?" she whispered.

Roman shrugged one shoulder. "The Tricking, apparently."

Shay closed the distance between them and sat down beside him. Roman didn't move; he just kept staring at the sky. Shay took a risk for a second time that evening and rested her head against his shoulder. His skin was cooled by the night breeze.

The gesture broke Roman's trance, and she felt him glance down at her. "You're very hot and cold," he observed.

"So are you."

He looked up at the stars again. "We balance each other well, then," he murmured. "When I'm cold, you can be hot, and when I'm hot, you can be cold. How does that sound, Miss Thief?"

She smiled. "Really good."

She studied the stars with him for a few minutes, his shoulder shifting under her cheek whenever he breathed. She found it comforting. Wind whistled through the palms, and far off in the desert, crickets chirped.

After another few minutes of listening to the sounds of the night, galaxies wheeling above them, she said, "Truth or lie?"

Roman tore his attention off the sky and blinked down at her. "What?"

"It's a game Anna and I used to play." She smiled wistfully. "I'll say something, and you can guess if I'm lying or telling the truth."

It took him a moment, but Roman said, "Okay."

"I dropped out of school when I was in eighth grade. Truth or lie?"

Roman's answer was immediate. "Lie."

"Nope, it's the truth!" She tipped her head back to grin at him.

"You're a dropout?"

"Sure am." She said it with pride; she'd hated school. Anna was the studious one with straight A's. Shay had barely passed any subjects outside of sewing and art class.

"Alright, truth or lie," Roman said. "*I* didn't drop out."

She squinted up at him as he looked down at her. "Lie," she decided.

"Truth."

"Damn."

"I graduated." He looked up at the stars again. "And I'm damn proud of it too." His lips spread with a proud smile that made Shay's chest warm with affection. "Your turn."

Shay brushed a piece of gravel away from her thigh, and it rolled into the pool with soft clacks. "I don't have any friends," she whispered.

"Pfft—that one's easy." He flicked her in the nose. "Everyone knows that, Shayla."

She slapped his muscular thigh. "Jackass." She snickered, and he laughed too. His was quiet and short-lived, but it was still a laugh. Shay hummed as she thought of another one. "I didn't expect to get along so well with you. Truth or lie?"

"What are you talking about, we don't get along," he teased, his grin so big it showed off that elusive dimple. "Lie," he declared.

"I'm going to pinch you."

"I'll bite."

Her smile made her cheeks hurt. "Your turn."

The humor on his face vanished as if a light had been switched, and the gold in his eyes darkened as he stared out at nothing.

Shay dragged her pinkie up his thigh, the denim of his pants tickling the pad of her finger. "Roman?" She watched as his throat shifted, his chest shaking with an inhale.

"I dream of killing my dad," he whispered. That voice was hoarse, and there was a cold, manic glint in his eyes, the one she'd seen the first couple times she'd collided with him. The face he wore when he stood on the world stage. The mask he rarely took off. His smile tipped down a bit, looking more like that baring of teeth—the shark's mouth—he always used to give her. Seeing it again sent a violent shiver up her spine. "Truth or lie?"

"Truth," she mouthed.

The corner of his mouth twitched with that same, dark humor that shone in his eyes. "Does that make me a bad person?"

The skin on her arms and legs pebbled. "No," she decided. "He's a bad person for making you feel that way."

SHAYLA SLEPT with Roman in his bed.

Roman had never been the type to actually sleep with women. He usually left the minute the fucking was over and done with, so it went against everything he believed in when he told Shay, "Come here" once they made it back into the motel room. The look on her pretty face told him she was expecting those words to come with the same benefits he'd given her the night prior, when he'd made her moan his name as she came on his fingers.

But she laid down with him anyway. And neither of them tried anything with the other. Roman just held her, her back against his front, her chest rising and falling under his arm.

She fell asleep quickly, and Roman did too.

Tonight, he didn't crave sex. He craved comfort—something he hadn't been given since before his mom died.

And so what if he barely knew Shay? So what if she'd stolen from him? So what if he had a reputation to uphold as Shadowmaster and Wolf of the Hollow? He was just a man, and out here in the desert, in this tiny, stuffy motel room, he'd managed to find something he'd spent twenty-seven years looking for.

He wasn't sure what to call it yet, but it filled that void inside him and made him feel whole.

There were a lot of cracks in his soul, though. So he knew the feeling wouldn't last long. But he decided he deserved to enjoy this moment, this slice of peace and comfort, before that strange *thing* filling the gaping hole inside him slipped through the cracks and left him empty once more.

57

ROMAN'S HOUSE
YVESWICH, STATE OF KER

Loren stood in Roman's kitchen, chugging her second glass of water in under five minutes. She drained the whole thing, and once the last drop was gone, she looked at the water dispenser on the fridge with longing.

It was morning. She had woken up several minutes ago with a thirst that was staggering. Her mouth felt drier than a desert, and from the moment she'd woken up, her stomach was assaulted with pangs so painful she had practically sprinted down here. The rest of the house was quiet, but she knew she wouldn't have been left alone.

"Thirsty?" said a quiet male voice from behind her.

She turned to see Tanner Atlas drifting into the kitchen in gray sweatpants and a baggy white t-shirt. He was watching her with a frown, brows pulled together. His wolf Familiar stood at his side, head cocked to the left.

"It's like I can't get enough," she admitted. She swallowed, her throat already dry and aching.

He held his hand out, the back of it facing her, and motioned toward her forehead. "May I?"

She set the glass down and nodded. He stepped closer, flattening his fingers against her forehead.

His frown deepened. "Do you feel cold?"

Feet pattered on the floor. Ivy walked into the room wearing exercise clothes, her hair tied up, Soot trotting beside her. The dog was a female version of Bandit—darn near identical.

Ivy slowed, her gaze flicking between them. She took out one wireless earbud. "Something wrong?"

"Loren's cold," Tanner said. "And she can't quench her thirst."

Ivy took out the other bud and walked over. "Can I see your tattoo? The Caliginous one."

Loren rolled up the sleeve of her hooded sweatshirt and showed them. Her skin was so pale, the blue of her veins showed through, but at least that wasn't anything new; she'd always had trouble keeping a tan.

The new ink was pulsing white, the light rippling in tune with her heartbeat, from the curve of the C to the loop of the heart and the zigzagging end.

The garage door banged open. Pounding feet and male voices drifted into the house.

"Darien!" Ivy called with an edge of panic.

"Don't freak him out!" Loren hissed. But it was too late.

All conversation stopped. Boots rapidly struck the floor.

Darien appeared, his eyes immediately finding Loren. Behind him, Jack and Kylar filed in. They were already dressed and ready; Loren wondered where they'd gone.

"Loren?" Darien's deep voice was tense.

Ivy snatched her wrist and held it up. "She needs to get to Silverway."

LOREN SHIFTED from foot to foot as Darien jammed his finger into the button on the elevator for a fifth time—the one that would take them to Caliginous On Silverway.

She stood in the elevator with him, Ivy and Tanner here too. Other people were in the building as well, having to redirect their steps toward the other elevators upon seeing them standing inside. Their group wore hoods, Loren included, but she knew the three Darkslayers still stuck out horribly, even if no one could put a finger on who they were.

"It's four o'clock," Darien growled. "There's no way they're closed."

A hellseher businessman walking by the elevators slowed, briefcase swinging in hand. "Are you trying to get to Caliginous?"

"Yes," Darien said tightly.

"They're closed."

"Why?" The word was a bark that echoed.

The man shrugged. "They canceled my appointment and didn't say why." He walked away.

Darien looked up through the floors with black eyes. Cursed under his breath. Loren knew the spells, distance, and many floors were probably blinding him. He practically punched the button again, causing the backlight to flutter.

"Darien," Ivy chided. "You'll break it."

Tanner added, "And then we won't be able to come here tomorrow either, and you'll be even more pissed."

He stalked out of the elevator. Loren followed, Ivy and Tanner on either side of her.

Darien spun on a heel. "Atlas, come here for a sec."

They stepped aside and spoke quietly for several minutes, leaving Loren alone with Ivy. Both of the guys stole glances at her every few seconds.

"What are they saying?" she asked Ivy.

"I'm sure they'll tell us when they're done gossiping." Her tone was teasing, but her smile was stiff.

And then Darien and Tanner were heading this way.

"In the car," Darien instructed.

They left the building and got in Darien's car. The snap of Loren's seatbelt buckling felt loud in the heavy quiet.

"Are you going to tell me what you're thinking?" Loren asked, bundling her fingers into her jacket sleeves. She knew Ivy's hellseher ears had picked up on what they'd discussed inside, but when Darien explained, he spoke as if his words benefitted everyone.

"We have a friend named Blue," he began. "You've met her before. She's powerful like you, but her magic is just blue. Back in Angelthene, our friend Dominic took her to the ocean to recharge her magic. Caliginous Chambers like Chamber Number Five recharge a person's magic. When you woke up out of a coma, it was only after every color—every type of magic—was poured into you." He must have noticed her shivering, because he started the car and turned the heat on. And then he held up his thumb and began ticking things off as he listed them. "You said you're cold. I believe it's because you need red magic—fire." His index finger joined his thumb. "You said you're always thirsty. Blue magic—water. What else? And don't hold back because you're afraid of causing alarm."

"I feel like I can't draw a deep enough breath." She rubbed at her chest that felt too small.

He added his middle finger. "Oxygen. Green magic." He dropped his hand and turned to look at Ivy and Tanner in the back seat. "Terra Firma."

Ivy said, "Terra Firma, Mist, and Inferno."

"What does that mean?" Loren asked.

"They're types of arcane magic," Darien said. He pulled his hood off and ran a hand through his hair, pushing the loose strands back flat. "Very old, powerful magic apparently lost a long time ago." He studied her. "Anything else?"

She nibbled on her lip.

"Don't hold back," he said gently, that intense gaze of his skating her features. "I need to know everything."

She inhaled, focusing on what her body was telling her, searching for anything that felt off. She shook her head. "That's it right now."

He put the car into drive and pulled out into traffic at lightning-speed, tires screeching. "Then let's get you back to Roman's. I have an idea."

58

MOTEL 58
STATE OF WITHEREDGE

Shay woke up in Roman's arms, in the exact same spot as last night. It made her wonder if the Wolf of the Hollow had moved at all while he'd slept.

A smile pulled at her mouth. But soon that smile was fading as she remembered that this was day number four, and she'd lost Roman's necklace.

This was a mistake. A road she should never have stepped onto. She had let Roman touch her, had initiated a kiss, and now she had spent the night in his arms.

She had never felt like such a fool. But even though this road led to certain destruction, and her brakes had failed, she had no desire to jump out of the vehicle.

She wanted to stay right here. Wrapped up in the strong arms of the Darkslayer she'd stolen from. The man who'd threatened her in that alley.

The man who'd surprised her in more ways than one.

He woke up a few minutes later, and when he stretched and flexed his body against hers, she felt his erection dig into her ass—and sensed that she was about to crash a whole lot sooner than she'd planned.

She rolled over to face him. His gold-flecked eyes were fixed on her, and she didn't miss the burning desire in that stare.

Men and their early-morning arousal. She supposed the timing was good, though, considering she was about to ask him something potentially dangerous.

"I need a favor," she said, trying not to breathe on him, well aware that she needed a toothbrush stat.

"Take your panties off."

Whoa. Her face got hot. She wet her lips, and Roman tracked the movement. "Not that," she said, though she questioned her own sanity for denying him. But he'd already done her a favor, and she still hadn't repaid him. Never mind that she was asking for a new, entirely different favor not of the sexual kind. "I need a sixth day," she told him.

The corner of his mouth pulled down, deepening his scar. "I'm awake for five minutes, and you ask me to be blackmailed for a sixth day?"

"I'll do something for you in return."

That red-hot stare dragged down her body, lingering the longest on the area where her thighs touched, and the hard peaks of her nipples that were showing through her pajama shirt. Technically it wasn't a pajama shirt. It wasn't even *her* shirt. It was Roman's.

Another bad idea. Wearing a man's clothes always felt like some massive commitment, like surrendering the one and only key to your heart to the guy whose clothes you were drowning in.

She was sure it wasn't that serious, but for some reason, with Roman, it felt that way.

Roman considered her offer. "No."

Shay bristled, unable to stomach the idea of being rejected by him—and she had to admit she was disappointed. After he'd gotten her off, it had only made her desire to take care of him in return intensify. "Why not?"

"If a woman is going to do something sexual for me, I want it to be because she *wants* to. Not because she has something to gain."

Okay, so maybe she had to be clearer with him.

"What if I have a different thing to gain?" She licked her lips; again, he tracked the movement with a stare that burned ever hotter. She knew exactly what he would ask her for, should he accept her offer. "What if I want to make you come?"

Roman was silent.

And then he swore, the word low and rough. He ran a hand through his tousled dark hair. "I can't handle you."

"Why not?"

"Because you say things that make me want to explode all over your face, Shayla."

He undid his belt—he hadn't undressed last night before getting into bed—and when she glimpsed his tan skin underneath, and his cock straining to be let out, she felt that area between her legs pulse with a need as strong as Roman's stare. He was big—he didn't need to take off his pants for her to tell. And she wanted every inch of him inside her. Now. Gods, she wanted it right now.

"Put your mouth on me," he commanded, his words soaking her panties, "and we'll talk about your sixth day after."

AFTERWARD, Shay walked into the bathroom and shut the door behind her. Faced herself in the mirror.

Her face was flushed, her lips rosy and swollen. Her eyes were bright with intensity, and parts of her still pulsed with the longing to be touched. But today was Roman's turn.

What was happening to her? She'd spent too much time in the desert with Roman Devlin, that was what. She bet he did this kind of thing with plenty of other girls—and was only bothering with her now because she had coerced him into shacking up with her for five days in the middle of nowhere. The man was probably bored out of his mind—and she was merely a toy for him to play with.

He'd warned her not to get attached, and she was intent on cooperating. There was no point in mulling over what they were doing out here, no point in fretting over the thought of him with other girls.

The man wasn't hers, and he never would be. Even if they wanted to be together, and even if being with him was allowed, they were too different. They were worlds apart, and as soon as she found her sister, she was leaving Yveswich. Roman Devlin would go back to being a stranger—a brief fling she would forget about after a few weeks.

As she brushed her teeth and washed her face, she had settled on two simple facts.

She was an idiot for getting physically involved with him. And no amount of weeks could ever make her forget about the Shadowmaster from the Hollow.

ROMAN WENT OUTSIDE FOR A SMOKE—AND to ask himself what in the hell he thought he was doing.

Getting involved with a Darkslayer from another house was forbidden. Doing so could get you killed—slowly and painfully. Death came for those who broke the rules, and the one who sent him was Donovan Slade. The man loved when his people broke the rules.

Had Roman been the only person involved in this screwup, he wouldn't have cared so much, but he wasn't breaking those rules on his own. And if anyone found out what he and Shay were doing out here, there'd be hell to pay.

Any other girl, and he wouldn't have cared. Would've thrown her to the wolves, because he was one himself. But he was beginning to realize that he was in over his head. He was drowning in Shayla Cousens, and the most concerning part was how much he enjoyed losing himself in the waves.

About an hour later, Shay was picking at the fruit and muffins Roman had brought into the room for her when she heard a car roll up outside.

A bad feeling twisted in her stomach.

She set the plate on the bed. Got up and crossed the room. Peeked through the curtains—

At the sight of the black car, the tall woman with strawberry-blonde hair, and the burly man who accompanied her, she dropped the curtain and backed up until the backs of her legs hit the bed.

The curtains swayed. Through the sliver of space between them, Shay watched as the couple evaluated the parking lot and tiny motel with shrewd gazes, their mouths twisting with disgust.

Shay's breakfast threatened to come back up.

Roman came out of the bathroom—showered and dressed in black jeans and a white shirt, hair wet, boots laced up. The plan was to go back to the Facility and have a better look around, and now that plan was wrecked.

Roman's dark brows lowered, throwing his honeyed eyes into deep shadow. "What's going on, pup?"

Shay couldn't find her voice.

"Pup?" He came closer, bringing that churning storm of energy with him. And that scent of his—the cologne, the body wash, *him*. That scent was all over her. All. Over. Her. He reached for her but didn't touch, his fingers squeezing into a fist in the air between them. "Shayla."

She faced him with wide eyes. "My mom is here."

There was no point in hiding. Shay had forgotten all about her little slip-up—how the motel room was registered under her real name. Hiding their auras, turning off their phones... All of it had been for nothing.

Because Athene Cousens had found her. She stood in the parking lot, her pencil skirt and blazer as blue as the ocean, her hair that was the same color as Shay's streaming down her back in perfect, glossy waves. The night they'd booked the room, Shay had been so sick of Roman's shit that her mistake hadn't even dawned on her. It was the kind of stupid slip she'd never made before.

And now, she'd wrecked everything.

She steeled herself with several deep breaths before reaching for the door knob—

Roman's voice stilled her hand. "Sure you want to do this, pup?"

She swallowed, her eyes stinging. "What other choice do I have?" Her voice quavered. "Tomorrow's day five. I guess I can consider myself lucky we made it this long."

"She's going to take you away fr—" He abruptly stopped. Shay heard him swallow. "From here," he finished.

"I don't have another choice," she whispered. She took a moment just to look at him, to feel his energy, trying to imprint Roman on her brain, just in case she never saw him again. She probably wouldn't. "I want to thank you, Roman," she whispered. "For helping me. For...not leaving me."

Roman's mouth became a thin line. "I can save you from her."

Shay gave him a sad smile. "No, you can't," she said gently.

And then she opened the door and walked out into the sunlight.

ROMAN KNEW he should stay put, but fuck it, he was notoriously bad at doing the opposite of what he should. Shoulda, woulda, coulda—fuck it all.

He walked out of the motel room after Shay, whose arm was already gripped by Athene Cousens's claws.

Athene looked up at his approach. Blinked. "Shadows." Her copper lips spread with a smirk. "How...unexpected." She redirected her poisonous smile at her daughter. "You're coming home—now."

Roman's hands curled into fists. "She's almost twenty years old, and you're treating her like she's your property."

"Donovan will be very interested to hear of your alibi, Devlin."

"I dare you to tell him," he spat. "I'm sure he'll be thrilled to hear that your daughter was hunting in a Gray Zone and stole directly from the House of Black." He knew it was a cheap shot—but he also knew that if Don found out about this from Athene's gossiping mouth, he wouldn't just hurt Shay, he'd torture and kill her. Better that she face the wrath of her mother than the vengeance of his psycho father.

Athene pulled Shay toward the car. "We're leaving—now."

Shay resisted, dragging her hiking boots and pulling her weight the other way. "Wait—my bags." She yanked on her arm, but Athene held tight. "Let go!" Shay's voice became desperate, the raw panic in her words boiling Roman's blood. "Let go—you're hurting me!"

Roman stalked forward, chest tight and aching with fury. "Let her the fuck go, Athene."

She pushed Shay toward the open back door of the car, shoving her so hard that she slammed into the door and made it rock on the hinges. "Balthazar, her things, please."

Her bodyguard headed for the room, and the moment Shay was in the car, door shut, Athene stepped up to Roman. Her ugly-ass stilettos put her at equal height with him as she lifted her chin, looking at him down her bony nose. "If you come anywhere near my daughter again, consider it an act of war."

"If you touch her again, consider it an act of war."

Athene's smile was venomous. "Whatever this is, it ends now. Do you understand me?"

"Do I understand you? Yes. Do I comply? That remains to be seen, Mrs. Cousens."

"If you don't stay away, you will be making a big mistake." She turned on a heel and strutted to the car.

Balthazar appeared, Shay's bags and jacket in hand. He looked like a drill sergeant with that haircut and square chin. He surveyed Roman with a gaze that could cut, and then he made the mistake of coming close—close enough to breathe on him. "You'd be wise to do as the lady says."

Roman hawked and spat in his face. "You'd be wise to get the fuck away from me."

Balthazar wiped the gob off his eyelid and cheek. Smirked. He shook the spit off his fingers, turned, and got in the car.

It took Roman an immense amount of willpower not to follow that car, not to flip it over and kill Athene and her pussy bodyguard and watch as the parched earth lapped up their blood.

Especially when he saw Shay turn to look at him through the back window, tears streaming down her face.

Shay never cried—she'd said it herself. Whether those tears were for him, the sister she hadn't found, or the mother caging her, he didn't know, but it didn't matter.

It still chewed him the fuck apart inside.

SHAY COULDN'T REMEMBER the last time she'd cried.

She sat in the back of Athene's car, her face wet. The tears had stopped, but she could feel them threatening to come again.

Possibly the worst part about them was understanding why they were happening. Was it because her mother had found her and was dragging her back to the Riptide? Was it because she still hadn't found Anna?

Or was it because of Roman? The look on his face when Athene had dragged her toward the car... That was pure, undiluted rage. No matter how long she lived, Shay would never forget that look.

It was the first time anyone other than Anna and their late father had fought for her. The first time anyone had cared enough to react the way Roman just did.

"You are never to see that boy again." Athene's cold voice cut into the car that reeked of floral perfume. She looked straight ahead, her eyes shielded by round sunglasses. Shay didn't bother pointing out that Roman was twenty-seven years old and the farthest thing from a boy. But when you could live forever, some parents tended to treat their offspring like children well into adulthood. "Shay? Do you understand me?"

Shay stared out her window. The backs of her eyes were burning, and another migraine was creeping in.

Athene's aura prickled like a storm cloud bursting with lightning. "You are never to look at, speak to, or sleep with Roman Devlin again. Am I being clear?"

"You're being unreasonable."

"Did you sleep with him?"

"No." It wasn't a lie.

"If I find out you're lying to me, there will be hell to pay."

Shay clenched her teeth. "Maybe, if you had been looking for Anna yourself, I wouldn't have felt the need to ask for a Shadowmaster's help."

"If you were the daughter I deserve, you would've trusted and listened to me."

"I'll never be the daughter you deserve—that was Anna. And you don't even care that she's missing—"

"Enough!" Athene's voice was so loud, it cracked. "I've heard enough, Shayla! You're coming back to the Riptide and you're staying there. No more sneaking away, no more ridiculous galavants in the desert." She

turned in her seat to glare at her through her sunglasses. "And no. More. Roman. Devlin." Her mouth was pinched, her pulse fluttering angrily in her neck.

She turned back around and flicked on the radio.

The rest of the car ride was quiet, aside from her mother's horrid taste in music, but Shay's mind was loud. Inside, she was screaming, as she had her whole life, only this time the screaming was different.

Instead of animalistic shouts and the rattling of bars no one but her could see, she was shouting out a name.

It was Roman's.

59

ROMAN'S HOUSE
YVESWICH, STATE OF KER

A shiver wracked Loren's body as she slowly lowered herself into the indoor swimming pool at Roman's house.

She wore a white one-piece bathing suit with peek-a-boo designs cut into the ribs. Darien had bought her the suit from a small surf shop in the Financial District; the new material smelled of all the sunscreen and coconut tanning lotion on their shelves. It reminded Loren of the summers she'd spent at the beaches in Angelthene with Dallas and Sabrine.

She missed them terribly.

"How are you feeling?" Darien's bass voice echoed in the cavernous room. He stood by the side of the pool, arms crossed over his broad chest, feet braced apart. He wore a black long-sleeve and black jeans, combat boots still on.

She sank in until the water lapped against her breasts. "Would be a bit better if it wasn't so cold." Her teeth chattered.

Darien dropped into a crouch and dipped his fingers into the water. Judging from the frown that tipped down one corner of his mouth, it wasn't nearly as cold as she thought it was.

"It's not cold, is it?" she asked him.

He stood back up and shook the water off his hand. "See how you feel after a few minutes. Tell me if anything seems alarming." He watched as she bobbed in the water on her tiptoes. It felt unsettling to be watched by him all the time, but she also didn't want him to go away. She wasn't sure what it was about Darien, but she felt safer when he was with her, as if he truly could stop anything bad from happening. "Why don't you try swimming for a bit?" he suggested.

"Do you want to join me?" Maybe she wouldn't feel so awkward if he got in the water too.

Or maybe she would feel worse because that would mean he'd have to take off his shirt.

Yeah, seeing him half-naked would probably make this way worse.

"Maybe another time," he said.

"You want to stay dressed and keep your boots on in case something bad happens to me, don't you?"

He didn't answer, but she knew she'd struck the nail on the head.

"Why are you doing all this?" Her voice was quiet and breathy, and her teeth chattered again.

He merely said, "Because I care."

They looked at each other for a moment that seemed to last forever. The undivided attention he always gave her made her heart skip beats.

He turned away suddenly, squeezing his eyes shut, a muscle working in his square jaw. When he reopened them again, Loren caught a glimpse of the black before it faded away.

"Are you okay?"

"I'm fine." He started pacing the length of the pool. "Just swim around for a bit. Pretend I'm not here." Pretending he wasn't here when he sucked the air out of every room he entered was pretty much impossible.

But she did as he'd asked, and for once he didn't watch her. He just kept pacing, squeezing his eyes shut every few minutes.

And then he stalked to the glass doors that led into the house, pushed one open, and shouted up the stairs. "Ivy!" A pause. *"Ivy!"*

It took her a couple of minutes to get down here, and when she did, they conversed in tones too quiet for Loren to hear.

And then Darien disappeared inside.

Ivy came to the edge of the pool. She tugged off her socks, rolled up her jeans, and dipped her feet into the water. "Darien will be back in a bit," she said with a tight smile.

But Loren was starting to be able to tell when they were hiding things, and she knew Ivy was hiding that something was wrong with him.

"You're addicted, aren't you?" Tanner asked.

Darien stood across from him in the kitchen, dripping Venom into his eyes. Jack and Kylar were here too.

"I think it's making my Surges worse," Darien said. He put the cap back on and shoved the bottle into the back pocket of his jeans.

Jack grinned. "Is that even possible?"

Kylar widened his eyes and said, "I don't really think now's the best time for jokes, Jack."

"But ill-timed jokes are my specialty." Jack's smile faded the moment he met Darien's stare. "Please don't excommunicate me."

Tanner looked concerned. "You might want to go easy on that," he said to Darien. "How many bottles did you get?"

"Three. More than I expected."

Jack said, "Hopefully he didn't dilute it."

"I don't think he would've been that dumb," Kylar said. "He might rip off other people, maybe, but not Darkslayers."

Jack stared at the thin, dark lines webbing away from Darien's shining black eyes. "Can you see anything when you're like that?"

"I can switch between regular vision and the Sight." He pushed off the kitchen counter and turned to look at himself in the reflection of the microwave.

Fuck, he looked like a monster—like the beast forever prowling in his soul. "I don't want Loren to see me like this."

"Still no memories?" Kylar asked.

Darien leaned in closer to the microwave and pulled down his lower lid to study all the black. Even the inside of his lid was gray and webbed.

"Why don't you show her yours?" Tanner suggested. "It might help her along."

The Hob was watching from the top of the fridge, though she hid behind the jar of coins and cereal boxes, fully ducking every time Darien looked her way.

"I'm not going to hurt you, Itzel," Darien said. "But I wouldn't mind if you were quieter tonight." Loren didn't know this, but Darien created sound barriers for her every night until she fell into a deep sleep. It meant less sleep for him, but he'd do it for her. Anything for her.

He turned back around and leaned against the counter. Ran a hand through his hair, his rings catching in the strands. "I don't want to do that," Darien said, answering Atlas's question. "Showing her my memories is no better than getting her to watch a movie—there are no feelings involved. I'd rather she remember on her own. Especially anything about me."

Jack nodded, a new idiotic grin on his face. "You mean the bang sessions."

The grinding of Darien's teeth was audible. "Everything."

"I think she'll remember," Tanner encouraged. "It's only been a few days."

Darien looked toward the stairs that led down to the pool; he could just barely hear the soft echo of Loren and Ivy's conversation. "Hopefully."

The stick of bare feet on the floor pulled his attention toward the hallway that led to the upper floors. Joyce was approaching, her body wrapped up in a pool towel, an extra bathing suit in hand.

Darien said, "Any doctor's tips for drug abusers?" He smirked.

Joyce noted the black eyes and webbing. "Don't use them."

Loren paddled around in the pool on an inflatable donut.

Ivy had put on the bathing suit Joyce had brought down for her and was swimming laps. Joyce lounged in the hot tub, arms spread out on the rim behind her, eyes closed and head back.

This was heaven. That strange, hot feeling in Loren's throat was gone, along with the stomach pangs. She didn't want to jinx it, but...she had to admit she was feeling much better.

The doors to the pool room opened, and Darien walked in.

Loren stopped kicking her feet and bobbed in the donut, her arms looped through the center of it. Her long hair was soaked and stuck to her back.

Steel-blue eyes went straight to her; it was like he only ever saw *her*. "How are you feeling?" His bass voice echoed.

"Better."

"Not thirsty anymore?"

She shook her head.

Ivy broke the surface of the water and pushed her wet hair back. "You're a genius, Daredevil. I never would've thought of this."

"I'm sure you would have," he countered. His focus returned to Loren. "What about the other things?"

Her hand drifted toward her chest—and the lungs that still felt too small.

He was speaking again before she could respond. "Your teeth are still chattering."

She didn't deny it.

"Why don't you come out, and we'll try something else?"

She swam toward the pool steps, pushed the donut aside, and got out, water dripping all over the floor. She walked with Darien to the closed doors of the sauna and steam room.

"Which one would you like to try?" he asked.

Ivy got out of the pool. "Wait, I'm coming too!"

Loren's eyes flicked between the doors. "The sauna." She didn't feel like being wet anymore.

Darien opened the heavy door for her, dry heat wafting out. Ivy hurried up, wet feet slapping the floor, her body wrapped in a fluffy towel. She passed a second one to Loren, and they walked into the sauna together.

Darien made to step in too, but hesitated.

Ivy said, "You'll roast in here in those clothes. Besides, it's already on and running fine. I'll stay with her, you wait out there."

Darien merely looked at Loren—one more time—before shutting the door.

The sauna was beautiful and lit with red light. It smelled of cedar in here, a sweet scent that owed its thanks to the tiered wooden benches. The walls were made of rock salt, and every so often a fan came on that blew ground salt into the room. Her lips already tasted like it.

They sat on the top bench and leaned back against the warm wall. Loren tucked her knees up to her chin and focused on breathing and the feel of the rock heating up her back, sinking into her muscles and loosening up the knots she hadn't realized were there.

"I think," Ivy began, her soft voice filling the room. She was resting her head against the wall, eyes shut. "I'm going to have to ask Roman if he needs a roommate."

Loren smiled. "This place is pretty incredible." She glanced toward the door. "He never goes away, does he?" She couldn't see Darien, but somehow, she knew he was there.

"Do you want him to?" Not at all.

Loren shook her head. "No. I just... I guess it's kind of weird for me to have people around who care so much."

Ivy opened her eyes and sat up straighter.

Loren continued, "Roark and Taega were never the...affectionate types. Dallas and I clung to each other a lot, but—" She stopped, her throat suddenly tight. Talking about Dallas made her heart twinge.

Dallas had never been the affectionate type either. But in a lot of ways, she was Loren's only family. Loren, on the other hand, had always felt as though she had a lot of love to give and no one to give it to. Maybe that was why she'd taken such a liking to plants and animals. They were always in need of love and never refused it.

Ivy was still watching her. Still listening to every word. Even when limned in red light, her face was truly breathtaking.

Loren inhaled the salty air and forced a smile. "I guess family for me was a little different than most. So I'm not used to all of this." She fluttered a hand toward the door—and the man she knew stood behind it.

"I know you can't remember everything yet," Ivy said, "but you're a part of our family. We love you as if you're one of us." Ivy's statement made her heart feel oddly full and empty at the same time.

Loren looked toward the door again, her mind spinning as she considered all that she'd forgotten from the past six months, the events that had turned the Seven Devils from terrifying strangers into family.

Ivy leaned back against the wall. "You've been talking a lot about repaying us for all of this, but believe me when I say you don't need to worry about that. We're doing this because we care, and because we're family—and you don't have to pay back family."

Twenty minutes later, she felt warmer than she had since the night she woke up.

Ivy pushed open the door, and Loren followed. They were fully dried off, aside from their hair.

Darien was waiting right there, just like she'd thought. Loren's eyes immediately magnetized to him, and his to her.

She shut the sauna door tight. "I think you might be onto something."

60

WITCHLIGHT
ANGELTHENE, STATE OF WITHEREDGE

Travis parallel parked across the street from Witchlight Alchemy and Archives. Jewels and Lace were with him, and rolling up into the free spot behind the car were Logan and Sabrine. The truck rumbled for a few seconds before Logan cut the engine.

They'd made the decision to come here after Tamika had expressed her fear of being watched. No one had spoken to Arthur in a while, not since before Darien and the others left town, so Travis wanted to check up on him. If Tamika was being watched, there was a strong chance that the former weapons technician for Lucent Enterprises was being surveilled as well. Especially after the old man had been canned for stealing blueprints of the Arcanum Well replica.

Travis looked in the rear-view mirror. Logan and Sabrine were watching him. Waiting. It felt weird to be *that* person—the one who was suddenly making all the decisions. That was Darien, and when it wasn't Darien, it was Max. And when it wasn't either of them, which didn't happen often, the authority shifted to Travis or Jack. He couldn't decide if he liked it or not.

"Coast looks clear," Lace murmured. Her eyes were black, and she was scanning the parked cars and businesses all around them. "No one seems to be lingering, and no one seems to be watching."

Travis shut off the car. "If there's anyone in danger right now, it's Arthur." At least Travis and the others had the means to protect themselves, but a human in his seventies? Arthur was practically a walking target. He opened his door. "Stay close."

They got out, Logan and Sabrine doing the same, and waited for a gap in traffic before crossing the street. It was just after noon, the block alive with activity. Pedestrians avoided them on the sidewalk, like usual, and the odd person slowed their car to get a better look. Typical Darkslayer life. You'd think they were celebrities.

They passed under the rickety wooden sign that read WITCHLIGHT ALCHEMY AND ARCHIVES, the wood cut into the shape of a grimoire, and pushed open the heavy, creaking door.

Travis had been with the Devils for such a long time that not much surprised him anymore, but he stopped short at the sight of the tall, red-headed man standing beside Arthur's table on the other side of the cluttered room.

Jewels wasn't expecting Travis to stop. She walked into him, smacking her face into his back.

Sabrine stepped around them. "Roark?"

The silence that descended upon the room—empty apart from Arthur J. Kind and Roark Bright, and now Travis and his group—was thick enough to cut.

Arthur was the first to speak. "Well." He sucked in a breath of air, and blew it out slowly. "This was bound to happen eventually," he said to Roark. "They're very nosey." His watery eyes flicked to the group by the door. "Come on in. Flip the sign and lock the door, please, Travis."

The others crossed the room and gathered around Arthur's side of the table. Travis kept an eye on Roark as he turned the deadbolt and flipped the sign.

Travis joined the others, taking up position between Lace and Jewels. Logan stayed close to Sabrine, the alpha emitting constant heat but thankfully not trembling.

Roark kept quiet while Arthur launched into an explanation.

"Roark has brought some...grave news," Arthur began. "For the first time since before Kalendae, the files containing the blueprints of the Arcanum Well replica have been accessed."

Silence descended. And then Travis said, "What does that mean?"

Lace added, her question for Roark, "Are you finally going to talk to us about all this bullshit, or do we need to keep guessing and running around in circles chasing our tails?"

Roark was unfazed. And still, he didn't speak.

Arthur said, "Roark is spelled. Like Erasmus. Shortly before the Phoenix Head Society broke apart, he and the other members were bound by a spell that prevented them from speaking of the things that happened in the society—especially not about the Arcanum Well."

Sabrine said, "Then how was he able to talk to you about the replica? How do you know all of this?"

Arthur clasped his wrinkled hands before him. "Because it is a replica," he replied with patience. "The silencing spell did not apply to replicas, it applied to the real thing." Sneaky.

"What about Taega?" Travis asked, remembering back to when Darien and a few of the others had paid a visit to the Bright penthouse before Kalendae. He said to Roark, "Taega was a member of the Phoenix Head Society—we saw her in a photograph we found in the tunnels below Angelthene Academy. She told Darien a bunch of shit about the Well and Loren before she got arrested."

A cool female voice floated through the room. "Because, Devlin, I was the first to leave."

Their group—all except Arthur and Roark—turned to see Taega walking through a doorway that led to the back rooms.

Her heels clicked on the floor as she crossed the room. When she reached the group, she took up position at her husband's side and folded her hands before her.

"Taega," Arthur began, "left the Phoenix Head Society before it broke apart. Roark stayed and was soon bound to secrecy. He could no longer speak of anything that went on in the society—not even to the woman who later became his wife." The old man gave Taega a warm smile.

"Did you know this the whole time?" Travis asked Arthur, unable to stop the betrayal prickling across his nape. "Why didn't you tell us?"

"Of course I would have told you, Travis, had I known," Arthur replied calmly. "After the Blood Moon, Roark and Taega decided to trust me with some secrets they have protected for years. And I took the liberty of trusting them as well. I think it's high time we all worked together. And so I told them," he concluded. "About Erasmus."

Travis couldn't read Roark's expression, but he swore the man's eyes tightened at the name of his old friend—the friend he'd believed was dead.

Taega spoke up. "The fact that the blueprints for the replica have been accessed tells us we have a big problem on our hands." She faced her husband. "Roark, if you'd do the honors of telling them."

The one thing Roark could speak freely about: The replica. "The files have been accessed somewhere in Yveswich," Roark began. "We don't have specific coordinates, but we are certain that whoever is accessing the files is there as we speak. And we have reason to believe it might be the imperator and his men." Travis watched as a muscle fluttered in Roark's cheek. He added tightly, "And we're afraid they are building another replica."

The blood drained from Travis's face. For a moment, their group was silent.

And then Logan said, "What would be the point? It blew up Angelthene the first time—what makes them think it won't happen again?"

Travis added, "And why Yveswich?"

"Yveswich is a very important place," Taega said. "It was the very first sealing point for the Veil, when it was first erected." She drew a breath that trembled, her eyes flicking to Roark. "The city also overlaps with the Void." Exactly like Tamika said. "It is directly overtop it—the mirror of a place in Spirit Terra known in history books as The Necropolis." An ancient language that translated to *City of the Dead*.

Travis's blood drained from his face, his thoughts immediately shifting to Paxton and Roman.

To Darien.

Roark scanned their group with a hard gaze. "Have any of you ever given the imperator a reason to want to go to Yveswich?"

61

MOTEL 58
STATE OF WITHEREDGE

Aside from a store that claimed to sell everything in the alphabet, Motel 58 was the only business around for miles.

Their group stood out front of the tiny motel—all except Blue and Dominic, who were invisible in the SUV. They'd decided it was a good idea to keep Blue hidden, and she hadn't argued; even simply being here set her on edge. From the moment they'd pulled up, she'd kept looking toward room number three with panicked eyes, and although Max couldn't see her right now through the spells, he had a feeling she was still doing it.

The employee they were speaking to was named Clark. A half-human warlock in his mid-thirties, who Malakai was about to lose his shit on.

"Did you," Malakai began slowly, speaking the same question he'd asked the guy twice already, "or did you not have a shift the day the police were here?"

Clark was staring into space. He blinked his bloodshot eyes and looked at the Reaper, as if finally noticing Malakai was there. "Huh? Oh—no. No, I didn't work that day, I just heard about it."

"Do you spend every day like this?" Malakai snapped.

The guy blinked again, mouth hanging open. "Like what?"

"High as a fucking kite!"

Aspen stepped forward. "Clark," she began, impatience simmering beneath her polite tone, "is there anyone else we might be able to speak to?"

Clark smiled goofily, as if finally understanding something. "Ohh—you're a Reaper!"

Aspen blinked. She was beginning to look as frustrated as Malakai.

"A couple other Darkslayers were staying here recently, y'know?" Clark said. "You guys are beyond cool. Vigilantism and all that." He gave a stupid nod of approval.

Max rolled his eyes.

"Vigilantism?" Malakai growled. He pointed a finger in Clark's face. "Don't ever insult me like that again—"

Max stepped forth, knocking Malakai's arm aside before he could get them all arrested. "What'd they look like?"

Clark blinked. "Huh?"

"The Darkslayers!"

"Oh. Uhhhhhh... He had a tattoo like yours—the guy." He scratched at his neck. "Couldn't tell if the girl had one."

"What do you mean you couldn't tell?"

He shrugged. "Makeup. Hair. Glamor. Who knows?"

"Which symbol?"

Clark was staring into space again. "Huh?"

"Which," Max gritted out, "symbol?"

He shrugged. "My eyes are bad. I need glasses, but they're not covered by my extended healthcare."

Max glanced at Malakai. "Think it was Darien?"

"Why the hell would Darien be here?"

"Darien Cassel?" Clark cut in with one of his random, inexplicable moments of clarity. "Nah. I would've known if it was him. It wasn't your symbol." He gestured to his cheek. "It was here."

Max shared another look with Malakai.

"Yveswich," Malakai said. He faced Clark and beckoned with an impatient hand. "Give me your guest names."

A nervous laugh bubbled out of Clark's mouth. "Pretty sure that goes against some sort of policy—"

Malakai stalked forward. "How about the gun-up-your-ass policy?" he snarled, towering over Clark.

Clark blanched and stumbled back—

The door to the motel office swung open, and a lady in her sixties, a name tag that said 'Priscilla' pinned to her flowery blouse, bustled out. "What in heaven's name is going on out here?" Short as she was, she somehow managed to look down her nose at Malakai. Max was majorly impressed. "May I help you, sir?" she clucked.

Max spoke first. "We're looking for my little sister—she's missing. Is there any way you could give us a few minutes of your time, please? Just a few minutes, then we'll get out of your hair. Promise."

Priscilla looked him over with pinched lips, but her eyes were kind, and it was those eyes that told Max she was taking him seriously.

About damn time.

Clark side-stepped toward Priscilla. "Can I go for lunch now?"

Priscilla patted his arm. "You may go." He left immediately. As soon as he was out of earshot, Priscilla's eyes flicked about their group. "You'll have to excuse him, he's new."

Malakai said, "And zonked. I want what he's smoking."

Priscilla beckoned them into the office. "Come, come."

They filed in, the room hardly big enough to hold all five of them, and crowded around the desk as Priscilla plopped herself into a swivel chair behind it.

"Is this about Anna Cousens?" She put on the eyeglasses she wore on a gold chain around her neck.

Max's brow creased. "No. What makes you ask that?"

"A couple of hellsehers came looking for her." She frowned, peering up at him through the tiny, squeaky-clean lenses. "Don't tell me there's been another abduction."

Max considered his response. "Not a recent one, but I'm starting to think they could be connected. What can you tell us about these hellsehers?"

"Well, the law says 'nothing'," she said cheekily, folding her arms on the desk. Her smile turned her cheeks into red apples. "Why don't you tell me some details about what led you here, and I'll see if I can help?"

"A rental car," Max answered promptly, "and three men who came here with a girl with blue hair."

Priscilla's expression was telling. "That sounds an awful lot like the situation involving Anna Cousens."

"My sister went missing years ago," Max said. "I thought she was dead, but I have reason to believe she isn't. If you can tell us anything—anything at all—I would be indebted you. I just want to find her—that's all I want."

Priscilla mulled the situation over. She drew a deep breath and exhaled through her nose. "Well. I can tell you the same thing I told the others. Three men and a young, blue-haired lady checked in a few weeks ago. A second woman—Anna Cousens—eventually joined them. When they checked out, they only had the blue-haired one in their company. Twice I observed them leaving; the first time, they were heading that way." She pointed a wrinkled finger at the endless, empty desert shimmering under the sun. "The second time—the time when they checked out—they went that way." She pointed now toward Angelthene.

Max motioned toward the empty desert. "What's out that way?"

She pursed her lips. "Not much. A power plant and some scattered housing."

"Anything else?" Malakai clipped.

She frowned at him. "You are an impatient brute, aren't you?"

Dallas stifled a laugh with a hand to her mouth.

When Priscilla's gaze returned to Max, her expression softened—which was saying a lot, considering the lady was already softer than a mashed potato. "That's all, my dear."

He stepped forward and extended a hand. "Thank you. I really appreciate it."

She shook it, her hand warm. "You are most welcome."

They left the office. The late afternoon had turned impossibly hotter, and they'd only been inside for a few minutes.

Malakai mimicked in a squeaky voice, "'Thank you, I really appreciate it'."

Max glared. "Nobody fucking likes you," he retorted.

Malakai smiled. "I consider that a very, very big win."

Max opened the door to the SUV, being careful to keep Blue hidden. "We're going to have to rent a room," he said quietly. "It's getting dark." Another day with hardly any answers, but tomorrow they'd drive out into that desert.

Dominic's mouth was twitching with a smile. "Did Malakai totally wreck that for you, or what?"

"Almost," Max muttered. He turned to Dallas. "Can you glamor her?" he said of Blue.

Dallas took out her magic stave and climbed into the back with Dominic and Blue. "Hold still," she told Blue. "Let's give you a new hair color." She squinted. "How about pink this time?"

Blue eyed Dallas. "Red."

62

THE DESERT
STATE OF WITHEREDGE

The drive back to Yveswich was quiet—just the way Roman liked it. Only this time, the silence was different. And it sucked—big time.

Because Shayla Cousens wasn't here with him.

They'd made it to day number four, which was longer than Roman had expected either of them to last before going for the throat. He'd agreed to a sixth day—at least, he'd planned to, once he'd made sure Paxton was safe. But he hadn't got that far before Athene the-bitch Cousens pulled up.

Shay should be here right now. Bickering with him about the A/C and his taste in music and dots that kept getting farther away on screens.

And telling him that she needed to pee every twenty goddamn minutes.

The front bumper was still scuffed up from her shoe. He had no idea why he never bothered to clean it. He could have done it back in Yveswich, before this trip with her began. And now, he had even less desire to remove it. There was little logic behind it, but that mark was a reminder of her—and there was a shortage of those now that she was gone. The last four days felt like a dream. *She* felt like a dream.

He tried to force himself to think about something else, but she consumed his every waking moment. And now that he'd felt her gorgeous mouth on his cock, not thinking about her was an even harder task. Fuck, Shayla getting on her knees for him was an amazing start to his day. She was very good with her tongue, her lips. He'd never felt so wholly owned by a woman before—nor had he ever enjoyed it this much.

He sighed and slumped against his sun-warmed door, remembering for the first time in minutes that he was driving and should probably pay attention to the road. He'd always found it kind of funny how he could space out and still manage not to crash.

Sayagul came out of Roman's shadow and shook out her wings, black sparkly dust drifting through the car. She crawled up onto the dash, claws clinking on the vents, and spread herself out on her belly to sun.

'I miss her too, you know,' the dragon said, stretching her long neck out.

"You?" Roman scoffed.

She opened one green, reptilian eye. *'Yes, me. I was growing fond of her. Could have done without your endless pining, though. The girl's too. You're both insufferable and desperate. Couple of horny, insufferable, desperate fools.'*

"Are all Familiars made of sass like you? Or am I just that lucky."

'Maybe you should look within. We are merely a part of our people.' The scaled corner of her mouth inched upward, exposing a hint of black gums. *'Though your recipe might have given me more sass. The cap must have fallen off the sass shaker when you were being made.'*

He snorted a laugh.

'Perhaps the girl is not as bad for you as I thought.'

His hands tightened on the wheel, but he glanced at the dragon, who still eyed him with compassion and scrutiny. "Why do you say that?"

Sayagul puffed out a snout-full of smoke that smelled like candles—like magic. *'You were beginning to open up to her. You haven't done that with anyone since Kylar and Willow.'*

He stared out the window, sunbeams splintering across it. "Didn't do me any good in the end. She's gone."

'Who says it's the end?' Sayagul countered. *'She didn't want to leave, stupid boy.'*

"Doesn't matter, alright?" he snapped. He drew a breath, but his lungs felt like they were squashed. "She's gone. I can't have her." He forced his hands to loosen on the wheel before he could crush it. "She just wanted to find her sister, anyway."

Sayagul's eyelid slid shut. *'Perhaps she found something else,'* she said drowsily, *'that she didn't know she needed.'*

The dragon fell asleep. Roman mulled over her words for the rest of the long drive.

And prepared to face the shambles of his life back in Yveswich.

63

THE HOUSE OF BLUE
YVESWICH, STATE OF KER

Shay had only been back at the House of Blue for an hour, and she already felt like she was suffocating.

She sat on the edge of her bed in the single room that she could call her own. It was drafty in here and smelled of brine and mildew—scents that instilled a fear deep inside her, as opposed to smelling like home.

Her eyes flicked about the furniture—the dresser that had nothing on it but a hand mirror and a music box. Very few of her things were here; she kept all the important stuff at her apartment in the district of Zima—the apartment her mother didn't know about. The orange glow of the sunset streamed in through the blue glass of the windows, casting rectangles of sapphire light on the floor.

Shay stared at those rectangles for a long time. Not blinking. Not moving. Her bags sat beside her on the bed—untouched. The last thing she wanted to do was unpack. This wasn't her home, and no matter what Athene said or did to her, she wasn't staying.

She couldn't stop thinking about Roman. Couldn't stop thinking about the Facility. About Anna.

Had all of that been for nothing? Out in the desert, she'd had the feeling that she was drawing closer to Anna, closer to answers, but now that she was back, she felt as though she had squandered her time.

A part of her felt like those four days hadn't even happened at all.

The door to her room opened, and Pia stepped inside.

"Ever heard of knocking?" Shay's voice was flat. She continued to stare at those squares of color, her eyes drying out.

Pia sighed. "Athene wants to see you."

TEN MINUTES LATER, Shay stood in her mother's study, watching as the sky outside the windows darkened, the last stripe of orange on the horizon fading away.

Athene sat in the chair behind the desk, looking over papers as if Shay didn't exist—as if she hadn't personally summoned her to this hellhole.

"How much longer must I endure this torture?" Shay demanded.

Her mother's eyes flicked up. For several blinks, she stared at her. And then she let go of the papers, folded her hands on the desk, and smiled in a way that made Shay feel like she was going to throw up. She had seen that look many times; it was as much an omen as the call of a magpie.

"Shay," Athene began, her tone far too chipper. "I've decided I want you to pretend to be Anna until she comes back."

Shay's stomach dipped. Oh gods, she *was* going to throw up.

Had her mother finally found out that she shared her same elusive magic? Shay scrambled to think how that might be possible, but she came up empty.

"Pretend to be Anna? What do you... What do you mean?"

"You'll have my help, of course. I'll use my powers—no one will be able to tell the difference." The words should have eased her concerns, but they only made her feel worse as she realized what that meant.

Shay ground her teeth. "You're sick." Her head started throbbing.

The corner of Athene's mouth twitched. "You're dramatic."

"I won't do it."

"Shayla!" Athene barked, her name echoing hollowly in the cavernous room. "You will do this for your family."

"What family?" Shay seethed. "I don't see any."

She turned and made for the door Balthazar was blocking—the man Athene was taking to her bed. He was one of the few people in the Riptide who were trusted with the truth of Athene's illusion magic.

Her mother stood. "Where will you go, Shayla?"

"Don't talk to me." She glared up at Balthazar. "Get out of my way."

"To *him?*" Athene continued, referring to Roman. She strutted across the room. "He doesn't care about you like you think he does."

Shay whirled around. "Oh yeah? He cared about me a whole hell of a lot more than you do!"

"Roman Devlin is a very gifted actor. If you paid any attention to your city and took your role as a Selkie seriously, you would know that. That man is poison, and I am ashamed of you for opening your legs for that *disease*. I thought you were better than that."

Shay's nostrils flared. "I didn't open my legs for him."

"You can't lie to a hellseher, Shayla. His scent was all over you, and yours on him."

"What do you want me to say, Mother? That I fucked his brains out? Because I didn't."

"You did *something* with him, and it is never to happen again."

Shay erupted. *"I hate it here!"* she screamed. "I hate it here, and I hate you!" She pointed in her mother's face.

Athene's gaze scalded Shay to the bone. "That man used you."

"Gods!" Shay started pacing.

"He made a goddamn fool out of you. You'll be ridiculed for your idiocy, soon as word gets around! 'The Whore of the Riptide Opens Her Easy Legs for the Wolf of the Hollow'. If our lives were broadcasted, you'd be on the front goddamn page!"

"What do you want from me? Do you want me to say that I'm sorry? Because I'm not. I'm not sorry. I did what I had to do to find Anna."

She scoffed. "And *did* you? *Did* you find her? If you found her, do tell, dear daughter, because I certainly don't see her."

Shay stared at her mom, eyes burning, mouth tight and shaking. She turned toward Balthazar. "Let me out."

Balthazar's small, sharp eyes flicked to Athene.

"Let her go," Athene said, glaring at the back of Shay's head. Shay didn't have to see her mother to know that; she could feel it. She would know that hateful stare blind. "She'll be back."

Balthazar stepped aside, and Shay stormed out, down the drafty old hallways that were lined with windows of blue glass. Every breath she drew caught in her throat, but no tears fell—she didn't let them. She had already cried once today, and one time was too many.

Athene had said that Roman was a gifted actor, but Shay refused to believe it. He might put on a mask when he stood on the world stage, but she had seen the real side of him—she was sure of it.

She was sure of it.

64

THE HOLLOW
YVESWICH, STATE OF KER

Going to the Hollow should have felt like going home. Instead, simply the sight of it sent an icy prickle up Roman's spine.

The buildings here were old and dark, each house, lamp post, and winding, cobbled road a masterpiece that favored eyes that appreciated the strange and the unusual. The roofs were peaked like witch's hats, and every lamp post was carved with designs of wolves, bats, sickle moons, and spiderwebs. Every graveyard in the city was in these parts, headstones jutting up out of the earth like broken bones and jagged teeth. Magpies cawed without rest, and pockets of fog seemed to hang around perpetually in nooks and crannies that were never smiled upon by the sun.

Roman would have loved it, had his dad not taken everything from him.

His Grandfather Slade had died when Roman was young, so he never had the chance to get to know him. But Roman figured the man must've been a real prick to produce two horrible sons. He'd had a third, as well— Dean Slade. The one brother who'd never had kids but should have. Dean was the good apple—a take-no-prisoners fucking badass, but in a good way. Roman had admired him when he was a kid; on his tenth birthday, he'd wished on blown-out candles for Uncle Dean to switch places with his dad. To this day, Roman sometimes wondered where he'd be now, had Dean been the one to guide him instead of Donovan.

The House of Black loomed at the end of a street up ahead. Bigger and blacker than every other house on the block.

Sayagul was curled up on the dash. She lifted her head as Roman rolled the car toward the house. *'I can understand why you are reluctant to kill your dad,'* the dragon said gently, her slitted eyes weighed down with emotion as she stared at the house. *'But perhaps, instead, you could kill Athene.'*

Roman tried to smile and failed. Still, he joked, "Killing is your solution to everything, isn't it?"

'Sometimes,' the dragon said, *'it is the only solution. When a soul grows so black that it taints the light around it.'* She peered up at him with regretful eyes, warm breaths puffing out of her snout. *'You have had your light blackened, my dear Roman, and it has been truly haunting to watch. But you may still be able to help her.'*

Roman drew a shaky breath. "Maybe," he said softly.

The gates rolled open, and Roman drove in, hands squeezing the wheel, through the arches of bone that framed the mouth of the driveway like a giant's broken ribcage.

Sayagul climbed down from the dash and vanished into his shadow. *'I'll be right here with you,'* she said, *'if you need me.'*

Roman parked and cut the engine.

There were a lot of vehicles here—not surprising. Too bad the spells were so thick, or he would've checked for Paxton's aura before bothering to go inside.

Roman hoped the kid wasn't here—for Pax's benefit and his own.

With a steadying breath, he opened his door and got out. Crossed the dark yard on legs that felt like jelly. It was funny how he'd faced every monster known to man, and somehow it was the one in that house who managed to scare him the most.

He walked up the steps, swung open the creaky door, and strode inside. Head high, shoulders back. He ate up the corridor with long, determined strides, heading straight for the three men drinking on the leather sofa straight ahead.

Donovan's looks were the only thing he had going for him. He looked a lot like Randal, actually; aside from a few minor differences, the two could have been twins. Don's eyes were a brighter blue than Randal's, and he wore his hair longer, the dark, wavy strands slicked back, the ends dusting his collar. The Slades had good genes, Roman could admit that—the only pro that came with being born into this family. But good looks didn't make up for being sick in the fucking head.

The two men sitting next to Don were Trey and Simon—two big Shadowmasters in their early forties who were known more for their brawn than their brains.

Roman loathed them both, but mostly he loathed the man in the middle.

At the sound of his approach, Donovan looked toward the hallway, his cutting gaze dragging up Roman from head to toe. "So you finally decided to show up," he sneered. He stood, swigged from his beer, and set the bottle down on the coffee table with a *bang*. "Where you been?"

Roman's pulse was already hammering. "On a job."

"Is that right?" He flashed a manic grin. "And where's the money?"

"Haven't got it yet." He glanced around, sweat prickling on his palms and the nape of his neck. "Where's Pax?"

That demonic glint in Don's eyes intensified, the sight of it drying out Roman's mouth. "You would know better than me."

He had to go. He had to leave—now, right now.

Roman turned, his spine tingling as he left his back vulnerable to his dad.

Donovan was there instantly.

He gripped him by the shoulder of his shirt and slammed him into the wall so hard, he shook the hallway.

"Something's up with you," his dad hissed, breath that reeked of beer wafting across his face.

"Let go." Roman's heart was going to explode.

Don pushed harder, his knuckles bruising Roman's shoulder. The wall yielded under the pressure, a thin crack splitting up toward the ceiling.

The men in the living room laughed at something on TV.

Roman felt the gold of his irises darken, felt the shade of his hair deepen into black. "Let. *Go.*" The shadows in the room stirred in response to his rage, preparing to strike—but his dad's stirred faster, and Roman could hear them whispering.

Donovan smiled, black swallowing his eyes. "Make me."

Roman didn't; he knew better than to cross certain lines. Had Paxton never been born, he wouldn't even be here. Might have even killed his dad by now for all the shit he'd done to him.

Or killed himself—whichever came first.

Don's smile grew. "That's what I thought," he hissed, the tip of his nose nearly brushing Roman's. Roman tried to turn his head, but his dad kept mirroring him, forcing him to make eye contact. He came in close to his ear and whispered, "You're a pussy." He pulled back. Evaluated him, head tilting from side to side, scarred mouth twitching. "Do I have a pussy for a son?"

Words. These were just words. It was nothing compared to what

Donovan usually did to him, especially when piss-drunk like this. Words, he'd take. He just didn't want to be put in that room again.

Donovan leaned in. Gripped his shirt tight, twisting. "Pussy," he hissed. The shadows echoed him, their spine-tingling, otherworldly voices like the hiss of water thrown over hot coals. *Pussy*, they mimicked, the sound hollow and pure fucking evil. *Pussy.* Something akin to laughter threaded through the echo. "Say it," Don demanded, bringing his face in even closer —breathing on him. "Say you're a fucking pussy."

Roman growled, *"You're a fucking pussy."*

His dad slammed him into the wall again, the back of Roman's head banging into it so hard, he nearly bit his tongue. "One more wrong word from you," Don hissed, "and Paxton will be the one going into that room." His hot, yeasty breath drifted across Roman's face. "Now say it. Say it, or I'll break that kid in half, and I'll make you watch."

He looked his dad square in the eye. Flexed his jaw and said, "I'm a fucking pussy, Dad. Proud of me?"

Donovan's new smile was even colder than the last, and Roman hated that he saw a hint of himself in those genetics—the curve of his mouth, the angle of his eyes, the shape of his jawline. "Not the least fucking bit."

He let go with a shove that caused bits of the wall to dust the floor. He drifted back several paces, face still lit with a drunk, cocky smile, before turning around fully and heading for the living room.

Roman exhaled, realizing he'd held the air in his lungs nearly the whole time his dad had him pinned to the wall. His shoulder ached, and his shirt was still warm from his dad's grip.

He wanted to have a shower. Burn himself in the water.

"You make sure you bring that kid home when you find him," Donovan called. He picked up his beer and took a swig. Lifted the bottle as if in a toast. "He's got a few lessons to attend."

Like hell he'd bring Paxton to this place.

He left, not bothering to search the rest of the house. Pax wasn't here; he could sense it, could see with his Sight that his aura hadn't been here in a while. Days, maybe. If he was lucky.

Good.

As he neared the door, Donovan's woman, Clare Slade, came down the stairs. Paxton's mom. She was a Helen Devlin lookalike, right down to the freckles on her thin nose, her long, black hair. Clare had no idea that she was no better than a replacement—practically a clone. Donovan had burned every photo of Helen the day she'd died, refusing to tolerate any reminders of the woman he claimed to have loved.

Clare didn't say anything to Roman, though her closed mouth shifted as if she wanted to.

To hell with her. The woman had done absolutely nothing to help Pax since Donovan had started his magic lessons, had done nothing to stop the pain her husband inflicted on the poor kid. Roman couldn't give a shit if she died. A part of him hoped she would; it was a better fate than being married to that asshole. Roman sometimes wondered if Donovan beat her, choosing to hit her in the places her clothes covered. It would be easy to conceal the truth with the sound barriers a hellseher's magic could generate, but he wouldn't put it past his fucked-up dad to gag her too, just for fun. He was into shit like that.

Roman would know; he'd done it to his mother.

He walked out of the house that by all rights should be his, and got in his car to head to the one place in the whole world that he could *really* call his own.

But first, he had a stop to make.

65

THE RIPTIDE
YVESWICH, STATE OF KER

When Shay made it out of the House of Blue and down to the rocky coast of the island, she took out her shapeshifting bracelet and prepared to put it on. It would be a long swim, but aside from the motorboats and jet skis that were rarely used, it was the only way off this island.

Sea glass and stones that had been tumbled smooth by ocean waves clacked under her feet. She still wore her hiking boots, jean shorts, and a white tank—clothes that still smelled like the desert. Like Roman. It was cold out, and a storm was brewing, wind whipping through the trees and making the branches groan like dying animals. But it didn't bother her. Not when her blood was boiling and her head was about to explode.

Three figures appeared up ahead. Three beautiful women dressed in wetsuits and drenched in water.

Pia, Beatrice, and Kailani were heading this way.

Shay stopped short. It didn't take long before the three of them were surrounding her like vultures.

"Look who finally decided to show up," Kailani drawled.

"What do you want?" Shay bit out.

Beatrice's broad smile was as cold as the gusting wind tearing through Shay's hair. "You—gone for good." They circled her, stones shifting under their water shoes.

"Anna's dead," Pia said. "And I want her title."

"Who the hell told you that?" Shay snapped. "She's not dead—"

"It's been weeks, Shayla!" Kailani shouted over the wind. "She's not coming back."

"She's *not dead!*" Shay's voice was a thunderclap. The sky echoed it, the sound like boulders cracking together.

Shay felt it—the warning. Lightning prickled beneath her skin, and she gritted her teeth as it forked up her nape, digging deep into her skull.

Pia moved, quick as the lightning shattering the rain-bloated sky. She hooked her fingers through Shay's bracelet and pulled.

The elastic stretched and snapped. Mermaid glass flew through the air and tinkled across the rocks.

With a guttural snarl, Shay lunged for Pia—

A spear of lightning struck the air between them, the sound a clap that rattled eardrums and sent Pia falling back on her ass.

The other two girls stumbled away with wide, frightful eyes. Kailani pulled Pia to her feet.

Pia stared at Shay as if she didn't recognize her. "What the hell was that?"

Storm magic set Shay's eyes aglow as she panted through bared teeth, "Don't ever come near me again, or I'll burn you all alive."

They backed up, their panicked gazes flicking between the sparks in Shay's palms and the lightning threading through her teeth.

The Selkies fled.

Shay hurried out onto the dock and got into one of the boats. She only had minutes left before those three bitches would tattle to Athene—minutes before her life would end.

She started the boat and steered it out into the choppy waves.

THE OCEAN WAS TRYING to drown her.

The wind was icy and relentless. It cut through the water in slicing gusts, causing white-capped waves to rock against the boat.

Shay had nearly forgotten just how dangerous the ocean really was. Being a Selkie had spoiled her. The undersea held plenty of dangers of its own, but during a storm it was far safer under the waves than it was above them.

With the winds and waves hindering her, it took far longer than usual to spot the shores of Yveswich. When she finally glimpsed the twinkle of city lights, it was nearly suppertime.

Night was descending. She had to get to shore and call a cab to take her to her apartment—and she had to do it quickly.

The docks were growing closer when something slammed into the boat, the force of the blow nearly pitching her into the waves.

She planted her feet and gripped the rain-damp wheel with numb, slippery fingers. Peered through the rain sluicing the darkness.

The ridged back of a water serpent arched up out of the ocean.

"Oh shit," Shay hissed. She stepped on it, slamming her foot down on the pedal. "Shit, shit, shit."

The serpent followed her, its scarred, scaled body diving up and down, up and down. Every few feet, it veered to the right and slammed into the boat. And every few feet, Shay was nearly launched overboard.

She gripped the wheel as tightly as she could and pushed the boat at maximum speed. "Come on, baby. Come on, baby."

The docks drew closer. She was almost there.

The water serpent suddenly dove under the surface, its long tail lashing and spraying water through the air. That tail soon disappeared, too.

Shay didn't slow, but her gaze flicked about the murky water surrounding the boat, searching for dark shapes or the telling gleam of scales.

She was about to use her Sight when the serpent rose up again, winding its body around the front of the boat this time. The engine groaned in defiance, the propellers sputtering and splashing as the serpent stunted her speed with its long, powerful body.

"Gods." Shay looked up, squinting through the rain slicing from the heavens. Willed her magic to wake up again and incinerate this foul thing.

It did not answer.

The vessel groaned and shuddered under her feet. The serpent tightened its grasp, squeezing the boat in a crushing death grip—

The boat took a nosedive.

Shay steadied herself with a gasp, gripping the steering wheel for dear life. Her upper half banged into the wheel, and her feet slipped.

She couldn't kill it. Only something like a frost-tipped harpoon could take down a serpent this size.

With dizzying speed, the boat spun around—pointing south now.

The serpent slammed into her again. And again.

Fucked. She was fucked.

66

ROMAN'S HOUSE
YVESWICH, STATE OF KER

Loren had spent the rest of the afternoon flitting between the different amenities in Roman's house, constantly under the protective eye of Darien, Ivy, or Joyce.

The sauna had filled a part of her that Darien and Ivy explained was connected to red magic. Fire magic. The arcane term for it was 'Inferno', birthed by Ignis herself. The pool, on the other hand, had quenched her thirst and replenished her blue magic. The arcane term for that one was 'Mist', these gifts given birth by Caligo.

She came out of the sauna for a second time that afternoon to find Darien waiting for her, like usual, though this time he sat on one of the poolside chairs. Elbows on his knees, hands clasped between them. He had a way of commanding attention in any room, no matter what he was doing or who he was with. Both Ivy and Joyce were with her this time, and Jack had joined too. Tanner was playing video games upstairs, and Kylar had left to pick up Paxton and Eugene from an arcade in the Theater District.

"Still good?" Darien asked. Loren still couldn't put a finger on what was bothering him, though he'd disappeared for a second time about an hour ago.

She nodded and crossed her arms over her breasts, her skin pebbling from the change in temperature. "Still good."

"What do we do about green?" Ivy asked, using her towel to blot the excess moisture from her hair. She'd gone for another dip.

"Green?" Jack asked, looking lost, water dripping off his curls. "What's that mean? Someone fill me in."

"Loren has every color magic, right?" Ivy began.
"Okay?"
"Which is how we woke her up in the Caliginous Chamber."
"Okay?"
"Well, Caliginous was closed early today—"
"I heard."
"But Darien figured out another way to replenish her magic. She constantly feels thirsty, and thirst is connected to water and blue magic. So she went for a swim, and now she feels better. She was also complaining about feeling cold. The sauna helps with that. Fire magic equals heat—pretty obvious. But..." She chewed on her full bottom lip, eyes flicking to Darien, who looked as deep in thought as his sister did. "Green. Hmm." She tapped a finger against her chin.

Joyce got out of the hot tub and wrapped herself up in a towel she'd draped across a chaise lounge. "I have an idea." She pointed at the windows behind Darien. "The yard. Ever heard of grounding? 'Earthing' is another term for it."

Jack said, "Nope," while Ivy exclaimed, "Yes, Joyce!" She was grinning from ear to ear. "Yes, you are a genius! I'm in a house full of geniuses!" She grabbed onto her husband's tatted arm with enthusiasm and shook him until his teeth clacked together. "Geniuses!"

Jack said, "I'm clearly not one of them."

Darien stood. "What's grounding?"

Joyce tied her towel under her arms and crossed the room, hair dripping down her back. "Come with me."

She led the way to the glass door that would take them outside. She pushed it open, and they filed out into the twilit yard. It was cold out, a storm brewing over the city. A sprinkle of rain fell from the sky, and strong winds howled through the neighborhood, the temperature so cold it burned. The gusts turned Loren's wet hair into frosted whips that stung her skin.

"Grounding," Joyce began, turning to face them, "is when you stand on the earth in bare feet, and the energy in it electrically reconnects you to nature. People claim it helps with inflammation, blood flow, and sleep."

"It's worth a shot," Darien said. He looked a bit skeptical, but he said to Loren, "Go on, it won't hurt."

She walked out onto the lawn, the blades of grass cool under her sauna-warmed feet. She felt very seen as everyone—Darien especially, that stare of his more powerful than ever—watched her.

Ivy, clearly noticing that Loren felt awkward standing out here by herself, stepped out to join her. "I'll do it too," she offered. "I'm into yoga—I can get into stuff like this." She faced Loren. "Try wiggling your toes. Focus on how the ground feels under your feet."

Jack hissed to Darien, "This is cuckoo." Darien didn't respond.

Joyce said, "Try breathing techniques."

"I'm good at that," Loren said. She breathed in deeply through her nose...and slowly exhaled through her mouth. She did it all while facing Ivy, the two of them breathing in unison.

In... Out...

In... Out...

After a few minutes, that squeezing sensation in her chest subsided. For the first time since she had woken up in Yveswich, she felt like she could draw a full breath. She was still comfortably warm too, and not the least bit thirsty.

How very bizarre.

Darien said, "It's working, isn't it?" He looked...amazed. And relieved.

Loren nodded and drew another breath, relishing in the feel of her lungs stretching with oxygen, the organs finally sated. "It's working."

THEY ORDERED PIZZA FOR DINNER.

Darien finished his last piece—the first thing he'd eaten all day—and sat back in his chair, watching as Loren flitted around the table with Ivy and Joyce, the three having insisted on cleaning up tonight. Jack and Kylar were still pigging out, and Tanner was working away on multiple laptops on the other side of the table, a mess of cords draped across the floor.

"How's Hell's Gate?" Darien asked him.

"The spells are still perfectly faultless, if I do say so myself." At least they were able to check on the others that way.

Ivy's fingers closed around Paxton's plate—empty aside from some pizza crusts and a blob of buttermilk dip. "You finished?"

The kid was typing his passcode into his phone, clearly trying not to smear tomato sauce on the screen. "Yes, thank you."

Darien eyed Pax's long, baggy sleeves. "You cold, Pax?"

He propped an elbow on the table and put his chin in his hand, eyes still on his phone. "Nah, I'm good."

Darien was about to inquire further—minding his own business be damned—when the kid suddenly gasped so loudly he made Jack choke.

Kylar clapped him on the back as Jack started hacking, thumping a fist against his chest.

Darien began to ask Paxton, "Wh—"

"Roman's back!" Paxton's grin was contagious; Darien had never seen the kid smile that big. "He just texted me—he said he's got a stop to make, but then he's coming straight here!"

Kylar wiped his hands with a napkin as Jack, eyes watering, took a long drink of water. "'Bout damn time," Kylar said.

"Don't worry." Paxton was looking at Darien, that grin still present. "I didn't mention anything about you."

Somewhere outside, a siren began to wail. The sound was soon echoed by other identical sirens.

Civil defense sirens.

Darien was up out of his chair in an instant. The others followed, murmuring to one another, as he stalked to the windows that overlooked the backyard and the sparkling city beyond.

Kylar came up beside him. "Shit." His oath was quiet and shaky.

Darien faced him, noting the way Ky's throat shifted, his eyes gleaming with fear. "What is that?"

"Fog warning."

Darien stared out at the city. A thick white cloud was descending upon Yveswich, swallowing everything it touched. It moved too quickly to be ordinary fog, as if it were summoned from someplace...*else*. Pushed here by forces beyond anyone's comprehension.

Tanner asked, "What does that mean?"

"Demons," Kylar replied. "Lots of them. It's kind of like a Blood Moon, but...arguably worse."

Howls and guttural snarls cut through the city. And fuck, were there a lot of them—everywhere, in every damn street. Including this one, Darien realized, as he picked up on the bloodthirsty baying coming from out front.

His eyes snapped to Loren's, who stood at the back of the group. Arms crossed, her small hands buried in the sleeves of her hooded sweatshirt. Darien could hear her heart pounding.

Paxton tugged on Darien's arm. The kid was looking up at him, and when he spoke, his voice was a shaky whisper. "Roman's out there."

67

S. COASTAL DISTRICT
YVESWICH, STATE OF KER

The fog usually came with a better warning.

Roman screeched his car to a stop by the harbor and got out. He sprinted down the closest staircase that led to water level, thumped down the rain-drenched steps, and slowed when he got to the docks. He scanned the harbor, knowing he only had seconds—minutes, at best—to get the hell out of the fog.

Out on the choppy water was a single boat. A girl steered it, her long, strawberry-blonde hair whipping behind her in the wind. The boat rocked relentlessly, pitching her from side to side.

A serpentine back lined with cerulean spikes snaked in and out of the water. The great serpent was surrounding the boat—pushing it away from the docks and slamming into the bow hard enough that it nearly capsized.

"Shay!" Roman's voice shredded his throat. He hurtled out onto the dock, boots thumping on the wet wood. It had stopped raining, but the fall of night had brought lower temperatures that semi-froze the dock. It was treacherous, and the wind chill at fifty miles per hour burned his skin and made his eyes water.

"Perfect timing!" she called. She steadied herself against the wheel as the serpent slammed into the boat again. "This bloody thing won't leave me alone!" She tried to make it sound like a joke, but Roman had spent enough time with her to detect the edge in her voice. She was scared as hell—and rightfully so.

He thudded to a stop at the end of this stretch of dock—the longest stretch. He thrust a hand out, the sharp movement pushing his magic outside of his body. It stretched like an elastic, and he willed it not to snap.

He could feel his power as if it were an extension of himself, so he could sense when it wrapped around the serpent like ropes. Roman swept his magic out wider, casting it out like a fishing net. The monster's howl of defiance rumbled the ocean. It bucked and flailed, spraying water—

Roman swept his hand down and bent his knees, the action pulling the serpent deeper into the waves. "Hurry!" he gritted out.

He pushed himself back up, his magic confining the serpent to the ocean floor. Despite the cold, he was already sweating—and his magic would only last so long before the serpent snapped the restraints.

Shay drove the boat to the dock and leapt out. Her shoe slipped on the wet edge, and she nearly fell into the water.

Roman's hands closed around her arm, and he pulled her the rest of the way. She collided with him, her cheek glancing off his chest.

"What are you doing here?" she panted, tossing her damp hair out of her face. "Roman, I don't have the necklace with me—"

"That's not why I'm here. I'm here for you."

It was hard to hear the civil defense sirens over the howling wind, but her eyes widened the moment her ears picked up on them.

"Oh my god, Roman! It's a fog warning."

"I know." He grabbed her hand, lacing his fingers with hers. "We need to get out of here."

They ran down the dock, the soles of their boots fighting for purchase on the sparkling frost. The water here was deep by human and immortal standards, but the serpent was too big to go after them. It disappeared into the ocean with one final lash of its scaled tail, its bellow tearing across the water as powerfully as the wind.

They were almost there when fog swallowed the dock. They couldn't see anything but an opaque white cloud and distant, murky silhouettes.

"Shit, shit—Roman! I can't see." Shay gripped his hand like a vise; her fingers were cold and stiff.

"I know, I can't either. Keep going—don't slow down."

A shape appeared up ahead. A monstrous mass of a body.

Roman slowed.

Shay skidded to a stop beside him. Her boot slipped out, her free hand coming up to grab his arm.

Roman shook his head, not wanting to believe his eyes as the monster with the whip-like tail and spikes all over its back prowled along the shore.

It was the same thing that had attacked them in the Facility. The same thing that had nearly killed him.

Roman whispered, "Oh fuck."

Shay felt like she had no blood in her head as she stared at the creature pacing by the dock. Waiting for them. That smooth, skull-like head. That grotesque body with skin that looked more like dry bone. Those beastly feet and claws.

"We're going to have to use my illusion again," she whispered. She rallied it, her eyes turning as black as the monster's.

"Shay, that barely lasted two minutes last time, and I'm parked up there." Roman pointed. It would take them longer than two minutes to get there, even at a breaking run—even with a hellseher's speed.

The demon watched them with hollow eyes straight out of a nightmare. Triangular nostrils flared, breaths puffing in the air.

She swallowed bile. "Any other ideas, Shadows?"

Suddenly, the creature slithered into the water and disappeared under the dark surface.

Roman's whisper was a rasp. "Oh my god."

Shay squeezed Roman's hand. Together, they eased forward a step. Another. They peered into the rippling water, searching for air bubbles or movement. Shay couldn't see a damn thing—

"Why can't I see it?" he gritted out, his eyes dark with the Sight. "It has no aura—"

The dock erupted under their feet.

They were launched into the air in a spray of water and foam. Wood and metal flew as the dock was smashed into smithereens.

The harbor rose up to devour them, and Shay barely had a chance to draw a breath before they were sucked into the dark and icy depths.

68

THE HARBOR
YVESWICH, STATE OF KER

Shay's body cut through the water like a spear. Gravity sucked her under, ripping her hand out of Roman's grip.

Something sharp lanced her thigh. A scream ripped out of her, an explosion of bubbles rushing out of her mouth. The weight of the water was crushing her. She tried to move. To swim, but—

Where was the surface? Particles, seaweed, and driftwood floated around her, but it was too dark to see much else. She could taste the iron of her blood. Which meant the monster would be able to taste it too.

She glimpsed a skull-like head—a stone pulsing above pit-like eyes. Shay fought the urge to scream again as the monster tore through the water with the speed and force of a great white shark. Its mouth opened to devour her, double rows of sharp teeth glinting like shards of black glass—

Shay kicked with her good leg and swept her arms back, trying like hell to get away.

The demon bore down on her—faster now.

No, no, no, no—

The thing abruptly stopped, as if it hit an invisible wall. It thrashed and roared, just like the serpent had.

Shay wasted no time in moving.

She twirled around. Used her Sight to locate the shore.

There it was—there were the colorful spells shimmering on the buildings; there were the threads of the anima mundi flowing up into the telephone poles and street lights.

Quickly, she swam for the shore. It was right there, but it felt so far away. The auras of rainbow fish flitted about like spirits as she swam. She was so used to swimming in her aquatic form, able to breathe underwater, that at first she didn't recognize why her lungs were burning.

She broke the surface as soon as she was able, gasping down mouthfuls of frigid air.

Roman was there, clothes and hair dripping. He grabbed onto her arm and pulled her out of the water. "Hurry," he panted. "We have to run—now." The fog was still swallowing everything in sight; they couldn't see more than three feet in front of them, but Shay spotted the smoky glow of distant street lights.

She tried to keep up with him, but her bad leg collapsed under her, her knee bending fully to the ground. "I can't—my leg!" The bleeding still hadn't stopped.

Roman swore.

The demon burst out of the water behind them with an ear-splitting roar.

Roman grabbed her and threw her onto his back like he had in the desert. He pushed off the pavement and ran—

The creature was faster, lashing out with one brutal swipe of its long, sharp tail.

It slammed into them, the pain so bad Shay swore her spine cracked in half, and for several horrible seconds she couldn't breathe.

They flew through the air like dolls.

Roman lost his hold on her. He smacked into the stone wall, the side of his head cracking against it so hard it instantly bled.

Shay struck the pavement several feet away and rolled, the skin of her arms and legs ripping open. White-hot pain splintered across her vision as the wood that was stuck in her leg was shoved in deeper.

She fought it—the pain—and pushed herself to her feet just as the monster went after her.

Roman's magic was a force of nature as it swept out again, his attack smashing the creature into the closest staircase. Wood and stone exploded.

And Roman still hadn't gotten up.

He pushed himself to his feet with visible difficulty, blinking as if dizzy. Red streamed down the side of his face and neck, the blood running into his eye and partially blinding him.

The monster was up instantly, bursting out of the destruction of the stairs.

With a spine-chilling bellow, it snapped its tail through the air, launching a hailstorm of barbs right at them.

Roman ducked, and Shay dove the other way, the act putting more distance between her and Roman. The barbs thudded into the wall, stone cracking and bursting into dust.

The spikes instantly grew back with a popping that was foul, and it struck again with another crack of that whip-like tail.

Roman cursed, dodging again. One of the spikes whizzed past his head, while another tore through the short sleeve of his shirt.

"Roman!" Shay cried. Shit—she couldn't move. Her leg was going to buckle again, the muscles burning and torn—

The monster went for Roman.

It moved in a blur—almost too fast for hellseher eyes. It lifted Roman and slammed him into the wall, pinning him there with a deadly claw to the throat, like it had at the Facility.

Shay limped forward, injury be damned. *"Roman!"*

"Get out of here, Shay!" His voice was a crackle. "Get out of here, please—*go!*"

Shay grabbed a rock and threw. "Leave him alone!" Thunder rumbled overhead, but no lightning came to help her. *"Get away from him!"*

The creature tightened its claw around Roman's throat—

Roman's gold eyes snapped to her face—one last time. "Run," he begged with a whisper.

The sickening snap of bone cleaved the air.

Shay's stomach quaked.

The blood drained from her face.

"No." The word was a choked whisper.

No, no, no—please!

With an animalistic scream that ripped apart her vocal chords, she launched herself forward, not giving a flying shit if she died too—

The creature's head suddenly exploded.

Shay stumbled to a stop, staring with wide eyes as pulpy black blood and bits of bone sprayed through the air.

Roman fell to the ground, and a moment later the beast's headless corpse fell too.

Shay stood there in shock, bleeding and in pain and trying hard to understand—

A tall, dark silhouette leapt off the wall and landed on his feet near Roman.

A man with black, slicked-back hair and tattoos approached, bits of bone and debris crunching under his black combat boots. His hooded sweatshirt and jeans were covered in blood, dirt, and patches of sparkling frost. His strong features reminded Shay of Roman's—equally stunning and terrifying, the kind of face you wanted to look at but were too afraid to.

Where he knelt on the ground, his chest heaving with labored breaths, Roman blinked at the man as fiercely as Shay was blinking at him.

There was a small tattoo below the man's ear. A letter S with a horn on each end.

"Cousin," the stranger said with a dip of his chin, his deep voice just slightly winded. "You're looking a little worse for wear." He offered Roman a hand up.

Roman—drenched and shaking and soaked in blood—was still gaping as he gritted out, *"Darien?"*

PART FOUR
THE EYRIE

69

S. COASTAL DISTRICT
YVESWICH, STATE OF KER

Darien had pinpointed his cousin's location by following the sound of a woman screaming bloody murder. It wasn't his usual way of tracking, but it worked well this time around.

Roman had sent Pax a message before the fog warning, saying he was making a stop at the harbor. This simple bit of information had allowed Darien to narrow down his whereabouts—and when the woman screaming bloody murder had started shouting out his cousin's name, it had made finding Roman even more of a cinch.

All the Venom Darien had taken earlier that day had helped with the rest. The stores of the drug had simmered in his blood, waiting to be unleashed, apparently. He could hardly remember what'd happened from the time he got out of his car to the moment he jumped down to the seawall, but the blood on his clothes told him it had involved a lot of destruction. And a lot of monsters.

Darien drove through the fog now, Roman following in his car. They had to crawl the whole way, the fog making it difficult to see. Darien had taken a risk by speeding to get down to the harbor in time, using his Sight to see the spells on buildings and to keep from driving onto curbs or into storefronts. But now, he was pretty drained. So crawling blindly would have to do.

The demons were starting to move toward their dens again, the fog thinning. The end of it was near.

By the time they made it up to Roman's district, the fog had thinned again, so they were able to step on their accelerators. Darien periodically checked in his rear-view mirror to make sure Roman was still there; his cousin was bleeding badly, and had pretty well been blinded by all the blood in his eye by the time Darien had found him.

Roman's neighborhood wasn't far now. Darien used the rest of the drive to sort out his thoughts and figure out how to explain six months' worth of information to him.

And to break the news that they'd screwed up, and his home wasn't a secret anymore.

ROMAN WAS STILL HAVING trouble wrapping his mind around everything that just happened. He questioned his sanity a few times, and wondered how likely it was that he was dreaming or dead.

"So," Shay began. It was the first word either of them had uttered since getting in his car. She'd managed to stanch the flow of blood in her leg, but Roman could scent her pain permeating the car. It was excruciating. "Darien Cassel's your cousin."

Roman picked at the crust of dried blood around his eye, his vision still shimmering from when he'd hit his head against the wall. "Yup."

"That was...pretty fortunate," she offered. "You obviously had no idea that he was visiting?"

"Nope."

Silence stretched between them until she said, "Are you okay?"

"Not sure yet, honestly. That was all pretty fucked up. Still trying to convince myself that it happened." He glanced at her to see that she was studying him closely. "How are you feeling?"

"Well, I'm alive, so I can't really complain."

"How's the leg?"

"Do you want my honest answer?"

He grimaced. "Maybe not. We'll get you sorted at the house. You're okay with coming to my place for a bit?"

"I don't really have anywhere else to go. I mean, I have my apartment, but after all that," she fluttered a scraped hand in the direction of the distant harbor, "I don't really have any desire to be alone right now."

"Yeah, you and me both." Now, it was *his* turn to study her as she stared into space. "You want to talk about what happened at the House of Blue?" Considering how quickly she'd fled that place, something extreme must have happened.

But Shay said, "Not unless you want to talk about what happened at the House of Black."

Even just the thought of his dad made him twist the wheel in a crushing grip. "Maybe another time."

Silence returned. And then Shay whispered, "I'm glad you came for me." It was better than a thank-you from this stubborn, spitfire girl, and he took it gladly.

And even though it wasn't a thank-you, he still said, "You're welcome."

By the time Shay limped into Roman's house, her head felt light as a feather, her vision speckled with stars. She was too short to comfortably sling her arm across his shoulder, so she had to grip him by the waist instead. His arm was wrapped snugly around her waist too; had she been in less pain, she might have swooned over the simple gesture.

"You should just leave me here and bring me a towel or something," she said as they shuffled away from the garage. Darien had entered the house before them. "I'm going to bleed all over the place."

"You think I'm worried about that?"

She looked up at him out of the corner of her eye, but he was purposely staring straight ahead. He still looked slightly dazed, blood all over the side of his face and neck.

It felt like it took forever to get to the living room, and when they did, Shay was taken aback by how many unfamiliar faces were waiting for them.

Three more Devils, not including Darien; a Shadowmaster who Shay recognized was Kylar Lavin; two boys who looked to be about twelve; a female hellseher in her late thirties.

And...a human girl. Shay's age, by the looks of her. She had blue eyes, bright blonde hair that was waist-long and thick, and very soft, feminine facial features.

She was absolutely beautiful—an exquisite planet Darien orbited around. They were polar opposites, and he stood slightly in front of her like a bodyguard. After what Shay had witnessed of Darien at the harbor, it made her pity whoever might be stupid enough to get too close to this girl.

The female hellseher in her late thirties rushed forward. "How bad is it?" Her attention flicked between Shay's face and her bad leg.

Roman said, "Needs stitches, definitely."

"There's a bathroom just down the hall," the woman said as she took

Roman's place, sliding her arm under Shay's. "I'm Joyce—I'm a doctor from Angelthene. I can fix you up in no time."

"Thank you," Shay breathed, wincing as she pivoted toward the bathroom. With one last glance at Roman, who stepped toward her as if to follow, she limped down the hallway. Leaving bloody footprints everywhere, just like she'd feared.

ROMAN HAD JUST TURNED around to face the group of people in his living room when Paxton rushed forward and collided with him.

"I was so scared for you," Paxton whispered into his shirt, his thin arms squeezing Roman tight.

Roman hugged him back. He'd missed Paxton way more than he'd realized. "Scared? For *me*? I'm insulted."

Pax peeked up at him with shining eyes. "Did you see Dad?"

"We'll talk about that later." He unwound his arms from around his brother and gestured to the living room. "Let's go sit down, my body's killing me."

The others were standing—all except Eugene and Ivy. Roman had never been bothered by the weight of being stared at, but he found that it bothered him tonight. He could sense that his family had a lot to tell him— and he'd be willing to guess that at least some of it had to do with the blonde human in the group. Darien seemed stuck to her as though they were magnets, constantly positioning himself around her as if he were ready to destroy someone if they breathed in her general direction.

Roman hadn't been around these two for more than a few minutes, but he found it obvious. Maybe it was because he'd never seen his cousin act this way with anyone—ever. It was...weird. Darien, in a sense, had always been a lone wolf like Roman. Clearly, a lot had changed—and so had Darien.

"I get the feeling I'm about to be bombarded with a shitload of information," Roman said as he moved toward the couch, Paxton shadowing him. He eased himself down slowly, and Paxton sat beside him.

Ivy said, "We'll try not to overwhelm you, but..." She glanced at Darien. "It might be a challenge." She offered Roman a warm smile. "It's nice to see you, cous."

"Likewise." He glanced at Tanner and Jack, and gave them each a nod. "Atlas. Jack."

Jack's grin was exactly the same as Roman remembered it. "You look like you got your ass beat."

"I did." He threw a grateful look in Darien's direction. "I thought I might die."

The corner of Darien's mouth twitched. "What's life as a Darkslayer if you don't think you might die at least once a night?"

"You guys aren't here because of Travis, are you?" A pit opened in his stomach.

"He's alive and fine," Darien said quickly.

"Unfortunately," Jack added.

Ivy snickered and slapped his arm. "Stop saying that."

Now that Roman could breathe again, his attention snagged on the girl standing near Darien.

His cousin noticed immediately—no surprise there—and stepped aside so he was no longer blocking her like a wall of muscle and tattoos. "This is Loren. Loren, this is my cousin, Roman."

"Nice to meet you," she said. Her voice was quiet and as gentle as she looked.

Roman lifted his hand in a tired wave. "Hey." He used that hand to gesture between her and Darien. "You guys...?"

Darien's answer was immediate and firm. "No."

Roman lowered his hand.

Fuck that. There was no way there wasn't something going on between those two. But he'd let it slide for now.

He leaned back against the couch, knowing full well that he was about to ruin it with his damp, filthy clothes. "To what do I owe this extremely random pleasure?"

The others turned their heads to look at Darien, who said, "It's a long story." He drew a breath. "A really long story."

70

ROMAN'S HOUSE
YVESWICH, STATE OF KER

It took almost an hour to explain everything to Roman. Darien swore it was the most talking he'd ever done in his life. It probably was.

The Darkslayer named Shay Cousens wound up joining them toward the end of the explanation, looking a lot better than when she'd first limped in here. She managed to catch Roman's brief recap—the summary he was giving mostly for his own benefit—as she took a seat on the ottoman near the couch. Joyce came in behind her and claimed one of the armchairs.

"I want to make sure I got all this straight," Roman said. He was looking at Loren, who'd moved to the couch about a quarter of the way through the conversation to sit beside Ivy. "The Arcanum Well is real. It was created by your father, who used it to create hellsehers and then used it to create you. You have the Well's powers and the ability to track it, which makes you extremely valuable. Darien was hired to hunt you down in the fall, and when he found out you were human, he became your bodyguard instead."

He paused, and she nodded, looking like she was trying to absorb the information just as much as Roman was.

Roman glanced up at Darien. "Because that's *so* like my cousin."

Darien couldn't help but smile.

Roman continued, "You worked with Darien to find your missing friend, who was kidnapped and taken as ransom because the kidnappers wanted you instead of her, but couldn't get to you. This other piece-of-shit fake Darkslaying circle wanted the Well for themselves, and they were working for the imperator, who also wants the Well."

Loren nodded again, appearing more lost the longer Roman spoke.

Roman said, "That's a whole lot of Well wanters."

Jack actually stifled a laugh for the first time in his life.

"He wants to use the Well to create his vision of a perfect world," Roman continued, "pretty much abolishing mortals, and use the Well to heal people of the Tricking and to give himself unlimited magic—the selfish bastard. He tried to create a replica of the Well, but your dad," he pointed at Loren, "arranged for all replicas to be cursed, so instead it turned into a bomb that destroyed all of Angelthene. You used your gift from Tempus the Liar—"

Loren pinched her solar amulet and held it up for everyone to see. The gesture brought a slight smile to Darien's lips.

"—to reverse time. And then you used your aura to shield the city from the explosion. And *then*, a few weeks later, you found out the explosion tore a rip into Spirit Terra. The Blood Moon and the security breach that happened on TV was actually the Veil almost falling, but you closed it—again, with your magic. But your human body can't handle magic, so it stopped your heart. Darien got it beating again—apparently, with Malakai Delaney's help, which I find really fucking hard to believe—but you were stuck in a coma. And then these people—" he gestured about the room "—brought you here because Roark Bright, your foster dad, told Darien that one of the Caliginous Chambers might wake you up." He concluded, "And it clearly did."

Loren nodded again.

Roman glanced dramatically between her and Darien. "And you guys are not dating," he stated flatly.

Darien stiffened. "For fuck's sake, Roman," he bit out. "Is that all that stood out to you?"

"I'm just bugging," Roman said, but his tone was still serious and slightly sharp, his mind clearly lost in all the dangerous things they'd just told him about—and they still hadn't addressed the other issue, the one involving the two Shadowmasters who'd found out about this place—his home. Roman breathed in through his nose and slowly exhaled through his mouth in a rush. "Any other fucked-up shit you'd like to assail me with tonight?"

Tanner spoke for the first time in minutes. "We're probably forgetting some things, but that's the gist of it."

Roman's gold eyes locked on Darien's again. "And Randal's dead. But I already knew that. Was that you?"

Darien shifted his weight. "Not *technically*."

Jack said, "He led him into a trap."

"What sort of trap?" Roman asked.

"Blackgate Manor," Tanner said. "Demon," he added.

Roman's smile was wicked. "That was nice of you."

Darien smirked.

"No, I'm happy for you," Roman said. He glanced at Ivy now, who was tapping out piano notes on her knee, her mouth set in a thin line. "Both of you. That was long overdue."

Ivy inhaled deeply. "It's nice not having him around."

Roman's features sank a little. "Yeah, I bet."

The living room grew silent. Paxton picked at the loose threads in his sleeves.

Eventually, Ivy sat forward and smiled at Shay. "I don't believe we've met. I'm Ivy Cassel, and this is my husband, Jack." She pointed at Jack, and then pointed at Tanner. "That's Tanner Atlas, hacker extraordinaire." Atlas gave a little wave. "And that's Loren Calla, the remarkable young lady you just heard so much about."

Shay waved. "Shay Cousens. I'm a Darkslayer for the Riptide."

"Athene Cousens?" Tanner said.

Shay's smile was visibly forced. "That's my mom."

Roman looked like he wanted to commit mass murder. "Athene's a bitch." He told Shay, "You're welcome to stay here as long as you'd like."

Darien pounced on the opportunity. "Are you guys dating?"

Roman scowled. "Fuck off."

Darien chuckled.

"We're just friends," Shay said, though she watched Roman with a warmth that Darien could spot from a mile away. "Really good friends."

Jack offered up another of his famous grins. "A lot can happen when you're really good friends."

Roman shot to his feet and made for the kitchen. "I thought you guys had changed, but you're still the fucking same. Any food left in this house, or did you eat it all?"

"There's leftover pizza," Darien said.

Tanner added, "We've mostly been eating out so we wouldn't use up all your food."

Roman retrieved one of the pizza boxes and thumped it onto the counter. "I was bugging—you guys leave your senses of humor back in Angelthene or something?" He flipped open the lid—and frowned. "Who ordered pineapple on pizza?"

Loren and Ivy raised their hands.

Roman grimaced and closed the lid.

"There should be pepperoni there too," Darien said.

Roman was already moving, shoving the ham-and-pineapple box back in the fridge and taking out the pepperoni. He retrieved a slice and took a giant bite. As he ate, he studied their group. Asked Kylar, "Anything happen while I was gone?"

Kylar hesitated. Glanced at Darien.

Darien knew this had to happen eventually. So he told Roman, whose chewing had slowed, a crease forming in his brow, "Finish eating, and then I want to talk to you alone."

DARIEN'S BOOTS thumped on concrete as he walked into Roman's garage, his cousin following. The door slammed shut, and the pounding of Roman's boots joined Darien's.

The hotrods and motorcycles shone under the fluorescents, the bright chrome so polished it reflected the room like mirrors.

Darien stopped by the line of motorcycles. "You've got a really impressive collection here."

"And you've got an impressive way of avoiding telling me something that's gonna upset me." Roman stopped just behind him, and when he spoke again, his words were tight with reluctance. "It *is* going to upset me, isn't it?"

Darien turned to face him, recognizing that look on his cousin's face—the one that told him he was preparing for a hard kick to the nuts. This was going to hurt Darien just as much as it would hurt Roman; he could sense it.

He crossed his arms, his tongue suddenly having trouble finding words. Swallowed. Drew a slow, deep breath.

Roman lifted his hands in a helpless gesture. "Darien—"

"An accident happened while you were gone," Darien began, speaking evenly. "Pax and Eugene were coming to the house, and they noticed they were being stalked by a couple Shadowmasters. Blaine and Larina."

Roman's face paled.

"They had nowhere else to go but to the house. And Blaine and Larina followed them."

Roman stared at Darien. His face was blank, and his throat shifted with several swallows.

And then he started pacing, one hand slowly rising to rub the stubble on his chin. "Jeez, Darien—for gods' sake—"

"It was an accident—"

He spun to face him. "So they were in this fucking *house?*" He pointed at the garage door that led inside.

Darien nodded.

Roman dropped his hand, and it slapped his thigh. "Well, I guess that's it, then." His voice wavered, and he ran a shaking hand through his hair. The few shadows in the room began to stir.

"Roman—"

"FUCK!" He roared the word through bared teeth. He kicked the bumper of the closest hotrod, the clang of dented chrome ringing through the garage. "Fuck's sake!" His chest shook with heavy, trembling breaths, and he started pacing again. "I never should have left—"

"Why does Pax never wear short sleeves?"

Roman ground his teeth. "Don't even start."

"I *am* starting, and I'm not going to stop. Tell me why."

Roman kept pacing.

"Tell me why, Roman. What does your dad do to him?"

The pacing continued. "Nothing, as long as I'm there."

"What does that mean?" Darien's eyes flicked over Roman—and narrowed in on the weird scars on his arms and shoulders, partially hidden by tattoos and other, far more 'normal' scars. "Where'd you get those scars?" Silence. "Where'd you get those scars, Roman?"

"I'm a Darkslayer—all Darkslayers have scars."

"Not like those."

"Lay off it!" Roman barked, his boot screeching on the ground as he brought his pacing to a halt. "I don't feel like talking about this shit right now—okay? I've got bigger problems than some old scars."

"I bet not all of those are old."

"Look—" Roman struggled to breathe. "Just because you got your old man killed with some freak stroke of luck, doesn't mean you can talk to me as if I'm living my life incorrectly. In case you haven't noticed, I've been fucking stuck here. I've had everything taken from me, and I've only stayed because of Pax. I've only put up with my dad's shit because of Pax. You were just as afraid of Randal as I am of Don. So don't," Roman concluded, panting through his teeth, "talk to me as if you suddenly have all the answers."

Darien gave his cousin a moment to breathe. They faced each other, but while Darien stared at Roman, Roman looked at the floor.

And then Darien made his offer. "I'll do it."

Roman's eyes snapped up to his face. "Do what?" His voice was hoarse, the defeat in his eyes excruciating to see.

"Kill him."

"What, like I can't?"

"I didn't say that. I just want you to know that the offer's there, if you decide to take it. Just say the words, Roman, and I'll do it."

"And I'm supposed to feel good about that? I'm supposed to just let you walk into the House of Black and start a bloody war? Who's going to clean it up after, Darien, huh? Who's going to clean it up?"

"We'll deal with it when the time comes."

"Great," he said, his tone sarcastic and scathing. "Just peachy. You'll fight my battles for me, and I'm supposed to feel good about my dad's men hunting you down afterward? Because they would—you better believe they would. They are *lethal.*"

"I'm not afraid of them."

He scoffed. "You're not a god, Darien. You're just a man. But you're also my cousin, and despite all this shit you just unleashed on me, I care about you. And I would never ask you to face someone like Don." Roman breathed through flared nostrils. "Ever."

Darien stepped up to his cousin. Slowly—closing the distance between them in two long strides. Roman was no longer looking at him. Not even when Darien breathed, "I'm so sorry, Roman."

Roman's whole body was taut, and Darien heard the breath catch in his throat from the apology.

Darien continued, "I'm really sorry—I am. And my offer still stands— whether you want to accept it or not." Roman refused to make eye contact with him. Darien breathed in and forced his own fists to slacken. "And," he added, his tone dripping with menace, "if Don ever lays a hand on you or Pax when I'm around..."

Roman finally met his intense gaze.

Darien concluded through clenched teeth, "Game fucking over."

SHAY SAT on the bed in a guest room on the third floor, resting her bandaged leg. Ivyana Cassel had given her a tour of the house and choice of available rooms, and once Shay had selected one, Ivyana had left to give her some space.

She was still processing everything that had happened. Not just by the harbor, but everything that happened this week too. Her few days with Roman, the mysterious Facility, Anna's continued absence...

And Shay's growing feelings for Roman, the man who'd gone looking for her at the harbor—not for his necklace this time, but for something else. Shay wasn't sure what to call it, exactly, but Roman had come to her because he cared. And she wasn't sure what to do with that truth.

As if he'd read her mind, Roman appeared in the doorway. "How are you doing, pup?"

She studied him—the crease in his brow, the set of his scarred mouth, the sheer emptiness in his eyes. "The look on your face tells me I'm the one who should be asking you that," she said.

He made to step in, but paused. "Mind if I come in?"

She scootched over, gathering her clean, damp hair over one shoulder.

He came in and sat down on the edge of the bed. "At least tell me how your leg is."

"Getting better. Thank gods for our healing abilities." A few days, maybe, and it should be fully healed.

Roman didn't say anything.

Shay swallowed. "Now tell me how you are," she whispered. Something must have happened in the garage. Darien must have told Roman something he didn't want to hear.

"My dad knows." Roman's words were so quiet, they were nearly inaudible. Shay's stomach dipped, her mouth drying out. "About the house," he clarified. He stared at the wall, his throat shifting with repeated swallows. "A couple of his Shadowmasters followed Pax and Eugene here while I was gone."

While you were with me in the desert, Shay corrected in her head, guilt tugging on her heartstrings. And while Roman was doing her a favor, he'd lost something incredibly important to him. His sanctuary in the storm of his life. If Athene ever found out about Shay's apartment... Well, she understood very well how Roman felt right now.

"I'm so sorry, Roman," Shay whispered.

"He's going to find out," Roman said quietly. "If he hasn't already, I mean." He drew a deep breath and forced a smile. "It'll be fine," he said, but it was clearly a lie. "I'll deal with it."

Suffer for it, you mean, Shay almost said. Roman would suffer for the lie.

"It's okay to be afraid," Shay whispered. "Gods—I'm afraid of my mom. I can't begin to imagine what it's like to have Donovan for a dad."

"Hell," Roman said, turning his head to stare at the wall again. "It's hell, and he's the devil."

AFTER GIVING himself a few moments alone to calm down, his conversation with Roman affecting him more than he'd let on, Darien went inside the house.

It sounded like Roman was upstairs, speaking with Shay. The others were in the living room and kitchen, including Loren, whose focus went to Darien as soon as he reached the living room—

A Surge slammed into him so hard, it felt like his brain was going to blow up.

He grabbed his head with both hands and staggered into the wall, smacking his face and knuckles into it like he had that night in Angelthene, when he was with the Reapers in that alley.

Loren stood. "Darien?"

Ivy, Tanner, and Jack shot to their feet.

Darien spun and made for the garage. "Stay away."

They listened.

He pushed into the garage, fumbling for the light switch. It flicked on, but it did shit with the Sight blinding him.

The door opened behind him.

"Loren." The warning was ground out through clenched teeth.

"It's me." It was Kylar.

Darien was panting like he'd run a marathon. "I need to fight."

Kylar stood on the steps, one brown hand resting on the door handle. "Even after all that?"

"I have a problem," he said. "What was the name of that place? Snake something—"

"The Snake Pit? The fighting ring at the Black Market, you mean."

"Yeah, that's the one. Anything I should know about it?" He managed to rid himself of the Sight and saw the wary look on Kylar's face... The way his hand gripped the door handle tighter.

"A lot of people die there, so I'd tell you to be careful. You gotta pay to participate, but you'll win thousands if you don't get killed."

"You got a ski mask or something?"

Kylar pushed open the garage door. "One sec." He disappeared inside.

One second turned into seven painful minutes, and when the door opened again, it wasn't Kylar who stepped out. It was Roman.

He thumped down the few steps and offered Darien a black mask. The same type the Darkslaying messengers wore, but this was a wolf instead of a rabbit.

"What's this?" Darien panted, not taking it yet.

"I fight sometimes, and this is what I wear. I prefer to use the chambers now—they're easier on my body." Darien still didn't take it. Roman held it closer. "If you wear this, everyone will just think you're me. It's safer this way."

Darien took the mask. While the wolf's teeth and eyes were painted white, the rest was a deep black that faintly sparkled when you moved it.

Roman said, "Hopefully, the next time this happens, you can try one of the chambers instead."

Darien checked his pockets for his keys—still there.

Roman was studying him. "I know this isn't a good time for questions, but she's asking about you." He tipped his head toward the house.

"She's my girlfriend," Darien said. Speaking that truth aloud for the first time since Loren had woken up nearly brought him to his knees. "She lost all memory of the past six months when she woke up out of her coma." His voice shook. Gods, was he about to break down in tears? It fucking felt like it.

Roman's expression smoothed with understanding. "She doesn't remember you," he whispered.

Darien tried to swallow but couldn't. "I don't want to overwhelm her. I want her memories to come back on their own, so—please." He met Roman's stare, not realizing that he'd broken it, and whispered, "Don't say anything."

Understanding brimmed in Roman's gaze. "The fact that you'd be willing to wait for her instead of rushing it says a lot about you." He opened his mouth to say more. Closed it. "Look, Darien—"

"It's okay, Roman," Darien said softly—as softly as he could manage during a Surge. "I get it. And I'm still sorry."

"Don't be. It would've happened eventually, regardless."

"Still would've preferred if it wasn't while I was here."

He shrugged. "Shit happens." He gestured to his own eyes. "You've been talking for a few minutes without the..."

"It's still there—I'm not that lucky." As he spoke, black flickered in his vision, as if summoned. He lifted the mask and said, "Thanks."

And then he turned and made for his car.

"Sure you can drive?" Roman called.

"I do it all the time at home." He opened the driver's door and got in. "I'm sure I'll survive." He shut the door and started the engine.

Roman walked up to the wall and pushed the button to open the garage.

Darien reversed and spun the car around. As soon as the gates were open, he sped through them.

Different city, same train wreck of a life.

LOREN'S SECOND recovered memory nearly knocked her to her knees.

Darien had left, but Loren still stood in the living room, looking toward the garage door as if he might come back. But the growl of his engine had long since faded, and she knew it would be hours before he returned.

Ivy, Jack, and Tanner were on the couches. Watching her, she knew. They'd answered her questions about Surges—about Darien. He'd gone to fight at a ring called the Snake Pit. Fighting was his coping mechanism—something that worked better for him than therapy.

Knowing this deep and painful secret about such a strong and capable person who was feared the world over made Loren's heart ache.

What made it ache even more, however, was the memory that had assaulted her mind the minute he'd raced for the door.

It had come to her in pieces. A bright, beautiful foyer with flowers on a glass table; a set of big doors Loren rushed forward to block; the scents of a house that had become a home.

And the Darkslayer standing in front of her, duffel bag hanging from his shoulder. His ripped and bloodied henley and jeans, his worn boots, the look of anguish in his eyes.

Then came the memory of his hand resting in hers. She'd asked him to humor her, and he'd allowed her to tow him to the living room, where he'd sat on the couch, knees spread apart. She'd knelt on the floor between his legs, and had told him to walk with her to a sparkling ocean with a beach of white sand.

He had wiped away a tear on her cheek, and then had used his thumb to trace her chin, then her lips. She remembered his touch, clear as day, and swore she could feel it on her skin right now.

How had she ever forgotten that night?

"Loren?" Ivy's soft voice called her back to attention.

She turned, blinking away her recollections of the past.

Ivy and Tanner were both watching her. Jack was focused on the television, his eyes glazed, mouth slack.

Ivy said, "He'll be okay. This is normal for him. I'm sure he'll be back in a few hours."

Loren nodded. "Yeah." She sounded as pained as she felt. "Umm—I think I'll go have a shower." She drew a breath that got caught halfway up her throat. "Have a good night."

Tanner and Jack called, "Night."

She disappeared toward the stairs, Ivy and Tanner watching her go.

She stayed in the shower for a long time, wishing all the while that more memories would return.

But they didn't. So she was forced to wait and wonder what other extraordinary things she could have possibly forgotten about Darien Cassel.

71

THE SNAKE PIT
YVESWICH, STATE OF KER

Darien lost himself to his rage, just like when he fought back at home. He couldn't remember how much time had passed or how many people he'd felled, but he knew it was a lot—of both. At least four hours and two dozen bodies. Minimum.

By the time he snapped back into his dark and vile mind, there was only one opponent left in the Snake Pit. The hellseher was dragging himself across the concrete floor of the ring in an effort to get away, a wet, reeking stain darkening the front of his pants.

Darien stalked toward him in ripped jeans and black boots, no shirt on. He wore Roman's wolf mask; there were no eye holes, but the magic allowed him to see through it. In one hand he held a spiked bat. He dragged it behind him, the rusted nails catching on pits in the concrete. An audience that behaved more like animals than they did people surrounded the ring, foaming at the mouths as they fought among themselves, fuelled by drugs and alcohol and tempers as bad as his own.

As Darien walked, dragging the bat behind him, he caught sight of a familiar face in the crowd.

A brawny warlock stood in the front row, his features shadowed by a heavy hood.

Darien lifted the bat, got a firm grip on one of the blood-slick nails, and ripped it out, splintering the wood. With blinding speed, he threw—

Straight at Finn Solace's face.

The nail hit the wall of spells surrounding the ring with a searing crackle. Finn must have known there were spells in place, but he still flinched and fell backward, slamming into the rowdy crowds who were quick to shove him the other way. Finn barely caught himself against the ropes before the spells could chew through his skin—not enough to kill but to maim.

Darien returned his attention to the man on the ground—the victim he towered over. "Any last words?" Darien's deep voice was slightly muffled by the mask. He'd covered up his Devils' tattoo before joining the fight—with blood from his own hand. A quick cut across his palm, and then he'd dragged his hand down the sides of his neck, caking on the red.

The hellseher on the ground squeezed out, "You're crazy."

Darien nodded. "Yeah. I think I am."

He gripped the bat with both hands, wound it back over his head…

And struck.

Unleashing all that pent-up rage made Darien feel like a whole new person.

There was no place to shower here, not like at the Chopping Block or Perez's Pit, so he had to leave wearing the same clothes he'd fought in. He'd at least had enough sense to take off his jacket and hooded sweatshirt beforehand, giving them to the ring announcer for safe keeping, so it was only his pants and boots that were wet and heavy with blood.

He spotted Finn having a drink at a dilapidated bar near the Snake Pit. The warlock eyed the whiskey he swirled in his glass, clearly contemplating his decision to order a drink in a seedy place such as this.

Darien headed his way, people stepping out of his path as he moved.

The detective must've sensed Darien's approach. He turned, his eyes immediately finding his.

"Did you know there was a wall of spells there?" Finn's every word was taut, and he still looked as if he'd seen a ghost.

"Did you?" Darien countered. "You still flinched," he accused.

"You still threw."

"What do you want?"

"To talk."

"How'd you find me?"

"I asked myself where you'd be, and I have to say you're a bit predictable."

Darien said, "Another city, different fighting ring. What do you want to talk about?"

Finn's eyes flicked about the market. "I'd prefer to do it elsewhere."

Darien grunted. "I'd prefer to know what it's about before agreeing."

Finn glanced around again, well aware of the many eyes picking apart their exchange, and whispered, "The men from The Blood Queen."

They made the decision to talk at a rundown diner not far from the Black Market. The Hash House was one of the few places that dared to stay open twenty-four hours, and because of how late it was, they were some of the only people in here. There was a drunk at the counter, staring up at the boxy television with glazed eyes, and a homeless person passed out in the corner farthest from the door.

Darien and Finn sat across from each other in a booth by the windows. Hoods up, heads down. The long, sit-down counter was lined with cushioned stools the same blue-green as the booths. The menu boards above the counter boasted a wide selection of breakfast items, milkshakes, and bottomless coffee—the same coffee Darien and Finn had ordered. Weaker than water. No amount of cream or sugar could fix it.

"Two of the men who died at The Blood Queen were Gaven Payne's," Finn was saying. He sipped on his black, bitter water and fought a grimace. "It took us longer to complete the autopsies because there wasn't much left of the bodies by the time we dug them up."

"And you," Darien began, shoving his cup aside and folding his arms on the table, "are here to ask me if I'm the one who did it."

Finn set down his mug. "You or one of your own."

Darien glared. "If I wanted to kill Gaven's men, I'd do it in private, where I could take my time pulling them apart."

"You were at the hotel when it exploded," he challenged.

"And I nearly got killed, in case you didn't notice."

"You could have timed it badly. It's easy to make mistakes when it comes to raw magic—"

"Do I look like someone who makes mistakes?"

Finn slid his mug aside, smearing the coffee ring, and laced his fingers on the table. "I've got a lot of people breathing down my neck right now to find whoever's responsible."

"I hate to break it to you, but I refuse to be someone you frame."

"I wasn't planning on framing you. I just want to know the truth. And if it wasn't you, then maybe you could lend me a hand finding out why it happened and who did it."

Darien's brows shot up. "Another favor?" The words were razor-edged.

"You don't have to call it a favor, you can call it..." He licked his lips that were chapped from the cold. "Joining forces. You want Gaven and his men dead, and I want them behind bars. If we work together, we can bring them to justice quicker." Justice. Fuck. Darien's idea of justice was very different than Finn's—and absolutely did not involve allowing his victims to breathe any longer than he wanted them to. "And in the meantime," Finn continued, "find the person who really did this. A lot of innocent people died in that explosion—"

"Don't try to sell me a sob story, Finn—it isn't gonna work this time."

"Look." Finn's tone turned pleading. "You've got something to gain from this, and so do I. Whoever caused those explosions needs to be arrested, same with Gaven and his men—"

"Wait," Darien cut in. "*Explosions?* There was more than one?"

Finn nodded, his expression grave. "The second explosion happened this morning—a skyscraper in the Financial District. A couple of the men who died happened to be near the outskirts of the blast, so we were able to identify them right away. Both worked for Gaven."

Darien's mind raced as he tried to figure out how and why this was happening.

And how this person was finding Gaven's men so easily. Their auras were hidden the same way Loren's was hidden. Had Darien been able to track them, he would've already found them and slit their throats.

"The third," Finn continued, "happened this afternoon. A hotel on the waterfront. Three wanted criminals—two were Payne's."

"And the other?" Finn didn't reply. Darien prompted, "The other guy—who was he?"

Finn sighed. When he spoke again, his words were barely audible. "He was in the imperator's employ."

Darien clenched his teeth. "The imperator." He squeezed his hands that were resting on the table into fists. "Is he in Yveswich?"

Wouldn't that be a coincidence? If the imperator really was here, Darien couldn't help but wonder if the man had tailed him after he'd left Angelthene. The ambush at the hospital...that attack had been organized by Quinton Lucent.

But he had no reason to follow—at least, not until now, and not unless his purpose was strictly to retaliate against Darien. For all they knew, Loren was still in a coma, still utterly ineffectual as a pawn in his game.

Darien took comfort in that fact. But even the simple thought that someone could be after her again made him want to race back to Roman's house and make sure she was safe. Guard her. Die for her, if need be. If protecting her was his sole purpose in life, he'd die for her with pride.

Finn's attention flicked to Darien's clenched fists. "I don't know," he said quietly, selecting the same careful tone someone might use to soothe a feral animal. "But clearly, some of his men are."

"Would you say that's unusual?"

"Not necessarily. The imperator has men in every capital city, but they don't usually turn up dead like this." Finn rubbed the stubble on his chin. "Two times, and we call it a coincidence. Three, and we call it concerning." He studied Darien, a glint of hope in his eyes, the foolish fuck. For a detective, he wasn't very good at reading people. Or maybe it was just Darien who he couldn't read. "So, what do you think?"

"I'm thinking I'm not sure I want to trust you again."

"I'm not fucking with you, Cassel—"

"This time," Darien hissed. He barely resisted punching the table, instead pointing a finger at Finn, the horns on his steel monster rings glinting. "You may not be fucking with me this time, but it hasn't been that long since the last."

Finn's jaw flexed. "Is there anything I can do to change your mind?"

"You could try putting your gun in your mouth and pulling the trigger."

Finn stared at him for nearly a minute.

Darien stared back.

And then Finn slid out of the booth and took out his wallet. He threw down a twenty and placed a business card on the table before Darien, snapping down the cardboard edge. "In case you change your mind." He slid the card closer.

And then he left, the bells on the door chiming with his departure.

Darien sat there for a minute. Thinking. He sensed Finn lingering in the parking lot, standing outside the diner instead of getting in his car and driving away.

After another few minutes of thinking, Darien got to his feet and walked out.

Outside, the night was sodden with rain that pummeled the ground in heavy sheets. Demons stalked through the dark, the gleam of their eyes barely visible in the shadows, while others dug through the dumpsters at the side of the diner, crushing garbage in sharp teeth. They ate everything—glass, metal, you name it.

Finn was heading for his car, hands in his jacket pockets.

"Finn!" Darien's deep voice sliced through the downpour. The detective turned, squinting through the rain. "Meet me at the morgue tomorrow morning. I want to have a look at those bodies."

Her tea had gone cold.

Loren sat by herself at Roman's kitchen table. Everyone else, as far as she knew, was fast asleep. Which was understandable, considering it was almost three in the morning. Even Singer was asleep in their bedroom upstairs.

The house was quiet. The only sounds she could hear were the ticking of the clock and the soft snoring of Itzel in the snack cupboard. The Hob was apparently quiet and well-behaved whenever Paxton was here, but maintained a very dramatic attitude toward anyone who wasn't Paxton—even Roman. Loren found it kind of funny, though Itzel's tendency to turn up the television to the highest volume often woke her during the night.

The garage door rolled open, the sound carrying through the house.

Loren sat up straighter, listening to the growl of Darien's car as he pulled into the garage. The shudder of the door rolling shut came a moment later, and another minute or so passed before she heard the thud of a car door closing.

Loren fiddled with her pajama shirt, butterflies swarming her stomach.

Darien came into the house. She couldn't see him yet, but she recognized the way he walked—with pride, all the time. He wore his identity like a badge of honor. Loren would bet no one and nothing could ever make this man drag his feet.

He rounded the corner in the same clothes he'd left the house in—a black hooded sweatshirt and jeans. The denim of his pants was stained red —Loren didn't let her thoughts linger on what it was.

Darien froze the moment he saw her, looking equally concerned and surprised. "What are you doing up?"

She got to her feet. "I wanted to...make sure you were okay." That same memory from earlier that evening played in her mind.

I haven't been okay since I was fifteen, Darien had said.

But right now, he told her, "I'm okay."

She smoothed the hem of her pajama shirt. "Where did you go?"

Darien hesitated briefly before saying, "I had a few stops to make."

There was dried blood on the backs of his hands. Blood caked on his steel rings.

When he saw where her attention had gone, he slid his hands into the pocket of his sweatshirt. "You should get some rest."

"I'm not afraid of you," she said softly. "The others said fighting is your coping mechanism. Gods know we all need those."

He tore his eyes off her and walked into the kitchen. She didn't miss that he gave her a far wider berth than he needed to. His back was facing her as he opened a cupboard by the fridge and grabbed a glass. At this angle, she was able to see the blood on his neck too, thick smears of it concealing his gang tattoo. "Most people go to therapy or support groups," Darien said. "Fucked-Up Anonymous and all that." He filled the glass with water from the fridge.

"Ivy told me you've tried therapy."

"I did. They spat me out because I'm too fucked up." He drank, tipping the glass back until he'd downed it all, and then placed the glass in the sink.

"We're all flawed," she offered gently.

He leaned his arms on the counter. "Except you. You're perfect."

Her face reddened. "I'm not. I get jealous and insecure. I cry too much. I'm bad at standing up for myself."

A sad smile ghosted across his alluring mouth. "If you could only see how much you flew these last few months. You put me to shame."

Gods, her face felt like it was on fire. "I highly doubt that."

"We all may be flawed, but we're also strong in our own unique ways. And when your memories come back, I think you'll feel proud of the woman you've become."

She tucked her hair behind an ear. "One memory did come back, actually."

His mouth sank, those inky brows creeping together.

"I helped you," she said. "With a Surge. We were at your house...and I stopped you from leaving. I told you to picture an ocean." She stared at him, and he stared at her. She couldn't read his expression, but she swore he wasn't breathing. "Was that my magic?"

Darien's voice was a quiet murmur. "I haven't been able to figure that one out yet."

They looked at each other for a long time.

Until Loren broke his stare and cleared her throat. "What are we doing tomorrow?" Although she'd severed eye contact, Darien still hadn't looked away from her.

"Tanner's taking Joyce to the airport. The hospital called—they need her back at work. More Tricking cases, new strains." He scrubbed a hand down his face, a shadow of something Loren couldn't place flickering in his eyes. "I'll be gone for part of the morning. I'm going to the morgue to meet with a friend."

"A living one, I hope."

The smile he cracked was unrestrained. And very, very handsome.

"When will you be back?" A part of her wanted to go with him, but she was reluctant to ask.

"After a few hours, hopefully." That mouth sank again. "If anything out of the ordinary happens—"

"I'll tell the others." She smiled.

"I'm not trying to sound overbearing—"

"You're not. I...like it. This has all been a lot to take in, so having you take control and help me the way you have been is...well, I really appreciate it."

A twitch at the corner of his mouth. "You're welcome."

She pointed behind her—toward the stairs. "Maybe I'll go to bed now."

He merely watched her.

"I'm glad you're okay," she added. She gave him a wave. Turned and padded down the hall.

"Goodnight, Loren Calla." His bass voice was gentler than most people likely believed him capable of.

Including her.

When she reached the bottom of the stairs, she turned to look at him. He hadn't moved, and he still watched her, but his expression had shifted, this new one even more impossible to read than any of his others. "Goodnight, Darien."

72

ASS-FUCK NOWHERE
STATE OF KER

Malakai was sweating his balls off.

He downed the last of his water—hot and nasty—and crumpled the plastic bottle into a pulp. "There's nothing fucking out here!" he fumed.

They'd been wandering around in the desert like a bunch of idiots for what felt like a goddamn eternity. He'd taken off his shirt and stuffed it into the back pocket of his jeans, and when his Angelthene tan had started turning into a red, peeling burn, he'd resorted to slathering on some of Aspen's coconut-scented sunscreen.

Coconut wasn't his usual choice, but neither was sweating his balls off in the middle of ass-fuck nowhere.

"Would you quit complaining?" Max snapped, sweat rolling down his temples. "We're all as uncomfortable as you."

"Clearly not, or we wouldn't be torturing ourselves like this."

"I don't know, guys," Dallas panted. "I'm thinking we should drive farther—maybe check out that housing Priscilla mentioned."

"Blue said she came from a facility," Max said. "Not a house. My first thought was the Facility could be a bunker—out in the middle of the desert where no one would think to look for a door." It was smart—Malakai had to give him that. But smart thinking did nothing to help with this whole swass problem going on in his jeans.

Aspen shielded her eyes with a hand and looked out at the SUV. The vehicle was barely a pinprick from here, the windshield scintillating with sunlight. Dominic and Blue were in there. In air conditioning, probably.

Lucky Angel prick. "Too bad she was drugged when they finally took her out of that place," Aspen said.

"Yeah, no shit," Malakai replied, unable to douse his fiery tone. All of him was fiery—even his hair felt like it was burning. About an hour ago, he'd taken off his rings, the steel so hot it burned.

Dallas hummed. "What about a business or a factory or something? Maybe one's a front for this facility place."

Max chewed on his sunburned lip. "She mentioned cristala power plants."

Malakai gestured toward the SUV with wide sweeps of his arm, hoping this was the end of this shit. "Great, let's go."

Max frowned. "We haven't checked over there yet—"

Malakai pointed with his empty, crushed water bottle. "Or there. Or there. Or anywhere else. You want to die out here, Reacher? Because I'm about to crisp into a nice, tasty little piece of Reaper jerky."

He scowled. "You are the most annoying, dramatic person I've ever met."

"I'm not annoying, I'm funny." He bared his teeth. "Ha ha."

"You're not funny if you're the only person who laughs at your jokes."

"Creature laughs at them."

"Creature doesn't have a sense of humor."

The bat tore out of Malakai's shadow with an angry chirp. He flitted around Reacher's face, wingbeats stirring his hair. Malakai laughed.

Max waved him away. "Call him off." He ducked when Creature swept for his head. "Call him off, or I'll get Grim to eat him." He ducked again.

"I'd like to see him try." But Malakai whistled, and Creature retreated into his shadow with one last angry chirp.

Reacher glanced out at the land again—rippling under the heat, as if this whole place was a barbecue and they were the unfortunate hot dogs—and swore, *finally* realizing how in over his head he was.

Bout fucking time.

Malakai made for the vehicle, parched earth crunching under his boiling-hot, steel-toe boots. Aspen was soon following—at least *she* had a sense of self-preservation. "Let's go find these power plants," he called over his shoulder, his fist crumpling the plastic bottle flatter, "before we all die."

It was the second power plant that turned out to be worth their time.

Max rolled the SUV into the parking lot out front of the multilevel building. Everyone was crammed in the vehicle, which had made for a hot and tense ride full of sweating complainers. Dominic and Malakai were about three seconds from strangling each other when Max stopped the vehicle and cut the engine.

Malakai opened his door. "If I stay in here for one more second, you're going to have to bury me out here."

"Facility." Blue's voice was high and panicked. "That's the Facility. I-I can't—"

Dominic clasped her hand. "It's okay, it's okay—no one's here. See?" He pointed at the building. He was right—it was completely abandoned. "See? No one's going to hurt you, Blue. I promise."

Her breathing didn't slow. "I can't, you guys, I am sorry. Dominic—I can't go in there. I can't go back—"

"You don't have to. We'll wait here." He glanced at Max in the rear-view mirror, and Max nodded once. The Angel turned back to Blue, hatred for the Facility burning in his stare. "Okay?" he asked her.

She took several calming breaths. "You'll stay with me?"

"Yes," he promised. "I won't leave."

Malakai said, "Well, *I'm* leaving." He got out. "I've about had it with this trip." He stalked toward the building, shirt stuffed in his back pocket. "See you fuckers later."

Max opened his door. "Nobody *ever* let me invite him again."

"I heard that." Malakai's voice echoed as he approached the massive, empty building.

Max got out, Dallas and Aspen following.

"Careful," Dominic called.

Malakai was already inside.

Cursing under his breath, Max hurried after him, Dallas and Aspen right behind him.

The building—the Facility—looked like a tornado had gone through it. The place was littered with debris, most of the walls were smashed or blackened, and there were gaping holes in the roof. Sunlight streamed in through the holes, spreading patches of buttery gold across the concrete floor. It was cooler in here, though not by much.

Max couldn't stop staring at the blackened walls. He swiped a finger across one and rubbed the chalky black substance between his thumb and forefinger.

Soot.

"Max?" Dallas called. "You might want to take a look at this."

Glass and stone crunched and clacked under his feet as he joined Dallas and Aspen beside a big metal chamber.

Fire-resistant. An emblem of a flame was bolted above the door, and there were warnings in multiple languages—Ilevyn included—all over the exterior walls of the chamber.

Max called upon his Sight and checked for auras. There weren't many here—they had likely been hidden as thoroughly as this building—but the few traces that remained were filled with such anguish, they nearly bowed his knees. He didn't need to know who these people were to figure out that this here—this fire-resistant chamber—was a torture device.

He turned around to find Aspen studying a big aquatic tank nearby. The Reaper tapped a knuckle against a portion of glass that wasn't shattered and said, "How much you want to bet that our blue friend spent a lot of time in here?"

Max turned again toward the fire-resistant chamber...

Maya. Gods—

The door creaked.

Max drew his gun. "Where's Delaney?" he mouthed.

The girls didn't have a clue. They drew guns of their own, and together they crept toward the front doors, Max taking the lead.

Max eased around the corner, the girls watching his back.

He pointed his gun toward the doors. Scanned the hallway.

Empty. The door was still swinging slowly, as if pushed by wind. Sunlight flooded the entrance, but no one was there.

Max was about to turn when something slammed into the side of his head—

MALAKAI SAUNTERED through the second floor of the building, wiping sweat off his brow. Endless fucking sweat.

This floor was lined with dozens of cells. There were doors instead of bars, yeah, but it made no bloody difference. The place reeked of prison life. Malakai would know; he'd spent time in both Blackwater and Darkwater, but his sentences hadn't stuck. There were numbers above these doors, the rooms empty apart from beds and desks. Abysmal. Depressing.

"If someone tried to bring me here, I'd kill 'em," he muttered. "I'd kill 'em, and I'd do it slowly."

Voices shouted up from the ground floor. Bullets cracked through the building.

Malakai stopped. Turned.

More bullets cracked. Someone shouted out his name—

Aspen.

"Shit."

He took off running, footfall clapping against the walls. When he reached the crumbling staircase, he leapt off the top step—

Fire blasted his way—swallowing the space he was about to land in.

Oh shit, oh shit—

He snapped his magic into a shield in time to not be incinerated by the fire rushing toward him. His boots hit the floor with jarring impact, and as he caught himself against the wall, he spotted Max and Aspen—throwing themselves out of the way of the blaze.

Heat scorched the room; he could feel it as strongly as he'd felt the desert sun, even through the invisible wall of his magic.

The inferno grew, heading straight for Aspen and Max—

Malakai's magic lashed out like whips, and he used them to throw Max and Aspen into the fire-resistant chamber.

But he couldn't get Dallas in there. She was on the other side of the room—in hand to hand combat with a girl with shimmering gold hair. Throwing her toward the chamber would only put her in the path of the inferno. Dallas had lost her gun, and it was a good thing her wings were spell-hidden, or they would have already been singed off.

Using his magic as a shield, Malakai dove across the floor and slid to a stop in front of the chamber. He thrust a hand behind him, stopping Max from opening the door.

"Don't be an idiot!" Malakai roared, throwing his whole weight against the door. "Stay in there!" He could smell Max's fear—could feel it as strongly as the barrage of fire that wouldn't let up.

Max was screaming—howling Dallas's name, fists banging against the door.

She was still in combat with the other person in the room—an Elemental. And she wasn't winning.

Malakai winced, his magic fluttering. He wouldn't be able to hold it for much longer.

This was how he was going to die, wasn't it? Crisped into a piece of Reaper jerky, just like he'd said. Pathetic. He'd always wanted to go out with a bang, and this just wasn't it.

Magic—new magic—blasted through the room, sending the Fire Elemental crashing into the tank.

Black wings momentarily blinded Malakai as Dominic swept into the room.

The Angel offered him a hand up.

Malakai ignored him and pushed to his feet. "I still hate your guts." He wiped the sweat out of his stinging eyes.

Dallas cried out as the gold Elemental—what the hell was gold, anyway?—threw her into the stairs.

Dominic moved to her aid—

Flames swept through the room as the Fire Elemental recovered from Dominic's attack. His hair was all flame, his eyes burning like embers as he leapt out of the tank and landed on his feet like a freaking cat.

"Any ideas?" Dominic gritted out.

Malakai reinforced his invisible shields, Dominic doing the same at his side. Malakai swept his magic out toward Dallas, shielding her as she staggered to her feet. Blood streamed down her temple.

Both Elementals attacked this time, fire magic mingling with—

Gods. That was a full-blown storm gathering under the gold one's skin, lightning bolts shooting up her neck.

A wave of icy blue water slammed into the Elementals, throwing them both into the wall above the tank and pinning them there. Mist sprayed Malakai's skin, cooling the areas he hadn't realized were burning.

A female voice speaking Ilevyn floated through the room.

Blue walked in. "Don't," she said through clenched teeth, "hurt him. Them. Or I—" she panted, eyes electric-blue, "—will kill you."

The Fire Elemental had cooled off—literally. He and the gold one both stared at Blue in shock.

It was the male who gritted out, his voice coated with surprise, "Blue?"

She let them go, using the water to safely lower them to the ground.

Malakai bared his teeth at the fiery one, whose wide eyes flicked between their group and Blue. "Is it not hot enough outside for you, or what?" Malakai snapped. "Bloody fucking Ignis."

The guy's name was Blaze, and he was a Fire Elemental like Maya. Of course, if he knew who Maya was, he'd know her as 'Scarlet'.

As for the girl, her name was Gold, and she was a Storm Elemental. Her magic was of the Aether.

Max resisted the urge to tap his foot. No mention of Maya yet. No mention of where she went, or if she was even alive.

Finally, for the first time in minutes, Blue faced their group and translated something new. "Blaze says they...broke out."

Their group was crowded around the fire-resistant chamber, still sweating and out of breath from the encounter that had nearly incinerated them all.

Max's spine straightened. "Broke out? Ask him about Maya—Scarlet, I mean. Please."

Blue turned toward Blaze, who looked like he was ready to bolt for the doors at the first sign of danger. Blaze might have wreaked most of the destruction during the fight, but Max sensed that the girl—Gold—was potentially even more dangerous.

Blaze and Blue conversed for a few seconds in tense, quiet Ilevyn, Gold observing quietly at Blaze's side. Dominic listened the whole time, clearly trying to decipher, too.

Finally, Blue faced Max. "Scarlet was part of the group. The group that...escaped." She gestured to Max, speaking to Blaze and Gold now.

Dominic murmured to Max, "She's telling them that you're Scarlet's brother."

Blaze faced Max with reluctance, and when he spoke this time, he was addressing Max—in Ilevyn, of course.

"What did he say?" Max's attention flicked to Blue.

"Blaze says Scarlet mentioned you a few times." The ghost of a smile curved Blue's lips. "They tried to erase her memories, like...like they did mine." Sadness filled her eyes. "But she never forgot you."

Max's throat was suddenly too tight to breathe. All this time, Maya had been in this building. "Where is she?"

Blue's next translation was a bit shaky. "Blaze says that Maya and the others were on their way to Eve...Eve's...Witch?"

"Yveswich," Max said. He shared a glance with Dominic.

Blue nodded. "Yveswich," she said again. "They look for...family. For... homes? He did not wish to go with them. He and Gold came back to look for girl. They lost her during the..." Her voice trailed off, and she shook her head, frustrated with herself.

"The breakout," Dominic offered.

Blue nodded. "Breakout, yes. Aurora. Her name was Aurora."

Dallas murmured, "Aurora." Her eyes flicked to Max. Rainbow aura, if her name was any indication. And apparently, names meant everything around here.

Blue whispered, "He does not...he does not wish to say anymore. He— they," she gestured to Blaze and Gold, "wish to be free."

Malakai said, "And I wish to be free of this headache."

Max faced Blaze. "Thank you," he breathed.

He seemed to understand that, and nodded once.

They left the Facility after searching the top floors. There were more tanks, chambers, pools, padded rooms—a whole bunch of shit that gave Max full-body chills. But no sign of other Elementals. No sign of Aurora. Blaze and Gold must've realized this too; they disappeared sometime during their search with no indication that they were leaving.

By the time they got out to the vehicle, it was nearly noon, the sun beating down so hard, Max could feel it burning his skin. It gave him another chill that felt weird in the heat. He'd been *this close* to being incinerated in there—by the same magic that apparently ran through his own veins.

Dallas fell into stride beside him. She was limping slightly, and there were streaks of dried blood on the side of her face and neck, but aside from this, she was okay. Max had nearly lost it in there—when Malakai had refused to let him out of the chamber. Had anything happened to Dallas...

He swallowed, his throat tight. The thought of anything happening to Dallas made his blood boil.

"Where do we go from here, big guy?" Dallas asked him. "You tell me, I'll follow."

Max used the hem of his shirt to wipe the grime off his face. "There's nowhere to go now. Not unless we go on a wild goose chase in Yveswich." Which would mean going to the same place as Darien, which wasn't a part of the agreement.

"I said I'll follow," she vowed.

"You've got school, Dal. I'm not about to wreck your future." It wasn't just her school that made him reluctant to agree—it was what just happened in that damn building. She was a Fleet trainee, and she'd got her ass handed to her. Clearly, this path he was walking was filled with the kind of enemies none of them were properly equipped to handle.

"You're not wrecking anything," Dallas said. "This is as important to me as it is to you." She grabbed him by the arm, pulling him to a stop. "You are my future, Max," she told him. "I know how badly you want to find Maya, and I want to help you do it. Please let me help you."

He brought his hand up, his knuckles gently skimming the wound on the side of her head. "Dallas, you're a brilliant student. You're a kick-ass Fleet soldier—"

"Trainee," she corrected.

"With a huge opportunity ahead of you. If the Fleet doesn't kick you out for missing this much training, then your dad's gonna give you the boot."

Her throat bobbed. "I don't care."

"Well, you should."

"No one has ever asked me what I want. My whole life has been laid out in front of me in stepping stones marked with numbers. I've never been allowed to skip anything, never been allowed to set my own stones. I'm a witch—I've got centuries ahead of me. I can always catch up."

"Some opportunities don't come around more than once." And the love he felt for Dallas wouldn't come around more than once.

He couldn't lose her.

"Neither will this," she said. "I'm not throwing anything away—I'm just deciding what's most important to me in this moment, and that's *you.*"

"Goddamn." He swept a hand down his filthy face. "You can't say shit like that to me."

"Why?" She flashed him a playful smile. "Does it turn you on?"

"Actually, right now, it's making me want to cry. And I'm not supposed to cry—I'm a Darkslayer."

Her smile grew. "I don't think I've ever seen you cry."

"And you won't—not if I can help it." He gestured toward the SUV. "Get going."

They joined the others who were waiting either by or in the SUV, doors open.

Malakai said, "I can't follow you to Yveswich, if that's where you're going. I need to get back to Angelthene."

Max nodded. "We'll all go. We should speak to Travis—make sure everything's okay in Angelthene. I'll decide what I'm doing after." He glanced among the group. "Good?"

Malakai gestured for Aspen to get in the back seat. "Ladies first."

She snickered. "You just don't want to be stuck in the middle."

"I need access to a door so I can roll out if I decide I can't handle you guys anymore." He looked at Max over his shoulder. "The next time I tell you to stay in a fire-resistant chamber when some infernal asshole is going to town on us, you listen." Right—he was likely alive right now because of Delaney.

He owed him a thanks, but it wasn't something he wanted to acknowledge. Especially not when he knew the Reaper had thrown him in there because he was aware that Max was afraid of fire. Malakai had learned a lot about the Devils years ago, back when he and Darien were friends. But...

Max said tightly, "Thanks."

The Reaper merely nodded.

73

THE MORGUE
YVESWICH, STATE OF KER

Metal clanged as Finn pulled out a temperature-controlled mortuary drawer at the morgue. Cold air billowed out of it, partially obscuring the body inside until it dissipated.

"This one's from the Financial District," Finn said. "The explosion that happened yesterday morning."

Darien pointed at the body. "*This* is one of the more recognizable ones?" The skin was practically melted off, as if acid had chewed through it. Darien was reluctant to see what the others looked like.

"I'm afraid so." Finn studied Darien's reaction closely.

Darien had to resist the urge to punch him out for still viewing him as a suspect—as if he was capable of doing...*this*. If he were capable, sure, it seemed like a great way to make his enemies suffer until the bitter end. But these wounds were not...normal.

"Recognize him?" Finn prodded. "From your...time with Gaven?"

Darien shook his head. "He's got a lot of men, though. Let's see the other—the second guy from this attack."

Finn rolled the drawer shut until it slammed. He strode to the end of the locker of drawers and pulled out another. More of that cold mist billowed out.

Darien walked over and had a look.

Partially melted, just like the last guy. But—

"I recognize this one," Darien said. "He was in Angelthene. Why do you think so many of Gaven's men would be in Yveswich?"

Finn shrugged. Pushed the drawer shut. "Maybe you scared him away." Darien knew exactly what Finn was implying—that he was aware of the path of revenge Darien had been carving out in Angelthene. He didn't try to deny it, but he didn't confirm it, either.

"Cause of death is raw magic?" Darien asked.

"That's what we thought. What a couple of the deaths look like. But the incident at the waterfront hotel—it's called the Pearl—was pretty bizarre. We're still waiting for the results for those."

"Bizarre in what way?"

Finn's mouth quirked at the corner. "Maybe, if you actually agree to help me, I'll tell you."

"Maybe," Darien crooned, matching his brazen tone, "if you prove yourself trustworthy, I'll agree. The next attack that happens—call me. I want to have a look at the actual crime scene before your men get their hands all over it."

He crossed the cold room. Finn followed, but at a speed that told Darien he wouldn't try to argue today.

Good—Darien wanted to get back to Roman's. Back to Loren. He'd checked on her before leaving, but she was sleeping too deeply to notice him. The memory of her slumbering face melted the ice around his heart.

Darien added, "If you don't call me when the sirens are still going off, I'm not coming at all."

"You gonna actually answer my calls this time?"

Shit—his phone.

He paused by the door. "I'll set something up," he said. And then he pushed the door open and left.

Loren woke up later than usual.

When she cracked open her eyes, the clock on the nightstand read quarter after ten. She recalled someone coming in to check on her, but she didn't know how much time had passed since then. She also wasn't certain who'd come to check on her, but she had a feeling he had black hair and a lot of tattoos.

It took her a few minutes before she no longer felt groggy, but by then she had another problem to face.

Her throat was dry and burning, her stomach was twisting into knots, and intense chills were wracking her body.

She got out of bed, nearly stepping on Singer, who was curled up on the floor.

He lurched to his shadowy feet and bounded out of the way.

"I'm sorry, buddy," she said, staggering across the room. She grabbed hold of the doorframe, took a second to steady herself, and then hurried downstairs.

As soon as she made it to the ground floor, she grabbed her freshly laundered bathing suit and a towel from the laundry room and headed down to the pool. There was no point in stopping to drink a glass of water; she knew it wouldn't help. And voices were bouncing up from the pool room, which told her that almost everyone was in there. Everyone except Darien, she would bet. He was probably still at the morgue.

She nearly had the pee scared out of her when a male voice behind her said, "You okay?"

Tanner was coming down the hall. He still had his jacket and boots on, truck keys—Darien's—in hand. "What's going on?" he asked.

"My symptoms are back," she said. Her throat was so dry, the words were a crackle. "I need to go for a swim."

"I'll come with you." He hurried to her side and walked with her down the stairs. "Darien should be back soon."

"Is Joyce gone?"

He nodded. "I just dropped her off at the airport."

She walked slowly, Tanner matching his pace to hers. She couldn't remember much of her relationship with Tanner, but she could tell that he was worried for his mom. "She'll be okay, right?"

He shrugged. "Hopefully. I hacked the systems and changed all her info once she got through security." Impressive.

"Is that hard?"

"It's kind of second nature to me."

They entered the room that was loud with laughter and echoing voices. Jack and Ivy were in the pool, throwing an inflatable ball back and forth. Kylar was in the hot tub, and Eugene was paddling around on an inflatable noodle, his glasses speckled with water. No sign of Roman, Paxton, or Shay.

Ivy fell silent the minute she noticed Loren.

Jack threw the ball, and it smacked his wife in the side of the head with a wet slap.

Ivy batted it aside and swam to the edge of the pool. "Is everything okay?"

"I'm fine." Loren made a beeline for the single change room. "My symptoms are back, but I'm sure I'll feel better once I go for a swim." She disappeared inside the change room and shut the door, well aware that she was now the subject of conversation. She didn't need to have an immortal's hearing to know that.

She changed quickly, practically ripping her pajamas off. As soon as she had her one-piece on, she hurried out and got in the pool.

No one was talking anymore or playing ball. They weren't doing anything except staring at her. Even Eugene, his mouth hanging open as he floated on that noodle.

She felt like such a buzzkill.

"Don't worry," she said, sinking in until the water lapped against her chin. "I'll be fine." She waved a hand in dismissal. "Do your things."

Ivy grabbed the ball that was floating through the water and resumed her game with Jack, but Loren could tell that neither of them were into it anymore.

Nearly thirty minutes passed, and the problem wasn't going away—it was getting worse.

And her Caliginous tattoo lit up with a bead of light that didn't stop pulsing.

When Darien got back to Roman's, he followed the echo of his family's voices to the swimming pool.

He pushed through the frosted doors and into the room, where he found Ivy, Jack, Kylar, Tanner, and Eugene. All of them were drying off—aside from Tanner, who still wore his boots and jacket, and looked far too concerned for Darien's liking.

Darien was about to ask where Loren was when she drew the curtain on one of the stone rain showers and walked out in her bathing suit, a braid over each shoulder.

Nobody said anything, as if waiting for someone else to do the talking, which was exactly how Darien knew something was up.

"Someone tell me what's going on." His voice echoed.

Ivy said, "We have a teensy little problem."

Loren wrapped herself in a towel. "It's not a problem, I just—"

"Your tattoo." Darien stared at the Caliginous on Silverway tattoo—at the bead of light that ran from the curve of the C to the zigzagging line. "Get dressed—we're leaving right away."

Kylar spoke up. "Getting in *might* be a problem."

Darien checked his watch.

Shit—it wasn't even noon, and Tanya usually snuck them in right before close.

Darien told Kylar, "Text Roman. Tell him the bare minimum—make sure he meets us at Caliginous ASAP."

74

THE BOARDWALK (VIOLET ZONE)
YVESWICH, STATE OF KER

It was morning, and the air was brisk.

Shay stood beside Roman on the rocky coast, her stiff, cold-bitten fingers wrapped around the warmth of her hazelnut latte. Paxton was close by, skipping stones on the water. His puppy Familiar named Chance stood beside him on lanky legs, tail constantly wagging.

Out in the distance, barely a speck from here, was the Riptide's island and the House of Blue. Shay was surprised no one had hunted her down yet and dragged her back there. Athene had eyes everywhere, no matter the color of the zone. It was only a matter of time before one of her cronies spotted her and pounced.

"You ever going to tell me what happened?" Roman's quiet, gravelly voice sliced into her brooding.

She sipped on her latte, the velvety coffee warming her belly. "I told you: When you're ready to talk about what happened with Don, I'll talk about what happened with Athene." She kept her voice down for Paxton's benefit. He was a really sweet kid. It was hard to accept that he was a Slade; he was too good for such a soiled last name. Too good for someone like Don.

Roman said, "I went to the House of Black to find Paxton, and he wasn't there. So I left." He sipped on his own coffee. "Your turn."

She snickered, and then sighed. "Athene refuses to acknowledge that Anna is gone. She said some things that made me angry, so I left." If Roman was going to water down his story, she'd water down hers. But she found, now that she was opening up to him, that she wanted to tell him more—to get the worst part about that night off her chest. "Three Selkies confronted me on the beach," she confessed, her voice a hollow whisper, "and I accidentally gave them a little light show."

Roman froze mid-sip of his latte—half-sweet. "They know?" A muscle twitched in his sharp jaw—it was probably the first time she'd seen that tic without being the cause of it.

"If they didn't figure it out last night, I'm sure they have by now." She stared out at the island—her prison. "And they'll tell my mom. No doubt about that." Her fingers tightened around the cup.

"Flick your wrist more!" Roman called to Paxton. A gentle breeze swept down the beach, and Shay watched as it played in the soft waves of Roman's dark hair. She envied it—the breeze. Roman might have got his fill of touching her in the motel room, but Shay realized, aside from that one morning—when she'd had the pleasure of getting on her knees for Roman—she'd barely got to touch him.

Paxton demonstrated. "Like this?"

"Try it," Roman said. He did, but the stone plunked into the water after only one skip. Roman shook his head. "Pathetic."

Paxton scowled. "You try, then!"

Roman offered his cup to Shay. "Hold this?"

She took it, and he walked to Paxton's side.

Shay couldn't help but stare at Roman. She always stared at him, the urge to do so prompted by a deep-seated fear in her bones and blood—fear that every time she looked at him might be her last. He wore a black jacket and gray jeans that were ripped in the thighs—no surprise there—with fine chains attached to the pockets.

She couldn't deny it any longer, and she didn't want to.

She was absolutely obsessed with Roman. If she dared to admit it, she might even call it love.

But love was utterly terrifying. Roman had a lot of bad things to say about trust, but love was the real offender.

Love gave someone the power to break you. And now, if he felt so inclined, Roman could shatter her like a rock thrown at a house of glass. It would hurt, no doubt about that—but staying away from Roman would hurt even more.

How could one man have changed her so quickly?

"Watch and learn, little shit," Roman said.

Shay smiled. With the two brothers standing side by side like that, it was easy to see the resemblance. By the time Paxton grew up, he'd look a lot like Roman.

Roman stooped to find a suitable stone, his long, tattooed fingers sifting through his options.

Paxton complained, "You're making it easy on yourself like you do in Cryptic Crypts. Pick a stone already, and throw!"

Shay laughed.

Roman eyed him with amusement as he selected a stone and stood. He braced one foot behind him, heel up. Flicked his wrist—

Six skips, and then the stone plopped into the ocean, the water calm today. This was one of the best places in Yveswich for rock-skipping.

"Impressive!" Shay called.

Roman instructed Pax again, and the next time the boy threw, he managed to skip the rock four times.

Paxton grinned up at his brother. "Did you see that?"

"See what?" Roman teased. "Must have had my eyes shut." He mussed up Paxton's hair.

"Nice job, Pax!" Shay shouted.

Paxton's smile grew, and he ducked his head, trying to hide the blush Shay could see from way over here.

Roman came back, and she passed him his coffee.

"Yours is bland," she told him.

"You tried it?" He took a swig.

"Your taste buds are a bunch of snobs. I'll never cook for you—I'd be scared it would wind up in the garbage."

"I'd feed it to Sayagul first."

The dragon huffed, her words audible for Shay's benefit. *'I think not!'*

"I'm not that much of a dick," Roman told Shay. "If you cooked me dinner, I'd be thankful for what I got."

"How about liver and onions?"

He fake threw-up in his mouth. "I'll take a rain cheque." His phone buzzed. He passed his coffee to his other hand and took out his phone. As he read the message, his face shifted into a frown.

"What is it?" Shay asked.

"Pax!" Roman's rough voice ripped down the beach, causing several people to stare. Shay had learned that wherever Roman went, people tended to leave, the Shadowmasters more feared than the members of any other house. "Let's go. We're leaving." He put his phone away. "Something's happening," he said to Shay as Pax hurried over, his Familiar bounding after him on clumsy legs. "We need to get to Silverway."

DARIEN WAS ABOUT to lose his shit, which wouldn't be good for anyone. Especially not Tanya, who was testing his last nerve.

He stood with the others in the corridor that led to Chamber Number Five. Arguing with Tanya, who didn't want to let him in the room with Loren while she had her treatment.

But Loren, who stood closest to the chamber door, had asked him to go in with her. And she was the one person he always listened to—no matter what. She wore the Caliginous on Silverway one-piece, her gold hair loose and tumbling over her shoulders in waves.

The door to the corridor banged open, three sets of footsteps echoing against the curved walls.

About time.

"Tanya, Tanya, Tanya." Roman's husky, teasing drawl was amplified by the narrow space. He was heading this way, Shay and Paxton on his heels, the latter peeking around his towering brother to see better. "Are you arguing with Darien Cassel?"

Tanya's heart skipped at the sight of Roman, the reaction giving away her crush. "This is my job," she said, lifting her chin. "There are rules I need to follow."

Roman stopped at Darien's side, and tsked. "Aren't rules more fun if you break them once in a while?"

"Not if they could harm someone." She stuttered on the last word, her eyes darting between Roman and the rest of the group.

"What's the problem?" Darien asked Tanya, his jaw flexing. "I was in there with her before. *Twice.*"

Tanya spoke in a level voice. "The problem, sir—"

Jack snorted. *"Sir."*

"—is the chamber can sometimes pick up on the other person's energy and funnel it into the client. And not all energy is good energy." The way she eyed him was suggestive—and her implication that he wasn't *good* for Loren made his palms prickle.

"Tanya," Roman said, that teasing smile still coating his voice. "If the man wants to go in the chamber, you're going to let him go in."

Her wary gaze bounced among the group. "Are you guys forgetting that I'm the one who works here? I'm in charge. If I wasn't here, you wouldn't even be able to get the chamber on."

Kylar and Jack parted to reveal Tanner, who stood just behind them, gray eyes darting around in question.

Jack said, "Have you *met* Tanner Atlas?"

"Alright, that's enough," Darien said. "Let's not be dicks—we've done enough of that." *He'd* done enough of that, and he wasn't about to get kicked out of here. He faced Tanya, and when he spoke again he managed to take the edge off his tone. "I know I'm asking you for a lot, and I appreciate that you're helping me out. But she wants me in that room, and I'm not about to say no to her. It didn't hurt her the first time, it didn't hurt her the second time, and I doubt it'll hurt her now." If he had even the slightest doubt about that—if he thought he was *bad* for Loren—he wouldn't set foot in there. Wouldn't even breathe on the glass of the window, for gods' sake. He took zero chances when it came to Loren's safety, but this wasn't a chance—he knew that.

Again, Tanya's eyes flicked helplessly about the group. "It's a matter of conscience."

Jack said, "Take the dark road for once." He laughed at his own joke.

Darien softened his tone. "You're not the one making this decision, Tanya. Your conscience is clear."

She stared at Darien, but he sensed that the fight in her was leaving, the silver rings around her pupils dimming. "If something bad happens, I will not be held accountable." She squeezed between them, bumping her shoulder into Darien's, and left the corridor. The tap of her stilettos faded with distance, and the door slammed shut with her departure.

Darien pushed his hair back. He faced Loren, whose heart skipped a full two beats the moment his attention settled on her. She was trembling, her nipples poking against the slippery material of her bathing suit. Usually, Darien would have drooled over the sight of those perky breasts like a horny idiot, but today, he was worried sick. It was way too warm in here—warm enough to make him sweat in his heavy black jacket—for her to be so cold.

She wrapped her arms around her middle, a visible chill spreading across her arms. "If she thinks it isn't safe—"

"It's whatever you want," Darien said.

Now, it was *her* turn to look among the group. When she answered him, she shifted her focus to the chains around his neck—avoiding eye contact, just like she used to before they'd started dating. "I want you in there with me," she said quietly. "Please."

Darien heard the first three words more than he heard any of the others. And there was no way he was saying no to that—no way he was saying no to *her*.

He unzipped his jacket. "That settles that."

Loren sat on the levitating tabletop inside the chamber as she waited for Darien to finish getting changed.

She gripped the smooth edge and swung her legs as she glanced about, watching as the pearlescent walls shifted with points of color. It reminded her of an opal—of the dress she'd worn in the spirit realm.

The memory brought a violent shiver to her body and made Singer whimper in her shadow.

A shrill whistle of approval sliced through the air.

Loren looked up to see Darien coming down the hall—wearing one of the white bathrobes provided by Caliginous on Silverway. His feet were bare, and he wore no jewelry. The Caliginous crest was embroidered on the left breast of the bathrobe, the silver thread catching the light.

Jack was the one who'd whistled. "Looking sharp, big boy."

Darien punched him in the shoulder as he passed. "Shut the fuck up."

The others were smiling.

Tanner said, "White's not really your color."

"He wears white shirts sometimes," Ivy argued. "It looks good on him."

Jack said, "Yeah, but I bet they only have white shorts." He beckoned with inked fingers. "Come on—model them for us."

Darien gave a quiet laugh. "Fuck no."

Roman goaded him on. "Come onnnnn—fucking do it." Paxton echoed his big brother, though he omitted the curse word.

Darien turned to face the group, walking backward now, and opened his robe to show off the Caliginous shorts. White, clearly, judging from the answering catcalls and laughter.

When he got to the door, he slipped out of the robe and hung it on the hook by the door.

"I'm going for a session," Roman called. He was already halfway down the hall, a smile lingering in his voice. "Keep an eye on Pax."

Paxton whined, "I don't need to have an eye kept on me!"

"Yeah, you do," Roman replied. "Hey, Shay, Ivy—they do massages here. Go talk to Tanya. Put them on my bill." He was gone before either of them could reply.

Darien entered the chamber and shut the door. The room was soundproof, so they could no longer hear anything the others were saying.

Loren saw Ivy and Shay disappear in the same direction Roman had gone. The bounce in their gaits told Loren they were going to inquire about those massages.

But she stopped noticing what the others were doing, because Darien was walking this way.

"They're right," he said, his bass voice echoing, "white's not really my color." Those shorts were demanding to be stared at—and it had little to do with the color, which looked far better on him than he insisted, and a lot to do with the fit. It took every ounce of Loren's self-control not to let her eyes stray downward. The white really brought out his tan.

"I think it is." She added, "I don't know about the satin, though."

His laugh was deep and rich. "Me neither." He stopped beside the table, reached into his right pocket, and took out a pair of white leather gloves. "These are for you. You're supposed to cover up your conduit tattoos."

"Those look really tiny." She wasn't convinced they would fit.

"Your hands are really tiny," he countered. He gave them to her, and she slipped them on, squeezing her hands into fists. He was right—they fit perfectly.

Guess I'm smaller than I think, she said to Singer. The dog answered her with a wag of his tail.

Darien glanced over his shoulder—looking out the circular window in the door. Tanner and Kylar noticed him watching, and when Darien nodded once, Tanner stepped up to the panel beside the door and turned the chamber on.

Little balls of light winked through the air like stars, and shivering raindrops floated from floor to ceiling and ceiling to floor in zigzagging lines.

"Why don't you lie down?" Darien suggested. "I think you're technically supposed to, but clearly we don't like following the rules." He winked.

Her stomach felt jiggly. "What about you?"

"What about me?"

"There's not enough room."

"You can lie on top of me if you'd like."

Her face turned tomato-red.

"I'm just teasing," he said, a smile tugging at his mouth. He had a really adorable dimple that he didn't show off enough. It softened his face and made him—a bit—more approachable. He gestured to the table with a tip of his head. "Lie down. Get comfortable. I'll be right here."

She eased herself down onto her back, rested her arms around her middle, and propped up her knees. Her hair tumbled over one side of the table; she should have kept it braided. "Do you think Tanya's right?" she asked him. Now that she was lying down, Darien only looked taller and more intimidating.

Blood rushed to her face as she imagined what he would look like directly on top of her, instead of off to the side like this.

Darien said, "About what?"

"That this could hurt me? Or you?"

"It won't hurt me," he said with resolution. "And I've already been in here with you twice. I don't know if it's related, but you didn't wake up until I was in the chamber with you." He stared at her with the kind of intensity that rivaled the magic in the room. "So I'm not really worried about it," he concluded.

She nodded. "Okay." It smelled like fresh-squeezed oranges and rainy earth in here. "Did anything interesting happen this morning?"

"With my dead friend?" He leaned a hip against the table. "Not really. I recently made an enemy out of a weapons dealer named Gaven Payne. He burned down my mom's restaurant the same night you fell into a coma. I went on a bit of a...revenge spree." His dark smile sent a chill up her spine. "Hunted down a bunch of his men in Angelthene. And now, for some reason, the rest of them are here. In Yveswich. And they're turning up dead."

"You're sure you're not the one doing it?" she teased.

He smirked. "Whoever it is, I guess I should thank them. It's one less problem I have to deal with."

"What's the cause of death?"

"Raw magic, as far as I can tell."

"Explosions?" Raw magic—the same type used for protection spells on buildings—could be fused into explosives that were very deadly and sometimes unpredictable.

"Mmhmm. Same way Gaven blew up Blackbird."

"Blackbird?"

"My mom's restaurant."

"Oh." She drew a deep breath. Little balls of light clung to her limbs, their touch comfortably warm and kind of fuzzy.

Darien was watching her intently.

"I already knew that, didn't I?" she asked him. Her teeth chattered around the words, but the shivers were lightening up. "About Blackbird, I mean."

"Don't feel bad for not remembering. I'm sure you'll be back to your old self in no time."

"Do you know if it's normal? Or is it just...me?"

He shook his head, a strand of dark hair falling in his face. He smoothed it back. "It's not just you. Roman and Tanner said memory loss is a common symptom of being in a coma."

"I hope they come back soon. I want to remember everything. I want to remember the others." Her attention flicked toward the door. "I want to remember...you. I feel like I know you a lot better than I think."

"We've pretty much been stuck together since we met, so...we got to know each other well." His reply felt loaded, but in what way, she didn't know.

She idly traced the stitching on her bathing suit. "I heard hellsehers can...show people their memories." She peeked up at him. "Is that true?"

A beat of silence. And then: "What do you want to see?"

She whispered, "The day we met."

75

CALIGINOUS ON SILVERWAY
YVESWICH, STATE OF KER

Allowing Darien into her mind felt...strange, to say the least. Seeing herself through the eyes of another person was...also strange.

The feeling was not exactly a good one—at least, not at first.

Darien must've sensed this, because he gently took one of her hands that had tightened into a fist and laced his fingers with hers.

She looked up at him in question, that uncomfortable pressure in her mind—the memories that didn't belong to her—still there.

"Touch helps," Darien explained, his voice whisper-soft. "But if you want me to stop, I will stop." She didn't know what he meant, exactly—whether he was referring to the hand-holding or the memory-sharing.

But she whispered of both, "No. I'm okay."

A crease of worry formed in his brow. "Try closing your eyes," he suggested. "Breathe deeply."

She took his suggestion, letting her eyelids slide shut, and inhaled. Even through the glove, Darien's hand was pleasantly warm, his thumb tracing comforting patterns across her knuckles.

Slowly and carefully, Darien clarified the images he was attempting to show her, and soon, those images became a motion picture.

She must have tensed again, because Darien said, "Breathe. It's just me here. Just us."

Again, she inhaled...

The air was hot. The sun beat down brightly, but the charm Darien wore on a fine chain around his neck kept him from overheating. The Avenue of the Scarlet Star was crowded, but he had his sight set on the girl—his target—who sprinted into the alley between Medea's Magic Tricks and an ice cream parlor called The Salted Caramel.

Darting into that alley was the girl's first mistake. Her second was staying there—fumbling her phone out of her jeans in the middle of a dead end. Phones were a distraction; whoever her parents were, they should have taught her that. A girl like her should have grown up with better instructions on how to be aware, how to defend herself in a city as dangerous as this one. Prevention was everything for someone like her.

When he reached the mouth of the alley, he slowed. Cocked his head to one side.

The girl was punching in the emergency number, her back facing the entrance to the alley—her third mistake. She was no better than a defenceless little kitten—mewling for help while a predator with bigger claws stalked her in the shadows.

There was nothing threatening about her. No weapons—nothing. She was clueless and tiny—brittle like a bird. Snapping her bones would be like snapping a pencil—easy.

She brought the phone to her ear. "I need help." Her voice was a gentle crackle, and her hand was shaking so badly she nearly dropped the phone.

Darien crossed the alley in under half a second. He wound an arm around her throat from behind, and pressed the muzzle of his handgun against her temple.

She dropped the phone. It hit the cobbles and cracked.

The girl—his target—wasn't breathing. And he swore she might collapse as he hissed in her ear, "Make one sound and you die."

The memory shimmered and sped up. A few minutes must have passed before the memory slowed again and sharpened into focus.

In the memory, Darien had spun her around to face him, the movement so quick she teetered in her high heels—

Her face sucked the air right out of his lungs. His hellseher eyesight hadn't done this girl justice.

For a moment, as she blinked up at him with eyes the darkest blue, he forgot why he was here—what he was doing. What he was supposed *to do.*

Collect her and turn her in, take the money and go. No questions asked. It was how he handled all his jobs—how he'd earned his reputation and status as leader of the Seven Devils.

Somehow, this girl made him forget all of that. That face. That hair.

He wasn't the only one staring in stupid silence. The girl was staring, too. Taking him in feature by feature, as if he were a work of art instead of a cash-hungry, coldblooded killer pointing a gun at her.

Her fourth mistake—and her last, if he decided to follow through.

If. If? What had gotten into him? This shouldn't even be a question, but—

"I don't believe it," Darien murmured. "You're human."

The memory rippled, as if it were a painting doused by water, the colors of that alley smearing into a blur.

Loren opened her eyes to find Darien staring down at her from where he leaned against the table.

When he spoke, his words were a husky whisper. "Are you okay?"

And when she spoke, hers were shaky croaks, just like that day in the alley. "You're pretty scary."

He made to let go of her hand—

But she tightened her fingers around his. "I'm not afraid of you," she whispered. "Not anymore."

"Good." His throat shifted with a swallow. "I don't want you to be afraid—not of me." Steel eyes scanned her face. "I would never hurt you."

No, he wouldn't. He'd had his chance, and he hadn't taken it.

She whispered, "What happened after?"

"I killed four people who were looking for you."

She inhaled deeply, and said on the exhale, "Did I faint?"

He shook his head. "No. You invited me for lunch." The corner of his mouth twitched, and she smiled.

"Did I try to run from you?"

"At first."

"You would have caught me. Easily."

His brow twitched with thought. "I don't think I would've tried. But I might have followed you around to make sure you were safe. Looking back, I don't think I would've been able to leave you alone, even if you hadn't asked me out to lunch." He winked.

"Why?" The word was barely audible.

"I was curious about you."

"Curious about *me*? Why? You're much more interesting."

He hummed. "I beg to differ." He studied her for a moment. "I also have a soft spot for humans, I guess. My mother was human." He drew a breath that sounded shaky. "Human, and fresh out of luck." He smiled a little, but it was a sad smile, not a happy one. "Just like you." He didn't need to add that no one had been around to help his mother the way he'd offered to help Loren.

She realized, then, just how lucky she was. Had anyone other than Darien found her, she'd be dead by now.

The chamber whirred as it shut down, and the little balls of light winked out.

Loren began to slide her hand out of Darien's, but he kept his fingers laced with hers.

"Let me help you up," he said. "You're tiny." He gestured to the distance that stretched between the floating tabletop and the floor.

"Like a bird?" she joked.

He gave her a smile—a real one. "Like a bird."

EVERY TIME ROMAN used the Caliginous Chambers, he felt like a whole new person the minute he stepped out.

Loren had finished her treatment about ten minutes ago. She was already dressed and ready to leave—Darien, too—but they weren't done here. Roman had managed to convince Darien to try Chamber Number Seven, and he wasn't leaving until his cousin got the hell in there.

Darien stood outside the door that was marked with a seven, shrugging out of his jacket and hanging it on the hook on the wall.

"Jewelry too," Roman said. "All of it has to come off."

Darien tugged off his rings. "I just put this shit back on. Couldn't have told me sooner?" Roman smirked. Darien set the rings on the small shelf and unclasped his three necklaces.

The sight of his jewelry—especially the wing-shaped locket Roman's Aunt Elsie had given him—reminded Roman of his own. He still felt naked without it resting around his neck.

He looked over his shoulder at Shay, who stood in the waiting area with Loren. She sensed him watching, and turned to look, but by then, Roman's back was facing her again.

"Boots too?" Darien asked.

"No. You're good to keep those on."

He shook his head. "Weird."

The door shot open with a hiss.

Darien stepped into the doorway, bracing a hand on either side, and looked into the pitch black.

This was the only dark place in Terra that didn't trigger Roman's phobia. His first session was the most challenging, by far; he'd panicked so badly, he'd thought he might wind up sedated and strapped to a gurney in the hospital. But once his body had adjusted, and his mind had recognized that this place was the farthest thing from a threat, the chamber had turned into a cradle instead of a snare. Now, his body craved it like it used to crave fighting. Only this was the kind of addiction that didn't have a million terrible repercussions attached to it.

Darien said, "Anything I should know?"

"Just jump in and relax. You'll feel brand new after. It's kinda like having several orgasms in a row." Roman's lips twitched. "It's fantastic."

Darien smirked. "Fuck, that's what I need."

"You could just tell her instead of continuing to torture yourself."

Darien's head turned his way in a flash. "Voice *down,*" he warned in a harsh whisper.

"She can't hear me. Now get the fuck in there so we can have a break from your attitude."

"*My* attitude?"

"*Go.*"

Darien let go of the doorframe and leapt into the chamber.

The door slid shut behind him, and an automatic lock clicked into place. The image on the wall-mounted screen changed from a green checkmark to a red X.

"I can't believe you actually convinced him to go in." Kylar's voice bounced down the hall. He was heading this way, the others trailing behind him, Eugene practically stepping on his heels.

"It'll be good for him," Roman said. "He needs it even more than I do."

Shay said, "I should try it sometime." Her hair was all messy, and her skin smelled like almond massage oil.

"Do you get Surges often?" Ivy asked her. Those two were hitting it off really well.

"Too often," Shay admitted, her eyes flicking to Roman. The look on her pretty face told him her thoughts had strayed to the same place as his—that night in Motel 58...his hand between her legs. "*Way* too often."

The whole building shook, as if with an explosion. Shay and Loren steadied themselves against the wall. The lights above their heads flickered and droned like hornets.

Nobody said anything.

Roman turned toward the chamber—

Another boom. The floor trembled under his boots.

Tanya rushed this way, the coil of keys on her arm jingling. "What's going on? Who's in there?"

Ivy said, "Darien. What's happening? Is he okay?"

Tanya pulled the coil of keys off her arm. "We should shut it off."

Roman blocked her with a hand in front of the scanner. "Leave him," he said, his focus on the chamber. He could *feel* the energy—it was a full-blown storm in there. A smile ghosted across Roman's mouth. "That's incredible."

Jack chuckled. "Until he brings the whole building down."

Another explosion of energy rumbled the floor. Darien's rings rattled on the shelf.

Loren said, "Is he okay?"

Tanya strutted up to the scanner. "Move, please, Roman."

He stepped in front of it, fully blocking her. "Tanya, Tanya," he crooned. "Calm down, sweetheart. You are way too high strung. When was the last time you got laid?" She huffed, the tops of her cheeks reddening. "Your chambers are built for this, no?" She had no answer to that. Her eyes darted between the faces in their group, as if searching for backup. "Just relax," Roman breathed. "He's not going to break it."

Tanya rolled the coil back up her arm. "You guys are going to make me go gray." She left, her stilettos tapping out a rapid staccato, and busied herself with the phones droning on the desk.

Jack said, "You sure he's not gonna bring the building down?"

Roman gave them all a wicked smile. "I'm not sure at all."

DARIEN WAS SURPRISED to find that Roman wasn't exaggerating.

This was fucking phenomenal. Never had he experienced this kind of relief from his magic—not unless he had a really rough, near-violent sex marathon that threatened to kill him. And even then, sometimes that didn't always work.

This, though?... He could stay in here forever.

There was no sense of time in this place. No light. It was just him and the stars. The dust motes and the constellations generated by the bursts of magic vacating his body.

Speaking of his body... It felt buoyant in a way that could only be described as delicious. He felt like a million bucks. He never wanted to get out of this thing.

He wondered how much it would cost to get one installed at Hell's Gate. That would be money well-spent.

As he floated, time lost all meaning. By the time the session ended, he had no idea how many minutes or hours had passed, but he knew that it wasn't enough. It would never be enough.

The chamber shut off with a jarring shudder. One by one, the galaxies his magic had created winked out, the absence of light plunging the room into darkness once more.

The return of gravity hit him like the snap of an elastic band.

He fell, deeper into the chamber, and landed in a black net that stretched all the way across the room. The ropes were tough and didn't have much give; they'd fuck up a mortal body, for sure. It was still dark in here; he couldn't see anything. There was no way of telling where the roof or floor was.

The door slid open. A beam of light fell into the room, illuminating the net he was lying upon.

Roman filled the doorframe, the others forming a crowd behind him.

"You," Roman said, his mouth stretching into a feral grin, "are one powerful son of a fucking asshole."

76

THE FINANCIAL DISTRICT
YVESWICH, STATE OF KER

"Your brain is out of this world," Darien said to Tanner, looking over the hacker's shoulder as he clicked away on his tablet.

The elevator—near full capacity, their whole group crammed inside—plummeted toward the ground floor of the skyscraper at a speed that would disorient any mortal. And it was that speed that caused Darien to stay extra close to Loren, in case she were to lose her balance.

But she was doing a lot better after her treatment, thank fuck. He'd checked her aura before leaving Caliginous—before she'd put her talisman back on. All her colors were equally bright, and her cheeks had a healthy flush. Even her eyes were filled with energy.

Whenever he made it back to Angelthene, he owed Roark the biggest thank-you.

"You don't like compliments," Tanner replied with a murmur, his sharp eyes scanning the codes on his tablet, "and neither do I."

The numbers on the elevator screen fell away one by one; they were almost there.

Tanner said, "Three...two...one...aaaaaaaaaand..." He pressed a button on the side of the tablet, and the device went to sleep. Gray eyes that were brimming with amusement snapped to Darien's face. "Check your phone," Atlas challenged, fighting a smile.

Darien pulled it out of his pocket and turned on the screen.

"Anything?" Tanner asked, his tone cocky.

"Nothing." The corner of Darien's mouth twitched, and he dropped the device in his pocket. "Thanks, Atlas." Finn would be able to message him now—from the number on his business card—but no one else.

The doors slid open. Darien was about to lead the way out of the elevator when the sight of a familiar face coming in through the revolving doors made him stop short, an icy spear of dread shooting up his spine.

He pushed back in, shoving Roman inside and yanking Tanner back by the arm. Questions bounced through the elevator, but Darien ignored them, blocking the way out with an arm, as he punched the button to shut the doors again. His heart was pounding.

Jack said, "Who'd you see?"

"One of Gaven's men. At least one—there might be more—"

"We can't just stand here," Kylar said, his voice tense. "If they press the button, we're done for."

Shay squeezed her way to Darien's side, weaving around bodies and dodging feet. "I have an idea, but you guys have to trust me."

Darien glanced at Roman. "What the hell does that mean?"

His cousin said, "Do what she says. No questions." But a muscle feathered in his jaw, and Darien couldn't place that look in his eyes.

Shay ducked under Darien's arm and opened the elevator with a poke of a button.

Darien hissed, *"What are you doing?"*

"No questions," she said firmly. "Follow me. Stay *close.*"

The imperator's men were *right there*—three feet away from them as they waited for an elevator. They looked right at their group as they walked out of the elevator and crossed the room. But—

They didn't react.

Darien blocked Loren from view, one hand outstretched toward her, the other grazing the gun that was tucked into the front of his pants.

He glanced over his shoulder.

The men were filing into the elevator. They didn't look his way again, and neither of them showed signs of having recognized them, regardless that *both* of those pricks worked for Gaven.

They made it out of the building, into the biting cold of the late afternoon. While the others hurried for the vehicles, Darien lingered by the revolving doors, watching the floor numbers tick away on the elevator.

Once he saw what he wanted to see, he joined the others at the vehicles. They were already in their seats, but a few of the doors on each were open, so when he stopped at Roman's car, everyone could hear him speak.

"How'd you do that?" he demanded, his eyes on Shay. She was in the passenger's seat, Paxton in the back.

The Selkie's mouth became a thin, bloodless line. She tugged on her jacket sleeve, as if hiding something.

A conduit tattoo, Darien would bet.

What the hell did she just do? *Disguise* them?

"Shay...," Roman began, leaning forward and resting one hand on the steering wheel, "has a very rare gift. She can explain it to you back at the house—" When she leveled him with a hard look, he amended, holding his hands up in surrender, "If she wants to, fuck."

Ivy poked her head out of Darien's car. "Where were they going?" she asked Darien, keeping her voice low. "Gaven's men?"

Darien looked up at the skyscraper—the top floor way, way above—and said, "Caliginous on fucking Silverway."

Loren was about to shut the truck door when she paused.

Darien had stopped on the sidewalk to check his phone. Roman, Shay, and Paxton were already gone, and Jack was about to drive away in Darien's car with Kylar, Ivy, and Eugene. Tanner was the only one in the truck with Loren.

A gust of biting wind howled through the street, nearly drowning out Darien's words as he shouted at the car, "Meet me back at the house—I've got a stop to make." And then he was rounding the truck and getting in the driver's side.

Tanner said, "Finn already contacted you?"

Darien turned on the truck and pulled out into traffic at a speed that yanked Loren against her seat. "Another hotel just caught fire."

"More of Gaven's men?" Loren guessed.

"Maybe. Probably." His eyes landed on her. "You okay to come with us?" The look on his face told her he'd rather she didn't, but they didn't have a choice.

So Loren nodded.

The hotel was only a few blocks away, on a busy street choked by smoke, the acrid smell floating through the vents. By the time Darien lurched to a stop at the doors out front of the building, police and fire trucks were just arriving.

A burly warlock—a detective, Loren realized as she glimpsed his badge —approached the truck. He seemed to recognize the vehicle, though Loren knew he couldn't see anything through the spells.

Tanner said, "We're waiting here, I'm guessing?"

Darien opened his door. "Keys are in the ignition. If anything happens, or if I don't come back after fifteen minutes, get her to safety." He was gone before either of them could reply.

Loren watched as Darien disappeared inside the building. It was no longer burning, which struck her as odd; the fire trucks had only just arrived, so how was the fire already out? Smoke plumed toward the overcast sky, and a large portion of the building was clearly burned, but...

No flames.

"Who put the fire out?" Darien asked as he walked with Finn through the hotel corridors that were choked with smoke. They had minutes, at best, before a plethora of cops and detectives poked their noses into this shit.

"Don't know," Finn said, using his hand to shield his eyes against the thick smoke. "Your guess is as good as mine—and your guess is why you're here, so try to be quick before I lose my job."

They reached the hotel room—room number two hundred and forty-two—that had suffered the attack. It was stuffed with so much smoke, it was almost impossible to see.

Black flooded Darien's eyes, his Sight revealing streaks of auras. Faint wisps of color threaded through the room—from the doorway to the two beds and the bathroom. Cleaning staff and room service, by the looks of them. The men had ordered food last night—and some strippers, if the colors of these auras were any indication.

Finn coughed. "Anything?"

Darien walked deeper into the room. "Room service," he said, "and a few strippers."

Three bodies were strewn across the floor—burnt to a crisp. A fourth was slumped against the air conditioning unit, only his lower half burned.

Darien stalked to the body, ash and smouldered wood crunching underfoot, and crouched down, studying the upper half with eyes that stung from the smoke.

The man's mouth was stuck open in a scream, and there were red, fern-like marks fanning out under his eyes. Another cluster of lines ran up the side of his neck and into his jaw.

Finn hovered just behind Darien, murmuring into his radio. He switched it off and said, "The others are coming up. You gotta get out of here."

Darien's attention was glued to those red marks—scars. The kind that were caused by only one thing in the whole world.

"Riddle me something first," Darien said. "What are the odds of being struck by lightning while *inside* a fucking building?"

Darien glanced about the smoke-filled room.

Fire. Lightning. He knew exactly who was doing this.

Loren waited with Tanner in silence.

Nearly ten minutes had passed, and Darien wasn't back yet. Cops, fire fighters, and detectives were filing into the building, a few of them already inside.

The radio flicked on with a burst of static that made her jump.

Tanner leaned forward in his seat to listen, an intense look of concentration on his face as the radio jumped between stations—

On its own. This was beyond freaky.

And it got even freakier when the words drifting through the speakers —all in different voices as the channel kept changing at rapid speed— formed a sentence: "I miss you losers."

Loren turned in her seat to look at Tanner, and mouthed, "Are you as weirded out by this as I am?"

The hacker's mouth twitched with a rare smile. "I would be, if I didn't know who it was. You don't have to worry, it's just our Hob," he explained. Amplifying his voice, he said, "We miss you too, Mortifer."

The channels switched again, and Loren listened closely as the audio formed another sentence in all different voices. "Where. Is. Dare. I. An."

Tanner said, "He's busy right now, but I'll tell him you said hi."

Loren whispered, "How's he doing this?"

Before Tanner could respond, music blasted through the speakers—a celebration song—startling the heck out of her.

Tanner gave a low laugh. "Yup, she's awake."

Loren gaped at Tanner. "That was for *me?*" She poked herself in the chest.

Tanner nodded. "He's very fond of you."

Mortifer flipped through the channels again. "I am. Running. Out. Of. Ice."

Loren didn't think she'd ever seen Tanner smile so big. "Pretty sure that's not how freezers work, pal," Tanner replied. "Where are the others?"

Static flooded the vehicle, followed by one word: "Ignoring."

Loren frowned. "Aww."

The channel changed again to an audio clip that sounded like a whimpering dog.

And then the truck went quiet.

Loren said, "Is he gone?"

"Sounds like it."

The driver's door opened, and Darien got in, keeping his face hidden in the shadows of his hood. "Sixteen minutes," he said, buckling up. "I'm disappointed you didn't drive away." He shot Tanner a look in the mirror.

"We received a call from Mortifer."

Darien turned still as a statue. "Is everything okay?"

"He said he's running out of ice."

The tension in Darien's body visibly melted. "Pretty sure that's not how freezers work." He put the truck in drive.

"That's what I said. What'd you find?"

"Most of the bodies were burned, but one had lightning scars."

"Elementals?"

"I'd bet money on it." He glanced out at the group of cops and detectives by the front doors. "We need to get out of here—that detective hates my guts." He turned the wheel and pulled into traffic.

Tanner stared out the back window. "Is that the guy who arrested you?"

Loren blurted, "You got arrested?"

"I was at a different hotel when it exploded—this was before you woke up," Darien explained. "Jacky and I were in the wrong place at the wrong time, so we were taken in for questioning." He drove slowly, clearly trying not to attract any attention, his eyes flicking between the mirrors and the road.

"So," Tanner began, "if Elementals are going after Gaven and the imperator's men… Why?"

"Revenge spree. Remember the aura magic in Gaven's warehouses? He was killing Elementals for those. Siphoning their magic until they died, I bet."

Tanner mused, "Fire and lightning… Do you think—"

"You bet I do," Darien said, his eyes meeting Tanner's in the rear-view mirror. "Maya's in Yveswich."

77

SOMEWHERE IN YVESWICH
STATE OF KER

Gaven Payne sat alone in his SUV in the northern districts of Yveswich, glancing between the band of pale skin on his finger, where his emerald ring had once sat, and the incoming call on his phone screen.

UNKNOWN NUMBER.

The phone had buzzed so many times, he knew it was about to go to voicemail. He also knew precisely who waited on the other end of the call, and would bet money on what Quinton Lucent was about to say.

With a steadying breath, he swiped his thumb across the screen and lifted the phone to his ear.

The minute the call connected, the imperator's deep voice snaked through the speaker. "Darien Cassel has been spotted in Yveswich. Poking his fucking nose around the crime scenes with the MPU." A beat of hostile silence. "Did you know about this?"

Gaven swallowed. "I've heard rumors." Cassel had survived the attack at the hospital—the one designed to kill him and take his human prize. But they'd had no idea where the Devil had gone from there. Closer than any of them had thought, apparently.

The silence that followed Gaven's reply was like the press of a blade to the throat, and he found his hand drifting toward the silvery ring of scars around his neck, tracing the ridges with shaking fingers.

"I want you to send him a message," the imperator said. "His friends and family who are still in Angelthene? Kill them."

Gaven stared out at the cars cruising by on the highway—people heading to and from work or home. "Yes, sir."

"And Malakai Delaney—I want that motherfucker dead, too. Same with that old guy Cassel's so fond of—that Arthur Kind. Show off a bit—make it brutal. I want my message to sink into Cassel's thick fucking skull. Think you can do that for me?"

"Yes, sir."

"Good."

Gaven made to hang up—he always had a firm idea of when the imperator was finished with him—but Quinton's voice cut through the speaker again.

"One more thing," Quinton said.

Gaven returned the phone to his ear.

"His house..." Quinton mused.

Gaven waited for instructions.

"Burn it down."

The line went dead.

78

ROMAN'S HOUSE
YVESWICH, STATE OF KER

When Darien pulled up to the gates to Roman's house, he slammed his boot on the brake the moment he caught sight of the jeep idling out front—the vehicle he'd hoped never to see again, especially not while Loren was with him in the truck.

The red of the jeep's taillights darkened as the driver cut the engine.

Tanner leaned between the front seats and murmured, "No way."

Darien was grinding his teeth so hard, he swore they'd crumble to dust.

Blaine and Larina Barlowe got out of the vehicle, the latter turning to give him a little wave.

"Who are they?" Loren's question was breathy and strained.

Darien shook his head, glaring at the back of Larina's as she ascended the front steps with a haughty little bounce in her gait. "Motherfucker."

DARIEN KEPT CLOSE to Loren as he entered the house through the garage, Tanner following closely behind her. There was no way of hiding her, no way of avoiding this shit—their only chance of that was Shay Cousens, who was nowhere to be seen.

Roman had likely insisted she hide the moment the jeep pulled up on the street. It was bad enough that Roman was keeping this house a secret from Donovan; if he found out his son was also involved with a Darkslayer from another circle...Darien loathed to think what the prick might do.

The moment Darien entered the living room, where the others were gathered—all except Shay—the group fell silent. Larina's eyes immediately landed on Loren, her open expression shifting into something icy and sharp —exactly like he'd suspected.

He'd seen this shit happen a lot—had been involved with enough women throughout the years to spot jealousy whenever it reared its ugly head. But never had he cared enough about anyone to take sides.

Now, though? Now, he cared enough that it could get him into serious fucking trouble.

Larina cocked her head and gave Darien a tight smile. "Wow, Darien," she crooned. "You weren't exaggerating." She pinned Loren with her venomous smile. "She looks just like me." Of course she'd put different words in his goddamn mouth, the bitch.

Ivy launched into introductions before Darien could start decapitating people. "Larina, Blaine, this is Loren. Loren, this is Blaine and Larina Barlowe. They work for the House of Black."

Loren didn't cower as she stepped forward and shook hands with them —Blaine first, and then Larina, who held onto Loren's hand way longer than Darien liked. Black flickered at the edges of his vision, the beast in his soul foaming at the mouth.

Larina's smile was pure poison, her grip visibly tightening on Loren's hand. "You are beautiful," she fake-gushed. She dropped her volume and added, "For a human, I mean."

Loren was unfazed; she might not be able to remember much from the past six months, but her spine was still reinforced with steel. "Thank you, you're far too kind." She slid her hand free of Larina's and returned to Darien's side.

Roman stepped into the center of the group, walking directly through Larina's sharp gaze that was still fixed on Loren. "I'll show you around," he said, his voice level and cool. Roman was gifted in not giving away his true thoughts and feelings; you had to know him really well to see through his facade, and he didn't give many people the pleasure of knowing him.

Blaine and Larina stayed for over an hour—a painfully long amount of time, the tension in the house thick enough to cut.

Roman was—rightfully—pissed; as buried as his emotions were, Darien could see the hatred simmering in his cousin's eyes. And beneath that layer of pissed-the-fuck-off was a glimmer of fear. Fear that this little visit would prompt the two Shadowmasters to finally tell Don about the house Roman was keeping from him.

They were in the shooting range, deep in the basement, their group attempting to keep the visit civil. But Darien was a ticking time bomb; if they didn't get the hell out of here soon, he was going to blow, and it wouldn't be pretty.

Blaine and Larina had taken several shots of hard liquor, insisting the others do the same. Darien didn't down a drop; the last thing he wanted was his senses muddled while these two were around, especially since they were firing bullets while under the influence. Ivy was strategic in disposing of her own liquor; she was sober, but she had a very convincing way of pretending not to be.

Loren had joined Shay in the attic—both of them hidden with the spells Itzel put in place. Darien checked on those spells every few minutes; had Morty been here, he wouldn't have felt the need to. But Darien had no idea how reliable Itzel's spells were, so he refused to take chances.

The unsolicited visit was going well, all things considered.

Until Blaine said something he shouldn't say.

"Why don't you come sit down?" Shay suggested. She sat on the couch in Roman's attic, stroking Nugget's velvety fur for comfort.

Loren had been standing by the door since they'd come up here. She was stiff as a board, her slender arms wrapped around her middle. She wore an Avertera talisman, so Shay couldn't read her aura, but the worry on her face gave away her thoughts.

Loren sighed. "I wish they'd leave."

"You don't like Larina, do you?" Shay ventured. She'd seen the way the female Shadowmaster looked at Darien—with a level of lust that was borderline predatory. Had she given anyone other than Darien—anyone who couldn't handle themselves—that look, Shay might've considered calling the cops on her. That girl was big trouble.

Loren fidgeted. "I don't like either of them, but if I had to choose, I'd pick her brother over her." With another sigh, she uncrossed her arms and came to sit beside Shay.

"How'd your treatment go?" Shay asked, attempting to distract her.

"It was fine. How did you do that, anyway?" She squinted her big blue eyes. "What kind of magic do you have?"

"It's illusion. It's very mysterious. I've never met anyone else with it." Aside from her mom, but she didn't feel like talking about Athene. Talking about her felt like summoning her, and that was the last thing she wanted to do.

"I've never heard of that before. Is it hard?"

"Not really. I just have to picture the illusion I want to cast, and then it's there. I've been doing it since I was a little girl, so it's kind of second nature to me. Like riding a bike or tying my shoes."

Loren glanced at the door again.

"You're very special yourself," Shay said. "Every color magic is pretty impressive."

"Thanks, but it doesn't feel like it. Not when I can't even use it." She stared down at her open palms—the tattoos on them.

"Are those conduits?"

"Yeah, but I haven't used them yet. Is that one?" She gestured to Shay's —the fish skeleton tattoo.

"It is."

"Any tips for when I use them?" She looked again at the sun and moon inked on her palms.

"As soon as you feel your magic waking up, concentrate on the feel of your hands. Steer your magic toward the tattoos, if that makes sense."

Loren nodded. "I think it does." She tucked her feet under her and laced her fingers in her lap.

Shay's immortal hearing picked up on a male shouting.

She stiffened, her head turning toward the door.

Another shout ripped through the house. And when Loren's head turned this time, Shay knew this one was very loud if a mortal could hear it.

Loren whispered, "Was that Darien?"

"Where'd your little fucktoy go, Darien?" Blaine asked, his cocky tone suggesting he knew exactly what kind of fight he was picking.

Darien stilled.

"She coming back down?" Blaine continued, a threat gleaming in his eyes. "Or is she too good for us?"

Darien stalked up to him. "The fuck did you just say?"

Blaine held his arms out in challenge. "What? She is your fucktoy, isn't she? The only thing half-life girls like her are good for."

Darien pushed him so hard, he staggered back three paces. "Get out."

"Don't push me."

"I'll do much worse than push you," Darien snarled. He shoved him again, and this time he staggered four paces. "You gonna do something, or just stand there and get pushed?" He shoved him again. Blaine nearly fell.

Larina rushed forward. "Whoa, whoa, whoa, he was just making a joke—"

"No, he fucking wasn't," Darien said without looking at her. He closed the distance between him and Blaine and pointed at the doors. "Get out."

"This isn't your house," Blaine barked.

"You're right," Roman said, stepping up to Darien's side. "It's mine. And I say get the hell out."

Thick silence fell. Blaine and Larina glanced among the group.

"You guys have overstayed your welcome," Jack chimed in, rifle still in hand. His finger teased the trigger. "And you are majorly outnumbered."

The sudden tension in the room was so thick, it felt like shrugging on a jacket. The tension might've warned lesser people to back off, to stop before things could escalate.

Not Darien. He lived for this shit.

So he stared Blaine down. "This is your last warning," he said darkly. He bared his teeth, pointed again at the door and snarled, "Get...the fuck...*out.*"

LOREN PUSHED to her feet and crossed the room, heart sprinting at the sound of the angry voices floating up from downstairs.

Shay jumped off the couch and followed her. "Hold on."

Loren crouched to open the door. "I'm going down there."

Shay crouched beside her, stilling the door with a slap of her palm. "At least let me check first." With a heavy blink, the Sight swallowed her pale green eyes with black.

"You can see through the spells?" Seeing through spells wasn't easy, which was why Darkslayers were so deadly. But there were some that were difficult for even the best slayers to see through, and Loren was certain Roman's spells were the best on the market.

"I can see through a lot of things," was Shay's only reply, her words washed with a tone Loren couldn't place.

Loren watched Shay as the Selkie stared through the floor, at whatever was happening several floors below. Watched her all-black eyes flick about, clearly following movements Loren couldn't see.

Finally, Shay whispered, "I think they're leaving."

But Loren's heart continued to race. Because she could hear those voices again—the shouting, the snarling, the threats. Darien was the one doing most of the threatening, Roman and Jack chiming in once in a while.

Kylar and Tanner made attempts to defuse the situation, but none of them worked.

As soon as Loren heard the slam of what she assumed was the front door, Shay lifted the hand that was blocking their exit and helped her pry up the attic door.

She descended the ladder, Shay following behind her.

DARIEN STOOD at the closed front door with the others, looking through the frosted windows as the jeep drove through the gates.

Two sets of footsteps sounded on the stairs, and Darien turned in time to see Shay and Loren coming down.

Kylar was the first to speak. "They didn't tell him." A mixture of surprise and relief coated his words. He looked at Roman. "They haven't told Don."

Roman started pacing. "They will now."

Paxton piped up. "How do you know? Maybe they won't—"

"They will, kid," Roman said, working to control his tone. "I have no clue why they haven't already, but I can tell...I can tell just by looking at that bitch Larina, that the first thing she's gonna do now is tell Don."

"It's because of Darien," Ivy said quietly. Her eyes were on him, her mouth set in a frown. Roman and Shay stared at her in confusion. Ivy explained, "Larina has a thing for him—I think that's why she didn't tell Don the first time. Now, though..." Her eyes flicked toward Loren.

Jack said to Darien, "You could always take one for the team and have a quickie with her."

"Absolutely not," Loren piped up, the words razor-edged. "I mean... that's not the answer, that's not...a solution. He shouldn't have to do that—"

"I'm not," Darien cut in softly. He leveled Jack with a hard look. "That's not the answer."

Roman waved a hand in dismissal. "It wouldn't even matter. She's probably tattling to Don as we speak." He scrubbed his hands over his face. "I'm going for a smoke." He turned and headed for the balcony at the back of the house. No one followed him, not even Pax.

But only a few minutes went by before the kid left, too—heading toward one of the training rooms. Darien blinked the Sight into his vision —easy, considering he was fighting a Surge—and read Paxton's aura as he stomped away.

Pax was hurting—suffering far more than he was letting on. He was a shaken bottle of emotions, just waiting to explode.

Darien would give Pax a few minutes, and then he'd be in there to check on him.

Darien found Paxton striking a punching bag in one of the training rooms. His aura was coated with so much pain that when Darien entered the room, it felt like a blow to the stomach.

The kid didn't notice him—not even with all the mirrors on the walls. Not even as the distance between them shrank with Darien's every long stride. There were tears in Pax's eyes—angry moisture blinding him.

Darien announced his entry with a low whistle. "I wouldn't want to get between you and that bag."

Paxton froze and dropped his fists to his sides. He ducked his head, strands of dark hair falling in his vision. Whenever he did that, he was a spitting image of Roman when he was his age. The sight reminded Darien of his childhood—the rare visits with his cousins, back before they'd stopped entirely. Back before Travis had moved to Angelthene.

Darien joined Paxton by the punching bag. "Can I give you a tip?"

Paxton wiped his cheek with the back of his fist. "Sure."

"Throwing power comes from your lower body," Darien began, "so stance matters." He demonstrated, positioning his feet apart. Paxton watched, immediately captivated, and mirrored him. "Keep your feet under your shoulders. Your dominant foot goes behind you."

Paxton shifted so his left was behind him.

Darien said, "Are you left handed?"

Paxton shook his head.

"Then switch feet. Dominant goes behind you—your dominant is your right." He pointed.

This time, Pax got it, shifting his right behind him, and his left forward.

"Good. Now for the fist." Darien held up his own. "Your thumb goes on top of your other four fingers." Paxton proudly held his up for assessment, and Darien nodded once. "Right—good. Roman taught you that?"

Paxton nodded, a little smile pulling at his lips, though his eyes were still heavy with sadness, guilt—and a level of hatred Darien remembered seeing in the mirror when he was Pax's age.

"Rest your thumb over your middle knuckle," Darien said. "Like this."

Paxton copied, and Darien continued, "Keep your wrist as straight as possible—never bend it when you hit your target. Got it?"

Pax nodded again.

Darien gestured to the bag. "Go."

Paxton struck.

"You hesitated," Darien accused.

"I didn't!" The kid's voice echoed.

"You did. Bend your knees a little—a little, not a lot." Paxton readjusted. "Bent knees make it harder to get knocked over if someone punches you back." He gestured to the bag. "Try again."

He threw another punch—a bit harder this time.

"You're still hesitating."

"I'm not!"

"If it gets to the point where you need to punch someone, you need to go all the way. No hesitating, no backing out."

Paxton punched again, but he still wasn't getting it. Hesitating—he was still hesitating, lightening up on his throwing power in the last second before his knuckles hit the leather. Mercy—the kid had mercy. And mercy couldn't exist when you were dealing with bullies.

"What's the name of that kid who had you pinned in the alley?"

Paxton glared at the barely-swaying bag. "Zac."

"Zac's a jerk, isn't he?"

"Yeah."

"I want you to pretend that this bag is Zac. How tall is Zac?"

Paxton's eyes flicked up and down the bag. "A little taller than me."

"So aim up here." Darien gestured. "And knock him the hell out. Go."

Paxton hit again.

"You're still holding back," Darien said. He could see Paxton getting visibly frustrated.

Good. This was what he needed.

Darien said, "Do Zac and his friends call you names?" Paxton's answering frown was telling. "Do they call you a pussy?"

Paxton sniffed. "Yeah." He wiped at his nose.

"Come here—face me. Dominant foot back again." Paxton did as he said. "Both fists up. Rest your right slightly against your cheek—like this." Darien pressed his own against his cheek, showing Paxton, who was quick to copy. "It'll help you keep it tight," Darien explained. Paxton held his position as Darien lifted both of his own hands—open, this time—so they were at roughly the same height as Zac's face. "This hand," he tapped his right palm, "this is Zac's mean fucking mug. Hit him."

Paxton struck, but Darien barely felt it.

"Again. Put more power into your legs."

Another punch.

"You're still holding back. Are you a pussy, Pax?"

"No," he said thickly. He struck again.

"You sure? Because I feel like a pussy is hitting me."

Breathing heavily, he struck again, splotches of red blooming across his face.

"Pussy."

Paxton hit—harder.

Darien reached out and shoved him in the shoulder, the surprise nearly knocking him on his ass. A brief spell of alarm lit Paxton's eyes.

This was hard, but it had to be done.

Darien spat, "Fucking pussy."

Paxton lunged forward and struck.

Darien shoved him in the shoulder again, pushing him back a couple feet. The kid stumbled on the mat, but didn't fall. Good. "Coward," Darien growled. This time, when Paxton's eyes lit up, it wasn't with fear or sadness—it was with anger. "You're a pussy—"

Paxton hit harder—several times. More times than he could count, his knuckles smacking Darien's hands—*smack, smack, smack, smack*—

And then he started punching him in the gut instead. Garbled, animalistic screams tore out of him, his raw, broken words echoing sharply against the walls. "I hate you, *I hate you, I HATE YOU!*"

Darien pulled him into an embrace, knowing full well that Pax's words weren't for him, knowing Paxton had kept them bottled up inside for who knew how long. "It's okay."

Paxton sobbed, his fists resting against his stomach, "I hate them, I hate them! *I hate them!*"

"Shh. It's okay, it's okay."

Paxton's arms closed around his waist. "They all call me that," he cried. "Zac and his stupid friends." He sobbed harder, arms shaking. "And dad," he added in a thick whisper.

Darien held him tighter, his own blood boiling.

He'd kill him.

"You are *not* a pussy," Darien said. "I don't care what they say, or how many times they say it, you are none of the things that they say you are. And I *never* want you to believe them—not for one second. *They're* the pussies. Do you understand me?"

Paxton nodded against his stomach.

"I want you to promise me something," Darien said as Paxton continued to cry into his shirt. "The next time Zac or one of his friends gets up in your face..." Darien grabbed Paxton by the shoulders, gently pulling him back until the kid was looking him in the eye.

Pax blinked, tears rolling down his face.

Darien said, "You knock them the hell out."

LOREN HADN'T MEANT to see this. She'd followed Darien down to the training rooms, and when she'd caught a glimpse of him and Paxton in front of the punching bag, she hadn't thought much of it—not at first.

Until she'd realized that Darien was teaching Paxton how to deal with school bullies.

Until she'd seen Paxton pummelling Darien's stomach and sobbing about how much he hated those bullies.

And one of those bullies, she'd come to realize, was his own father.

She backed up into the hallway, but her heel caught on something—a boot—and she stumbled.

Roman stood just behind her. Staring into the training room with dead eyes, where Darien held Pax in a tight embrace. The kid was still shaking—still crying. Completely unaware that Loren and Roman were watching.

Darien's eyes locked on Loren's first. And then they shifted to Roman, who now wore the same furious expression as Darien—almost identical.

Roman tipped his chin up—gesturing toward the upstairs.

Darien nodded once, but did not let go of Paxton.

Loren couldn't read auras, but she could feel a lot in this one space. A lot of hurt, yes, but there was love, too.

These people loved each other. And she could tell, simply from the look in Darien and Roman's eyes, that both of them would go down fighting for that twelve-year-old boy crying over school bullies.

Crying over his dad.

Her throat was so tight, it felt like someone was choking her, and the backs of her eyes began to burn.

She stepped around Roman and left, taking the stairs quietly.

DARIEN FOUND Roman on the roof. He was sitting on the highest peak, his boots dangling over the edge, his gold eyes fixed on the glimmering spread of the city. Roman didn't look up as Darien crossed the roof, his steps echoing hollowly, and sat down beside him.

"Bullies?" Roman asked.

Darien gave a stiff nod.

Roman's smirk was cold, his attention still fixed on the twilit sprawl of Yveswich. "As if it isn't bad enough already."

"He didn't want to tell you. He was worried you'd kill them."

"Those assholes are doing it for status. They think it somehow makes them look tougher if they can get away with bullying Donovan Slade's kid."

"Damn rights. But not anymore."

"You really think he'll follow through?"

"Do you?" Darien countered. "If not, you just keep instructing him until he does. Those bullies are the one thing he can deal with on his own, and he's gonna deal with them."

They sat for a while in silence. It was milder tonight—still cold, but not as biting, the wind just a quiet breeze.

Darien said, "You gonna tell me what he does to Pax?" As soon as the question was out, he sensed Roman tense. Darien stared out at the city, giving Roman the chance to breathe and think—and hopefully answer—without the weight of being watched.

Finally, Roman spoke on an exhale, the cold turning his words into ghosts. "Same shit he does to me." He drew a shaky breath. "Less hands-on garbage, but same shit. He doesn't let anyone hit Pax—only he's allowed to do that, but we've been lucky enough that he's only done it once. Doesn't stop him from having a firm grip, though." That explained Paxton's reluctance to wear anything but long sleeves. "Me, though?" The corner of Roman's mouth twitched. "I'm the lucky one. He saves all the hitting for me. Sometimes, he doesn't go as hard, if he needs some extra bills paid." That cold smirk spread. "Other times, Pax's lessons piss him off so badly that he beats me till I can't walk for a few days." The smirk fully faded, and his throat bobbed with a tight swallow.

"How strong is Pax's magic?"

Roman shrugged. "Don doesn't even know it's manifested yet. I put Pax on suppressants several years ago—before Don could find out he had magic. He's convinced Pax is going to be as strong as me—maybe stronger. And every day that passes without his magic showing up, he..." Another swallow. "...gets more mad."

Now, it was Darien's turn to focus on breathing. He braced his hands on the roof behind him, flattening them so he couldn't form fists.

Although it was milder tonight, the roof was icy, the feel of it grounding him.

When Roman spoke again, he set his eyes on Darien for the first time since he'd come up here. "I'm not kidding when I tell you that my dad is a nightmare. Randal was powerful, I know, but Don, he's..." Roman shook his head. "I don't know. He's changed a lot these last few weeks. I've never seen magic as terrifying as his. Closest I saw was yours, honestly. Which I guess is how I ended up like this—" He gestured to himself, rings glinting. "Most notorious Darkslayer in Yveswich, and I can't even stand up to my dad." Fuck, Roman was speaking the thoughts that'd dominated Darien's mind every waking moment, back before Randal died.

"I was the same as you when Randal was alive. And you were right—it *was* a freak stroke of luck that killed him."

"What happened, anyway?"

Darien stared at the forcefield. "He was threatening Loren's life." The muscles in his arms hardened from the memory. "So I led him and his men into a trap. Blackgate Manor, it's called. An old house with a demon that'll kill you if it can smell your fear."

"And it killed Randal?"

Darien nodded. "It killed Randal."

Roman was studying him with something like admiration. "But not you."

Darien said, "I wasn't afraid of it. Wish I could've said the same about my dad."

Roman shook his head and stared out at the city again. "Regrets upon fucking regrets."

"You got that right."

They breathed for a while in silence—just sitting together, not saying anything, the ghosts of their breaths their only company.

"I come up here by myself sometimes," Roman said a few minutes later, his voice whisper-quiet. "It's funny—whenever I look at something like the night sky, I'm reminded of how small me and my problems are. We're all made up of our own little worlds—some just have less stars."

79

ANGELTHENE
STATE OF WITHEREDGE

"Call me if you need anything, hey?" Dominic said as he got out of the SUV, black wings gleaming like oil as the street lights in the Financial District buzzed to life. The sun was setting; businesses would be closing soon.

Max was pulled over in front of the skyscraper that housed the Death's Landing penthouse. Blue waited nearby on the sidewalk, disguised by one of Dallas's spells. Dal was getting better at using magic; her glamors were lasting longer than they used to.

"Will do," Max called.

Dominic shut the door and took Blue's hand as they made their way into the building—walking instead of flying up to the penthouse like they usually did. Max knew it was because Blue had complained about feeling carsick from the long drive. They'd barely stopped driving from the minute they checked out of Motel 58 until they got to Angelthene. Max was beat, and he needed a shower, pronto.

"They are so cute, they make me sick," Dallas said with a grin as she watched the Angel and the Elemental disappear through the sliding glass doors at the front of the building.

Max pulled out into traffic. It was just him and Dallas now. Malakai and Aspen had made it back to the city before them, the leader of the Reapers too impatient to drive at Max's speed.

"Are you coming to Hell's Gate, or do you want me to take you to the academy?" Max asked Dallas as she let out a big yawn.

"I'll come to Hell's Gate," she decided, eyes watering. She flicked away a tear that escaped one corner. "I need a nap."

He was about to reply when something slammed into the SUV's left side, ramming the vehicle clear across two lanes.

Max's heart lurched up his throat. He cranked the wheel, but he couldn't stop it.

The SUV careened into the concrete barricade and flipped.

TRAVIS HAD MADE A HUGE MISTAKE.

He had eaten way, *way* too much food. He'd taken Jewels on a date to the Lakehouse—a restaurant not far from Werewolf Territory—and now they were gorging on ice cream at a tiny parlor just down the street.

Aunty May's, it was called. Ice cream flavor? Cookie dough. His favorite.

"How's the bubblegum?" Travis asked Jewels, who sat across from him at one of the outdoor tables. It was a nice night—almost warm enough to not need a jacket. Darkness was falling, so aside from a few families packing up in the parking lot, they were the only customers left.

"So good," Jewels gushed, taking another giant lick of her cotton-candy colored ice cream. Travis fought the filthy urge to imagine she was licking something else. "This was my favorite ice cream when I was a little girl. I can't remember the last time I had it."

Travis finished off the last bite of his waffle cone and wiped his sticky hands on a clean napkin. Jewels was almost done too, though she kept having to fend off strands of her hair that were stirred by the wind.

Another one floated into her face and glommed onto her ice cream. "Ugh," she grumbled, peeling the purplish-blonde strand off the dessert. Travis couldn't help but laugh. "Sometimes I hate having long hair."

When Jewels was done, they stood, taking their napkins to the garbage bin by the front door.

"I gotta say," Jewels began, rounding on a heel to face Travis as the street lights in the parking lot flared to life. She looked up at him, coming close enough that Travis could feel her aura. "That was a great date." A smile played with her lips; the sight of it made Travis's heart speed up.

"Dinner and ice cream? Seems pretty cliche, if you ask me."

Her smile grew, the sight so pretty it made Travis's blood thrum. "Did you just insult yourself?"

Travis shrugged. "I've never done the dating thing. I'm more of a…" He gave a little smirk. "Maybe I should stop insulting myself."

Her eyes sparkled, and she stepped closer, walking her fingers up the zipper in his jacket. "I think I like you."

Travis's heart began to pound. "How much?"

She held up her thumb and forefinger, a small gap between them. "This much."

He gave a low whistle. "Wow. That's a lot—" Travis stopped talking, a prickle climbing up his spine.

Something wasn't right.

Jewels's eyes locked on something behind him. "Travis." Her hand drifted toward the pistol tucked into the back of her jeans.

Travis got his own gun out, and Jewels got out hers, both of them moving blindingly fast.

But Travis couldn't turn to see what had caught her attention, because something else had caught Travis's. He pointed his gun behind her—at the men approaching, their own guns raised—while she aimed hers at something behind him, covering his back just like he covered hers.

More men. He could sense them now, felt their auras.

Travis's heartbeat staggered into a sprint.

They were surrounded.

Surrounded and out-fucking-numbered.

THE SILENCE that followed the initial collision was severed by the deafening crunch of metal on concrete.

The SUV flipped through the air, striking the busy highway on the other side of the barricade repeatedly.

Tires screeched.

Horns blared.

Dallas screamed, the sound drowned out by the smashing of glass and the earsplitting compression of metal.

Icy shock speared through Max's body, his hellseher reflexes kicking in barely on time.

His magic belled out with an umbrella of protection, softening the last few strikes of the SUV as it kept flipping.

And flipping.

And flipping.

The last strike popped two of the tires and sent the vehicle spinning round like a top, the back end smashing into the barricade separating traffic.

When silence fell again, Max's world was swimming, his head drowning in shock so intense it was paralyzing as he attempted to gather his bearings.

"Dallas?" His own voice was muffled by the ringing in his ears. His head weighed a thousand pounds, and warm moisture trickled from his nostrils, a line of wet dripping from his brow, too.

Dallas was dazed—bleeding from the side of the head. "Holy shit." Had she whispered? Or were her words muffled because Max couldn't hear anything?

"Dallas," he said again. The screeching in his ears intensified, and his stomach roiled. He fought the urge to vomit.

Dallas pointed. Shouted out a warning he saw more than heard.

Max spun in his seat. Fumbled his gun out. Fired.

He didn't hear the shots, but saw the spray of blood as bullets tore into the bodies of three men, and knew he'd aimed true.

A fourth came from the back of the vehicle, firing a shot through the shattered window—through the spells that had ceased to function.

The bullet ripped through the leather back of Max's seat. The shot grazed his arm, the pain like a butane torch passing over his skin.

He barked out a curse word as the top layer of his skin was torn off.

Grim leapt out of Max's shadow with blinding speed, pouncing on the gunman and tearing into him with teeth and claws. But the Familiar, too, was rattled by the accident, and another man who Max didn't see at first came up behind Grim and gagged him with a shadowy rope that had a noose at one end.

"*Grim!*" Max wrenched on the door handle, but it wouldn't open. He wound his leg back and kicked the door, but it was so crushed it didn't even budge.

And Grim was being dragged across the highway.

"Dallas—*Dallas, get Grim!*"

She fought with her own door, and soon she was shattering the last of her window in an effort to get out.

Max did the same on his side. He dove head-first through the narrow opening, landing hard on his shoulder on the pavement. Glass and gravel bit into his bare arms.

He got up and rushed toward Grim, who was being hauled by two men toward the open doors of a nearby car.

"*Grim!*" Max's voice cut through the night like a knife. He fired again, killing two more men. They dropped like stalks of wheat, blood misting the pavement.

Something hot bit into the muscle at the back of Max's shoulder, and he went down.

"Exarmaueris!" Dallas shrieked, waving her magic stave through the air. A smattering of magic swept down the highway, incapacitating another two attackers as she sprinted to his side. "Max!" She grabbed onto his shoulders, keeping him from falling. He blinked fiercely, the pain of the gunshot rippling through to the front of his chest. *"MAX!"*

Sirens bounced down the highway. Grim was no more than a limp, black blur as the men wrestled him into the back of the car.

There was a glowing red collar around Grim's neck. The Familiar kept fighting, but his efforts were visibly strained, as if something was holding him back.

Max was shouting—screaming himself hoarse. *"Grim! GRIM!"* The rust of his own blood filled the air as Max pushed to his feet and sprinted after the car.

The driver sped away, tires screeching. Max tried to speak to Grim through the Spirit Bond, but it was like there was a wall there, and he couldn't break it down.

He crashed to his knees again, gray fogging up his vision.

"No," he wheezed. "No, no, no, *Grim—*"

Grim was gone. Max's vehicle was crushed, his back wet with blood. And that splintering, blistering pain—

The last word that left Max's mouth was a name: Travis.

He had to get home. Had to find Travis and Lacey—

Spinning pavement rose up to meet him as his world went black.

TRAVIS HAD BEEN in enough fights—fists, guns, you name it—to know that they all started the same way. Not for the same reason, not that—but with an eerie beat of silence that reminded him of the calm before a storm.

For a moment, just one, the only sounds were the wind hissing through the palms and the distant beeping of car horns.

Then came the bullets.

He acted quickly—firing shots at the six men spreading out to form a wall as they pulled their triggers on him.

Travis's magic snapped out—obliterating the bullets flying this way, bits of shrapnel zipping through the air.

Blood sprayed. He'd felled two men, but the others were still coming.

Travis shot again. *Bang. Bang.*

Bangbangbangbangbangbang.

Behind him, more men fell. More blood sprayed.

A hand latched onto his arm. *"Get down!"* Jewels's voice sliced through the night like an arrow.

He ducked. A blade nicked his ear, but he didn't feel the pain.

Travis turned and threw himself in front of Jewels. Grabbed a knife that was strapped inside his leather jacket.

He threw. The blade spun, hilt over tip.

It found its mark in a hellseher's forehead, the force behind Travis's blow burying the blade right to the hilt.

Travis's next throw thudded into the soft hollow at the base of a warlock's throat. A squirt of thick blood shot across the ground, and the body hit the asphalt with a thud that echoed.

A third cut through a man's jugular.

A fourth speared into a different warlock's eye. More blood sprayed, and the warlock collapsed, gun clattering on the pavement.

Jewels took down a fifth—hand lashing out to grab one of Travis's knives.

With impressive strength, she threw—

The blade cut the hellseher's neck. He fell.

And then there was silence.

Travis's rasping breaths, combined with Jewels's, were the only sound that filled the night air.

That was the last one, Travis realized. They were all dead—all fourteen of them.

Fourteen bodies.

Holy shit.

He allowed himself a minute, and then he stood, pulling Jewels to her feet with him. "You okay?" He brushed the hair out of her eyes and cupped her face with his hands.

It took her a minute, but she nodded. "Yeah." She swallowed, a pale hand coming up to press against her pulse pounding in her neck. "Yeah, I'm good."

Travis grabbed her hand—the one that was pressed against her throat—and laced his fingers with hers. "Let's get in the car." He tugged her into motion. "Come on, hurry."

They crossed the lot hand in hand, their footfall clapping through a parking lot that suddenly looked darker than before. Travis used his Sight to ensure no stragglers were left alive as he brought Jewels to her door, helping her in. With one more sweep of the parking lot, he rounded the car and got in his side.

Once he was in the car, door shut, protective spells rippling into place, he allowed himself another few seconds to slow his heart. But he found it sprinting anew as his mind drifted to the reason why those men had come here tonight—and who else might be a target.

Travis's eyes landed on Jewels at the same moment hers landed on him. And when Travis spoke, she spoke too.

But while Travis uttered the name 'Lacey', Jewels said another.

"Malakai."

MALAKAI WAS JUST LEAVING the Umbra Forum when his phone buzzed in his back pocket.

He'd come here alone after dropping Aspen off at the House of Souls. He'd hesitated to tell her that he was itching for some Venom, but he'd admitted it anyway. She already knew he had a drug problem—she lived with him, for gods' sake—so there was no point in lying. Besides, if he was going to pursue Asp, he wanted to do it right—no lies, no secrets. He'd made enough mistakes in his life, and he refused to allow a woman like Aspen to be another.

The name JEWELY BEAN flashed across Malakai's screen.

He answered and lifted the phone to his ear. "You miss me?"

"Malakai, we need help!" The panic in his little sister's voice sent an icy prickle up his spine.

Malakai quickened his pace; the bike was parked up ahead. "What the hell's going on? Are you okay?"

"Travis and I were attacked. We're fine, but—" She was panting. "We need you to go find Arthur."

"The old fucker? *Why?* And where?"

"We believe he could be a target, too. We're on our way to Lacey—"

"Wait, wait—you want me to go save Arthur's ass, and not come to *you?*"

"Malakai, we *need* him—you need to help him! Please."

Malakai growled. "Fine. But be careful, got it?"

"I will—"

"Wait, wait, where is he? Arthur."

Travis's voice drifted through the background. "Witchlight Alchemy and Archives."

Malakai hung up and got on his bike. He started it and hit the accelerator, heading for Angelthene's downtown core.

He pushed the bike to its limit, weaving in and out of traffic and blasting through yellow lights. As he neared the district where he'd find Witchlight, he blinked his Sight into his vision, guided only by the glow of spells on the buildings, vehicles, and streets.

There was a mass of raw magic up ahead. It was underground—barely visible through the spells. Anyone other than a Darkslayer, and they wouldn't have been able to see it.

It was a bomb.

Malakai sped up, taking his chances as he zipped through a red light. Trucks and cars swerved; one crashed into a telephone pole.

He parked a block away—out of the path of the bomb, if it were to blow before he got out of Witchlight. He got off the bike and ran.

Gunshots cracked through the night.

Malakai ducked, the window of a car to his left exploding. "Motherfucker, they want me dead too?!"

Another shot popped through the night. A street light shattered.

Malakai got out his pistol and fired over his shoulder. Heard a wet gurgle, followed by the thump of a body hitting concrete. Saw the lump of a corpse peeking out from behind a car.

Malakai sprinted across the street. Pedestrians shouted in alarm and dove out of his way. Cars swerved and screeched to a stop.

He threw open the door to Witchlight, snapping the deadbolt, and ran across the room, holstering his gun as he moved.

Arthur was at the far end of Witchlight—staring at him in shock, a neat stack of papers in his wrinkled hands. "Malakai? What is—"

"No time to explain—we gotta go." He thumped to a stop beside Arthur and reached for him.

The old man swatted him away with the papers as if he were a fly. "What in heaven's name do you think you're doing?"

"This place is gonna blow." He could feel it—the bomb. It was below the floor—barely three feet under their shoes. They had ten seconds before this whole business would be blasted sky-high. "I need to carry you."

"You will do no such thing!"

Malakai ripped the papers out of his hand and threw them.

"I will walk," Arthur tried.

But Malakai was already picking him up.

Arthur tried and failed to shove him. "Malakai, I swear to the gods, if you pick me up, I will never forgive you!"

"I can live with that," Malakai grunted as he threw Arthur over his shoulder like a sack of potatoes. "But you dying? No can do."

And then he was running. Across the business, through the doors.

He tore, fast as a bullet, across the sidewalk, down the street, heart thumping like an anvil—

Witchlight exploded.

Malakai was blasted off his feet.

He threw his magic out, shielding Arthur, who flew off Malakai's shoulder and rolled across the concrete.

Malakai slammed into a parked car, triggering the alarm system that was drowned out by the noise of the explosion. He managed to land on his feet in a crouch, watching as Witchlight Alchemy and Archives was devoured by flame and colorful raw magic that looked like fireworks.

Arthur was hunkered down nearby—lying on his stomach, his hands fluttering above his head as he gaped at the burning building.

"Any broken hips?" Malakai shouted.

Arthur kept gaping, his watery eyes reflecting the glow of the explosion.

Malakai said, "That could've been you!"

Finally, Arthur met his stare—and frowned. "Thank you for pointing that out, Mister Delaney."

Malakai just fucking grinned.

80

WEREWOLF TERRITORY
ANGELTHENE, STATE OF WITHEREDGE

Lace Rivera's car idled in the Silverwood District, purring like the cat Familiar curled up on her shoulder as she loaded her pistol with Morstone bullets.

'When do you think they will be back?' Cinder asked as she licked her paw, her fluffy tail flicking over Lace's shoulder. *'It has been days.'*

"Soon," Lace said, but she wasn't certain of that. Without the ability to check in with each other as frequently as they were used to, she had no idea when Max and the others would be back. And she especially had no idea when Darien would be back. The only good thing that came with Darien's continued absence was the knowledge that something must be going right for him over in Yveswich. Had things ended badly, he would have already returned. Lace added, "I thought you liked having a break from Bandit. Don't tell me you miss him."

Cinder stopped licking her paw and twitched her tail with attitude. *'Miss Bandit? Never in my life have I heard something so preposterous.'*

Lace snickered. She slapped the magazine into place and holstered the gun. She was about to shut off the car when her phone started ringing.

She took it out and checked the caller identification. As soon as she saw his name, she answered immediately.

"Travis?"

"Lacey, where are you?" Travis's voice was edged with panic, and she heard his engine growling in the background.

"Silverwood," she said, her brow creasing. "I'm by Queenswater Rapids—"

"Are you in your car?"

"Yes, why? What's going on?" As she spoke, movement caught her eye, and she looked out at the street that looped through Queenswater Rapids to see several dark vehicles approaching, the beams of their headlights slicing between the trees.

Ice dripped down her spine.

"Jewels and I were just attacked," Travis said, his words barely audible through the bubble of adrenaline socking in Lacey's mind. "We believe you're a target, too."

Her phone shook in her hand as the vehicles spread out—blocking her in. "Travis," she whispered, "I think I've been baited." The job she was hired for, the job she had accepted earlier that afternoon...

It wasn't a real job.

Silence. And then Travis barked, *"What the fuck is going on?"*

"I need to get out of here. I'm being surrounded. Hold on." She set the phone in her lap, put the car in drive, and gunned it.

The vehicles attempted to block her only way out, and she barely squeezed between them on time, nicking the left side of her car on a bumper. She pulled the e-brake, car drifting to the side, and then lowered the brake again, pushing the vehicle as fast as it could go.

Her eyes flicked to the rear-view mirror.

They were following her.

"Travis!" she shouted. "Travis, they're following me!"

"Get to Logan's house!" His shout crackled through the speaker. Lace pushed the car faster, the needle on the speedometer fluttering. Cinder jumped off her shoulder and disappeared into her shadow. "I'll meet you there!"

One of the SUVs slammed into her.

She pushed the car faster. "Travis, *Travis*—they're trying to run me off the road!"

"I need you to try to use your magic!" The groan of the engine was so loud, Lace could hardly hear him. "Try, okay? Use it like Darien uses his— you can do it, Lacey. *Do it.*"

Lacey took several deep breaths, concentrating on rallying her magic as two vehicles slammed into her back end, attempting to steer her off the road. She pushed the car faster—

And pushed the black into her eyes.

With a guttural scream, she willed a sparking mass of her magic outside of her body—willed it to crash into the vehicles behind her with the force of a battering ram.

Two of them careened and spun before colliding. One crashed into the barricade, another flipping into the trees of Queenswater Rapids and bursting into flames.

"Lacey!" Travis was shouting. "Lacey, what's happening?"

"I'm good," she called back, her heart pounding. "I lost a few of them, but another three are on my tail."

"How far are you?"

"I just passed the Lakehouse."

"I'm almost at Logan's. Stay on the phone, okay?"

Her eyes flicked to the mirrors.

The vehicles were gaining on her.

Travis had never driven so fast in all his life.

He ripped the car through Werewolf Territory, blowing through stop signs and red lights. Logan's neighborhood wasn't far; another few minutes, and he should be there.

Logan and Sabrine weren't answering their phones. Travis fought the urge to throw up, trusting that they were alive—that the imperator or Gaven, whoever was behind these attacks, had not targeted the wolves.

"Travis," Jewels exclaimed with alarm, pointing ahead, "Travis—that's smoke!"

Shit. Thick smoke was billowing out of a street up ahead—Logan's neighborhood.

Not just Logan's neighborhood—it was his house. Flames spiralled toward the sky, and in the distance sirens wailed. People were rushing out of their houses to stare.

There was hardly anything left of Logan's home.

Travis pushed the car faster, but it was at its limit, the engine groaning in defiance.

Up ahead, he caught sight of a red convertible, the top up.

Lacey.

Behind her, right on her ass, were three SUVs. They were slamming into her repeatedly—crushing up the sides and back of the car.

Another came up behind her. Another SUV, this one faster than the others. But instead of slamming into Lacey, it slammed into the people who were chasing her, sending one into a fire hydrant and the other into a telephone pole. The pole shuddered, magic sparking. The fire hydrant exploded, water jetting into the air. People screamed and ran.

"Who the hell is that?" Jewels shouted.

"Who cares?" Whoever it was, they were helping. He'd deal with the specifics after.

The last remaining SUV hit Lacey's convertible with enough force to flip it over.

Travis slammed on the brakes and swerved, barely missing Lacey's car.

The convertible tumbled like a leaf in a gust of wind, the noise deafening.

Travis's tires squealed as his car finally skidded to a stop, narrowly missing a speed sign.

Travis threw open the door and got out, Jewels following, and sprinted for Lace. "Lacey!" His voice was raw and broken, his heart shattering into a million pieces as he tore through the night, jacket whipping around him like leathery wings. "LACEY!"

A blonde head appeared. Lacey wiggled herself through the crushed window, blood streaming down the side of her face.

"Lace!" Travis sped up. "Hold on! Hold on—I got you!" His boots slid on gravel as he stopped beside her and helped her out, his grip on her arms slipping from the blood coating her skin. "You okay? You okay?" He lifted her to her feet, Jewels coming in on his other side, her hands outstretched toward her in case she was needed.

"I'm fine." Lace blinked. Swayed. "I'm alive."

A vintage truck rumbled to a stop beside them. Logan got out, followed by Sabrine. "Chrysantha?!" the alpha thundered. He ran toward the burning house. *"Chrysantha!"* His voice was a broken, thunderous roar. "CHRYSANTHA!"

Lace was staring elsewhere—at a dark figure walking this way. A tall male vampire with golden hair. "What," Lace began, panting, "is he doing here?"

The figure had gotten out of an SUV—the same SUV that had rammed Lacey's attackers off the road.

It was Jaden Croft.

And hurrying after him was his sister, Emilie, her white-blonde hair more silver than gold under the fall of night.

Logan was stalking back this way—heading toward Jaden, his whole body vibrating as he fought the Shift.

"What did you do?" Logan spat. "Where's Chrysantha?"

"I can explain—" Jaden tried.

"Where is she?"

"Logan!" shouted a husky female voice. A young woman got out of the SUV—Jaden's SUV—and sprinted this way. "Logan—stop!"

Logan's legs visibly shook, his features smoothing with relief as Chrysantha ran down the street, her curly dark hair whipping behind her, her eyes painted with the same fiery brush as her brother's.

And then the alpha's fist lashed out, punching Jaden in the face.

THE ONE GOOD thing about being shot in Angelthene was the ability to remove the bullet quickly with the aid of magic.

When Max came to, he was in the back of an ambulance. Surrounded by a trio of paramedics and a Healer. Dallas was in here too—peering between the bodies of the healthcare workers, alarm in her eyes. The wails of the sirens were piercing, the ambulance turning corners sharply.

Only minutes must have passed. Minutes since he'd fainted on the side of the highway—minutes since those men had tried to kill him.

Minutes since those men had stolen Grim.

Travis.

Lacey.

Max lurched to his feet.

"Sir!" the Healer cried.

"Sir, please—you have to sit down!" said a paramedic.

He was at his jacket in an instant, grabbing his gun that sat on top.

Max spun to face them and aimed. Clicked the safety off. "Stop the ambulance." His torso was bare and covered in blood, his face filthy and sticky with sweat.

Their hands shot up. But no one moved.

"STOP THE AMBULANCE!"

The Healer radioed the driver.

Seconds passed. The ambulance didn't stop.

Max aimed at the back doors, ignoring the bite of the wound as his muscles shifted, and pulled the trigger.

One of the windows shattered, glass spraying. The Healer screamed.

Max pounded a fist on the wall that separated the driver from the cluttered space in the back. *"Pull over!"* He could see the driver through the tiny window—throwing glances through the glass, head tucked into his shoulders like a turtle.

The man cranked the wheel, dust billowing over the ambulance, and slowed, tires spinning on loose gravel.

As soon as they'd come to a full stop, Max thumped to the doors, gesturing for Dallas to follow, and forced them open. He stepped out, sucking down breaths of night-cooled air. Dallas jumped out behind him, his shirt in hand. He took it from her and fought to put it on without ripping his wound open wider, the pain agonizing.

People on the sidewalk stared as Max stalked up to a warlock who'd just finished putting money in a parking meter.

"I need your car," Max said. The man gaped at him, his aura washed with fear. "Give me your keys—now."

He surrendered them and stepped back, lifting his shaking hands above his head.

Max opened the driver's door, and Dallas got in the passenger's seat.

"Where are we going?" she asked him as he started the car and put it in drive. "Are you okay to drive?"

He merely said, "Hell's Gate," and slammed his boot down on the accelerator.

81
HELL'S GATE
ANGELTHENE, STATE OF WITHEREDGE

Hell's Gate was destroyed.

As soon as Max got down the driveway, he threw himself out of the car and sprinted inside—through the doors that had been kicked off the hinges.

"Lacey?" he roared as he tore into the foyer, her name breaking on its way out. Heart lurching up his throat with every beat, he stalked through the room, over broken furniture, shattered glass, and splintered picture frames. The glass table was in pieces, crushed flowers and Crossroads coins scattered across the floor. *"TRAVIS!"*

No answer.

Footsteps crunched behind him. He whirled, but it was only Dallas—pale-faced and tearing up as she took in the house that looked like a tornado had gone through it.

Max was going to vomit. Every step he took sent shots of terror deep into his bones—terror that he would catch a glimpse of blood or body parts in the ruins of his home. Pieces of his family.

Fuck.

Fuck.

"Morty?" This time, Max's voice was barely a choked sob.

His legs threatened to buckle as he stepped into the living room. Swept his gaze across the couches, the broken television, the shattered glass all over the place, the overturned table with the art of a winged devil burned into the surface.

Max's breathing slowed, but the sick feeling didn't go away. He might not have found any evidence of death yet, but he still had the rest of the house to search and—

And Mortifer was gone.

A low whine came from behind the sofa.

Grim climbed out from under pieces of broken wood. He was limping, his dark body speckled with slivers of glass.

Max crouched down. "Grim, buddy, hey." He beckoned, and Grim crept closer, his neck still cinched with that goddamn glowing collar. As soon as Grim got closer, Max used both hands to get a firm hold on the collar and pulled.

Nothing. He pulled harder. "Come on," he muttered, sweat prickling on his temples.

It snapped—

And burst into flame.

Max let go and recoiled, nearly falling on his ass as the collar disintegrated. Within seconds, there was nothing left of it but a small pile of ashes on the wood floor.

Grim sat down, head hanging low, and whimpered, tail curling around his front legs. *'They took him, Maximus.'*

"Who?" Max asked, bile coating his tongue. "Morty?"

Grim nodded. *'They forced me to let them in,* he whispered. *I couldn't stop them—I had no control. I am sorry.'* He said again, *'They forced me. Mortifer, he...he was so scared.* Grim whined. *And I could do nothing.'*

"That was why they took you," Max said. "To get in the house."

To get past the spells that were programmed to keep intruders out...

And allow only the owners and their Familiars inside.

Shit.

Nothing like this had ever happened before. Until today, Max had no clue it was even possible to steal a Familiar.

Max pulled Grim close, wrapping his arms around the mountain lion's thick, fuzzy neck.

Grim buried his face against Max's shoulder, his lean body trembling, each shaky breath whistling through his black nose. *'I'm sorry. I'm so sorry.'*

"It's not your fault," Max said, holding him tight. "It's not your fault."

The crunch of tires on the gravel driveway had Max pushing to his feet. He grabbed his gun and took the safety off...pointed toward the busted front door as the sound of rapid footsteps drifted into the house—

Travis was the first to come in, followed by Lace and Jewels.

Max lowered his gun. *"Travis?"* His voice was a broken sob, and his legs shook so hard he almost fell.

Travis lowered his own gun, Lace doing the same at his side, and bit out, "Max?"

"Fuck you!" Max shouted, pointing between them. Tears stung his eyes, blinding him. As he spoke, Travis crossed the room. "Fuck you both," Max went on, chest heaving, lungs scalding, "I thought you guys were dead—"

And then Travis was there, pulling him into a hug. "No," Travis said, squeezing him tight, "but they gave it their best shot."

Max held his friend—his brother—tightly, his heartbeat still rapid and painful, his gunshot wound aching like a son of a bitch. After a couple minutes, and after reality had set in enough that his heart was no longer bursting with dread, he pulled back. "Who did this?" he asked, gesturing with his gun to the destruction of their home.

Now, it was Travis's turn to look like he wanted to throw up. "The imperator, I think. Gaven, maybe?" He shrugged one shoulder. "Jewels and I were attacked, and Lacey was hired by some fucking fakes."

Lace crossed the room, Jewels behind her. "It was a close one," Lace said, reaching out to give Max's hand a squeeze. Max squeezed back. "I almost fell for it." There was blood all over one side of her face, and her hand was shaking. Gods.

Max's gaze swept through the destroyed house. "This was not what I expected to come home to."

"Did you find Maya?" Lace asked him.

"No. But we found the facility where they were keeping her—her and Blue. I'm going to Yveswich." There was no point in staying here anymore, not after this. They were better together, and wherever Darien was, was where they needed to be.

Travis said, "To find Darien?"

"And Maya. A couple Elementals were at the Facility." He still couldn't catch his breath. "Nearly killed us. They said Maya and a few of the others staged a breakout and were on their way to Yveswich." His gaze flicked between Travis and Lace. "You're coming with me. There's no way you're staying here—not after this."

Travis was staring at the fridge—at the empty space on top of it. The tipped-over cereal boxes, their contents scattered across the kitchen floor among shattered glass.

The rumble of a motorcycle drifted into the house. Whoever it was, they were programmed to get down the driveway. Malakai, probably.

"Where's Mortifer?" Travis's free hand curled into a fist, his other tightening on his gun.

Max felt like he couldn't breathe as he forced out a reply. "Gone."

When Travis's eyes snapped to Max's face, they were burning like embers. *"Gone?"* he snarled.

Max nodded. "They fucking took him."

"THAT," Arthur said as he staggered off Malakai's bike, shaking a trembling finger in the air between them, "is the last darned time I will ever get on one of these blasted things!"

Malakai couldn't help but laugh as he propped the bike up on the kickstand. "You can't tell me you didn't have even a little bit of fun, old man."

"Fun?" Arthur repeated, his face ghostly pale. *"Fun?* This is reckless! Public endangerment, is what it is—"

"Arthur?" Max's voice cut through the front yard. He came down the steps, followed by Travis, Lace, and Jewels. Half of his white shirt was soaked with blood, the other half smeared with it. Lace and Travis didn't look much better, their faces scraped and filthy. "What's going on?"

Malakai said, "I just saved this old bastard, and he's giving me shit for my taste in vehicles." Max looked like he was in a daze, so Malakai explained, "Jewels called me after she and Travis were attacked—she had a hunch that Arthur was a target, too. Sure enough, Witchlight lit up like it was the Kalendae festival." His gaze flicked again to Max's bloody shirt. "You get shot or something?"

Max said, "Nobody thought to call *me?*" He poked his own chest.

"We were getting around to it," Travis said. "We didn't even know you were back—Jewels took a risk in calling Malakai."

Malakai noticed the house, then—the busted door, the mess in the foyer. "What the hell happened here?"

Max had never looked so mad. "The imperator—or Gaven's men, we don't fucking know who... They broke in. Stole Grim to do it—"

"Stole Grim?" This question came from several mouths, Malakai's included.

Max ran a bloodstained hand through his hair, causing it to stand on end. "I don't know how they did it, but... Dallas and I were in a car accident —we were attacked. Someone put a glowing collar on Grim and took him. They were able to use him to get through the spells. They took our Hob." His jaw flexed, eyes wild with revenge.

"Burning Ignis," Malakai growled, squeezing his hands into fists. His eyes snapped to Jewels. He scanned her from head to toe, searching for damage—the kind that didn't come from the Tricking. "You okay?"

"I'm fine. Thanks to Travis." She reached for Travis, as if to grab his hand, but stopped at the last second, lacing her fingers before her instead. Not a mark was on her—which was exactly the reason why Malakai, for the first time in his life, found himself feeling grateful for Travis.

Fuck, he hated *feeling* things. Feelings were gross.

"Have you talked to Sylvan and Valen?" Malakai asked her, his mind going to Aspen, who he'd dropped off at the House of Souls.

Shit, he shouldn't have left her. If anything happened to her, and he wasn't there to help—

But Jewels said, "I just talked to them. They're all fine." She tucked her hair behind a pierced ear. "Whoever did this, I think they wanted you. And the Devils, obviously." Her eyes flicked to Travis's face, lingering on the drops of dried blood, the purple and yellow bruises.

Max interrupted. "We're going to Yveswich," he declared. With a blood-stained, shaking hand, Max gestured to Malakai. "And you're coming."

Malakai's brows flicked up. "Oh I am, am I?"

Max ignored him and pointed at Arthur. "You too," Max said.

The old man was frowning. "I suppose I don't have much of a choice, do I?"

"If you want to live?" Max asked. "Sorry, Art, but I don't think so."

"Well, I've got one thing to say about that," Arthur clipped. "I am not riding on this blasted motorcycle again!" He waved a disapproving finger at the bike.

"Where are Dom and Blue?" Lace asked. "Has anyone talked to them?"

Max got out his phone. "They're at Death's Landing. I'll call them now."

A truck pulled up to the gates, followed closely by an SUV. Logan and Sabrine jumped out of the truck, and when Emilie, Chrysantha, and a blond male vampire got out of the SUV, Travis stepped forth. "We've got some interesting news," he said, crossing his arms.

Max growled, phone frozen in his hands, "From Jaden Croft?"

Travis nodded. "Trust me—I was just as surprised as you."

Jaden claimed that he was on their side.

Max was reluctant to believe him, for good reason. But he had to admit the vampire and heir apparent to the House of the Blood Rose had a very convincing story.

He also had a key—one of the keys they'd seen in the photograph of the Phoenix Head Society. The keys worn on necklaces by six members.

"This," Jaden said, holding up the thin silver rectangle that was attached to a fine chain, "is the Key of Ignis."

They stood in the ruins of Hell's Gate, most of them covered in blood and looking like they hadn't slept in days. Jaden, too. Which was part of the reason why Max was beginning to wonder if Jaden might actually be telling the truth.

If he wasn't, if he was lying, then nearly getting himself killed by flipping over vehicles in Werewolf Territory was a damn convincing way of making a bunch of people believe you.

Max and the others had multitasked in the time since Jaden and the others had rolled up, using some of the time for explanations and the rest for packing. They were ready to go—to leave Angelthene and find Darien in Yveswich. Max and the others had changed into clean clothes, but they all had blood on them still. No time for showers or rest—that would come when they made it to Yveswich. So would sleep, but Max was about ready to drop dead, exhaustion weighing heavily on every bone, every muscle, his gunshot wound still burning like hell.

"And what is it?" Sabrine asked Jaden. "We saw these in a photograph of the Phoenix Head Society. Logan's dad was wearing one."

"Your dad was killed because of one of these keys," Jaden said to Logan, who was somehow managing to contain his wolf temper, his curiosity winning over the primal urge to Shift—to tear apart his enemy. "My mother was after the keys. The murders that were happening on your land—that was her attempt at starting a war so she would have an excuse to go looking for your father's key. The keys are for the Arcanum Well—the Phoenix Head Society created them to protect the Well and keep its powers from being used by the wrong people. People like my mom." He grimaced—another convincing reaction. "Six members of the society were entrusted with protecting the keys when the Well was hidden away. If someone has all six keys, they can use the Well without needing the girl."

"Loren," Dallas breathed, her eyes flicking to Max.

"Loren is the Skeleton Key," Jaden explained. "Which means Loren is the only person who can use the Well without needing these." He shook the key in illustration, causing it to rattle. He extended it toward Max. "This is for you," he declared.

Max stared, his attention flicking between Jaden and the key swinging in his hand. "You're giving this to me?"

"I told you: I'm on your side. I killed my mother so I could put a stop to her tirades before she started a war with the wolves."

Logan said, "And we're supposed to just believe you?"

Chrysantha placed a hand on her brother's arm. "The deaths have stopped," she said gently, her fire-painted eyes beseeching. "The murders. They stopped after Calanthe was killed."

"Not right away," Logan argued. "We found Desiree Denaldi at Silver Claw—she had been drugged. And another vampire was killed *after* your mother died. Explain that, Jaden," he spat.

"I don't expect you to trust me," Jaden said calmly. "After her death, I had to weed out the corruption without giving myself and my true motives away. And I am *still* weeding it out, which is why I attacked my own sister—to get her out of the Blood Rose and out of harm's way." The attack that had prompted Emilie to show up at Logan's house while Darien was there. She'd sought sanctuary, and the alpha and his sister had taken her in.

In his peripheral vision, Max saw Emilie absently reach for her throat—bruises that had long since faded. Bruises from her own brother's hands.

Jaden continued, "Some of Calanthe's people were still acting in her stead immediately after her death—going forth with the orders she'd put in place. The orders I didn't know about—and the ones her people assumed I would be backing. I've since put a stop to her plan to get into Werewolf Territory, but...it's been hard, truthfully. They're after the Key of Sapientia—your father's key, Logan."

"If you're expecting me to tell you where it is," Logan began, "I have no clue, and I wouldn't tell you, anyway."

"That key could be a fake," Malakai said, his eyes fixed on the key in Jaden's outstretched hand.

"Touch it," Jaden challenged.

The crowded room blinked at him.

Jaden said again, "Touch it. You'll see that it's not ordinary."

Max shifted on his feet. "You first."

Jaden reached out, pinching the rectangle between his thumb and forefinger. He rolled it around in his grip, and then let go, the key tinkling like silvery bells as it swayed. "Go on."

Max kept his stare on Jaden as he took hold of the key—

And nearly fell to his knees. It made him feel sick—like his stomach was churning, and the acidic bite of bile rose in his throat, sweat prickling on his back.

He let go. "What the hell was that?" he bit out.

"It's the magic," Jaden said. "I've never felt anything like it."

Neither had Max. Not even magic staves felt like that.

Max took and pocketed the key, only touching the chain this time. "I'm far from thanking or trusting you," he warned.

"Understandable. I'm sure you'd all like some time to yourselves, so I'll be on my way." He strode through the group, slowing as he passed his sister. He dipped his chin. "Emilie."

The female vampire said nothing, her fingers still idly stroking her throat.

Jaden left—by himself, no guards, nothing.

The group stood in silence, listening to the sound of Jaden's crushed SUV starting and sputtering away.

No one had told the heir to the Blood Rose where they were going. No one had made any indication that they were leaving at all. They'd managed to change clothes and pack, but they'd kept the bags out of Jaden's line of sight.

Now that he was gone, they were able to speak freely.

Logan drew a deep breath and said, "You're leaving?"

"We're going to Yveswich," Max said. "If we stay here, we're no better than sitting ducks. And if the imperator hired those people to kill us, he'll be going after Darien next."

"If he hasn't already," Lace said with a shudder. She looked like she wanted to throw up.

That made two of them.

Sabrine faced Dallas. "You're going with, aren't you?"

Dallas nodded, and the wolf stepped forward to embrace her friend.

Max said to Logan, "I'd offer for you to stay at Hell's Gate, but I'm not sure you want to be here right now."

"I can stay with the Guardian Pack," Logan said. "I've got a lot of options." As alpha of all wolf packs, he could stay with any he wanted—and could have moved into his father's mansion after his death, but had chosen not to. The Guardian Pack lived in that mansion, guarded it. It would be an obvious place to look for the Key of Sapientia, but—

"What about the key?" Max asked Logan.

Logan drew another deep breath, visibly working on calming the tremors now tearing through his thickly muscled body. A wolf could only go so long without shifting; he would have to do it soon. "Knowing my dad, he did a really good job hiding it. But I'll look."

Max's eyes swept over the group, lingering on Lace and Travis. "You just about ready?"

Malakai made his away across the room, toward the front doors. "I need to swing by my place and talk to the others. You want to meet me there, and we'll head out?"

Max nodded. "Sure. Sounds good."

Malakai's gaze snapped to his sister. "Jewely?"

She walked to his side, throwing a backward glance over her shoulder at Travis—a glance everyone in the room noticed.

Things were changing—in more ways than one. Before they'd branched out and made these new, unlikely friendships, they'd already had a lot to lose, but they had even more at stake now.

82

ROMAN'S HOUSE
YVESWICH, STATE OF KER

The following evening, Loren lounged in an armchair in Roman's living room as the sky darkened outside.

This romance novel was *really* good. She was about two hundred pages in, so roughly halfway. She had reached the point where she wanted to savor the story, but at the same time couldn't resist binging it. When she'd first plopped down in this chair and cracked open the paperback, she'd found her floral bookmark saving her place in chapter twelve. She'd started from the beginning, of course, since she couldn't remember reading this title. But the more pages she turned, flipping past the twelfth chapter, the more the story picked at her brain.

She *had* read this before—the whole thing. More than once.

The page crackled as Loren flipped to the next one. It was peacefully quiet in here. The others were scattered throughout the house—doing target practice in the shooting range, playing video and board games in the attic. All of the usuals were here, including Paxton and Eugene. The only person who wasn't here was Darien, who'd left to run errands. Loren had the lamplit living room all to herself, and she was quite enjoying it, a mug of chamomile tea steaming on the coffee table. This was glorious.

Darien walked through the front door, snow cone in hand. But she didn't mind; if anyone was going to disrupt her, she'd prefer it was Darien.

As soon as he spotted her, he stayed quiet as he crossed the room, boots thumping, and sat down on the leather couch across from her.

Loren peeked up at him, book still open in her hands.

"You ever had a snow cone before?" he asked her. He dug the plastic spoon out of the dome of fruit-flavored crushed ice and took a bite.

"I can't say I have."

"They're really good." He seemed to be speaking louder than he needed to, and when Darien added, "They're made of crushed ice," Loren saw a shadow on top of the fridge move, saw Itzel sit up, her neon pink eyes peering from the darkness like two rosy fireflies.

"Ooh, ice! That sounds yummy," Loren said, playing along. "What flavor did you get?"

Itzel crept closer to the edge of the fridge, the bright, swirly flames on her head flickering. The tiny Hob reminded Loren of a cupcake with a body.

"Cherry and blue raspberry," Darien said, licking the spoon. Everything this man did was insanely attractive. Was it weird of her to be jealous of a plastic spoon? "I could eat ten of these—"

Itzel appeared beside him on the couch in a puff of sparkling smoke.

Darien wasn't even fazed by her sudden appearance, though Loren spotted humor pulling at the corner of his mouth. "You ever tried this before?" Darien asked the Hob, waving the spoon in front of her.

She reached for the cup with a tiny hand and missed.

"I'll share it with you," Darien began, "but you need to promise me something in return."

Itzel glared up at Darien, impatient and suspicious.

Loren pressed her lips together to fight a smile.

Darien said, "You need to be quieter at night. *Every* night, not just when Pax is here."

Itzel's grabby hands strained to reach the cup—

Darien moved it out of her reach. "Uh-uh," he said, dark hair gleaming as he shook his head. "You don't get any of this unless you agree."

Itzel folded her arms, plopped down on the cushion, and scowled.

"You can still watch TV, but you need to keep the volume low. And no pots and pans orchestra on Tuesdays. Deal?"

She glowered at a corner of the room, the pink flames on her head burning hot.

Darien taunted her by lifting the spoon to his mouth, moving it as if it were an airplane. "Mmmm, so good—"

Itzel relented and smacked the couch cushions, bleating noises floating from the mouth she opened in a wide O.

"Is that a 'yes'?" Darien prompted.

Itzel nodded with enthusiasm, the motion sending pink sparks flying.

"Here." He passed the snow cone to her.

Itzel took it, dumping some on the couch with a splat, the cup too big and heavy for her. She made an attempt to pick up the melting ice, pinching it with her fingers and licking them clean.

Loren couldn't help but smile. When Darien noticed, his eyes locking with hers, she dropped her attention to her open book.

"What are you reading?" His deep voice made her shiver.

"A book," she said, still fighting a smile.

The sound of wet crunching filled the room.

"I can see that." Darien was fighting a smile, too; she could hear it in that voice of his that kept making her shiver. "What's it about?"

"Just a romance."

"Let's see the cover."

She held up the book, her face turning red as he studied the male abs on the cover. To make matters worse, Itzel pointed a finger and started squeaking and twittering like a squirrel. The Hob was *laughing*—giggling around the mouthful of fruit-flavored ice she devoured with vigour.

Darien's mouth twitched, his steel eyes dancing. "Let me guess: small-town cowboy romance. The guy's closed off and arrogant, falls for his childhood sweetheart who got away."

Loren frowned. He was good. "There's more to it than that," she said, a bit defensively, "but that's the gist of it." Itzel was still chittering.

"How long's your necklace been gone?" All the humor in Darien's voice had vanished.

Loren's hand shot to her throat—to the bare skin dusted with gold. "I just felt it like twenty minutes ago," she said, still groping. But there was nothing on her neck but powdery bits of gold. That and the conduit she always wore—the solar amulet her biological father had given her. "Did it fall off?" She started searching the cushion of the armchair—

"No," Darien said. She stopped looking. He explained, "The necklaces disappear once the magic has been used up."

"Oh."

Black swallowed Darien's eyes with a heavy blink, and she found herself blushing anew as he scanned her aura. Whenever his eyes turned black, Loren couldn't decide if she found it sexy or frightening.

It was a bit of both.

Darien blinked the black away and reached behind his head to unclasp his own Avertera talisman—the only gold chain he wore, the three others made of silver. "Here." He stood, stepped around the coffee table, and crossed the room.

Loren sat forward and set the book in her lap. She scooped up the tumbling waves of her hair as Darien bent down and looped the necklace around her neck.

"What about you?" she asked him as he did up the clasp with deft fingers. Once he was finished, she let down her hair and tipped her head back to see his face.

"I have another one upstairs." There was a little crease in his brow; Loren fought the desire to reach up and smooth it. "Your colors are looking a little dim." He gestured to the hall. "Come with me?"

She got up, placed her book on the coffee table, and followed him down the stairs to the swimming pool. The sound of the Hob's chewing faded with distance as they walked.

Loren's bathing suit was already down here, the white one-piece draped over a shower head to dry. They had the whole space to themselves, the room quiet, save for the bubbling of the waterfall.

As she stood on her tiptoes to grab her bathing suit, she kept her back facing Darien and forced out the question she was dying to ask—and dying for him to say yes to. "Do you want to swim with me?"

A beat of silence. For a second, Loren wondered if Darien had left, but she turned around to see him standing in the exact same spot, his expression impossible to read.

And then Darien said, "Really?" As if it was the greatest honor to be invited to swim with her. For someone so scary, he sure was adorable.

She fiddled with the bathing suit. "I mean, if you want to—"

"Of course I want to." He drifted toward the doors, walking backward and somehow managing not to fall in the pool. Had she tried that, she'd have tumbled in head-first. "I'll be right back."

She nodded. "Okay."

With a wink that made her stomach freak out, he turned and left, and Loren waited until the door swung shut behind him before hurrying into the change room. She got into her bathing suit quickly; it was dry, and it smelled like chlorine from the last time she'd worn it.

When she was done, she opened the change room door, the creak of the hinges echoing wide, and tiptoed out, the floor icy cold against her bare toes.

Darien still wasn't back. Even just the thought of him made her stomach flipflop again. Gods, she had a major crush.

Loren crossed the room, padded by the waterfall, and found her favorite inflatable donut crammed in a metal basket brimming with water toys. She pried the donut free and used the steps to enter the pool.

Darien came down a few minutes later in nothing but black shorts, bare feet slapping the floor. One measly look at him—at those tattoos and impressively muscled physique—made Loren's face turn into a tomato. Maybe inviting him to take his clothes off wasn't such a good idea.

Gods—*take his clothes off?* She had to get a handle on her thoughts! He was dressed for swimming—it wasn't like he was naked. Her mind pitched itself into the gutter every time this man came around.

Can you blame me, though? Loren asked Singer, who was just waking up from a nap in her shadow. *He's gorgeous.*

Singer merely wagged his tail.

Darien dove into the water at the deep end. Loren was floating on the donut in the middle of the pool, her lower half in the water. The inflatable toy was jostled about by the waves Darien generated by diving in. Loren watched, bobbing in place, as the Darkslayer swam under the clear, rippling surface. With every stroke of his arms, he got closer, and closer...

He collided with her lower half—on purpose, she knew. When his hands closed around her thighs, she shrieked, the piercing sound echoing.

He resurfaced with a splash and pushed the black hair out of his face.

"You scared me," she accused with a smile as Darien rested his dripping arms on the donut. She fought a shiver when his hands grazed hers, and she wondered if he'd done it—touched her—on purpose.

"What an asshole, hey?" he said with a wink. But he grew abruptly serious as he asked her, "How are you feeling?"

She thought about it. "I'm okay."

He tipped up a brow, water beads rolling down his face. "Promise?"

"Promise. Look." She showed him the Caliginous on Silverway tattoo, no droplet of light pulsing through it.

"Good." He smoothed back a stubborn strand of his hair.

"I've been...meaning to tell you something," she began. She had spent a lot of time mulling over the memories Darien shared with her in the chamber yesterday, and she had a few questions. "When you showed me your memory of the day we met...you saved me from other slayers. And I'm just wondering—who were they?"

"An unauthorized circle. Unauthorized means they aren't allowed to work Angelthene soil. They call themselves the Phoenix Head Society."

Her stomach dipped, her mind catapulting back to her time spent in Spirit Terra—in the past.

Singer whined, slinking deeper into her shadow.

"I know that name," Loren mouthed. "I...I saw them...when I was in a coma."

Darien's steel eyes tightened. He swiped the water off his face. "What do you mean you saw them?"

"I was...," she swallowed, "in between. I was seeing things that happened in the past. I saw them create the Arcanum Well."

"You *saw*?"

Loren nodded, her heart breaking at the memory of the Staring Teenager. Poor William. "They...the founders of the society visited a Nameless creature in a cavern somewhere. A giant serpent. The serpent gave them access to the prima materia, but...they were only allowed to use it to create one thing. And the serpent warned them that every time they used the Well, a life would need to be traded. For payment." She choked on the last word.

It was abhorrent. The Phoenix Head Society was nothing but a group of murderers.

"Who are 'they'?" Darien asked, his bass voice echoing, those eyes burning with intensity. "Did you get names?"

"One was a woman named Helia—she lived in the Old Hall at Angelthene Academy." Darien was always hard to read, but Loren could tell he'd heard this name before. She continued, "Erasmus Sophronia and Elix Danik found her there—" Loren abruptly stopped talking, an epiphany striking her like lightning. "Oh my god. Elix Danik is *Roark*." That memory slammed into her so hard, she felt her gut pitch downward. Now that she was reflecting on her time spent in Spirit Terra, and now that she had regained some of her lost memories, she recognized Elix Danik's face.

That was her dad—the man who'd adopted her from the Temple of the Scarlet Star. A much younger version, yes, but Elix and Roark were the same person.

Loren scanned Darien's face. "Did you know this already?"

"We did," he said, looking like he wanted to say more, but didn't. There was still so much to know, so much to be filled in on, and it was very clear that he didn't want to overwhelm her.

Loren stared at the water rippling under the lights, looking but not seeing. Thinking.

Erasmus had used the Arcanum Well to create her—to give her life. But the serpent had warned that life and death were the natural order of things; one could not exist without the other.

Loren's blood chilled. "That means..." She swallowed. "Someone must have been sacrificed for me." Her words were so quiet, they were nearly inaudible.

Gods—*who?* Had someone died—been killed—for *her?*

Darien stroked his thumb across her wrist. "What do you mean?"

"I saw them... The society lied to people—they sacrificed innocent students to the Well," she explained, her tone panicked. "They *killed* people, Darien—"

A piercing *beep* cut through the house. The sound was so sharp, it sliced into Loren's eardrums.

The room plunged into darkness. The trickle of the waterfall went silent. She was blind, the house eerily quiet without power running through it.

"Darien?" Loren ventured.

His hand slid across her wrist, fingers gently squeezing. "It's okay, I've got you," he said. "The power must've gone out."

It was nearly pitch-black in here; she didn't like it. Moonlight bled softly through the yard, and as the minutes wore on, and the power remained off, Loren's eyes began to adjust. She saw Darien's head turn, saw him studying something out in the yard.

"Should we get out?" Loren whispered.

Darien didn't answer. He just kept staring out at the yard.

At the protective spells over the house, she realized. The wall of magic mortal eyes couldn't see.

Darien was using his Sight; if she looked hard enough, Loren could see the black gleaming in his eyes.

"Darien, what—"

Water splashed, startling her, as Darien began to push her toward the edge of the pool. "The fucking spells are down."

83

ROMAN'S HOUSE
YVESWICH, STATE OF KER

Roman led the way out of the shooting range, Jack and Kylar following. The house was pitch-black, so Roman was guided by nothing but memory and the Sight. Regardless that this was his home and he knew it like the back of his hand, his skin prickled with chills, and his heart beat harder than normal, the darkness threatening to swallow him whole.

He drew a deep breath in through his nose…blew it out through his mouth. He focused on the voices of Jack and Kylar bouncing through the house as they spoke to each other, willing their conversation to ground him.

They made it upstairs and into the kitchen just as Tanner, Ivy, and Shay were coming down the hall from the top floors. And thumping down the stairs after them were Paxton and Eugene, the latter tripping on the last step with an, "Oof!"

Tanner, no more than a silhouette that made Roman's scalp prickle, said, "The spells are out."

"It's a blackout," Roman said, the words tight. He was sweating. He blinked rapidly, willing his eyes to adjust quicker.

"Does this happen often?" Ivy asked.

"Once in a while," Roman said, blindly heading for the control panel set in the wall. "But they don't usually stay out for more than a couple minutes." And they'd better not, or he'd fall straight into a panic attack. Which meant he'd be useless if anything worse happened. He dug out his keys and found the small one shaped like a microchip. "We can usually get them back on if there's nothing obstructing the anima mundi."

"We call them rifts," Kylar explained to the others as Roman slid the key into the slot at the side of the panel. "It's when the flow of magic is severed and the threads need to be stitched back together, so to speak."

"Fractures, you mean," Tanner said. "Those have happened a few times in Angelthene." Roman felt like the words were loaded, but he kept his focus on the screen that gradually came awake by battery.

"How can there be so many names for the same thing?" Jack laughed.

Roman felt the last of the blood drain from his face as he deciphered the columns of symbols on the black screen. The runes were transparent, every symbol a muted shade of gray. No white, no colors.

Tanner stepped up to his side, scanning the codes over his shoulder, his eyes as black as Roman's. "There's no feed," Tanner breathed, concluding the same thing as Roman. "There's no magic coming in at all..." Not just a rift, a fracture—something that could be mended.

There was no fucking source, no pool of magic to cast a line to.

"Roman?" Shay called. She stood by the big windows in the living room, her form silhouetted by the moonlight.

She pointed at the backyard—at the opaque wall of white fog swallowing the neighborhood.

Oh fuck.

Shay whispered, alarm choking every word, "What kind of fog is that?"

LOREN STUMBLED up the steps of the pool, water splashing, her hand clasped tightly in Darien's. The moon illuminated only one section of the long, dark room, silvery beams falling across the towel racks, the line of rain showers, the lounge chairs set up by the windows.

Darien let go of her hand long enough to grab two towels. "Dry off," he said, passing her one. She started blotting the water off her body immediately. "We should find the others."

"What do you think is happening?" she asked, lifting one foot after the other to dry them. "Is it like a Blood Moon or something?"

"I don't know," he said, aggressively scrubbing his towel through his hair. He shook the strands out of his face and threw the towel onto the closest lounger. When he looked her way, his face was barely visible in the dark. "You good?"

She was dry enough not to slip, so it would have to do. And she was about to reply, about to drape her towel across the lounger when the limited light in the room abruptly waned.

A mass of white fog had swallowed the yard. It blotted out the moon like a thick wad of cotton; no light could get through.

The bone-chilling wails of civil defense sirens sliced through the neighborhood, echoed by others that were farther away—every siren in the whole city crying out the same warning.

Darien had just reached for Loren's hand when murky shapes began to move among the fog. Dozens of them. High baying and keening howls cut through the night, and in the distance, people screamed.

Without warning, every window in the room shattered.

No—*exploded.*

"Watch out!" Darien grabbed her, throwing her behind him as broken glass zipped through the air. She felt Darien wince, breath drawn through his teeth, as a volley of glass fragments buried themselves in his back.

As soon as the glass stopped, the last of the shards tinkling across the floor, Darien whipped around to face the yard, still using his body to shield her as he kicked the towel she'd dropped out of the way.

Loren peeked under his arm to see a pack of bloodthirsty demons stalking into the house on all fours.

THE LITERAL DEFINITION of the word 'slayer' was someone who killed a person or creature in a violent way.

Roman had spent so many years as a Darkslayer, he'd lost count of how many lives he'd taken. Roman knew death so well, had met with the Grim Reaper so many times, he could almost call it a friend.

He could feel death stalking through the shadows of his house now, could feel it consuming people throughout his street and the next one over. And the next. The next. Death had an appetite that was never sated.

But despite how familiar he was with Obitus and the god's dark devourings, Roman's whole body prickled with goose bumps at the screams of the frightened, the moans of the dying, the wet gurgles of lungs choking on blood.

Not in his house—not yet. And not at all, if he had anything to say about it.

Fog warnings were always bad—but never had the spells malfunctioned like this, leaving a city of over ten million people vulnerable to demon attack. The fog was like a Blood Moon—it drew every monster out of their dens and thrust them into a frenzy. They had only one need, one purpose: Feed. Without magic to stop them, the monsters could get into any street, any house, no matter how filthy rich the occupants. No amount of money could save you. The rich would die with the poor.

Only the strongest, only the most skilled in magic, would make it through this night.

Glass shattered somewhere downstairs. A deep voice ripped through the house.

Darien.

"Get to the panic rooms," Roman said to Paxton and Eugene. "Right now—*go*."

The kids bolted, but they didn't even make it three feet before the windows on either side of the front door were smashed out, shards of glass flying. Eugene screamed.

Translucent-skinned demons shoved their way through the window frames, their eyes glowing like suns. More swarmed behind them. All different breeds, but they had one thing in common.

There was a stone pushed into their foreheads. A black stone that pulsed like a long forgotten star.

Deeper in the house, more glass shattered. Guttural snarls, deep baying, and the clicking of otherworldly forms of communication filled every corner, every room. Feet scuttled on the roof, and claws began to rip at the siding on the house, gouging lines and holes.

Paxton rushed to Roman's side, the gleam of his frightened eyes showing in the dark. *"Roman."*

He pulled his brother behind him. "Stay behind me."

Ivy said, "We need to get upstairs. Darien has a blade in his room—it's made of black adamant. It's our best chance at killing these things."

"Uhh, what about a *gun?*" Roman asked.

Tanner explained, as their group began to spread out, moving as a single unit, everyone protecting each other's backs, "These are Veil monsters. They're almost impossible to kill."

Of course—the stones pushed into the heads. Those stones were the same thing he'd seen in the head of the demon that had attacked him at the Facility, the harbor. These demons were smaller, yeah, but they came from the same cursed place: Spirit Terra. The land of the dead.

It made perfect sense—how could you kill something that was already dead?

"We'll cover you," Roman said to Ivy. He stalked to a drawer at the kitchen island and took out the pistol he always kept in there. So what if guns wouldn't work? It was better than empty hands. "It's better than nothing," he said to the others as they looked at him in question. "I'm not going up against them empty-handed."

"Magic works best," Jack said, his eyes darting between Roman and the monsters creeping closer, teeth bared and hackles raised. "Are you good with your shadows?"

"I'm a Shadowmaster—what kind of question is that?"

"Now's not the time for egos, guys," Shay chimed in. She said to the others, "Roman can use them like restraints."

Jack said, "What about making heads explode?" He chuckled.

Like Darien, Roman added mentally. He'd never done that before—never seen anyone other than Darien use their magic like that.

Darien...and Donovan.

But Roman said, "I can try."

Kylar drew his own firearm, and Jack pulled a meat cleaver from the knife block by the stove, the wide blade hissing against the wood. He held it up, the steel reflecting his smile. He gave a low whistle, and his jaguar Familiar came out of his shadow, the others doing the same—Sayagul, too.

Ivy said, twisting the blade in her hand, "If you can't land a hit, just shield. Wait it out."

Roman met Shay's stare as the demons crept closer. He hated to ask her this, but— "Shay?"

"I can buy us enough time to get to the second floor," she said, practically reading his mind. She checked her wrist tattoo like she would a watch, and said, "On the count of three."

The monsters in the immediate area moved like a pack of wolves, the others that were farther down the hallway scrapping with each other—fighting for the meal they all wanted. They surrounded them on all sides, eyes glowing, mouths dripping with foam, those stones in their foreheads pulsing with the darkest magic. If Roman looked too long, he felt the beginning pangs of a headache between his brows, and his eyes shimmered as if with tears.

"Three," Shay began, rallying her magic. "Two."

The demons came closer. Downstairs, furniture broke. Bone snapped. Water splashed, and someone—Loren—screamed Darien's name.

Shay closed her eyes. A moment later, they shot back open, gleaming like black pits.

"One."

Loren stood at Darien's back, shielded by his muscular body as his magic cut into the packs of monsters prowling into the house. There were so many of them, he must have already killed at least two dozen.

But he was tiring—Loren could tell. He'd said something about Venom, but she didn't know what that meant. Blood streamed down his back from the glass wounds, the lines of crimson gleaming in the trickles of moonlight that barely made it through the fog.

Darien's hand lashed out, the force of his magic sending three wolflike demons smashing into the wall, their bones breaking on impact. They fell to the floor in a heap, one of them still twitching but paralyzed.

"You okay back there?" Darien said, panting.

"I'm fine," she gritted out, but her heart was sprinting like mad.

"We need to get upstairs—"

Something charged them from behind—

Fear locked Loren's muscles in place as two translucent-skinned, vaguely humanoid monsters barreled from somewhere deep in the house.

She stumbled against Darien, felt the dampness of his blood slip across her arm—

His left hand swept out toward her, an invisible wave of his magic blasting those two demons clear across the room, where they died on impact against the doors of the sauna, hitting the wood with sickening thwacks.

A third came down the stairs that led up into the house.

A fourth followed.

A fifth.

And there were still more coming on Darien's side.

Darien cursed, and suddenly he was planting a hand against her upper back and pushing her.

The move was so unexpected, she stumbled several feet and fell, barely missing a pale-skinned monster that dove for her head. Had Darien not pushed her, it would've torn her throat open.

"Up—*up!*" Darien shouted, lashing out constantly as more and more creatures charged into the house, their hunger driving them to move faster—to attack without thought or hesitation. Bandit worked alongside Darien, attacking the ones that got past Darien's magic, the dog's lean body hardly more than a black blur. "GET UP! *Back with me!*"

She got to her feet, but the thing that had attacked her scrabbled after her, the other two from the stairs flanking it, moving like a pack of wolves—stopping her from getting into Darien's bubble of protection.

A monster that resembled a decaying canine leapt on Darien, its teeth latching onto his forearm.

Darien's shout of pain echoed, the sound chilling Loren's blood. "Bandit, Bandit—*get Loren!*"

'Going, going! I'm coming!' The dog leapt for her, but was knocked off course by another decaying canine. The dogs smashed into a corner in a spray of black mist and blood.

Loren bolted—away from the monsters that were separating her from Darien, baiting them away from the Darkslayer. Around the swimming pool she ran, sprinting for the sauna and steam room.

She heard a thud, and turned to see one of them falling as a spear of Darien's magic tore through its skull, blood misting the tile.

But the other two were still coming.

Loren slid to a stop in front of the steam room, bare feet squealing, her left barely missing the bloody lump of the dead creature Darien had thrown against the sauna. Her momentum sent her slamming into the wall by the temperature dial, the impact bruising her shoulder.

Claws screeched.

They were gaining on her.

She grabbed onto the door handle. Pulled it open—

And spun around, planting herself in the doorway. With one hand propping the door open, opaque clouds of rose-scented steam fanning her back, she faced the demons barreling at her full tilt.

At the last second, she let go of the door and rushed out of the way.

The monsters didn't have time to stop. With keening yelps and sharp barks, they tumbled into the benches inside the boiling-hot steam room, the slam of their bodies echoing loudly.

Loren threw her whole weight into the door, pushing it shut—trapping them inside. It was still so hot in there, even without power, that Loren wondered if the sauna had a backup power source.

The thought gave her an idea.

The demons attacked the door, throwing their bodies against it in effort to get out. She twisted the deadbolt, praying it would hold, and moved to the temperature dial bolted to the wall—

With a twist of her fingers, she cranked it.

She must have distracted Darien, because he was knocked off his feet as two four-legged creatures, their bodies limned with rippling green flames, leapt on him.

He landed on a pool chair with a grunt of pain, wood snapping under him.

Loren ran back his way, lungs burning. She leapt over corpses, her bare feet slipping in blood.

"*Darien!*" she screamed as he held one wolflike creature back by its jaws, its claws tearing into his chest. "Darien, there's more coming!"

With a sharp twist of his hands, Darien snapped the thing's neck.

And then Darien turned his head, eyes locking on hers as he shoved the monster's corpse off with an upward push of his legs. *"Loren, Loren—look out!"*

Loren barely saw the blur of the humanoid demon as it charged at her from the stairs.

It smacked into her, jarring every bone in her body.

She crashed into the pool, the creature's weight pushing her down deep.

"Shit," Shay muttered as the tattoo on her wrist stopped glowing.

That was it. Her magic was up. Until the tattoo lit up again, she wouldn't be able to use her magic.

Thanks to the illusion she'd generated, she and the others had made it to the second floor—barely. They were at the top of the staircase now, their surroundings thick with darkness.

"Which room is Darien's?" Shay gritted out, sweat prickling on her brow.

Ivy pointed. "That one."

Monsters swarmed every hallway, every room.

They were surrounded.

Shay felt Roman come up the stairs behind her, felt his magic stirring inside him like a thundercloud.

"As soon as they're out of the way...," Roman began, his deep voice fraught. Shay knew this was hard for him—to be utterly blinded in this house, with nothing to guide them but their Sight—the Sight that was pretty much useless, since these things didn't seem to have auras. "Get that fucking sword," he concluded.

And then both of his hands lashed out, fingers curling like claws.

The shadows in the room came alive under Roman's command. Blackness lashed out like whips and nets. The monsters yelped and howled as those shadowy whips latched onto their legs and necks—

And literally pulled them apart.

The sounds—the grotesque tearing of sinew, the wet squelch of bones being ripped out of joints—made Shay want to throw up.

But no matter how impressive his magic, no matter how brutally his shadows could maim, Roman couldn't handle all of them, so Kylar and Jack used their guns and blades on the others. Paxton and Eugene kept close to Tanner, Shay, and Ivy, the kids' fear thick enough to cut.

"Aim for the ankles and wrists!" Jack barked to Kylar as he ducked, dodging an attack, his meat cleaver slicing through the thin skin at the back of an ankle—one of the weakest areas, the rest thick like armor.

Endless blood sprayed, soaking everything. Endless bodies fell.

As soon as they'd cleared a path down the hallway, Ivy ran for Darien's room, dark hair streaming behind her.

Shay bolted after her, breaths rasping in the dark.

They had almost made it when a massive creature with antlers like a deer charged out of the room next to Darien's.

Ivy grabbed onto the doorframe and swung herself into Darien's room—

But it was too late for Shay. The demon was upon her, swiping a massive, branchlike claw her way—

She ducked, sliding on the floor past the monster that stood on two legs, and sprang back to her feet.

The thing lunged for her, its claw snagging in her hair.

Shay bolted—

And collided with a wall of hard, pale flesh, a pair of eyes glowing white in the dark.

A beautiful, vampiric creature stood before her, the hallway so dark Shay could hardly see her.

Like the others, this thing had no aura. And she smelled like...death.

How very sweet you are, the monster purred, her vast wings beating.

Shay paled.

It could *talk*.

CHLORINE BURNED Loren's nose and throat as she fought to disentangle her limbs from the monster's bony ones. She heard shouting going on above the surface, heard the crack of breaking bones and the crunch of exploding skulls. Heard Darien shouting—calling her name.

She had to get to him.

Claws ripped into her bathing suit, gouging the flesh on her hip.

She cried out, bubbles exploding out of her mouth. Red clouded the water, and the thing immediately scented it, tearing toward her through the pool like a shark, eyes feverish with intensity.

Loren fought to get away, every sweep of her legs sending more blood through the water.

When she blinked, she found herself in a memory.

The pool at Angelthene Academy, a male student pushing down on her head, trying to drown her. In the memory, clear blue stretched all around her, just like it did now. And the pool vibrated with a thud, just like it did now, magic blasting through the water in many colors that looked like spilled paint.

Loren opened her eyes to see the same thing happening in the present—clouds of sparkling magic tinting the pool, the shades so vibrant that to look upon them felt like staring at the sun.

The monster that had attacked her was no longer moving, its blank eyes bolted open in death. It floated in the colored water, wisps of black blood streaming out of its gaping jaws.

Loren swam, gritting her teeth against the searing pain in her hip, until she broke the surface with a gasp.

Darien had dove into the pool. He was only a couple feet away from her now, swimming straight for her as more demons crept toward the broken windows of the house. There appeared to be less of them now, the fog finally thinning. Darien's back and arm were bleeding badly, a pool of red clouding around him.

"Are you okay?" Darien's panicked voice echoed sharply, his eyes wide with alarm. "You okay?" He wrapped an arm around her waist.

"I'm fine," she said, clinging to his shoulder. "I'm okay."

"I got you," he said, holding her close. "I got you, you're going to be okay—I promise."

"Are *you* okay?" she asked him around chattering teeth.

"Don't worry about me."

He pulled her toward the ladder at the deep end of the pool and helped her up, his hands gripping her waist and lifting her onto the ladder.

She caught sight of her reflection in the chrome handrails. Her eyes were wholly white, no irises or pupils visible.

The sight startled Loren so badly, her hands slipped on the rails, Darien's grip on her waist the only thing that kept her from falling.

"You okay?" he called, supporting her weight as she stepped up to the last rung.

"My eyes are white."

"It's normal."

"It *is?*"

"Baby, you're bleeding." Darien's voice echoed even louder now as she pulled herself onto solid ground.

"I'm fine." It wasn't deep enough to need stitches, but it was terribly painful, and the chlorine made the sting worse.

Darien got out of the pool, water splashing—

Bullets popped through the upper floors. Monsters shrieked. Bodies fell, and they had no idea who or what they were.

"Shit. Fuck." Darien's eyes swept around the room. It was clear that he was torn on what to do, where to go, who to help. Loren could almost see the question flashing in his mind: Stay down here and stop the monsters from getting into the house, or go upstairs and help the others?

"ITZEL!" Darien thundered. More creatures charged inside, and Darien felled them with more waves of his magic. "We need you to get the spells back on!"

Loren heard Itzel's frightened voice chattering from one of the upper floors. Her tiny words were saying, *I don't know how.*

"She says she doesn't know how," Loren said.

Darien's head whipped her way. *"What?"*

Loren's face smoothed with surprise that mirrored Darien's.

"You can understand her?" Darien breathed.

"White eyes are normal and this *isn't?*" she shrieked. Gods, just how much had they not bothered to *tell* her?

But there was no time to think about it further, because the lights in the house came on and started flickering. The flashing was so fast and so intense, it was worse than steady darkness. It changed from blinding brightness to blinding darkness, blinding brightness to blinding darkness.

And every time the lights came on, more monsters appeared.

Lights out.

Lights on.

Lights out.

Lights on.

The monsters were coming, their every move lit up with flashes of light that made it look like a movie constantly put on pause.

Darien's power cut into them without fail, his eyes blacker than the night outside, but there were too many for him. And every time the power went out and came back on, more appeared—getting closer every time.

The next time the lights came on, Loren thought she saw someone else in the room. More people.

Darien grabbed her arm, pulling her down to the floor with him and narrowly avoiding an attack. *"Stay down!"*

She did as he said.

Darien got back up—

Loren shouted out a warning as a monster with leathery wings collided with him, and he slammed into the ground.

THE WINGED, vampiric creature picked Shay up with a hand to the throat.

So beautiful, the thing crooned, a black, scaly tongue lashing out of its hideous mouth. *So juicy.*

"Shay!" Roman's voice was a furious roar. She heard bones snapping, heard bodies being whipped like sandbags into the wall as Roman used his magic like a battering ram, fighting his way to her.

Shay couldn't breathe.

The monster's forked tongue flicked out again between rows of razor-sharp teeth—

And licked up the column of her throat.

Shay's stomach quaked, her limbs turning to jelly.

She fought harder, kicking her feet against the creature's iron-clad stomach, but it did no good, and she had gone too long without oxygen. She could feel her face turning purple, eyes shot through with veins.

Roman screamed her name again. Shay sensed his shadows barreling down the hallway like a dark storm.

A different type of darkness began to set in, carrying Shay somewhere else...

A blade swept down from above, cutting the winged creature's head right in half.

The monster let go, falling to the floor in two perfectly cut pieces, its otherworldly skin steaming where the black adamant had butchered it.

Shay dropped to the floor with a *bang*. She sat up right away, clutching at her aching throat. Blood slicked her skin, but the wounds were shallow—no stitches needed. She gasped down mouthfuls of air, lungs screaming.

Ivy stepped in front of her, a shining black sword in hand. Using her wrist to wipe the sweat off her forehead, she said to Shay, "Sorry that took so long."

When Shay replied, her voice was a croak, and she used her sleeve to wipe the slimy saliva off her neck. "That was disgusting."

THE BACK of Darien's head smacked against the floor so hard, he couldn't tell up from down. The only thing he knew was that something was perched on his chest, a claw encircling his throat as leathery wings flapped above him.

Loren. He had to get to Loren. He couldn't even tell where she was, what she was doing, if she was okay—

Feeeed, said a primordial, slithering voice.

Oh fuck.

This was the same breed as the one under the Strangler Fig. The same monster that had chewed through his shields of magic by shooting acid out of its mouth.

His hand went to the claw around his throat. He tried to pry it off so he could draw some air, but the creature wouldn't let go.

This was it. He was going to die like this, wasn't he?

Black nails pierced his skin, sinking in deep. Darien thrashed, blistering pain shooting through his neck. The creature's eyes flared brightly, its mouth opening to reveal green acid bubbling at the back of its throat—

Blood sprayed Darien's face as something sharp burst through the creature's left eye from behind, the tip of it shining like a star. That blade stopped barely three inches from Darien's own forehead. Any closer, and he'd be dead too.

Darien's arms shook as he held the creature aloft—as it went limp with death. The light in the monster's eyes went out like snuffed candles, leaving behind two black holes in its face, one skewered by a sword of—

Black adamant.

Heart pounding, whole body screaming in pain, Darien shoved the dead creature aside with an exhausted roar—

And looked up to see Malakai Delaney standing right there.

The Reaper smiled like a fiend and offered him a tattooed hand. "Bet you're glad to see me."

84

ARDESIA
YVESWICH, STATE OF KER

Malakai had to admit, it was funny as shit to see Darien gaping up at him like an idiot, rendered speechless for once in his stupid fucking life. Behind him stood Loren, hardly a mark on her tiny body, most of the blood that was drying on her skin or clumped in her damp hair not her own. As a hellseher, Malakai could scent the difference.

Cassel had won. Not just against nearly a hundred monsters that were lying in bloody heaps around the swimming pool, a few mangled corpses floating in the water—but he'd also won in waking Loren up.

Malakai's grin grew. Son of a bitch. Was there anything this asshole couldn't do?

"I cannot say," Arthur began as he shuffled through the room, his eyes sweeping about the wreckage, "that coming to Yveswich was the safer option." He cringed away from a particularly brutal kill, his pale throat bobbing.

Finally, Darien snapped out of it and took Malakai's outstretched hand, grip trembling. He sat up, wincing in pain. Malakai pulled him to his feet.

Darien stared at the group behind Malakai with a dazed expression.

Arthur. Jewels. Aspen. Lace. Travis.

Maximus and Dallas were last to come in through the shattered windows, the former tucking his pistol into his back waistband.

As soon as the witch caught sight of Loren, she shrieked. Grinned.

And then she took off running, making a beeline for Loren.

The mortal stumbled forward to meet her, Dallas's name floating off her lips in shocked whispers. *Dallas, Dallas, Dallas.*

The witch collided with Loren with a slap, nearly knocking the human right off her feet.

Malakai glanced at Darien, who looked like he wanted to kill something.

And Malakai couldn't help it—he laughed. And laughed and laughed.

Darien punched him in the arm. But soon, the rage on his face was thawing, because Loren was crying and laughing, Dallas too, the girls talking over each other, saying, "I missed you" and shit like that. Dallas was sobbing so hard, she started snorting, wiping the snot from her nose.

"Yard's secure," Max declared, his voice echoing. He took in all the gore, the blood and bodies in the pool that was tinged with pastels. "You okay?" he asked Darien.

Darien still looked like he wondered if he was dreaming—still looked like he wanted to save Loren from the clingy, sobbing witch.

But he nodded and said, "Could it have killed you to show up a few minutes sooner?" He took a step—and hissed, a hand drifting over his shoulder. "I need someone to get this glass out of my back."

Several heads turned toward Arthur, who looked like he needed a really long nap and an extended vacation.

The old man sighed. "I suppose that someone would be me."

THE SPELL SYSTEM had been restored, a thick coat of magic covering the property once more. As soon as it'd come back on, Roman's stomach had twisted with the same nausea he experienced whenever he passed through the city's forcefield. Time seemed to pause before lurching forward to catch up, yanking his soul out of his body and pitching his stomach about like a ship tossed by violent waves.

The lights were back on, thank gods. Outside, the fog had faded away, leaving the visibility throughout the city perfectly clear.

Now that his home wasn't choked by darkness, Roman could see the destruction better. And damn, was there a lot. Too many dead bodies to count, and so much blood and guts, it coated the floor like thick, reeking paint.

The others were still catching their breath, putting away their weapons after checking corners, closets, and rooms. The second and third floors were secure—

Roman's stomach dipped.

Darien. Loren.

He rushed to the staircase, feet pounding, and launched himself over the railing. The others sprinted after him as he barreled down the hallway—

They nearly ran right into him as Roman stopped short at the sound of voices bouncing up from the pool. Some of those voices sounded like...

No. No, it couldn't be.

The others spread out on either side of him. Staring in the same direction. Waiting, listening. Shay claimed her spot at Roman's right, the back of her hand grazing his. Roman hooked his pinky through hers. Held his breath.

Darien came up the stairs first, soaked in blood and water. Loren limped up the steps at his side, her bathing suit stained red, and behind them filed a line of people Roman hadn't seen in a long time.

Probably the most shocking was Malakai Delaney. Just behind him came an auburn-haired female Reaper—Aspen Van Halen, who spoke to Lace Rivera like they were gossiping in a hair salon.

Behind Lace was Arthur Kind, a weapons technician and former doctor. Roman had met him only once before. Maximus Reacher was right behind Arthur, a witch with long red hair and white wings walking at his side. Roman didn't recognize her.

Then came Jewels Delaney, Malakai's younger sister.

The last person to enter made Roman's heart stop dead in his chest.

Paxton's gasp echoed. The kid stumbled forward in shock.

Travis met Roman's stare. Smiled a little—a smile that made Roman feel like he was looking in a mirror. "Hey," Travis said, tossing him a sheepish wave.

Roman ground his teeth, his free hand curling into a fist. "Travis, I'm going to *fucking* kill you."

A LOT HAD HAPPENED BACK in Angelthene. A lot here in Yveswich, too, Ivy recounting everything that'd happened on their side, giving Darien a chance to breathe, to work on loosening his sore, taut muscles.

Where he sat at one end of the dining room table, Darien tried to focus as the others launched into their explanations, Ivy having finished with theirs a few minutes ago. Tried to think through the exhaustion fogging up his mind. The others had the habit of speaking over each other, so Darien only caught bits and pieces of information—enough to conclude that his family had made the right decision in coming here. They were better together, and had they stayed in Angelthene after the imperator and Gaven had made attempts on their lives, it wouldn't have been good.

Loren was perched on the seat beside Darien's, her hands clasped in her lap, the charms on her bracelet glimmering like rosy stars. She was still in her bathing suit, though he'd given her one of his clean shirts to wear for the time being, her body drowning in the fabric. As for himself, he'd pulled on a shirt too, after Arthur had removed the glass from his wounds and stopped the bleeding. No one else had any injuries that needed more than a few stitches or bandages, thank fuck.

As he listened to his family and friends, he kept an eye on Loren, his attention drifting every now and again to the bandages taped to her hip— the claw marks from that demon. It was already dead, but Darien felt like finding its wretched corpse and ripping it to bloody shreds with his bare hands. Loren, at least, hadn't needed stitches—the best possible outcome from this shitstorm of a night, and his inability to get to her when she'd needed him most. But he still couldn't stop worrying about her, couldn't stop staring at her like some stalker. Every once in a while, her big eyes would meet his before darting away again, blush dusting her cheeks.

"Hold on," Darien said, interrupting a loud argument that'd started between Travis and Malakai—a stupid one that served no purpose, other than to apparently give Darien a splitting headache. "Where," Darien said, his gaze picking apart the group, his breaths coming faster, "is Mortifer?"

Nobody had time to answer.

Because three vehicles pulled up outside. And Roman's face paled.

"Would you look at this?" boomed a deep, husky voice. A voice Darien hadn't heard in many years. "Would you just fucking look at this."

Donovan Slade stood in the doorway, flanked by nine Shadowmasters. He looked so much like Randal, Darien couldn't stop his stomach from twisting into knots, his heart beating just as rapidly as it had the moment Loren had baited those monsters into the steam room. When she had crashed into the pool with one on top of her.

He faced his uncle in silence. Not knowing what to do, how to react, whether to talk through whatever bullshit accusations came their way or just start ripping into Donovan and his men and hope for the best.

But this was the worst timing for option two. Darien's body was spent, his mind ready to shut down, his bloodstream screaming for a hit of Venom. If he had to fight again, he wasn't sure he would win.

But he had people to protect. He stood at the head of the group, the others—Ivy, Tanner, Jack, Kylar, Lace, Maximus, and Dallas—flanking him. At the back of the group, partially hidden from sight, were Paxton and Eugene. Roman had taken the opportunity to hide Shay and Travis, insisting Arthur, Malakai, and Jewels hid, too—with Loren, of course. There was no chance in hell Darien was letting Donovan set his eyes on Loren, the only mortal in their group and the light in Darien's life.

Roman still hadn't come back. Darien trusted his cousin was doing a good job concealing the others from Donovan's prying eyes.

"Is this a fucking family reunion or something?" Don's harsh voice scraped through the room—another thing that reminded Darien of Randal. And from the sound of Ivy's heart skipping a beat, his sister felt the same way. Donovan added, the words coated with a threat, "And no one thought to invite me."

Max tried, "We just got to town an hour ago—"

"That's not what my people tell me," Donovan challenged. Behind him stood Blaine and Larina Barlowe. When Darien met the latter's stare, her sensual lips curved with a smile as cold as Donovan's.

Bitch.

"Where," Don said, his hostile eyes sweeping about the group, "is Roman?"

No one said anything.

Darien was the one who answered—speaking before Don could detonate. "In case you didn't notice, we just had a blackout," Darien said, hoping to buy Roman some time without completely offending his uncle right off the bat.

Of course Donovan would *choose* to be offended by such a simple statement, his mouth curving with a cruel smile.

Great. Just great.

"I noticed," Donovan said with deadly, exaggerated patience, his eyes fixed on Darien. "Do you want to know what else I noticed more? That my sons," his upper lip curled in disgust, "failed to inform their father about this house." He spread his arms. "This beautiful, magnificent house."

A beat of tense silence fell.

"Chose," Donovan continued, the volume of his voice growing with every word, "to keep it a secret from me."

Nobody dared speak. Not even Darien.

"Where," Donovan repeated with a baring of teeth, the many hearts in the room pounding like drumbeats, "is Roman?"

When Roman had sensed Donovan coming up the driveway, he'd grabbed Travis by the collar and dragged him to the back door, out of sight of their asshole dad and his small but powerful army of Shadowmasters, Blaine and Larina Barlowe among them.

Now, they stood in a far corner of the attic, breathing heavily, the others in their group—Shay, Arthur, Jewels, Malakai, Loren—hidden with spells in the living room a few feet away. They'd gotten in here by climbing up to the roof and slipping in through a window, barely avoiding being seen.

And barely avoiding Malakai Delaney's ego giving them away. The idiot wanted to fight, but sometimes being smart enough to know when to run served just as well.

"I need you to stay up here," Roman hissed.

"Fuck that—"

"Travis," Roman snapped, being careful to keep his voice down. "Trav, if you care about me at all, you will stay put and stay the hell out of sight." He swallowed the dryness in his throat. "Can I trust you to do this for me? To not completely blow everything?"

"It's been years, Roman," Travis said in a hoarse whisper. "Years since I saw you, years of me running away—"

"We can talk about that after," Roman hissed. "But I'd prefer not to watch my brother get butchered before I even have a chance to hear about the past few years of his life."

"*Me?* Butchered?" Travis snarled. "What about you? Look at your scars, Roman! You think I didn't notice?"

"*After*," Roman insisted. "We'll talk *after*."

Travis's throat bobbed. His mouth shifted with the words he wanted to say, but he didn't set them free.

Roman clasped his brother on the shoulders with both hands and leaned in, resting his forehead against his. "Do not leave this room," Roman whispered. "No matter what you hear."

He was gone before Travis could reply, hoping like hell that the brother he'd saved would not be stupid enough to come downstairs.

Loren buried her hands in the folds of Darien's shirt. It was so big on her, she was drowning in the black fabric, but it helped keep her warm. And it smelled like him—his cologne, body wash. The calming scent helped her stay level-headed.

She was on the couch in the attic, Shay, Aspen, and Jewels beside her. Arthur sat in the rocking chair while Travis and Malakai paced the length of the room, the two of them so tall, their heads nearly brushed the low ceiling.

Shay said to Malakai, "You're making me dizzy."

"This is bullshit," the Reaper spat. "There are enough of us here—there's no reason why we should be hiding from that prick."

Travis rounded on him. "If Roman tells us to hide, we hide. You don't know my dad. He's a hundred times worse than Randal."

The name brought back a vivid memory in perfect detail—Darien's father, Randal Slade, holding Loren aloft in the tunnels under Angelthene with the wicked hand of his magic.

And Darien—begging his dad to let her go. Begging for her.

Loren blinked, goose bumps prickling across her body.

"We stay put," Arthur declared, somehow managing to sound authoritative over two terrifying Darkslayers. "And Malakai Delaney sits down."

The Reaper scowled, but threw himself onto the other couch. His eyes snapped to Shay's face.

She stared back at him. "What?"

"Weren't you missing?" He glanced at Aspen. Pointed a tattooed finger at Shay. "Wasn't she missing?"

The female Reaper tilted her head, her blunt mahogany bob swishing against her chin. "I never saw the photo."

"You must mean my sister," Shay said. "Anna. We look alike."

"What happened to her?" Loren asked, the words prickling with dryness. The chlorine had really done a number on her.

"She was abducted." Shay picked at a thread in her pants. "But I don't really want to talk about that right now."

"THERE HE IS," Donovan drawled, his smile wide and wicked as Roman walked into the crowded space. "I was starting to think you wouldn't show."

"Since when have I ever run?" Roman replied, his tone betraying no hint of the fear coursing like ice through his veins.

Roman stopped at Darien's left. His cousin still smelled of chlorine and blood, still emanated a bone-deep exhaustion and a clawing need for something Roman recognized as drug addiction. If Don made the decision to strike, they'd all be done for.

"What do you want?" Roman bit out.

"What do I want?" Don spat. "I want a son who doesn't lie. And I want another son who isn't a spineless pussy—"

"That's *enough,*" Darien barked.

Don's eyes went black. He stalked forward—

Roman moved, coming between Don and Darien. "Stop." The word echoed. "I'll go with you. That's what you want, isn't it? I'll go. Happy?"

Don stepped back, beckoning with a hand. "Paxy—"

Roman's blood cooled. *"No,"* he snapped.

But Paxton was already walking, squeezing between the people who looked torn on what to do, afraid of making the wrong move, of crossing a line Roman didn't want them to cross.

There were many.

Roman stopped Paxton with a hand on his shoulder. Said to Don, "He's staying here."

"I can do this all night, Roman," Donovan threatened. "Either you both come to the House of Black...or we end this family reunion. Right here. Right now." His eyes flicked to Darien again—and gods, that threat in them, that promise of death, was enough to make Roman want to hurl.

Roman stared at his dad, well aware that everyone in the room was looking at him.

There was no point in fighting tonight—they wouldn't win.

So Roman took his brother by the hand. "Fine. You win. Like always."

Donovan smiled. "Wise choice."

"Roman..." The whisper came from Ivy.

Roman's eyes locked with hers. "It's okay," he lied. He scanned the group behind him—the faces of his friends and family.

Darien's expression was livid, his eyes flickering with black. "Just say the words, Roman," he urged.

Roman dropped his attention to the floor. Swallowed the lump in his throat. "Not today," he whispered.

He tugged Paxton out the door, silently vowing to guard him as he always did in their personal hell.

TRAVIS LASTED TEN MINUTES. Ten, and then he said screw it and sprinted down the stairs.

He thundered to a stop by the open front door to find everyone standing quietly in front of it.

Don and his Shadowmasters were gone. And so were—

"Where are they?" Travis said, breaths tearing apart his lungs in wild gasps. He stepped into the group, shoving his way through, his eyes picking apart the foyer, the empty living room beyond. "Pax?" His breaths came quicker, head spinning. "Roman?"

Footsteps sounded on the steps behind him. One by one, the others appeared. Loren, Jewels, Malakai, Arthur, and Shay.

"Gone," Darien said. His voice was hollow and quiet, his eyes a shining black as he stared out at the empty driveway, not a trace of Roman and Pax in the area. "Don took them." He scrubbed a hand down his face. Pushed his hair back. "And I don't know what to fucking do."

Travis knew from the look in Darien's eyes, his tone of voice, that Roman *chose* to leave. Knew that Darien found himself at a crossroads for really good reason.

Because going after Roman could have even deadlier consequences than not.

85

THE HOUSE OF BLACK
YVESWICH, STATE OF KER

Roman held Paxton's hand as they walked together up the steps of the House of Black. Donovan took the lead, his Shadowmasters fencing Roman and Pax in on all sides. Near the perimeter of the enclosed yard, Don's pet wolves observed from the shadows with gold eyes, a few pacing along the chainlink of their pens.

The pounding of Pax's heart was audible, his breathing ragged. Roman gave his hand a gentle squeeze, willing himself to be strong for his brother.

No one would touch Pax—not if Roman could help it. And he always did, taking the brunt of anything Don threw their way. But it never made it easier on Pax—not by much. Emotional and mental scars sometimes ran deeper than physical ones.

One by one, they filed into the House of Black—the mouth of the beast. Roman kept Paxton close, but the moment they got down the hall, Larina shutting the front door, Don gave Simon and Trey a stiff nod.

Simon grabbed Paxton by the arm, pulling so hard he ripped the other out of Roman's grasp.

"No!" Paxton shrieked.

Roman moved, stalking forward just like one of those wolves his dad chained in the yard. *"Don't fucking touch him!"* he snarled, eyes going black.

His magic swept out, pinning multiple Shadowmasters to the walls.

But Don's top cronies were stronger than Roman with their magic, and they blocked the storm of shadows with their own. Darkness exploded through the foyer—so thick, it was blinding.

Trey used the advantage of the darkness to land a fist in Roman's gut. Another across his face, the impact splitting his brow open.

Paxton started screaming.

Sayagul tore out of Roman's shadow with a screech. But the dragon was soon pinned to the wall by Blaine's owl Familiar, talons skewering her wings.

A blow across the back sent Roman crashing to his knees. He stopped fighting, knowing it was no use. This night would end the same way as the others—with suffering, pain. *His* suffering, *his* pain.

"Romaaaan!" Paxton's scream of anguish rattled the windows. "Leave him alone! Don't touch him—" His pleas were silenced by a wicked twist of his arm, sick delight on Simon's face.

The sight of Paxton in pain boiled Roman's blood.

"Let," Roman growled, the shadows in the room stirring anew, his eyes and hair solid black, "him go."

Simon did not. Just one more little twist and Pax's arm would snap like a tree branch.

So Roman reined his shadows in. Looked up at Donovan from where he knelt on the floor, his back throbbing where Trey had struck him. "It was me," Roman declared. "My fault. My decision. I told Pax to keep his mouth shut about the house. Do whatever you want to me—just don't touch him. Please."

Donovan measured him with soulless eyes. Although the shadows of their magic had dissipated, it was still dark in the house—a shadowy den perfectly fitting for a shadowy creature. "You're so pathetic, Roman." Don's cold words echoed. "Begging like a pussy." But he said to Simon, "Let him go."

The prick released Paxton immediately.

Simon and Trey moved toward Roman—

Roman stood before they could lay a hand on him. "I'll walk."

They merely smiled, Don included.

And so Roman walked to his fate.

THEY TOOK their sweet time beating him, like usual. Roman was used to it—the pain, the humiliation, the torture. But worse than his suffering was the sound of Paxton screaming.

Not in pain—not that. And thank gods it wasn't. Had they laid a hand on his little brother, Roman would've fought to the death, would've razed this house to the ground to get to him. Protect him.

Paxton's screaming was for Roman's benefit. He was on the main floor, yelling his lungs out at Don and the other Shadowmasters, begging them to let Roman out of this room—this damp cave deep below the earth. The kid was even offering himself in Roman's place—taking after his big brother in all the ways Roman did not want him to.

The room he was in was literally a torture chamber. This house had been built centuries ago, in a time when certain practices had not yet been outlawed. It had belonged to an ancient, royal bloodline of witches and warlocks who had used this room to torture the innocent, the disrespectful, the traitors.

Roman had the utter misfortune of feeling their souls every time Donovan ordered his men to drag him down here. The auras of the tortured had long since vanished with death, but there were faint echoes of their suffering left behind, the kind of stain that could not be scrubbed clean with any passing of time. The soul-cutting anguish of those tortured people —visible only with a sixth sense—not only mirrored Roman's own, but doubled it, making the hurt so much worse. Every strike had double the force. Every blow to the gut, every wooden paddle taken to his back, every searing lash of a belt.

Donovan liked to shackle him. The long chains were fastened to the high ceiling, the rusting cuffs so sharp they pierced Roman's skin, biting in deeper the longer he hung here like some dead animal. Don let Simon and Trey have their fun with him first, and as soon as Roman was battered and blue to his liking, Don would come down for his own share.

Roman couldn't wait until it was done. Until he could walk out of here and calm down Paxton. Dry his tears. Give him a hug or ten.

The kid did not deserve this.

Another scorching blow of the paddle across Roman's back, and he damn near stopped breathing. Thick blood stringed out of his slackened jaws, and his eyelids drooped, threatening to shut. He fought the urge to pass out, willing himself to stay awake in case Donovan dragged Paxton down here to see. He'd done it before, several times. Taking delight in his youngest son watching his eldest suffer. Submit.

He had to stay awake.

His surroundings shimmered. His ears rang, his nostrils so plugged up with blood, he was forced to breathe through his mouth.

Fog swept in, darkening the already dark room—

Sometime ago, Trey and Simon had left. Minutes, maybe, or hours.

Roman wasn't sure. But when he opened his eyes again, chains tinkling under his weight as he swayed in place, feet barely touching ground, he saw a beam of light cut across the winding stairwell. Boots pounded, and Roman could tell from the pattern, the gap between steps, that his dad was coming down here.

His personal devil was coming.

Roman's fear was so intense, darkness slammed into him—

He must have passed out again. He came to when a hand roughly nudged his face. His eyes slowly cracked open—

At the sight of Don standing before him, Roman recoiled, thrashing against the chains.

"You're even more pathetic than before you fucked that Selkie out in the desert." Donovan's harsh voice slithered over the walls, his shadows echoing every word.

Pathetic, the shadows giggled. *Fucked that Selkie.*

Shit. Donovan knew.

Donovan fucking *knew*.

Shayla—

"Stay with me, son," Donovan said, the words that would've sounded kind coming from anyone else's mouth contrasting sharply with that awful, mocking, *hateful* tone. "I'm through with you yet."

No. No, not this—*please,* not this.

'I'm here,' Sayagul said from his shadow, but even she sounded terrified. *'I'm here with you, my dear Roman. I'm here.'*

Invisible claws pierced his mind, so sharp they felt like knives thudding into his skull with wicked force. Donovan's magic dug in deep, and as they pushed even deeper, sinking into the center of his brain, awful, heartbreaking images flashed through Roman's head.

His mother—lying dead on the bedroom floor in a pool of blood.

"Stop," Roman ground out, spit and blood dripping from his lips.

Donovan's claws did the opposite—digging in deeper.

Roman winced. Thrashed against the restraints.

And then the shadows in the room exploded into a massive storm—a literal storm of writhing darkness, so petrifying it made Roman almost piss himself.

Floating in that storm were the same images Donovan was forcing into his mind—making Roman see these memories with his eyes closed *and* open.

Helen Devlin, her gold eyes bolted open in death.

Flies crawling across her dead body—the corpse Donovan hadn't bothered to clean up for days. Roman remembered the reek of his rotting mother as if he'd smelled her just yesterday, recalled vomiting all over the floor when he'd stumbled in to find her there, lying beside the four-poster bed where she'd conceived her two sons.

"Stop." The single word was a hoarse whisper. Roman's aching body shook so hard, the chains rattled. Sayagul wept in his shadow. The dragon had been just a baby when Helen had died, but she remembered it as clearly as Roman, had cried just as hard. "Please."

"Open your eyes," Donovan hissed, bringing his vicious face in close to Roman's. "Quit being a coward and open your goddamn eyes."

Roman forced them open. Donovan's face was close—too close.

Donovan pointed at the mass of shadows spinning through the room like a hurricane. Evil incarnate. "Look at her."

Roman didn't.

Donovan grabbed his chin, his grip bruising. *"Look at her."*

Roman looked—at his mother's crying face.

And then at a different memory—Helen bleeding from the eyes after Donovan had used this same magic on her. This same torture.

"Your fault," Donovan hissed, shoving his face away. "She died because of *you.*"

'He's lying,' Sayagul said gently, consoling, still weeping. *'Do not listen to him.'*

Roman knew it wasn't true, but Donovan had poisoned his thoughts for years—twisting reality around until Roman believed the lie without question or argument.

It had worked, for a time. Years of therapy had shed light on the corners of his life that Donovan had shrouded in shadow with meticulous, resentful hands.

So Roman kept looking, knowing he had to if he wanted this to end, if he wanted to get to Paxton, who he could still hear screaming and sobbing upstairs, his tiring fists banging on the locked door.

'Stay, Roman,' Sayagul pleaded with a sniffle. *'We must stay awake.'*

But as Roman stared at the many images of his dead mother in the swirling storm of shadows, Don's magic sliced deeper.

He began to bleed from the nose. The ears. And finally, from the eyes, but by the time that happened, he had passed out.

When he woke back up, Donovan was gone, those otherworldly shadows gone too. The nightmare was over—for now.

He wished he could say forever.

ROMAN'S BREATHING wouldn't slow. He hung from the chains, not knowing how much time had passed since he'd last opened his eyes. He'd fallen unconscious for a second time after his dad left the room, and without any windows down here, it was impossible to tell the time.

His whole body was screaming in pain. The shirt he wore was stuck to his back, his blood acting like glue. The skin of his wrists was chafed, and his mouth tasted of the blood that had dripped from his nose, drying in thick lines on his lips and chin.

Roman opted to keep his eyes shut. There was no point in staring into those shadows. He was stuck here until Donovan decided he was done with him. Sometimes, he came down for another round. Roman prayed it wouldn't happen this time. If it did, he wasn't sure he'd survive it.

Quiet footsteps shuffled on the steps. Too small to belong to an adult.

Roman forced his eyes open.

Paxton was coming down the stairs, blindly groping the curved stone wall, his Familiar following on quiet paws that swirled with black mist. Roman had no idea how the kid had gotten in. He hadn't heard the door open, hadn't seen any light streaming in, hadn't picked up on the jingle of keys. Don always locked him down here like he would a true prisoner, keys and all.

"Pax," Roman gritted out, his tongue fat and clumsy, teeth caked with blood. "Pax, please, buddy. You gotta go. I don't want you to see me like this, okay? I'm fine."

"Look what he did to you," Paxton whispered, stepping closer on shaking legs that reminded Roman of bean poles. He was too young for this. Too innocent.

How was any of this fair? Kids didn't get to choose their parents, their siblings. Every child came into the world the same way, but were dealt different cards. Pax should have been born into a different family, should've had a father who loved him, and a mother who fought to protect him, the way Roman fought.

'It is not fair,' Sayagul agreed, the dragon as beaten down as Roman. *'Many suffer, and it is not fair.'*

"Pax," Roman gasped around the pain, "go. Please."

But Pax was too stubborn. Roman supposed he got that from him.

He came closer.

And took out a set of keys.

"Pax," Roman bit out, wincing as the muscles in his back spasmed again. "Don't tell me you stole those. Please don't tell me you stole those."

"I didn't steal them."

"Don't lie to me."

"I'm not. *I* didn't steal them." Paxton backed up, craning his neck and squinting to see the shackles. "I need to grow a few feet."

"Pax, I need you to go." Roman's heart sprinted with fresh fear. "I need you to take those back. If Dad finds out you took them..." He swallowed bile and blood. "Please, just go."

Paxton's eyes shone in the dark. "Look at your face," he croaked.

"I'm fine. I don't need you crying over me, okay? This is bad enough." He shut his eyes tight. Tried not to cry himself. "Please, Pax, just go. You'd be doing me a favor." He added in a quieter whisper, "Please."

"Fine," Paxton sighed, "I'll go. You can stay."

Had Roman been in a better mood, he would've laughed. His brother was always cracking ridiculous jokes, some of them not even funny, but he loved him for it. "Very funny, you lippy little shit."

Silence.

"Pax?" Roman opened his eyes.

Standing in his place was Shayla Cousens, and drifting toward the stairs on silent feet was Pax, who shrugged and said, "I let her in."

"Shay," Roman breathed.

She smiled, though her mouth wobbled, her pale green eyes gleaming with tears. "Hello, Prince of Shadows."

SHAY SNUCK Roman and Paxton out of the House of Black and into her tiny apartment in the district of Zima.

She helped Roman into the shower, helped him out of his bloody clothes, even kneeling to shimmy off his jeans.

"You don't have to do this," he said, bracing a hand against the bathroom counter as he lifted one leg at a time, every movement careful.

"You'd do it for me," Shay said, tugging his pant-leg and sock over his left foot. She peeked up at him. "Wouldn't you?"

His throat shifted, his blood-crusted, gold eyes darting toward the running shower. "This is embarrassing."

"What's embarrassing is that your dad gets off on beating his sons," Shay said softly, helping him lift the other foot. "He's the embarrassment. Not you."

She stood, scooping up his filthy clothes, and placed them on the counter. She'd do laundry tonight. Bleach the blood out of them, erase every trace of Donovan and his awful men.

Roman stepped toward the shower. Every movement made him wince, pained breaths drawn through his teeth. Dried blood streaked his cheeks like tears, his ears full of blood, too.

Shay couldn't decide if she wanted to scream or cry, but she knew one thing for certain.

She wanted to kill Donovan. Make him suffer for hurting Roman. Pax. There was no excuse for this nightmare.

Donovan Slade was a monster.

Once Roman was in the shower, Shay left so she could make a bed for Paxton on the couch. The apartment was small, only one bedroom, but she had enough spare blankets and pillows to turn Pax's little area into a fort.

"Do you have everything you need?" Shay asked him as she flicked off the kitchen light. Pax was snuggled up under piles of blankets on the couch, his eyes fixed on the television, an empty cup of hot chocolate on the coffee table. Shay had used a spare sheet to create a canopy above the couch, draping the sheet across the end of it like a curtain—a door for his blanket fort.

"I think so."

"If you get thirsty during the night, there's juice and water in the fridge. I also have chocolate chip cookies. Help yourself to anything you want, okay?"

"Okay." His voice was small.

"Goodnight, Paxton." She padded across the room, reaching for the single lamp that was still lit—

"Shay?" Paxton called. She turned to see him sitting up on the couch, fresh alarm in his eyes. "Can you leave the light on, please?"

Shay nodded. "Sure. I'll keep it on." She dropped her hand, turning her head so Paxton couldn't see the look on her face—the emotions that were threatening to tear through her careful restraints. "Goodnight, Pax."

Blankets rustled as he laid back down. "Night, Shay."

Fighting the sob building in her throat, she walked down the hall, heading for the single bathroom again to check on Roman.

Her phone buzzed in her pocket.

She took it out to see the name DARIEN CASSEL flashing across the screen. They'd exchanged numbers before she'd left Roman's house—after she'd declared that she was going to the House of Black and no one was to follow her.

Darien hadn't argued, which was probably a first. But everyone knew it was for the best. The leader of the Seven Devils wasn't in any position to fight more battles tonight, and if he tried, there was a risk he wouldn't win.

No one wanted to take that risk.

Shay read his message, then typed up a reply.

DARIEN
How's he doing?

SHAY
He's okay.

DARIEN
And Pax?

SHAY
Tired but good. I just tucked him in.

DARIEN
Good. Let me know if you need anything.

SHAY
I will.

Shay put the device to sleep at the same time she heard the shower shut off.

She crept down the hallway, opting to wait right outside the door, giving Roman some much-needed space. She had left some loose clothes on the counter for him to change into—gray sweatpants and a baggy white shirt Paxton had grabbed from the House of Black. Easy enough to get on without her help, hopefully. But she listened quietly, in case he needed her. A few minutes passed before the door slowly opened, and he limped out.

Roman forced a crooked smile. "Pathetic, hey?" He took another step, limping again.

"Your dad? Yeah, he is pathetic."

Roman smirked. "Where am I sleeping?"

"With me."

Roman stared at her.

"If you want to," she said quickly. "I don't have a guest room, but I can make up a bed for myself on the floor—"

"Your room is fine."

Shay drew a breath. "Okay. Right this way." She walked down the hall, moving slowly for Roman's benefit. The Shadowmaster braced a hand against the wall with every step, his eyes downcast.

It took him a few minutes, but he finally made it into the bedroom.

He paused in the doorway, his gold eyes sweeping about her room, lingering the longest on her collection of bizarre art sculptures. Her favorites were made of soda cans. "You're artsy," he said.

Shay flushed. "That's funny."

He picked up on her reaction, his eyes snapping to her face. "What?"

"Most people who see my apartment call it trashy. A junkyard. They don't have any appreciation for vintage collectibles."

"Have you let many people see your apartment?"

"No." She eyed him. "I feel like your question is coded."

"Everything I say is coded."

She gestured to the bed. "Lie down. Make yourself comfortable."

He took a step. Winced. Another step. Winced. "Where are you going?" His eyes found hers as she drifted toward the door.

"To do some laundry. I'll be back in a few."

She left before he could reply or offer to help. Walking quietly in case Pax was already asleep, she grabbed Roman's bloody clothes from the bathroom and hurried into the laundry room. The space was tiny and always humid, the washer and dryer stacked. As she scooped the bottle of detergent off the tile, she resisted the urge to pinch herself.

Roman Devlin was in her bedroom. Not in good condition, but still.

The Wolf of the Hollow was in her bedroom. In her bed.

Another, different reality hit her right after the last: The man with such a feared reputation as Head of the House of Black was not as bulletproof as he led the world to believe. Athene had called him a gifted actor, and while she'd meant it in a negative way to imply that Roman was selfish and dishonest, she had been correct in calling him that. He was not selfish, nor dishonest, but he wore a mask, and he played his role convincingly. A gifted actor who allowed very few people backstage.

Shay was honored to be one of those people.

As soon as the laundry was in, Shay grabbed the basket that was full of clean clothes she hadn't bothered to put away before going out to Motel 58 and carried it into her bedroom.

Roman was still awake—lying on top of the covers. He stared at her as she set the basket on the bed.

"I said make yourself comfortable," Shay said. "That doesn't look comfortable."

"I'm comfortable," he argued.

"You're not even under the covers."

"I don't like restriction." He eyed the basket. "Don't tell me you're folding laundry at this hour."

She pulled a bath towel out of the basket and folded it. "I won't tell you, then."

He sat up.

She dropped the t-shirt she'd just grabbed. "Lie down." She pointed.

"Don't tell me what to do, pup." He tried to stand three times before finally succeeding, then shuffled around the bed. "If you're folding laundry, I'm helping."

She grabbed one end of the basket and pulled it away from him. "I'll do it tomorrow."

His hand gripped the other end, pulling it back his way. "We'll do it together."

She blinked up at him. "Fold laundry?"

"Mm-hmm."

"I don't know if folding laundry is your thing."

"Why? Because I'm a man? Fuck gender roles." He plucked something out of the basket—and her face turned scarlet as she realized it was a pair of lace panties. "Besides, I get an excuse to ogle your underthings."

She snorted. "My *underthings?*"

He folded the panties and set them aside. "Are you going to stand there and watch me, or are you going to help?"

Shay relented with a sigh. "Fine. But if you get the towels wrong, you're fired."

Roman's answering smile showed off his dimple and made the gold flecks in his irises come back to life. "Deal."

86

ROMAN'S HOUSE
YVESWICH, STATE OF KER

This night fucking sucked. For more reasons than Darien could count.

He was going to explode. Explode or puke, whichever came first. Because he kept getting slammed with one thing after another, and eventually, he was going to break.

Eventually might come tonight.

He paced in Roman's kitchen, the others crowding around Tanner at the oak table. The hacker's laptop was open, the screen displaying the security camera footage at Hell's Gate.

The footage that showed Gaven and the imperator's men trespassing on Darien's property, entering his house and destroying everything, the home he and his family had built together.

The destruction wasn't even the worst part.

The men had stolen Mortifer. On the screen, the Hob hid behind the cereal boxes. Darien could see Morty visibly jump with fright when one of the men threw aside the cereal boxes and grabbed Mortifer as if he were a rag doll—as if he had the *right* to touch him.

He'd stuffed Mortifer into a canvas bag, cinching it shut.

And then he'd punched the fucking bag.

"Turn that off!" Darien snapped, his words cutting through the tense, quiet room like a knife. "I don't need to see it a third time!"

Tanner snapped the laptop shut.

"Was that Lionel?" Malakai asked, the question dripping with rage—with vengeance. "I swear I saw Lionel—"

"It was," Lace said, her voice thick and wobbling. "The imperator's buying everyone out." The Huntsmen. The Wargs too, probably. Lionel, Channary—they had already been bought, Darien would bet. And whoever the imperator couldn't bribe, he aimed to kill. The Angels...they weren't safe—

"Has anyone talked to Dominic?" Ivy asked, practically reading Darien's thoughts. None of their friends were safe.

But Max said, "He's fine." The reassurance allowed Darien to draw a breath. "He's coming here too, but he's a couple days behind. I think Quinton planned on sending the same men after him once they'd come for us." He shared a look with Dallas.

"But the asshole didn't anticipate us killing them," Travis chimed in.

Darien paced faster. "They did it while I was gone." Stole Mortifer while Darien wasn't there to stop them. He squeezed his hands into fists. Loosened them. Squeezed again. "Motherfucking cowards."

He needed air. Needed to peel his own skin off his bones.

Roman was gone. Probably had the shit beat out of him by Donovan before Shay was able to get him out of that hellhole. Darien didn't even want to consider what that prick had done to Paxton. If he let himself think about it, he might start a war with the House of Black. A war he was in no position to finish. They might've won a battle against the demons of the fog tonight, but they had been thrown straight into another fight against different, far worse monsters.

Story of his fucking life.

"Darien...," Tanner tried. The room had fallen silent, everyone watching him with wary gazes.

With Loren in the room, perched on one of the chairs near Tanner, Darien worked hard to control himself.

He failed.

With a guttural roar that made multiple people jump in alarm, Loren included, he grabbed a free chair, lightning-fast. Whipped it across the room—

It hit the wall with an earsplitting smash and exploded into smithereens.

Nobody said anything.

He stalked out onto the back deck, slamming the door shut behind him, and sucked down breaths of icy air. Hours had passed since the fog had cleared, but ambulances were still hard at work throughout the city's many districts, the sirens slicing through the night.

A couple minutes passed before the door opened behind him.

Darien whirled around, the bomb in his soul just waiting for one last spark before detonating—

Ivy stepped out onto the deck, tears glimmering in her eyes. Quietly—so quietly compared to the noise he'd caused in the room, she closed the door.

"Ivy," Darien choked out, his blood boiling, heart pounding with pure, undiluted rage, "I need—"

She conquered the distance between them with several quick steps.

And threw her arms around him. "This," she whispered, squeezing him tight. "This is what you need."

Darien's body was tense, but he felt himself gradually melt as his sister held him, defusing that bomb inside him like she used to when they were kids, trapped in the nightmare of their childhood.

The same sort of nightmare Roman and Paxton were still stuck in. The cage they couldn't break out of.

His arms closed around her.

And he let the tears fall. All those emotions he'd bottled up since Loren had fallen into a coma...since he'd got her back only for her to not remember him, to *still* not remember him...he set them all free.

The tears turned into sobbing, each breath rattling through his chest.

It hurt. Everything hurt.

"We'll get him back," Ivy vowed, her own tears wetting his shirt.

"Yeah," Darien agreed thickly. He squeezed her tight, unable to get that awful image out of his head—the one of Mortifer being stuffed into that bag. The Hob's terrified face, no one around to help him, his family gone. The sight of that asshole punching the bag to stop Mortifer from thrashing.

The way the bag had fallen still afterward, either from Morty's fear or because...

Darien didn't want to think it. So instead, he vowed, "Fucking rights we will."

"I promise I'm not an alcoholic," Travis said as he crumpled another empty can of beer. He sat on the roof of Roman's house, Jewels Delaney walking quietly across the peaks to join him. She placed one foot in front of the other, as if walking a tightrope, her hair blowing in the wind. Travis continued, "I just literally cannot afford to be sober right now, or I might do something stupid. Like try to kill my dad."

She sat down beside him, swinging her sneakers over open air. "I'm in no position to judge," she said, her hands gripping the frosted edge of the roof. "I turned to some pretty bad things back when my stepdad was around. Drugs, alcohol, vandalism, you name it. I was the definition of juvenile delinquent. I know how you feel...and thought you might want someone to talk to." She peeked sidelong at him.

"Thanks," he said, but he didn't talk.

"If you need anything, Travis, I'm here. Even if you just want to sit together in the quiet." She drew a breath, staring out at the sprawling city, and said again, exhaling out a puff of breath in the cold, "I'm here."

"I need a new dad," Travis blurted. "I need to know my brothers are safe. I need to be able to see them whenever I want to. I need justice." He paused. "And I need another beer." He reached into the case beside him and wrenched one out. Cracked it open. Guzzled half.

The burp he let out echoed across the yard.

Jewels snickered. "That was disgusting."

"Made you laugh, though."

She nodded. Smiled. "Yeah. Yeah, you did."

"I need...," Travis continued, circling back to his former list of needed things, "to get so rip-roaring drunk that I forget I'm even alive."

Her happy smile changed to a sad one. "Then go ahead and get rip-roaring drunk," she said softly. "And I'll be right here to make sure you don't fall off the roof and break your neck like an idiot." She inched her hand across the roof, but abruptly froze, tucking both hands between her thighs instead.

Travis lifted the beer in a toast. "To Jewels Delaney. My dream girl—" He swayed, nearly falling—

She grabbed onto his arm. "Whoa, easy there." She huffed a nervous laugh. "I think you might already be rip-roaring drunk."

"That's one thing off my list. Next stop: Kill Don."

Her attention snagged on something behind him. She patted his thigh, and the next thing Travis knew she was swinging her legs onto the roof and pushing herself to her feet. "I'll be back in a few."

"What about the whole making sure I don't break my neck thing?" he called. "Sick of me already?"

But Jewels was already gone, and a different shadow with a heavier gait sat down beside him, swinging his boots over the edge.

"Give me a beer," Malakai grumbled.

"What do you want?" Travis demanded, squinting at him through the haze of his drunken mind.

"A beer." He beckoned with a curl of his fingers. "Give me one."

Travis dug around in the case and shoved one into Malakai's waiting hand, missing twice. "Is Jewels really gone," Travis slurred, vision shimmering, "or am I so drunk that I can't even tell the difference?"

Malakai cracked open his beer. "If you're that far gone, then I pity you. The more you drink, the prettier people are supposed to get."

"You're right, I can't be that drunk. You're ugly as hell."

Malakai paused mid-sip. "Watch it, or I'll push your dumb ass off this roof and tell Jewels you fell to your drunken death."

Travis was wasted enough to laugh at the threat.

The silence that fell afterward would've been really damn awkward if Travis was sober.

"I had a stepdad just like Don," Malakai said out of the blue.

"That's what Jewels was saying."

"Shut up and let me tell my story." Malakai sipped his beer. "He was a prick. A real big prick."

Travis waited. Seconds turned into minutes. "Is that it?" he blurted.

"Yup."

"I thought you said you had a story to tell."

"That *is* my story. Once upon a time, I had a big prick for a stepdad. The end."

Travis shook his head. Smirked. When silence fell again, to his horror he began to sober up, his hellseher genes allowing him to filter out substances a lot quicker.

"You took care of Jewels while I was gone," Malakai said. "She told me you saved her."

Travis grunted. "She helped cover my ass too." He cracked open another beer, not wanting to be of sound mind so soon.

"She's pretty adamant that if you hadn't been there, she'd be dead."

"And?"

"And what?"

"It sounded like you were going to thank me."

He snorted. "Gods no. I don't do thank-you's." He studied the beer in his hand, moonlight glinting off the rim. "I *do* steal beer and drink it, though." He sipped again.

Travis hummed. "Well, just for the record, you're welcome."

"Eww." He got to his feet. "Try not to fall, it's slippery up here. Or do —I don't care." His voice faded with distance.

Travis laughed under his breath. "You're a weird one."

The night fell quiet. And Travis sat there. Alone, beer in hand.

He lifted it to his mouth, but paused. Set it down on the roof beside him.

And chose to watch the stars instead.

THEY HAD CLEANED up the house in the time since Roman and Pax had left. Dumped the demon corpses on the street for city officials to clear away. Used their magic to piece the windows back together, though a few were too difficult to mend and would need to be replaced. The Hob got rid of all the blood, the place almost like new again. Good enough to sleep in, anyway. They'd take care of the rest tomorrow.

Darien found Loren lying awake in her bedroom, her beautiful face illuminated by the orange glow of her salt lamp. Singer was curled up in a tight ball beside her, a back paw twitching as he dreamed.

Loren blinked up at Darien as he appeared in her doorway. "Are you okay?" she whispered, her words crackling with exhaustion.

"I came here to ask you the same thing." He'd showered and changed into black sweatpants and a white shirt, his hair wet again but no longer reeking of chlorine and blood. His back still burned like a son of a bitch, but was well on its way to healing.

"I'm okay," she replied. "A little rattled, but fine."

"Mind if I sit with you for a minute?" He drifted into the room, his need to be closer to her setting his feet into motion before she could reply.

She sat up and scootched over as he took a seat on the mattress beside her.

"I want to apologize," Darien began, "for startling you."

A little crease formed between her sandy brows. "When did you startle me?" But then her face smoothed. "Oh—you mean the chair."

He grimaced. "My temper gets the best of me sometimes."

"You have a right to be upset," she said gently. "What they did to your house... To..." She shook her head, her eyes shining, her thoughts clearly on Mortifer. "What they did was wrong."

Darien drew a breath. "I'll fix it," he declared. "I'll get him back."

They sat in silence for a few minutes, Darien listening to the sound of Loren's heartbeat, her breathing. Even simply being alone in a room with her calmed him down in a way nothing else could. Not the fighting, not the slaying, not the drugs. He didn't know how he ever got by without this girl. His miracle. His angel.

"Hellseher healing is very impressive," Loren said, those stunning eyes scanning the wounds on his face. She reached for him...

Darien held his breath, wanting—hell, *needing* her to touch him—

But she abruptly stopped, leaning over to grab a small tin off the nightstand instead. Her healing salve from Mordred and Penelope's.

She twisted the lid off and dabbed her finger into the salve. "May I?"

Darien's answering nod was immediate.

She slid closer, blankets bunching up around her waist, and carefully dabbed some salve that smelled of peppermint and eucalyptus to the cut in his brow, the touch instantly cooling the searing pain.

Darien watched her the whole time, her beauty mesmerizing him. What he wouldn't give to finally touch her. Hold her. Kiss and taste her—

Loren dropped the salve, the tin clattering across the floor.

Darien got up. "You okay?" He bent to scoop up the tin that was spinning like a top, his damp hair shifting into his face.

"Yeah," she breathed, looking dazed. She tucked her hair behind her ears. "Have we done this before?"

Darien froze.

Was this it? Was she finally remembering?

Loren blinked up at him. "Sorry, that's a stupid question."

"No, it's not," he said softly. His heart began to race, that spark of hope in his chest spreading into an inferno. "Loren..."

"I'm really tired," she said suddenly, the words rushing out. "I think we're both tired." She took the tin right out of his hand. "I'll see you in the morning?"

Darien just stared at her, the words dying to come out. But he said, "Yeah, okay." She wanted him to go—he could see it in the way she avoided his stare, her shaking hands continuously smoothing her hair behind her ears.

So he made for the door, desperate to make her happy. "If you need anything, come and get me, okay?"

She managed a nod.

Darien left, closing her door halfway.

She was remembering. And it clearly scared her. Confused her.

He'd pick the right time, and he'd sit her down and tell her the truth.

Tomorrow. Or the next day—no later.

And hopefully, once he told her, he would get her back. He couldn't handle waiting any longer. He needed her to know the truth.

But that didn't stop him from being afraid. Afraid that he'd lose her in a different, far worse way.

Because as long as she had no memory of him, of their history together, he was nothing more than a stranger. There was no love there, just facts. Cold, hard fucking facts.

It took Loren a while to fall asleep after Darien left. She found herself staring at her door. Hoping he would come back.

She'd practically demanded he leave, and she felt sorry for the way she'd just booted him out like that.

But another memory had come back. One of her kneeling on the floor between his legs as she applied a healing salve—the very same tin that now sat by the salt lamp—to some cuts on his chest.

The chest that had calla lilies tattooed on it. The ink was made up of more than just lilies, but... She couldn't help but wonder.

And then a second memory had come to her, one of her dabbing that same salve on the wounds on his handsome face. They were in a big, beautiful bathroom together, him staring up at her with affection from where he sat on the lip of a deep bathtub.

Just how *close* were they?

And why was no one telling her if it was closer than she thought?

"This," Dallas hissed, poking Max in the chest, "is the stupidest thing any of you idiots have ever done!"

They stood across from each other in one of the guest rooms on the top floor of Roman's house, arguing about Darien's decision to not tell Loren that they were dating, fucking. To not overwhelm her before she had the chance to remember things on her own.

She'd lost her memories. Max couldn't believe how much that girl had gone through in less than a year. The explosion on Kalendae, being blackmailed by the imperator, saving everyone's ass during the Blood Moon, dying and being resuscitated, falling into a coma...

And now amnesia. Partial, yeah, but still.

When the hell would it end?

"It isn't our decision to make," Max said for the hundredth time, working to keep his voice down. Delaney, who was staying in the bedroom next to theirs, had already bitched to him once about being too loud, and once was more than enough. "It's Darien's—"

"And he's choosing wrong!" Dallas's whisper was more a shout.

Sure enough, Delaney drawled, his words muffled by the wall separating their rooms, "Shut. The fuck. Uppppppp."

"She's going to remember, and she's going to be pissed," Dallas went on. "He's not doing himself any favors—"

"Then let him find out his way."

Dallas scowled at a painting that hung on the wall. She shook her head, ponytail swinging, the silver rings around her pupils burning brightly. Max knew he was asking a lot of Dallas. Loren, after losing her memories and being thrust into a life that Dallas and Sabrine were temporarily not a part of, would surely want to speak to her adoptive sister the moment she woke up. He only hoped Dallas would find a way to either dodge Loren's questions or avoid interacting with her entirely.

Again: Asking for a lot.

"Dallas?" Max prodded.

She shifted her scowl from the painting to him. "What?" she bit out.

Max's brows flicked up. "Are you going to tell her?"

"I *should* tell her," she warned. "I'm her sister. She trusts me to be honest with her." Max could understand that, but...

"Don't you think we owe Darien a little more loyalty than that? Loren's awake—alive—because of *him.*"

"And I'm awake because of you," Malakai called.

"Quit eavesdropping!" Max snapped.

Dallas returned to glaring at the wall. "I won't tell her," she decided. She pointed a finger up at him. "But I'm warning you, she will not be happy with him—with *any* of us—when she finally remembers."

A chuckle came from Delaney's room. "You got that right, Crimson."

Max couldn't argue with that. But he'd do what his best friend wanted, even if he wound up paying for the lie in worse ways.

87

SHAY'S APARTMENT
YVESWICH, STATE OF KER

Shay woke up the following morning to the smell of something burning. She was so tired, it took her a while to recognize what it was.

And even longer to remember why a male arm was draped across her waist, twitching every now and again as the Shadowmaster dreamt.

Her eyes shot open to see Roman's doing the same.

Roman blinked, the gold flecks in his irises brightening.

And then his nostrils flared, and his arm tightened around her, his fingers curling in her shirt. *"Pax."*

They were on their feet and running into the kitchen in no time.

Well, *Shay* ran. Roman limped.

Paxton stood in the sunlit kitchen, waving a dish towel to clear the smoke billowing out of a frying pan on the stove.

"Pax?" Roman called from behind Shay. When his hand slid across the small of her back, she shivered. "What are you doing, bud?"

"Making breakfast." He flicked off the burners—all on high.

The kitchen was a mess, the counter strewn with breakfast items—bagged frozen hash browns, a loaf of bread, a carton of eggs, jugs of juice, spatulas and whisks.

Paxton wiped soot off his cheek. "You can sit down. I'm almost finished."

Shay and Roman shared a glance.

"Sure you don't want help?" Roman asked.

Paxton grabbed a stack of plates from the cupboard, and Shay cringed as one slid to the side, nearly shattering on the floor. "I'm good."

Roman kept gaping at his brother, looking like he couldn't decide whether he was concerned, shocked, or proud.

Shay took the Shadowmaster's hand, threading her fingers through his, and tugged him to the kitchen table, being careful to move at his pace.

Roman's back must've started bleeding again during the night, the white material of his shirt stained with streaks of dark red. He was still limping, still wincing every few seconds, but Shay could say with confidence—and relief—that he wasn't suffering as badly as last night.

They'd slept with the light on. Shay had flicked it off about an hour after Roman had fallen asleep, only for him to jerk awake like a bomb had gone off.

"Shay?" he'd rasped into the dark room. "Shay, turn the light on. Please."

Of course, she hadn't argued. And of course, she'd felt bad for not cluing in sooner, her own exhaustion and preference for dark rooms causing her to forget.

Roman was afraid of the dark. And now that she was remembering back to her time spent with him in the desert, she realized she had never actually *seen* him sleeping.

Hindsight now told her he'd stayed awake every night, unable to fall asleep in the black motel room. When they'd eaten breakfast together that first morning, he'd claimed he hadn't slept because he didn't trust her.

What a good liar he was. He played his part as Shadowmaster and Wolf of the Hollow very well.

As she sat down across from Roman, she locked eyes with him.

And she vowed—silently, to herself—that the rest of the world would never know. She would keep his secret as carefully as she kept her own.

Pax served them each a plate of scrambled eggs and toast. He filled their glasses with orange juice, and then grabbed the pan of hash browns off the stove and carried it to the table.

He paused by Roman's chair. "I burned them." He frowned at the charred potatoes, his lower lip jutting out.

"What are you talking about, they're perfect," Roman said, offering Pax his plate. "Load me up, chef."

Paxton's frown turned into a smile, and he dumped some on Roman's plate. "Want ketchup?"

"Please," Roman said.

Paxton turned to Shay, pan in hand. "You don't have to eat them if you don't want to."

"Of course I want to," Shay said, holding up her plate. Paxton scraped some hash browns out of the pan. "You're spoiling me. Thank you, Pax."

"Welcome." He went to the fridge to find the ketchup.

As Shay set her plate before her, she caught Roman staring.

He winked—with the eye that wasn't as puffy as the other.

The breakfast was very good, hash browns aside. When she was finished, Shay thanked Paxton a third time as she scraped her plate clean and started tidying up the kitchen.

Roman watched her from where he sat at the table, hands wrapped around a mug of green tea. Paxton was jabbering to his brother about Cryptic Crypts, his voice as cheery as the sunlight streaming in through the windows of the tiny apartment.

Shay liked having them here. It felt less...lonely. She could almost pretend she had a family. People she could call her own.

And she liked that Roman's face had healed a bit during the night, the bruises fading. His skin wasn't as swollen, the cuts healing.

His back, though...those wounds would take longer.

"Can I have a shower?" Paxton asked suddenly.

"Of course you can," Shay said, filling the sink with hot, soapy water.

Paxton pushed his chair out. "Thanks." He skipped down the hallway, his puppy Familiar coming out of his shadow to chase after him and nip at his heels. The sound of Paxton's laughter bubbling through the apartment warmed her heart.

Shay smiled softly and watched the water foam up from the soap, her tired eyes glazing over. She needed another coffee.

"Thank you." Roman's husky voice filled the usually silent, lonely kitchen.

Shay looked up to see Roman watching from his spot at the table, his golden eyes heavy with emotion. Shay knew he wasn't thanking her for cleaning up.

He drew a breath. "'Thank you' doesn't even begin to cover it—"

"It covers it just fine," she interrupted gently. "And you're welcome, Roman."

88

ROMAN'S HOUSE
YVESWICH, STATE OF KER

The house was alive with activity. There were so many new faces here, Loren found it a bit overwhelming to keep track of them all.

She sat at the kitchen table, sipping from a cup of velvety matcha, as the others finished eating breakfast all around her. A few of the slayers had to sit at the island or in the living room, not enough chairs for everyone at the table. Arthur insisted on eating in the living room, in an armchair that was far more comfortable for someone his age.

Loren could sense Darien watching her from where he sat at one end of the table, but she tried her best not to look at him, still not sure what to think of everything that happened last night. The new memories…and her fear that he was keeping things from her.

As if he could tell that she was thinking about him, Darien said, "If you need more painkillers, I can get them for you."

She stared straight ahead as she sipped her matcha. "I'm fine."

Darien only kept watching her. Still, she did not look at him.

Loren had been waiting all morning for an opportunity to talk to Dallas alone—to ask her sister questions about what *really* happened these last six months. But Dallas was avoiding her the same way Loren was avoiding Darien—never making eye contact, never speaking directly to her. It made this whole situation even worse, because Loren could feel more memories making their return. Bits and pieces of things filling in the gaps in her mind.

A memory of the one named Malakai Delaney pointing a gun at her and Darien under the crimson wash of a Blood Moon.

A different memory of his sister Jewels yelling at him in the House of Souls about a botched date, Dallas and the Devils standing around Loren.

The unexpected recollection of these events made her feel nauseous and off-balance, as if a tidal wave had slammed into her, ripping her off solid ground. Never mind that she felt alone, no one able to relate to what she was going through, nor were they able to explain things properly without knowing exactly *what* was missing in her mind and what wasn't.

The others had more to discuss this morning, so she mostly listened instead of spoke. During their time apart, Travis, Lace, and Jewels had gone with Sabrine and Logan to a place in Angelthene called Witchlight Alchemy and Archives, where Arthur, Roark, and Taega had told them they believed a new replica of the Arcanum Well was being created. And all replicas, Loren's biological father had ensured, would be cursed, a fact that made a replica of the ancient artifact something to fear.

"Why, though?" Ivy was saying as she grabbed Jack's plate and stacked it on top of her own. "It didn't work the first time. They wouldn't be that stupid, would they? To risk building another one? It's suicidal."

"And if they are, why bring it to Yveswich?" Max added. He sat beside Darien, Dallas in the chair on his left. "Makes no sense."

"Tamika had something interesting to say, actually," Travis said. It was the first thing he'd said all morning, his mind clearly occupied by his brothers who were still absent. He looked like he hadn't slept.

Darien cocked his head. "You went to see Tamika?"

"She was doing research on the Veil," Jewels said. "Her late dad was fascinated with the history of Spirit Terra, and she felt she owed it to him to pick up the research he never finished. She seemed particularly interested in the Void overlapping with Yveswich." She shared a glance with Travis.

"Overlapping?" Kylar asked. "Chew with your mouth shut," he hissed to Eugene before continuing, "The dimensions are on top of each other or something?"

Arthur spoke from the armchair in the living room. "Picture a color wheel." Heads turned to look at him. "Now picture the world of Terra being divided into different sections on that color wheel. There is a region in Spirit Terra called the Void, where dark magic reigns supreme. If you were to take that section and place it overtop a map of Terra, the coordinates would put the Void right on top of Yveswich."

"So basically, if the Veil falls, Yveswich is screwed," Jack said, "since the worst monsters are probably in there. Lucky us."

"Roark and Taega were pretty concerned about this, too," Lace added, "with, you know, the Well replica supposedly being here." She shuddered.

Jack chuckled. "A literal *bomb?* I'm concerned too."

"Yeah, but *why?*" Malakai cut in, lifting the tattooed arm that was slung across the back of Aspen's chair in question. The female Reaper was finishing off the last of her pancakes. "Bring it here to blow up Yveswich instead of Angelthene?" He scoffed. "Not very smart."

Something picked at Loren's brain. A memory.

She fidgeted.

Where he sat at the head of the table, arms crossed over his chest, Darien's mouth shifted into a thoughtful frown. "The Well only turns into a bomb if Loren's magic triggers it. If they don't have Loren, they can't turn it into a bomb. It's just a useless replica. So I highly doubt we need to worry about *that* right now."

Malakai persisted, "Okay, so they're doing all this shit for nothing? They can't use a replica to heal themselves or make a mortal immortal, and they can't force Loren to use it without turning it into a bomb. Why build it at all, then?"

"You're right," Jewels said, nibbling on her lip. "It doesn't add up."

"And," Tanner added as he clicked away on his laptop, "if they know what we know—that Yveswich and the Void overlap—they wouldn't want to risk blowing a hole in it, no?"

Tanner's comment was enough to slide the last puzzle piece in Loren's mind into place.

"I know what they're doing," she cut in.

Everyone fell quiet.

When Loren shut her eyes, the faces around her disappeared, and she saw the memory in her mind, clear as daylight...

With a deep breath, she faced ahead. Her feet slowed to dragging at the sight of the structure materializing out of the mist.

A massive tower—a pillar—pierced the sky. It looked just like the two framing the entrance into Spirit Terra, except bigger, larger than the Control Tower. It was made of the same black, glasslike material as the pillars under Angelthene, only this one was shot through with veins of oozing black instead of rainbow. There was no color here. No color at all.

Beyond that pillar was another Veil. An endless black wall that looked like undulating ink. The temperature here was so cold the ground was covered in frost, the plants glazed with ice that made them look like glass.

One of the men faced the imperator. "The Void, sir."

Loren wasn't sure why, but the statement made her blood run cold, her heart crackling, as if the same ice that coated the plants was spreading into her body. Her hand drifted toward the sensation in her chest—toward the amulet whose heat she could no longer feel.

"What's the Void?" she asked, that strange metallic tone of her voice carrying far. The desolate land whispered her words back to her with a series of echoes.

Quinton stepped up to the pillar. Tilted his head back, peering all the way up to the top. The peak of the pillar was lost in a brewing storm. Teal light glowed within that storm, the color outlining the short silver hairs on the imperator's head.

"What is the Void?" she said again.

There was movement beyond the Divide. A rippling of shadow.

Something was pacing on the other side of that wall.

Loren's boot scraped as she stepped closer, squinting her eyes to see, a frozen tree branch snapping under her foot. The closer she got to the pillar, the more hollowed out she felt. A wind carried her hair back, and her teeth buzzed in her mouth, eyes watering. If she felt this terrible when she was still several feet away from it, she feared getting closer.

The men surrounding her readied their guns, pointing them at the misty wall, eyes peering through crosshairs.

One of those men glanced at Quinton, tossing his head in the direction of the Divide. "Shucca," he said, voice hushed.

Loren stepped back. "What's a Shucca?"

The man smiled at her. "You'll do best to shut your eyes if you hear their howls, girl."

Erasmus was watching her, eyes wide with fear. "Are you c-certain this is where we should go, Loren?"

Loren shook her head. "I don't know, I— Can someone please tell me what the Void is? What are we looking at?"

"The V-void—," Erasmus began.

Quinton interrupted. "The Void is just another of the many sections in Spirit Terra." He faced her. "If this is where you say we will find the Well, then we need to lower this wall."

The memory vanished with the opening of her eyes.

"It's my fault," she said.

Darien uncrossed his arms and sat forward.

"I remember now," she whispered. "I didn't want to tell the imperator where the real Well is, so...I lied." She swallowed, her heart tripping a beat as she concluded, "I told them the Well was inside the Void."

When Roman walked through the front door of his house, Shay and Paxton at his side, he had the sense that he was interrupting something important.

The others were crowded around the kitchen table, either sitting or standing, Darien reaching for Loren as if to touch her.

Of course he didn't, opting to rest his fist on the table instead, torturing himself in good old-fashioned Darien style.

Loren was staring at her hands that were folded in her lap, her eyes downcast, bright blonde hair hanging in her face like a curtain.

Roman shut the door. "What'd I miss?"

Travis shot to his feet. "What did *you* miss?" Rage transformed his features, hands curling into fists at his sides. *"What did you miss?* What the *fuck* happened to your face?"

"Dad beat the shit out of me, Trav," Roman stated matter-of-factly. "Don't act surprised. Are we really going to argue about this right now, or are you guys going to tell me what the hell's going on and why you all look like you're afraid the planet's going to blow up?"

Malakai pushed out from the table and stood, picking up his and Aspen's plates as he went. "Way to hit the nail on the head, Devlin."

Roman blinked. "Okay—explain. Now."

"The Arcanum Well," Tanner began, his eyes bolted to his laptop, "is the only one of its kind. All replicas are cursed. It was a replica that blew up Angelthene on Kalendae. The imperator has created another replica and brought it to Yveswich. We need to find it and make sure he doesn't turn it into another bomb, or it'll cut through the Veil and...well, we're screwed if that happens."

"Why would someone *want* to blow through the Veil?" Shay asked.

"Because they believe the real Well is in Spirit Terra," Darien said. "In the Void, to be precise."

Roman said, "Okay, and what's the Void?"

Darien gestured to the living room—to the old man sitting in the armchair, reading the Daystar paper as if life as he knew it wasn't about to end. "Arthur can explain it better than me."

Arthur looked up. Folded the paper. "I'll get my color wheel." He heaved himself out of the chair and set the newspaper on the coffee table.

"Color wheel?" Roman and Shay blurted in unison.

Darien merely said, "It'll make more sense when he starts explaining."

"You might want to have a seat," Tanner advised without looking up from his screen. "It'll probably take a while, but as soon as we're done, we should go to Silverway." His eyes flicked up to Darien, who stared at him in question. "I have an idea."

All this shit about color wheels and Spirit Terra was enough to make Roman's head spin.

Now that Arthur was finished with his explanation, Roman was out front of the house, having a smoke by the garage while he waited for the others to get out here. They would be heading to Caliginous on Silverway so Tanner could plant a bug in the security system—one that would give him view of the areas in the building where cameras didn't cover. The plan was to not just catch Gaven and the imperator, their men included, but to see what they were doing at Caliginous—if there was a reason they were going there that didn't involve the same reasons Roman and countless other hellsehers went. For appointments to relieve their Surges.

The front door opened, and voices drifted out. The others began to file to the vehicles that were parked in the driveway, figuring out who was going with who, etcetera. Arthur and Kylar would be staying behind with Paxton and Eugene, but everyone else would be going. Darien and Loren were the only ones who weren't out here yet.

Travis had just determined that he'd ride with Jewels on his bike when he turned on a heel and started heading Roman's way.

"Fuck," Roman muttered, the hand that was tucked in his jacket pocket tightening into a fist.

"Did you just swear under your breath?" Travis accused. When Roman didn't answer, Travis said, "Stop giving me that look."

"What look?" Roman flexed his jaw.

Travis paused several feet from him, shifting his hands into the pockets of his jeans. "Like I'm not supposed to be here."

"You're not," Roman bit out, taking another drag. "The fucking agreement, Travis," —he blew a stream of smoke at the sky— "was that you wouldn't come back here."

Travis winced. "I haven't seen you in years, and the only thing you're capable of talking to me about is how I shouldn't be here?"

Roman stared out at the gates. Paxton lingered near Shay, who stood near Roman's car—listening. Both of them were listening, Roman could tell. In a world of immortals, privacy was hard to come by.

"Roman?" Travis prodded. His steel eyes were scanning the bruises on

Roman's face, only partially obscured by the shadows beneath his hood. "You never told me it was this bad," he said quietly.

"You didn't need to know," Roman snapped.

"I'm your brother. I *should* know—"

"Travis—" He took one last drag and flicked the cigarette aside. The sky started spitting rain, fat drops drumming on his hood and speckling the pavement. "This—" he waved a hand at his own face "—is precisely the reason why I got you the fuck out of Yveswich. So that *this*—" he waved again "—would not be you. Is it so hard to understand why I'm pissed?"

"Go ahead and be pissed, then, but I'm not leaving," Travis said. "And I'm not going to let *that*—" it was Travis's turn to wave "—happen anymore."

Roman couldn't find words in the heat of his rage. Since Travis had left the city, and Roman had cut all ties between them, he'd wanted nothing more than to have a relationship with Travis again. *One day,* he'd always told himself. *One day,* when Don was dead in the cold ground.

Travis had come back too soon. Travis, the one brother he'd saved, had come back too fucking soon. And Roman knew, the minute Don found out his middle child was back, in the city he'd abandoned...

Black pushed at his eyes, and he squeezed both hands into fists.

"You're worried," Travis said. "And I get it. I'm worried, too—I admit it. But I'm not a teenager anymore, Roman—"

"It doesn't matter how fucking old you are, Travis!" Roman barked. "I'm twenty-seven years old, and I couldn't beat Dad in a fight if my life depended on it!" His voice ripped through the yard, silencing the conversations of the others who stood by the vehicles. "And it fucking has," Roman continued, breathing heavily, working to lower his voice and failing. "But, by some grace—or curse—of the gods he hasn't killed me yet. *Yet,*" he enunciated, nostrils flaring. There had been several close calls, most of them in the last twelve months. Paxton was Roman's only tether back to life, the thought of his brother being alone in the House of Black keeping his heart beating day after day.

It was either that, or the gods were punishing him. Giving him a personal hell right here in Terra before he went to the next after death.

Darien came out of the house, then. He thumped down the front steps, keys in hand, Loren trailing behind him. She pulled up the hood of her white jacket, her full lips moving with a question Darien answered with equal quiet.

Travis's throat worked with a swallow. "I'm not leaving, Roman. And he," Travis said, pointing now at Darien with a hand that slightly trembled, "is not leaving, either." Fuck, they'd talked—clearly.

As if his name had been called, Darien glanced their way.

"This isn't his war to fight," Roman said, tearing his eyes off Darien, but speaking loudly enough for his cousin to hear, too. He wouldn't drag any more people into this than the ones who *had* to be in it—himself, that was it. What he preferred. No Travis, no Darien—and as soon as Pax was old enough, Roman would throw him the hell out of this city, too.

"You're right—it's not," Travis said. "But you have people who care about you. People who are really fucking pissed that you watered down how bad it was over here. I'm going to let Darien talk to you himself, and you can go ahead and try to convince him not to help and see if you win. But you're not winning with me—not this time. I'm here to stay."

With a steadying breath, Roman stalked up to Travis, who'd grown nearly to his height. Ignoring the many faces watching their exchange, he growled, "Then I guess I'll have to bury my brother, after all, won't I?"

He walked past Travis before he could reply—and before he could feel the weight of his words in the colors of Travis's aura. He knew this wasn't what Travis had expected to come home to, but Roman hadn't expected him to come home at all. He was an adult, and he could make his own decisions, but Roman feared he was choosing wrong.

And feared he'd literally have to watch his own brother be killed right before his eyes. In Yveswich, a Darkslayer abandoning his house was a crime that demanded punishment. And now that Travis was back on Yveswich soil, a Devil walking a zone that didn't belong to him, Don had free rein to enact that punishment any way he wanted.

And Roman knew he'd aim exactly where it would hurt the most: at Roman.

89

CALIGINOUS ON SILVERWAY
YVESWICH, STATE OF KER

Loren watched the droplets of water zigzag through the air above her head, the chamber at Caliginous on Silverway whirring around her. She breathed in deeply, her lungs filling with the scent of citrus and rain.

Her treatment was timed for twenty minutes. Already, she felt better than she had last night, her heartbeat steady and strong, her mind clear.

She was in here by herself this time. Dallas, Ivy, and Shay were out in the hall, peeking in at her every once in a while. The others who'd decided to come with were elsewhere, helping Tanner carry out his plan in whatever way they could, whether it was distracting Tanya or keeping watch down on the street in case anyone of interest showed up.

After Caliginous had been closed a few days ago with zero explanation as to why, and after Darien had recognized several of the imperator's men coming up here, Tanner thought it was worthwhile to investigate—to find out if there was a potential connection between Caliginous on Silverway and the imperator's plan, whatever it was.

The others had insisted it wasn't her fault. That she couldn't have known the imperator would be so daring as to cut a new doorway into the Veil. But she couldn't help but feel responsible. She had given them reason to want to get into the Void—the most deadly and terrifying place imaginable. And if they succeeded...if another doorway was opened, and Death and his demons were free to enter their world...

She focused on her breathing. Inhale... Exhale...

The session ended, and the chamber shut off with a rolling shudder.

Loren sat up and tugged off the white leather gloves. She turned her left hand palm-up, studying the tattoo in the center of it.

She might have been imagining it, but she swore she didn't feel quite as replenished as she did when Darien came in here with her.

Loren sighed and swung her legs over the side of the tabletop. It was probably her imagination—the crush that kept her from wanting to be away from him.

She needed to talk to him. Hopefully tonight.

"So you were sick that day?" Darien said, his arms folded on Tanya's desk. "That's why you were closed?"

She hung up the phone with a heavy sigh. He'd started hounding with her questions the minute she'd said goodbye to the client on the other end of the call, not giving her a chance to put the phone on the receiver first. "Yes. I took a sick day. Do Darkslayers not have sick days?" She typed on her keyboard.

"Hellsehers don't typically get sick. Neither do veneficae." Not unless it was the Tricking. Colds and flus were a mortal thing.

Her manicured fingers froze on the keys. "I had a few drinks the night before," she said, her silver-ringed eyes downcast. She started typing again. "I was hungover."

Darien grunted. He threw a glance at the corridor that led to Chamber Number Five. Loren's treatment ended two minutes ago. Behind him, Roman paced in the waiting area, phone glued to his ear. Travis and Jack sat across from each other, tossing something between them. They were the only people in here, the other clients having checked out before Tanya took the last call. Atlas was still gone—and luckily, Tanya hadn't noticed he'd disappeared.

Suddenly, she shot to her feet. "Hey!" she exclaimed.

Travis and Jack froze, the latter catching the pink blur of an object in a hand he held palm-up in his lap.

"Is that my stress ball?" Tanya fumed.

Jack held it up. "Is that what this is?" He squeezed it, making it flex. "I need to get me one of these." He tossed it up so high, it hit the ceiling.

Tanya pushed her swivel chair aside. "Alright, that's it—give it back."

A door opened, and Darien turned to the sound of female voices. One in particular—the sweetest voice he'd ever had the pleasure of hearing.

Loren was coming out of the corridor to Chamber Number Five, Ivy, Dallas, and Shay with her. Loren's eyes found his...

And immediately darted away.

Fuck, he needed to talk to her.

Jack whipped Tanya's stress ball at the desk. The squishy pink orb struck a bottle of essential oil and knocked it over.

"Whoops," Jack chuckled.

"I *need*," Tanya gritted out, her face red with anger as she leaned across the desk to stand the glass bottle back up, "you guys to leave."

Another door in the room—this one by the elevators—opened, and Tanner walked out.

"What is he doing?" Tanya blurted. "What were you doing?" She glared at Tanner as she snatched up the stress ball, squeezing it tight.

Tanner shut the door. "Using the washroom."

"That's the maintenance room!"

Tanner glanced at the door he'd just shut. "It is?" Darien bit the inside of his cheek to keep from laughing.

Tanya, tiny but fierce, rounded the desk, stilettos tapping. "What were you doing in there?"

"I got lost."

She crossed her arms, the coil of keys on the left jingling. "Tanner Atlas, one of the smartest people in Terra, can't read a sign that very clearly says *Maintenance Room?*"

Silence.

Jack wheezed a laugh.

Tanya exploded. "That's it! I've had it. You guys need to leave. Now!" She thrust an arm out, pointing at the elevators.

"Tanya," Roman tried as he got off the phone.

"Don't 'Tanya' me!" she shrieked. "This is where I draw the line. You all need to go, or you're going to get me fired."

"Tanya, just a sec—" Roman tried again.

"Out!" She waved her hands in a 'shoo' motion. "Now! Unless you want me to ban you—for *life*, Roman. Get out!"

Darien picked up on the faint whistling of sirens. Quickly, he crossed the room, bypassing a glaring Tanya, and looked out the wall of windows at the street far below.

Fire trucks and ambulances were speeding by. And in the distance, there was smoke, plumes as black as soot ballooning out toward the heavens.

Darien made for the elevators, boots pounding loudly on the polished floors. "Let's go—now."

The others hurried after him, asking questions he didn't answer.

Tanya breathed a sigh of relief and muttered, "Finally."

THE ELEVATOR RIDE felt like it took a million years.

As soon as the doors opened, Darien sprinted through them, where he met Max, Malakai, Aspen, and Lace out front.

"We need to head to that fire," Darien said.

"Which one?" Max asked. "And why?"

Shit. There was so much to fill each other in on, Darien had completely forgotten about his theory that Maya had something to do with these attacks.

Wait—Max had asked *which one*.

He scanned the area. The smoke was coming from two separate sides of the city—two different fires.

They would need to split up.

"The imperator's men are turning up dead," Darien said, the words rushing together. "And I think Elementals are behind it."

Max's face went white. "Maya?"

"You take that one," Darien said to Max, pointing south. "I'll take the other." He spun around, his eyes finding Loren's. "Loren—with me. Roman, Tanner—you too. Let's go."

They split up, Darien taking his car. Loren squeezed into the back seat with Tanner, ignoring Roman about how she should take the front.

And then they were off.

WHEN THEY GOT to the burning building—another hotel with a conference room on the ground floor—Darien and Roman split up while Tanner stayed in the car with Loren. Darien planned on meeting Roman from opposite ends of the corridor where the attack happened, hopefully cornering any of the imperator's men—or Elementals—who might still be in the area.

Darien sprinted up the stairwell now, through the thick smoke choking the interior, eyes black with the Sight.

He had almost reached the thirty-eighth floor when a blur ran right into him, crashing into him so hard he was knocked off balance.

A shout of surprise—female—echoed in the stairwell.

Gravity sucked him into his grip, too quickly for him to stop it, to reach out and grab the railing.

He fell backward down the stairs, the female falling with him—

They smashed into the landing a floor down, the girl on top of him.

Darien looked up through the smoke to see a young woman with red hair pushing up off his chest.

She pulled a knife on him.

He grabbed her wrist, twisting it.

A cry of pain shot through the stairwell. The knife clattered to the carpet.

Through the swirling smoke, he saw eyes light up like embers. Saw the red hair that tumbled over the girl's shoulders start to glow—

And then her whole body transformed into flame. Literal flame, no flesh, her form glowing so brightly she was almost blinding.

"Maya?"

She froze. The flames cooled. And through the smoke, he recognized her—the girl who used to play catch with him when they were kids. The girl who got bubblegum stuck in her hair one summer, and Darien had to cut it out.

"Maya?" he said again, his question a whisper now instead of a shout. "It's me. It's—"

"Darien?" The inquiry was a choked sob.

A door banged open several flights below.

Maya got up and bolted—throwing herself through the narrow window on the landing, glass smashing.

Darien shot to his feet and ran to that window, catching himself against the frame as he stared out at the rain-drenched street far below.

There was no sign of her.

Detectives and cops were coming up the stairs. The same goof who'd arrested Darien caught sight of him.

"What's he doing here?" the detective thundered. "He's hindering the investigation!" he shouted at no one. He whirled on Darien. Pulled a gun on him. *"What the hell are you doing here?"*

Darien jumped through the window. Wind whipped past him, catching in his open jacket like a sail.

He landed on his feet with jarring force, knees bending to absorb the impact. He straightened. Looked both ways, searching for Maya.

No fucking trace of her.

Voices shouted from the floors above. One was Finn's.

Darien bolted. Around the building. Still no sign of Maya, but—

There was a black car parked by a side door that led into the hotel's restaurant, back doors open.

Filing into the car were three faces he recognized—two of Gaven's men, the third the imperator's.

Darien took off after them.

The last one to get in the car spotted him. Swore under his breath as he ducked inside. "Drive!" the man bellowed. *"Go!"*

Tires screeched, and the driver took off, nearly hitting pedestrians who screamed and scattered.

Cops came up behind Darien, running after him on foot.

"Freeze!" one of them shouted.

Another said, "Put your hands in the air!"

Darien sent a wave of magic behind him, knocking the cops and detectives off their feet—just enough to slow them down.

The black car had pulled over by the hotel entrance up ahead. The back door swung open, a fourth man hurrying toward it, briefcase in hand.

Darien bolted, eating up the distance between him and the car in several powerful strides.

He skidded to a stop beside the still-open door, hand lashing out to grab the hellseher inside—

He saw it coming half a second too late.

The door slammed shut—shattering the bones in his fucking hand.

White-hot, searing pain exploded through bone and muscle, fragmenting his vision— *"MOTHERFUCKER!"*

Through the white wash of his surroundings, and the blood roaring in his head, Darien barely saw the car speed away. Barely heard the screech of tires over the high-pitched ringing in his ears, the labored inhales and exhales sawing through his tight, aching lungs.

He doubled over, right there on the sidewalk, cradling his hand to his chest. Nausea eddied and swelled in his gut. He retched. Almost threw up—

Roman rushed up to him, gold eyes lit with alarm. "Darien?"

"Fuck, *FUCK!*" The pain was agonizing. Debilitating. Blistering, *burning* as if he'd thrust his hand into an open flame— *"FLIP THE CAR, ROMAN!"* he managed to bellow.

"Which one—"

"The black car—*FLIP IT!*"

With a strike of his arm, as if he were throwing something, Roman's magic barreled down the street, the force of it shattering street lights and fire hydrants.

It slammed into the black car.

And sent it spinning through the air.

90

THE FINANCIAL DISTRICT
YVESWICH, STATE OF KER

Roman could not begin to imagine the pain his cousin was going through. To have your bones shattered was excruciating, no matter how it was done, but when magic was involved?

Gods, he felt sick just thinking about it. It was the kind of splitting, burning pain that would have brought a lesser man to his knees.

But somehow, Darien stayed on his feet and kept his head up as he walked at Roman's side, holding his broken right hand against his chest—keeping it slightly above heart level to help with the swelling and pain. The slight tremor in Darien's breaths was the only indication that he was suffering.

Up ahead, the black car Darien had told Roman to flip lay on its roof in the middle of the street, haloed with shattered glass and a spray of blood. Cars had pulled over, the drivers, passengers, and few pedestrians on the sidewalk staring. They only had a few minutes before the cops would be over here.

The longer they walked, the more irregular Darien's breathing became, the more frequently he doubled up before steeling himself and resuming his determined pace.

"You okay?" Roman asked him quietly.

"Fine," Darien replied, but the word was coated in agony, and beads of sweat dotted his face, his skin pallid.

They stopped beside the car, and Roman got down beside Darien as he crouched to look inside.

All the men were dead—no one they could take in for questioning.

Darien banged his good hand against the car. "Fuck."

Loren knew something was wrong the minute she caught sight of Darien and Roman heading this way, the former cradling his hand against his chest.

Where she sat in the back seat of Darien's car, Tanner beside her, she straightened, the hacker uttering a low oath she seldom heard on his lips as he did the same.

Darien and Roman had just made it to the car when the same warlock detective who was at the last crime scene approached, stopping them. They were close enough for Loren to hear their conversation.

"What the *hell* are you doing?" the detective fumed. Loren remembered Darien calling him 'Finn Solace'. "You're going to get me in trouble—"

"You're the one who asked me to help you," Darien cut in. "And I am *done*. I'm not your grunt."

"You saw who did it, didn't you?" Finn persisted, making the mistake of following as Darien and Roman made for the car. "Cassel, if you withhold information—"

"What?" Darien barked, rounding on a heel and getting up in Finn's face. "You'll *what*, Finn?" The detective's throat bobbed. "Stay away from me and my family. No more favors, no more working together—that's it." He cut his gaze to a different detective—the one who'd arrested him and Jack—storming through the front doors of the conference center. "And keep that motherfucker away from me, or I'll kill you both." The threat sent a chill down Loren's spine.

Darien got in the car, Roman taking the driver's seat this time. The Devil didn't say anything as he doubled up in his seat from the pain of the hand Loren realized was broken, except one word: *Drive.*

The spells on the car had wrecked Darien's hand so thoroughly that Arthur had to set quite a few of the broken bones using a process called open reduction, where he made incisions in the skin so he could insert pins and plates.

From the sound of Darien's muffled screams slicing through the house, the pain was unbearable. Excruciating.

Loren paced in the living room, eyes stinging, her throat too tight to swallow. Ivy sat on the couch beside Jack, her hand squeezing her husband's in a death grip. For once, Jack had no jokes to crack, his expression more solemn than ever. Kylar and Tanner stood in the kitchen, silent and stiff as boards. Roman was out front, having a smoke, he'd said. He hadn't even come inside. And as for the rest of them who'd gone with to Caliginous on Silverway, they had yet to make it back.

An Angel of Death named Dominic Valencia and a girl named Blue were here now. Let into the house by Arthur while the rest of them were at Caliginous. They stood together on the back deck, Blue unable to stomach the sound of Darien's pain.

Loren could hardly stomach it either, muffled as it was. He was likely biting into something—wood or leather. Had magic not been involved in the breaking of his hand, the consequences for a hellseher wouldn't have been nearly this bad—and neither would the pain, the others had told her. When magic was involved, bolts of it were left behind in the fractures, so when the bones were reset, the magic was released, forcing the victim to relive the pain a second time. Tenfold.

Nearly fifteen minutes of utter quiet passed. No one spoke or breathed too loudly, not even Jack. No further sounds came from the room Darien and Arthur were in—no bloodcurdling screams, no hoarse shouting, no cursing.

Eventually, Loren heard the quiet mumble of conversation.

And then the door clicked open, and Arthur walked out.

Darien came down the hall behind him, cradling his wrapped hand against his chest. He looked pale, and there were beads of sweat on his face.

"Someone," Arthur began, looking a little pale too, "needs to drive Darien to the hospital."

"I can drive myself," he mumbled, for once not bothering to fix the strands of hair hanging in his face.

"I'll drive him," Tanner offered. "Are we going to see a Healer?"

"Yes," Arthur said before Darien could argue, his tone resolute. The old man shot Darien a stern look. "If he doesn't get a Healer to look at it, he could be living with this for at least a month. A Healer's touch can lessen the recovery time by half."

Tanner was already moving—grabbing the car keys off the table. "Let's go, then."

But Darien didn't budge. And when Loren lifted her eyes to his face, she found that he was already staring at her.

Ivy extracted her hand from her husband's and sat forward. "The imperator already knows we're here," she said softly. "It doesn't matter anymore if anyone sees you. You need medical attention, Darien."

The whole time his sister spoke, Darien didn't take his focus off Loren, though his face was lined with so much suffering, he looked like he might faint. "You'll be okay while I'm gone, or do you want to come with?" he asked her, the words thick with agony.

"Darien," she said gently, his concern for her warming her heart, "I think the only person you should be worrying about right now is yourself."

"I'll always worry about you." His words caused a memory to slam into her so hard, the room spun—

Loren didn't speak until the parking lot of Angelthene Academy came into view.

"How very kind of you to think this through before you led me on like you did," she said, her words thick and wobbling. She turned her head to look at him, tears flooding her eyes. "I don't suppose I get any say in this, do I? You're the one making all the decisions about us, as if what I want doesn't matter—"

"This is your life, Loren!" Darien shouted so loudly, he startled her. She blinked in surprise, a warm tear slipping down her cheek. "Forgive me for trying to protect you. I will protect you from anything—even from myself. Always."

She jerked back to the present, eyelids fluttering.

Darien was staring at her. *Everyone* was staring at her.

The leader of the Devils stepped toward her.

"Go," she bit out. "Deal with that," she gestured to his broken hand, "and we'll talk when you get back." She didn't mean to make it sound like a threat, but it did, even to her own ears.

But it was too late to take it back, too late to say anything else.

Because Darien was walking away, swallowing repeatedly, as if he was going to be sick. Gods, the pain he must be in.

Ivy stood. "Do you need help getting your jacket on, Darien?" she called, following them into the foyer.

"I'll be fine like this." Darien's reply was coated in so much pain, the words were hardly comprehensible—and that black long-sleeve was hardly warm enough in a city like this, but no one argued.

He and Tanner left, and Loren went upstairs to lock herself in her room, where she could mull things over without anyone watching.

She walked back and forth, trying desperately to remember, Singer peering at her from where he was curled up in a misty ball on the neatly made bed.

Everything—she wanted to remember everything, not just pieces.

Darien might not be in good condition to talk about this right now, but she was tired of waiting, wondering. It was clear that they had a history together—more than anyone was letting on, and she had no idea why.

As soon as he came back, she would confront him and find out the truth.

Maximus pulled up to the gates to Roman's house in time to see Darien and Tanner walking out the front doors. Roman sat on the edge of the big fountain out front of the house, elbows on his knees, cigarette burning in hand. Max nodded at him in greeting as he drove by, but Roman did not return the gesture.

Dread curled in Max's gut.

"Did something happen?" Shay wondered aloud. She was in the back with Lacey, Dallas in the front with Max. He knew she was mostly speaking to herself and not really expecting an answer. They hadn't spoken to any of the others yet, so no one could know what'd happened.

As Max stopped the SUV—a brand new black one he'd bought before leaving Angelthene, his other too wrecked to fix—his attention snagged on the bandaged hand Darien held against his chest.

What the hell?

He cut the engine and got out, Dallas, Lace, and Shay following.

"What happened?" Max asked the moment he was out. The slam of his door was echoed by three others.

"He ran into some of the imperator's men at the fire," Tanner replied. "He went after them and got his hand caught in a car door."

Max's face leached of blood. "Shit."

Darien managed to choke out, "I found Maya."

This time, Max actually swayed. "What?" he whispered. The fire he'd gone to had yielded nothing of interest, but the other...

Max's must have been a decoy. If he'd gone to the other one...if Darien had sent him to that one instead of going himself... Fuck, for one, Darien's hand wouldn't be broken. And two...

Max would've got Maya back. Would've seen his sister again.

"It was her," Darien said, forcing a swallow. "She ran, though. I couldn't catch her." He winced, nearly doubling over. "I need to get to the hospital."

The street beyond the gates rumbled with a motorcycle's approach. A moment later, Malakai pulled in, Aspen on the bike with him. That made Jewels and Travis the only people who weren't back yet.

As Darien and Tanner made for Darien's car, the front door to Roman's house opened, and Dominic appeared, Blue at his side.

"Oh my god," Shay exclaimed, gravel crunching under her feet as she approached the front steps, her green eyes fixed on Blue.

Blue shrank under the scrutiny, the eyes of the Angel at her side flicking warily between Blue and Shay.

Behind Max, further down the driveway, Roman got to his feet.

And the Shadowmaster began walking over, gravel crunching under his swift boots, the minute Shay choked out, "You're that girl."

ROMAN GLANCED between the blue-haired girl tucked against the Angel's side...

And Shay, who had never looked more terrified and confused.

When he'd made it back to the house, he'd opted to stay outside and smoke, where he couldn't hear the sound of Darien screaming. Call him weak, but his own night had been so awful, he couldn't stomach any more suffering, especially not when the person suffering was someone he cared very much about. And because he'd opted to stay out here, he hadn't yet been introduced to the Head of Death's Landing—Dominic Valencia—and his blue-haired tagalong.

So he'd had no idea. No idea that the girl the cops were looking for was right here in his own house. No chance to prepare Shay or find out what in the hell was going on.

"You're that girl," Shay repeated, the yard silent. No one spoke, though a few glanced at each other in confusion. Even Darien and Tanner were lingering, car doors open—waiting to see how this would unfold. "You're wanted—you...I've seen you on TV."

The Angel wound an arm around the waist of the blue girl. Everything about her was blue—eyes, hair. Even her nail beds. "Everything they've said about her is a lie," said Dominic Valencia. He spoke calmly, but Roman recognized the warning in his eyes and the twitch of his wings. "She's not dangerous, I promise."

The blue one was the next to speak, those electric-blue eyes glued to Shayla. "Anna?" The inquiry was hushed. Timid.

Roman heard Shay's heart stop. Stumble. Hells, Roman's stopped too.

The blue girl edged around the Angel. "Are you…Anna's sister?" she ventured, every word lilted with a thick accent Roman couldn't pinpoint.

"Yes," Shay choked out, her body visibly trembling. "Yes, I am." She took a step. "Do you know where she is? Is she okay?" Silence. "Where can I find her?" Her next step brought her closer to Roman—so close, he could feel the sheer agony and pure, desperate hope ripping through her.

This was going to hurt real fucking badly.

"Please." Shay's voice turned thick and wobbling. "Please—I've been looking all over for her. Please, can you help me find her? I'm so worried about her. I just want to bring her home—please."

"She was there," the blue one whispered. "At the motel."

"Yes," Shay urged, the word cracking like glass. Roman's heart cracked with it. "Yes, that's right—she was at the motel. Where did they take her? Where is she?" Shay's lip wobbled, and tears began to fall.

The sight of her in pain was a knife to Roman's gut.

"I'm so sorry," the blue girl whispered, her own eyes filling with tears.

Roman felt Shay's reaction as intensely as if it were his own. Felt her heart splinter into too many pieces to count.

Roman stepped toward her. "Shay—"

Shay turned and bolted down the driveway.

"Shay!" Roman took off after her, gravel shooting under his heels. "SHAYLA!" he screamed, her name ripping his throat apart.

She rounded the fountain—

And literally disappeared.

Roman cursed but kept running. Shouting her name. *"Shayla!"* He thumped to a stop by the wrought-iron gates that were still closed, the magic having not picked up on her illusion. "SHAYLA!" His head swiveled, eyes wild as he looked for her, breaths raking through clenched teeth. "SHAYLAAAAA!"

But she was gone.

And when she'd fled, she had not bothered to look back.

91

YVESWICH GENERAL HOSPITAL
YVESWICH, STATE OF KER

Going to see a Healer was quite possibly the best advice Arthur had ever given Darien.

He sat in a chair in a private room on the third floor of Yveswich General Hospital, his hand cradled in the careful touch of the young brunette Healer kneeling at his feet. Tanner was keeping watch out in the waiting area—and probably playing that retro frog game again, if Darien knew Atlas at all. They'd left for the hospital shortly after Shay had learned that her sister was dead—and had sprinted off Roman's property too quickly for anyone to stop her. Darien and Tanner had stuck around long enough for Roman to fill them in, telling them that he'd gone with Shay out to the desert to search for Anna Cousens, who, as it turned out, had been at Motel 58 with Blue and the same men who'd turned up dead in Angelthene.

Small fucking world. Small, bizarre fucking world.

Roman would be going after Shay soon enough, Darien knew. It was what Darien would do if it were Loren who'd ran, Loren who'd needed comfort. Roman could lie through his teeth all he wanted, but Darien could tell that he'd fallen really hard for that girl.

Darien stared at the clock on the wall, listening to it tick away. They were halfway through the procedure. The Healer had taken the bandages off his hand, needing skin on skin contact for the magic to flow properly from her aura into his. The gray mat she knelt upon was covered in runes that glowed all different colors, the magic emitting a hum that reminded Darien of hornets.

"How are you feeling?" the Healer asked him as she gently tipped his hand, using her nails to apply pressure to the tips of his fingers. It was a bit like acupuncture, but without the needles. And far more enjoyable.

"Way better," Darien said. "What's the mat for?"

"It helps me draw energy up from the anima mundi. The higher the floor we're on, the harder the magic needs to work to travel. If we were on the ground floor, I wouldn't need to use a mat." She tilted his hand the other way, the movement causing her wedding ring to catch the fluorescents, the diamond winking like a small star.

"Did you pick that ring out yourself, or did your husband choose?"

She smiled up at him. "I dragged him to a few jewelry stores before he proposed. Gave him an idea of the style I liked." She rubbed her thumb up his palm, little ripples of warmth curling lazily through his hand. He almost groaned with pleasure. This was heaven compared to the setting of his bones. The pins and plates Arthur had inserted had already been dissolved by magic, no longer necessary now that his healing process had been sped along. Having Arthur set his bones beforehand had saved Darien from spending extra time here in the hospital, though the process had been painful as hell without morphine. "The rest," the Healer concluded, "he did himself."

"Is there a name for that style?"

"It's just a round-cut diamond." She rubbed the muscle in his thumb with the tip of her own. The firmer pressure caused Darien to tense, a bolt of splintering pain zipping up to his wrist. "Sorry," she said. Her eyes flicked up to his, filled with apology. "We're almost done. There must have been a spark of magic left in that spot."

He drew a steadying breath through his nose. "It's fine."

"Do you have a lady you're thinking of proposing to?"

"It's crossed my mind. I saw your ring and thought the style would suit her." He'd done a lot of thinking—fantasizing, really—about engagement rings after finding his mother's in Blackgate Manor, but he didn't know the first thing about proposing, and there were so many cuts of diamond, it was ridiculous. How was he supposed to know what to choose?

"I would take her to a few jewellers," the Healer advised. "Or, if you want to surprise her, maybe see if her friends can find out what she likes." She let go of his hand and got to her feet. "Wait right there."

As she rummaged through drawers and cupboards on the other side of the room, Darien turned his hand palm-up, studying it. Then turned it the other way, examining the other side.

It already looked way better, the bruising and swelling all but gone.

The Healer returned with what looked like a compression glove. "Give me your hand, please."

He extended it to her, and she carefully tugged the glove onto his hand, shimmying it down and securing the velcro strap around his wrist. The glove was black, the stretchy material ending just beyond his major knuckles.

She stepped back, and Darien held his hand up to take a look, resisting the urge to form a fist to test the glove's flexibility. Fuck, not making a fist was going to be a challenge.

"Can I punch someone if I'm wearing this?"

The Healer frowned. "What kind of question is that?"

"The wrong one, apparently." He sighed, lowering his hand to rest it in his lap. "How long until it's fully healed?"

"For a hellseher? I'd say two weeks. Three, worst case scenario." She eyed him. "If you punch someone, it'll definitely take three. Maybe four."

He grunted in irritation.

"I'm assuming this is a problem because you're a Darkslayer?"

Darien didn't say anything.

"Use your left as often as possible. Try not to bend your fingers more than you need to. The worse breaks are lower down, in this area—" She demonstrated on her own hand. That explained why she'd opted for a glove that didn't cover his fingers. "If you need to use a firearm, a basic handgun is your best option. A knife works too. Anything that requires two hands is going to be a challenge for you until the fractures are fully healed." That sucked.

"I got one more question," he said. "Can you do anything for a patient who suffers from amnesia?"

She blinked at the turn in conversation. "Full or partial?"

"Partial."

She grimaced. "Ooh, that's a tough one. Full is easier than partial because we know all memories are missing, so we can fill them in fairly quickly with little risk. If it's partial, the process can take longer."

"How long?"

"Weeks, at best. Worst-case scenario would be months, and in rare cases, years. There are other risks involved, too, such as overwriting memories that are perfectly fine and intact. It can cause serious damage to the patient's brain—can kind of scramble it in a sense. So we need to be very careful with partial cases." She studied him. "Who has amnesia?"

"My girlfriend." He got to his feet. "Thank you."

"You're welcome." As he made for the door, she called, "And good luck."

Darien didn't know if she was talking about his hand, the amnesia, or the conversation they'd had about proposing. He didn't bother asking her to clarify.

ROMAN DESPERATELY WANTED to go after Shay, but he also knew she wanted space. She'd made that very obvious the minute she'd used illusion to stop him from following her.

About an hour had passed since then—since Shay had bolted, and Darien and Tanner had left for the hospital. Roman and Kylar stood in the kitchen with Dominic and Blue, the former explaining the origins of his blue-haired friend. How the Devils' paths had wound up crossing with Blue's, where she'd come from, how her magic worked. She was known as a Blue Elemental—someone who possessed the magic of the Mist. Someone who Max, Lacey, and Tanner had picked up one night after finding her standing in the middle of the road with a tracking device in her arm. A device she'd cut out.

This shit explained so much about the Facility. About what little Roman and Shay had learned from Doctor Rowe before he'd been gutted by that monster from Spirit Terra.

About what happened to Anna Cousens.

"I believe you, too, are an Elemental," Arthur said to Roman. "Kylar as well." The old man sat at the island, sipping a cup of black tea. Aspen and Malakai were in here too, sifting through the cupboards and fridge and bickering about whether to cook something for dinner or order takeout. It was getting to be that time already.

And if Shay didn't come back, she'd be spending tonight alone.

Roman blinked. Forced himself to breathe. "What do you mean?" he asked Arthur. "How can we be Elementals when we weren't...modified?" Blue'd had her magic honed in the Facility—the same way as the other Elementals, all of them named after the color of their magic—their auras.

"You can bend shadows, yes?" Arthur asked, eyes flicking between Roman and Ky.

"Yeah, but we can't summon them out of nothing," Roman said. Not like Blue could summon water—literally out of thin air. Roman had seen it with his own eyes only a few minutes ago—watched her demonstrate, a snake of water twirling up her wrist and threading through her fingers, her eyes glowing the brightest blue. There were a few hellsehers who could bend the elements the way Roman and the other Shadowmasters could bend shadows, but they'd never been given a specific title before—never been called *Elementals*.

"I believe you are an Elemental, but your powers are on a slightly smaller scale," Arthur said. "And I believe Blue was just like you two, once, except with the ability to bend water instead of shadow." Bend water, but not summon it.

"He's probably right," Dominic offered. "Blue didn't spend her whole life in the Facility, but she began going there as a child—back when she was too young to understand what was happening or have the ability to say no. Long story short, she wound up living there when she was in her teens, and the people who ran the Facility worked on her mind over the course of many years. Making her forget everything. Even her own name." He scowled in disgust.

"Shit." Roman's eyes flicked to Blue. "I'm sorry."

"I've been remembering, slowly," she replied, every word coated in an accent Roman now knew was Ilevyn. "I remember that my parents were murdered the last time they brought me there, when I was a teenager. Killing them was how the people in the Facility were able to keep me." She swallowed, a haunted look in her eyes. "And stop...having to pay them." Selling your child—deplorable. Apparently, the same damn thing had happened to Max's sister, Maya Reacher. Sold by her mother when the wrong people had discovered she had fire magic. People who wanted to use her for their own gain, essentially torturing her in the Facility.

"Was your hair always blue?" Kylar asked, bending to lean his elbows on the counter, his long fingers wrapped around a glass of whiskey. "Or was that some sort of side effect to the shit they were doing to you?"

Blue looked to Dominic for the answer.

"Side effect," the Angel said. "The eyes, the hair, the nails—all the result of modification."

"Your eyes," Kylar said, speaking to Roman now. "Your eyes always go dark when you're using your magic."

"In a different way than the Sight?" Aspen asked.

"Yeah, the gold in his eyes goes dark."

"My hair, too," Roman said, raking a hand through it.

"I also believe," Arthur said, addressing both Roman and Kylar, "that you could teach yourselves to summon shadows. Not the shadows that already exist in a certain space, but the shadows *inside* you." He sipped his tea.

"You're one of us," Malakai cut in, thumping yet another cupboard door closed. "By that, I mean Darien and me. We have shadow magic. When the Veil almost fell, it switched from being invisible to being black." He glanced at Aspen. "Let's just order pizza—there's nothing here."

"So did Travis's," Dominic cut in.

"Who cares about him?" Malakai said with a black look.

Dominic's wings flared out, wind stirring through the room. "I was simply pointing out, *dickwad,* that Travis and Roman are brothers, so they have the same damn magic."

Travis walked through the front door then, as if summoned. Jewels came in behind him and shut the door.

"Bout fucking time," Malakai growled. "Where you been?"

Travis bent to unlace his boots. "We got hungry."

Malakai ground his teeth. Said to Aspen again, "Let's just order pizza."

Aspen sighed and grabbed her phone off the counter. "Pizza it is."

Roman got out his phone too—checking the screen again to see if Shay had answered the lone message he'd sent her.

She hadn't.

"Have you heard from Shay?" Ivy asked as she and Jack walked into the room in workout gear, Jack bobbing his head to the music drifting through his earbuds.

"No." Roman made for the door, ignoring Travis's probing stare as he passed. He'd let the others explain. "But I'm going after her." He had no idea where she was or how he could find her when she was gifted with illusion, but going to her apartment was a good place to start.

OVER TWO HOURS had passed since Darien had left for the hospital, and during that time, Loren had not set one toe outside her bedroom. Dallas had brought her some pizza, which she'd had to force herself to choke down. She didn't have an appetite.

She lay on her back on the bed, solar amulet in hand. She tipped it this way and that, watching as the metal rays caught the amber light of the sunset streaming in through the bedroom window.

With a sigh, she dropped the amulet and got to her feet. She crossed the room to the dresser and sifted through the contents of her bag that sat on top. If she was going to stay in here until Darien got back, she figured she may as well read. But she couldn't find her book—the small-town cowboy romance about the arrogant guy and his childhood sweetheart, as Darien had described it. Where had she put it?

As she dug around, she wound up opening a side pouch, her fingers closing around a device. Her cell phone.

Loren looked toward the closed door. Looked back at the device in her hands. It was powered off, but it didn't surprise her, not for how long she had been in a coma, and not when Tanner had disabled cell phone use. It likely didn't even have a battery charge.

She stuffed her hand back into the pocket of her bag—

And found a charger.

Her heart broke into a nervous sprint. She stood there for a few minutes, thinking it through. The cons, the risks.

And then she walked to the outlet closest to the bed and plugged it in. She sat down on the mattress, knees bouncing, teeth worrying her lower lip.

After a few minutes, the device came on. The lock screen appeared. The symbol on the top-right corner told her Tanner still had communication disabled. That was fine—she didn't need communication.

With the press of her fingerprint to the scanner, she unlocked the screen...

And tapped on the photo album.

It was true what they said about pictures—they really were worth a thousand words.

As she sat there on the side of the bed, fingernail clicking on the screen as she scrolled through rows upon rows of photographs, her vision blurred with tears.

Most of these pictures were of her and Darien. Every photograph she looked at prompted a new memory to return, filling in the gaps in her mind one by one.

The day they'd met. Their lunch date at Rook and Redding's.

The first night she'd spent at his house—how terrified she'd been, and how angry Darien had become when he'd found out the other Devils—Travis, Max, Lace—had been rude to her.

The graveyard called Dusk Hollow.

How he'd flirted with her in the dining room, stroking her with his magic. That sultry laugh when he'd realized she had been fantasizing about him. The way he'd pulled back the moment he'd sensed she was uncomfortable—and how, despite her nerves, she hadn't wanted him to. Had wanted him to keep going until her core that was tight with need—need for *him*—unravelled.

By the time the memory of their first kiss struck her like a bolt of lightning, she was crying so hard she had to put down the phone. She got to her feet. Crossed the room and threw open the door. She stomped down the hallway, down the stairs, heart racing. She was not angry about the truth—not at all. Not when it explained so many things, so many feelings.

She was angry that no one had told her. Had opted to keep something so important a secret from her, instead of helping her to remember.

Instead of helping Darien, who—looking back now—had clearly been suffering this entire time.

She found Ivy, Dallas, Max, and Jack lounging on the couches in the living room. Pizza boxes and soda cans were scattered across the coffee table.

"When were you going to tell me?" she fumed, blinking the tears out of her eyes.

Slowly, Ivy stood, as if approaching a wild animal. Loren felt like one.

Loren rounded on Dallas, who was stuffing her face with a pint of ice cream, spoon frozen halfway to her mouth. "Even *you*, Dallas?" she prodded, her tone scathing. *"Really?"* Dallas had nothing to say, though the look on her face told Loren she had not wanted to go along with this.

But she was too furious to care as she bit out, "Darien and I are *dating?*"

TANNER DROVE them back to the house.

Now that the procedure was over and done with, Darien felt way better. He was well enough to have driven them back himself, but in all honesty he was glad to have a break from being behind the wheel. Glad to be given the opportunity to tune out the traffic and focus instead on what he was going to say to Loren.

He was going to tell her. The minute he got inside, he'd ask her if they could speak in private. And then he'd tell her—everything. Even if the truth overwhelmed her, even if it drove them apart for a while, she deserved to know. Only a few days had passed since she'd woken out of a coma, but it felt like forever, and he couldn't take it anymore. He had to tell her.

Twilight was falling, turning everything into a monochrome blur of grays, the buildings and street lights glimmering to life all around them as they drove through the gates to Roman's property.

Tanner parked out front this time. As he shut off the car, he said, "You're going to tell her, aren't you?"

Darien's fingers stilled on the door handle. "How'd you know?"

The hacker shrugged. "You're quiet. I figured you've been acting the whole thing out in your head."

Darien smirked. "You're right—I was." He stared out at the house, the windows aglow with light. And then he sighed and opened his door. "Let's hope this goes the way I'm wanting it to."

Tanner got out on his side. "I'm surprised she hasn't already figured you out. You slipped up a couple times and called her 'baby'." He shut his door.

"Shit, really?" He had, hadn't he? Every time she'd nearly died right before his eyes, he'd called her 'baby', 'sweetheart'...

Tanner's lips curved upward. "Mm-hmmm."

As they made their way into the house, Darien drew several deep breaths, walking at a far slower pace than he needed to.

Fuck, he was...nervous. So damn nervous. She was the only woman who'd ever managed to make him feel this way. The only woman who ever would.

There would be no one after her. So he really hoped he wasn't about to fuck their relationship up. If he did, he'd grovel. Would get on his knees like he'd told her before. Crawl for her—anything.

Loren held his heart in her hands. She'd held it since the day he'd laid eyes on her in that alley on the Avenue of the Scarlet Star. He had belonged to her since the moment he'd chosen to kill for her—and back then, she didn't even know it. And neither did he.

"What's in it for you?" she'd asked him at Rook and Redding's that first day.

You, Darien said in his mind now. *You're in it for me.*

You're it for me.

He had just opened the front door and stepped inside when Loren came into the foyer, his friends and family who were present—Ivy, Jack, Dallas, and Max—trailing behind her, all wearing identical expressions of concern.

Darien's heart started pounding at the sight of the shine in Loren's eyes, the hurt and betrayal etched deeply into her sweet face—the betrayal that told him he was several hours too late.

Fuck.

Jack said, "I hope you're feeling better." His grin was a nervous one, and he lifted his hands in a gesture of prayer. "Because god-fucking-speed."

"We need to talk," Loren bit out, her nostrils flaring with furious, shaking breaths. *"Alone."*

92

ROMAN'S HOUSE
YVESWICH, STATE OF KER

Loren walked swiftly down a hallway in the lowest floor in Roman's house, Darien shadowing her about a dozen feet behind. She'd asked him if they could speak in private, and when he'd agreed, she had immediately come down to the place where they were least likely to be overheard—the floor with the training rooms, the shooting range, and the armory.

Most of the lights down here operated on a motion sensor, so she didn't need to flip any switches until she pivoted into one of the training rooms. She hit the switch and walked out onto the black mats covering the floor, the material sinking under her socked feet. The mirrors lining the walls showed several of her all at once, but she didn't look at any of them. She had no desire to see how pained and confused she looked; feeling it was bad enough.

The sound of Darien's heavy footsteps drawing closer made the butterflies in her stomach rapidly flutter their wings. She hugged her middle and paced across the mats, only stopping once the Devil walked inside, and she could not hold back her words any longer.

She faced him. "Why didn't you tell me?" she demanded.

Darien stood just inside the doorway. He still wore his boots, his right hand in a black compression glove. He looked...tired. Wary. She hated that this needed to happen tonight, after what he'd just gone through, but...

Had he told her sooner, instead of withholding the truth for whatever flimsy excuse he had, this wouldn't have happened.

"I was going to," Darien said. The reply was hoarse and brittle.

"When?"

"Tonight."

"How convenient," she scoffed. "Exactly when I've already figured it out on my own!"

"I'm not lying."

"Why?" she asked him again. "You still haven't told me why! And don't you dare say it was for my protection."

"It was," Darien said anyway.

She threw her hands up. "Gods."

"Loren, you were overwhelmed. You were scared as hell. You couldn't even wrap your mind around the fact that you were friends with us—that you *knew* us at all. What was I supposed to do, be like, 'Oh, by the way, you're fucking me too, hope you don't mind'?"

"Yes!" she exclaimed, her heart pounding at that naked truth. Although plenty of memories had come back upon seeing the photographs in her phone, everything that followed their first kiss was still shrouded in a fog of mystery.

Except one memory. Just a piece of one, really. Her, lying flat on her back in her bed at Hell's Gate on Kalendae—her birthday. And Darien, hovering above her, a masterpiece given life, her bare thighs tightening around his waist as he thrust into her—

She blinked the memory away with a fluttering of her lids, her face warming.

She'd lost her virginity to Darien Cassel. And the man who everyone was afraid of had handled her with such care.

Now, Darien Cassel was staring at her. "Yes?" he asked in disbelief.

"Yes," she said again, the word barely a breath. She started pacing again, idly rubbing her hands against the thighs of her jeans, needing the physical contact to ground her—to pull her out of this anxious bubble she was trapped in.

"I'm sorry." Darien's apology was loaded with emotion. "I guess I made a mistake, didn't I?"

"Yeah," she fumed, her voice cracking. "Yeah, you did."

"No matter what you think of me, I did it for you."

"Lied?" she croaked, her hurt overpowering her anger. "You're saying you *lied* for me?" She poked herself in the chest.

"If you want to call it lying, then yes, I lied for you. Because I thought it was best to give you some time—a few days, even, to get comfortable before I threw a truth that heavy on you. Everything that I do, Loren," he paused to breathe, chest shuddering with the inhale, "is for you." His words were sincere, but she still felt so blindsided, so betrayed by his decision not to tell her something this important, that she was hardly hearing him.

"Gods, I feel like such an idiot! *Everyone* knew about us—everyone except *me*. Do you have any idea what that feels like?" She glared at him, his face blurred by tears. "To be blindsided by the truth because everyone who claims to care about you was just...*lying?*"

Darien's breathing was now as ragged and audible as hers, his eyes brimming with as much pain as she could feel in her own. When he spoke again, his tone turned desperate. "You want truth, Loren? You want truth—I'll give you the truth." The hurt on his handsome face only intensified as Darien practically shouted, the three words clapping through the cavernous room, "*I love you.*"

Loren's heart stopped.

Restarted.

I love you more than anything in this world, Darien had said to her in his house on Kalendae, when he'd pinned her to a wall and kissed her tears away—

"I slept with you every night in that hospital," Darien went on, every word raw with emotion. "For ten days, I slept in that bed with you. And then Roark came to see me—told me about the Caliginous chambers, how they might be able to save you. I left that night. And guess what? Your heart stopped along the way. And I woke you back up—that's what I was doing, when you said you were drowning? When you said I helped you breathe again? That was me resuscitating you. I did all of that for *you*, Loren." His throat shifted with a swallow. "Because I love you, sweetheart. I have no better excuse. I guess I plead insanity because I am insanely in love with you, and I have no better excuse for this."

Loren couldn't speak. Couldn't move. Couldn't even blink.

And those three vulnerable words shot another memory into her mind.

The Control Tower. The ring Darien had slid onto her finger—forfeiting his life so he could save hers.

And it was that memory that finally made her see clearly. See *him* clearly.

Suddenly, she was no longer angry with him for the same reasons as before. Now, she was angry because they could have been together sooner—could have skipped all this hurt he'd unleashed upon himself. The pining, the stolen touches. He'd done all of that—tortured himself—for her.

He was right—everything he ever did, he did for her.

"We aren't just dating, we're in love with each other," Darien continued. "I fucking love you, sweetheart. You can hate me all you want, but it doesn't change anything. I've wanted you since the moment I laid eyes on you. I love you when you're angry. I love you when you're sad. I love you when you're happy. I love *you,* Loren, and I will love you for the rest of your life—"

She was moving before he got out the last word.

They collided, her mouth meeting Darien's so quickly that for a second she forgot who had moved first.

His hands wrapped around the backs of her thighs, and he lifted her up, hooking her legs around his waist. Loren didn't know how it happened, but suddenly her back was pressed against the wall, Darien pinning her there with his hips. He kissed her like he was drowning and only her lips were his salvation, his hand disappearing up her shirt to grip her waist, her breasts, the other fisting her ass. He touched her the same way she touched him—as if it was the first time and the last.

"Show me," she gasped between kisses. When Darien pressed his groin into her, she felt him against her core—how hard he was for her. She wanted him inside her—wanted every inch of him filling her up right now, fucking her raw. "Show me something."

The memory Darien chose swept into her mind like the swift fall of night.

Him on top of her, her heels on his shoulders, one of his hands on her waist while the other gripped her thigh.

Even more impactful than the visual were the feelings that went along with it—Darien's feelings, emotions.

He loved her. He loved her so much, she could physically feel it, the rawness of his attachment so great it nearly broke her. Broke and healed her.

"I want that," she said, kissing him harder, crushing her lips against his. "I want that—you—right now."

"Thank fuck."

He tugged her shirt over her head, and then went for her bra, unlatching it with one deft movement. Her pants and underwear were off so quickly, she hardly registered it happening, and then her own hands were moving to his belt buckle as Darien ripped off his shirt, the fine chains around his neck jingling with the force, and threw it aside.

As soon as their clothes were off, nothing separating them, he hoisted her up again, sheathing himself inside of her with one swift, forceful movement that made her gasp.

"Fuck," Darien groaned. He filled her right up, spearing her deep, and gods, it was the best feeling in the world. So was the warm press of his skin against hers, the beating of his heart under her palm as she flattened her hand on his broad chest—needing to feel him, claim him. "Fuck, I needed this, baby—I needed you so badly."

Darien wasted no time in moving—fucking her against the wall with brutal intensity, showing her exactly how badly he needed her. She used that wall for leverage, pushing back against it so she could fuck him back. She deepened every movement he dealt to her body, sharpened every thrust, and it still wasn't enough. She wanted him—needed him—more than she needed air.

"Gods," she managed around a breathy whimper. "Is this what I've been missing?" If he'd only told her sooner, the truth would've saved them both so much pain—and given them so much pleasure.

Darien smiled against her mouth. "You like that?"

"Yes."

"We fuck all the time," Darien growled, kissing her again as he pounded into her, the wall unyielding against her spine. "We can't keep our hands off each other. We're always fucking, and your tight little pussy is always making a mess on my cock."

"Oh gods," she gasped, clawing at his broad back. With every hard thrust, his muscles shifted under her grip, and gods, she loved it—loved the feel of him. She touched him with greed, pulling him closer, raking her nails across his smooth skin.

As he kissed her, his thrusts never slowing, he showed her another memory—one of her riding him on a beach somewhere. The sight of him underneath her, completely taken by her as she moved above him, made her inner walls flutter, release shimmering right there. But she fought it, because she didn't want this to be over yet—*ever*. She wanted this to last forever.

And then she saw herself in the same memory—from Darien's mind—and realized the first part was her own. Another memory coming back, and with it the emotions she'd lost.

Her love for Darien—the love that knew no bounds. The truth her heart had been screaming at her since she'd awoken in that chamber, the truth her mind had forgotten. The truth she hoped never to lose again.

"That turns you on, doesn't it?" Darien's deep voice was as decadent as chocolate, his mouth so close to hers that she could feel the words as much as she could hear them.

"More," she gasped, "show me more."

His mouth covered hers, swallowing her voice. He gave her what she wanted—more images of them tangled up in each other in beds and on couches; in his truck and car. Her mind flashed between the present and the past, every memory vivid and breathtaking, but it wasn't enough—she wanted more of this Darkslayer, wanted this incredible man to be her present, her future.

Her forever.

Three more strokes that were so deep she felt each of them in her stomach, and she shattered around his cock, his name floating off her lips in a breathless whimper. Darien supported all her weight as she dissolved, right there in his arms, drawing out her orgasm with quick, sharp movements, the room echoing with the slap of their bodies.

And then he spun, lowering her to the mat, where he settled heavily between her thighs, not missing a beat as he fucked her right there, the angle so deep and so good that she instantly came again, tipping her head back with a high cry the room answered with an echo.

An erotic groan rose deep in Darien's throat. "Fuck, I love that," he panted, thrusting with all his weight into her hot and swollen center. "I love *you.*" When she felt him throb inside her, she knew he was close.

"Darien," she whimpered. She was raw and full of this Darkslayer, every stroke pushing her higher, each dexterous roll of his hips teasing the taut bud of her clit. "Darien—" she gasped. "Gods, please, don't stop—"

His movements sped up and deepened. He fucked her so hard, she couldn't figure out where she ended and he began. She was lost in him, and he in her. She clawed at his back and kissed him deeply, teeth and tongues clashing. He tasted like everything she'd ever wanted. She was drunk on him.

"Fuck, Loren." His pace quickened with a frenzy of need. "Fuck, baby, I need—" He rested his forehead against hers. *"Fuck,"* he hissed again, the word fanning her mouth. He slid a hand under her ass, grabbing a fistful of it as he pounded into her.

And then he came so hard his eyes turned black, her name floating off his stunning mouth. She lifted her head to kiss him, claim him, sucking and biting his lower lip as he spilled himself inside her with such force, his cum dripped out onto the mat.

His movements gradually slowed, and he relaxed on top of her, being careful to keep his weight off her chest, his heart pounding heavily against her breast. Her body was spent, her legs trembling on either side of his waist, heart thumping just as hard as Darien's.

Although the room was empty apart from the two of them, it felt so full in here. So perfect.

"You love me," she whispered, needing to hear that truth on her own tongue.

Darien kissed her brow. "We love each other," he said, the deep rumble of his voice traveling from his sweat-slick chest into hers.

"I'm alive because of you," she whispered.

Darien corrected, "I'm alive because of you." He bent his head to kiss her softly on the mouth. The gesture was so gentle compared to the frantic, intense need that had just overtaken him, it stole the last of her breath.

For several minutes, Darien stared down at her—speechless.

She reached up to push back his hair. "Are you okay?"

He shook his head, but then nodded. "Yeah, just—" he panted "—trying to convince myself that this is actually happening. That I'm not dreaming."

"You're not dreaming," she whispered, tracing the strong edge of his jaw with her fingertips. "This is real."

"Even before tonight, even for weeks, *months* after I met you, I had to stop and ask myself if you were even real. I wondered what I did right in a lifetime of wrongs to deserve someone as perfect as you." The sight of him hovering above her blurred as Loren's eyes stung with tears.

"You're making me cry," she said around a wobbling sob, though her lips spread with a smile. Sadness and joy were a strange combination.

He kissed her between the brows. "Sorry, I'm just so happy I got you back. So happy you're home." He kissed the tip of her nose.

"I hope they come back," she panted as he pressed his lips to hers this time. "The memories," she clarified. A blink of her eyes sent a couple tears down her cheeks, and Darien softly wiped them away. "I want to remember you—all of you, not just pieces." She swept her hands up his muscled shoulders, winding her arms around the back of his neck and slipping her fingers into his silken hair. "I want to remember everything."

"If they don't come back," Darien said, still catching his own breath, his eyes roving her face with affection so deep she could feel it, "then I'm up for the challenge."

She cupped his cheek. "What challenge?" she whispered.

He started moving inside her again, grinding his hips into hers, burying himself deeper with a sexy groan. Gods, her heart was still pounding, her lungs desperate for air, and yet he was ready to go for another round, every inch of him still hard as granite inside her. This man would be the death of her. "Making you fall in love with me again," Darien said, his movements quickening. But there was no challenge there.

He had already succeeded.

93

ZIMA
YVESWICH, STATE OF KER

Night had fallen sometime ago.

Roman stood out front of Shay's apartment building, cupping his hands over his mouth and shouting for her to come down—*please* come down—if she was in there.

"Shaylaaaaa!" he called again, panting. No answer. People were beginning to peer out their windows, and while Roman knew he should care, he didn't. All he cared about was Shay. He needed to see her. Needed to know that she was okay. If she asked him to leave, he would. But until then, he couldn't not try.

He was all too familiar with grief. How it chewed a person up inside, leaving nothing behind but raw and bloody scraps of soul. A ghost of a person's former self. He refused to leave her alone in this.

A small, dark blur sped through the night sky, leathery wings flapping wildly. Sayagul.

'The spells are too strong,' the dragon said. *'And her blinds are drawn.'* She flapped down to perch on Roman's shoulder.

He swore under his breath. Called for her again. "SHAYLAAAAA!"

A man shouted out his window for Roman to shut up. Roman shouted back, his words so aggressive and colorful, the man was quick to disappear inside and latch his window.

Roman shouted for Shayla again, not giving a shit if someone called the cops. Maybe they should so he could let off some fucking steam.

A taxicab rolled up to the curb, and a middle-aged witch got out, studying him with silver-ringed eyes. "You looking for Shay?" the woman asked him.

"Yeah, is she in there?" He was out of breath. "Can you let her know I'm here? We're friends."

"She's not here, honey." She fished a cigarette out of her overflowing purse, a sugar glider Familiar peeking out. "Left a couple of hours ago in a cab. Looked like she might be gone a while." Those last words were a swift kick to the nuts.

Gone a while. Had she left with suitcases? Boxes?

Was she coming back?

"Did she say where she was going?" Roman choked out.

She shook her head. "I didn't have a chance to talk to her."

"Thank you." He got back in his car, and after he called Kylar to let him know where he was going, he sped out onto the interstate.

BEING BACK in room number nine in Motel 58 came with a lot of emotions that were difficult to swallow.

Shay sat on the edge of the bed closest to the door—her bed—surrounded by the ghosts of her and Roman. This room had seen thousands of guests, had housed thousands of stories.

This tiny, ordinary room had brought her closer to Roman—the man she'd left back in Yveswich. Left without saying goodbye.

Her bags sat on the table by the door. Her whole life was crammed in that duffel and backpack. She didn't have much to show for over nineteen years of life, but if Shay had learned anything this month, it was that the important things in life could not be bought or borrowed, but were found on the inside.

Nugget sat beside her on the bed, peering up at her with sad eyes, a flipper laid softly across her thigh in comfort. The room was so quiet. So... empty. Her heart was split in half, the jagged pieces weighed down by the lack of not one person, but two.

Roman and Anna. Shay had lost her sister, and in trying to find her had wound up falling for the last man she had ever expected to lose her heart to. And now, they were both gone.

Shay blinked, warm tears rolling down her cheeks and dripping into her lap. She opened her fists that were resting on her knees and watched the tiny bolts of purple and yellow lightning crackle across her palms, setting aglow to the teardrops like beads of glass struck through by sunbeams.

Shay sighed. "You want to go for a swim?" she asked Nugs.

The Familiar cocked his fuzzy head in question. He may not be able to speak, but Shay knew what the Familiar was asking: How could they possibly go swimming when the pool was dry?

As if in answer, thunder cracked outside, and a flash of lightning sliced through the curtains.

Shay got up and crossed the room. She unzipped her duffel and sifted through her clothes until she found the yellow bikini she'd bought from Everything but the Kitchen Sink.

She parted the curtain. Drew a deep breath as she stared out at the monochrome landscape. And whispered, "Let's see what my magic can do."

TEN MINUTES LATER, Shay stood outside in her bathing suit by the empty pool, a towel clutched under one arm.

Her most sobering moments had taken place right here in this desert, a stagnant, barren landscape so different from the busy city and her busy life. She had failed to notice it the first time she'd come out here, but she noticed it now—how quiet and still it was out here in the desert, her mind sighing in content at the emptiness. No noise fell upon her ears except the wind. No skyscraper in sight. Just land. Just peace.

With a heavy blink, she summoned her magic, her eyes darkening to the deepest black. She pushed that magic outside of her, covering the motel with spells that would muffle any noise, the people in those few rooms sleeping soundly.

No one would know.

When she opened her eyes, she tipped back her head, staring up at the clear sky studded with stars.

And she let herself feel.

She cried. Hard. She thought of Anna, thought of the future she'd lost, the best friend she would never get back. Her sister, her other half. She was alone now. Alone and lost, and missing relationships both old and new. Tears streamed down her face, blinding her vision of the night sky.

But she saw the clouds the moment they arrived—a rumbling mass that blotted out the stars. Veins of brightest yellow and palest lilac carved the sky into pieces, throwing the hazy layers into stark relief.

Deep inside her, her magic strained to be let out, stretching like an elastic band.

Shay let it snap. And as she let it go, she sucked in a deep breath and screamed.

Thunder cracked. Lightning flashed brightly enough to blind, turning night into day.

And for the first time in its life, the desert saw rain.

94

THE DESERT
STATE OF WITHEREDGE

Roman drove out to Motel 58 with the windows down. Balmy air gusted into the interior of the car, his shirt billowing like a sail. The closer he got to the motel—to the red dot on the navigation screen—the wetter the air felt. And it smelled like...

Rain. That damp, earthen scent was rain.

Roman leaned forward in his seat and peered up at the sky. There were no clouds—just a perfect, star-flecked canvas of black. But there was no mistaking that fragrance, the one thing no one in the world could replicate, no matter how hard they tried.

Another ten minutes passed before Roman caught sight of the glitching neon sign welcoming him to Motel 58. It was just a building, just a shoddy motel, but the sight of it caused his hands to tighten on the wheel. His stomach flip-flopped, and his heart shifted into a pounding sprint.

No one had ever managed to make him feel this way—no one except Shayla Cousens. The incredible, extraordinary, and utterly beautiful woman who'd walked into a house of monsters and set him free.

He pulled into the parking lot, slowing to a stop in one of the stalls along the perimeter, and cut the engine.

This was it. Maybe he was crossing a line, maybe she didn't want him here. Maybe she would scream at him to leave the minute she saw him. But he wouldn't know until he tried, and he couldn't stomach driving away without knowing, so he opened his door and got out.

As he walked, he sensed Sayagul watching from his shadow, the dragon filled with pure, innocent hope. If Shay wasn't here, if she'd already left, or if she wound up yelling at him to give her space, this would crush them both.

'*Be positive,*' Sayagul said gently, a phantom wing curling around Roman's soul like a hug. '*I can feel her. She is here. She is hurting.*'

Roman quickened his steps, his boots crunching on dry earth. He rounded the building, following his gut—the instinct that told him he'd find her out back. By the pool.

He was right. Shay sat on the slick edge, swishing her feet through the water. The pool was so full, it was overflowing. She wore that same yellow bikini that had driven Roman crazy the first time he'd seen her wearing it, her tan lines peeking out under the straps.

She looked up at the sound of his approach, blinking her big, pretty eyes in shock. "Roman?" Water splashed as she got to her feet.

Roman kept walking, not stopping until only a foot separated them.

"What are you doing here?" Shay breathed, staring up at him as if this was a dream. Little did she know, she was *his* dream.

"I couldn't do it," he admitted, his throat tight and aching. "I couldn't just let you go, knowing how hard this must be for you—how much you're hurting. If you want me to leave, I will. But I couldn't not try." He scanned her face, noting the shine in her eyes. He felt his own burning as he added, "I needed to see you."

"Roman," she croaked, the girl who never cried visibly battling the tears welling in her eyes. "I... Roman, I didn't plan on going back. To Yveswich, I mean. I packed my things." The words were a blow to the stomach, and for a second, Roman couldn't breathe.

She'd left, and she hadn't planned on going back. He was not entitled to her friendship, not entitled to anything Shay had to offer, but he couldn't stop the hurt, the feeling of betrayal.

Everyone always left. All under different circumstances, and not always by choice, sure, but somehow he always wound up alone.

Shay was scanning his expression. "Does that upset you?"

"If I said 'yes', that would be selfish of me. So I won't say it. You had a life and dreams before me, and I have no right to take those away." He heard her heart speed up and skip, felt her aura warm and soften. "But I'm going to be selfish about one thing, if you'll let me." Shay waited, and Roman said, "Give me one night. Just one. A night where it's just us—no one else, no regrets, no thoughts wasted on other people. I promised you five days, Shayla. And I don't break promises."

Shay's mouth wobbled. "It's all so wrong," she whispered. She inhaled, the deep breath hitching in her throat. "Who are they to tell us who we can and cannot love?"

That four-letter word stopped Roman's heart. Shay's face smoothed with a level of surprise that told him she hadn't meant to say it.

But it didn't matter, because the word was already out. And those four letters broke the last of Roman's self-control. Fuck his life, fuck his dad, and fuck anyone who dared to tell him that this was wrong. Shay was right for him, and even if he could only have her for this one night, he'd take it, and he wouldn't regret a fucking thing.

So he moved, sweeping her into his arms.

And crushed his lips against hers.

SHAY DIDN'T KNOW how it was possible, but every kiss she shared with Roman was somehow better than the one that came before it.

Her legs were around his waist, her hands in his thick hair. She kissed him as if it might be the last time, because she was afraid it would be.

Roman kissed her back with matching intensity—because they both shared the same fear, the same story. Before she'd met Roman and blackmailed him into coming out to this magical desert with her, she had believed the two of them couldn't be more different.

How very wrong she was. They were both tortured and trapped. Both desperately in need of someone to love and understand them.

She loved and understood him.

Thunder rumbled overhead, and when they broke apart to come up for air, black flickered in her eyes, and she knew Roman saw it.

"Is this a normal Surge or a zappy one?" he asked her.

"Normal," she said, nipping at his bottom lip. She had spent all her magic an hour ago—her emotions exploding out of her, thunder and lightning cracking the sky like an eggshell. "Don't tell me you're scared," she taunted.

"I'm not."

"Then prove it."

He did—crushing his mouth against hers, his big hands fisting her ass, tongue diving into her mouth. She broke the kiss long enough to tug his shirt over his head, and then she ran her hands across the smooth planes of his chest…over his muscled back, feeling the ridges of all those scars, all that pain. She would heal him if she could—would take it all away and mark up her body instead. Roman was a giver. He took care of people, but who took care of him?

She vowed right then and there that she would.

She would.

Roman set her on her feet long enough to get his pants and boots off. He didn't stop watching her that whole time, his stare so potent she could feel it. Those eyes were for her—all for her.

Shay backed up, her lips twitching with a playful smile.

She dove into the water. Clear blue stretched all around her—rain water. The rain of her magic, the curse she was beginning to see as a gift.

When she broke the surface a moment later, Roman was there, pulling her against his hard, damp body. From the moment she'd met him, she was well aware of how big he was, but pressed against her like this, their bodies flush, it was much more apparent. And gods, if she didn't like the difference between them.

"Truth or lie?" Roman breathed, the words husky, his eyes devouring her body. He gathered her to him, supporting her weight as he gently spun her through the water, moving her until her back was pressed up against the wall. He crowded her against it, bent his head, his nose skimming hers, and declared, "I think I'm falling for you."

She cradled his face in her wet hands. "Truth," she said, tipping her head up to brush her mouth across his.

He nodded. "Truth." The word was weighted with emotion. He leaned in…and pressed his mouth solidly against hers. The water was cold, but in Roman's arms she felt perfectly warm. And she felt even warmer when Roman broke the kiss and added, his breath caressing her mouth, "Definitely truth."

His hands went to her bottoms, and Shay's heart sped up as he tugged them down to her ankles. She kicked them off into the pool, and he hoisted her legs up, water swishing, and took his cock out of his boxers—the only article of clothing he still had on.

Shay held her breath as Roman positioned himself at her entrance. She watched as he gripped his cock, his inked fingers circling the thick shaft… and rubbed the crown up and down her center.

"Gods," she breathed, her back arching against the pool wall. Her core was already wet and aching for him, but he took his time with her, and when the broad head of his cock rubbed up against her clit, grinding her piercing into that sensitive bud, pleasure sparked, and Shay's legs twitched around his waist.

Roman's eyes darkened with arousal, the gold flecks in his irises winking out.

Gods. He was the most breathtaking man she'd ever seen.

"Roman," she begged.

His mouth twitched with a smile—like a wolf ready to bite, to sink his teeth into her. Devour her. "You know exactly what I want, pup," said the Wolf of the Hollow, the words coated with approval.

He bent to her level, locking his lips with hers...and pushed himself inside her.

Shay's breathy cry mingled with Roman's deep moan as he buried himself in her heat, right to the hilt, that burning stretch so good. Gods, she'd never felt anything like this—like Roman—before. Her core was wound up so tightly, so deliciously, and it coiled even further as Roman pulled out several inches, and then plunged back in, as deep as before.

And then deeper, stealing an extra inch.

Roman broke the kiss, but kept his face close to hers as he began to fuck her with deep, methodical strokes, the cool water lapping around them. "Tell me what you want," Roman said, the muscles in his arms flexing with every thrust, "whatever you want, and I'll give it to you. The world, anything—I'll give you anything, Shayla Cousens. Just fucking name it."

But the one thing she wanted was the one thing she couldn't have.

But she said anyway, "Just this." The words were breathy with pleasure as Roman came in deep, his body trembling with restraint. "Just you." She flattened a hand over his pounding heart. "Like this."

Forever, she wanted to add. So what if she had known him for less than two weeks? In those few days, Roman had given her more than what most people got in a lifetime. And love, she'd learned, did not have time limits or rules. Love was boundless. Boundless and infinite.

Rain began to fall, the drops splashing all around them. Roman kept his thrusting slow and deep, his attention flashing between her face and the area where their bodies were joined.

Shay used the pool wall for leverage, pushing back against it to sharpen Roman's movements that turned frantic and rough, both of them sprinting toward that same, delicious end.

Roman held onto her tightly, a hand on the small of her back, pushing down on the base of her spine as he thrust in and out of her, their bodies slapping together. He bowed his head to kiss her neck, his lips leaving a trail of heat up the side of it, all the way to the sensitive spot just below her ear. As they neared climax, his breaths became heavier and rougher, his strokes deep and swift. Water sloshed around them, and Shay felt Roman throbbing inside her as he neared his release, her ass slapping against the wall.

"Roman," she gasped, digging her nails into his back, his rock-hard length grinding into her inner walls with every thrust. "Don't stop."

He moved faster, angling himself so his pelvis rubbed into her clit with every roll of his hips.

"Yes," she whimpered, crying out his name again. *"Yes."*

She climaxed, her inner walls squeezing him tightly. The feel of him moving inside her was almost too great, too much.

"Ah—*fuck, Shayla.*" Roman came with an erotic groan, letting off deep inside her. "Shit—fuck," he panted, his body trembling with release, "I'm sorry, I couldn't stop."

"It's okay," she gasped, running a hand through his wet hair. "It's okay—we're good." She couldn't catch her breath to explain any further, but she knew he understood what she meant.

He reached up to brush a strand of wet hair out of her face, and then cupped her cheek, thumb stroking as he looked at her. Just looked.

Shay stared up at him, too, as he held her there against the wall, and asked herself a question: Truth or lie?

She was hopelessly in love with Roman Devlin.

There was only one right answer. It had barely taken a week for this man to win her heart, and it would take even less time for him to break it, if he felt so inclined.

They had promised each other this night—just one. But it wasn't enough for her. And that truth terrified her to her core.

No amount of time with Roman would ever be enough. Every moment spent together was stolen time. She was a thief who'd stolen minutes and moments with a man she couldn't have.

And that time was up.

95

ROMAN'S HOUSE
YVESWICH, STATE OF KER

Loren maybe got three hours of sleep that night.

Darien was ravenous for her, and her for him. They didn't leave that room, but they changed positions often, and by their third time, Darien switched to where they were both lying on their side, her back to Darien's front. He fucked her slowly and deeply this time, taking his time with her, lifting up her thigh to nestle in as far as his firm, hot length could go.

This man was exquisite. Exquisite and all hers.

"Are all hellsehers like this?" she asked him. A whimper as taut as her body slipped out of her as he picked up speed, her breasts bouncing with every firm thrust.

He bent his head, pressing his lips to the space just below her ear, his rough, panting breaths warming her skin. "You'll never find out," he replied, every word edged with insatiable lust. He kissed the edge of her jaw. "Because you're mine, sweetheart," he said with a husky whisper, teeth nipping her ear. He pounded into her harder, his fingertips digging into her hip. Loren clawed at the mat, her core tight with carnal need. "All. Fucking. *Mine—*"

His words—his claiming—were her undoing. She cried out his name, her inner walls fluttering around him as she was struck with a surge of ecstasy, her body unraveling like a spool of thread.

"Goddamn," he growled, breath fanning her ear, his cock jerking inside of her, his release close.

And then Darien's arms were circling her waist, gripping her to him.

He flipped over so he was lying flat on his back, Loren now upside-down on top of him, spread out over his lap. His hand fisted her hair, the other gripping her hip, positioning her so she was lined up with him, her head resting against his shoulder. She arched her back over him as he drove his hips up.

Deep. Deep. Deeper. He dipped his good hand between her legs, rubbing her wet, swollen clit.

"Fuck, you're perfect," he growled, fucking her ruthlessly. "Most beautiful thing I've ever seen."

Pleasure sparked again, and she clenched around him, her body and blood heating—

She tipped her head back with a moan as another orgasm ripped through her, her heart beating so fast it was more a hum. Gods, she hoped her tattoo wouldn't act up, because she never wanted him to stop.

"Good girl," Darien murmured, kissing the side of her head as he drove himself in faster, grinding the head of his cock against a deep, sensitive spot that made her legs twitch. "Such a good girl."

"More," Loren squeezed out, her toes curling on the mat.

"How do you want it, baby?"

"Harder. As hard as you can."

He obliged her. His movements turned frantic. Animalistic, carrying her over the edge again, hitting that spot way inside her in tandem with his fingers rubbing her clit. She soaked him, her insides squeezing him so tightly it made him swear colorfully. Groaning deeply, he went over the edge too, finishing himself off inside her with several brutal, uneven thrusts, panting her name as he spilled himself deep in her deliciously aching body.

"Fuck, baby." His movements slowed, his heartbeat strong against her back. "I'm so addicted to you."

"Likewise," she panted, turning her head so she could kiss him.

"How's your back?" he asked her, pressing his lips to her cheek. Her brow. The tip of her nose. When he loved her like this, she couldn't get enough.

"I'm sure I'll feel it in the morning." Her heart was pounding everywhere, the pulse between her legs gradually fading.

He gave a soft laugh.

"How's your hand?"

His lips moved to the side of her neck now, the tip of his nose skimming the space just below her ear—an area he seemed to give attention to often, her curiosity making her wonder if it had to do with his tattoo. His identity. His past and present. When he kissed that spot, his tongue sweeping out to taste her, she shivered, her reaction making him twitch inside her. "I'm sure I'll feel it in the morning," Darien said, the rumble of his words traveling through her back and chest, settling right in her heart.

Afterward, Loren lay on her side, facing Darien as he looked at her. Just looked at her, his hand cupping her face, thumb grazing her brow. He'd dimmed the lights so only the row closest to the mirrors were on, the rest of the room dim, and he'd given her his shirt to wear. He'd put his jeans back on, but Loren had a feeling those would be off again in no time, given how the last few hours had gone. It was late now and the house was quiet, and she was here with Darien, alone in their own perfect bubble.

"I'm sorry I didn't remember you," she whispered.

His thumb dipped to her cheek, tracing the freckles scattered across the top of it. "And I'm sorry I didn't tell you."

"Don't be. I understand why you did it. I didn't before—understand, I mean—because...I couldn't remember everything. And I was just... confused. And scared." Not remembering anything was more frightening than she could possibly explain. To have your life ripped from you, so many important moments that had defined her scattering to the wind, the feelings scattering with them...

It was something she wouldn't wish on even her worst enemies. It made her mind feel like it belonged to someone else, like it had somehow betrayed her, turning her into a stranger in her own life.

"You had good reason for reacting the way you did," Darien said, his words as equally quiet as hers. "I'm just glad you forgave me." A smile tugged at his mouth.

One tugged at Loren's in return, and Darien's attention briefly lowered to her mouth. "I can never stay mad at you for long." She took his hand into hers, joining their fingers, and used her thumb to trace the symbols and ancient numerals on his knuckles. "Do you think we'll ever get to experience a normal life together?" she wondered, unable to disguise her concern.

"Of course I do," he said softly. Quietly. "This can't go on forever, sweetheart." He said it with the same level of hope she felt sparking in her own chest. "But if it does, I'll be there with you every step of the way. Even if it takes forever, you have me."

She felt her mouth sink, her heart sinking with it. "My forever will be a lot shorter than yours." It was a truth that haunted her every waking moment. Since the day she was born, she had been identified by her mortal status, her inabilities outweighing her few abilities like a shadow constantly stalking her in the dark. A human lifespan was a mere blip in the grand scheme of things. It was rare that a mortal ever made an impact on a world like Terra. They died quickly, most never leaving so much as a trace of a footprint after a measly seventy, eighty years at best.

Darien was frowning, the blue of his eyes gray in this light. "Don't say that, baby. Please don't say that."

She swallowed the tightness in her throat. "It's the truth—"

"And it kills me." His deep voice echoed, sending a shiver from her spine to her nape. "Rips me apart inside." He gently squeezed her hand. "Live in the moment, okay? This right here." He came in for a soft kiss. "You and me, right now." Another press of his lips. "Just us." And another. "This moment." One more, and her heart all but melted.

"I love you," she told him with a whisper.

He lifted her hand to his mouth and kissed the back of it. And then he let go so he could come closer, pushing up onto an elbow so he was hovering over her. The pendants he wore caressed her chest, the silver warm from his body heat. His mouth locked on hers, tongue spreading her lips, leaving no part of her mouth untouched, unclaimed.

This man's kiss was a beautiful thing. Intense. Captivating. Irresistible. There was nothing better than this, nothing better than Darien.

He took her again, right there on the floor. He made love to her slowly this time, moving carefully right up until the end, showing her the side of Darien Cassel that no one but Loren ever saw.

She may be mortal, may be doomed to say goodbye to him eventually, but she still considered herself the luckiest woman in the world.

She would not trade Darien's love for anything. Not even immortality.

THE REST OF THE NIGHT—WHAT was left of it—brought back more memories. Until, eventually, she sensed that her mind was finally as full as before she had fallen into a coma.

They were all back—the pieces of everything she'd lost, back where they belonged, nudged into place every time Darien showed her another of his own memories.

With Darien lying beside her, sleeping soundly on the mat, his touch lingering on every part of her body, she had never felt so whole.

96

MOTEL 58
STATE OF WITHEREDGE

It was late, and the motel room was quiet.

Shay lay on the bed in Roman's arms, the blankets and sheets tucked around them, her left hand pressed flat against his right. He watched her face, marvelling at her features while she marvelled at the sight of their hands flattened together.

"Truth or lie?" Shay whispered. When Roman tilted his head slightly in question, she confessed, the words so quiet they were nearly inaudible, "I lost your necklace."

Shay waited for his response, her heart pounding in the quiet.

Slowly, the corner of Roman's mouth sank, deepening the small scar on the one side. The response made Shay's heart beat even faster. But those gold flecks in his irises remained bright like bits of glitter, and Shay didn't know what that meant, how to read him.

She swallowed, the pounding of her heart shifting into a nervous sprint, her stomach winding up into tight knots. "Roman, I'm so sorry—"

But Roman snaked his hand under the collar of his shirt, pulling up one of the silver chains he wore around his neck.

The same necklace she'd stolen from him in the alley. A wing-shaped locket—an antique made a very long time ago, only a handful of them existing in the whole world. Engraved on the back was the phrase, *Love must always win.*

Shay's mouth fell open, words eluding her. *How?* And how had she not noticed him wearing it?

"Truth or lie?" Roman whispered, his gentle yet husky voice raising a chill on her back, yet at the same time setting fire to her blood. He tucked the chain back under his shirt. "I stole it back." His lips quirked with a cunning smile, the dimple in his cheek showing off.

"When?"

"The first night."

"Our first night?" she gasped. *"Here?"* She looked pointedly around the room. "But...you could have just left." Taken off while she was sleeping or in the shower and never seen her again.

He shrugged and took her hand back into his, threading their fingers this time and setting their joined hands in the soft sheets. "Guess I didn't want to."

She stared at him. Minutes passed, and as the silence continued, Roman began to look worried.

He traced his thumb across her knuckles. "Shay—"

"You're full of mysteries," she whispered. "You're literally a walking mystery, Shadows."

He gave her a little smile, but it didn't reach his eyes. "Are you disappointed to learn that the Wolf of the Hollow isn't the predator everyone made him out to be?" Something told Shay her answer meant more to him than he was letting on.

"No," she mouthed. "I don't find you disappointing at all." She pushed up onto her knees, and as Roman shifted to lay flat on his back, his eyes already darkening with arousal, she swung one leg over his waist to straddle him. "I find you addicting," she said, speaking another of her confessions. He was still a predator—a very intimidating, accomplished predator, but the kind that chose his prey wisely instead of killing without need. She slid her hands up his shirt and over his chest, feeling his heart speed up with anticipation under her touch. "And I find you wonderful, Roman Devlin."

She pulled her shirt over her head, and then proceeded to show the Wolf of the Hollow precisely how wonderful she thought he was.

Roman left before sunrise.

Shay was still asleep, her face smooth and relaxed, her soft features suffused with the glow of the street light sneaking in through the curtains.

As he stood by the door, keys in hand, he couldn't help but look at her.

He'd never felt this way before. There was a deep pull in his heart, a need that had no logic or common sense. His life before Shay had come along was so small, so simple. A girl wasn't something he'd felt like he was missing, but now that he'd come to know Shay, he couldn't imagine life without her in it.

He didn't know what to call it. This feeling, this...hurt.

'It's love,' Sayagul whispered softly from his shadow. *'You love her.'*

'I can't have her.' His soul was so broken, even his internal voice cracked.

'We don't have to leave just yet—'

'She had a life and dreams before me. I have no right to take those away.'

'But she loves you too.'

Roman swallowed. Unlocked the door. *'Then she knows where to find me.'*

He walked out, locking up behind him.

As he got in his car, he looked at the door to room number nine. One last time. Vision blurring, he said into the quiet night, "I love you, Shayla."

But she was better off without him. Because so long as they belonged to different houses, and so long as they continued down this forbidden road, they'd both wind up dead. And Roman would rather suffer from a broken heart than suffer knowing he had anything to do with Shay being killed.

SHAY TREASURED those precious moments between wake and sleep, when reality was fuzzy and she could imagine, for a time, that her life had not been shattered into pieces. That she hadn't lost Anna. Roman.

It was the thought of Roman and the memory of the night before that made her eyelids flutter open.

It was dawn. And the room was empty.

She sat up. "Roman?" she called.

Had he been here at all? Had she dreamt it?

No. No, it was real. She could still smell him, feel him, the colors of his touch lingering all over her body like painted handprints. If she used her Sight, she could see them, his claiming everywhere, all different hues. She brushed the tips of her fingers across her lips that were slightly swollen from all the kissing, her skin still tasting of him. Already, she missed it. Missed *him*.

She whipped the blankets aside and sprinted to the door. Unlocked the deadbolt and threw it open.

Warm desert air that smelled of sage and dry earth gusted in. Shay shielded her eyes from the sun and stared out at the parking lot of the tiny, rundown motel that had changed her life.

Roman's car was gone. He'd left.

Her heart was at a crossroads. Before she'd met Roman, she'd had a plan. Dreams. And a sister with whom she'd strived to make those dreams come true. She'd lost everything, but as her life had crumbled around her, she'd found something she didn't know she needed. It had come in the form of someone entirely unexpected, but perhaps was not a bad thing.

She had a different dream to chase after now, if she dared.

As she stood there, staring out at the sunrise, she made her decision.

97

ROMAN'S HOUSE
YVESWICH, STATE OF KER

When Loren woke up the following morning, she took in her surroundings with several slow blinks.

Roman's training room, sunlight streaming in through the big windows lining the far wall. Mirrors covered every wall that didn't have windows, making the room feel extra bright and open.

And there was Darien, sleeping beside her. He'd grabbed a spare black mat during the night and had dragged it over for them to use as a pillow. He was lying shirtless on his stomach, hands lightly grasping the mat, one knee bent to the side.

No matter how many times she saw him sleeping, the novelty never wore off. There was something so vulnerable about trusting someone enough to sleep in their presence. For her and Darien, it worked both ways. Had anyone outside of their friendship circle seen them together like this, they would've surely thought her a fool for trusting a Devil—a leader, no less. As for Darien, there were many people out there who considered him an enemy, and so he trusted few. Loren knew she was very fortunate to be one of those few.

As she lay there beside him, birds chirping in the backyard, she studied his ink and scars, like she did so many mornings and nights. There was a particularly brutal scar by his hip—one she'd looked at a thousand times but had never asked him how he got it. A knife wound, probably—

"What are you looking at?" Darien's deep, husky voice raked up her spine.

She lifted her eyes to his face to see him watching her with affection. "Your scar," she said, the words cracking from early-morning fatigue.

"Which one?"

She reached across the mat and traced her fingernail along the puckered line. And then she flattened two fingertips against it, feeling the ridges.

"Mmm. I thought you were looking at something else." He gave her an impish smile, and her eyes skirted down...down—to what he *thought* she had been looking at. If he hadn't been sprawled on his stomach, she would've noticed *that* a lot sooner. Especially considering he'd slept with his pants undone. "Apparently," Darien began, "someone sensed that the love of my life is finally sleeping beside me again and is ready to go." When he dipped his hand under his body to adjust it, she gulped—loudly. Darien gave a dark laugh. "You're probably sore."

"A little," she admitted. *A lot,* was more like it. Darien Cassel was insatiable when it came to sex—to her. She wished she didn't feel so achey, because she wanted him again right now—

To her horror, her stomach growled. *Wrong kind of hunger,* she told it.

Darien was instantly reaching for her, pushing up her sleeve and dragging his thumb across the tattoo on her forearm. The medical symbol was pulsing with red light that reflected in his rings and watch. "You need to eat." Before she could object, he got up and did up his pants. And before she had a chance to stand, he was stooping and picking her up.

She wound an arm around his neck. "You like carrying me around, don't you?" She used the other to rake her fingers through his silken hair—just the way he liked.

"I love anything as long as it involves you." He picked up the rest of their clothes on the way out. Loren helped him carry some of them, overly aware as he started heading upstairs that the shirt she wore—Darien's shirt—barely covered her ass in this position.

And she heard voices floating down from the higher floors.

Her face turned red and warm. "They're going to know what we were doing!" she hissed, her arm tightening around his neck, the other fisting the clothes she carried.

"They already know, sweetheart. We disappeared downstairs last night and never showed our faces again—I'm sure they made assumptions quickly." He gave her a wink.

"Maybe they think we fought to the death," she teased.

He frowned, boots pounding as he ascended the steps.

His attention shifted to the black dog standing at the top of the stairs, whose red eyes narrowed into accusatory slits.

'Finally!' Bandit fumed, black nose twitching. *'We have been waiting hours for you! There has been an emergency.'*

Darien's arms tensed around Loren. "What kind of emergency?"

'The female demon-monkey has stolen Cluckles!'

Darien rolled his eyes. "Oh for fuck's sake."

LOREN SAT down at the kitchen table with a bowl of cereal as Darien worked on convincing Itzel to surrender Cluckles.

Itzel was on top of the fridge—a hiding place that seemed to be the norm for House Hobs. She had taken the rubber chicken hostage, the chewed-up toy nearly as big as her. From the sound of Darien's murmuring, he was trying to figure out why she had taken it—while also trying to keep Bandit, who stood beside him, from losing his cool and destroying the fridge, which the sassy dog had already threatened to do. More than once.

Everyone was scattered throughout the kitchen and living room, but mostly the living room. Roman and Shay weren't here, and neither were Paxton and Eugene, who were likely in school. But aside from them, everyone else was present. The big coffee table and the carpet it sat upon were cluttered with weapons, tools, and laboratory glassware. Loren was surprised Arthur was comfortable setting up the glassware around someone like Jack, who crouched nearby, looking all too interested in the glowing liquid bubbling through the coiled tubes.

As Loren dug into her cereal, observing the many faces crowded around Arthur at the coffee table, she put two and two together.

"You're making swords?" She took another spoonful, far hungrier than she'd realized. She had her night with Darien to thank for that.

She glanced at the slayer in time to see his steel eyes flicker to her, as if sensing where her thoughts had strayed. But then she realized...

Her talisman—she wasn't wearing it. He'd taken it off sometime last night, because he liked to feel her in every way possible—body and aura—when they were being intimate together. His mouth twitched with a smile that told her he was reading her again now.

"Right you are, Loren," Arthur said. He was giving instructions to Tanner, Kylar, and Malakai, the Darkslayers holding swords of black adamant across their laps, all three of the slayers shirtless. "I'm teaching them how to reinforce our little miracle weapons." The only blades that could cut through the monsters of Spirit Terra with ease.

"He made us new bodysuits too," Dallas said from where she sat by the windows, an arm draped across Max's knee. She held up an onyx ring. "We've all got one now." In her other hand, she held up another—a pearly white one. "Yours is white." With a flick of her wrist, she threw it. It soared over Loren's head, too quickly for her to put down her spoon and catch it.

Loren got to her feet as the ring clattered into the foyer. *"Dallas,"* she huffed. She knew better than to throw things at her; she had terrible hand-eye coordination.

"Sorry," Dallas called.

"Am I the only one who doesn't have black?" Loren asked as she retrieved the ring.

"Mine's red," Ivy said.

"Jack's is pink," Travis chimed in with a poker face. Max and Tanner laughed.

"Hey—I'd rock pink better than you assholes," Jack said.

Loren came back to the table, the ring in her fist. Her eyes snagged on Darien again, who finally got back the rubber chicken. "There's a lot of shirtless men in here," she said quietly, unable to resist gawking at *her* shirtless man. Darien, Malakai, Tanner, Jack, Kylar—they were all shirtless. What was this, some kind of no-shirt party?

"And one pants-less lady," Malakai said. "You into orgies, sweetie?" Aspen snickered and pinched him.

Loren's face warmed. "No, thank you." She added, "I've got my legs full with Darien." That earned her a laugh from several people and an impressed smile from Darien.

"You sure?" Malakai pressed. "We can get Arthur in on it too. It'll be wild."

Arthur's gray brows shot up. "Alright, I think I've had enough of Mister Delaney for one morning." He stood with mild difficulty. "You all seem to be doing well enough without me. Finish those blades —I'm going for a stroll. I'll grade your work upon my return." Loren couldn't tell whether he was joking about the last part.

"Art, be careful out there," Darien said as he tossed the chicken to Bandit, who caught it in his teeth and immediately began tearing into the toy. "Atlas, you feel like doing a store run?"

Tanner twisted around. "What for?"

"Itzel wants a snow cone. It's her price for giving the chicken back."

'Her price,' Bandit chimed in, biting down on the chicken hard enough to make it wheeze, *'should be a fight to the death.'*

Malakai said, "You guys let those creepy little fucks dictate you?" Itzel hissed like a cat and flung a piece of cereal in Malakai's general direction.

"Looks like Morty's going to have himself a girlfriend," Jack said.

Travis sighed through his nose. "If we get him back."

"We will," Darien vowed.

Arthur was in the foyer, shoes on. "I shall be back in a while."

"You want anyone to go with you?" Lace called.

"I enjoy solitude." He opened the door. "Which means no Jack or Malakai. If any girls want to come with, you are welcome to join me."

Jack said, "You could just walk up and down the driveway instead so no one gets you."

"No one is going to 'get me', Jack," Arthur grumbled. "And I will not be confined to the driveway like some pet." He padded out the door.

Lace pushed to her feet. "I'll go with him." She got her shoes on and disappeared after him.

Darien helped himself to some cereal and sat down beside Loren. "How are you feeling?"

"I long for the day when you don't have to ask me that."

He took a bite. Chewed. Swallowed. "Can you answer me, please?"

"I'm fine." She slid her hand across the table to give his forearm a light squeeze. "I promise."

"Good."

She finished the last bite of her cereal. "And I'll let you know if anything changes," she hurried to say, before Darien could voice the request himself. "Beat you," she said, winking before he could beat her to that, too.

His smile showed off the dimple in his cheek. "I'll beat your beautiful ass for being cheeky to me."

Loren's mouth popped open. A few snickers from the living room were the only indication that anyone heard them.

"Later," she mouthed to Darien.

"Finish eating," he said, that dark look in his eyes hinting that 'later' would be coming very soon.

LOREN WAS in the steam shower getting ready for the day, rinsing the last of the conditioner out of her hair, when a knock came at the door.

"If you're Darien, you can come in!" she called, wringing her hair out.

The door cracked open, and Darien walked into the bathroom.

"Mind if I join you?" he asked as he pushed the door shut. What a ridiculous question. She never minded anything, as long as it involved him.

"No," she told him, her heart already pounding as she watched him undress.

When he opted to brush his teeth before getting in the shower, she knew exactly where this was going. And a different, more intimate part of her body began to throb with anticipation, beating in time with her heart.

Gods, she was so glad her memories had come back.

He opened the glass shower door and stepped inside. Gave her a little smile. "Hi."

"Hi."

He stepped into the water, soaking his hair and pushing it back. "How are you feeling?" She knew he wasn't referring to blood sugar this time.

"Better."

"Good." He stepped closer, his left hand coming around to the small of her back, and bent to kiss her. "I swear I've never been happier," he breathed between kisses. "I'm so happy to have you back, sweetheart. I can't keep my hands off you." When he grabbed a fistful of her ass for illustration, she whimpered, a sound he was quick to swallow with another kiss.

"Pretty sure you couldn't keep your hands off me before, either," she breathed against his mouth, barely able to get the words out as he kept kissing her as if he were starved.

"Still got that naughty mouth on you." He picked her up, making her squeal in surprise, and wrapped her legs around his waist. "But it's that mouth that made me fall for you."

He took her to the bench with him and sat down, placing her in his lap, her back to his front. He spread her legs so one was draped over each of his knees, and she felt the hard press of his cock against her spine.

And then his hand came around her waist, dipping between her thighs, his middle finger circling her clit. Gods, he was so good at this, her muscles were already tightening in anticipation.

They tightened even more when Darien asked her, "Are you too sore from last night, or can I play?"

Her back was arching against him, her toes curling in open air as he swirled the wetness—not all of it from the water—around her clit. "You can play," she whispered.

So he spread her open, sinking his middle finger inside her.

They groaned in unison. She was a bit sore, but she didn't care. She just couldn't get enough of him.

He dipped his finger in and out of her, only going up to the second knuckle. When she began to get desperate for more, squirming in his lap, he added another finger and pushed them both in all the way.

"This gives me some practice with my left hand," he said, his breath fanning her mouth as she turned her head to look at him. She leaned closer, catching his bottom lip between her teeth, kissing and nipping in a way that made him groan, low in his throat. "Fuck, you're so beautiful." He quickened his pace, and as he finger-fucked her, she felt phantom pressure on her clit—a teasing and rubbing that varied between feather-light and a firmer touch that sent pleasure sparking through her in white-hot bolts.

"What is that?" she gasped, knowing full well he wasn't using his other hand—the broken one.

The corner of his mouth twitched. "My magic."

"Have you ever used it on me before? Aside from that time at—" Gods, her legs were shaking— "the school?" When he'd assaulted her body with it, and she had literally fallen to the grass from the staggering force of the orgasm he'd given her.

"Only in the dining room that one night." She remembered that night very well. "I wanted to make you come so badly. You were such a filthy girl, fantasizing about fucking me. I didn't want to stop." He kept dipping his fingers in and out of her, using the heel of his hand to rub her pulsing clit, his eyes devouring every face she made. "I liked how you squirmed for me. I wanted to lay you back on my table and watch you come from my magic. And then I wanted to get on top of you and fuck you raw. I was already down so bad for you, you drove me insane."

"Why didn't you?" she challenged, her lust winning over her words and thoughts.

He gave a dark chuckle, pressing a kiss to the space below her ear. "Baby, you know why." Yes, she did, but she didn't want him to stop talking about that night—the details he had never given her before. "You weren't ready for that. But you made me so fucking horny, I had to take care of myself after." His hand quickened between her legs, fingers dipping in and out. In and out. "I thought about you the whole time. Your gorgeous face. Your perfect body." He pushed both fingers in deeper. Moved them faster, her inner walls fluttering with every movement. "That smart, beautiful mouth. I came so hard, baby, I saw stars—"

Her orgasm ripped through her, and Darien covered her mouth with his, carrying her through the throes of it with swift, brutal movements.

And then he lifted her up and set her down on his cock this time, and she cried out in pleasure as he pushed her right down to his base.

"Tell me what you thought about that night," Darien breathed, gripping her by the waist and bobbing her up and down. Up and down. The friction was so good, she couldn't stop panting, every upward thrust of his hips striking her deep. "In the dining room. I want that sweet mouth to finish me off."

"I thought about you fucking me," she admitted, barely able to get out the words as another wave of pleasure began to crest. She gripped his thighs, fingernails digging into muscle. "I fantasized about how your face would look between my thighs." Darien swore, moving faster now, as deep as he could fit. "And..." She wet her lips with her tongue, biting down on the lower one, her expression darkening Darien's stare. "I fantasized about what you would look like when you were coming—"

"Fuck." He moved her even faster. Lifting her up and down, slamming into her all the way to the hilt, her breasts bouncing with every thrust. Water splashed around them, and a few minutes later, she felt his cock throbbing inside her, and he barked out her name, the warmth of his release shooting deep and dripping out of her.

"Like that," she panted, watching as that mouthwatering expression lingered on his face, his eyes a shining black. "Even better than I imagined."

"You're even dirtier than I thought," Darien crooned, still bobbing her up and down, movements gradually slowing. "My filthy fucking girl."

She leaned in to capture his mouth with hers, biting and sucking on his bottom lip. "You are insatiable," she mumbled against his skin. She swept her tongue out, tracing the curve of his mouth and making him groan. Pulling back slightly, she whispered, "But I wouldn't have it any other way."

Darien gave a little smile and kissed her—softly this time.

And then he lifted her up, pulling out of her. But instead of letting her get to her feet, he set her back in his lap. His arms came around her from behind, holding her against him.

Hugging her. Once upon a time he'd told her he wasn't much of a hugger, but gods was he good at it. "I love you," he told her, burying his face against her damp shoulder, his wet hair dripping on her skin.

"I know," she teased. When she felt him lift his head, she tipped hers back so she could see his face.

He scrunched up his nose.

She scrunched hers in response.

And then his tongue darted out, licking the tip of her nose.

She shrieked and laughed. "Did you just lick me?" She lifted the back of her hand to her face—

"Don't you dare wipe it off." His bass voice echoed in the big bathroom.

She froze. "Staking your claim, are you?" she snickered.

"I staked my claim the minute I met you," he said, his heart still beating heavily against her back, their sweat-slick skin stuck together. "The minute I killed for you." It was amazing how that one decision had led them here.

"I'm glad you showed me—the memory, I mean."

"I'll show you anything, all you have to do is ask," he said, smoothing a strand of wet hair off her cheek and tucking it behind her ear. "Speaking of the day I killed for you..." A smile pulled at his mouth, showing off the dimple she hadn't seen in a while. "There's this place I've been dying to show you since I got here."

"What is it?"

"You're not going to believe it, but they've got a street just like the Avenue of the Scarlet Star."

98

THE AVENUE OF THE WANING MOON
YVESWICH, STATE OF KER

Darien wasn't joking when he'd said there was a street in Yveswich just like the Avenue of the Scarlet Star.

They were in an apothecary called Harriet's Spells and Things, waiting for the witch who stood behind the counter to finish bagging their items. Loren was stocking up on some extras—teas, essential oils, contraceptive tonic. Of course, Darien paid, but she didn't really have another option, since no one had packed her wallet. It was funny to look back at everyone's behavior, now that she knew the truth—how Jack had told her Darien was her wallet. He, for one, hadn't lied.

Having Darien pay was probably for the best, though, given how many shifts she was missing. She would need to call Mordred and Penny soon and let them know she was okay. It was strange to think that her life was completely on pause back at home. She wondered what everyone thought of her absence—how much they knew.

When they walked out the door to the apothecary, under a sky that began to sprinkle with rain, Darien said, "I hate how everyone looks at us like that."

She peeked up at him. "Like what?"

"Like I'm wrong for being with you. Like I'm somehow hurting you by being your boyfriend."

She took his hand, loosening his fist and lacing their fingers. "You're the one who always says it doesn't matter what people think," she said softly, watching as a muscle feathered in his jaw. "And it doesn't."

"I know." He sighed. "I guess I just get my back up about it because I'd never raise a finger against you."

"They don't need to understand, Darien. Besides, we're kind of in our own private club this way, and..." She shrugged and tucked a lock of hair behind an ear. "I like it." It was true—she liked what they had. She never wanted it to change.

Darien lifted their twined hands and kissed the back of hers. "Let's cross here," he said, using their hands to gesture to the crosswalk. "There's this place I want to show you."

"Okay," she said, walking now with a skip in her step.

It turned out to be a bakery with what Darien claimed were the best cinnamon buns in the world. When they picked a table by the windows and sat down to eat, Loren knew from the first bite that Darien had not been exaggerating. These were amazing. Melt-in-your-mouth amazing.

Just like the Darkslayer sitting across from her.

This right here—this life with Darien—felt like home. It didn't matter that Angelthene was miles away. The city didn't matter—*he* was her town, her home. Darien was all she needed. And when he leaned across the tiny table to kiss the sugar off her lips, she melted just like the icing.

Singer and Bandit were sprawled under the table by their feet, eating Murktreats. Bandit scarfed his down faster than Singer ate his, then proceeded to stare at Singer in challenge.

When Loren was finished, she sat back in her chair and rested her hand on her stomach. "That was so good. I'm so full."

Darien pushed their paper plates aside and folded his arms on the table, his eyes briefly dipping to the hand that was resting on her stomach. "Do you think you'll ever want kids?"

"Whoa there, Daredevil," she breathed. "The only baby bump I want right now is from a cinnamon bun."

He fought a smile.

She leaned forward to rest her arms on the table. "Where is this coming from?"

"Just a question," he said quickly. "I don't mean anything by it, but I think about our future a lot. And..." He inhaled. "I just want you to know how much you mean to me. And that I'm in it with you for the long run. No matter what you want in life, no matter what comes our way, I'm with you." His use of the term 'long run' made her heart give a painful thump.

Long run...as if they had all the time in the world. As a hellseher, Darien did, but a mortal like her...

She swallowed, staring down at the checkered tablecloth. Now that all her memories were back, she couldn't help but recall one in particular.

Her conversation with the Widow. The spider had told her that she was not meant for Darien, had urged her to leave and stop breaking her own heart. Had told her they were fighting against chains unlikely to be broken. Perhaps the one thing the Nameless beings were good for was their honesty. Anything they said, a person could trust. But the truth was not always kind.

Darien dipped his head to try and catch her eye. "Baby?"

She lifted her gaze to his face. "Do you want to be a dad?" she wondered.

His expression turned grave, his eyes filling with warring emotions. "I don't know," he admitted. "I'm scared I wouldn't be any good at it." To hear Darien say those words—'I'm scared'—was so...bizarre. There wasn't a lot that scared this man. "Especially if I had a son," he added.

"Because of Randal," she said quietly.

He gave a stiff nod, his eyes as cold as glass.

She leaned forward and reached for his hands, and he gave them to her, the tension in his left melting under her touch. "Just for the record, I think you'd be an amazing dad."

Darien's gaze softened. "And I think you'd be an amazing mother. You're kind and selfless. Patient. Mild." He smiled a little. "And utterly perfect."

She snickered. "You're the perfect one."

That little smile faded. "Hardly."

She eyed him. "Do you bring this up because you're worried you won't be able to offer me what you think I want?" Maybe their thoughts weren't so different after all. She was afraid that she wouldn't be able to give Darien what he wanted, but perhaps he feared the same in a different way.

He shrugged. "It's always been a fear of mine, since the moment I realized I had fallen for you. I want to give you anything—anything you want."

"I already have everything that I want," she told him gently. The guarded expression in his eyes thawed. "Anything else is just a bonus. You're my real gift."

"Pretty sure you're the gift."

"Pretty sure you don't see yourself clearly," she volleyed back.

"Pretty sure you don't either." He winked.

"I can do this all day, Darien," she warned with a smile.

"Good, because we've got a lifetime." He gave her hand a gentle squeeze.

And there was that shadow of a thought again—the one that reminded her of the mortality constantly breathing down the back of her neck.

"We'll take a rain cheque on the kids conversation," he said. He was watching her closely, no doubt picking up on her concern.

She forced a smile. "When we're ready. And when I'm not twenty and practically a baby myself." It was a joke, but something...strange entered Darien's eyes, and she had no idea what it was. A shadow darker than anything she'd seen on his face in a long while. Darien hid it quickly, and before she could ask him what was wrong, he moved on to another topic.

They sat at that little table and talked for a long while. About everything that'd happened while Loren was in a coma, about Maya Reacher. Everything Loren hadn't been filled in on before, she was filled in now.

And then it was her turn to do the talking.

"You said you *saw*," Darien began, "Erasmus and Roark in the spirit realm."

She nodded. Drew a breath. "I saw them create the Arcanum Well. They were both human—both attending Angelthene Academy thousands of years ago. They made a trade with a Nameless creature so they could use the prima materia."

Darien's brow lined with confusion. "How did a couple of mortals have something worthy of a trade of that magnitude?"

"They didn't," Loren said. She glanced about the bakery. "They made friends with Helia. She was the one who made the trade."

"Your mom." Darien had been with her that day at Erasmus's townhouse—when Loren had asked Erasmus what her mother's name was. He'd told her it was 'Helia'—he and Cyra had *both* told her it was 'Helia'.

"She bargained with the Nameless, so she could keep her friends with her forever. But—Darien... Cyra is Helia." Her mother had been right under her nose. This whole time—right under her nose.

Darien stared at her, looking as shocked as she still felt as he tried to make sense of it—why Erasmus had aged, and Cyra hadn't. Why Erasmus was human again, and Cyra wasn't. Why neither of them had told her the truth. Erasmus was spelled—Loren knew that much. She figured Cyra was too. It was the only reasonable explanation for the many secrets they'd kept. The secrets they were *still* keeping.

"Cyra is my mom." Her voice cracked on the last word.

Darien stood in a phone booth, listening to the line ring as he watched cars roll by on the Avenue of the Waning Moon. Loren was here with him in the drafty booth—tucked against his side, her big blue eyes flicking up to meet his every once in a while.

Something was bothering her, and he didn't know what—whether her silence was due to thoughts of her mother back in Angelthene or a fault of Darien's own. Maybe he should've kept his mouth shut about kids. She was probably thinking too deeply about his words, the way he so often thought about hers. Thinking could ruin so many moments.

"You okay, baby?" he said quietly as the line kept ringing.

She gave him another of the same smiles she'd given him in the bakery, after they'd finished filling each other in on what they'd learned—a forced smile. "I'm fine." She dropped her gaze to the ground, hands in her jacket pockets, hair falling in her face like a curtain of light.

Yeah, it was definitely what he'd said in the bakery. Goddamn it.

'Look what you've done,' Bandit grumbled from his shadow. *'We just got her back and she's already distancing herself.'* He gave a low growl.

'Can you mind your own business?' Darien shot back.

'It's hard to mind my own business when we share a head.'

'She's not distancing herself, she's just overthinking.'

'Kind of like someone else I know,' the dog said with a brazen snort.

The line finally connected, and someone breathed on the other end.

"It's me," Darien said.

A beat of silence, and then the Butcher growled a laugh. "Hey, kid. Still kicking, I see."

"Still kicking."

"To what do I owe this pleasure?"

"That demon you caged. The one that destroyed the carnival. What'd you use to down it?" After Darien had seen the others reinforcing the blades of black adamant Arthur had rushed to create during the Blood Moon, smoothing out the jagged edges and giving them proper hilts, he'd remembered back to the carnival. To the Butcher's men having caged that powerful monster. They only had three swords of adamant, and three was not enough. Not if the creatures of Spirit Terra were going to keep showing up like this.

The line crackled as the Butcher breathed on the other end. "Morsian darts," he said, his voice barely a rumble. "It's a tranquilizer made from the venom in Hound quills." A tranquilizer was better than nothing.

"Any way you could line some up for me?"

"I'm going to assume you are where I think you are." Darien didn't say otherwise. The Butcher took his silence as a yes. "Stop in at Tekram later tonight and find a man named Alfie. He'll bring you Below to get you what you need. Don't linger, don't ask any questions—you know the drill."

"Got it," Darien confirmed. "And thanks."

"Don't mention it."

Darien made to hang up—

"Hey," the Butcher called. "Tell Bright I'm gonna tan her ass." Loren must've heard that, because her brow creased, and she tipped her head at Darien in question.

"What for?" Darien asked.

"Why don't you ask her yourself." He hung up, and Darien put the phone on the receiver.

Tekram—market. Next stop, the Black Market.

99

THE BLACK MARKET
YVESWICH, STATE OF KER

"You created a dating profile for Casen?" Loren gasped later that night as she walked with Dallas through the Black Market, Darien just slightly ahead of them. The sun had set a couple of hours ago. As soon as darkness had fallen, and they'd filled up on leftover pizza for dinner, they'd made their way here. Max and Kylar were here too, the latter leading the way through the maze of tents, booths, and ramshackle buildings while Max followed closely behind Dallas and Loren, a lethal, hooded shadow of a bodyguard.

"I thought he deserved to find love," Dallas said proudly, her features and hair concealed by her heavy hood. Her wings were hidden tonight too, allowing her to wear the kind of clothing that wasn't specifically designed for wings. "He's always so grumpy—when was the last time the man got laid?"

Max chuckled. "Fuck, Red. I'm pretty sure he doesn't struggle in *that* area." He said to Darien, "How mad was he, anyway?"

"He hung up before I could find out." Darien turned mid-stride to grab Loren's hand, tugging her up so she was right beside him as the crowds around them thickened.

"The profile's already gone, so I'm assuming he's majorly p.o.'d," Dallas said. "I tried signing in, but it said the account doesn't exist. I'll wait a bit before making him another one." She waggled her copper brows.

Kylar's husky laughter trickled from up ahead. He turned, the diamond in his tooth winking with a dimpled smile. "You're asking for it."

A few minutes later, they reached a small shop with a red wooden door, a round window of bubbled glass cut into the wood. Kylar opened the door, and with an elaborate flourish of his arm, he held it for everyone to file through.

Loren clamped down on the urge to cough as she ducked inside, the reek of hot tar stinging her eyes and clawing down her airways.

A hulking warlock stood behind a spell-protected counter, thumbing through a wad of paper bills he'd just received from the customer waiting on the other side. The dealer's dark, silver-ringed eyes flicked up to observe their group as they entered. As soon as he was finished counting the cash, he tapped the stack against the counter, smoothing the jagged edges, and slid a bottle of Venom through the wall of spells.

The customer took it and left, head down. The door creaked and slammed shut with his departure.

Darien stepped up to the desk, his hand still wrapped around Loren's.

The warlock looked him over. "You're here for Venom," he said, tucking the money into a cash box, a pair of yellow eyes peering from the shadows inside.

"As much as you can give me," Darien confirmed.

But the warlock shook his head. "I got nothin'. I'm all out."

"You're out *again?*" Darien snapped.

"Who's buying this shit?" Kylar chimed in.

The man merely said, "Bring me tar. I'll get you your Venom."

Darien cursed under his breath, but turned to face the others. "Let's go." He twisted to address the man again. "How long are you here till?"

"Four."

"How quickly can you make it?"

"An hour. Two, tops."

"Fine," Darien bit out. His fierce blinking told Loren he was fighting a Surge. "I'll be back within the hour."

They left the dealer's and moved onto the next stop on their list: Morsian darts.

"Do you need to go and get tar?" Loren asked him with a whisper.

"Right after this," he confirmed, his words still taut with lingering anger.

"Am I coming?"

He glanced down at her. "I'd prefer if you didn't, but I won't stop you." He tugged her slightly to the left, out of the path of a drunk werewolf who was fighting the Shift, tremors running through his body from head to toe. "The pits are infested with Hounds," Darien explained. "We got attacked the last time we went there."

"I'll ride with Max back to Roman's, then," she decided. They'd brought two vehicles here—Max's new mammoth of an SUV and Darien's truck. Malakai was currently in the latter, keeping an eye on the vehicles, this market crawling with criminals. Darien had told her carjacking was a big problem in these parts.

She stuck close to Darien as Kylar once again led the way through the squalid, overcrowded market. This place was a giant puzzle, the abundance of meandering paths enough to muddle anyone's bearings. Compared to the Umbra Forum, this market was densely packed, which meant more threats to watch out for, more reasons to watch your back. But the many vampires, veneficae, werewolves, and hellsehers crowding the space were wise to clear a path for the Darkslayers, who hid their identities with hoods yet still managed to demand respect with presence and vibe alone.

When they reached an outdoor fighting ring, Kylar pushed deep into the crowds surrounding the roped-in square. Darien followed, Loren's hand still in his, Dallas and Max coming in close behind. Loren kept her head down as they walked, careful not to look at the many faces picking apart their group, most of the stares lingering on her and Dallas. She knew that if she gave them the satisfaction of looking up, they'd take it as an invitation. A challenge.

Wild cheering and the ear-splitting squall of a bullhorn tore through the night, the ring announcer declaring a victor. All around them, the crowd erupted with excitement, jumping and clapping and stamping their feet.

Someone slammed into Loren hard enough to bruise, the force of the collision nearly ripping her hand out of Darien's grasp.

But Darien did not let go, and he was quick to shove aside the man who'd bumped into her, the look on Darien's face so lethal, it could pass for a weapon all on its own. *"Come near her again, I'll cut your goddamn heart out,"* Darien snarled through bared teeth. Black eyes that were truly terrifying shone in the shadows beneath his hood.

The man backed up, hands shooting into the air. The few people in the immediate vicinity retreated too, murmuring to one another in fearful tones.

Darien tugged Loren closer and kept walking, wrapping a strong arm around her waist this time, putting her partially in front of him. No one could bump into her now unless they hit Darien too, and no one in their right mind would want to do that. "You okay?" he asked her, that razor-edged tone still present in the question. The crowd was so loud, she could hardly hear him.

"I'm fine."

"Anyone else touches you, I'll slit their throat." The threat sent a shiver up her spine.

She peeked up at him, tracing his scarred knuckles with her thumb. "Are you okay?" she whispered, noting the black lingering in his eyes.

Darien took a second to answer. "No one can touch you, sweetheart, or I lose my shit." Loren knew that was true, but there was something in that deadly stare he used to pick apart the crowds—*daring* people to come too close—that told her something else was going on here.

She decided she would ask him tonight—when he and Malakai finished their errand and got back to Roman's.

"I love you," she told him, the words so at odds with their violent surroundings.

The declaration made the black in Darien's eyes disappear with one blink. He kissed her hand and plowed on.

No one touched her after that.

They found the man they were looking for in a covered seating area overlooking the fighting ring. It was less crowded over here, but Darien still hung onto her as they ascended the steps, their feet thumping hollowly on wood that sagged with moisture and age. Loren resisted the urge to look down at the gaps between the benches, where an unnatural darkness lurked. She could feel many eyes watching her, could hear whispering as the creatures tried goading her into looking down.

Look down, they whispered with hissed, razor-edged chuckles. *Don't look up.*

Watch out, another giggled. *Don't trip.*

Won't you play with us?

We're so lonely, another wept.

Such sweet, human blood.

"Head up," Darien warned.

She nodded. Drew a steadying breath, focusing on where she was placing her feet, never looking directly at the dark, swirling gaps between the wood, the unworldly blackness sparkling with faint colors. "What are those things?" she asked Darien.

"Exspiravits. They suck the breath out of people." Loren heard Max explaining the same to Dallas a short ways behind them. "Two more steps," Darien said. "I got you." He helped her up, his hold never faltering.

Kylar had already reached Alfie, both men smiling as they spoke. Alfie was a warlock in his early forties, his inflamed eyes and pallid skin suggesting he was sick with the Tricking. As he spoke to Kylar, he stared out at the match, his lips moving around the thick cigar trapped between teeth that were yellowed from drug use. Their exchange was so quiet, only immortal ears could hear.

"Alfie, this is Darien," Kylar said, gesturing with a brown hand adorned with spider- and phantom-shaped rings.

Alfie took the cigar out of his mouth and used the other to shake hands with Darien. "Cassel—pleasure."

"Likewise."

As Alfie's eyes flicked between the others in their group, glinting with curiosity as he took in Loren and Dallas, Max stepped forward and extended a hand. "Maximus Reacher."

Alfie shook it. "Pleasure. You're right on time." He put out his cigar and stood, a couple of warlocks who were seated in the tiered benches farther up doing the same. Bodyguards, Loren realized. "Follow me."

He led them down the steps and around to the back of the wooden stands, to a door illuminated by an acid-green bulb mounted to the exterior wall. It was the only light source in the area, the shadows and lack of activity behind the stands creating the same atmosphere as a Crossroads—a supernatural one. The darkness was pressing. Cloying. A buzzer sounded as Alfie opened the door, and hazy lights flicked on with a motion sensor, revealing a treacherously steep staircase that dove deep into the earth.

"Wait right here," Alfie said to his bodyguards, his voice barely a mumble.

Loren followed Darien inside, and as she felt the air peel back, she realized—

What she had felt a moment ago wasn't her imagination. This place was hidden by magic. The same way the blood farm at the Umbra Forum was hidden, the spells keeping law enforcement from digging up the people responsible for the heinous crime of farming blood from the unwilling.

Her heart sped up as they descended the concrete steps, deep into the underground that reeked like a tomb. Darien, sensing her distress, gently squeezed her hand, and then lifted it so he could press his mouth against the inside of her wrist, his steady breaths warming her skin that was suddenly icy cold.

At the bottom of the steps was a network of corridors, all lit with acid-green bulbs that made everyone in their group look sickly. There were so many closed doors down here, they reminded Loren of cells. She shuddered to think what lay beyond them. Alfie brought them to the third door to the left and pushed it open. One by one, they filed in.

The door shut behind them, and Alfie strode up to a row of metal lockers, all latched with padlocks. "Martel said to get you as many as I have on hand," Alfie said, back facing them as he slid a key into a padlock. It clicked open, and he swung open the locker doors to reveal stacks of black boxes.

"Right," Darien confirmed, completely at ease down here. Gods, how many places like this had he walked? Loren could *feel* things lurking in the air, even in a room as unfurnished and wide-open as this, no shadows to be seen, no closets. Just a few simple lockers and a single table in the center of the room. It unsettled her to imagine sleeping down here, especially when she heard distant screaming from a room deeper in, and a squawking that sounded like a cross between bird and human.

Alfie slid out the third box from the bottom and brought it over, thumping it onto the table that rattled under the force. He slid a thumb into the cardboard latch at the front of the box and opened it, revealing rows of small pointed missiles. "Two thousand Morsian darts," he said, bloodshot eyes flicking up to meet Darien's. "That's all I got, but more's coming next week."

"How much you want?"

"Ten thousand," Alfie replied.

Darien let go of Loren to get out his wallet. As soon as his hand was no longer holding hers, she noticed Kylar and Max were standing very close to her—fencing her and Dallas in, their faces lined with tension.

They, too, must have sensed something was down here.

Dallas's silver-ringed eyes flicked toward the door—toward the bird-like screaming that kept getting louder. "What is that?" she mouthed to Loren, who shook her head in answer, her whole body covered in goosebumps.

Darien handed over a wad of bills. "Fifteen," he said. Alfie took it, a question in his eyes. "Consider this a down payment. I want the others you're bringing in next week," Darien explained. "All of them."

Alfie nodded once, clearly pleased. "They're all yours."

DARIEN WAS ITCHING for a hit of Venom. Dying for one was the better word. The line between need and want was starting to blur.

They were nearing the truck, the clamor of the Black Market fading behind them, when he let go of Loren's hand and opened the passenger's-side door of Max's SUV for her. Malakai stood on the sidewalk, phone glued to his ear. It sounded like Tanner was on the other end. Another two minutes passed before the Reaper hung up.

"What's happening?" Darien asked him.

Malakai slid the device into his pocket. "Nothing yet. Atlas got the spell feeds set up."

Finally. Spell feeds could tell them what was happening in Caliginous on Silverway in the areas where cameras didn't cover. They couldn't see visual feeds, but the spell feeds acted like a blueprint for energy—showing the layout of Caliginous and lighting up with colors whenever someone was present in certain areas of the building. It was a hack the Devils frequently used to track targets who were hard to find, though for a number of reasons, it didn't always work. While it detected energy, it didn't identify the facets of an aura the same way as the Sight, leading to a lot of educated guesses as opposed to the certainty that came with remotely tracking someone.

"He said Tanya's still there," Malakai added, "doing closing duties."

"All clients are gone?" Max asked.

"Apparently." Malakai shrugged one shoulder. "Where to now?" he asked Darien. "You got the Venom?"

"They were out." He watched Loren get into her seat, her teeth chattering in a gust of wind that tore down the road. "We need to get more tar and he'll make it for us. You up for coming with me?"

"Sure," Malakai said, making for the truck. "Why not? I'm bored as shit—there's not enough excitement around here."

Darien turned his attention to Loren as she buckled up. "How are you feeling? You cold?"

"I think it's the normal kind."

He took her wrist and pushed up her jacket sleeve. The tattoo for Caliginous on Silverway was ordinary black ink, no bead of light running through it. He lightly squeezed her wrist and let go. "I'll see you back at the house?"

She nodded, and he shut her door. He got into the driver's seat of the truck, waiting until Max had driven away before he fired up his own vehicle and sped out to the tar pits.

100

THE THEATER DISTRICT
YVESWICH, STATE OF KER

Roman had made it back to Yveswich in the late-afternoon. He'd driven the speed limit for once, fighting the urge to turn around and go right back to Shay.

Now, he sat in his car out front of the movie theater, waiting for Paxton and Eugene's show to end. The others were currently at his house or the Black Market. Roman would have gone with Darien to get the Morsian darts that could take down the demons of Spirit Terra, but he'd wanted to be here to pick up his little brother. Paxton had texted him with an update a few minutes ago, saying the show got out in ten.

They were approaching fifteen when Roman's phone buzzed in the cupholder. He grabbed it and typed in his passcode, assuming it was Paxton saying they'd stopped to play an arcade game or to buy extra candy. Instead, he saw a name he hadn't expected to see again for a long time. Maybe ever.

SHAY
> Truth or lie?

Roman's idiotic heart skipped two full beats. He waited, watching the typing bubble, *dying* to hear what she said next. He knew he was a goddamn fool for getting his hopes up. But—

SHAY
> I came back.

Roman's heart was no longer skipping—it was racing. With excitement, with relief. With joy. He even felt a smile pull at his mouth for the first time in hours. He'd literally cried on the drive back—sobbed like someone had died. And he wasn't even ashamed of it.

Shay Cousens had managed to change him in such a short amount of time—had literally stolen his heart from him like the incredible thief she was. He'd slept with too many women to count, most of the experiences now nothing but blurs, but last night?

Last night was a dream. *She* was a dream—the best thing that'd happened to him in years.

His phone buzzed again.

SHAY
> I couldn't leave.
>
> I was hoping we could talk, if you're not busy.

ROMAN
> You're one of those one-line texters, aren't you.

SHAY
> Where
>
> Are
>
> You?
>
> 🖤

ROMAN
> I'm picking Pax and Gene up from the theater.
>
> Where
>
> Are
>
> You?

SHAY
> My place.

ROMAN
> If you don't mind a couple of termites tagging along, I can swing by in a few.

SHAY
> I'll prepare the bug spray 🖤

ROMAN
> 🖤

He'd never sent a heart symbol before, but there was a first for everything.

Shayla had already been his first for so many things. He hoped there would be plenty more where that came from.

'There will,' Sayagul said gently, the dragon sounding as relieved as Roman to learn that Shay was in Yveswich again. *'She came back.'*

Yeah, she did. She sure fucking did. For *him*. Damn, was he lucky.

Groups of people began to file out of the cinema, carrying bags of popcorn and fountain drinks. The Theater District was lit up better than most of the others in Yveswich, the road lined with super bright LED street lights, so Roman spotted Paxton with ease. Eugene walked at his side, soda and popcorn in hand, and coming up behind them were—

Simon and Trey.

Roman ground his teeth. "Shit."

Paxton's eyes found the car, and fuck, the kid looked scared for his life. So did Eugene.

This was not part of the plan.

Roman started the car, but before he could even put it in drive, Simon and Trey herded Paxton and Eugene into a black van parked by the curb. They got in, Simon standing by the sliding door to make sure Paxton didn't try to get back out. And when Pax poked his head out the still-open door, craning his neck to see Roman, Simon shoved him inside and slammed the door.

"Motherfucker," Roman growled, blood boiling. Simon deserved to have his hand cut off for that.

His phone buzzed in his lap. Keeping an eye on the van, he checked the message.

DON

Follow the van.

Roman didn't know what to do—what sort of trap he was about to face. But Simon and Trey had the kids, so he'd walk into anything, no matter how bad.

Another message came through.

DON

You'll be wise to do as I say.

The van started driving.

Roman drew a deep breath and followed.

Shay had never considered Yveswich her home. She'd never had a reason to want to be here, aside from Anna, and even when she was alive, they'd plotted to get out of here as soon as they could.

A few weeks and one Shadowmaster later, and she had a reason to be here now, a reason to want to come back. She would have made it back sooner, had she not needed to wait for a taxicab to get all the way out to Motel 58. She had tried bribing the driver to break the speed limit in exchange for a generous tip—from the funds she'd stolen from Roman—but to no avail.

She stood out front of her apartment door, her body weighed down by all her bags, the extra pounds making the scar tissue from her injury burn with a vengeance. She shimmied her keys out of her back pocket, found the one for the front door, and wrestled it into the lock. The spells softened. The key clicked. She twisted the door handle, pushed open the door—

And flipped on the light to find her mother sitting cross-legged on the couch.

She stopped short. "Mom?"

On the couch beside her, throat slit from ear to ear, her corpse propped up like a doll's, was Shay's neighbor—a witch with a sugar glider for a Familiar.

Athene gave Shay a venomous smile. "Hello, dear daughter."

101

ROMAN'S HOUSE
YVESWICH, STATE OF KER

Loren had just finished brushing her teeth and getting into her pajamas when Ivy intercepted her in the hallway.

"You doing okay?" Ivy asked.

"I'm fine," Loren said, wrapping her arms around her middle. She felt cold again, but the tattoo on her wrist was still dark, the ink ordinary. She chalked it up to nerves and exhaustion and asked Ivy, "How come?"

"Darien said you seemed like something was bothering you."

Oh crap. Was she being that obvious at the bakery?

Loren drew a breath, her lungs feeling tight again. "No, I'm okay, I just... I noticed that he's acting a bit funny." Well, it wasn't a lie. Ever since she'd gone with him to the Black Market, she'd been dying to know what was up with him. The edge to him was unfamiliar—something not even his Surges had caused. And, come to think of it, she had noticed it before her memories had come back, too—that time he'd switched places with Ivy while Loren swam in the pool. She'd never figured out where he had gone, what was bothering him. "Is *he* okay?" Loren prodded.

It was Ivy's turn to take a steadying inhale. "He's addicted to Venom," she said. Loren's face smoothed with understanding. "I figured I can tell you because I know he won't keep it a secret from you for long. I think the reason he hasn't told you yet is because he just got you back. Typical Darien not wanting to bother other people with his problems, you know?" She waved a manicured hand.

Loren nodded. "Yeah." She studied Ivy. "Can we help him?"

"Not unless he can get off the Venom, and...well, I don't think he's getting off of it anytime soon, with the way things have been going." She grimaced.

Loren chewed on her lip.

She'd had no idea. He'd protected them all by taking Venom to maximize his output of magic, and he was already paying for it.

Ivy said, "Now will you tell me what's bothering *you?*"

Loren met her searching gaze. And after everything that'd happened lately, after the thoughts that had assaulted her mind at the bakery—during that quiet moment with Darien that was supposed to be nothing but peaceful—she found that she wanted to talk. So she confessed, "It's something the Widow said."

102

ZIMA
YVESWICH, STATE OF KER

This was worse than anything Roman had imagined. Far worse.

The black van Paxton and Eugene had been herded into led him straight to Shay's apartment. Simon and Trey parked right out front—in the same spot where Roman had parked just last night.

Had they followed him here yesterday? Had he caused this?

Another buzz of his phone had his mouth drying out.

DON

> Why don't you go see if your girlfriend is home?

"Shit." Roman's heart was punching through his chest. He looked up at the windows of Shay's apartment.

They were aglow with light.

Fuck.

Fuck.

'What do we do?' Sayagul whispered, the dragon trembling in Roman's shadow.

'We make sure she's okay.'

And not dead. Not fucking dead.

With a deep breath, he slid his phone into his pocket and got out.

He crossed the street, heading for the van, wishing like hell that he had more than just the lone pistol strapped to his hip.

He was so focused on getting to Shay that he didn't see the people coming up behind him until it was too late.

Until he was being choked by fishing line and dragged into the shadows of the alley beside the apartment building.

"Mom," Shay said again, the word a hollow whisper. Her eyes flicked to her neighbor, Claudia, propped up like a dummy on the couch, blood streaming into her lap. Her eyes were bolted open, the silver rings around her pupils already dull. Shay swallowed the urge to retch. "What did you do?"

"I had to get in here somehow," Athene said with a cluck of her tongue, her tone implying she thought Shay was stupid. "What did you expect me to do, wait outside in the cold until you came home?" She tutted. *"Home."* A harsh laugh scraped out of her, and her eyes darkened with the Sight— something Shay seldom saw in her mother's eyes, but never failed to frighten her, the black so at odds with her striking face. "Have you created a home for yourself here, Shayla? Is the House of Blue not good enough for you?"

Shay was shaking her head. "That's not it."

"How long have you had this place?"

"Three months," she lied.

"There you go again with the lying."

"I'm not lying," she said, but it was no use. Her mother had taken her by such surprise, she could not even call upon her magic to aid her tonight. No lightning would save her, and neither would illusion. Her mother was gifted with the same magic as Shay, and therefore had immunity to its effects; if Shay cast an illusion, her mother would be able to see right through it.

"I paid a visit to your landlord," Athene went on. "That tubby warlock in apartment number forty-three. He gave me this big, long *boring* spiel about tenant privacy, so I decided to take matters into my own hands." A beat of tense silence. "You don't have a landlord anymore, Shayla—if you'd like to see him one last time, you'll have to go dumpster diving out back. Hopefully the demons haven't already picked his bones clean."

Shay's hands curled into fists, temples pulsing. "You're sick."

"If sick is what I have to be to get things done, sick I shall be," she said, those eyes so black, that expression so hateful, Shay hardly recognized the woman who'd birthed her. This...*thing* sitting on her couch was no mother —she was a threat. As much a demon as the ones feasting out back on her landlord's body. "Now that that waste of skin is gone," Athene continued, "with the pull of a few strings, this sad excuse for an apartment building will be mine, and I shall sell it." She gave her a hard stare, those eyes glinting like black holes. "Any objections from my least favorite daughter?"

"Your *only* daughter," Shay corrected, the reality of that statement silencing her words to barely a breath. "Anna's dead." Saying the truth aloud felt like punching herself in the stomach.

Athene did not react. If Shay didn't know any better, she'd think her mother already knew—had known this whole time.

Maybe she had.

Athene uncrossed her toned legs and rose with one fluid movement. "This is the last time I'll say this," she began, stilettos clicking sharply as she crossed the room. "You are never to see Roman Devlin again. And if you do..." She stopped barely a foot from Shay. "I will see to it that Donovan has him tortured and killed in whatever creative way he finds fitting."

There was a lump in her throat, and she couldn't swallow it. "I haven't seen Roman—"

"You don't really think Claudia didn't talk before I slit her throat, do you?" Athene interrupted, glaring down at her. "The bitch saw him standing outside last night. Said he came here looking for you. He was shouting up at your window like the heartthrobs in all those tacky romance movies." Those eyes shone blacker.

"It's a lie," she tried.

"You're the only one who's lying, Shayla." She strode past, wafting her with that syrupy perfume. "And your lying will be the death of that Shadowmaster if you don't wisen up." She opened the front door. "Pack your things. I expect you back at the House of Blue full-time starting tomorrow."

She left, leaving Shay alone in her apartment with a dead woman.

ROMAN STOOD in the alley beside Shay's apartment building, fighting to keep his footing as Adham—one of Don's men—kept choking him with that fishing line. He felt his face turning purple, felt the wire cutting into his skin, his fingers uselessly grasping for it, trying and failing to get space between the wire and his skin. Space to breathe. The van idled nearby, Paxton and Eugene banging on the glass of the window. Screaming their lungs out.

Gravel crunched under boots as Don stalked up to Roman, so heavily wreathed in shadows he was nearly invisible. Several more of his men hung back, watching the scene unfold with sick amusement.

"Hello, Roman," Donovan said, as if they were taking a walk in the damn park. Behind him stalked his two-headed wolf Familiar, a hulking beast with glowing crimson eyes.

Roman couldn't get a breath down. Couldn't move. Couldn't respond.

Don beckoned to Adham, who let up on the wire—barely enough for Roman to suck in a thin stream of air. Adham kept the wire poised, pressing deep enough that the slightest of movements would cut off his oxygen again.

"I figured you'd be coming here tonight," Don said. "So I decided to join you. As a family instead." He cast a look of sick delight at the van, where his youngest son continued to pound on the window. "Isn't this wonderful?"

"What do you want?" Roman managed to bite out. His question caused Adham to tighten up again.

"What do I want?" Don chuckled, the sound short and harsh. The shadows wreathing his hands spread up his arms, threading around his neck and head like snakes waiting to bite. "I want a son who respects me. Who *listens* to me," he hissed through bared teeth. "What did you think was going to happen, Roman? Did you think I wouldn't find out? Did you think you could somehow get away with breaking one of the most important rules in my city without my knowing about it?"

Even if Roman had wanted to reply, he couldn't—Adham had tightened his hold again, the wire cutting in. Sharp as a knife.

Don stepped up, getting right up in Roman's face like he so often did, and began with a whisper his shadows echoed. "Here's what's going to happen. If you step out of line again, she," he pointed a finger up at Shay's window, "will be raped bloody by several of my men."

Roman fought, but the wire only tightened.

He'd kill him. He'd fucking *kill him*—

"And then they'll string her up, just like they do you," he pointed now in Roman's face, "and squeeze her little brain until she's bleeding from the eyes and ears. Just like they do you." His mouth twitched with a smile. "See where I'm going with this? Except—plot twist." He flourished his hands, black mist swirling. "They'll do it till she stops breathing. And you're gonna go in afterward," he poked him in the chest, "and clean up her blood." For several beats, Don stared at him in disgust. "Do you want to hear what I'll do to Pax if you don't listen this time?"

Adham slackened his hold enough for Roman to hiss, *"No."*

But Don wet his lips. "For Pax, I've got a bit of a different plan—"

Roman thrashed, the wire slicing a line into his skin. "I fucking said *no!*"

Don smiled, but his eyes were burning coals. "Let him go." He waved a hand at Adham.

The wire was lifted, and Roman had to resist the urge to collapse to his knees, instead bracing a shaking hand against the cold wall. "Pax and Eugene," he squeezed out. "You let them go—I'll stay away from Shay."

Don sized him up—studying him to see if he was lying. Smiled a little —a cold and deadly thing. "Fine." A whistle cut through Don's lips.

Trey got out of the van and came around to open the sliding door. Pax and Eugene stepped out, eyes bolted wide with fear.

"Shouldn't have kept that house from me, Roman," Don said. He made to leave, but turned back, coming back for more. He always came back for more. "Oh—about the house. I'll be selling it and keeping all the money. Better enjoy it while you can; I've already got a few offers lined up."

Fuck him.

Fuck. Him.

"Pax's got a magic lesson next weekend," Don called as he made for the van, reaching out a hand to muss up Paxton's hair as he passed. Don threw Roman a smile over his shoulder. "And you're gonna watch."

103

THE TAR PITS
YVESWICH, STATE OF KER

"I seem to remember," Malakai began, unable to resist, as he and Darien filled up several vials with tar from the bubbling pit they were crouched beside, "the last time we were working together, you said you'd show me some naked photos of your girl." He fought the urge to smile, already sensing that Darien was going to detonate. Cassel was a walking bomb, and if you wanted to set him off, all you had to do was poke him with a little stick labeled 'Loren'.

And damn, was it fun to set him off.

"Don't even start," Darien warned as he capped the vial and filled up another. Moonlight trickled through the park, limning the edges of their black clothing with silver. Fog—the normal kind—hugged the bluffs at the outskirts of the grounds, while dark, otherworldly smog that was typically found in monster habitats hung out in the dips and hollows in the earth, creating the perfect hiding spots for the lesser breeds of demon.

"You were the one who said it," Malakai crooned.

"Don't put words in my mouth," Darien snapped, his eyes turning black under his hood.

"Dude, your inability to keep your voice *down*," Malakai hissed, casting a pointed look at the Hounds scattered throughout the park, some of them sleeping in pits or waterfalls, others gorging on prey that might've been human, "is going to get you dragged into one of these pits, and I will not save your ass if that happens. All I'm saying—"

"I didn't fucking say that," Cassel bit out, quieter now, eyes still black with the Sight. Malakai knew he was itching for Venom; Ivy had filled him in on a lot since he'd got to Yveswich, and she hadn't left out the little tidbit about Darien being addicted to Venom. The longer Malakai hung out with this asshole, the more they had in common. Cassel continued, "And you will not see a single one."

Malakai grinned. "So you *do* have some."

Darien merely glared and resumed filling up the last of their vials.

When they made it back to the Black Market and found the dealer in a tiny tin shop deep in the maze of stalls, the warlock told them he would need some time to make the Venom, but confirmed they'd brought enough tar to get triple the amount Darien had bought from the guy last time—enough to feed their addictions and their magic.

Perfect.

"Come back in one hour," the warlock said as he took the glass vials into a meaty hand. "I'll have your Venom."

They were walking through the Black Market, back toward the truck, when Cassel slowed, his eyes drifting to a fighting ring nearby. A black sign painted with a white snake was nailed to the base of the enclosure, the wood warped from the weather. The roped-in square was surrounded by spectators, and inside the ring, men and a few women of every species aside from human fought to the death, their faces concealed with masks that ranged from black adamant to the kind they wore on ski hills.

Darien threw Malakai a look. "You feel like fighting to kill some time?"

"If this is your way of asking me if I want to fight you to the death, the answer is yes."

"Not me, motherfucker," Darien said. Malakai chuckled. "They alternate to matches involving teams after ten p.m.," Darien explained. "Next match is two against two. Yes or no?"

Malakai grinned. "Hell yeah. Is that even a question?"

Cassel's answering grin was just as wicked. "Let's see what you got."

ROMAN DROVE BACK to his house in silence. He didn't say a word, and neither did the kids. The only sound to fill the silence was heavy, ragged breathing and the pounding of three hearts.

They were nearing the district of Ardesia when Pax broke the silence. "Do we have to say goodbye to Shay?" he whispered.

Shay had already sent Roman several messages since Don had threatened him. Those messages were the reason he knew she was okay—and the reason he hadn't sprinted up there once Don had left. Now, his phone that rested in his lap buzzed with another.

As he drove, Roman glanced down to read the messages.

SHAY

> Please tell me you're okay.
>
> A thumbs up, even.
>
> Anything.
>
> Guess I really am one of those one-line texters.

Roman sighed. Scrubbed a hand down his face. This was going to hurt, but it needed to be done. It was just a matter of when, and what words he'd use. He hated the idea of hurting Shay, even if it was only verbally, but he needed to make it convincing. She was stubborn and rebellious, and if he didn't convince her to leave Yveswich like she'd planned, she was carrion.

He should never have went after her to Motel 58. If he hadn't, she'd be long gone. Long gone and safe.

"Roman?" Pax whispered.

"Yeah," Roman breathed, finally answering. "Yeah, we need to say goodbye to Shay, bud." He glanced at Pax to see him frowning down at the crumpled-up bag of popcorn in his lap. "For now," Roman decided to add, to lighten the blow. And maybe because he needed to hear those words too.

For now.

He could see her again after he dealt with his dad—however the hell he was going to do that. He had no plan yet, but he knew one thing for sure: He couldn't keep going like this.

This could not continue.

Once they got back to the house, Roman parked out front and got out. He sparked a cigarette, needing a moment to himself before he went inside. Eugene vanished into the house, but Paxton lingered.

"You okay?" he asked Roman.

"I'm fine," Roman said, taking a drag and blowing the smoke away from Paxton. "It's just a scratch." He gestured to the cut in his neck.

Voices drifted from inside the house. The door swung open, and Kylar appeared.

The minute Roman saw the dread on Kylar's face, he put out his smoke and started moving. "What's going on?"

"We have a problem," Kylar breathed. "Have you heard from Darien?"

"No, why?"

"He needs to get here—*now.*"

Darien and Malakai were heading back to where they'd parked the truck, both of them covered in blood but feeling like a million bucks, when Darien's phone rang in his pocket.

Darien answered without checking the identification. "Cassel."

"It's me," Atlas said on the other end.

Darien slowed. "What is it?"

"I found them," Tanner replied. Holy shit. The imperator, Gaven. Finally.

"They're at Caliginous on Silverway," Tanner added. The tension in Atlas's voice put Darien on high alert.

"Atlas?" he ventured.

"They took Tanya hostage."

104

ROMAN'S HOUSE
YVESWICH, STATE OF KER

Darien stood beside Loren, the others spread out in a group behind them, watching the screen on Tanner's laptop at the dining room table. The camera feeds for Caliginous on Silverway.

The interior lights of the business were all at full brightness. Tanya stood in her usual spot behind the desk, squeezing a stress ball at her side, her very posture exuding tension. Men with guns stood all around her, and heading down the corridor that housed chambers one to four and six to seven were—

"That's the imperator," Darien breathed. Now that he was seeing him with his own eyes, now that he knew for certain that it wasn't just Quinton's men who were here in Yveswich, but Quinton as well, Darien's blood thrummed with vengeance.

He'd kill that fucker. Make him pay for this bullshit he'd put them all through. There was no sign of his son, Klay, but the minute Darien ran into him, he'd get revenge on that prick too. Beat him black and blue and slit his throat for coming near his girl, for grabbing her hand against her will that day in the hospital. Before, Darien had refrained from acting, for Loren's sake. Her safety.

Now, he'd kill him. Cut off his hands for touching her.

As if sensing his rage brimming over the edge, Loren stepped closer to him. Darien drew a breath, focusing on the comforting feel of her aura.

"There's Gaven, too," Tanner announced, using his mouse to circle the man who walked at Quinton's side.

As if they somehow heard them, the imperator looked toward the camera that pointed down the chamber corridor—the lens their group was currently looking through.

Loren's hand drifted to Darien's wrist, her fingers circling it. Darien took her hand, threading his fingers through hers.

One by one, the cameras went black.

"We need to help Tanya," Tanner murmured, clicking to enlarge the spell feeds again—their only way of monitoring what was happening within the walls of the business, now that they didn't have cameras. "Right now."

Roman paced in the living room, phone pressed to his ear as he tried calling Tanya's cell phone for the fifth time in under three minutes.

Even from several feet away, Darien could hear when Tanya's answering machine picked up again. "Hi, you've reached Tanya—"

Roman cursed and hung up. "Nothing," he declared as Kylar and Darien glanced his way.

"She's probably not answering because someone's in earshot," Darien said. He took off his jacket and pulled his shirt over his head. "Get your shit on—bodysuits, as many weapons as you can carry," he told the others. "We need to go right away." He'd kill the imperator and every person working for him, would get his revenge for the destruction they'd done to his house, the attempts made on the lives of the people he cared about—

And for stealing Mortifer. As soon as he got the Hob back, he'd give him all the shave ice in the world.

"We should split up," Tanner suggested. "Take a look here." He zoomed out on the spell feeds until the entire blueprint of the skyscraper was in view. With a click and a drag of the mouse, he spun the skyscraper around. "The imperator's men have been going into chamber seven, but get this—I haven't seen them come back out. It's like they disappear."

"What are the chambers made of?" Malakai asked.

"Adamant," Roman replied. He took off his hoodie, leaving the tight-fitting shirt he had on underneath—clothes that would fit more comfortably under the bodysuit. "The same thing as the rabbit masks. Which means—"

"The chambers don't show up on spell feeds," Darien cut in. Only the flip-side did. Roman nodded, and Darien faced Tanner. "What are you thinking?"

"I'm thinking the chambers lead to a network of tunnels. Remember how they were storing the first Well replica in Angelthene underneath the city?" Several people murmured in answer. "Why not do the same in Yveswich?"

"It's a good guess," Lace said as she began strapping weapons to her body, suit already on. Jewels and Aspen were doing the same in the living room just behind her. "What better place to hide a bomb than underground where no one could stumble upon it by accident?"

Tanner went on, "I can't view anything that's covered in adamant, but look here," he dragged the mouse, gesturing to the vague, colorful lines running underneath the skyscraper, along with a shaft that seemed to abruptly end before picking up again near the bottom of the screen, just a sliver of a colored line. "I think this is the maintenance elevator."

"So," Max said, "some of us go in through Caliginous while the rest of us go in through the elevator?"

"You'll need an employee code and print to use them," Tanner said, pulling up a different screen. "Give me two secs and I'll get them for you."

"What about the Necropolis?" Kylar asked.

Heads turned to face him.

Darien said, "What necropolis?"

"It's a city below the city," Roman replied. "A place they used to write stories about. A city of the dead—literally."

Kylar added, "It's a bunch of old tunnels and catacombs they sealed off a long time ago to help control the underground demon populations."

"Where were the entrances located before they sealed them?" This question came from Travis, who was helping Jewels fasten her weapons belt, much to the dismay of a glaring Malakai.

"By the tar pits," Roman said, speaking to his brother for the first time in hours.

"So...," Jack began, sliding a knife into the sheath by his ankle, "some of us should take a look in case they've reopened an entrance?"

"Exactly," Kylar confirmed, eyes bright with adrenaline.

"Block them in from all sides," Dominic smiled. "I like it."

"Okay, so three groups, then," Ivy said. "Who's going to the tar pits and who's going to Caliginous?"

Eyes scanned the group, most of them looking to Darien for the answer.

"Me, Roman, Jack, Tanner—chamber seven," Darien decided. "Max and Dallas—maintenance elevators. We'll meet where the tunnels intersect." He turned to Tanner. "How close are they?"

He hummed, bringing up the blueprint again, and shrugged. "Can't tell. Might have to wing that one."

"Alright," Darien said. "The rest of you—tar pits." There were a few people in the group who were staying behind—Arthur and the kids, obviously, and Dominic and Blue, who'd volunteered to stay at the house in case any protection was needed here. Darien had managed to convince Malakai to stay too—for Loren. If Darien couldn't be with her himself, he'd pick the strongest person to guard her. The Reaper had argued—vehemently. But had ultimately accepted.

Now, the Reaper grumbled again about having babysitting duty, but didn't argue. Instead, he stalked up to Aspen to help her with her weapons.

"Where's Arthur?" Darien asked, scanning the room full of people.

The old man was coming down the hallway in his pajamas. "Here. Got your blades." Wrapped up in a towel, he carried the three swords, reinforced and complete with proper hilts. In his other hand, he held the rest of the rings. He passed them out and gave instructions to the few people who didn't know how to use them. "Where is Shayla?" he asked, scanning the room.

Roman's eyes fell to the floor. He turned the ring on his finger, the black suit shooting out to cover his body, magic shimmering over his face. "Not here." He cleared his throat. "And not coming."

Arthur offered him the navy blue ring he'd made for Shay. "Take it anyway. Just in case."

Roman didn't.

"I will," Ivy said. She stepped forward and took the ring.

Darien glanced at Tanner's screen again—one last time. The innocent woman they could no longer see, thanks to the cameras being cut. "We need to hurry."

A FEW MINUTES LATER, Darien stepped into one of the spare bedrooms upstairs with his sister, who he'd asked to speak to Loren while he was gone—to find out what had been bothering her since he'd brought her to the Avenue of the Waning Moon. He knew he could ask Loren himself, but he'd already tried—and sometimes, women were more open to each other in ways not even their boyfriends could get them to be. And fuck if he was going to let anything drive them apart. He'd just got her back—he needed to fix this.

Whatever *this* was.

"So?" Darien asked, keeping his voice down. He was ready to go—bodysuit on, blade of black adamant strapped to his back. Although he couldn't use most weapons without causing himself a great deal of pain, he'd still strapped a couple to his hips and thigh, an automatic rifle fastened to his back alongside the sword. Better to have them than not. If he needed to break his hand again to save his own life or the life of one of his family members, he'd do it. Gladly.

"It's exactly what you suspected," Ivy said, speaking with equal quiet, her bodysuit a deep scarlet that looked like blood in the lamplight. "She's bothered by the future and the fact that she's mortal and you're not." Fuck —not again.

"How did that whole conversation go? Does she want to break up or something? What's the solution here?" He wasn't an idiot—he knew her mortality would pose a problem one day. But he lived in the moment in a way Loren couldn't seem to. And he loved her too much to bear the thought of ever losing her.

Natural death was the one thing he couldn't protect her from. And death always won.

"Of course she doesn't want to break up," Ivy said. "She's just...keeping you in mind, mostly. Your happiness. Your future. She thinks she won't be able to offer you the kind of life you deserve." Kids, if they decided to have any—a life she was cursed to not be a part of forever.

'I told you,' Bandit grumbled.

'Not a good time,' Darien warned.

'We aren't ready for pups.'

"For fuck's sake," Darien muttered, ignoring Bandit. He swiped a hand down his face, the material of his bodysuit scraping the bridge of his nose.

"She's been through a lot lately," Ivy offered. "I'm sure she'll be back to her old self in no time."

"Yeah, until she decides to be bothered by this shit again."

"So let her be bothered, then. If you want my opinion, I think it's normal for her to think about this every once in a while. You guys are opposites—it's only natural for her to feel stuck because of her mortality."

Darien sighed. "Yeah, but there's no solution to it—nothing I can say that'll make her stop thinking about it." Nothing that would fix it. When something was making her upset, it boiled his blood, made him want to strangle whatever the problem was with his bare hands. And he hated that he couldn't fix this. "Even if she thought breaking up was the answer, to 'give me freedom' or whatever the fuck reasoning she has, it wouldn't make a difference. My fate's tied to hers."

Ivy gave several rapid, exaggerated blinks of shock. "Don't be dramatic, Darien," she scolded.

He didn't answer.

Slowly, as silence stretched between them, her features fell. "Darien?" she bit out, her breaths thinning out. "You *are* just being dramatic, aren't you?" He could almost see her piecing it together in her head—the details he'd never told any of them about his visit with the Widow.

"Am I ever just being dramatic?" Apparently, that was the wrong thing to say—the wrong time, too. But he'd kept this secret bottled up for so long, he knew it was only a matter of time before it slipped out.

Ivy's features transformed with horror. With a shaky whisper, she asked —*demanded* of him, "What did you do?"

LOREN FELT like someone had punched her in the stomach. She couldn't draw a breath, couldn't even remember how to breathe.

"Tell me it isn't true," she whispered as she drifted into Darien's former room upstairs, hands balling into fists at her sides. She couldn't believe what she'd just heard—he *had* to be lying. It *had* to be a lie. She wouldn't accept anything less. "You tied your fate to mine?" She glanced between Darien and Ivy, both of them loaded up with weapons, his sister looking like she either wanted to strangle someone or burst into tears.

Loren felt the same.

She pressed, "Is that what you traded the Widow?" He'd never told her —never explained the details of the bargain he'd made to get her dog back. When Singer had died, Loren had known so little about hellsehers, the Crossroads, and the deals that magic-born people had the power to make, but she'd never believed for one second that it would be something this bad.

Darien didn't answer, but he didn't need to. The look on his face was answer enough.

He would die the minute she did. This powerful, amazing Darkslayer, who so many people loved and depended upon, would die the minute her mortal life ended.

And the thought of that broke her heart.

She stomped forward, vision blurring with tears—and shoved him in the chest. "How *could you?*"

He was so caught off guard by her reaction that he stumbled. *Actually* stumbled.

"I love you, Darien," Loren squeezed out around the sob building in her throat. "I love you so much, I want you to live! I want you to have everything that I can't. I want you to *live!*" she said again, her broken voice slicing through the room like glass.

"And I want *you*, sweetheart," Darien tried. "I want to share all of that with you." He tried to step toward her—

She stepped back. "I hate you for doing that." That vile word was out before she could stop it. She was angry. Crushed. She had always been more than grateful for his sacrifice, but she had never understood the magnitude of it.

Because he hadn't told her. He'd kept this a secret from her, and now she was blindsided by it. Blindsided and heartbroken.

"What if the roles were reversed, Darien?" she squeezed out, her question broken apart by splintered breaths. "How would you feel? How would you feel if I forfeited my life—"

"I'd be pissed," he snapped. "I'd be fucking livid."

"Right. And I'm pissed." Tears washed the room as if with rain. "I'm livid. And I don't want to talk to you right now, I don't want to see you." She made to leave the room, but turned on a heel to face him again, more words exploding out in the heat of the moment. "Why would you do that?" she demanded. *"Why?* No one in their right mind would do that, Darien—just trade their life away like they don't care about themselves at all! What about Ivy?" She waved an angry hand at the sister who looked torn between rage and despair—torn between staying in the room or stomping out. "What about the others? Your family?" She pointed downstairs—where she was certain multiple people were listening, the sudden silence suggesting she was right. "What about them?"

"I did what I felt was right in the moment—what I felt like I wanted."

"Killing yourself, basically," she said flatly. "For *me?*" She gestured to herself in a what-am-I-worth gesture, warm tears slipping down her cheeks.

"I've struggled with this shit my whole life, Loren—about feeling worthy, about not knowing if I want to be dead or alive. And if I was going to lose you—not in the sense of breaking up, okay? I'm not talking about that, I wouldn't put a gun in my mouth over that like some psycho—"

Ivy abruptly left the room, stunting Darien's speech. "Ivy!" he called, but she didn't come back.

Darien swore under his breath. Continued, "If I was going to lose you—the only shred of happiness the universe has given me since my mom died—I wasn't going to live with that. I can't. Call me weak, but I can't."

Loren swallowed. Forced herself to soften her tone—trying desperately to see this from his perspective. But she was so lost in the feeling of her heart being ripped out of her chest, that it took everything in her power not to yell and scream her lungs out. "Darien—"

"You want to know what the Widow told me?" he said suddenly, his throat shifting with a swallow. "Do you want to know?"

She merely waited. Crossed her arms over her chest.

"The Widow told me..." Darien had to pause to breathe, his good hand curling into a fist at his side. "Fuck." He glared at the wall.

Her blood ran cold. Rarely had she ever seen Darien like this. "Darien?" she prodded, the question a hollow whisper.

"The Widow told me...," he began again, his eyes snapping back to her face, "that you wouldn't make it past the age of twenty-one."

Loren felt her heart stop dead in her chest. Felt the blood leave her head, rushing down to her feet. She had never been more aware of her pulse than she was in that moment—her cursed, mortal heartbeat.

"How old are you, Loren?" Darien looked like someone had punched him, looked like he didn't have air—looked like he was dying. Exactly how Loren had felt only moments ago, when she'd learned he'd traded his life. Darien's jaw flexed, eyes shining. "How old are you?" He already knew the answer, but he said again, "How old are you? Tell me."

"Twenty." The answer was so breathless, she could barely hear herself.

"Do you know what that means?" His words were strained as he fought the emotions rising inside him, his black lashes dampening with the tears he was holding back. "That means you're going to die in less than a year. And if I can't save you—" He looked away, jaw clenching as he focused on breathing. He did not finish his sentence.

And Loren didn't know what else to say.

Another few seconds passed before Darien spoke. "Hate me all you want. But the decision was—*is*—mine. I did what I felt was right at the time, and I'd do it again in a heartbeat. If you die, Loren—if someone like you, who has such a good heart, just dies at twenty-one, that's..." He threw his hands in the air. "I don't have the words. And I also don't have time right now. We can talk about this when I get back."

He breezed past her before she had a chance to reply, her hair streaming over her shoulder with his swift departure.

And she wondered if that was what the Pale Man had meant when he'd said the Devil—Darien—would die. Ever since she'd learned of the abhorrent creature's premonition, she'd vowed to make sure it never came true.

Little had she known that Darien himself had put the gun in his own mouth, and she was powerless to stop him from pulling the trigger.

Roman was heading to the vehicles with the others—aside from Dallas and Max, who were already gone—when a female voice stopped him dead in his tracks.

"Glad to see you're okay."

Roman shut his eyes. Cursed under his breath.

Slowly, he turned around, his stomach twisting with guilt and self-loathing.

His heart stalled at the sight of Shay standing several feet away from him. Her arms were crossed, her back stiffer than a board. Her pretty face was filled with hurt and confusion—an open book so different from the thief he'd met in the Onyx Skull.

"You shouldn't be here," Roman bit out, well aware that he had the attention of everyone in the yard.

And the heart of the girl who'd come looking for him.

Hurt flickered across her face, the look so raw and vulnerable, and he hated himself for putting it there. "I wanted to make sure you were safe—"

"I'm fine, pup." With a gloved hand, he gestured to himself. "See? All in one piece."

The look she gave him in return suggested that what he said hardly constituted as being fine.

"You need to leave," Roman urged. He looked out toward the shadowed street beyond the gates—the many places where someone could hide. The many places where Don's men could hide, waiting to take her the minute they saw her here. To rape her bloody and kill her, just like Don had said. "This thing that's going on between us—" With a thick swallow, he forced out, "It needs to end."

Shay stared at him. Tightened her arms over her chest. "End?" she whispered, those green eyes flicking about the yard and the people lingering by the vehicles, Darien halfway inside the driver's door of Roman's car. "What do you mean end?" Quieter, she said, "I came back for you." Sayagul was watching from Roman's shadow, the dragon sniffling quietly—a sound only he could hear.

It always ended like this—every relationship he and Sayagul ever had. His mother, Travis...

And now Shay.

"You made a mistake," Roman said, his throat tight and aching. "And so did I—I should never have gone after you. Besides, isn't that what you wanted? To leave Yveswich?"

Again, she tightened her arms, fingers curling in her jacket sleeves. "What if I don't want to anymore?"

Roman didn't have words. This—her coming back—was what *he'd* wanted. *Shay* was what he wanted. But more than that, he wanted her safe, far away from the savage hands of Don and his men.

Shay persisted, "I never had any reason to stay before..." A swallow. "Before..." She didn't finish her sentence.

Me, Roman thought, his shoulders sinking. And that was fucking bad.

"My sister and I planned on running away," Shay went on, "but now that she's gone...now that she's gone, I don't really want to leave anymore. And it's because..." A pause. And then she choked out, "Because of you."

Roman kept his face empty of expression as he stated, "That's stupid."

"*What?*" she snapped, reeling back as if he'd slapped her.

"You're giving up your dreams for some guy? That's the dumbest thing I've ever heard. I didn't think you were that fucking stupid, pup. This—" he gestured between them "—is a fling. It's a crush. And a mistake. You don't throw away lifelong dreams for a fling, Shayla."

Shay was barely breathing. "Yeah, well, sometimes...dreams change," she tried, every word, every hard-spoken confession ripping Roman apart. "And you're not just a crush, Roman, you..." Her eyes darted about the yard and the people in it. Settled back on Roman. "You're my dream." Her breath hitched, and Roman felt his heart stall again. "My new dream."

Now, Roman couldn't breathe. Still, he managed to speak—managed to sound like the heartless wolf he'd always painted himself to be. "I'm not your dream, Shay. I'm not puppies and rainbows and fluffy clouds. I'm a goddamn nightmare." He hardened his voice with every word. "I'm sharp teeth and black eyes and things that go bump in the night. You think your life is a wreck now? Find out what it becomes if you stick with me. You'll be running for the door by the third night, I guarantee it."

She turned away—so he couldn't see her face, Roman knew.

He drew a breath. "You're getting out of here, Shay." He opened the passenger's door of his car. "You're getting out of Yveswich and you're following your dream, which is. Not. Me. End of story."

"He threatened you," Shay whispered, whirling around to face him, tears shining in her eyes. "Didn't he?"

Roman didn't answer.

"Don threatened you," she pressed.

"You need to leave."

"My mom did the same to me, Roman. She showed up at my apartment." She swallowed. "Killed my neighbor and my landlord." A blink sent a lone tear sliding down her cheek, and Roman fought the urge to wipe it away. To care for her, the way he once had. "She told me to stay away from you."

"I'm sorry that happened." Gods—he sounded like such an asshole. He'd always played his role convincingly, had worn a mask he rarely took off.

He should never have taken it off for her. This was what he got for his slip-up: Heartache. Pain.

"That's it?" Shay bit out. More tears dripped to the driveway. The girl who never cried was crying for him. "You're *sorry?*" She shook her head, staring out at the quiet street he'd soon have to say goodbye to. "If you don't stand up to him," she said, her voice whisper-quiet, "he will kill you one day."

"That's for me to worry about," Roman replied, that cold mask and flat voice disguising the real him. "And for you to get the fuck out of here."

Several long seconds passed as she delayed, clearly hopeful that Roman would take back everything he'd said.

He didn't.

So she backed up several paces, arms still crossed. "Have a nice life, Roman," she gritted out, voice breaking on a stifled sob.

She was gone before Roman could say anything else.

"You just broke that girl's heart," Darien said a few minutes later as he sped down the driveway. They were in Roman's car this time. The others had left too, taking Darien's truck to the tar pits.

"Better a broken heart than one that isn't beating," was all Roman said, the words coated in ice.

"So you're never going to allow yourself happiness—"

Roman exploded, his shouts stretching the car. "Don't fucking talk to me about happiness—not after what I just heard between you and Loren!" he snapped, nostrils flaring. "And not after all that bullshit you just put yourself through."

Darien squeezed the steering wheel. The beast in his soul began to pace, foaming at the mouth, his blood begging for a hit of Venom. He was a fucking joke, and he knew it—right back to being addicted to drugs not long after getting off of them. Right back to fucking up every relationship in his life—and all but destroying the most important one.

The apple didn't fall far from the tree, indeed.

"I heard the whole thing," Roman said, his words still razor-edged. "We all did. And I'm not going to berate you for your decision to bargain your life away, but I *am* going to berate you for walking out on her like you just did."

Darien stared out the windshield, gripping the steering wheel, boot pressing the accelerator flat to the floor. For several minutes, neither of them spoke, not even Jack or Tanner, who were in the back seat, holding so still they were barely breathing.

When Roman spoke again, he used a slightly softer tone—trying, just like Darien, to control himself. His temper. "You're a lot like me, Darien," Roman began. Darien kept staring at the road ahead, not seeing it, instead picturing Loren's crying face in his mind. How broken she'd been. "You're a lot like me," Roman went on, "and that is not a compliment. But you've managed to get something right in your life, and that's her." He pointed behind them—at the house that had been swallowed up with distance too quickly. The girl Darien wanted nothing more than to race home to. "You have a choice—I don't. And I just listened to you completely fuck that up."

Roman spoke the hard truth. Leaving Loren like that—in any condition other than perfect—was not like him. She was upset, and she had a right to be. Loren was correct in thinking he'd be livid if the roles were reversed—if he'd learned that she had traded her precious life for his.

Maybe he had made a mistake in bargaining with the Widow. But it hadn't felt like a mistake in the moment, and it didn't feel like one now, neither had it felt like one the moment Loren's heart had stopped during the Blood Moon. Darien had only managed to outlive that one because Loren had not gone past the point of resuscitation.

"I didn't fuck it up," Darien said. He drew a deep breath in through his nose, but it didn't help at all. His muscles were rigid, heart pounding with rage. With regret. "I'll talk to her after."

"If you're not dead."

Darien ground his teeth. "I think I'm done waiting for your permission."

"Permission for what?" Roman snapped back.

"Killing Don. We haven't had a chance to talk since all that shit happened at the House of Black. He do that to your neck too?" His eyes flashed to the fresh cut across Roman's throat.

"Doesn't matter right now."

"Why—because we need to hurry? Because someone else always matters fucking more? I thought I was a martyr, Roman, but you're terrible." Roman stared out the windshield, jaw flexed. Darien sensed that Jack and Tanner wanted to jump in on the conversation but were holding back.

"We're going to help Tanya. And as soon as she's safe, I'm helping you. And you're not saying no again."

"Darien—" Roman drew a ragged breath through flared nostrils, hands in tight fists. "You can't."

"Fuck you mean I can't? He can't keep doing this, man—"

"Fuck—*listen.*"

"I'm listening," Darien said, but the beast in his soul was pacing faster.

He needed to kill. Needed to find something to rip apart so he didn't do it to his own family.

"I saw you kill that demon by the harbor, okay? I saw you kill hundreds of them in my house. And you killed even more when the Veil almost fell. Right?"

"What's your point?" Darien barked.

"My point is," Roman said, black swallowing his eyes as he, too, fought a Surge, "the only other person I've ever met with magic anywhere close to yours is my dad."

Fuck Don. Fuck him.

Darien's heart pounded harder, each beat driven by uncontrollable hatred. For himself, for the imperator, for Don.

"I saw what you're capable of, and it's fucking incredible," Roman went on. "But I'm not going to lie to you." His pitch-black stare settled on Darien. "Darien, if you try to kill him, you will lose."

Loren was too late.

She threw open the front door and sprinted outside, lurching to a stop on the front steps just in time to see the glow of the tail lights on Roman's car disappearing down the street.

Upset didn't begin to cover how she'd felt to learn that Darien had traded away his life. But she was even more upset that she'd allowed their conversation to end like that.

Every couple was bound to fight. To disagree on things once in a while. She wasn't so blind as to think she would always see eye to eye with Darien. But if something bad happened tonight...and that was the last time she ever got to speak to him...

She stared out at the dark neighborhood, at the street lights bleaching the pavement.

And wished she could take it back.

105

THE FINANCIAL DISTRICT
YVESWICH, STATE OF KER

Roman pressed his phone against his ear as Darien sped through the Financial District, blowing through red lights and stop signs. It was still dark out, but workers were beginning to make their early-morning commutes, clogging up the roads with the most piss-poor timing in the world.

He was about to hang up again when the line finally connected.

"Roman?" Tanya's voice, brittle with fear, floated through the speaker.

Roman's fingers tightened around the device. "Tanya. Tanya, what's going on? We saw you on the security cameras. Are you okay?" In the back seat, Jack and Tanner leaned forward to listen, while Darien's gaze continuously flickered between Roman and the street flying by under the tires.

"I can't talk for long." Her words were muffled, as if she had the device pressed right up against her mouth. "They...they're going to come back."

"We're on our way—"

An oath cut through the speaker, silencing him. Tanya's shaking inhale rattled the phone.

"Tanya, are you safe?" Roman pressed. "Is there any way you can get out of there?"

"They're guarding all exits," she whispered. "Roman, I—I'm afraid. I want to go home." The confession was a punch to the gut. She may be a grown woman, but in that moment she reminded Roman of Paxton. Stuck in a situation she couldn't get out of, didn't deserve, and all she wanted was to get out of it.

"I know, Tanya, we're coming. We're on our way as we speak. Just hold on for a little while longer, okay?"

Something like a whimper cut through the phone. "I have to go, they're coming."

Roman gripped the phone tighter. *"Tanya—"*

The line went dead.

His eyes snapped to Darien's face, his own skin going white. "They're going to kill her."

"No, they're not," Darien said, pushing the engine faster. "No, they're fucking not."

IT TOOK a matter of minutes for them to get up to Caliginous on Silverway once they'd parked. Minutes that felt like years when an innocent woman's life was on the line.

The imperator and his men had been manipulating Tanya for who knew how long. Darien only hoped they still deemed her useful enough to keep alive. That they weren't too late.

The elevator doors slid open with a hiss.

Darien walked through first, taking the corner with caution. His eyes were a shining black, the skin of his cheekbones and temples webbed with black lines from the Venom. Roman and Tanner flanked him, and Jack came up behind Darien, covering his back.

They'd all taken a hit of Venom—all except Tanner—but Darien was the only one who'd doubled his dose. Not by choice, but because he had to. He'd not just developed a dependance on the drug, but a tolerance as well. Now, he had to take a higher dose to experience the same effects everyone else got with only one hit. A much higher dose.

He knew what he was doing was dangerous. But so was walking straight into this minefield without Venom sparking through his blood, waiting to ignite his magic to its fullest potential. Risk over reward, and all that shit.

Together, they walked deeper into Caliginous on Silverway. The sword of adamant was strapped to Darien's back, the blade faintly rattling as he walked. It felt weird to come in here without a weapon in hand, when the others who were with him had theirs raised, eyes peering through scopes, fingers poised on triggers. Darien's only weapon tonight would have to be his magic.

The interior of the building was eerily quiet and empty. Only the soft gurgling of the diffusers on the desk and the tinkling of classical music filled the silence. No droning of phones, no clicking of fingers on a keyboard, no hum of an occupied chamber. And no employees or clients in sight.

Darien directed the others with several waves of his hands, mouthing where they should go and what they should do.

They spread out, Tanner and Jack hanging back to check the rooms by the elevators. Darien kept an eye on them as he and Roman walked deeper into the building.

A phone on the desk rang. And rang and rang.

Roman kept his feet light as he approached, walking heel to toe—

He froze in shock, paling. The automatic rifle in his hands drooped as he beheld the scene before him.

Darien ate up the distance to his cousin in three long strides—

And saw Tanya. Slumped in the chair behind the desk.

A bullet in her fucking head.

PART FIVE
THE LABYRINTH

106
CALIGINOUS ON SILVERWAY
YVESWICH, STATE OF KER

Roman stared at Tanya with speechless rage and shock. At the blood leaking from the bullet wound in her forehead, the trickle of crimson streaming down the sides of her dainty nose. The once joyful, flirtatious eyes, now flat with death. Empty.

Darien stepped up to Roman's side. "Let's go," he urged quietly.

"She's dead," Roman choked out, unable to draw a full breath. He couldn't help but feel responsible for this. Maybe the imperator would have killed her anyway, but Roman and the others had asked so much of Tanya, had asked her to break the rules so Loren could use chamber five. If he hadn't been so blind and selfish, he might've looked into Tanya's recent change in behavior—the attitude she had never given him before. Not just the attitude, but all the overtime as well.

Tanya was not the only employee here at Caliginous. She wasn't even the owner. And yet, for the past couple of weeks, she was the only person they'd seen working here.

What the actual fuck. They'd all majorly screwed up—

"Roman," Darien tried.

Roman shook his head to snap out of it, tearing his eyes off that bullet wound deep in Tanya's skull. Darien, Jack, Tanner—they were all staring at him as he stared at Tanya.

He gripped his firearm tighter. Approached Tanya to get the keys off her arm. Bile rose in his throat as he shimmied the coil down her arm, keys catching in her blouse.

This was a death that hit close to home. Tanya was practically a friend

—someone he'd come to know in recent months. Someone who'd struggled financially and worked overtime to support herself. Someone Roman had lent money to.

Someone who was now dead.

Keys in hand, Roman looked at Tanya one last time. Brushed a knuckle against her smooth cheek. Mouthed, "I'm sorry."

He turned, deliberately not looking at the others as he made for the hallway—the one he'd walked a hundred times. At the end of the hallway was chamber seven, where they'd find the imperator.

Once a sanctuary, now a tomb.

"I'm surprised he doesn't have anyone standing guard here," Dallas said as she stood beside Max in front of the maintenance elevator on the ground floor of the skyscraper.

Max chose not to reply, instead focusing on keying in the passcode Tanner had given him. The screen that was mounted on the wall beside the elevator emitted faint beeps with every tap of his finger. His reason for ignoring Dallas had nothing to do with not agreeing with her—it was the opposite. He *did* agree with her. And simply the thought of the imperator leaving the elevators wide open like this was...unsettling. And made him fear they may be walking into a trap.

They'd move forward with the plan, though. Unless something drastic deterred them. And the plan was this: Block all exits the imperator and his men could use to get away, push further inward until they found the Well replica, and meet the others there. While Max and Dallas took the maintenance elevator to the tunnels, Darien, Tanner, Roman, and Jack would go in through chamber seven. And Lace, Ivy, Travis, Jewels, Aspen, and Kylar were currently heading to the tar pits, where they would do one of two things: Guard the tunnel if they couldn't find the way in...or, if they found out how to get inside, they'd come and meet at the Well replica.

Max extended his hand to Dallas. "Fingerprint, Red."

She retrieved the glass slide from the back pocket of her bodysuit and passed it to him. He unstuck the glass pieces, peeled off the thin plastic sheet that bore a fingerprint—one that belonged to maintenance staff—and flattened it on the scanner.

A cheery beep sliced through the screen speakers. A moment later, the elevator doors shot open.

"Green light of approval," Max breathed. He and Dallas stepped into the elevator. On the screen inside, he keyed in another code—another Tanner had given him. The code that would prevent anyone but Max and Dallas from coming down or leaving.

Once that was done, he turned to face Dallas. "Ready?" he asked her, hand drifting toward the buttons by the door.

She squared her shoulders and nodded once. "Ready."

Max jammed his finger into the button that read BASEMENT, and they began their descent.

THEY RAPPELLED down to the bottom. While jumping was an option for hellsehers, the chambers were deep, and Darien didn't want to risk injuring themselves over something so reckless and easily avoided.

Darien touched ground at the same time as the others, all of them moving at the same swift pace. Buckles clinked as they took off their rappelling gear and set it aside. Weapons again at the ready, they started walking.

The tunnels were so deep below the earth that by all rights it should've been pitch-black down here. But there were bioluminescent glow worms all over the walls and ceiling, the clusters of insects casting ethereal blue light on everything. The tunnels were made of adamant shot through with silvery veins of cristala, the valuable material that had kept this place hidden from everyone except the few people who'd already known about it. Stalactites and stalagmites were everywhere, the mounds and tapering columns sparkling with bits of cristala that looked like shattered mirror.

"Look at these here," Tanner said. Despite the low volume of his voice, his words resounded through the tunnels. He pointed at the thin, colorful lines forking through the floor. Everywhere they stepped, those lines flared with colored light, illuminating the path ahead with a rainbow-like glow.

"What are they?" Roman asked, his gravelly voice carrying farther than Tanner's.

"Channels for energy," Tanner replied, his boot lighting up as he took another step. "The anima mundi, maybe." *Hopefully*, was what Tanner looked like he wanted to say. But Darien didn't let dread get the better of him as they carried on, guided by nothing but their Sight, the bioluminescent insects, and the veins of energy lighting up and warming under the soles of their boots, suffusing their bodysuits and faces with many hues.

Eventually, they reached a massive cavern with a ceiling too high up to glimpse. There were eerily realistic statues of animals and people everywhere, frozen in place like pieces on a chess-board. No two were alike, but they all held one similarity that stuck out to Darien in a way he couldn't ignore: They looked terrified, as if they had spent their final moments facing off with something so petrifying that to merely look upon it had instantly stopped their hearts.

Darien fought the chill building at the nape of his neck, Bandit breathing heavily in Darien's shadow.

'Those are Familiars,' Bandit said with a low growl. Dogs and cats, wolves and lions, birds and aquatic animals...

As Darien walked, deeper into the underground chamber, the air seemed to peel back, like a gate swinging open with enough force to cause a sharp breeze. The temperature dipped alarmingly quickly, his breath instantly fogging before him. The floor was no longer lighting up from the anima mundi, the veins below their feet dull and colorless and cold.

Darien's good hand curled into a fist at his side, the long blade that was strapped to his back emitting a hum of warning, as if sensing the same thing Darien sensed.

The Nameless beings that inhabited pockets of the in-between throughout Terra usually required payment from their visitors in advance. Without payment, a person could not enter. But there were a few beings that had eked out a living for so long, they had carved out their habitats more firmly than the newer creatures, existing in such a way that unsuspecting prey could stumble upon them without coin or blood. Without payment. Without planning, nor premeditation.

And this? This deep cavern that felt more like the belly of a beast...

It was a fucking Crossroads.

"Shit." The low oath came from Roman, who gripped his gun tighter, beads of sweat forming on his temples. "Faster." He gestured with his gun to the arched doorway at the other end of the cavern—the only way out, aside from the door they'd come through.

Something dripped from the ceiling.

Splash.
Splash.
Splash.

A drop dripped in Darien's hair. On his cheek. He wiped it off, smearing it between his thumb and forefinger. The liquid was too thick to be water.

He tipped his head back, scanning the deep, supernatural darkness way up top. It felt like gazing into a pit, except...upside down. Dizzying.

A crumbling staircase wrapped around the perimeter of the cavern, spiraling all the way up to the top. Overturned pillars of bone and obelisks of polished adamant were crisscrossed from one side of the vast chamber to the other in fortuitous bridges, all the way from floor to ceiling, the latter carved with bygone runes. The moldering bits of staircase and fallen pillars became invisible closer to the ceiling, the churning gloom at the top gulping them down like a black hole. But it wasn't the pillars, nor the sinister darkness shifting across the ceiling that snagged Darien's attention. It was the thing that dwelled here.

Draped across the forsaken structures was a mass of scales. A giant serpent, only parts of its limbless body peeking out of the gloom, thousands upon thousands of black scales catching the light of the bioluminescent creatures that dared to linger here.

Darien's stomach twisted into a knot, his heart speeding up to a painful sprint. He wordlessly urged the others to move faster, all while rallying his magic. Venom sparked in his blood, waiting to be unleashed.

Good—he'd need it.

"Oh *shit.*" Jack's whisper bounced through the room as he spotted the curve of the serpent's enormous body, lying motionless in the dark, way above their heads. In a pocket between worlds, its place of origin far darker and colder than this.

A place of evil. Terror.

"Keep going," Darien said, the words tense. "Don't slow down. Don't look back." *No matter what you hear,* he almost said.

Because he knew what that thing was. Knew that not everyone would be making it through that doorway.

Knew the demon called the Basilisk had chosen him. He could sense it.

So he slowed his pace, and as soon as Jack, Roman, and Tanner made it through the doorway, safe on the other side, he slowed again—

Just as the massive serpent lowered part of its body down, slithering over both doors. Blocking him in. Its thick body scraped across the cold stone floor, the sound as it dragged itself leisurely across the stone reminiscent of water thrown over hot coals.

The others shouted his name. But they could no longer get through, their panicked words muffled by that ginormous body—the body that, according to legend, could swallow creatures twice its size. Whole.

Darien stood very still.

"What an absolute delight this is," said the serpent, its voice coming from somewhere way up high—the darkness that didn't have an end. That voice was ancient and cold, consisting mostly of whispers and hisses—very fitting for a primordial serpent. "You shall make for a delicious challenge, oh haunted one."

According to the screen on the inside of the elevator, they were about halfway to the bottom.

It was very quiet in here, only the whir of the elevator and the tinkling of vintage music breaking the silence.

Max knew Dallas was nervous, and so was he. They had only a slight idea of where this led, knew that in a matter of minutes, they'd be walking into pitch-black tunnels that could be crawling with demons.

Scratch that—they *would* be crawling with demons. That was a given.

As he watched the progress of their descent tick away on the elevator screen, Max adjusted the sword strapped to his back. Arthur had only enough material for three swords, so Darien had divvied them up between each of the groups. Max carried one, Darien carried another, and Ivy had taken the third to the tar pits.

The percentage on the screen that showed their descent—no floor numbers, since the basement was the last stop to the bottom—began to slow, ticking down from three seconds passing between numbers to greater than ten.

Dallas's silver-green eyes flicked up to his face. "Why are we slowing down?"

The elevator was jarred with a massive boom, the force as the structure came to an abrupt standstill nearly knocking them to the floor. The music cut out. The lights buzzed and flickered.

Dallas reached for his hand, and he gave it to her, holding onto her tightly as he stalked up to the control panel.

The screen said fifty-one percent.

"Max?" Dallas ventured, her breath showing in the air. It was suddenly freezing.

And they were trapped halfway down an elevator shaft.

107

THE CAVERN
YVESWICH, STATE OF KER

Funny how the one Crossroads Darien always swore he would never visit would be the first he'd stumble into by accident.

"You're the Basilisk," Darien said, watching as that mass of scales continuously shifted around the room, never a head or tail showing. Just the horrifyingly large body, bony plates gleaming with a strange black light.

"And you," the creature replied, that hideous voice still coming from somewhere way up high, "are Darien Randal Slade."

"It's Darien Cassel now," he said, his left hand forming a fist at his side, knuckles cracking as he squeezed.

"You can rid yourself of a name, but you cannot rid yourself of your blood. Your history. Your father is in you. You will never be rid of him."

"Is that what you specialize in?" Darien drawled, tipping back his head to peer up at that swirling darkness, so reminiscent of a black hole. "Insults?"

"I specialize in truths. I operate much the same as a mirror. Mirrors do not lie, and neither do my words. It is not my fault if you refuse to accept yourself as you are, Darien Slade. Self-love eludes you, and should you continue to let it, it shall be your downfall." How fitting. How fucking fitting, given the conversation he'd just had with Loren.

What he wouldn't give to turn back the clock and bite his tongue about fate. If he hadn't slipped up and let that secret out, he never would have fought with her or his sister.

"I appreciate the warning," Darien said, blood simmering in his veins, "but I've got places to be. Is there something you want from me?"

A brief spell of silence descended. Darien sensed the creature was amused by his daring. "I would like to propose a trade." The statement was a hiss that came from everywhere all at once, followed by a quick, unsteady burst of sound—a rattling.

This was a fucking pit viper. The biggest, most vicious of all serpent kings.

Darien felt a prickle of fear, but fought it like he always did, his reply immediate and firm. "No." The cavern clapped back the word with a series of echoes, and those echoes were succeeded by another rattling. A warning.

"It would be wise to hear my offer before you decline," the Basilisk said, its words dripping with malice.

"You feast on memories," Darien said. "You rot the brain from the inside. I have no interest in making a trade with you when it'll only destroy me in worse ways."

"Do you not wish to be free of your mother's death? The pain. The suffering..." Something akin to a sigh raked through the room, skittering up the length of Darien's spine—another sound that came from everywhere. Where the fuck was the head? "So much suffering, Darien Slade. Just a poor, helpless child you were." The Basilisk tsked. "It need not hurt anymore. I can take away the pain."

"Fuck no," he said again, the retort echoing even louder than before.

"Very well," the serpent breathed. The temperature dropped again, cooling the bodysuit and turning his breath into ghosts. Darien hadn't even realized it had spiked. "I shall let you go. But...I wish to give you a premonition first."

"Let's hear it then." He wanted this over with. Figured the snake would give him the same prediction as the Pale Man.

He was not expecting something worse.

"Should you outlast the Pale Man's prediction," the Basilisk began, "your road will still end in death. Beware the girl you love. Sometimes the strongest of us are broken by the people we least expect."

He clenched his teeth so hard, his jaw popped. "Are you telling me not to trust the woman I love?"

"I tell you to be vigilant. Had she come with you tonight, I would have given her the same warning. The course of a person's life is a swift and ever-changing river; different decisions lead to different paths." Darien had held onto this truth since the moment the Widow had revealed to him that Loren would not live past the age of twenty-one. There had to be a way to defeat that ugly prediction—to save her from such a young death. And he was certain there was a way to change it; the Pale Man's prediction was enough of a hint. If Loren died, Darien died—such was the deal he'd made with the Widow. But the Pale Man had said that Darien would have to die so she could live—a different road, one he was intent on setting foot on.

"Yours and Liliana's, however," the Basilisk continued, "are painted in blood. Who pulls the knife and lands the mark remains to be seen."

Darien bristled. "I would never hurt her." His words rang through the cavern like a struck bell.

"This is my warning, Darien Slade. Are you accusing me of being dishonest?"

"I prefer the term 'full of shit'," he spat. The blade hummed at his back, the adamant emitting the same strange light as the snake's scales, limning the edges of his bodysuit in faint shades of fluorescent. "That's what creatures like you are made of: fucking shit."

The mass of scales shifted faster. Darkness fell in a heavy shroud, the bioluminescent insects winking out. "Do you wish to take that back, Darien Slade?" the Basilisk challenged, a hiss skittering over the walls.

"Actually, I wish to kill you." The sword sang as Darien drew it with his left hand. "And I wish for you to stop calling me *'Slade'.*"

IN THE THICK darkness just beyond the Crossroads, Roman stared at the bulk of scales covering the arched doorway. Chest so tight he couldn't draw a full breath, he thought only of his cousin. Trapped on the other side with no way out. If the Basilisk had blocked this entrance, it had sure as shit blocked the other.

"He'll be fine," Tanner panted, glancing between Roman and the serpent, the hacker's body as visibly tense as Roman's, "right?"

Jack persisted, as if to convince himself, "They don't usually kill people like him."

When Roman finally answered them, his voice was flat. Hopeless. Just like his eyes, his expression. "Do you know what that is? That's the fucking Basilisk." He stared at the mass of scales continuously shifting over the door, faintly glowing with black light.

The Basilisk was a serpent king with a lethal gaze—one that could turn any living thing into stone, an ability it hardly needed when it had a body that could crush a ship, a mouth that could swallow monsters twice its size. Many legends had been written about this demon, and while legends could be muddied by the passing of time, there was one that had held on throughout the years, as true today as it had been when it was first uttered hundreds of years ago.

Roman spoke the truth aloud now in a brittle whisper. "No one has ever survived it."

108

THE ELEVATOR
YVESWICH, STATE OF KER

Max had never been fond of elevators. In fact, he hated them. Once, when he was a kid, he'd got stuck in one with Maya. Only five minutes had passed before the hotel staff had got the doors open, but those five minutes had felt like a lifetime to two young kids.

And Max and Dallas were already going on ten.

Dallas jammed her finger into the button again, to no avail. She swore and spun around to face Max. "Anything?"

Max put his phone away. "Nothing." He couldn't get a bar down here, and when he tried his watch, all he got was static.

With panting breaths, Dallas scanned the ceiling—the emergency escape hatch in the top. "What about climbing out?"

"That'll take forever." They were way too far below the earth to even attempt that, and regardless, there was nothing to grab onto, the shaft sheer and smooth.

Dallas's wings twitched. "We could fly."

"*You* could fly," Max corrected. "You can't carry me." He was too heavy.

She cursed again. "I'm not leaving you." She chewed her lip. "What about your magic? Can you push us—"

The elevator shuddered.

Sank a couple inches.

Max held his breath. He grabbed onto Dallas with one hand, pulling her close, the other grasping the handrail that was so cold, it felt like an icicle, even through the glove of his bodysuit.

The lights began to flicker.

"Max?" Dallas's question, strained with fear, was barely a whisper. "Max, what's happening—"

Max's stomach hollowed out, and Dallas screamed at the top of her lungs as the elevator dropped at light-speed.

109

THE TAR PITS
YVESWICH, STATE OF KER

Shay followed the others out to the tar pits. Riding in the back of Darien's truck was not her preferred method of travel, especially not when Travis drove it as if he'd stolen it, every speed bump and corner jarring her bones, but circumstances called for this.

The others had no doubt believed she'd left the moment Roman had told her to, but the bodysuits they all wore, Roman included, had only piqued her curiosity—and her concern.

Something was happening. And whether Roman wanted her help or not, it didn't matter. She wasn't leaving. Not until she at least found out what was going on. Where they were going, why they were dressed in those magically-enhanced bodysuits—the suits designed specifically for use in the most dire of emergencies.

Travis parked Darien's truck at the tar pits. He and the others got out and began walking across the dark grounds.

Shay held her breath and listened carefully, sensing that not everyone in the group was gone.

Ivy was still here. Her boots crunched in the grass as she walked the length of the truck, as if looking for something. For a moment, Shay thought she might be spotted; her illusions could only hold for so long.

Before Ivy had a chance to look too closely at Darien's truck bed—and Shay lying right there, her illusion gradually wearing off—Travis and Lace called for her in hushed tones.

Shay dared a peek over the side of the truck to see Ivy reaching into a zip pocket in the thigh of her bodysuit. She dug something out and placed it on the hood of Darien's truck, casting one last glance about the grounds before running after the others.

Once Shay was certain she was gone, she sat up in the truck bed, crept to the side and leapt out, landing on light feet in the rain-damp grass. Quietly, she walked to the hood to see what Ivy had left behind.

A navy ring. One of the bodysuits Arthur had designed.

Shay stripped off her jacket, picked up the ring, and slid it onto her finger, turning it counter-clockwise until it clicked.

The bodysuit encased inside the ring shot out, covering her from neck to toes. A coat of magic covered her neck and head, shimmering faintly across her vision. She held up her gloved hand, turning it from side to side.

And gave a quiet, impressed laugh. "Awesome."

Guns and knives now strapped to the built-in weapons belt, she set off across the old park, crouching close to the ground to keep the Hounds skulking about from noticing her. Many were feasting on prey, the wet sound of muscle and sinew being torn into ribbons carrying through the crisp early morning. The sun would be rising soon, but it was still dark out, the stars only just fading into a predawn sky.

It took her a short while to find the tunnel where the others had vanished, the narrow entrance tucked away behind foliage and an outcropping of rock.

Bracing a hand against the mouth of the tunnel, she peered inside with her Sight, scanning the energies of tree roots and insects. She could no longer see or hear the others, but she found that she didn't feel fear as she ducked into the tunnels and went after them.

TRAVIS WALKED at the head of the group, through the network of tunnels at the tar pits.

It was pitch-black in here, the beams of light from their firearms barely cutting through the gloom. The place was packed with the bones of animals and men, scraps of clothing and jewelry among them. It smelled disgusting in here—of rot and blood.

Twice already, the tunnel had spit them out in a different corner of the park, forcing them to turn around and go back inside in search of another route.

It happened again now, bringing Travis and the others to a confused standstill.

Jewels and Ivy murmured in question.

"This doesn't make any sense," Lace said with a sigh, blinking away the Sight that had proven useless during their trek.

"No, it fucking doesn't," Travis agreed. They had taken every possible turn they'd encountered, and none of them had yielded the correct route.

Kylar said, "Maybe they fully sealed the entrance with rock, not just magic?" Hundreds of years ago, the city had supposedly used an invisible shield of magic to stop anyone from entering these tunnels, working to keep the underground demon populations from bleeding into the city streets.

"Wouldn't it be obvious if they did?" Aspen wondered aloud. "There should be a bunch of rubble or something to show where they sealed it, right?"

"I might be able to help," said a female voice.

Everyone turned to see Shay coming down the tunnel, eyes black with the Sight, her bodysuit a deep shade of navy that looked black in this lighting.

Ivy full-on grinned, looking happy for the first time since they'd left Roman's. Since learning of Darien's bargain with the Widow. Travis still wasn't sure what to make of that.

Or of the girl slowing to a stop before them. The girl his brother had very clearly fallen for.

"Didn't Roman break up with you?" Travis blurted.

Shay winced. "We were never really dating, but sure, yeah—he broke up with me." She gestured to the tunnel at her back. "You walked right past the entrance."

"What?" Lace and Aspen snapped, glancing at each other.

"Illusion," Shay said matter-of-factly.

"I thought your power was rare," Ivy said.

"It is. There's only one other known illusionist in the city." With a grimace, she said, "My mother."

110

THE CAVERN
YVESWICH, STATE OF KER

The Nameless creatures spent most of their unholy existence in solitude. Talking was something they rarely had the pleasure of doing, so when given the opportunity, they talked a fucking lot.

All the better for Darien, though. He needed time, needed to make it to higher ground. Needed to give the Basilisk a reason to expose its throat.

With swift feet, he ascended the crumbling staircase that wrapped around the cavern, leaping to close the gaps between the broken structures. Putting as much power into each jump was vital; with a sword in his good hand, the other too broken to hold his weight should he need to grab onto something, he had no other choice. He needed to land on his feet. Every. Single. Time.

The massive serpent observed with humor. Curiosity. Darien felt it peering down at him from that storm of darkness way up top, its thick body hissing with constant movement.

Darien reached another ledge and jumped, feet moving in open air as if he were running. He landed on the next platform with enough force to jar his bones and teeth. Vaulted over a curve of the serpent's body, those hideous scales glinting like liquid night. Kept moving. Running as fast as he could.

"You amuse me, slayer," said the Basilisk. "You really think you have a chance, don't you?"

"So long as I'm alive, I have a chance." He sprinted and leapt again, flying through the icy air, feet striking ground on the next decaying piece of staircase. Higher—he had to get higher still.

"They all believed the same," the serpent said solemnly, referring to its many guests down below, eternally trapped in stone. Rumor claimed their souls lived in the statues, cursed to observe in immovable silence as countless others wandered in here to be met with the same terrible fate. Stuck here for eternity, never to move on to the afterlife. Never to find rest. "So filled with hope," the serpent went on. "With want for life."

"You almost sound sincere," Darien shot back, his breaths puffing out before him like ghosts.

The next ledge was so far, Darien had to push himself faster, taking it at a sprinting jump. He soared through the air, gravity poised to suck him into its swift grip.

He barely made it, and when he landed, part of the staircase broke off under his boot. Bandit swore, and Darien barked out a curse word of his own, his alarm ringing through the cavern as the chunk of stone fell to the floor way below and burst into dust.

The Basilisk chuckled. "Close one."

He pushed up and kept moving, heart pounding, tripping, skipping. He sensed his time was coming to a close. The Basilisk was preparing to strike, its foul presence shifting faster in the preternatural darkness above his head. Darien had fought enough monsters in his lifetime that he could *feel* hunger.

And this monster was starving.

Another jump, another ledge later, feet jarring with another forceful landing, and Darien picked up on stealthy movement somewhere behind him—a different kind than the continuous shifting of that endless body draped all around the room.

'Watch out,' Bandit warned quietly.

He brought up the blade so he could see into the flat side. The material shifted from black to reflective glass right before his eyes, as if adapting to what he wanted—needed—it to be.

A mirror.

And in that mirror, he saw part of the serpent's body loop down from up high. Saw the head materialize out of the gloom that writhed just like the snake, every bit as alive as the monster.

Fuck, it was terrifying—the darkness *and* the Basilisk. The serpent's thick snout was bursting with razor-sharp teeth, the jagged shards speckled brown with rot. The vicious, scarred head was crowned with spikes all different lengths, as if some had been broken by past opponents, evidence of its many victories. Its eyes glowed red like rubies struck by sunlight, the slashes of black in the centers embedded with pinholes of color—

The serpent struck like lightning.

Darien ducked, using the reflection to his advantage, missing those powerful jaws by a hair's breadth.

It struck again, even quicker this time, coiling its body around to block his path.

Darien bounded to the left, launching himself straight into open air, the wind of his fall whipping at his eyes and hair—

He landed on his feet on a fallen obelisk that stretched from one side of the cavern to the other like a bridge. The surface was so smooth and dusty, the soles of his boots failed to find purchase. No footfalls, nothing to grab onto. He leaned forward to keep his balance, and ducked again with a shout of alarm, barely missing another attack. The snake was so quick, he hardly saw it moving, its body so long, it was hard to sense which part of it would act next, where the attack would come from.

Darien ran up the length of the obelisk, pouring all his strength into his legs to make the ascent, calf and thigh muscles burning with exertion.

Movement again from behind.

He brought the blade up in time to see a curve of the snake's body looping down—

He jumped off the obelisk, landing on another section of staircase about a dozen feet down, boots skidding down the jagged steps. His feet stilled mere inches from open air, loose gravel shooting out and trickling to the floor below like hail.

Fuck, this was tiring.

"You are quick," the serpent said, coiling back up—protecting its throat, just like he thought. The one and only place a person must strike to have a chance at killing it. "Very quick."

He sensed movement again, and rushed toward the next ledge. "You like to play with your food, hey?" he asked the snake. It would be the death of it—Darien would make sure of that.

A quick glance in the flat side of the blade—still reflective, as if sensing that its wielder needed a mirror—told him the snake had retreated back above, its head no longer visible.

Games. Endless fucking games from this thing.

Little did it know, Darien was intent on playing. Its games would be its demise.

So he hurtled to the edge of this broken section of staircase. Leapt into open air—

And smacked his face against rock.

"What the fuck!" he barked, eyes watering and stinging.
Not rock—part of the snake's body had materialized out of thin air.
It could fucking camouflage.
But he had no time to think about it anymore.
Because down he was falling, straight to the floor far below.

III

THE ELEVATOR
YVESWICH, STATE OF KER

This was, possibly, the single most terrifying thing Max had ever lived through, second only to the house fire he'd believed had killed his sister.

And whether or not he lived through this remained to be seen.

The elevator plummeted to the basement so quickly, Max couldn't feel his body. The lights above their heads flickered at a dizzying speed, the descent creating a loud shrieking noise that shredded his eardrums. Max held onto the railing for dear life, the sheer drop threatening to peel his feet off the floor.

"Hold onto me!" he shouted to Dallas.

She did.

And then he swept his hand out, forcing the Sight into his vision and his magic outside of his body.

The ground was approaching quick; he could see veins of magic in the anima mundi down below. Three seconds—that was all he had, the only chance he had to do this.

Quickly, he covered the base of the elevator with his magic—and pushed.

Up. Up. Up...slowing their descent and cushioning the impact—

The elevator still smashed into the ground with jarring force, knocking both Max and Dallas off their feet. He landed hard, cracking his head against the floor, the bodysuit lessening the blow. One light panel remained intact, the others shattering from the crushing force. Glass tinkled around them, showering their clothes like sleet.

Silence stretched for several long heartbeats. He panted, chest pumping, the ceiling of the elevator spinning like a top.

As soon as his surroundings stilled, Max got up. He pulled Dallas to her feet, brushing strands of hair out of her face. "You alright?"

Dallas nodded. "Yeah. Yeah, I'm good."

"We're at the bottom," he said. He couldn't decide if that was a good thing or not, but at least they were no longer stuck halfway up the elevator shaft. He crossed the tiny space, pried open the elevator doors—

And froze at what he beheld in the dark tunnels just beyond.

Demons. Thousands of them.

112

THE CAVERN
YVESWICH, STATE OF KER

Darien pushed himself up onto his hands and knees.

He'd fallen to a part of the staircase below—smoking his face against the stone so hard, he'd briefly fallen unconscious. A syrupy line of blood trickled out of his mouth, the color black in this light.

Bandit was standing at attention in his shadow. *'You alive?'*

'Barely.' He spat out a mouthful of blood, and with mild difficulty he stood. Gathered his bearings.

He hadn't fallen far; he was still closer to the top than he was the bottom.

And the snake was still watching him, amused and hungrier than before he'd fallen, the smell of his blood permeating the cavern. The shadows swirling about the ceiling began to whisper, stirring at a swifter pace, as if the smell of blood had pulled them out of their eternal slumber.

"Your blood tastes of my place of origin," the Basilisk said as Darien wiped his nose on the arm of his bodysuit. He bent to grab the sword he'd dropped, the blade scraping on stone. "Of night and stars. Death and decay."

"Are you ever going to show your face?" Darien asked with a biting edge, staring up into the gloom. The rusty tang of his blood filled his nose. His throat. "Or are you that much of a coward?"

The serpent did not answer, so Darien started moving again. He sprinted toward the next ledge. Jumped.

The faraway floor of the cavern seemed to spin below the soles of his airborne feet, his vision zooming out and in, out and in. Had he really hit himself that hard? The jump seemed to take forever, but finally, he landed—

A piece of stone broke off underfoot, and he slipped.

"Shit!" He grabbed onto the ledge with the hand that held the sword, fingers digging into the stone to stop his fall. His legs kicked in open air, body swinging with momentum, nearly sucking him down. With a growl of determination, he hoisted himself up, his surroundings shimmering and wobbling, and crawled onto the landing.

Fuck, what was going on? Two mistakes now—that was two mistakes.

He rarely ever made one.

'The mist,' Bandit said as Darien pushed to his feet. *'It's the mist—it's toxic.'*

Darien braced a hand against the cold, rough wall. Lurched up the steps, his surroundings bouncing, feet dipping. He shook his head, but it wouldn't clear, and his ears began to feel plugged, every scuff of his boots and rasping breath muffled and distant.

'It's poisoning you,' Bandit said.

The closer Darien got to the top of the stairs, the harder it became to breathe, to concentrate, to aim correctly when he reached the next ledge. On feet that were clumsier than they'd ever been, he backed up several paces to take a running jump.

As soon as he started sprinting, he knew Bandit was right.

But he couldn't stop now, not when he was so close. He had to get that thing to expose its throat. So he jumped, stomach pitching endlessly along with his mind and vision.

He managed to put enough force behind the action to land in the middle of the next broken structure, but his thoughts were even more muddled than before. Everything spun, even the hand he held out before him, reaching for the wall for balance—

He missed. Dropped forward onto the ground, kneecaps popping on stone.

"Fuck," he panted. He pushed back up. Swayed and staggered into the wall. Blinked fiercely. *"Fuck."*

The snake that was wrapped around the room began to shift faster.

'Look through me,' Bandit said. *'My eyes. I am not affected by the mist.'*

Gods, he didn't know if he could. But he tried, shifting the lens in his mind from his own eyes to Bandit's—

And saw clearly.

'If this works,' Bandit said, licking his chops, *'you owe me a new chicken.'*

'Deal. Just let me kill this thing first.'

'Waiting.'

Darien shoved off the wall and ran again, leaping onto the next piece of staircase.

And the next.

The next, all the while looking through Bandit's mind instead of his own, having no clue how this was working but glad that it was.

The darkness—the poisonous black mist—way up top was getting closer.

Darien raised the blade again, forcing his eyes to focus on the reflection.

The serpent came down from its habitat above, preparing for another strike—unaware that Darien was no longer affected by the mist.

Darien pushed himself faster, hurtling along the ledge, toward the next jump that was farther than any he'd already conquered.

'It just camouflaged,' Bandit warned. *'Jump left!'*

Darien reached the edge and leapt left instead of straight, landing instead on another obelisk. Sure enough, a camouflaged portion of the snake's body reappeared.

It struck, and Darien jumped, off the obelisk and onto another platform, boots skidding. He caught himself with a hand against the wall. Crossed the length of the platform in three powerful strides, heart pounding as the Basilisk prepared to bite. To devour.

This was it.

'Make it count,' Bandit said.

'For the chicken?' Darien joked, despite his pounding heart, the sweat trickling down his back.

'For our girl,' Bandit said.

Darien would.

He reached the edge—the second-last one—and launched himself forward with all his might, straight into open air.

Time seemed to slow.

In the reflection of the blade he held aloft, the serpent came in for the kill, eyes flaring silver. Preparing to turn him to stone, into a prize trapped here forever. "You've put up a good fight, Darien Slade," it hissed, that voice so near, Darien could feel it on the back of his neck. "But you are mine now."

Like hell.

The final ledge from the top—his only opportunity—neared…

And neared…

Instead of landing *on* it, he tipped back in midair and flattened his boots against the edge—just like he'd planned.

With a mighty roar, he bent his knees and pushed back off the stone, launching himself into a backflip that propelled his body over the serpent's spiked head.

The Basilisk didn't have time to turn back.

Its face collided with the staircase, stone exploding with an earsplitting *smash*, shards of rock slicing through the air like shrapnel.

"You!" the serpent seethed, whipping its head about, dust and bits of stone flying off. Its voice was so loud, the cavern shook, debris raining down as Darien soared through the air. *"HOW DARE YOU ATTEMPT TO KILL A NAMELESS, DARIEN SLADE—"*

Darien landed on the back of its neck.

The serpent screamed and bucked, launching Darien eighty feet into the air—straight into that swirling, poisonous mist that no longer whispered with cunning but balked. As if bowing to him.

Its new master.

Using the Venom to his advantage, his magic sweeping out to hold the mighty serpent in place, Darien leaned into the fall, angling the blade behind his head. "IT'S DARIEN FUCKING *CASSEL!*" he roared, eyes black with magic, blade poised to kill—to slay.

The Basilisk screamed, its thrashing body nearly bringing down the cavern as it tried to flee.

"And you," Darien snarled, the earthward plummet weaponizing him, "are fucking *dead.*"

He cut the snake's throat.

113

ANGELTHENE
STATE OF WITHEREDGE

The weight of that spell was so heavy that the moment it was cut, Cyra sucked in a sharp, gasping breath, her body so light she felt like she was levitating.

She set down her book and lurched out of bed, her feet catching in the blankets. Bracing her hands against the wall for balance, she searched for Erasmus. The room spun around her in a blur, every step she took like bouncing on a trampoline.

Many long years had passed since their tongues had been frozen by that gods-awful spell. After Loren was born, they had gone back to the Basilisk —the serpent king that ruled the tunnels below Yveswich—for one final trade.

Little had they known the Nameless creature had been waiting patiently for the moment they came back—the moment it would have the opportunity to curse them. It had taken so much from them—their freedom of speech, Erasmus's immortality. Only the beings of the Void had the ability to take advantage of the loopholes in a bargain.

It had not hesitated to strike.

"Erasmus?" Cyra called, his name cracking on its way out. She was weightless as a balloon—a planet drifting out of orbit. "Erasmus?" With shaking fingers, she pushed open the bedroom door—

And nearly bumped into Erasmus. He was breathing just as heavily as Cyra, his eyes lit with hope.

"It's happened," Cyra whispered on a sob.

Erasmus took her by the hands.

Cyra squeezed them, tears of joy flooding her eyes. "The spell is broken."

It took an incredibly powerful person to kill a serpent king—a task they had believed impossible, and had given up hope in thinking it would ever happen.

But it had. Someone had slain that fell beast.

And Cyra and Erasmus were finally free.

114

THE CAVERN
YVESWICH, STATE OF KER

Darien hit the ground in a crouch. Panting and soaked in the Basilisk's reeking black blood, the sword dripping with it. That blade hummed as if with pride, magic rippling through the adamant from hilt to vicious tip in veins of neon.

The snake was dead. The statues of the people the creature had killed had burst into dust the moment Darien had severed the head from its serpentine body, all those souls that were trapped in stone freed at last.

'Well done,' Bandit said, panting proudly in Darien's shadow. *'I expect payment come tomorrow.'*

'How about something quieter this time? Like a sock monkey?'

'Chicken,' Bandit growled. *'A deal's a deal.'* But a moment later, the dog added, *'What's a sock monkey?'*

Darien rose out of his crouch. Lifted the sword behind his back to sheath it.

And winced. Fuck, his hand. He'd made the mistake of wielding the sword with both as he'd dropped down on the Basilisk, and now the nerves were burning as if he'd thrust his hand into open flame.

But he didn't have time to waste on pain.

He crossed the room, boots splashing in a lake of the Basilisk's sticky blood, and prepared to face his next challenge.

"It's not moving." Tanner's hoarse whisper scraped against the walls, the words full of raw, desperate hope. Slate eyes darted between Roman, Jack, and the serpent.

Minutes ago, the mass of scales blocking the door had stopped shifting. And not long before that, a horrid scream had ripped through the tunnels, nearly bringing down the roof and shattering their eardrums.

Roman stepped up to the blocked door—

The serpent began to move.

"Watch out!" Roman shouted, pulling Jack and Tanner back.

Slowly, the limp body of the serpent rose into the air, scales catching the trickles of moonlight.

Roman blinked in disbelief, taking in the scene before him as it appeared in stages.

Black boots. Bent legs that slowly straightened as the serpent rose higher—

Darien stood in the doorway, arms lifted above his head, those arms barely straining under the weight of that massive creature.

With an upward push of his hands, and a slight bending of his knees, he threw the Basilisk—literally *flung* its corpse as if it weighed nothing.

It soared behind him and crashed into the ground with such force, the three of them were nearly knocked on their asses.

Darien used the arm of his bodysuit to wipe the black blood off his forehead, Bandit coming out of his shadow to stand boastfully at his side. "You guys okay?"

"Holy gods," Tanner choked out.

Roman swallowed the dryness in his throat. "Remind me never to get on your bad side."

"What'd it do to piss you off?" Jack asked with a nervous chuckle.

And although Jack had clearly intended for the question to be rhetorical, Darien said as he stepped through the doorway, Bandit's eyes glowing red in the dark as he walked beside him, "It called me 'Darien Slade'."

Max was tiring.

From the moment he'd pried open the elevator doors, he and Dallas had not been given a single opportunity to catch their breath, the demons coming in droves. The creatures had been starved down here for centuries, living off gods-knew-what, probably resorting to eating each other. They had gone feral the moment they'd caught sight of the witch and the Darkslayer standing in the elevator, practically being served up on a silver platter. Max had given Dallas the sword, opting to use his other weapons, his magic acting like an invisible coat of armor.

Now, that armor keeping him and Dallas safe waned—

Max shouted out a warning to Dallas as a winged creature crashed into him, claws ripping into his bodysuit—the only thing, aside from that shield of magic that had slipped, that was keeping him alive.

He smashed into the back wall of the elevator. Reached behind his head to grab onto the demon—

He pulled it over his shoulder, the magic protecting his head crackling as the wings flapped, the pointed ends dragging along the shimmering bulwark of power.

With both hands, he ripped the creature in half, disembowelling it from right shoulder to left hip.

And then he whirled around, intercepting another winged demon before it could get to Dallas, who was panting from the effort it took to wield the sword of black adamant. This one, he sliced open from throat to navel, dagger dripping with black, fizzing blood.

With a roar, Max grabbed another fell creature, whipping it into the wall so hard its skull cracked open, blood misting the air.

Something with brute strength crashed into him from behind, and suddenly he was on the floor. He flipped over, blocking claws that swept for his throat—

And saw a pulsing stone in a translucent forehead. A stone shining black, the sight of it hypnotic.

The demon sprayed acid, the droplets melting holes in Max's bodysuit.

He shouted in pain as the acid burned his skin, blistering it—

With a scream of fury, Dallas punched the sword through the monster's head, skewering it. Max shoved its corpse aside with an upward push of his knees—

Piercing, otherworldly screams sliced through the air, followed by a blast of heat that had Max instantly sweating. He risked a glance through the doors of the elevator to see fire engulfing the tunnels, burning through the hundreds of monsters swarming the area until not even bones remained.

And Max couldn't breathe, a single word blaring in his head like an alarm.

Fire. *Fire.* That was fire choking the tunnels from floor to ceiling, swelling and roaring and blasting through everything in its path—

And then Dallas was there, hovering over him where he lay on the ground, her wings fanning out above him like an angel's embrace.

"I got you," Dallas was saying. Just behind her, the inferno roared, suffusing her grimy, freckled skin with an orange-and-red glow. "I got you, Max." She cupped his cheek, the glove of her bodysuit warm with heat. "I'm right here—I'm not leaving."

Max forced himself to breathe. Kept looking into Dallas's eyes, praying for that fire to stop. Blocking out the memory of Maya screaming, the flames that had singed his hair and skin, the smell of burning flesh.

A few minutes that felt like a lifetime passed, and then the fire vanished, and so did the memory, leaving the tunnels dark once more.

"I got you," Dallas said again.

And then she eased back onto her haunches, helped Max sit up. Together, they looked toward the tunnels beyond the warped elevator doors—

And saw a young woman standing there in the dark. Fire given life.

Max stared. And stared and stared in disbelief.

It was Maya. Little Maya Jane, all grown up. Flanking her were more Elementals, all of them glowing with the colors of their magic.

Their souls.

DARIEN LED the way deeper into the tunnels, toward the Well replica he could sense somewhere up ahead. No light was in these parts, no bioluminescent insects. Just the tactical lights on the firearms the others held, and the veins of the anima mundi lighting up under the soles of their feet. The blackness here held a likeness to the swirling mass above the Basilisk's habitat, almost oily in feel, glomming onto their skin as if it were alive.

The tunnels snaked on for miles. And just as they reached a sharp bend, Darien saw a light glowing beyond.

The lack of armed guards alerted Darien to the magnitude of the problem at hand before he saw it—the Well replica glowing in the very center of an underground chamber even bigger than the last, the walls and ceiling shining black with a thick crust of adamant. This replica, to Darien's horror, was far more advanced than the one on Kalendae, as if nurtured for longer, like some kind of pet.

It had sunk into the floor like a manmade lake, carving out a permanent place for itself in the earth. The waters glowed teal, and floating about were tiny balls of light the same shade. Fireflies.

The Well's first call of magic nearly brought them all to their knees. It ripped through the tunnels, a sound only immortal ears could hear, making them grit their teeth, their blood vibrating with the sheer force of it.

Just like Darien predicted, there were no guards here—none of the imperator's men in sight. No one but them.

As soon as the magic took its claws out of them, Tanner straightened out of his crouch. Staggered in place. Panted, "We need to get out of here." With a shaking hand, he pointed at the veins of the anima mundi below their feet, constantly pulsing with every shade of the rainbow. "We're too late—they've already activated it. Look."

Those veins were channels. They ran from the chambers at Caliginous on Silverway...all the way into the Well replica.

And Loren—the Skeleton Key—had used those chambers. Her magic had been running through these channels since Darien had brought her to Yveswich, feeding the replica. Nurturing it. And with the imperator's men nowhere in sight, the blacked out cameras stopping anyone from seeing that they had left—

Darien bit out, "They've led us into a fucking trap."

115

ROMAN'S HOUSE
YVESWICH, STATE OF KER

Loren looked up from where she lounged on the pillows on her bed, trying to distract herself by reading her romance novel, as Malakai drifted into her room.

For the third time since the others had left.

"I'm so fucking bored," he complained, ripping a frustrated hand through his shoulder-length hair.

"Malakai," Loren sighed, flopping her book into her lap. "Must I entertain you every few minutes?"

"The others are boring. Arthur's teaching Dom and Blue about science shit. Blegh." He leaned against the dresser, the handles on the drawers rattling as he nearly knocked it over. "What are you reading?"

Loren glanced down at her open book. Back up at Malakai. Gave him a cunning smile. "A romance novel. Want me to read it out loud to you?"

"Eww, no."

She flourished the book before her.

He stepped back as if it were a spider. "Get that thing away from me."

She snickered.

The speaker on Malakai's watch crackled.

He turned the face until it clicked. And then he held it up to his ear, listening. Loren listened too, nerves twisting her stomach into tight knots.

This was the first form of communication the others had given them since they'd left. But she couldn't pick up on anything except bursts of static; she couldn't even tell who was speaking.

Malakai cursed and walked out into the hallway, watch still lifted to his ear.

Loren sat up, holding her breath, willing her mortal ears to pick up on what the person on the other end was trying to convey.

The minute Loren recognized Darien's deep voice coming through the speaker, barely audible and intercepted with static, she closed her book and got up, following Malakai on quiet feet.

It had taken her a while to stop crying after Darien had left. And although she was still upset about his decision to bargain away his life, they had a different problem to deal with tonight, one that was approaching immediately instead of within the next ten months. No one's fate was certain; different decisions led to different destinations. The Widow might have said she would die by the age of twenty-one, but she could not accept that Darien would die, too. There must be a way out of that bargain—a way out that would save him, even if she still had to die.

The Reaper was standing just outside her door, watch raised to one ear, a finger pressed against his other.

Loren stood in the doorway. As she listened to that horrible truth coming through the speakers, every word broken up by static, her pounding heart lurched into a painful sprint.

The city was going to blow up. The replica had already been activated by the flow of magic from the Caliginous Chambers.

Which meant *she* had done this. Her treatments at Caliginous on Silverway had been feeding the monstrosity below the streets.

And if she didn't act now, she would be responsible for ten million people dying. Ten million deaths pegged on her.

And some of those deaths would be the people she loved. Dallas, Ivy, Tanner. Jack, Max, Travis.

Darien.

She couldn't let this happen. She wouldn't.

"Malakai," she said quietly.

It took him a minute to turn around. He flicked off the watch, nothing coming through now but static. "We need to go," he said, face bleak, his green eyes more haunted than she'd ever seen them. "Leave Yveswich, I mean. Atlas estimates less than thirty minutes before the replica blows."

Less than thirty minutes. Gods.

But Loren wasn't running. Not anymore, and not when it meant abandoning the people she loved. Abandoning Darien. "I'm not leaving." She turned and went back into her room. "We need to get to the Control Tower."

"Fuck that noise," Malakai bit out, storming in after her, the dresser rattling from his heavy footfall.

Loren pulled her pajama shirt over her head, causing Malakai to whip back around, his back now facing her, though he didn't leave the room. She had to get that bodysuit on and get out of here—quickly.

"We both know what happened last time," Malakai said, still facing the other way as she shimmied her shorts down to her ankles and stepped out of them. "You almost died."

"Thirty minutes isn't long enough for them to make it out of those tunnels," Loren said. She grabbed a baby-blue t-shirt and a pair of black leggings and put them on—clothes that would fit most comfortably under the bodysuit. "They'll be too close. They'll either die from the blast, or they'll wind up stuck in the tunnels."

"And how are we supposed to stop a literal bomb from going off?" He peeked over his broad shoulder, and once he saw that she was dressed he turned to face her. "Might I remind you again that the last time you poured your magic into the Control Tower, your heart stopped beating. I refuse to be responsible for that happening again."

"It won't. I have *these* now." She held up her hands, showing him the conduit tattoos on her palms, the sun and crescent moon shimmering as if with glitter. "These will help, won't they?" She studied him closely, but he was good at not giving himself away. "Do you have any?" she pressed.

He begrudgingly showed her the hooded Reaper tattoo that wrapped around his right forearm. "Sure fucking do," he muttered, but he was still frowning, clearly not wanting to admit that her plan might work.

And that was exactly what gave Loren the last of the confidence she needed. There was no fear left in her anymore—just adrenaline. "Okay— what does it feel like when you're using your magic?" The white ring Arthur had made for her sat on her dresser. She grabbed it now and put it on. With a twist, the bodysuit shot out, covering her from head to toe, the magic blowing her hair back.

"It starts to hurt when you get close to your...limit," Malakai said, every word tight with reluctance. That was good enough for her.

"Get your suit on," she said, walking past him and out the door. "I won't be able to save everyone, but I'll be able to shield part of the city."

He stopped her with a hand on her arm, pulling her around to face him. "Loren..." He held onto her, emotions warring in his gaze. "I can't let you do this. I can't be responsible for you dying."

"And I can't be responsible for *them* dying." She pointed out at the city.

Malakai had nothing to say to that. But he kept holding onto her, quarreling with himself.

"I spent so many years being afraid," Loren whispered. "I'm done with fear."

"It's not about fear," he argued. "Sometimes it's smarter to know when to run." She knew he was trying to save her, knew he must've made an agreement with Darien. But she couldn't—wouldn't—leave.

"Do you want to walk away from here knowing they'll die?" she asked him.

He frowned. "Of course not."

"Then let's go."

It took him a minute, but he finally loosened his grip and sighed. "Lead the way, Blondie."

116

THE TUNNELS
YVESWICH, STATE OF KER

Darien bolted through the underground chamber, away from the Well bellowing out its ancient, horrible song. Every wave of magic it released raked along his bones like claws and set fire to his blood.

"Faster!" he shouted. He kept his pace slower than the others', hanging back just enough to ensure Roman, Tanner, and Jack would make it out. They had minutes if they were lucky—minutes to put distance between themselves and the replica. Enough for their bodysuits to have a chance at saving their asses.

They had almost reached the mouth of the tunnel when Darien caught sight of a blinking red light above the archway. He scanned the ledge and crevices as he ran, his stomach dipping the moment he spotted the wires and the bulk of cylinders that had no business down here.

"GET BACK!" Darien roared. The others skidded to a stop, shouting out questions.

Darien swept his magic into a shield of protection just as the explosives went off—

And the tunnel collapsed right before their eyes.

Heat and light seared the air, temporarily blinding them.

They stumbled back as a group, cursing and muttering and coughing as dust choked the area. Debris showered down around them, bits of rock rolling down the bulwark of shadow that had belled above them like an umbrella.

Shadow—Darien's magic was visible again.

Roman lurched toward the tunnel—toward the rubble blocking them from getting through. "No," he gritted out. *"No."*

That was their only way out.

Unless they could find another exit, they were trapped.

117

THE TAR PITS
YVESWICH, STATE OF KER

Travis and the others were lost.

He couldn't reach Darien or Max. He'd tried several times, with both watch and cell phone, but to no avail. There was no service in these tunnels, no frequency on his watch.

And there was no way of navigating, either, the screen Aspen had pulled up on her tablet yielding nothing. These tunnels were supposed to lead them to Darien and the others, but Travis was certain they were going around in circles. When Aspen cursed under her breath, the soft glow of the screen showing the frustration on her face, Travis knew he was right. This was no use.

Another ten minutes must've passed when a burst of static came through Travis's watch.

"Travis?" Darien's voice cut through the speakers, broken up in places by bad reception. "Travis?"

Finally.

Travis held the device up to his mouth. "I'm here," he said, speaking loud and clear. "What's going on?"

"Where—y—"

"We're in the tunnels—" Another burst of static interrupted him. He could feel the others watching him, listening. "Darien?" He waited, but no reply came through. "Darien, can you hear me?" Silence. "We are in the tunnels—"

"Get the f— out—" Darien was suddenly shouting. "Well is— the— *explode!"*

Travis's face leached of blood. He whirled to face the others, who were gaping at him in silence.

The next words Darien uttered were staticky screams, as if he were praying Travis would hear. *"GET OUT OF THE TUNNELS—NOW!"*

After that, there was nothing but static.

And Travis realized, since the minute they'd walked in here, that something about these tunnels was off.

Long ago, they had been sealed with magic to trap the demon populations down here.

And there were no demons, as if they had all fled from a far worse predator.

A bomb.

Travis's command was a fierce whisper. *"Run."*

"You trying to choke me out, girl?" Malakai shouted over the rumbling bass of the motorcycle as they raced through Yveswich. Dawn was coming, washing the streets with the silvery light of a crisp early morning. Wind tore at her eyes and hair, their surroundings passing by in blurs.

Loren slackened her arms that were squeezing the Reaper's neck, her legs doing the same to his waist. "Sorry," she said. She hadn't realized how hard she was squeezing. "I've never been on one of these before."

"You don't say."

The Control Tower was only a few blocks away. The arrival of daylight had brought more cars and pedestrians to the streets, slowing their efforts. Still, Malakai blew through red lights and stop signs, barely avoiding causing accidents. Horns blared everywhere they went, the screech of tires and the smell of burnt rubber slicing through the air.

They were shooting under another intersection glowing red when Malakai abruptly swerved, the bike veering so sharply to the side it nearly tipped over.

Loren clung on tightly to his neck, her stomach pitching left with the bike. "Are you okay?" she shouted.

Malakai's shake of his head was not in answer, she knew, but as if to rid himself of something. "I don't know what happened." He pushed the bike faster, his pulse suddenly thrumming against her wrists.

Loren felt the next one—a deep, rolling shudder, as if an earthquake struck the city, the eerie call of the Well replica blowing through the streets like a horn. A sound only magic-born people could hear—an audible attack that was paralyzing.

The motorcycle careened to the left again as that wave of otherworldly magic incapacitated Malakai—

Loren's stomach flew out her ass, Malakai's name leaving her mouth on a piercing scream as they crashed into a telephone pole and went flying.

SHAY COULD NOT EVEN BEGIN to imagine living through this nightmare more than once. But the people running on either side of her through the dark tunnels had, to her horror, already lived it.

The Well replica was going to explode. She had no idea how likely it was that they would survive the blast, considering how close they were to where it slumbered, but she didn't have the courage to ask. Everyone in the group ran as fast as they could, their eyes lit with alarm, with a desperate hope for survival. She wouldn't crush them with a question no one would want to hear or answer.

So she ran, fighting to keep up, the winding tunnels seeming to go on forever. Each corner only led to more stretches of tunnel that gave way to yet more corners. It felt like running through a fever dream.

She had the feeling they were halfway there when Travis skidded to a stop at the front of the group, bringing the others to a jarring standstill, bodies slamming together.

The way out was blocked. By four towering, roaring Hounds.

HAD Loren not been wearing the bodysuit, the motorcycle collision would have surely killed her.

The bike was pulverized. Glass and metal glittered on the sidewalk and road as she pushed herself to her feet, Malakai doing the same several feet away. Her body ached, but it wasn't nearly as bad as it would have been without the suit. Cars had come to a stop, idling nearby, a few drivers and pedestrians either calling the emergency number or heading this way to see if they could help.

"You okay?" Malakai called. He came her way, shaking off the pain with only a slight limp in his step. "You hurt?"

"I'm fine." The suits were a gods-damned miracle. She peered down the street, at the Control Tower shining like liquid silver at the end of it. "We need to hurry." She offered Malakai her hand, and he took it, swinging her up onto his back.

"Try not to choke me like you did on the bike," he joked, securing her in place with wrists hooked under her thighs.

Loren merely held on and said, "Show me how fast you can run."

Minutes had passed, and even with the sword of black adamant, they'd only managed to kill one of four Hounds.

Shay was thrown into the tunnel wall with brute force, the oxygen leaving her lungs in a whoosh. She crumpled to the ground, gasping for breath, her diaphragm burning as the others fought all around her, as winded and in pain as she was.

They couldn't keep doing this. If they couldn't get past these Hounds, they were all done for.

"Shay!" Ivy called, her voice breaking with exhaustion as she drove a blade into the back of a Hound's skull. Bone crunched, and the demon roared, angrier now than before. "Can we use illusion?"

She almost answered in truth. Almost slipped up and told them that Hounds were one of the few breeds of demon that could not be fooled with illusion, a fact she had learned the hard way as a teenager, when she and her foolish friends had wandered out to the tar pits to smoke Boneweed.

Shay pushed to her feet. "I can buy us three minutes." *I can buy you three minutes,* she corrected mentally.

"Hurry!" Travis shouted, driving the black blade Ivy had tossed him through a second Hound's head. Even with that blade on their side, these things were hard to kill. They were fast, strong. Menacing.

Shay drew the dagger that was strapped to her thigh and cut her neck.

It was just a small cut. But Hounds went into a frenzy over any amount of blood, no matter how small. And because she'd dealt the injury to her body herself, the magic of the suit did not stop it from happening.

All at once, the Hounds whirled her way.

"Now," Shay declared. The wound in her neck stung, trickles of blood warming her skin. "Run—now."

The others did. Bolting straight for the tar pits.

Shay watched them go—just for a moment. Watched them believe that her cutting herself was the illusion they'd asked her to cast.

She gave a little smile and started running the other way, the remaining Hounds following behind her with hungry roars.

And she found that she did not feel afraid.

THE CONTROL TOWER WAS MASSIVE. Even bigger than the one in Angelthene. It stood in the center of Yveswich like a proud tree, the roots of the anima mundi tunneling deep into the earth. Pulses of color flowed through the channels, sipped up by the base of the tower.

As soon as they were close enough, Loren leapt off Malakai's back and ran the rest of the distance to the tower, the cristala shining like liquid silver.

"You sure you know what you're doing, girl?" the Reaper panted as he sprinted beside her.

"I'll figure it out when I get there," she answered.

Another wave of the Well replica's magic forced Malakai to a halt. He clapped his hands over his ears. Bowed his knees.

Loren twisted around to face him. "Malakai—"

"Go, go!" He waved her away. "Go—I'll be right there."

She did not have time to get to the first platform like she had during the Blood Moon. She would need to pour her magic into it from down here and hope for the best.

With her conduit hanging from her neck, the tattoos on her palms shimmering as she rallied her magic, she stepped up to the humming tower. Shut her eyes...

And slapped both palms onto the cristala.

TRAVIS and the others ran like hell for the way out.

Dawn had arrived, so he was able to see its glow coming from a bend up ahead. They were close, but even if they made it out of these tunnels, that didn't leave them much time to get the hell out of this city. Either way, people were going to die. Whether they were in this group or not. The thought sickened him. Paxton, Roman... Darien, Tanner, Jack... Would he ever see them again?

"Faster!" Travis shouted, his breaths rasping through the tunnels. He grabbed Jewels by the hand, pulling her at a faster pace.

Another ten bounding strides, and they were through, sucking down the fresh air of an early morning. They didn't stop for a rest—there was no time. They had to get to the truck.

He ran, pulling Jewels with him—

"Wait!" Ivy called.

He skidded to a stop, the others thumping to a standstill as well.

Ivy's gaze tore wildly among the group, searching.

Someone was missing.

She exclaimed, voice ringing with alarm, "Where is Shay?"

118

THE ELEVATOR
YVESWICH, STATE OF KER

Since the night Max found out Maya was alive, he'd dreamt of this moment, this reunion. He'd thought about it so many times, he was convinced that when the day came, it would play out exactly like it had in his mind. He'd dreamt he would run to her, swoop her up into his arms and give her one of his bear hugs she'd always complained were crushing her.

Reality was, words escaped him, and so did his feet. Stunned into silence, heart beating all throughout his body, he lifted himself up off the ground, staring through the warped elevator doors at the sister he'd believed he'd lost.

Maya 'MJ' Reacher had grown up. She had lived in Max's memories for so long that for some reason he'd not clued into how she would have grown and changed with the passing of time. She was no longer a teenager but a woman, and she was extraordinary. Her body was all fire, her hair spiraling upward like flame. Ignis in the flesh.

Beside her, the other Elementals took their own blazing forms, an assortment of colors all glowing in the dark. Yellow, violet, green, magenta... and the red one, burning at their center like a heart.

Beautiful. Ethereal. All deadly in their own unique way.

"Maya." Max spoke her name with barely a breath, and once it was out he found he couldn't draw another.

His sister was alive. MJ was alive, and she was right there, looking at him just like he looked at her. All this time...

All this fucking time.

Tears blinded him. A sob rose in his throat, clawing out and echoing into the now-silent tunnels. Nothing was left of the demons, their bones incinerated by the fire, the ground still hot beneath Max's feet.

His sister's fire. Maya had done this—saved him. His little sister.

Max blinked away the tears, watching with an eager heart as the caution on MJ's face gradually subsided. Her flames cooled. Flesh replaced fire, and her hair settled down, tumbling over her shoulders in the same reddish-brown waves Max remembered, the hair she'd fought with every day before school, cursing the frizz and the tangles and wishing she had been born with more manageable hair.

Maya spoke so softly, the single word was nearly inaudible. "Max?"

That was when the bomb hit.

SHAY HAD LED the Hounds deep into the tunnels—toward the Well replica beating like a heart deep within.

Now, she ran back the other way, her lungs and muscles screaming, head pounding with a vicious headache.

Behind her, the Hounds continued their search. She'd managed to lose them in the network of tunnels, by some miracle. She likely had the Well replica to thank for that, its long, loud peals as effective on demons as they were on Shay.

She sensed that she was running out of time. The replica continued to emit those horrible, blasting calls, each one slicing through her bones and vibrating her blood.

Another call sounded now, louder than the ones that had preceded it. It sent her staggering into the wall of the tunnel, the magic protecting her face shredding against the stone.

She clapped her hands over her ears and kept running.

Shay, you're slow, Roman had once told her in the desert. It was true—she had no hope of making it out of here alive. And she was so close to the Well replica, it would be a miracle if her suit managed to save her.

Still, she sent a quiet prayer up to the gods she had never paid much attention to before, hoping with all her might that they heard her now.

"Anna's gone," she croaked into the dark, tears burning her eyes as that horrible truth left her tongue. "I'm certain she would have prayed to you in her final moments, just as I am now." She kept running, clapping her hands over her ears again as another blast rang through the city, the gap between pulses so much shorter now, like a clock ticking down. "I pray not for myself but for my...my friends."

They *were* her friends, weren't they? She hadn't known them for long, but they had given more to her in that short time than anyone at the Riptide ever had.

Tears spilled down her cheeks, sparkling under the magic of the bodysuit as she whispered, "Give them a chance—please."

Give Roman a chance, she added mentally. She was convinced she had never met a person who had suffered more than Roman, one who'd sacrificed so much for the people he loved and had been given so little in return.

She thought only of his handsome face as the replica detonated, heat and light blasting through the tunnels—

As quickly as it had brightened, Shay's world went dark.

IN THE TUNNELS below the city, so close to the Well replica, Darien sank to his knees.

He sensed the replica's power was coming to a head. It was only a matter of seconds now before it exploded. Before more than ten million people died. Including Darien. Including his family. His friends.

There was no other way out of here. No use in trying to dig through the rubble choking the tunnel. There was far too much of it, and far too little time.

Darien's heart was pounding so hard, it hurt. Nausea ebbed and flowed in his gut, his blood alive with not just his own magic, visible once more, but the calls of the Well. Each toll as it counted down the seconds till his death clanged through his bones, his skull. He was so close to the replica, he couldn't hear himself think, couldn't move, as if this moment was no more real than a dream.

He thought of her, though—Loren. Pictured her beautiful face, her bright smile, in the whirlwind of his thoughts. He prayed Malakai had followed through with his promise—had taken her to safety the minute Darien had given him the warning. Prayed she was already miles away from this doomed city.

Roman, Jack, and Tanner continued to dig at the rocks strangling their way out, their skin shining with sweat, eyes feverish with determination. Darien didn't have the heart to tell them it was no use.

The call of the replica grew to a blood-curdling shriek that blew up like a pipe bomb between Darien's ears, sending him curling over himself on the ground. His shoulders tensed up from the hit, his hands shooting up to flatten over his ears. His mouth opened with a scream he couldn't hear or feel, his eyes flooding with tears of pain. He ground his face into the stone, tasting dirt and blood, needing to get the fuck away from that monstrosity bellowing out its ancient song just behind him.

His teeth sang. His muscles twitched and vibrated. Where he lay on the cold, hard ground, unable to move, he angled his head and saw the others doing the same, blood mixing with Venom as both leaked from their eyes.

By the time the wave of magic receded at last, Darien had almost passed out from the immense force of it. He blinked the blood and fog away to see the others struggling up from their various positions on the ground, looking as disoriented as Darien felt.

One by one, they staggered to their feet and came to join him. Lurching into pained crouches on either side of him. Darien pushed himself up so he was kneeling, and without saying a word, they took each other's hands.

Panting, blood streaming from his nose, ears, and eyes, Darien tipped his head back, feeling something...*else*...rippling over his skin. Being on the flip-side of the adamant, he could see through it. Up to the city way, way above. Saw where the two cobbled streets intersected—the massive Crossroads where the Basilisk had once lived.

And, for a reason he couldn't place, found himself looking toward the Control Tower...

Just as the replica exploded.

119

THE CONTROL TOWER
YVESWICH, STATE OF KER

Using her magic gave her an all-seeing ability.
Loren could feel her many-hued power rippling through the streets, as if she were reaching out and touching them with hands dipped in paint.

She stood there at the Control Tower, head bowed, both palms flattened against the cristala that thrummed and vibrated as it drew magic up from the anima mundi—drew magic from *her*. She saw the city in her head like a map, saw different streets and buildings and districts light up with the protection of her magic—the shield that would save as many people as she could from the replica's explosion. She prayed it would be everyone, but...

Truth be told, she was already fading. The glowing tattoos in the center of her palms were dimming and cooling, the conduit that hung from her neck threatening to turn into a useless pendant, its heat waning too. The pain began, just like Malakai had warned her, a burning in her hands that spread up, and up, and up at rapid speed.

And she had not even managed to cover a quarter of the city.

Either way, the Well replica was going to explode. It was going to kill a large majority of the people who lived here, those people currently unaware that their world was about to end. Whether they were heading to work, just waking up, or deciding to sleep in, they had no idea what was about to hit. And it broke Loren's heart.

With a raw, desperate cry that might've been from determination or defeat, she pushed her magic out farther, hoping with all her might that her conduit tattoos would keep her alive, acting as a buffer the same way as a magic stave, and give these people a chance. Another shot at the life that was about to be snatched out of their reach, if she failed to stop it.

She sensed the Reaper behind her, guarding her back while she poured her magic into the tower.

"Loren," he warned.

"I know," she gritted out, pushing herself harder, stretching that bubble of protection to its limits. She covered the northern districts, tunneling into the underground where Darien and the others might still be. She couldn't feel them, but she hoped she would reach them with her shield. If she didn't...

She did not finish her thought.

Out, her magic poured, rippling through more streets and districts farther out, the shield thinning the farther she pushed it. The Well rumbled the concrete, stones clacking. The glass of nearby windows tinkled like wind chimes. As the tower shuddered, she thought of Darien, picturing that face she loved so much, *needing* to save him—

She had reached just over a quarter of the city, her face streaked with tears and dirt, when the replica detonated.

When the bomb went off, Darien lost his hold on the others.

The eruption was so horrific, he couldn't breathe, not even with the protection of the bodysuit. Heat and light were everywhere, raw magic ripping through the chamber like a hurricane.

Roman, Tanner, Jack—he couldn't see any of them. There was nothing but brightness and heat and terrible power.

And then the Veil fell.

120

UNDERGROUND
YVESWICH, STATE OF KER

The Void swallowed everything like a fucking black hole. Darkness blasted through the chamber with as much force as the bomb, threatening to rip Darien's flesh right off his bones.

After the horrific, otherworldly might of the initial blast, Darien had no idea how he was still alive. It had torn his hands out of the others' grips and launched him blindly into a wall hard enough to knock the wind out of him. Hard enough to bruise to the bone.

Now, he was hunkered down beside that wall, arms thrown over his head, waiting out the collision of dimensions as darkness triumphed over light, suffocating everything it touched.

Finally, the falling of the Veil and the sheer force of two worlds blending into one stopped like a window shut against a storm. There was nothing now but an eerie silence and endless, choking darkness.

Nothing but blindness.

With a roar of pain, he pushed rubble off his body and staggered to his feet, a part of him wishing, as he blinked fiercely at his surroundings that had disappeared, leaving nothing but flat black, that he hadn't survived the blast.

Because this darkness that was choking the tunnels... It felt thicker than tar. Colder than ice. It pressed on Darien like a weighted blanket, not even the vaguest of shapes visible in the endless gloom, no matter how hard he blinked or squinted. A hellseher, blind for the first time in his life, even his Sight unable to glimpse a single thread of color. What irony.

Worse than the darkness was the silence. Roman, Jack, Tanner... Where the hell were they? He could hear nothing but the odd clack of debris, the pounding of his heart and his rapid breaths, so warm against the sudden chill.

No other heartbeats. No one else breathing.

"Roman?" he called, the word crackling with exhaustion. With pain.

No answer.

"Roman!" he called again. His shout echoed as if he were stuck in a bell.

The eerie sound that followed was a faint groaning and creaking, as if the walls themselves were stretching, the throat of a beast poised to devour.

"Tanner," he tried, chest pumping with labored breaths. He tried using his Sight again, but it showed him nothing. Just endless velvet black that made Darien wonder if this wasn't the Void at all, but maybe he'd gone blind during the explosion. His breaths came faster, and his next shout was a desperate roar. *"JACKYYYYY!"*

Nothing.

"Fuck. *Fuck.*" Darien reached over his shoulder, his skin and muscles screaming in agony from the blast, his bodysuit ripped from head to toe, and grabbed the automatic rifle.

The tactical light bobbed before him like a spark as he pointed the firearm into the black shroud. Not blind. He wasn't blind, but—

No light could penetrate it. The lightbulb just flitted about uselessly like a firefly, emitting no beam to cut through the dark.

A cold sweat broke out across his back. His heart stumbled two beats.

The Veil had fallen. He had no idea where his friends or family were, if they were even alive—

And, for the first time in his life, he was utterly blind.

ROMAN COULDN'T TELL up from down, left from right. The darkness pressed on him, relentless and suffocating. It was closing in—

'I'm here,' Sayagul said. *'Stay calm. Find Darien. We need to find Darien—'*

"Darien," Roman panted. He got to his feet and staggered through the dark, following the sound of his cousin's shouting.

"Roman!" Darien's deep voice cracked with relief. "Roman, where the fuck are you?"

"Here," Roman squeezed out, moving faster, the toes of his boots catching in rubble. He tripped and smacked his face against stone—a wall, the skin of his cheek ripping open. He pushed off the adamant and kept walking, focusing on the sound of Darien's footsteps. Blood trickled in lines down his back, warm against the icy air inside the chamber. "I can't see." And if he couldn't see, then what did that mean for Pax? Kylar? Shayla? Were they even alive? Fuck, he had to find them.

"Neither can I." Darien's voice was closer now, the shift of rock under boots getting louder.

Roman's lungs were too small; he couldn't draw a full breath. They shrank further, squeezing and burning and shriveling—

'Stay calm,' Roman, Sayagul urged, though her words were also edged with panic, her mind flashing between their surroundings and thoughts of Paxton. Shay.

Roman tried to take her advice, but he couldn't breathe, his phobia gripping him in sharp claws. He couldn't fucking *breathe*. *"I can't see—"*

"I know." Darien's voice was strained. A hand settled on Roman's arm, and Roman flinched, breaths drawn through clenched teeth. "It's me—I'm here," Darien said. "I'm right here. You hear me? You listening?"

Roman nodded. Swallowed. "Yeah." The burn of bile surged up his throat, and he swallowed again, his gut roiling. "Yeah, I hear you."

"I'm going to need your help. So I can't have you passing out on me, okay? I can't do this without you." Darien gave Roman a few seconds to breathe, to calm down, and Roman took them, grounding himself. Usually, he took in his surroundings bit by bit, but when darkness was everywhere, he had to do it another way. Breathing in, out... Inhale... Exhale...

Once he'd calmed down enough, he squeezed out, "What do we do?"

A beat of silence. And then Darien admitted, "I don't know."

"How did the tunnels not completely collapse?" It made no sense. They should be buried under rubble, not standing here breathing.

Another beat of silence, this one weighed down with something Roman couldn't place, and then Darien said again, "I don't know."

Roman stared into the pitch; he had a feeling Darien was doing the same, searching for something, *anything*. But that darkness just wouldn't bend, no matter how hard Roman willed his eyes to adjust. And as long as they were blind like this, they were no better than sitting ducks. Even his Sight did fuck-all; he couldn't see anything.

Rock clacked nearby.

"Jack?" Roman called, quietly. "Atlas—" He was silenced when Darien's grip tightened on his arm in warning.

Roman held very still, Darien doing the same at his side.

Something in that darkness hissed. The sound was echoed by others just like it, along with the guttural roars of beasts.

They were not alone.

121

THE CONTROL TOWER
YVESWICH, STATE OF KER

Even with Loren's magic shielding parts of the city, the explosion razed countless structures to the ground. It snuck through the apertures in her coat of protection, leveling almost the entire north end.

Blinding white light swallowed Yveswich in one fell swoop. Seismic waves erupted through the earth with horrid force, buckling the asphalt in violent ripples that could be felt in all corners of the city. Everywhere her magic failed to cover, destruction was wreaked.

Power lines snapped. Bridges and overpasses disintegrated. Vehicles cracked into pieces, as if they themselves were bombs, bits of shrapnel carving the torrid air apart like bullets.

With the suit protecting her, keeping her alive when by all rights she should have died the minute the bomb went off, Loren saw it all. And it was a nightmare.

It was Kalendae all over again, only—impossibly—worse. Because she did not pass out like last time; she was forced to witness the catastrophe in full.

A fitting punishment for someone who'd failed. Someone who had been birthed by the same monstrosity that had just killed millions of people —countless souls added to the replica's ever-growing death toll.

She lay on her stomach among the wreckage, the force of the blast pinning her there, as that bright light continued to rip through the city. It had no end—it just kept going. Blasting with such force, she worried her magic would not hold.

She could already feel it bending. Felt her body warm under the weight of all that heat. That raw, horrible power that had no master.

Her nose began to bleed, red dripping to the pavement—what was left of it. Her eyes watered and burned. The back of her bodysuit heated up and began to blister and peel, exposing her back to the magic of the bomb—the weapon threatening to do the same to her flesh.

And she still couldn't move, the blast immobilizing her, destruction tearing around her like a hurricane. It was utterly terrifying.

And Malakai was nowhere to be seen.

The people of Yveswich didn't even have a chance to scream—to feel fear or even recognize that there was a threat. The explosion incinerated them, leaving not even bones behind—nothing to bury.

As quickly as it had come, the bright light of the eruption was swallowed up by something far more powerful.

Night. Thick, choking night. Or was it smoke?

The longer she lay there, squinting into the dark, the faster her heart beat. Had she gone blind?

With a wince, her very bones screaming in agony, Loren pushed to her feet among rubble, blinking fiercely into the sudden blackness.

No, that wasn't smoke.

That *was* night—shadow.

The Void. The dimensions had collided, the preternatural blackness of that other realm invading their own.

And within that blackness, horrible things began to bay. Jaws and teeth and bones clicked. Claws scraped on rubble and clinked on shattered glass. Fell things scuttled in the dark, some of them hissing, others snuffling in search of prey.

"Malakai?" Loren called, the word as brittle as she felt. Using her magic had hollowed her out, and while the explosion had not killed her, it had still taken its toll. Her heart felt weak, her head heavy, limbs buzzing as if it were acid flowing through her veins instead of blood.

Every part of her body hurt. The bodysuit was all but shredded, and she felt something wet and warm trickling down her arms and legs. Her back.

She reached over her shoulder, wincing as her fingertips grazed the shredded flesh of her back. That warm wetness was blood, the rusty scent of it calling out to the creatures she could sense nearby, the monsters swarming the streets all around her. The creatures she could not see.

Something moved to her left. Breathing noisily in the dark.

Scenting her.

Heart shooting into her throat, she turned toward the sound. Backed up several paces, rock clacking underfoot. "Malakai?" she called again.

It was the otherworldly cry of a creature that answered her. The rasp of claws on stone.

She held her breath. Choked down her scream. She staggered through the dark, hand held out before her to keep from bumping into things, the other poised to grab her gun, should she need it. It might not be able to kill most breeds that had come through the Veil, but it was better than having nothing.

Through the darkness, she walked, covering barely any distance, the eruption of pavement nearly impossible to maneuver when she couldn't see. The darkness was pressing, as if someone had pulled a blanket over her head.

A dry cough cut through the eerie quiet.

"Malakai?" she said again, hushed now.

"Loren?"

"I'm here," she said, her words choked with relief. She stumbled toward the sound of his voice, her feet catching in rubble.

"Where?" he rasped.

She closed the last few paces to his side. Her toe caught in a crevice of rock, and she crashed to the ground beside him, pain splitting through her kneecaps. Loren felt around for him, her hand at last closing around his searching fingers. "Here," she said, feeling the raw skin of his callused fingers, the blood coating it. "I'm right here."

"I can't see anything, girl."

"Hold on—hold on, I've got an idea." She had one bead of magic left—just one. She could feel it humming in her core, a tiny spark waiting to gutter out.

She closed her eyes, resisting the urge to tremble when it made no difference to her surroundings...and pushed her unusual Sight into her vision, like she had that night at the carnival.

When she reopened them, she could see again—not as if the darkness was gone, but...as if she were a hellseher.

Quickly, she scanned the Void. The auras and energies; the spells rippling over the buildings, the magic sputtering with the effort to keep working. Her protection had kept the Control Tower from fully coming down, leaving the buildings that remained standing with at least partial protection.

Nobody in the immediate area was still alive. The only sentient creatures that stalked among the rubble were different breeds of monster, all of them equally terrifying.

"Loren?" Malakai ground out. He blindly felt around for her in the dark.

"I can see," she whispered. She grasped his other hand, holding them both now. "I can see," she said again.

"How?" His hands squeezed hers. "Did I go blind?"

"No." She shook her head. "No—it's the Void. It's swallowing everything." There was a lump in her throat, and she couldn't get it down. "Can you see with your Sight? Anything?"

A brief delay. And then, "Fucking barely. Just the spells on some buildings."

"Not the monsters?"

Another beat of silence. And then he admitted: "No."

For several minutes, they crouched there together, their rasping breaths filling the eerie quiet. Neither of them had any idea what to do—it was obvious in their reluctance to move, fear and blindness freezing them both.

And then the baying began anew. The howls and the roars—all sounds that curdled her blood and made her stomach quake with fear.

Malakai laced his fingers with hers. "Don't let go of me," he ordered.

"I won't," she whispered.

"Promise." His breathing was as ragged as her own. "You have to promise. If we lose you, we're all dead."

She nodded—a gesture he couldn't see.

With a deep breath, she tightened her fingers around Malakai's. Faced the writhing darkness...the many monsters hunting within, howling at the sunless sky—calling together a hunt that would decimate what was left of a once-proud city. "I promise."

122

ISLEY RESIDENCE
ANGELTHENE, STATE OF WITHEREDGE

The rattling of the teacups on the serving tray caused Tamika Isley's head to turn toward the window.

Was this an earthquake?

She picked up the tray that sat on the bed beside her ailing mother and carefully slid it onto the nightstand. On quiet feet, she got up and walked to the window that overlooked the Victoria Amazonica District. With hands that slightly trembled, she drew the curtain.

Tamika stared out at the skyline glimmering in the distance, her breaths quickening as memories of the Blood Moon slammed into her.

The forcefield was still functioning; she could see its greenish hue bubbling above Angelthene. The city was calm—no sirens.

Angelthene was secure. Safe. They were *safe*.

Pressing a hand to her racing heart, she drew several slow, deep breaths and worked on loosening her taut muscles.

Behind her, the bed creaked as her mother stirred, and a pained groan sliced through the room. Her mother always had fitful sleeps; the Tricking had kept her from getting proper rest for years. Tamika did not want to admit it, but her mother's time was coming to an end.

"It's okay, Mom," Tamika said quietly. She knew she wouldn't get an answer; the Tricking had robbed Charlene Isley of her speech, too. But Tamika couldn't handle never saying a word to the woman who'd raised her, so she still spoke as if her mother might reply. Tamika turned. "It must have been a minor earthquake—"

Tamika froze.

The bed was empty, the sheets creased by her mother's body—by the woman who hadn't moved from that bed in months.

Charlene Isley was nowhere to be seen.

Tamika's heart stumbled. Her throat dried out.

"Mom?" she called. She took a step toward the bed, the floor creaking underfoot.

The power went out. The room plunged into darkness.

Silence fell like a cloak—heavy and thick.

"Mom?" she called again, quieter now. A chill spread across her body, pebbling her skin.

The power flared back to life. The lights flickered on. The ceiling fan resumed its spinning—

The last thing Tamika saw was the glint of a knife.

Gripped by her mother's pale hand.

EPILOGUE
ANGELTHENE, STATE OF WITHEREDGE

Cyra could not remember the last time she had felt fear this strong. Her heart was pounding, her stomach churning like a whirlpool as she watched the news channel with Erasmus in their townhouse.

The screen went black as the camera in the heart of Yveswich was swallowed by a deadly explosion of shadow.

It's happened, she thought. Her hand fluttered to her mouth.

The Veil had fallen.

It was only a matter of time now before the rip between worlds spread wider. Yveswich was a sealing point—the most vital one. The cold, historic city, with its waterfalls, canals, and ancient, labyrinthine tunnels, was the place where she had funneled her magic all those years ago, stitching the seam separating dimensions. A lifetime ago.

Back then, she had gone by a different name: *Helia*. The name, like *Cyra*, meant 'sun', though *Cyra*, in some languages, could also mean 'moon'. Both names were fitting, given her history.

> *Sun, Moon*
> *Moon, Sun*
> *What are we but two sides to the same coin?*
> *The same but different*
> *Different but the same.*

Cyra had left that identity behind—a decision made with the best intentions. Had she known that it would lead to this—to tragedy and destruction—she never would have done it.

Her daughter was there—in Yveswich. Her sweet Lily.

"Loren is there." Cyra's hoarse whisper was choked by panic.

Erasmus clasped her hand, his own trembling. "She'll be alright," he said gently. "She's with *him.*" Her husband's words did no good. Nothing and no one would be able to save their daughter—save any of them—from this. Not even Darien Cassel. Not anyone. This was something far bigger than Darkslayers. Far bigger than their world.

"We have to help them," she said.

"How?" Erasmus croaked.

Now that the spell was broken, they could speak freely to others about the Phoenix Head Society instead of just to each other. Now, they might stand a fighting chance. Might be able to right their many wrongs.

But neither Cyra nor Erasmus were the same as they once were. They were different now, their powers long gone.

Still, Cyra whispered, "We have to try."

The live newsfeed was still black. The camera kept recording, but there wasn't one lens in the city that wasn't blacked out by the Void. The news anchors were fleeing—she could hear them shouting and screaming as they abandoned their jobs and made a run for it. Howls and baying ripped through the speakers, along with the spitting of rapid-fire gunshots and the raw, desperate screams of the people as they were eaten alive.

Cyra swallowed. "He will be coming."

Erasmus's eyes locked on hers, his fear mirroring her own. He knew exactly who she meant.

He was coming. And the moment he got here, this world she had fought so hard to protect would not stand a chance.

CAST OF CHARACTERS

THE SEVEN DEVILS

DARIEN CASSEL — Head of Hell's Gate and lead Darkslayer in Angelthene. Formed the Seven Devils when he was nineteen. He is Randal Slade and Elsie Cassel's son, and Ivyana Cassel's twin brother.

MAXIMUS REACHER — Darien Cassel's Second. He is Maya Reacher's older brother. Max has been best friends with Darien since childhood.

TRAVIS DEVLIN — Darien Cassel's cousin. Also known as the 'Devlin Devil'. He has two brothers: Roman Devlin and Paxton Slade. He was born in Yveswich but moved to Angelthene at the age of seventeen.

JACK STEELE — Ivyana Cassel's husband. Jack is the newest member of the Seven Devils and the family jokester. Before he joined the Devils, he made a lot of enemies as a compulsive gambler and swindler.

IVYANA 'IVY' CASSEL — Darien Cassel's twin sister, born seven minutes after Darien. She is the daughter of Randal Slade and Elsie Cassel. She's been married to Jack Steele for two years.

TANNER ATLAS — Hacker for the Seven Devils. He is Doctor Joyce Atlas's son. He and Darien became friends after Darien stood up for him against school bullies.

LACE RIVERA — Niece to Lionel Savage. Former member of the Huntsmen, though it was never made official. She was Darien Cassel's first serious girlfriend.

THE REAPERS

Malakai Delaney — Head of the House of Souls and Right Hand of Darien Cassel. He is Jewels Delaney's older brother.

Valen Hayes — Malakai Delaney's Second.

Sylvan Wolfe — Malakai Delaney's Third. Named after Sylvan the god.

Aspen Van Halen — Best friend to Lace Rivera, and twin sister of Clover Van Halen. Assists Clover with hacking spell systems, databases, etc.

~~Brodie Verlice~~ — Twin brother of Macen Verlice and former Reaper. Died during the events of *City of Souls and Sinners*.

~~Macen Verlice~~ — Twin brother of Brodie Verlice and former Reaper. Died during the events of *City of Souls and Sinners*.

Jewels Delaney — Malakai Delaney's younger sister. She is sick with the Tricking.

Clover Van Halen — Aspen Van Halen's twin sister. Hacker for the Reapers.

THE HUNTSMEN

LIONEL SAVAGE — Head of the Hunting Grounds and former Right Hand of Randal Slade. He is Lace's uncle and Harley's father.

HARLEY SAVAGE — Lionel Savage's son, and Lace Rivera's cousin.

SETH MARKSMAN — Second to Lionel Savage.

COLTON ADLER — Third to Lionel Savage.

ARCHER SAVAGE — Nephew of Lionel Savage. Lace and Harley's cousin.

SHEPLEY MARKSMAN — Hacker for the Huntsmen.

XANDER PRICE — Assistant hacker to Shepley Marksman.

NATHAN RHODES — Newest member of the Huntsmen.

THE ANGELS OF DEATH

DOMINIC VALENCIA — Head of Death's Landing and former member of Angelthene's Aerial Fleet. Conrad Valencia's brother.

CONRAD VALENCIA — Dominic Valencia's brother and Second. Former member of Angelthene's Aerial Fleet.

HANLI SHADID — Third to Dominic Valencia and former member of Angelthene's Aerial Fleet. Aided the Devils during the Well explosion at the end of *City of Gods and Monsters*.

DYLAN REED — Hacker for the Angels of Death. Former member of Angelthene's Aerial Fleet.

GWEN REED — Assistant hacker to Dylan Reed, who is also her brother. Former member of Angelthene's Aerial Fleet.

THE WARGS

CHANNARY GRAVES — Head of the House on the Pier. The Wargs have an assortment of rare magical pelts that are enchanted with shifter magic.

LUMEN GRAVES — Channary's daughter and Second.

UMBRIELLE GRAVES — Channary's daughter and Third.

~~VALARY STERNBERG~~ — Darien's former friend with benefits. After threatening Loren in *City of Souls and Sinners,* Darien had her excommunicated by Channary. Presumed dead after the events of *City of Souls and Sinners.*

CHRISTA COPENSPIRE — Recently moved back to Angelthene from the city of Skylen. Her relationship with Darien Cassel was long-distance and solely physical. It nearly changed into a serious one, but things ended badly between them before this could happen.

JACINTHA COPENSPIRE — Christa Copenspire's sister, and assistant hacker to Isabella Moss.

ISABELLA MOSS — Hacker for the Wargs.

RYLEIGH WITT — Sister to Vanessa Witt.

VANESSA WITT — Sister to Ryleigh Witt.

THE VIPERS

JUDE MONSON — Head of the Den of Vipers. Former friend of the Devils. He had a fall-out with Darien Cassel in *City of Souls and Sinners* when Darien gave Malakai Delaney a promotion.

NADIA MONSON — Jude Monson's fiancée.

JESSA GILCHRIST — Darien Cassel's former friend with benefits. Aided the Devils at the end of *City of Gods and Monsters*.

SAGE MONSON — Hacker for the Vipers. She is Jude Monson's sister.

CARTER MCKENZIE — Jude Monson's cousin and Second.

IVAN GILCHRIST — Jessa Gilchrist's cousin.

RACE HUNTER — Jude Monson's Third.

JASMINE ROSE — Member of the Vipers. Assistant hacker to Sage Monson.

DARKSLAYERS OF YVESWICH

ROMAN 'SHADOWS' DEVLIN — Shadowmaster and Head of the House of Black. Known as the 'Wolf of the Hollow'. He is Darien's cousin and Travis and Paxton's older brother.

SHAYLA 'SHAY' COUSENS — Member of the Riptide. She is Athene's daughter and Anna's younger sister.

KYLAR 'KY' LAVIN — Second and hacker to Roman Devlin. He has a little brother named Eugene.

DONOVAN SLADE — Head of all Darkslaying circles in Yveswich. He is Randal and Dean Slade's brother, and the youngest of the three. He has three kids: Roman, Travis, and Paxton.

ATHENE COUSENS — Head of the Riptide. She has two daughters: Shay and Anna Cousens.

ANNA COUSENS — Second to Athene Cousens. She is Athene's daughter and Shay's sister.

PIA — Third to Athene Cousens. Anna's friend.

LARINA BARLOWE — A Shadowmaster who answers to Donovan. She is Blaine's sister.

BLAINE BARLOWE — A Shadowmaster who answers to Donovan. He is Larina's brother.

BEATRICE — A Selkie who works for the Riptide.

KAILANI — A Selkie who works for the Riptide.

WILLOW ADAMS — Third to Roman Devlin.

HELLSEHERS

THE TERRAN IMPERATOR — The most powerful person in all of Terra. His real name is Quinton Lucent.

KLAY LUCENT — Quinton Lucent's son. He was instructed to watch Loren in *City of Souls and Sinners*.

~~RANDAL SLADE~~ — Former Head of all Darkslaying circles in Angelthene. He is Darien and Ivyana's father, and Elsie Cassel's husband. Died during the events of *City of Gods and Monsters*.

GAVEN PAYNE — A weapons dealer and one of Randal's former business partners. He is under the imperator's employ.

JOHNATHON KYLE — CEO of Lucent Enterprises.

HELIA SOPHRONIA — Loren's mother, and Erasmus Sophronia's wife.

CYRA — The rabbit messenger who hired Darien to find Loren in *City of Gods and Monsters*.

BLUE — An Elemental with the magic of the Mist.

JOYCE ATLAS — Tanner's mother. She is a doctor at Angelthene General.

MAYA 'MJ' REACHER — Max's younger sister. At the end of *City of Souls and Sinners,* Blue revealed that Maya is still alive and goes by the name 'Scarlet'.

PAXTON DEVLIN — Roman and Travis's little brother.

EUGENE LAVIN — Half-human hellseher. Kylar's little brother and Paxton's best friend.

BLAZE — An Elemental with the magic of the Inferno.

GOLD — An Elemental with the magic of the Aether.

~~TYSON GELLER~~ — Former Reaper. Killed by Darien in *City of Gods and Monsters*.

~~HELEN DEVLIN~~ — Roman and Travis's mother. Deceased before the events of *City of Gods and Monsters*.

CLARE SLADE — Paxton's mother. She is married to Donovan Slade.

KYLE — Tattoo artist and owner of Diablo.

~~KORAY AND XANDER~~ — Rogue hellsehers. Killed by the Seven Devils in *City of Gods and Monsters*.

~~LIAM~~ — Former Reaper. Killed by Darien in *City of Gods and Monsters*.

IAN GRAY — A Reaper who was excommunicated by Malakai in *City of Gods and Monsters*.

GIOVANNI — Tattoo artist and owner of Giovanni's Tattoo.

DEAN SLADE — Randal and Donovan's brother.

HUMANS

LOREN CALLA/LILIANA SOPHRONIA — Daughter of Erasmus and Helia Sophronia. After her father created her with the Arcanum Well, she ended up being gifted with its magic and able to track the Well. When she was a baby, her parents left her on the steps of the Temple of the Scarlet Star, where she was soon adopted by Roark Bright. It was Taega's choice to give her the last name 'Calla', so she would have some connection to her real name.

ARTHUR J. KIND — Former doctor and weapons technician for Lucent Enterprises. When Elsie Cassel first moved to Angelthene to be with Randal, Arthur became her doctor and very close friend.

ERASMUS SOPHRONIA — Creator of the Arcanum Well and Loren Calla's father. Founder of the Phoenix Head Society.

~~ELSIE CASSEL/EMBERLEY SLADE~~ — Darien and Ivy's mother and Randal Slade's wife. When she moved away from home to be with Randal, she changed her name from Elsie to Emberley. Died before the events of *City of Gods and Monsters*. Her death was ruled as suicide, but Darien and Ivy suspect she was killed.

WITCHES AND WARLOCKS
(VENEFICAE)

DALLAS BRIGHT — Roark and Taega's daughter. She is a student at Angelthene Academy and a trainee in Angelthene's Aerial Fleet. She is Loren's best friend and adoptive sister.

CASEN MARTEL/THE BUTCHER — The lead Blood Potions dealer in the state of Witheredge. Runs the Umbra Forum in Angelthene. Has a daughter named Chloe.

TAEGA BRIGHT, NEE TINE — Roark's wife and Dallas's mother. Former member of the Phoenix Head Society.

ROARK BRIGHT — The Red Baron and General of Terra's Aerial Fleets. He is Taega's husband and Dallas's father. His real name is Elix Danik, and he was an original member of the Phoenix Head Society.

FINN SOLACE — Head Detective for Angelthene's Magical Protections Unit.

TAMIKA ISLEY — An optometrist at Angelthene Optometry.

TANYA — Receptionist for Caliginous on Silverway.

MORDRED AND PENELOPE — Owners of Mordred and Penelope's Mortar and Pestle.

ALFIE — A drug and weapons dealer who works at Yveswich's Black Market.

BENJAMIN — A grave robber who lives in Dusk Hollow cemetery.

CAIN NASH — A criminal who was after the Well in *City of Gods and Monsters*. Darien helped Finn put him behind bars.

~~IVADOR LANGDON~~ — Former Headmaster of Angelthene Academy. Died during the events of *City of Gods and Monsters*.

DENNIS BOYD — Owner of Puerta de la Muerta and Chrysantha Sands's former employer.

MILES OSBORN — Headmaster at Angelthene Academy.

AGATHA — Hedgewitch and owner of Agatha's Post-Secondary Education for Botany.

ETHAN, CHAD, AND GARRETT — Students at Angelthene Academy.

ANTONIO PEREZ — A mob boss who owns the Pit.

GRAYSON PHIPPS — A teacher at Angelthene Academy.

CHLOE MARTEL — The Butcher's daughter.

WEREWOLVES
(LYCANTHROPES)

Logan Sands — Head of the Silverwood District and alpha of all werewolf packs in Angelthene. Also known as Shadowback.

Sabrine Van Arsdell — Best friends with Loren and Dallas. Logan turned her into a werewolf in *City of Gods and Monsters*.

Sebastian — Second to Logan Sands. Also known as Cryo. Member of the Guardian Pack.

Chrysantha Sands — Logan's sister. Also known as Tundra. Member of the Guardian Pack.

Cash — Third to Logan Sands. Also known as Silverrain. Member of the Guardian Pack.

~~Bleddyn Sands~~ — Logan's father. Died before the events of *City of Gods and Monsters*.

Big — Head Chef for Silver Claw.

VAMPIRES
(LAMIAE)

~~Calanthe Croft~~ — Head Vampire of the district of Drakon and former Head of the House of the Blood Rose. Died during the events of *City of Souls and Sinners*.

Emilie Croft — Calanthe's daughter and heir to the House of the Blood Rose.

Jaden Croft — Emilie's half-brother.

Baylor — Former manager of the Devil's Advocate.

Viktor — Member of the House of the Blood Rose.

Lenora Aldonold — Member of the House of the Blood Rose and Calanthe Croft's Second.

Desiree Denaldi — Heir to the House of the Silver Torch. She has a twin sister who is also an heir.

COVENS, PACKS, AND HOUSES OF ANGELTHENE

VENEFICAE COVENS OF ANGELTHENE

- Upper West
- Lower West
- Northwood
- Farhallows

WEREWOLF PACKS OF ANGELTHENE

- Guardians
- Queenswater
- Eastside
- Black Mirror

VAMPIRE HOUSES OF ANGELTHENE

- Blood Rose
- Silver Torch
- Corpse Flower
- Hammer Orchid
- Blue Lily

FAMILIAR SPIRITS

BANDIT — Darien Cassel's Familiar. Short-haired dog with cropped ears and a cropped tail.

SINGER — Loren Calla's shepherd dog Familiar. Brought back from the dead by the Widow, a deal made by Darien Cassel, who paid for the dog's return with years off his immortal lifespan. The number of years and the conditions surrounding the agreement are unknown.

MORTIFER — House Hob of Hell's Gate. Formerly owned by a mob boss before he was rescued by Darien Cassel.

CREATURE — Malakai Delaney's Familiar. Bat with an arrowhead tail. Favorite food is bananas.

TWITCH — Jack Steele's Familiar. Jaguar with facial tics.

SOOT — Ivy Cassel's canine Familiar. Nearly identical in appearance to Bandit.

GRIM — Maximus Reacher's Familiar. Mountain lion.

GHOST — Dallas Bright's Familiar. Winged tiger.

SILVER — Tanner Atlas's Familiar. Wolf with a sweet tooth.

NOBLE — Travis Devlin's Familiar. Mastiff dog.

CINDER — Lace Rivera's Familiar. House cat with sapphire eyes.

PEBBLE — Sabrine Van Arsdell's Familiar. Crow.

ITZEL — House Hob. Belongs to Roman Devlin.

SAYAGUL — Roman Devlin's Familiar. Small dragon. Loves gummy bears.

NUGGET — Shay Cousens's Familiar. White seal pup.

CHANCE — Paxton Slade's Familiar. Puppy.

THE NAMELESS

THE WIDOW — A giant spider. She built her home in the Crossroads known as the Wishing Fountain. Her real name is Araneae.

THE PALE MAN — A humanoid creature who lives in a gilded den beyond the Chalk Door. He is fond of riddles and has the ability to predict the future.

THE FAUN — A horned creature who walks on cloven feet and lives beneath an old fig tree in Angelthene National Forest. Darien paid a visit to this creature when he was fifteen to see if he could make a trade to have his mother back.

~~THE SOUL-EATER~~ — A creature who guarded the Crossroads under the Strangler Fig in the community of Whitebridge. Killed by a creature of the Veil in *City of Souls and Sinners*.

THE BASILISK — Information about this creature is extremely limited. There have been no documented sightings of the Basilisk in hundreds of years.

Miscellaneous

Mr. Crispy — A plant that lives on the windowsill at Mordred and Penelope's Mortar and Pestle. Mr. Crispy helped discover the antidote for the curse in *City of Gods and Monsters*.

Miss Prickles — A plant that lives at Mordred and Penelope's Mortar and Pestle. She developed a crush on Darien Cassel after hearing his voice in *City of Gods and Monsters*.

Cluckles — Bandit's rubber chicken and the bane of Darien's existence. Darien purchased the toy from Whisker's Pets and Things on the Avenue of the Scarlet Star.

ACKNOWLEDGMENTS

I'm going to try to keep this short, because holy cow, this is a long book (are we really surprised? I don't think we're surprised). But I had so much fun writing this. I'm not exaggerating when I say this is possibly the most fun I've ever had writing a book. I hope you enjoyed the adventure as much as I did.

To my husband. I dedicated this book to you because you really were my leap of faith. I had no idea how much my life would change after we met, but they have all been good changes. Thank you for standing by my side through everything, and for always giving me support when I need it. Love you always.

To Sarah, for another kick-ass cover (and for the special edition covers too!!!). You are insanely talented, and I could not be happier that I randomly stumbled upon your website when I was just a baby author. I hope you know you're stuck with me for my whole career.

To my agent, Kim Whalen, for taking a chance on an indie author. Thank you for helping me make my dreams come true. I could not be more grateful for your guidance and support!

To Rachel, for never saying no when I slide into your DMs with a new dumpster-fire first draft for you to read—and, of course, for being such an amazing friend. P.S. Thanks for the tea rec! You have officially converted me to the peppermint vanilla tea club.

To my beta readers and ARC team—you are all amazing.

The biggest thank-you to my family. Words can't express how grateful I am for all of you. For over a decade, you've watched me fight to make my dreams come true, and you never once doubted me. Thank you for everything.

Last but not least, a personal thank-you to *you*, the reader. Your support means the world to me. Thank you for loving Darien, Loren, and their found family of Darkslayers, and for finding a second home in the city of Angelthene. For the comments, the messages, the emails, the fan art—

everything. We are three books into this series and still have a ways to go, but to each and every one of you who have journeyed with Darien and Loren and made it this far...thank you. Your support is appreciated more than I could ever express. See you right back here in Yveswich in 2025!

On a station platform, with nothing to read,
and a four-hour train journey stretching ahead of him...

That's where the story began for Penguin founder Allen Lane.
With only 'shabby reprints of shoddy novels' on offer,
he resolved to make better books for readers everywhere.

By the time his train pulled into London, the idea was formed.
He would bring the best writing, in stylish and affordable
formats, to everyone. His books would be sold in bookstores,
stationers and tobacconists, for no more than the price
of a ten-pack of cigarettes.

And on every book would be a Penguin, a bird with a certain
'dignified flippancy', and a friendly invitation to anyone who
wished to spend their time reading.

In 1935, the first ten Penguin paperbacks were published.
Just a year later, three million Penguins had made their
way onto our shelves.

Reading was changed forever.

—

A lot has changed since 1935, including Penguin, but in the
most important ways we're still the same. We still believe that
books and reading are for everyone. And we still believe that
whether you're seeking an afternoon's escape, a vigorous debate
or a soothing bedtime story, all possibilities open with a book.

Whoever you are, whatever you're looking for,
you can find it with Penguin.